STEEL DRAGON 3

STEEL DRAGON 3

STEEL DRAGONS SERIES™ BOOK 3

KEVIN MCLAUGHLIN

MICHAEL ANDERLE

First US Edition, February 2020
Version 1.01, February 2021
eBook ISBN: 978-1-64202-778-5
Print ISBN: 978-1-64202-779-2

Kristen Hall had always enjoyed going to the gym. She was athletic by nature, so it provided a place to both exert herself when there wasn't a sport to play and a way to hone her body for when it was time to go back onto the field.

Being a dragon only heightened that appreciation. Instead of sports, she now hunted criminals, but the drive was the same. This was a place to build, grow, and sculpt herself into the next better version of who she could be.

Although, admittedly, there were differences in being a dragon when it came to exercise. Training her human body had direct effects on her dragon form so she still worked out in the shape of a human, but her abilities could only be described as supernatural.

While before, she might have been able to bench-press a hundred and thirty pounds a few times, she was now well beyond her own weight as a measure. She did reps of hundreds of pounds regularly and currently, did reps of ten with two hundred pounds of weight. Melissa Heartsbane spotted her—not smiling and possibly not helping if she needed it, depending on how she felt in the moment.

Despite her pretty platinum-blonde-girl appearance, Heartsbane was tough. Her namesake came from her dragon power of aura, which was stronger than most. She could overwhelm almost any human's emotional state and replace their feelings with whatever she wanted them to feel. This ability extended even to some dragons although the two had trained closely together ever since Kristen had been falsely accused of killing a dragon. Heartsbane didn't trust easily —in her youth she'd been betrayed by her own powers into giving others false feelings too many times—but she'd come to trust the Steel Dragon.

Although that didn't mean she would help out with a spot.

"Come on, human, is that all you have?" she snapped and flashed her aura so Kristen felt a wave of disappointment surge over her. Heartsbane probably didn't feel that way but she often seemed to think tough love was the way to strengthen someone. It could be exhausting at times but right now, with two hundred pounds pushing down on her for the thirtieth time, she appreciated it. She wouldn't disappoint anyone—not Heartsbane, not the rest of her team, nor the humans who'd raised her as their own daughter.

"Yeaaaarrggh!" she shouted as she shoved the weights up and straightened her arms. Heartsbane grinned and guided them to their place on the rack. "Flames on, girl. You did good."

"Thanks." Kristen sat, wiped her sweaty brow and the bench she'd lain on, and stood. "But I still don't see the point of all this. I can lift over eight hundred pounds in my human form and way more than that when I'm a dragon. What does it matter if I can lift two hundred pounds thirty times?"

"Was it easy?" her companion asked.

"No, not at the end, but most of what we do here is more—"

"Practical," John Emeraldeyes cut in. Everyone called him Emerald and in his dragon form, he was green and gifted with no unusual powers. He could fly, breathe fire, and use his dragon aura, but that was the limit. As a result, he was called a common by other dragons, something of a derogatory term although Kristen didn't see why. Emerald still had powers beyond what any human had and was committed to training. He was young for a dragon—barely a century —and had spent his life pushing his abilities to the limit. She had abilities he would simply never possess and yet she wouldn't dare take him on in a real fight.

Although sparring was exactly what he wanted her to do now.

The two teammates donned headgear and light gloves, climbed into a boxing ring, and began their bout.

Kristen had never seen the point of boxing or sparring with gloves. She thought martial arts and especially mixed martial arts made more sense, but much of what the dragons did to train involved limits. It was a necessity given that they could all transform into dragons and simply incinerate any workout gear they didn't like.

Emerald's right hook caught her across the chin and made her pay dearly for her wandering mind. Her sense of balance almost failed her, but she caught herself and tried to keep his dreadlocked head in the center of her vision.

"Are you all right?" Emerald asked. He didn't sound jovial—he never sounded jovial—but there was amusement there.

"I'm fine. Let's go," she said and decided she really wanted to punch him in his emerald green eyes.

She pressed an attack and he blocked and let her fists connect with his forearms.

"Good…good attack," he coached as she tried to penetrate his defenses.

He blocked her blow to his gut and caught her across the head hard enough to knock her off her feet. It was easy to overdo it when one fought with dragon strength. Instinctually, her skin turned to steel.

"Shit, sorry," she said and pushed to her feet. The limits they applied to themselves included restraining powers and abilities like her steel skin.

"It's all good," Emerald said. "Although I'd appreciate it if you turn it off before you hit me."

"You got it." Kristen transformed into her regular, pinkish, freckled hue. Her hair changed from steel strands to fiery red. That was her unique ability and why she was known across the world. Not only had she been raised by humans and grown up thinking she was merely a regular girl—albeit unusually fast and strong—but her power had never been seen in dragon society. Kristen Hall—Kristen Steel to the dragon community—could change her skin to steel when she was in human or dragon form.

The steel was malleable enough to still grant her a full range of motion and strong enough to shrug off grenade blasts. In both her bodies, it made her heavier, but in her dragon form, she could still fly while covered in steel, although she was more sluggish and less maneuverable.

"Don't worry so much about turning your steel reflex on like that," Stonequest said. He was the leader of their Dragon SWAT team and the dragon she'd known the longest.

"I don't want to rely on it." Kristen raised her gloved hands again and resumed sparring with Emerald. Dragons were expected to be able to multitask. She had filed reports while running laps and been drilled on dragon manners while performing aerial acrobatics in her dragon form.

"You don't. I've seen you turn it off many times when it makes sense to do so, but there's no point in acting like you don't have the ability." Stonequest would know. He could turn his dragon body to stone—a beautiful marble, in fact—that granted him some of the protection her abilities granted her. It was real luck that she had grown up in Detroit, where his team regularly patrolled. If she'd had to transition from human to dragon with a different mentor, she could only imagine how much more difficult it could have been. Stonequest continued to give orders despite the fact that her partner continued to strike at her. "If you get hit, turn to steel. Make your enemy have to work to hurt you unless there's a reason not to."

"Yeah, like maybe you don't want me to break my hand," Emerald said before he swung another punch at her face. She dodged and somehow—miraculously—managed to catch him in his mouth.

She'd aimed for his eye, but she'd take it.

"Damn, Steel." He spat blood. "Good hit."

"Thanks."

Despite all her time with Dragon SWAT, it was still weird to train with them. When she'd been a police officer on the human SWAT team, drawing blood while sparring was definitely considered extreme and was generally avoided. Dragons were different. If she and her opponent went a whole round with neither bloodying the other, it was assumed neither had really tried.

It kind of made sense, though. It could take a human a week to heal from a split lip. Emerald's was already back to normal. Along with all their other powers, dragons had healing abilities that could mend their wounds in a fraction of the time it would take a human to heal. Even broken bones weren't much of an issue for dragon kind. A split lip was practically nothing.

"If you knuckleheads are done pummeling each other, join us for some tai-chi."

Kristen was glad to take the advice from Lumos and step out of the ring. She was exhausted—the bench presses had been the last of a long series of weights that Heartsbane had insisted on—and the bouts with Emerald were always exhausting.

She walked across the gym, chuckling to herself at the absurd amount of weight that seemed to be the default setting for so many of the machines in the gym. The amount of iron they lifted casually in there would have put most human bodybuilders to shame, and yet that was what it meant to be a dragon. It was a privilege, an undeniable privilege, to have so much power when humans simply did not.

No one was more aware of that than Lumos. He was old—thousands of years old—and by far the oldest member on Dragon SWAT. Despite that, he wasn't arrogant as so many of the ancients seemed to be. He didn't even seem to be particularly ambitious. He respected Stonequest as their leader and never challenged him for dominance of the group, even though he was literally centuries older than the Stone Dragon.

Lumos cared more for humans than most dragons did, an impressive characteristic given that he—over the course of his long life—had probably seen more die than almost any other dragon on the planet. He had an ability to glow—illuminate was what he preferred it to be called when the other dragons weren't ribbing him—that was useful against certain other dragon abilities but didn't seem to have much advantage beyond that. In his human form, he looked like an old, spry white man with an impressive mustache and pointed goatee. Someone might have compared him to Colonel Sanders if the dragon hadn't been millennia older than the fried-chicken icon.

Currently, he led the last member of the team in a tai-chi sequence.

Erin Timeflash was the member of Dragon SWAT Kristen liked the most despite spending the least amount of time with her. In her human form, she was a caramel-skinned woman with dark curly hair and an affinity for purple. Her yoga pants currently featured a cosmic purple design. In her dragon form, she was a gorgeous purple dragon with the most unusual ability Kristen had ever encountered.

The dragon could restore broken things to the way they originally were. Her powers were limited so she couldn't fix an entire city and she couldn't mend anything living, only inanimate objects. Still, her ability was like something from a fantasy movie. If a car had been crushed in a battle, Erin could unwind the damage done to it. If a historical building was demolished by two dueling dragons, she was often called in to put it right.

This ability gave her an affinity for humans because it was their objects she so often repaired. Dragons didn't build things per se—why bother when there were millions of people to do the work for them? —So Erin was quite familiar with architecture, design, and the pinnacles of human construction in a way most dragons simply were not.

This made her empathetic to people and a soft-spoken champion for the mages who often helped her restore the damage her dragon kin wrought in the world. Because of her abilities, she was away quite regularly so it was a treat when she was around.

Kristen fell into step with her and followed Lumos's lead. Stonequest, Emerald, and Heartsbane joined the exercises too.

There was a time when the Steel Dragon might have dismissed the movement of energy that Lumos spoke of while he guided their cooldown, but now that she was a dragon, it all seemed so obviously true. Her body possessed rivers of energy. How else would she be able to transform? Working with Lumos and his tai-chi exercises had given her a fluidity of control she had previously lacked, and she relished them now and went through the motions with ease.

A knock at the door to the gym unfortunately disturbed the measure of peace the routine brought.

That someone knocked at all was odd. The gym filled most of the fifth floor of Dragon SWAT Headquarters. As such, it was used by all the dragons who worked there. Even now, others who weren't part of their team labored away at various machines.

A knock was intrusive and basically conveyed the message that they intended to interrupt, which meant it wasn't a dragon at the door but a mage.

Lumos ignored it, as did everyone else in the gym. Kristen watched out of the corner of her eye as the mage opened the door and approached their mat. He smiled nervously as he watched them go through the flowing motions of tai-chi. In his hands, he held a package wrapped in brown paper.

He stood awkwardly until finally, one the dragons couldn't take it any longer

"What the hell do you want?" Heartsbane demanded. It wasn't at all surprising that she had been the one to crack first. She had little patience and even less for humans.

"A delivery ma'am. For...er, Heartsbane."

The situation struck Kristen as decidedly odd. She didn't know this mage but that in itself wasn't unusual. A vast network of them existed across the United States as well as the world, and they often moved to different places in search of better jobs exactly like regular people did.

What was odd was that he didn't know he was already speaking to Heartsbane. Practically everyone knew her by virtue of her reputation. She'd chewed out everyone who worked in the paper dungeon— the office that handled most of Dragon SWAT's paperwork—so it was an unconnected mage indeed who didn't know who the scowling, platinum-blonde beauty was.

"Yeah, well, you fucking found her." Heartsbane snorted. Despite the dragon having no love for mankind, she was an undisputed master of their swear words. She often made Kristen think of Hernandez, a previous human partner on Detroit SWAT. Even the thought of what a conversation would sound like between the two of them made her smile. If it played on the radio, there would be five minutes of bleeped-out expletives and nothing more.

"Stop torturing the boy and take your mail," Stonequest said to Heartsbane before he turned to the rest of the group. "Everyone else, take five and get water. We'll do stretches after this and move into training in dragon mode."

Everyone went to retrieve their water bottles while Heartsbane approached the man with her package.

"Who is it from?" she demanded.

That too caught Kristen's attention. She turned to watch the exchange and after a moment, wandered closer to see that the package was, in fact, unmarked.

Her teammate snatched it out of the mage's hands, who—now that he no longer had a purpose—began to walk quickly toward the door.

"Wait a second, you little whelp. Get back here in case I need to send this back," Heartsbane said, finally lost her scowl, and broke into a grin. "Something tells me this is some kind of practical joke from one of you losers. So help me, if there is lingerie in here, there will be bloodshed."

The other members of the team laughed, but the mage only swallowed nervously—although he did furtively study Heartsbane a little more closely at the mention of lingerie. Not that anyone could blame the poor guy. She was attractive, as most dragons were, but her features seemed to compliment her aura exceptionally well. On top of that, she wore little of anything, as uniforms weren't particularly conducive to working out.

Still, the mage should have known better. He would have if he had known who Heartsbane was. She cast a cruel smile at the kid, whose emotions were no doubt no longer his own, and ripped the paper of the package.

Inside was a wooden box like something an expensive bottle of wine would come in.

"I gotta say I like this a hell of a lot more than cardboard." She smiled and opened the lid with a flourish.

In the next moment, the container exploded.

CHAPTER TWO

Kristen was saved by both her dragon abilities and her human training. Her time on Detroit's SWAT team had teamed her with foul-mouthed demolitions expert, Lyn Hernandez. The woman had tested the team many times on what bombs looked like when they detonated.

At the time, the Steel Dragon had often grown impatient with the repetitive grilling on information she didn't expect to need very often. Now, however, it paid dividends. She glimpsed a tiny flash and instinctively turned her skin to steel as she flung herself prostrate. The force with which she landed on the mats where she'd done tai chi was such that she actually cracked the floorboards beneath them.

Fire and compressed air rolled across the room, scooped people up, and hurled them against workout equipment or walls.

She used the moment of the explosion to thank God, the universe, her lucky stars, and anything else out there listening for what she was. If she hadn't been trained by the right people and possessed dragon abilities, she had no doubt she would have been catapulted into one of the walls or wrapped around a piece of workout equipment.

Her next reflex was to survey the scene and make sure it was safe. She couldn't exactly lead a rescue or check on victims if the roof would collapse on their heads. Dragon SWAT headquarters were located in the Capital Square Building in downtown Detroit, a building that had been built in 1897. It was entirely possible that a bomb would weaken the brick structure to the point where it caused a collapse.

Thankfully, she didn't think that was likely to happen. The building had been heavily reinforced by its dragon occupants and this floor especially. After all, dragons trained there and often leapt into the sky only one floor above. Steel beams supported the ceiling and although one of them was dented and bent slightly out of shape, none of the others were. That meant the ceiling and the sixth floor of the building wouldn't collapse onto the scene of destruction that already defined most of the fifth floor.

Kristen moved her assessment to the room itself as she pushed to her feet. Almost every piece of equipment was either upended or damaged. It seemed only the boxing ring had escaped the serious effects and that was probably because the force and shrapnel from the bomb mostly went straight through between the ropes.

Fires had started around the room, though. The top rope of the boxing ring was aflame, as were workout towels, floor mats, and a wicker basket used for dirty rags. The sprinkler system seemed to notice this at about the same time she did. An alarm bleated and water was released to extinguish the blazes and douse everyone in the process.

Her lightning-fast assessment moved to the victims. Instinctively, her first reflex was to check for the mage who'd brought the package. After all, he was human, while everyone else working out were dragons. They had a much better chance of survival than a human did, even a magic one. Dragons were tougher, stronger, and had healing powers, after all.

But there was more than simple concern in her mind. She also wanted to question him. Where had he come from? Where did he get the package? Who had given it to him? It wasn't unrealistic to think he'd been sent by someone, given how unfamiliar he had seemed to be with Heartsbane's reputation. Dragon SWAT Headquarters didn't actually have the strongest security. A building filled with shape-shifting dragons and magic-wielding mages wasn't exactly a good target for the average criminal. It was possible the mage had snuck in, hiding behind his magic abilities to simply blend in.

She realized she would never get the answer to her questions, though, as she finally found him. He was a bloody smear on the wall closest to where the bomb had detonated. Tatters of his robe and his boots were all that were left to positively identify the man. She grimaced. It must have been quick, which was a tiny comfort and the barest relief, but to go in such a grisly fashion wasn't what she'd choose for anyone, whether they had been a spy or unwitting accomplice.

Kristen shifted her focus to the dragons in the room. Most seemed to be recovering—they moved groggily, struggled to their feet, and checked on each other—but one was not.

Heartsbane was down and bleeding.

Both she and Stonequest rushed to her side and reached her at the same time.

He seemed fine, protected by good luck and by apparently being behind some workout equipment when the package exploded. A large lump on his head had already begun to shrink as his dragon abilities kicked in. His rapid healing only highlighted the fact that something was really wrong with their teammate.

She was unconscious, for one thing—which was extremely unusual for dragons—but the blood that soaked her workout clothes was of much greater concern. Wounds were visible across her chest, gashes of varying depth that together, released copious amounts of blood from her body. Her face was a mess too but with her eyes closed, it was impossible to see if they had been affected.

"Melissa," Stonequest said sharply and tried to drag the dragon back to consciousness with his authoritative voice. "Melissa Heartsbane, hear me. You need to focus your healing on your torso. You need to stop the bleeding. You can fix your pretty face later."

That she wasn't healing was obvious. Even the smallest lacerations on her body continued to bleed, and the larger ones were a truly fearsome sight.

"She'll bleed out," Kristen said without intending to. She had never heard of a dragon bleeding out. It simply didn't happen. Their healing abilities were quite adept at prioritizing near-lethal wounds. To kill a dragon, you basically had to chop their heads off or destroy their hearts. Even damaging the heart or the lungs didn't always work. They were simply too powerful and their bodies were quite capable of restoring themselves.

"Heartsbane, damn it—Heartsbane, wake up! Why isn't she healing?" Stonequest asked the room as if someone would be able to answer him. Kristen had never heard that raw edge in a dragon's voice before, much less her team leader's. His freaking out told her how serious this was. He was normally calm and collected, even in the midst of battles with other dragons. But he'd never witnessed something like this—a friend dying in his arms while he could do nothing about it.

"We need to stay calm and we need a mage who knows how to heal," she said.

Stonequest didn't hear her. He was too focused on Heartsbane. Kristen had never asked any questions about their past, but she wondered now how long they'd worked together and if there had been more to their relationship than simply a team bond. He seemed to be losing it and going into shock.

"Lumos!" she shouted and flexed her aura to show fear and concern.

He stumbled toward her, clutching his leg. "The cursed thing stung me good. Something's not right about the wound," he said through clenched teeth.

"We need a mage who can heal—now," she said.

"Of course." He rushed toward the door with a burst of dragon speed. She spared a glance around the room to locate the rest of her team. Emerald held an arm that wept blood. Erin seemed fine and she was checking on him. Okay, so it was Heartsbane they needed to worry about. She knew she should feel some relief that the others were all right, but confronted as she was with the bloody mess that was Melissa Heartsbane on the floor in front of her, it was hard to feel anything but panic.

But she had to stay calm. Stonequest was losing it, which meant she had to be a rock to his crumbling stone.

A mage would be there soon, she knew that, and yet she couldn't simply sit and watch the dragon bleed out. She had taken basic first aid and seen her fair share of wounded people so she checked the body once more, looking for a clue as to why the woman wasn't healing.

She noticed a gash on Heartsbane's shoulder and a piece of shrapnel protruding from it. Carefully, she removed the sliver of debris and made sure to not disturb her battered body.

"What the hell are you doing, Steel?" Stonequest roared and flashed his aura to show her how angry he was. "Don't touch objects embedded in wounds. Even I know that!"

"It was only her shoulder. She won't bleed out from her shoulder." Kristen tried to keep her tone level but it did nothing to calm him.

"You don't know that. Maybe that's how it works for a person, but you don't know that about dragons. You can't. If she can't heal from this, you might have permanently damaged her wings in dragon form."

She didn't think that was the case, not when she realized what the piece of shrapnel in her hand was. Still, she put pressure on the wound she'd removed it from, hoping to calm Stonequest, as she examined the object.

It was a dragon scale, she confirmed with growing horror.

The bomb had been filled with dragon scales.

That was why Emerald's arm and Lumos' leg weren't healing. Dragons could inflict great damage on each other. Their claws, teeth, and spiked tails were the best weapons against their opponents. Recently, however, someone had learned that even once removed from the body, dragon parts could be used to hurt dragons, especially if repurposed into bullets. She had already seen multiple dragons killed with the lethal tech.

It seemed that it had now climbed to a new level and harnessed the power of bombs.

Every wound on Heartsbane was caused by a piece of a dragon, which was why none of them were healing.

The implications were staggering, but Kristen couldn't exactly get into them now. It didn't matter who had made the bomb at the moment. All that mattered was that she was now quite certain that Heartsbane's wounds could prove to be fatal. She wouldn't be able to heal until every last sliver of dragon scale was out of her.

Calmly and quietly, she told Stonequest, who only moaned. He knew as well as she did about the dragon-based weapons someone had made. While he'd argued that a dragon had to be behind it, she had steadfastly believed humans were the masterminds. Thankfully, neither had the opportunity to resume the old argument as Lumos returned with a mage.

A short woman in a white robe emblazoned with a blue staff entwined by a single serpent hurried across the room. Her hands were already bathed in blueish light. She was Dragon SWAT's healer and if anyone could help Heartsbane, it would be her.

"What happened here?" she asked. Kristen couldn't remember but thought her name was Sarah or maybe Sareth.

"Heartsbane is hurt," Stonequest told her sharply. "Do something!"

"He's in shock," Kristen said. Sareth—it crystallized in her mind now—nodded. She'd no doubt seen this reaction before in people and mages.

"A bomb?" the woman asked and held her hands over Heartsbane. The blue light intensified and seemed to reach out to the gory chest.

"Yes, but the shrapnel is dragon scales," she replied.

Sareth nodded and breathed deeply. The blue light that emanated from her hands intensified even more. Now, phantom hands shaped by the glow reached carefully into the lacerations and tried gently to remove the pieces that prevented Heartsbane from healing. First, there were only two of these hands made by magic and Sareth's mind, then there were four, then eight, then more than Kristen could count. Half tried to grasp and remove the shrapnel while the others hovered over Heartsbane's chest to provide her with some kind of energy.

Unfortunately, neither of these efforts seemed to bring results.

Sareth reshuffled and tried to make all the hands retrieve the fragments, but the glowing fingers seemed to grasp ineffectually at nothing. "It's dragon, you said?"

"Yes." Kristen nodded and held up the scale she'd taken from the shoulder wound. Seeing it wouldn't really do much to help, but she wasn't thinking completely clearly either.

"My magic can't get hold of it. I...I can't feel the difference between Heartsbane and the foreign pieces. Normally, these kinds of wounds are metal."

"Are you saying there's nothing you can do?" Stonequest demanded.

"If I can develop a spell to separate one dragon from another, I will!" Sareth spoke quickly with a definite note of desperation in her tone. She no doubt felt his wrath. "But that will take me hours—maybe a day. She doesn't have time for that."

"Are you saying she'll die?" he asked.

The mage stared at him in consternation. Clearly, that was what she thought, but medical training—both magical and pedestrian—kicked in and she shook her head. "No, not if you can get her to the hospital. A human surgeon could get all this out. It'll be a race against time, though, and she'll need a transfusion of dragon's blood, which can be tricky."

"Can you do it?" His tone was abrupt but she managed to remain calm.

"The transfusion? Yes, but it'll have to be in the hospital. I don't have the hands for this kind of work," Sareth confessed. It seemed an odd turn of phrase given that her healing magic had taken the form of hands, but maybe that was exactly what she meant.

"We're wasting time, then," Stonequest said and transformed into his dragon form in a cloud of stony dust.

Perhaps changing into his dragon form—his true form, as he doubtlessly thought of it—did something to calm his mental condition and he didn't snatch Heartsbane up like Kristen feared. Instead he gently— even tenderly—scooped her up in one of his claws.

"Stonequest, wait a minute! Let's send Erin for a surgeon and do it here in Sareth's ward," Kristen said.

The woman didn't react, so she'd got her name right.

Emerald grunted and Kristen looked over to see he'd removed the dragon scale from his arm. "I can go too," he said. He really did have a chip on his shoulder. Despite being injured by an insane technology, he was ready to spring into action. It didn't escape her notice that none of the other dragons in the gym had been so willing to help, despite the fact that many of them had emerged unscathed. But that made sense too. Kristen and her team were the field team for Detroit. They were all hard-wired to spring into action.

"We don't have time to wait. Getting a surgeon here from a hospital is two trips instead of one. Plus, we might not have everything they need. We go now." Stonequest moved to one of the walls of windows in the gym. He could have shattered it with the spikes on his dragon head but obviously didn't want to subject Heartsbane to that kind of jostling. Instead, he broke a hole for himself in the wall between two of the pillars.

"Stonequest, don't go!" Kristen tried to show that she was calm with her aura, but she had no idea if he could even feel it over his own that was riddled with fear and fueled by the dragon equivalent of adrenaline. "We have to assume this bomb was made by the same people who have used dragon weapons to target dragons. It was delivered by a mage and they have mages. It used dragon parts to hurt a dragon and also targeted dragons who have a significant influence on human affairs."

"All the more reason to get Heartsbane to a doctor so we can hunt these apes," Stonequest retorted. Kristen frowned at the use of the word apes. Dragons referred to humans as monkeys or apes or rats when they denigrated them. He didn't normally use such language, which was merely more evidence of how upset he was.

"No, Stonequest, think about it. Constance and the team behind her have never relied on simple attacks. They are coordinated, understand how dragons think, and know how to use our actions against us. This was a bomb, but we know they have dragon bullets. If Constance and her mages can afford to spare dragon parts for a bomb, think of what else they could be armed with."

"Now is not the time for your damn conspiracy theories!" Stonequest turned from her and faced the aperture. "We have to save Melissa."

With that, he leapt through the hole he had created. No sooner had he cleared Dragon SWAT headquarters than gunshots rang out.

Illuminated as he was in the sun, she clearly saw blood erupt from his chest and holes appear in his wings as bullets struck home. Instead of flying away to safety, Stonequest plummeted with Heartsbane still cradled in his claw.

CHAPTER THREE

It was Kristen's turn to spring into action, heedless of the danger posed to her. Part of her thought back to the conversations she'd had with Constance. Few and tense though they had been, the woman had consistently displayed a reluctance to kill her. She'd said she thought of her as her own daughter, that she wanted the Steel Dragon to join their side, and that she could be an ally to the mages who threw themselves against the status quo of hidden rule by the Dragon Council.

But would that still hold true? After all, the last time she had seen the woman, she'd actively stopped her from killing a dragon who had admitted to eating dozens of mages during the second human rebellion. Would Constance forgive her for that, or was it finally enough to turn the Steel Dragon into a threat?

And did any of what had happened between her and Constance truly matter? She still didn't know for certain if the assassin was truly in charge of the cabal of mages who seemed so intent on killing dragons. She might only be their weapon, a powerful killer with ideas of her own that weren't supported by the rest of her organization.

It didn't matter. Right now, she had to stop her teammates from plunging to their deaths. With dragon shrapnel—and now dragon bullets—in their bodies, the impact with the street five stories below could be enough to kill them.

She vaulted from the window in her human body and transformed into a dragon.

It had happened without conscious thought and although she'd transformed quickly before, she'd never attempted it like this.

To onlookers below and those lucky enough to catch the entire process on their smartphones, it appeared as if a human leapt from the window in pursuit of the dragons and was then enveloped in a cloud of silver from which a dragon emerged. Kristen would be dumbfounded later when she realized the speed with which she'd transformed. The videos would make it look like she'd vaulted into a cloud of silver and that a dragon had come out of it.

Obviously, all that tai chi with Lumos had helped.

At the moment, though, none of that was important. What mattered was that she had to reach Stonequest before he struck the tarmac.

The only thing in their favor was that he wasn't completely unconscious. His wings tried weakly to catch the air, which was enough to slow his descent.

Kristen pumped her wings once, then tucked them as she dove after them and gained speed like a peregrine falcon. Over the roar of the wind and the pounding of her own heart, she heard more gunshots. So much for Constance convincing the rest of the dragon-killers to spare the Steel Dragon.

But the shots missed—or worse, weren't aimed at her at all and had instead been an attempt to wound Stonequest even further—and she was able to ascertain more or less where they were coming from even as she plummeted toward her teammates.

Her talons lashed out and grasped his wings before she spun them into a barrel roll. She weighed more than he did in her steel form so had the momentum to swing him above her as she tried to guide the three of them around the building and out of the shooter's line of sight.

They cleared the corner as a fusillade of gunfire followed them but now, she was completely upside down and essentially trapped by Stonequest's body above her. There were dragons who could have performed the same maneuver she had and pivoted into a clean landing, but she was definitely not one of them.

Rather than right herself, she only pumped the air and achieved nothing since she was inverted. In moments, she plowed into a row of cars parked along the sidewalk. Her steel body was long enough that she was able to crush three separate vehicles.

She registered the contacts as the metal frames and broken glass scratched her steel skin, but they were tiny superficial wounds. They'd heal by the time she was back on her feet.

Carefully, she rolled onto her side but didn't release her hold on Stonequest's wings until he sprawled on the street. Only then did she let him go and clamber off the damaged cars. With luck, the owners would have them repaired by Timeflash, but given everything else that had happened, she hoped the people had insurance.

"Stone, are you all right?" she asked the crumpled form of her team leader.

"Heartsbane… We have to help…Heartsbane," he mumbled. He was delirious and clearly losing blood virtually by the gallon.

"We will, Stonequest. We will help her, but I need you to transform into a human right now," Kristen implored.

"No chance…hospital… Get Heartsbane to…hospital."

"I will, Stonequest. I swear to you that I will, but I can't leave you here for those bastards to harvest. I need you to transform. Otherwise, I won't be able to carry you to the hospital."

He groaned an agonized protest but slivers of stone flaked from his body and he began to change. It took a long time for him—almost half a minute—and as he shrank, his body seemed to drag across the street which exacerbated his injuries. His healing abilities did nothing at all for his chest wound, and the scrapes he earned from the street showed no sign of fading. But at least there were two human bodies in the street instead of a human and a dragon. Stonequest passed out from the effort, but he'd finished his transformation. She could work with that.

Timeflash flew overhead, no doubt to come to their aid, but more gunshots forced the dragon to veer away. She understood the danger as well as anyone. Most of their team was now injured and she couldn't risk being hurt any more than Kristen could.

Although it seemed that not getting hurt was no longer an issue as the gunmen who'd shot Stonequest rounded the corner and began to fire at her.

Still in dragon form, she reacted instinctively and used her wings to envelop and protect the two wounded human-shaped dragons. It seemed the right thing to do, even though she knew that if their attackers used dragon bullets, they'd tear through her steel skin like a normal bullet would through a human.

Kristen also brought her tail up as Stonequest had taught her. Against dragons, it was a formidable weapon as it gave her reach and power and was tipped on one side with an ax-blade and spikes on the other.

To her surprise, the spikes launched free and rocketed toward the two gunmen at a speed only her dragon-enhanced vision could see.

The spines drilled into the shooters—as well as the car they'd come to stand in front of—and they fell.

Nothing like that had ever happened to her before. She'd never seen another dragon use anything like it either. It was fortunate that it had eliminated the gunmen, but if there had been innocent bystanders around, it could have really hurt someone. If a new ability had manifested, she'd have to train with it, but now was obviously not the time. There could be other gunmen, and Stonequest and Heartsbane were losing more blood by the second.

Kristen took each of them carefully in her back talons, called to Timeflash to bring Sareth to the hospital, and took to the air.

She wanted to get above the city and take a direct route to the hospital, but she couldn't. Unfortunately, her precious passengers meant that she had to remain low between the buildings and make sure no more attackers could target her.

Her path was both hasty and a little frantic as she veered between buildings at breakneck speed and dodged unseen attackers. Every car backfiring sounded like a gunshot to her, and she wondered if every gust of wind was caused by hidden mages determined to eradicate this team of dragons who had so diligently thwarted them.

In her dragon form, she couldn't really check on her injured friends. She held them in her talons but didn't dare lift them to her face for fear of aggravating their injuries. Furthermore, it wasn't like she'd be able to hear them breathing over the rush of the wind or feel their pulses with all the banking and turning she had to do.

She located the hospital and circled a few times before she summoned the courage to land—her paranoia might have got the best of her for a moment—and reminded herself to do so as gently as possible. With extreme care, she transferred the wounded to her fore talons to free her legs to take her weight.

It occurred to her that she had never taken a dragon to a hospital before. Now that she considered it, she wasn't sure if anyone had besides her friends when she had been injured. She also had no idea if she could land on the roof like she did at Dragon SWAT Headquarters. Rather than take the chance, she chose the front door instead and a little old lady who had walked out at the wrong moment screamed and passed out. She dearly hoped she hadn't given the woman a heart attack.

"I need help!" Kristen roared in dragon form, her voice so loud it shattered the glass of one of the floor-to-ceiling windows at the front of the building.

Three figures hurried out with a stretcher. The nurses appeared professional but the doctor looked perturbed that a dragon had bellowed loudly enough to shatter glass and obviously intended to ignore the line in the waiting room for the ER. When she saw the condition of Stonequest and Heartsbane, however, she seemed to forget about the inadvertent destruction completely.

"Get them both on stretchers and straight to surgery. Call Doctor Chakrabarti. We'll need his hands."

"Yes, Doctor Gilead," one the nurses said, retrieved a cordless phone from his pocket, and hurried into the ER for another stretcher.

Kristen laid Heartsbane tenderly on the one they'd already

brought out and the nurse and Dr. Gilead both secured her. The gurney was already on its way to surgery by the time the other one returned to transport Stonequest.

She lowered her team leader carefully onto the stretcher and the doctor and male nurse secured him.

"We'll contact you when we get them stabilized," Dr. Gilead said. She was a middle-aged white woman with short, light-brown hair who looked like she was quite used to confronting dragons.

"That won't work," she said and promptly shocked herself and them when she transformed into her human form in the blink of an eye. One moment she was a dragon, and in a flurry of silvery glitter, she became a human once more. Her training with Lumos really had made a difference. She now felt she could transform as fast as dragons who had changed shape for millennia, not that this was the moment to gloat.

Dr. Gilead didn't even blink. "Ma'am, don't tell me how to do my job and I won't tell you how to protect your friends. They've clearly lost considerable blood. We'll stabilize them and go from there."

Kristen almost admired her boldness and wanted to tell her so. It took guts to face a dragon and tell them they'd messed up, but there was no more time for that than there was for anything else. "You have to operate now. They are both dragons and were injured by—" Her mouth suddenly went dry. Stonequest wanted the details of the weapons kept secret. He didn't want the world to know that dragon body parts were being weaponized, but she couldn't simply say nothing either. "Heartsbane—the woman—was hurt by shrapnel from a bomb, and Stonequest by a gun."

"I've seen victims of explosion and guns before. We'll make sure they don't bleed out before we move on to treating the injuries." Dr. Gilead turned to go.

She put a hand on the woman's shoulder and flexed her aura to implore her to listen to the words and to make her feel like she needed to know what was being said. "Dragons have healing powers, right?"

"Sure." The doctor nodded. Obviously, her aura had affected the woman.

"Well, neither one of them can heal until you get every last sliver of that shit out of them. Besides, if they need blood, it'll need to be dragon blood."

Dr. Gilead nodded and apparently took the information at face value. "It sounds like we'll need you in a bed then. Nurse!"

A staff member responded with alacrity and approached them.

"Get this woman in a bed and go ahead and take two pints and bring them to surgery. I'll page you if I need more."

"Yes, ma'am."

"Now, if you'll excuse me, I need to save your friends' lives."

Kristen nodded and sighed as Dr. Gilead hurried away along the same hallway that Stonequest and Heartsbane had vanished down.

The nurse guided her to a different part of the hospital, sat her on a bed, and began to take a pint of blood. Excitement and the loss of her friends still had her on overdrive, so she filled the bag quickly. The nurse put another one in to be filled but she didn't manage to watch that one.

By that time, she'd already passed out, exhausted from the events and a little lightheaded from the bloodletting. As she lost consciousness, her mind swirled around her friends and her mad flight. She had made it to the hospital without incident, but only time would tell if she had made it in time.

CHAPTER FOUR

Kristen was awakened much later by a doctor. She wanted to reach for her phone to check how long it had been, but the urgent look on his face told her she needed to wait to satisfy what was really her own unimportant curiosity.

"Hello, I am Doctor Chakrabarti. I don't know if you remember me, but I removed a bullet from your shoulder a while back." The doctor wore scrubs and a surgical mask around his neck, but the appearance of him being human ended there. His hair was disheveled and almost looked like spikes, and he had a mustache even more impressive than the one Lumos sported. More than that, though, she sensed his aura pouring off him in an attempt to make her feel calm. Chakrabarti was a dragon and she had thought bringing her friends to a hospital would only work because there would be human surgeons.

"I...we never met," Kristen said lamely. "But thank you."

"Your friends are not healing. I need to know why," he said matter of factly.

"I told the woman—"

"Her name is Dr. Gilead and your friends would be dead without her, so I suggest you show her some respect," he snapped and revealed a little of the ferociousness many dragons possessed. At the same time, he clearly demonstrated that he was unusual in that he defended people. Dragons continued to be more diverse and less culturally homogenous than Kristen had assumed.

"I told Dr. Gilead that you guys need to get that shrapnel out of them or they won't heal."

"Lady Steel," Dr. Chakrabarti said placidly. His use of her dragon name told her very clearly that he knew exactly who she was. "We have removed most of the shrapnel from their organs and major veins. Every dragon I have ever treated would already be healing, yet they are not. I even tried to introduce some of your blood to Heartsbane, and she will not take it. I still have the two pints on hand but would prefer not to waste it so need to find out why before I try again. If you choose to give me the runaround, I will not argue. Stay here while your friends continue to bleed to death." It wasn't exactly the Hippocratic oath, but he was a dragon and maybe that was how they interpreted it. Somehow, she wasn't surprised.

Still, she hesitated. Stonequest had been so clear that the bullets were classified. Surely the bomb was an even bigger deal, as it seemed an even larger waste of dragon parts. He believed knowledge of these weapons reaching the public would cause a panic in dragon culture and could precipitate a war. She didn't see how a room full of surgeons, nurses, and hospital staff knowing about these things could stay a secret.

His aura shifted and she felt a touch of his fear and concern for his patients but nothing more.

It was enough to convince her to tell him. Her friends' lives were more important than keeping this all secret.

"The bomb that injured Heartsbane was filled with dragon shrapnel. Scales, I think. Stonequest was shot with a bullet made of dragon parts as well, similar to the one that shot me."

Dr. Chakrabarti seemed genuinely surprised as she felt his aura pulse with shock. "The bullet I removed from you was quite different from the one we took from Stonequest—a composite between lead and something else. Are you telling me it was dragon and that this one is too?"

"They were used by different shooters, merely parts instead of the whole thing. Was the bullet you took from Stonequest cream-colored?" He nodded. "That's what we saw last time."

"Last time?"

Kristen cursed. She hadn't meant to say that. Keeping this under wraps was not going well. "Stonequest was shot in the wing as well as the chest. You'll need to get both out for him to be able to heal."

"And Heartsbane?"

"She was actually holding the bomb when it detonated. I think if you get all the pieces out, even the ones that are only superficial, she'll be all right."

Her mind raced as soon as he had left. Had she done the right thing? Of course she had. Stonequest and Heartsbane were more important than a secret, she told herself but apparently, she didn't believe it. Dread crept constantly into her mind at the thought of the whole world knowing how easy it would be to kill a dragon.

Her nervous anxiety had driven all thoughts of the time from her head and she was only pulled from her reverie by another knock on her door. This time, she glanced at her phone. It had been four hours since they'd started their workout. Was that enough time to know the fate of Stonequest and Heartsbane?

It seemed she wouldn't get her answer immediately. Instead of Dr. Chakrabarti as she'd hoped, the dragon inspector Windlock entered her room.

"Steel," he said by way of introduction. "Do you have time for a few questions?"

"Yes, of course," Kristen said and straightened. The last time she'd seen him, she hadn't really had a good look at him, what with them being at a crime scene and everything. Now, she took in his features without making her scrutiny too obvious.

He was handsome with a strong nose and hard mouth or he would have been if his face wasn't pockmarked. It immediately made her think of Heartsbane. Hopefully, she wouldn't end up with scars like that. It was a petty thought and she pushed it away. Windlock's eyes weren't cold, exactly, but certainly calculating and he looked like a man who didn't miss much. He wore the same long trench coat he'd worn when she'd last seen him, although he removed his hat and held it in his hands while he worked at the brim in what looked like a habitual fidget. She wondered how many of those he'd gone through.

He was almost a complete opposite of the man who poked his head into the doorway behind him.

"This is my associate, Larry Brockton. You remember him." Windlock said it as fact, not a question, and yet Kristen nodded.

"It's nice to see you again, Lady Steel. It's not often we talk to living dragons if you see my meaning—on account of all the dead ones we see." She had forgotten that one of the man's magical abilities seemed to be able to speak endlessly without any need for oxygen.

The inspector appeared about as impatient with it now as he had the last time she had seen the two investigators—or investigator and servant. She didn't know the nomenclature for dragons and their human assistants. "Damn it, Brockton, get the scroll going and save the poor woman's ears."

Despite the harsh words, Brockton complied immediately and without complaint. A roll of parchment streaked into the room, followed by a floating ballpoint pen. She had the sense that the two of them had worked together a long time and that the mage tolerated Windlock's standoffish nature as much as the investigator tolerated Brockton's non-stop talking.

"All right, first things first. How did Heartsbane get hurt?" the inspector asked.

"It was a bomb filled with dragon scales."

"How do you know that? Are you a forensics expert or a doctor?"

"No, sir, actually…" Kristen dug in her pockets and pulled out the scale that had been in Heartsbane's shoulder. "I have a piece right here."

"This came from the bomb?" he asked.

"Yes, sir."

"Brockton, bag this." No sooner had he given the order than a plastic evidence bag darted into the room and swallowed the piece of dragon scale.

"Are Stonequest and Heartsbane okay?" she asked.

"I'm asking the questions," he said.

At almost the same moment, Brockton launched into a response. "Yeah, they'll be fine. That's what Dr. Chakrabarti said and I'm inclined to believe him seeing as he did the surgery himself. Stonequest is doing good. Apparently, he only had the two wounds and once both bullets were out, he began to heal, although the doctor made it very clear that it'll take a while. Heartsbane is stable but still unconscious. She might be dead already if you hadn't given her that pint of blood. At first, her body rejected it, but with most of the slivers out, they were able to transfuse it successfully and they have the last one on standby if it's needed."

"Enough, Brockton," Windlock said and effectively silenced the mage, who winked.

The interaction between the two definitely had an amusing side. The man could have told Brockton to shut up at any time during his explanation, yet he hadn't. Logically, it meant he wanted him to tell Kristen about her friends and by extension, that he wanted her to know they were okay. It also meant he wanted to appear as a gruff investigator burdened with a chatty mage. She realized that the pretense made him both seem meaner than he really was and less competent, which in turn would distract the people he was questioning and make them more likely to say things they otherwise might not. Honestly, it was all very clever. She couldn't help but like this team of near opposites who played their roles so well.

"Next question. Who delivered it?" Windlock asked and betrayed no hint that he had purposely let Brockton say all that he had.

"I didn't know him but it was a mage, I can tell you that. He had the tattoos and robes of a mage anyway, but he didn't work in our building."

"And he's…" He raised an eyebrow to prompt her to continue.

"Dead." Kristen confirmed the unfinished question. "He might have known what was inside the package because he did try to make a fairly rapid escape. Honestly, though, Heartsbane has that effect on many people, so I don't really know. She called him back and I guess he, uh…well he wasn't as strong as a dragon."

Windlock nodded as Brockton used the ballpoint pen to write this all down. She wondered about that too. Surely digital notes would be better, so was the scroll also designed to make criminals feel this team wasn't as sharp as they actually were?

"What about Emerald and Lumos? Both of them were hurt."

Again, it was Brockton who answered, although this time, Kristen paid closer attention. The inspector flashed his aura at the mage to make him feel something like consent.

"They're all right, Lady Steel. Both had a few gashes but nothing serious. The mages at the station are working to get it all out of them."

"When I saw Emerald, he'd already removed a shard. Is he healing okay?" Kristen cut Brockton off and felt a little bad about it, but that seemed the only way to get him to stop talking.

"He had a few more but nothing fatal. Although…well, uh…" Brockton glanced at Windlock, which essentially betrayed the whole act for what it was.

"They're healing but it's slow going."

Brockton—permission granted—took it from there. "We're worried there are still tiny pieces of…the foreign contaminant in there and don't want them doing anything for a few days, but they'll probably complain about it more than anything else. Dr. Chakrabarti said that based on what we saw, they don't need to come in."

"How long for Heartsbane and Stonequest?" Kristen asked.

The two men shared a glance and Windlock answered. "We can't say and simply don't know. But I can say they wouldn't have had a chance if you hadn't stepped up. You're a very brave dragon, Lady Steel. Risking your life after you saw those gunmen do that kind of damage to Stonequest is above and beyond the call of duty."

"What about those two gunmen? I…uh, I hit them with spines from my tail."

Again, she sensed the pulse of aura from Windlock to his assistant to tell the mage to unleash his floodgates of words.

"Eyewitnesses said they were dead," Brockton began and rapidly gained steam. "But their bodies were gone by the time we got there. So were your spines, by the way, but we did see the punctures they'd made in a car. That's quite a tail-hook you have there."

"Do you think they were dead?" Kristen asked Windlock.

Unsurprisingly, Brockton answered. "Based on the amount of blood we saw? Yeah, they're dead. Wicked dead. Maybe if they were dragons, they could have sustained that kind of damage, but there is no way humans could have."

"And you're sure they were human?"

Windlock stepped in. "Of all people, I'm surprised you'd ask that question. I've spoken to Stonequest about your pet theories on all these dragon murders. The way he says it, people are behind all of it."

"And yes, we know they're people. Dragon and human blood are different enough that I can sense it," Brockton explained. "Which is why Heartsbane really does owe you one. Without that blood, she'd be in a bad way."

Kristen looked from one to the other and wondered how much Stonequest had told them and if she could trust them. Still, she felt like she already had the answer to the second question and couldn't help but trust them.

She decided to enlist their help. "I can tell you some theories but first, I want to point out that someone went to tremendous effort to incapacitate the entire Dragon SWAT field team. That bomb was a huge risk, and I have a feeling that the mage knew something about what was happening. He seemed too nervous to think it was a gift or whatever inside. Beyond that, they had gunmen ready outside the building. That means they were hoping we'd flee or wanted to be ready if their first plan went wrong. They lost lives and risked revealing their dragon bullets and the dragon bomb."

"Do you have a name for me?" Windlock asked.

"There's a woman…Constance Vigil. She's been involved in these cases before." She looked at his face. He didn't seem surprised and she said as much.

The inspector shrugged. "It's not my job to make theories without facts. However, I am interested in what you think."

Kristen almost told him there and then that Constance had called herself her mother and had refused to kill her on multiple occasions despite having the opportunity to. She didn't want Windlock to think she was involved—at least that was the reason she told herself—but really, she felt like she owed something to this hidden assassin who was so willing to upset the order of dragon culture.

Pushing that aside, she continued. "Whether it's Constance or not, I think this was more than simply an attack. They took massive risks to hurt most of Dragon SWAT. If it is Constance, this is a level she and her team have never attempted before, and if it's someone else, they have even more resources than she does. I think eliminating Dragon SWAT was merely the first step of something big. My guess is that whoever did this is planning more, and now that none of dragon SWAT is dead, they'll act soon before the team is on its feet again."

"How would you like to work with me for a while?" Windlock asked, seemingly out of the blue.

Kristen was flabbergasted and momentarily speechless.

Brockton was more than willing to fill the void in the conversation. "He's saying your theory makes sense and he's impressed that you came to the same conclusions we did. Not that any of it's proven, of course, but it seems that if a group wanted to hurt dragons, the last ones they'd choose would be those trained in self-defense and who regularly mete out justice to the dragons who hurt people. It doesn't make much sense as a target unless they needed something else to happen. So anyway, what do you say? Your team will be out for a week and like you said, it's more than likely that if anything happens, it'll be soon."

"Are you sure?" she finally managed to ask and felt a little foolish.

Windlock shrugged. "Nothing's ever sure in this line of work. Except for putting a body into the ground."

"It's only...you're way senior to me. You're above Stonequest if you've read all his reports. Those were classified and he's hounded me to not say a damn thing outside official channels and you seem to know it all."

"Are you scared?" the inspector asked and flashed a smile.

"Think of it like prom. Did you go to prom?" Brockton asked and continued without waiting for a response. "Sure, it's weird to have a senior ask a freshman out and can be creepy too, depending on the people involved. But it's kind of an honor—a chance to see into a world you wouldn't otherwise have access to for years. Plus, there's no obligation to make out, not as a freshman unless the guy is a real creep, and we're not." Brockton smiled as if he'd paid her some kind of compliment.

"The fact is I could use your help. You have experience with all this, and with a human background, you might notice things we don't," the dragon added.

"I resent that," the mage whined. "I'm human."

"Brockton, if you use magic to open bags of potato chips, you don't really count as a normal human anymore."

"That's only because I spent so much time working in a convenience store. Do you know how many bags of chips I opened for kids and old ladies? More than a man should have to open in his life, that's for sure. I used to have bad dreams about them, in fact. I'm only trying to level the playing field. If anything, me opening bags would make me more human!"

"Okay, I'll help," Kristen agreed hastily and didn't bother to even take time to think about it. For one thing, she knew she had to do it—she was too curious and besides, whoever had done this, Constance or not, they had targeted her and her friends—but she also wanted Brockton to shut up.

Windlock smiled and nodded. He seemed to know exactly why she had made her mind up so quickly.

"Well, if you're ready, let's go to the crime scene and have another poke around," he said.

"Right," Kristen said and stood from the bed. "Wait—there's something we need to do first. You said Heartsbane used a pint of my blood. As in only one?"

The two men exchanged a glance. Finally, the inspector nodded and unleashed Brockton's gift of the gab.

"Yeah, I believe that's what the doctor said. I'm sure of it, in fact.

He said they only needed the one and that she was stable and he didn't think she'd need more."

"Can I get the unused one back?" she asked.

"Do you feel weak or something?" Windlock asked in reply.

"I went to prison because there was a ninety-percent DNA match to me on multiple dragon crime scenes. You tell me two men are dead because of my spines—a power I might point out I didn't even know I had—and the spines are gone as well, and you expect me to leave a pint of blood lying around? Yeah, right."

"She has a point," the mage said.

"I know she has a point, Larry," his boss replied.

They sent for a nurse who protested the odd request but ultimately acquiesced. After all, it wasn't every day that two dragons and a mage demanded blood. Honestly, it didn't seem like a good time to say no.

When it was placed in Kristen's hands, she thanked the nurse and went to see Stonequest and Heartsbane.

Windlock had said they were okay, but she had to see them for herself. It turned out to be something she regretted. Heartsbane was still unconscious and severely injured. The traces of dragon scales had all been removed from the wounds but it was still hard to see her like that, lying under a sheet like a human who'd been hurt.

It was the weakest she'd ever seen the fierce dragon and she didn't like it.

Stonequest's condition was better and he was conscious at least. When she told him what she planned to do, he didn't argue like she had thought he would.

Instead, he told Windlock to mind himself because she was as tough as nails and didn't take shit for an answer.

"I'm counting on it," the gruff investigator said, which only made Kristen like him even more.

Once outside, the older dragon waited while she transformed and incinerated the pint of blood with dragon's fire.

She would help them solve this case but in doing so, she had to be damn sure no one else would be able to use her against her friends. It was already very possible that the shrapnel in Heartsbane would match her DNA by about ninety percent. There was no way she would leave anything her enemies might be able to use while she tried to rescue her sibling from Constance and her cabal of mages.

That done, they took to the sky. It was time to catch the people brazen enough to attack Dragon SWAT.

CHAPTER FIVE

They returned to the scene of the crime without delays or detours. Kristen and Windlock were in dragon form and Brockton rode atop the investigator's back, thus cementing their relationship in her eyes. Dragons didn't let people ride their back unless they respected them, liked them, or wanted something from them. He could have carried the mage in his talons and the fact that he was allowed on top meant they were partners.

When they reached Dragon SWAT headquarters, the entire block was cordoned off and dragons—many of whom she recognized as staff from her building—scoured the area for evidence. At first, she didn't think they would allow her in as this was well above her pay-grade, but when Windlock flashed his badge, they gained admittance without question.

They walked down the street, beyond where Kristen had defended Stonequest and Heartsbane from gunfire, then past the two red stains from the men she had inadvertently killed with her new powers.

By this time, they'd taken human form and walked beside Brockton. She didn't understand the full extent of his powers. When it came down to it, she didn't understand much about mages at all as she'd been so focused on learning her own dragon abilities and navigating dragon culture that she hadn't spent much time with them. Brockton could control a parchment and pen and seemed to be able to lift things from a distance, but he also seemed to have some kind of forensic ability.

When they moved past the bloodstains, Brockton paused, held his hands out, and cast a faint but visible light over the area.

"Magic?" Windlock grunted and waited.

The man shook his head. "I sense the presence of a dragon—Lady Steel's spines I think—but nothing else. If these guys were mages I—wait, wait. I'm getting something. Yeah, there was magic here but I don't think it was combative. No…no, I think maybe magic was used to remove the bodies? We never got a lead on how they left and maybe that's because the mages whisked them away."

"Is that common—for a mage to not use their powers in a fight and then use them after?" Kristen asked.

Windlock only shrugged but nodded to his partner to explain as they continued past the area.

"It all depends, really," Brockton said and took a breath before he launched into one of his explanations. "You see, every mage has innate gifts. My ability to sense magic and auras is kind of unusual. It's why Windlock keeps me around, I think."

"It's definitely not for your banter," the investigator said, flashed a badge at the dragon who stood at the entrance to headquarters, and led them onward.

"So mage powers are like dragon powers? Like every mage is born with certain things and training can only enhance them? Your ability to sense magic is like my steel skin?" Kristen asked.

"Eh, not really," he corrected quickly. "Any mage can basically learn any power. Some of them are really difficult—healing, for example, can be wicked hard. That's why I'm not much good at it, but I could learn it if Windlock didn't keep me so busy. Most of us can do the simple things—illusions, levitate objects and maybe some basic elemental stuff like gusts of wind, make water flow uphill, flashes of fire, or whatever. It takes practice to hone one's skills, though. I can't do much beyond sense stuff because that's all I ever do."

"Because you're lazy," his boss quipped.

"Because I'm lazy," he agreed with a grin.

"So you're saying these mages not using any of their powers in a fight with dragons doesn't mean they didn't have any?" Kristen tried to assimilate the important facts so she had something to work with.

"Don't make assumptions," Windlock warned.

Brockton nodded in agreement. "Be careful about guessing at motives for individual actions—one of Windlock's rules. It's better to look at the big picture and remember that people can make mistakes. These mages might not have powers that can kill dragons or they might have wanted to make us frightened of their guns. They could have powers that might be used to safely remove their people and maybe they even intended to but were…uh, surprised by your spine attack."

She nodded and tried to keep up with the thought process her two companions seemed to follow. It probably made sense to not guess at motives but at the same time, she didn't think she'd listen. After all, the two men both were quite capable of distancing themselves. There really was no point in her doing the same given that she would be less experienced with it. They'd asked her to join their investigation for her perspective, not theirs, although she would try to keep her opinions to herself in mixed company. That seemed especially important in light of the fact that somehow, the mage who'd done the delivery had entered Dragon SWAT with an unmarked package.

They reached the fifth floor and went to the gym, now full of mages being led by Timeflash.

"Erin—oh, thank goodness you're okay!" Kristen said and hugged the only dragon on her team who hadn't been hurt.

"How's it going in here?" Windlock demanded.

"It's going all right. We're looking for clues about what dragon sent the package via that mage. I don't think it could have been my team, but I have to assume someone could have had a contact. It's a nightmare, honestly. I want to put everything back into place—it feels so wrong to have been attacked in our headquarters—but haven't done so yet because I assumed you would want to investigate."

Kristen didn't say that she was almost certain that people were behind this. She hadn't said much about her theories in front of Erin, mostly because the other dragon was away so often. But Stonequest had also never wanted her to talk about her theories with anyone and she respected him enough to comply.

"Do you guys have any leads?" Timeflash asked and sounded exasperated.

Windlock shook his head and glanced meaningfully at Kristen. He obviously didn't want her to say anything either.

The woman nodded, either unsurprised that they didn't know who it was or accustomed to the higher-ups keeping their investigations under wraps.

Brockton wasn't able to find anything other than what they already knew. It was a bomb, not something magic, and had been filled with dragon scales turned into shrapnel. No other evidence of magic existed as far as the explosive was concerned.

They moved to the sixth floor once the investigator had seen all he needed to and set up interviews with the mages.

While they waited for Brockton to fetch the first one, Kristen used the moment to ask why Windlock wanted to continue the pretense of dragons being involved. "I simply don't understand. You told me not to make assumptions and yet you're comfortable with the fact that everyone assumes dragons are behind all this."

He nodded, obviously unsurprised by the question, and held a finger up. "One reason. There is no guarantee that a dragon isn't behind the humans doing this."

"But there's also no guarantee a dragon is involved."

"Right, which is why we brought you on. The human angle is one I'm interested in but I see no value in collapsing other avenues of investigation, especially if they'll rule our theories out at any point."

"Wouldn't it be better to have them working with us?"

"Maybe, if we were sure, but Lady Steel, I'm still not convinced. Humans and especially human mages have done dragon bidding before, remember. But that's not the only reason I want you to keep this all hushed." Windlock held up a second finger. "I'm sure

Stonequest made it clear that spreading the word about humans with dragon-killing weapons would inspire fear and panic in dragon kind. We've come a long way from people trying to get into our castles and cutting our heads off."

"But surely dragons can't be that afraid of people?"

"You're right, dragons aren't that scared. They don't like to be that scared either, and that's the problem. If they are even a little spooked, they'll be pissed-off. And pissed-off, skittish dragons are no fun to be around when you're small, pink, and squishy."

Kristen sighed. "Do you really think they'd hurt people without knowing for certain what's going on?"

Windlock laughed darkly. "I do. Dragons hurt each other without knowing their reasons, as do people. I don't want to throw fuel on that fire. If you're right, we'll have to go public with this, but the only way I see that working out for people is if we come to the dragons with the people behind this already apprehended. If we expose the threat and prove it's been taken care of, there won't be retribution. If we do only the first part—" He mouthed the word "boom" and mimicked an explosion with his hands.

She nodded although she didn't like it, but it made sense. Obviously, she also wanted to avoid a war, which meant the investigation should be done as quietly as possible. And yet, even the logic failed to ease her concerns.

"But the word is getting out. Think about today. Those gunmen took Stonequest—a battle-hardened dragon on SWAT—out of the air with two shots, plus we have a trail of dead dragons leading us to this point. More will hear about it with every new attack."

"Which is all the more reason to find these killers soon," Windlock said to end the conversation when Brockton arrived with the first of the mages.

The team garnered little information of any value from those interviewed. Kristen knew most of them, but she didn't reveal this until after each interview. Nevertheless, he drew the same conclusions she had. Those who worked in the building were loyal to the dragons who employed them. It seemed unlikely that any of them were part of the attack and it would have been virtually impossible to lie, given that both Windlock and Kristen probed their emotional state as they spoke with them.

What was interesting was that the mages confirmed that all the scales came from the same dragon—or seemed to anyway as they were all the same cast-iron color. Dragon scales were fairly homogenous. In other words, one's scales all looked much the same, and none of the pieces retrieved stood out.

One mage was a little more nervous than the others, though. When he walked in, his gaze seemed drawn to Kristen but at the same time, he wouldn't look at her directly. He glanced continually at her and then away.

"You're in charge of DNA forensics, correct?" Windlock asked.

"Yes, sir. That's correct, sir," the mage said far too quickly.

"Have you run any of these scales yet?"

"Yes, sir. Only one but I'm working on more as we speak."

"Well?"

"It's…uh… That is, it…uh… Well, it matches the DNA from the… uh, samples found in the other deceased dragons. It might not be identical but it's close—real close. Above ninety percent."

That immediately explained his behavior. She smiled sweetly and focused on him. "Was it you who discovered that my DNA was a close match for the dragon bullets?"

Now, the mage was visibly sweating. "Yes, ma'am. And I'm sorry about that, ma'am. Really. It's merely that ninety percent…well, that's extremely high. We normally don't get that and…well, I shouldn't have said anything."

"No, you absolutely did the right thing," Windlock said. He smiled a little. "Stop smiling at him like you intend to eat him, Lady Steel."

Kristen laughed and the mage managed a response that was more a grimace than a smile. It was painfully awkward and he wiped his brow.

"It's fine. I know you were only doing your job. We're doing the same to you guys, after all. It sucks when this stuff looks like it's internal." She stopped smiling with her teeth visible, which seemed to help.

The mage sagged and the tension leached from him. "I didn't want to lie about it so I told Stonequest and that was that. I'm sorry, I really am."

"It's fine," she said.

"But we'll need you to run a closer analysis," Windlock said.

"Sir?"

"A ninety percent match isn't good enough. I want to know the color of this dragon's eyes and if it shares the steel ability with Lady Steel. Hell, I want to know if his mother's father was colorblind. Do I make myself clear?"

"Uh…well, that is—"

"You did good," Kristen said. "Now do better."

That seemed to be the mage's language as he nodded enthusiastically.

Windlock dismissed him, the mage thanked them—Kristen wasn't sure for what but maybe not eating him?—and he returned to work.

"Right," the investigator said briskly. "What are your thoughts?"

"I thought you said to not make assumptions," she replied.

"Not in the open on a crime scene. But now, we've gathered evidence. It's time to swap theories and rip each other's ideas apart. So, your thoughts." His tone brooked no argument.

His focus on her didn't make her uncomfortable at all. She had theories and might as well share them. "The mages confirmed that the bomb used C4. That's generally a military-grade explosive. I know there's newer stuff out there but still, it seems to point to a certain kind of background."

"How so?"

"Well, it's possible that whoever did this obtained C4 without a military contact, but I find it unlikely."

"Because of the C4?"

"Partly, yes, and because those two men I hit with my spines didn't have pistols but military-style assault rifles."

"This is America. Everyone has military-grade assault rifles," Windlock countered.

"Right, but the weapons plus the C4 point to the military. I could be wrong, but I'd definitely say military weapons if a little dated and old. Whoever was involved might have contacts in the armed forces."

The investigator nodded. "I'm impressed. You might be wrong, of course, but we'll have to disprove you at the very least. Do you have any other points?"

"That whatever will happen now will be soon."

She wished he had told her she was wrong on that count, but he only clenched his jaw and nodded agreement.

CHAPTER SIX

From there, they went to where the gunmen had probably waited for those dragons who survived the bomb. There were two locations—possibly more, but Windlock seemed confident that the team that scoured the scene had done a good job of confirming the positions of all the shooters.

What surprised Kristen was that the two areas were on opposite corners of Dragon Swat headquarters. Each watched two sides, so no matter which way Stonequest might have chosen to exit the building, he would have been visible. It showed a level of coordination even more efficient than she had imagined.

"How do we know they were here?" Windlock asked one of the dragons they found guarding one of these locations, a room in a nearby building.

"Based on where he was shot, we extrapolated their positions. It took a little time but we're fairly sure this is the place," the dragon explained.

"Fairly sure?" The investigator frowned and looked around.

The guard grimaced. "There's nothing left behind, sir. No fingerprints, no bullet casings—nothing like that."

"How do you know this is the place, then?" Kristen asked.

"It smelled like gunpowder when we arrived. I know it's not much but it's all we have. Plus, this is downtown Detroit—fifteen years ago, this entire building might have been abandoned, but this is the only apartment on this floor facing HQ that doesn't have a tenant. The previous one moved out last week—in something of a hurry, apparently, and cited only a family emergency as the reason."

She nodded as the apartment was, in fact, completely empty. It could have been simply fortuitous, but her instincts told her otherwise. While they had no idea how or why, it was possible that the tenant had been compelled to vacate or simply been frightened enough by something to leave. Or it could simply have been rented by one of their team who moved out on schedule. In turn, it meant that Constance—if that was indeed who was behind this—had possibly planned this attack very carefully and taken steps to ensure the location was vacant and accessible.

"And the other location?" Windlock asked.

"It's much the same as this—the middle floor with good coverage of two sides of the HQ. There was no gunpowder there, of course, but that fits with no shots being fired. We found it unlocked. I'm reasonably sure those two monkeys you killed were the guys from that building," the dragon said with a sneer.

"Don't call them that," Kristen said in response to the slur.

The dragon startled. "Do you prefer murderers?"

"Attackers is the most accurate," Windlock said, although he didn't sound like he cared. For all Kristen knew, that was merely part of the character he played so she chose not to read anything into it.

"Whatever you want to call the bastards is fine with me," the guard said, obviously annoyed.

"Brockton, do you sense anything here?" the investigator asked briskly.

The mage extended the silver glow from his hands in an attempt to sense if magic had been used in the room. After a long minute during which tendrils of light from his fingertips scoured the entire room, he shook his head. "No magic was used here, sir. I have a feeling that if these were mages, they were given very specific orders to stick to pedestrian means."

"Do we have anything else?" Windlock asked. He didn't sound frustrated, at least not to the casual observer, but Kristen could detect something beneath his gruff veneer. This whole situation worried him. It didn't feel good to be outsmarted by two dead men.

"Actually, sir, yes." Brockton sounded excited. "While you were asking questions, I managed to catch Lady Steel's little exchange with these fellows on a closed-circuit television one of the other dragons commandeered from a downstairs store. It gave me a little peek at how those spines work, Lady Steel, and I gotta say you are a dead-eye. You were a good fifty yards away and still managed to fell them both with one shot! It's not easy, that. You must have played sports, huh? Baseball? Lacrosse maybe?"

Kristen sputtered a yes, but it was Windlock who steered the conversation in a meaningful direction. "Where's the footage, Brockton?"

"Right here, sir." He handed his boss a tablet.

It was a low angle from a convenience store so it didn't show everything, but it did show Kristen catch Stonequest and Heartsbane seconds before her teammates struck the ground and her twist to impact with the parked cars. Gunshots followed the dragons but almost too quickly, two men emerged from around the corner. That seemed to indicate that once she had come through the side of the building—or maybe when Stonequest had—these shooters had already begun to move. Obviously, they were in contact. It was annoying to think she might have been able to overhear them if she'd had a walkie-talkie.

The camera was located behind the men, so no faces were visible. One guy had light skin and the other dark, but that meant next to nothing in Detroit.

Kristen sucked in a breath as she saw herself beg Stonequest to transform. That moment had truly been the most pivotal of the entire fight. If she hadn't convinced him to change, she could never have carried him to the hospital and would have either had to abandon him or stay and let Heartsbane bleed out—an impossible decision.

The men on the screen interrupted her thoughts when they drew their weapons and fired at her. She squinted to focus more clearly when she responded with a flick of her tail that eliminated the enemy and wedged spikes in the car.

"Your file doesn't say anything about you having projectiles," Windlock said.

"I didn't know I had projectiles," she replied.

"Really? You really never practiced with them before?" Brockton demanded excitedly.

She shook her head.

If Windlock was surprised, he didn't show it.

The footage continued as she scooped Stonequest and Heartsbane up and took off. She was about to declare it useless from that point, but tires squealed and a black van drew up beside the two men as soon as she rounded a corner and vanished from the feed. Four people poured out of the van, their motions smooth and practiced. They were dressed entirely in black with ski masks. These seemed more careful than the shooters had been. One of them leaned down to check the pulses of the dead men and shook their head, obviously disappointed to lose their soldiers. The motion dislodged a lock of blonde hair that protruded from the bottom of the mask.

"That's Constance," Kristen said, touched the screen, and paused the video so Windlock could see the blonde hair. The quality of the footage was poor but it was obvious the hair was blonde or perhaps silver. "That's the woman who has assassinated the dragons."

"How sure are you?" the investigator asked.

"Damn sure. It's the only thing that makes sense. Who else could it be? A Russian spy with a ponytail?" she retorted.

"You're jumping to conclusions. Think it through—how does this match your perp's description? The hair is one thing. Do you have anything else?"

A little irritated, she touched the screen to continue the feed and watched the person shake their head and get back in the car. She rewound it to watch another two times. "I guess... I guess I can't be sure. The size is about right and the figure works. Constance is slim and that body fits, but we're talking about a woman of middle height with breasts small enough to hide beneath tactical gear and long blonde hair. It isn't exactly the rarest human shape."

"What about her movements?" Windlock enquired.

"I don't see any ticks or anything, but she's obviously in charge and obviously cares. That fits Constance, in my mind. She's always been involved but she's also been...empathetic?"

"How do you mean?" he pressed, his eyes sharp with the kind of interest that probably made him good at his job.

Kristen decided she had to tell him. "She's had chances to kill me and hasn't. I think she doesn't really want to hurt people and truly believes she does this to make the world a better place. The person in this video looks like they regret those deaths, that they weren't simply nameless soldiers with no value. That seems like Constance to me but you're right, I can't be sure."

Windlock nodded. "Now you're talking like an inspector," he said. "We can't be sure it's this Constance of yours, but the details you identified are good clues."

"Watch the rest of the video." Brockton sounded excited.

They resumed play of the footage. After the woman—Constance, Kristen was convinced it was her—checked the bodies, she got back in the car and the others with her rushed forward, bagged the two dead men hastily, and pried the spines from the car they had struck. They loaded them into the vehicle with little ceremony, slammed the back doors, and accelerated away.

"Do we have leads on the other people?" Windlock asked.

Brockton looked at Kristen and raised an eyebrow, obviously pleased that the dragon investigator had missed something so very visible to human eyes. He seemed to be playing his own little game of cat and mouse, though, as he said nothing in response to the question. It was, she decided, as if he were waiting to see what she would say or if she would notice.

"We have a license plate number," Kristen said, amused to see the dragon's eyebrows raise in surprise, then crease in embarrassment. He'd missed the clue, obviously. Brockton would no doubt have pointed this out, but she was pleased he'd let her have the honor of showing the inspector that he didn't know quite as much about the world as he thought he did.

"Zoom in," she said and Windlock obliged. There it was—Detroit plates, no less, and as clear as day.

Obviously, license plates weren't totally foreign to dragon kind. As soon as he had noted the seven digits, he called the number in and issued orders to both dragon and human law enforcement to be on the lookout for it.

"We have a BOLO going out with all eyes." Brockton brimmed with excitement. "I have a feeling we'll catch these bastards before the day's out. Like a dolphin caught in a net made for tuna, this van will be found."

CHAPTER SEVEN

With the crime scene fully investigated, Windlock and Brockton moved to the dragon's office. Kristen was surprised that it was in the Dragon SWAT headquarters building. She had sometimes seen him there but it was a rare enough occurrence that she'd always assumed he was merely visiting. More surprising still was the shabby condition of his desk.

It was obviously pressed wood—something from Ikea—and looked like it had survived a few different owners. The office itself was pleasant—or it should have been since it had windows on two walls—but it was so crammed with file folders and books on law and what appeared to be dragon history that it resembled a real dump. The windows were more obscured than visible, which was entirely crazy in her mind. Her office was located somewhere in the middle of the building with no windows and no natural light, only fluorescents.

"Do you have a problem?" Windlock asked, his tone not entirely friendly.

"No, it's fine," Kristen replied almost reflexively.

"It's a dump in here, Windlock. I'm not the only one to notice it, merely the most patient." Brockton cleared himself a chair buried beneath paperwork. At least, that was what she thought he intended at first, but she realized he had simply moved a stack of papers so he could sit on the bottom half of the pile. She tried to create a similar place for herself and sat gingerly.

"Is that it?" the inspector asked.

"Yes," she confessed. "From what I understand, investigator is a fairly high rank. I would think you could have someone clean for you—we have any number of mages who can move papers without even touching them. Plus…well, honestly, your desk looks like it's one cup of spilled coffee away from collapsing into a pile of sawdust."

He chuckled at that. She wondered if he would have even shown that much personality if the door to his office was open.

"You're right," Windlock began. "Investigator is ranked fairly high and I've had various bureaucrats offer to upgrade my desk on the taxpayer's gold coin. I like to keep it this way to keep them on their toes. It's fun to watch paper-pushers squirm."

"I guess," she conceded dubiously. "I expected more than this, though. It's not very impressive," she persisted.

"Well, be that as it may, I like to work here to escape all the other nonsense. I report directly to the Dragon Council of North America and have a fancy Washington DC office with a teak desk and everything else you'd consider impressive."

"Mahogany," Brockton interjected, although—thankfully—he kept the interruption to only one word.

"I don't like working there, though. I'm continually surrounded by politics—all bullshit, to use the human word for it. I prefer being in the thick of things so I use my clout to keep offices available to me in every city around North America. Right now, Detroit is the place that needs me. It's not every day that we have a team assassinating dragons."

"You're saying this is the biggest case in North America right now?" Kristen asked.

"North America?" Brockton sounded incredulous. "More like the world. Windlock is based here but he's even reported directly to *the* Council before—the big one. The worldwide conclave of the most powerful and influential dragons in the world."

"Brockton came too. Don't let him think he's doing anything except talking about how great he is."

The mage stood from his pile of papers and made an extravagant bow as his boss rolled his eyes.

"Will it be a problem that I don't have real wood to support the paperwork for this investigation?" Windlock asked.

"No, not at all," she responded quickly when she noted the edge of sarcasm to his tone. "Really, I think I could grow to like it. When I was on human SWAT, I swear I did my best work on my laptop in the lounge so with that in mind, maybe it's better to spend time being effective than it is to spend time looking fancy. Honestly, if you had a fancy office filled with expensive knick-knacks, I don't know if I'd be as comfortable."

"See, I knew we would get along," Windlock replied, retrieved an aging laptop, and booted it up.

Kristen grimaced instinctively. The device didn't look like it could run a spreadsheet, let alone stream a video.

"I know, I know," Brockton agreed and gestured toward the computer. "I get his argument about the crappy desk, but the laptop is another thing altogether."

"It works." Windlock waved the complaints away. He struck a few keys and looked proficient despite the aging machine. After a few moments, he looked at them. "We have no hits yet. The van has yet to be located."

She waited only long enough to take a deep breath before she said quickly, "It might be time to bring additional help in."

The inspector's expression clearly indicated that he understood exactly what she intended. And he did, of course, because he was smart and was familiar with her career. He knew her allies and that they were committed to helping her. Hell, the last dragon's life Kristen had saved successfully was only because her team had arrived to offer assistance. He made no mention of any of this, however, and merely leaned back in his chair instead and asked, "What do you recommend? Your SWAT team is out of commission."

"Right, and the dragons we have left at HQ aren't really trained in the kind of thing we need."

"What do you mean by that?" he pressed.

"I mean that when shots were fired, I was the only one who went to help. Many of the dragons here aren't accustomed to risking their lives, and despite you wanting to keep everything hush-hush, word will get out."

"Again, what do you want to do?"

"Well, dragon SWAT isn't an option but my old human team is more than capable and always willing to help."

Windlock's smile told her he'd known she would mention her team long before she said anything.

"These are human shooters, right?" she continued when the silence seemed to indicate that he wanted her to do so. "Brockton didn't detect any magic, which means that if they are mages—and that's a big if, given that we don't want to make assumptions—they're using regular human tactics. My old team knows a hell of a lot more about dealing with shooters than dragons do. After all, they're used to taking cover from bullets and don't care if they're made of dragon, lead, or goddamn silver. They hurt people all the same."

Again, the old investigator remained silent. Kristen had the sense that he wanted to know more of what she thought of her team, so she obliged him. "Honestly, we probably should have brought them in sooner. When I worked there full time, Drew knew full well I was a dragon but he wouldn't let me fight like one. I trained like a human, worked like a human, and faced criminals like a human."

"Most of the time," Brockton interjected. "I saw the footage your buddy posted of you wrapping a thief in metal bars like they were twist-ties."

Kristen chuckled. "Well, I said I received training. I didn't say I was the perfect employee. The point, though, is that they know how to work in these situations. They've defeated dragons and worked under pressure so are the right people for this. Plus… Well, this is rude…"

"Go ahead and offend," Brockton said. "Windlock can take it. I make sure to keep his skin thick, don't I, you old dinosaur?"

Windlock shook his head and gestured for her to continue.

"Well, again, no offense, but Heartsbane didn't know what she was doing with that package. For one thing, it was unmarked. That alone should have been a clue to proceed with caution, and she didn't. She simply opened that box thinking it was a joke. She even looked directly into it, poor thing. If I hadn't been trained to evade in that kind of situation, I would have been in much worse shape. My human team won't make those kinds of mistakes."

Windlock nodded and at least appeared to not to take any of it personally. Kristen decided she liked him more and more.

She pushed her argument. "You know, if we can't locate and arrest this group, it might be worth it for my team to train the dragons here."

Brockton laughed at that and threw his head back with such gusto that he almost fell on the floor. Windlock also smiled, which Kristen decided she would count as a victory.

What he said next surprised her, though. "I think you're right."

"You want Drew to train dragons?" She had to consciously close her mouth against her utter stupefaction.

"Well, that might be a somewhat hard sell so we should probably hold back on it for now, but your team is a good idea. I think we could use them for this case. If nothing else, they'll know what they're getting into."

"Uh...well, sure." Kristen hadn't been surprised that he had expected her to mention her team, but she was shocked he'd agreed to bring them on board so soon. "What about jurisdictional issues? I thought it was a big headache with the differences in the law between dragons and humans."

"Not if you're right and these are humans. Even if there is a dragon in command, these people used human methods to hurt dragons. This seems to fall squarely under human jurisdiction to me. Bringing them in is logical as they have more experience dealing with human criminals than I do."

"I'm merely...surprised, is all."

"How come?" Windlock asked.

"Well, it's refreshing, I guess. Most dragons treat humans like a liability, at best. It's nice to see a dragon who actually recognizes that we can be helpful too."

"And that," he said brusquely and pointed a finger at her for emphasis, "is exactly why I brought you on. You think like a human, grew up as a human, and have human experiences and thus perspectives no other dragons do. I think your team would only be an asset. They'll give us more access to the minds of the people you believe are behind this."

She could only agree and they relocated to the SWAT precinct building to further their investigation.

CHAPTER EIGHT

Kristen had made the flight from Dragon SWAT Headquarters to her old Detroit SWAT station many times. She'd often gone over there when frustrated with Stonequest and the other dragons or when she badly wanted to talk after a long day. There were other times she'd flown the distance when she'd simply needed a drink with friends. She'd never visited with a dragon as high-ranking as Windlock, though, and never with the expectation of official police business. While she'd recruited her old team innumerable times, it had always been under the radar.

If the flight felt different, the reception when they walked in the front door was a complete shock.

The woman who worked the front desk stood when they entered and even bowed. That alone was a shock as she usually grunted and relayed orders. This level of respect was something new, and despite her humanness, she discovered that she didn't mind it at all. The receptionist paged someone—obviously, they had a procedure in place for this because she did nothing more than press a button—and an officer arrived a moment later with a tray laden with coffee.

He saw Kristen, recognized her, smiled sheepishly, and offered to get her a donut. She smiled and recalled a time when she'd had

57

to fight for donuts. Although a part of her felt a little discomforted by the thought, she had to admit that she liked the welcome reception a dragon received when they were actually expected.

Another officer appeared and guided them to Captain Hansen's office. The woman stood in front of her desk when they entered. "Well, if it isn't my old firecracker, Kristen Hall. It's a real pleasure to see you like this."

"It's nice to see you too, Captain. I was half-worried you would be mad at me for ditching your team and joining dragon SWAT."

The captain smiled warmly. "I never begrudge an officer a promotion. Plus, you being out of the office has saved me a stack of paperwork."

Kristen laughed. Captain Hansen had always been obsessed with dotting her I's and crossing her T's.

"And who is your friend?" the woman asked and Kristen blushed a little self-consciously.

"Pardon me. I assumed you already knew Investigator Windlock." She smiled awkwardly when she realized she'd introduced the dragon without properly introducing him. "This is his investigative assistant. Larry Brockton is a mage who specializes in forensics."

"It's a real pleasure to meet you, ma'am. You may be the only person I know who still gives the Steel Dragon nightmares. We appreciate what you did with her training and everything. She has keen instincts and is able to hold them back for more than a few seconds. Our guess is that is your doing."

Captain Hansen guffawed at the mage's motor-mouth and turned to Windlock.

"You're with an investigator, huh, Hall? That's fast-moving—not that I'm surprised. I was under the impression that an investigator is higher up the dragon chain than SWAT."

"That's technically correct, ma'am." Windlock bowed slightly in greeting to show respect but also to acknowledge that she was, in fact, higher in the hierarchy of human law enforcement. Although the two agencies didn't often cooperate, everyone knew he held the real power in the room, despite Hansen controlling the most formidable police force in the state.

"Well, good for you, Kristen. At this rate, you'll soon be a lawyer for the Dragon Council of America," the woman said kindly.

The older dragon raised an eyebrow at that. "I must say, ma'am, I'm impressed that a human has bothered to learn so much about dragon culture. I don't know how you find time given that you have an entire city to protect."

"Well, aren't you the sweet-talker," she retorted. "Honestly, it's all Hall's fault. Having a dragon working under my command made dragon culture relevant in a way it hadn't been previously. I had worked with Stonequest before she came on board, but with everything that's happened since she was hired, I've made it a point to learn more. After all, it pays to know more about the folks you work with."

"Indeed." Windlock nodded. "I've only worked with Lady Steel on a temporary assignment, but the more I learn about her, the more I think a permanent transfer might be in order."

Kristen turned to him and barely managed to keep her jaw from falling open. This was the first time she'd heard about any possibility of promotion. She said nothing, of course, but Windlock noticed all the same. Most dragons were able to control their auras better than she could and she had revealed her surprise.

"He moves fast," Brockton said to fill the short but not unpleasant moment of silence. "I had about twenty-four hours to decide before I was brought on board. At least you were on Dragon SWAT's field team when we met you. When he met me, I worked in a convenience store. Do you know what that's like? To go from selling bags of chips and scratch-offs to investigating dead dragons and stolen treasure chests? It's a mind-bender, I tell ya. A real mind-bender."

"Brockton, you're doing it again."

"Ah. Yes, sir...sorry, sir." He nodded at the dragon and closed his mouth with a snap.

"Well, to what do I owe the honor of your visit? I know you're not here simply to gush over Kristen. Chatter on the radio says all the roads near dragon SWAT have been closed and mentioned something about an explosion. I gotta say, I wish my team was as good at locking scenes down as your kind is."

"You see, ma'am—" Kristen began before she felt a strong pulse from Windlock to tell her to stop talking. Dragon auras didn't use words so she merely felt a strong desire to be alone, but she understood what that meant—be quiet.

"May we sit?" the investigator asked.

"Of course." Captain Hansen moved to her chair behind her desk. She sat and gestured for her three visitors to follow suit.

Windlock sat, took a sip of his coffee before he set it down carefully, and seemed to transform into business mode. "The first thing I need you to understand is that everything said in this meeting is completely confidential. It cannot be shared with anyone—not loved ones or even officers who might find it interesting. No one."

"I understand operational and information security very well, thank you very much," she replied. A glimpse of the old captain—the one who could rip Kristen's head off if she broke the rules—revealed herself.

"Very good, ma'am. I merely wanted to be clear on that. Here's the quick and dirty version. An explosive was delivered to dragon SWAT under the guise of a package. Most of the team was injured and only Kristen's training here saved her."

Hansen frowned, both in concern and a little confusion. "I'm sorry...but shouldn't dragons be immune to such things? In Hall's first firefight, she shrugged a rocket off. I know she has steel skin, but I thought you all had healing powers."

Windlock clenched his jaw, uncertain of what to say.

Brockton bought him a little time. "You really do know a good deal about dragons. Many people don't know of the healing ability."

The captain raised an eyebrow. "Hall worked here, remember? We saw her beaten and bruised, only to heal over a night of pizza. A good captain needs to know things like this about her officers."

"Again, Captain—and please, I do not say this to cast aspersions on your integrity—I must reiterate that what we share here is absolutely top-secret," the investigator said.

"Understood."

He paused and almost seemed to dissect her with his eyes. Finding her trustworthy, he continued. "The attack involved a new type of weapon—a bomb that can injure dragons more than superficially. We were incredibly fortunate and I have no doubt that some of our dragons could have been killed. Obviously, we need to find who brought this into our headquarters."

"And you think humans delivered or developed this weapon," Hansen said with no question in her voice. She seemed as certain as Kristen was that people were behind this.

That surprised Windlock and it could even be felt in his aura.

"How did you come to that conclusion so quickly?" Windlock asked.

Hansen's smile was a little smug. "Because you came here," she said. "When you arrived, the only thing I could be sure of was that you were looking for a human. Why else come to human SWAT?"

The investigator smiled and nodded. "Kristen's impeccable instincts and police skills begin to make sense. She had a good mentor."

"Oh, please," the woman said and waved the compliment away. "Drew did most of the training."

"Well, I'm sure he learned from you. I wonder if he also has your sense of modesty."

"Investigator, you know as well as I do that the best way to do your job is to do it well enough to go unnoticed. Now, enough compliments. How can my team find these people and this bomb they have?"

Hansen asked Windlock the question, but he immediately turned to Kristen and nodded. This was her time to speak and tell the captain what she thought they needed. She appreciated the fact that he was willing to defer to her in this. After all, it was her expertise with humans that made her a true asset in this case so it only made sense to let her lead the recruitment.

"I would like my old team—all of them. Jim Washington too, even though I know he hasn't worked as long as the rest of them."

The captain rolled her eyes. She had obviously expected this.

"They're not really a detective team. You know they're more about breaking doors and skulls. What do you hope to achieve here—that Hernandez will out-bomb a bomber?"

"I know they're not detectives but I have a feeling that once all this is over, we will need to do a little door-breaking." She shrugged. "I want people I'm used to working with. We have an investigator and my old team has good reflexes. I could take twice as many other people but I honestly believe they are the best choice."

Hansen nodded. "You got them, Hall. I merely gave you a hard time for being predictable. I'll clear their schedule and put them on call for you. Plus, I'll give them temporary command status so if they need any other help from my office, they'll get it."

"Thank you, ma'am!" Kristen was surprised at the generous offer.

"Don't mention it. After all, if you're to be the bridge between dragon and human law enforcement, I'm more than willing to build a good foundation on our side."

"That's very generous of you, Captain," Windlock said.

"It's not because I'm trying to be politically savvy or anything." The woman frowned as if the very thought offended her. "If these are human terrorists attacking dragons, the sooner we catch them, the better."

Kristen swallowed hard at that. It was the first time anyone had used that word. Terrorists suddenly seemed even more sinister and dangerous. It was accurate, though. The people who'd done this— Constance and her team, she was all but certain—had used fear and murder to spread terror. The only difference was instead of crashing planes, shooting up movie theaters, or driving cars into protestors, this group targeted dragons. Their goal, however, was the same—to use fear to change people's minds.

"Are you all right, Hall?" Captain Hansen asked. She'd obviously noticed that she had paled visibly.

"Yes, ma'am. It's only—" She turned to Windlock but he didn't shake his head or use his aura to tell her to shut up so she pressed on. "It's only…okay, I know this is stupid, but I hadn't really thought of them as terrorists yet. I still called them serial killers in my head."

The woman clenched her jaw and shook her head. "I don't think that's a fair assessment. Serial killers are deranged and possibly obsessed. Plus, they don't work in groups and given the attacks, you are looking for more than one of these assholes. That doesn't sound like a serial killer to me. Terrorists, though? Well, it all fits. If this has anything to do with the other dragon murders that have plagued this city—and I'm not saying it does, I'm only saying I'm damn sure your team has considered that possibility—then this has all the hallmarks of a radical group trying to use violence to upset the established order. It stinks of terrorism to me."

Windlock nodded and Kristen was still amazed that Hansen's mind worked so quickly. She'd almost forgotten that.

"You're damn right," Brockton said. "I hadn't used those words either—as insulated as I am by dragon culture—but it does fit. I wouldn't be surprised to find out these crazy bastards think they're doing the good Lord's work or some other nonsense."

"What worries me"—Captain Hansen leaned over her desk—"is that I've been studying history."

"What aspects?" the investigator asked.

"The two rebellions," she replied conspiratorially.

He nodded. "It must be a tricky endeavor. Dragons aren't exactly forthcoming with information from those days and of course, you humans didn't have digital records back then."

She nodded. "The first rebellion is basically lost to myth. I couldn't find anything on it other than that mages created dwarves to fight dragons and although their war was lost, the newly created beings won Canada. Even the dwarves don't like to talk about it. Their history all seems to start after the founding of their country. I suppose they aren't too keen on the reality that they were made by crazy magic humans."

"I'm not sure if the first rebellion is completely relevant anyway," Windlock said cryptically. Kristen wondered immediately what he really knew.

Hansen probably had similar thoughts but she was able to hide it more successfully. "This makes me think of the second rebellion rather than the first. Again, mages were involved, and they created pixies to fight the dragons. It didn't work, obviously, because the pixies were—"

"Too volatile," Brockton interjected. "They have more magic than human mages do—as in much more—but those first pixies had a ton. Like, enough that they would light themselves on fire and turn themselves to crystals. From what I've read, it was a real mess."

"I see you've read the same records as me, then," Hansen said and looked at Windlock despite the fact that she spoke to Brockton.

The investigator only shrugged. "The Dragon Council is concerned primarily to maintain the peaceful coexistence of humans and dragons. It's been their policy for a long time to reveal as little as they could about the rebellions. We know there are humans who don't like us. Of course there are. Power imbalances are never fun, but the last thing we want is for people to get the idea that another war is in their best interest. To the Dragon Council, that means locking down information."

"Sure, but…I mean, that's un-American, but okay," the woman said and sounded frustrated for the first time in the conversation. "But there are still reports about how the war was fought. Humans could write and we have some of their texts."

"Not all of them, though," Brockton grumbled.

If Windlock was uncomfortable with where this conversation was going, he didn't show it. Kristen wondered if he humored Captain Hansen, was genuinely interested in her theories, or was simply curious about how much a human could really learn. She very much doubted it was the first option.

"The thing is, the mages didn't wage an all-out war. Even with pixies, they knew it wouldn't have worked. Dragons are simply too powerful. Flight, near-invulnerability, and breathing fire is a potent combination, plus there are the dragons like Kristen with extra abilities. They knew then that it was best to search for chinks in the armor, to single out weak dragons or potentially important figures and eliminate them as quietly as possible."

"Which is exactly what this group is doing," Kristen said and finally saw where her old captain was going with all this.

"Exactly. That means these mages probably know their history better than I do. They could be descendants of those rebels or see themselves as spiritual descendants, which could be even worse as it would mean they're less interested in facts."

"You can't know all that, though," Windlock said and sounded as if all this had occurred to him long before.

"Of course not, but it occurred to me after a little research into non-classified documents," Hansen said.

Kristen nodded. She understood and the implications were staggering. "You're saying that other people could come to the same conclusions you did."

The captain nodded. "I'm worried these terrorists might begin to radicalize the public. People love looking at the mythic past. If a major newspaper—or worse, a cable news channel—picks up this angle and reports on it, good or bad, it could be disastrous. We all know human and dragon relations are only ever temporarily peaceful. If the public at large began to suspect that another rebellion was in progress, people might choose to participate."

"But they'd lose," Kristen said. "There's no way people could kill more dragons than dragons could kill people."

"Ah, Hall, you've already forgotten what it's like to be a person." The woman shook her head.

"That's bullshit!"

"You still swear like one but you forget what it's like to live under dragons. People know we're expendable. Sacrifice is part of humanity, after all. We lionize soldiers and police not simply because they're brave but because they're brave enough to risk their lives. They're willing to die for what they believe in and that means a lot to many people. If you don't catch these terrorists, I'm afraid people might start to think along those terms."

"But millions could die," she protested.

"I know." Captain Hansen didn't look happy about the prospect. "But think about our own World War. I don't know a single American who thinks the lives lost fighting the Nazis were wasted. Sixty million lives were lost in that war—sixty million. They weren't all soldiers, obviously, and yet most people think winning that war was worth the cost. And they're right. But what happens when people start thinking about all the lives lost to dragons? It's far more than sixty million, I can tell you that."

"Damn, Captain Hansen," Brockton muttered. "You almost make me want to join these damn rebels."

"That's why I want you to catch these killers and bring them to justice," she said bluntly. "The potential cost to our world if they aren't caught before they set the whole thing on fire cannot be understated. Of course you can use your old team. You can use the whole damn force if you need it. Anything to stop it all from burning."

CHAPTER NINE

A short while later, Captain Hansen said goodbye and told them that the old team was training in the gym.

Kristen led Windlock and Brockton down the outdated and slightly grungy halls of the Detroit SWAT building. Part of her felt embarrassed to show this powerful dragon and his magical henchman —she regretted that label as soon as she thought of it—around the building that was obviously in need of an upgrade. The Capital Square Building where Dragon SWAT was located was much older yet far more appealing. It was kept in great repair and must have been restored much more recently than her old headquarters, despite its antiquity.

But if Windlock cared at all, he didn't show it. She reminded herself that his office had literally been the messiest room she'd seen at Dragon SWAT and he was unlikely to be one to wipe a glove on a surface and check for dust.

They reached the gym and she led them in without knocking.

For the briefest of moments, she had the same kind of nostalgic déjà vu one might feel when walking into their elementary school after years away. She recognized every machine and knew the rack of weights better than she knew her own pantry. The punching bag still had dents she'd made and stains on floor mats she'd helped put there. And yet, after spending so much time working out with dragons in their own state-of-the-art facility, this gym suddenly felt like it was for children.

The machines were a little outdated and seemed fragile compared to the ones the dragons abused. There weren't enough weights in total for Emerald to squat his maximum. She could tell that the punching bag was filled with foam instead of gravel like the one at dragon HQ was. The sparring area didn't look like an inferior version, though, which was odd because any dragon would be able to obliterate a human combatant in less than a second.

"Well, look what the fucking cat dragged in!" Hernandez shouted, dropped a pair of dumbbells on the floor, and earned a glare from Drew, who smiled at Kristen once he saw that the other woman had recognized and responded to his ire.

"It's the Steel Dragon!" Keith whooped.

"Well, I'll be a stuck pig. I was just thinking about you," Butters said, sat on a bench press, and wiped the sweat from his brow. She thought the overweight sniper might actually have lost weight.

Beanpole waved cordially from the top of Butters' bench where he'd been spotting him. The two were basically inseparable.

Jim Washington didn't say a thing. He merely turned his treadmill off, marched over, and gave her the sweatiest hug she'd ever received.

"It's nice to see you, Hall," Drew said. "Is this business or pleasure?"

"Obviously not pleasure now that Washington covered her in fucking body odor. Go take a shower. You stink," Hernandez said to the Wonderkid.

"Hi, everyone!" Kristen called and held the door wider for Windlock and Brockton to enter.

"Business then," Butters said when he saw her companions. Although the inspector was in human form and Brockton wasn't wearing anything that immediately identified him as a mage, it was obvious they were professionals. Windlock wore his rank and role like a badge and it was patently obvious that he was there on official business.

"This is Investigator Windlock, a dragon I'm working with on a new case, and Larry Brockton—"

"I'm a mage from Vermont and man, is it great to meet you guys. This is the team that made the Steel Dragon into a power to be reckoned with, huh? The forge, we could say. It's such an honor to meet you all. Do you know how many dragons can't stand this group of cops right here? You've done more to bring dragons to justice than any human in…shit…since the second rebellion, I guess."

"Brockton, you're doing it again," Windlock said.

"Oh, right." The mage mimed zipping his mouth shut, locking it, and throwing the key away. The irony of a loudmouth mage who could make things float tossing aside an invisible key he could simply levitate back to enable him to talk again was not lost on her.

"Do we have time for a shower or do we need to go now?" Drew asked and earned uncomfortable looks from his team. They'd all spring into action if he ordered it, but no one appeared particularly excited about sharing the back of a SWAT van at the moment.

Kristen deferred to Windlock on that. He nodded, probably because he didn't like the smell any more than anyone else did.

The three visitors waited in the lounge for the others to freshen up. She knew it wouldn't take long. The team leader had drilled them on efficient showers like he'd drilled them on everything else. She was about to help herself to a day-old powdered sugar donut when Windlock cleared his throat and spoke.

"I'd like to include them without telling them everything. We don't want the word of these weapons to spread any further than it already has."

Kristen didn't have to even think about her answer before she disagreed. "It's not possible, Windlock. They already know about all this shit. Washington knew about the dragon bullets even before I did. They've seen me shot multiple times by them, plus saw Death's corpse, who had been killed by this tech. They were even with me when I was shot at Amythist's mansion and also saw Obscura's corpse, which had obviously been killed with a gun."

"So what you're saying is that we can tell them anything we damn well please because they already know so this won't count as spreading anything," Brockton said in the span of fewer than two seconds.

"Still…let's limit the information about the bomb. They don't know about that yet."

"If you expect the team to be completely ignorant when they walk into a situation I can't protect them from, we have different ideas about how this entire collaboration is supposed to work," she said and tried not to snarl.

"Tell them it's a bomb, then, but not what's in it."

"They're not stupid, Windlock. They'll work it all out themselves without details from us. And if we don't tell them, they'll know we're hiding something. They might give me shit for that but they won't trust you if they think you're making me withhold information from them."

"Which"—Brockton held a finger up—"you totally would be if you insist that the Steel Dragon not tell her loyal knights about the threat we face."

"We don't have knights anymore," Windlock muttered before he flashed his aura to tell Kristen that he agreed with her. She took that to mean she should tell them everything.

The team arrived less than five minutes later—Drew really was a hard one when it came to schedules—and Kristen introduced them quickly.

"This is Lyn Hernandez, demolitions."

"And resident shit-talker," the short Hispanic woman said.

"That's Keith. We call him the Rookie."

"Which is totally unfair," Keith said before he somehow managed to topple the cup of coffee he'd fixed. He tried frantically to wipe it but only made the mess larger.

"Butters may not look it, but he's the best sniper in Michigan."

"Even if you count shots per pound," Hernandez quipped.

"Was that a fat joke? I declare war, young lady, war indeed," Butters said in his southerner's drawl.

"Beanpole works with Butters."

"Cheers," the tall thin man said with a wave.

"Jim Washington, aka the Wonderkid, helped defeat Obscura a while back. Amythist would be dead if not for his actions."

Jim nodded politely.

"Dragon kind owes you a debt, then," Windlock said formally.

"See? Fucking Wonderkid even gets accolades from a fucking dragon! No offense to the fucking dragon, obviously." Hernandez smiled at Windlock.

"And that's Drew. He's the reason I'm the cop I am."

Drew, tall, muscled, and with a hard jaw, nodded curtly before he said, "So what's the deal?"

Kristen told them everything that had happened. It was refreshing to know that Windlock now agreed she could tell them about the particulars of the bomb and the guns the assailants had used to attack Dragon SWAT HQ. He didn't speak or tell her to obscure anything and merely let her explain until she'd said everything there was to say. She even mentioned that the dragons she normally worked with were in the hospital as she knew it would be the first question she would ask in their place.

When she was finished, the investigator cleared his throat. "I would like to point out that this is not even need to know information. These are no one needs to know details. If rumors get out, we'll have a storm far worse than a few dead dragons."

"We understand that, sir, and given that no one knows about this tech even though we've known about it longer than you have... Well, I think I made my point." Drew cracked his neck as if in punctuation.

Windlock nodded. "I like this one."

"He takes no shit, that's for sure," Brockton added.

"All right...so, are you guys down?" Kristen asked.

Everyone looked casually at one another and nodded as if she had invited them to attend a party instead of to join an investigation into a cabal of people determined to murder dragons.

Drew finally spoke. "It's a little outside our purview as we aren't detectives. Once we find these folk, I have no doubt my team is the best equipped to bring them into custody or eliminate them if necessary, but finding them will be the tricky part."

"You know, I may have some ideas on that front," Jim said and carefully avoided the hard gaze of Windlock.

"What is this, fucking charades?" Hernandez demanded in her usual blunt way. "Do you have an idea or not?"

The Wonderkid smiled at that and shook his head, still avoiding the dragon's eyes. "Well, you guys know that I…uh, I used to have a serious grudge against dragons. I mean to the point where calling me anti-dragon was a fair shake of my politics."

"Yeah, it still is, except for hot red-headed ones with nice legs and freckles on their tits," Hernandez quipped and stuck her tongue out suggestively at him.

The Wonderkid blushed at that and now avoided Kristen's eyes as well. Hernandez had obviously seen her in the showers but Jim had as well. Maybe he'd mentioned something to the demolitionist once and she—as always—used it as a barb against him.

"Well, uh…all that aside. I used to spend considerable time on the dark web and tried to learn about anything dragons don't want us to know about like pixies' powers or dragon abilities. I might have found my way into anti-dragon forums back in the day."

"Dude, I've seen your profile. You have a power-ranking." Keith shrugged.

"Seriously, Rookie?" Jim hissed in frustration, even more embarrassed.

"We all have our biases," Windlock said. "For example, I'm not particularly fond of dogs. It's fine."

"It's really not." Brockton shook his head. "He doesn't even like corgis. How can someone not like a corgi? They're like happiness in a stretched and pointy-eared form!"

"They have cold noses and they stick them in crotches," the dragon intoned and earned scowls from the entire room. "The point is I won't hold anything against you. What do you have?"

"Well, after the recent murders, I went back to some of those forums. I thought if there was a pattern, the people there would have recognized it. Also, that the people who did this might very well post there. Many people post fantasies about how they'd like to hurt dragons and that kind of thing."

"Oh yeah, people?" Butters asked.

"Look, that was the old me, okay?" Jim looked profoundly uncomfortable. "I haven't been on those sites since Kristen saved my life probably a half dozen times. I only thought that if anyone knew anything about all this, it might show up there."

"What did you find?" Drew asked, ever the professional.

"Nothing at first, and nothing about the murders. There were theories about various things, obviously, but mainly the regular screwed-up shit. Losers took credit for something they thought was kickass, others came up with crazy ideas about pixies or a hollow earth that hides dragons—all the regular wacko stuff." Jim looked at Windlock.

"No hollow earth. Sorry, kid." The investigator chuckled.

"Yeah, I know." The Wonderkid nodded. "I simply thought that with magic making y'all transform, it might be possible that—never mind, that's not the point."

"Yeah, I was gonna ask if you had one," Keith said. Hernandez looked pissed that he'd said something before she could.

"I didn't see anything about the murders but I did have a sense that there's a new presence on the board. A couple of accounts that I, uh… hadn't seen before posted fairly often. Much of it was the regular anti-dragon crap, but every now and then, there were calls to action. Nothing specific, not like protests or anything, merely asking for help and saying to message them if interested. I had the sense they were recruiting."

"Forgive me, but it's hard to keep completely up to date with your human Internet," Windlock said, which drew a loud guffaw from Brockton. "How were they recruiting?"

"It's not that complicated," Keith interjected. "I spend time on the Internet and never post about work because it's all cop stuff but also because I've had people try to recruit me."

"What kind of people—dork conventions?" Hernandez asked.

"More like terrorist groups," Keith said and looked more uncomfortable than Jim had a moment before. "They use the Internet for recruiting and usually go to places where discontents hang out and talk, where they look for specific kinds of people. They mostly target those who are hurting, disaffected, or angry. At first, it seems fine. They reach out and offer health tips and self-help, shit like that, but then they ask you to come to meetings or join private threads."

"How many times has this happened to you, Keith?" Butters asked.

"Only twice," the Rookie said defensively. "I spend a huge amount of time online and like I said, I never mention that I'm a cop. Anyway, I posted all those videos of Kristen kicking ass, and some people think that means I don't like dragons, even though I am obviously a huge fan."

"Who tried to recruit you?" Drew asked and for a moment, curiosity overcame his normally brooding nature.

"You will never believe this, but I've been approached by both a white power and a death to America terrorist group. One was called Purify and the other Cleanse. I can never keep them straight. The weird thing is they both used the same damn rhetoric. Both loved posting pictures of their members holding assault weapons in one hand and religious books in the other. They were both nice but batshit insane and even invited me to a few events."

"And you went?" Beanpole asked.

"No! Once I got in deep enough to realize who they were, I stopped replying and they stopped bugging me. They don't want doubters because doubt is contagious. Anyway, my point is that's how it works. They look for people who seem to spend considerable time online instead of in the real world and go from there. It's never overt, at first."

"And you saw an anti-dragon terrorist group recruiting on these sites of yours?" Drew asked Jim.

Keith breathed a huge sigh of relief when the team leader turned the conversation away from him.

"Like Keith said, I can't really be certain," Jim explained. "It's not like these guys say we'll attack a dragon at such and such address, bring a ski mask, and we'll go out for beers later, you know?"

"Did you ever message any of them directly?" Kristen asked him.

"No, and like I said, I'm not too sure about any of this. I never wanted to go completely down that rabbit hole. If it got out that an officer of the Detroit PD was involved in that kind of crap, it could ruin the reputation of our entire force."

"Not to mention get mud on the Wonderkid's face," Hernandez said with a smile.

Jim's expression said that this too was a concern, even though he didn't verbally agree.

"You really don't have to worry about that if you use a properly encrypted machine," Keith said.

All eyes turned to the Rookie, who blanched.

"I never joined the assholes. I swear. I'm only saying that encryption is encryption."

"Well, Jim, it's good to know we have one smart mind on the force anyway," Drew said and glared at Keith. "It was the right thing to not get involved, obviously." He sent another glare at Keith. "But now, this is an open investigation with clearance unlike anything we've had before. You have permission to investigate this recruiting drive and make yourself some friends."

The Wonderkid shook his head. "Sir, really, with respect, I don't want to do that shit anymore. Humans and dragons need to work together—hell, everyone needs to work together be they dragon, human, mage, black, white, gay, whatever."

"Once this is all done, I'll be happy to pull my guitar out and sing 'Kumbaya,' but until then, your job is to get recruited. That's an order," the team leader said.

Ten minutes later, Jim was at a computer while Kristen, Windlock, Drew, and Keith all hovered nearby. The Rookie had insisted on cramming into the tiny room when he'd realized how woefully unknowledgeable the rest of them were about cyber-security. When the Wonderkid had asked if they should go to a library so they couldn't be tracked, Keith had lost it and refused to let them log on without him first giving the machine a once-over.

The other members of the team were still in the break room with Brockton. Kristen hoped the mage was getting along well with them, but she was sure he was. He seemed to get along well with everyone as long as they could keep up with how much he talked. That wasn't important, though. Right now, they had to keep their eyes on Jim and their mind on whoever was on the other end of his Internet connection.

"I want to remind you guys that this won't be a one-and-done," the Wonderkid said. "I haven't been online in a while and don't know how active my old circles are."

He logged in and scrolled through a few of the more recent posts that made vaguely disparaging remarks about dragons.

"Is this really what people think about us?" Windlock asked in real surprise. "Humans are afraid we'll eat you?"

Jim shrugged and grimaced a little awkwardly. "No…I mean, not exactly. We know dragons don't eat people anymore but that seems to sum up the whole sentiment. It fits with the cattle metaphor and the power imbalance. Look, man, I don't believe this shit anymore. I'm merely trying to sound like my old self."

"Your old self really had a thing for comparing napalm to dragon's fire," Keith remarked after his teammate added another comment to a meme showing dragons flying in a fighter jet formation.

"Yeah, well, the screen name is burnedblindsoldier7 for a reason, right? I saw shit in the war that wasn't supposed to happen. Men versus dragon flame is a hard thing to unsee. I'm only trying to stay consistent."

"You were in Central America in the late nineties?" Windlock asked, seemingly out of the blue.

"Yes fucking sir," Jim said.

"That was a real mess down there and totally inappropriate. If it makes you feel any better, we caught the dragon who did that to your friends. He's behind bars now."

"He should be six feet under, but I guess it's good to know I'm working with the dragon who saw an end to that shit," he stated.

The inspector looked like he intended to say more, but Keith interrupted.

"You have a reply. Who the hell is dragonzsuckmydick420?" he asked.

"He's an old anti-dragon acquaintance and has been on these boards longer than me."

"Do you think he's involved?" Kristen asked.

"I have no idea, but he'll know what I'm talking about for sure."

Jim replied to the other user. *Wish there was something we could do, you know? Sick of reposting memes.*

Dragonzsuckmydick420 replied a minute later. *Times are changing. Check out some of these.* He posted a few memes that were all more or less of groups of people injuring dragons in increasingly violent ways.

"I don't get it," Drew said.

Kristen was repulsed by it all and Windlock also looked rather uncomfortable.

"They are all posted by the same user," Keith said before Jim could. "Can you message him directly, do you think, or is that too forward?"

"It looks like I won't have to. I think Dragonz must've told him about me." The Wonderkid pointed to his private messages. He'd received a new one from humanpatriot2020, the user who'd posted all the memes.

"See if he has anyone you can contact in Detroit. Tell him you're worried about working online," Drew said.

"No way," the other man protested. "That's way too fast, even with my history."

"Are you sure about that?" Keith asked when another message appeared in the inbox. Humanpatriot2020 asked about meeting in person.

Jim told him he was in Detroit and received a smiling emoji in reply. A few seconds later, humanpatriot2020 asked if he was busy or if he could meet that week.

"This is going too fast, seriously," Keith said. "They would usually romance me a little before asking me out on a terrorist date."

"Could it be a trap?" Drew asked.

"It could be." Jim scratched his chin thoughtfully. "But I don't know. Some of the people on here know who I am. When I first got on, I was only a pissed-off soldier and I told people that. I posted a little when I first joined Detroit SWAT too before...well, you know, Kristen saved my ass, so they might be hoping to get a cop on their side too."

"Or they might want you to get to me," Kristen said.

"Either way, we need to act on it," Windlock said.

"Not right now we don't. Tell him you have to check your schedule," Drew said and immediately betrayed his complete lack of understanding of how people used the Internet.

"I don't want to pull rank but we don't have time to dither on this," the investigator protested.

"We're talking about one of my team's lives here, sir. With all due respect, we can take a few minutes."

"We'll say yes even if it is a trap," Windlock said. "These people attacked Dragon SWAT at our own headquarters. Lady Steel and I agree that they were merely paving the way for something bigger—something dragons would have been able to prevent. They probably wanted them all dead but they have to settle for incapacitated. It's a perfectly reasonable assumption that they also know about dragon healing speed, so they will have to work against the clock. All this simply means we don't have time to waste."

Drew turned to Kristen. "Is that really what you think?"

"I'm sure they're planning something. I don't know what, but Windlock's right. It's gonna be big and it will happen soon." She wished it wasn't true but that was what she believed.

"All right, then. Let's walk into these jaws," the team leader said. "Washington, are you all right with that?"

"Risking my tail to join an anti-dragon group now that I finally don't have a grudge against all dragons? Yeah, that's why they call me the Wonderkid." The sarcasm in his voice was palpable.

"It'll be fine," Windlock said. "We have wires that are beyond human tech. It's one piece of technology we got out in front of."

That didn't calm the man, though. "Oh, great. So not only will I try to meet potentially magic terrorists, but I'll have a nice little button so they know I'm a snitch?"

"We won't let you get taken," Kristen assured him. "We might not be able to hold sightlines, but we can be close."

"You can't," Windlock said.

"Huh?"

"Mages can sense auras. Not all of them, but there are many like Brockton who can sense a dragon as easily as you can smell a pie. You and I will have to keep our distance. Brockton too, probably."

"How is any of this supposed to make me feel better?" Jim grumbled.

"We'll be close," Drew said. Keith nodded enthusiastically.

Finally, the man nodded and agreed to meet humanpatriot2020.

The next message asked to meet him at Comerica park, at the Detroit Tigers home game they'd play the next day.

"Well, at least we'll be able to watch the game," Keith said.

No one else was particularly excited about the situation.

CHAPTER ELEVEN

Jim enjoyed baseball. Some said it was slow but that was what was so great about it. The sport let you relax, drink a beer or three, enjoy a hotdog or a pretzel, and merely watch a game. He loved the sounds of the crowd alternately cheering and jeering, depending on who was up to bat, and that it was hard to miss a play. If you heard the crack of the bat, you focused your gaze on the field. It wasn't like basketball where a blink could make you miss the game's best dunk, or football, where if you fell for the play fake you didn't know what was going on. Baseball was simple and even pure, a true American pastime.

Currently, he felt none of that, however.

He held a beer that had already gone warm as he couldn't bring himself to drink it, and his hotdog was unpleasantly cold. He sat in the mezzanine as that was where humanpatriot2020 had told him to meet, but even these seats—far from the action below—were crowded. The Tigers played the Toronto Bluejays, so the stadium was packed. In recent years, the two teams had developed something of a rivalry, and Toronto's proximity to Detroit meant that many fans had packed the stadium until it was almost unbearable.

Jim had assumed that humanpatriot2020 would have him wear a

Bluejays hat as that was the other team in the stadium, but he now saw it would have been a mistake. While he couldn't say half the stadium wore the bluejay and maple leaf, maybe a quarter did. If he'd worn that, he would have blended in enough to be all but invisible.

Instead, they'd told him to wear a New York Yankees cap.

It meant that not only did the Tigers fans hate him, but the normally polite Canadians also stuck their noses up at him. There was no good reason to wear a Yankees hat to this game. It was arrogant, rude, and plain insulting to the two teams playing, which made it even weirder that he wasn't the only person with one. Apparently, Yankees fans liked their team so much they even went to games in which they weren't playing.

Jim truly was in lousy company, as a man beside him was now quite drunk and had taken to simply insulting every batter who came up. Every. Single. One. And this despite them being so far away that there was no way any of them could hear a word he said.

Every time the inebriated lout yelled, people shouted in response and some even began to turn their ire on the innocent spectator beside him.

He was beginning to wonder if he should simply give up the entire endeavor—after all, he wouldn't be able to infiltrate anything or gather any information if he was assaulted by Tigers and Bluejays united in a common cause—when he noticed a woman moving toward him in a Tigers cap.

"I have incoming," he mumbled to the tiny hidden microphone he wore.

It was the seventh-inning stretch, so the mezzanine was about half full as many people had gone for snacks and beer. The woman sat beside him. He knew it was his contact right away and suspected it was the woman named Constance Kristen had talked so much about. Something in the way she held herself—like she was a viper ready to strike—set her at odds with everyone else in the stadium who simply tried to have a good time despite the Tigers being down two runs.

"Hey, how are ya?" he said to her by way of greeting and hopeful to keep things looking realistic.

For a moment, the woman said nothing and merely sat and stared at the field. Jim was beginning to wonder if she was the wrong person—maybe she was merely a wound-up Tigers fan—but before he could decide one way or the other, she spoke.

Her voice was as sharp as a razor blade. "Well?" she asked.

The Wonderkid wasn't sure how he expected a recruitment meeting to go, but this wasn't it. The woman was supposed to be the leader in the meeting. She should take charge and give him somewhere else to meet or an assignment—something beyond a single word that seemed to suggest the roles were reversed.

When she said nothing further, he finally asked, "Well what?"

"You asked for this meeting, Jim Washington. Former Marine and current member of Detroit SWAT. You worked for many months with Kristen Hall and even accompanied her on missions to protect dragons. So what did you want?"

Jim began to panic. This wasn't how this was supposed to go. He had hoped to appear as a random guy who wanted to rebel against the dragons. That was what his history on the anti-dragon corners of the web supported, after all. But that story obviously wouldn't work given that humanpatriot2020 was Constance herself.

From a crazy tangle of thoughts, he drew an idea. It would be a gamble and a big one, but what else could he do? She knew who he was and who his allies were, so he wouldn't be able to play dumb.

"I know who you are too—Constance Vigil."

"If you hope to arrest me, I assure you it's impossible. I have agents throughout the stadium—and none of them are wearing a Yankees hat." She sneered, which really pissed him off as she had told him to wear the offensive headgear. "Why are you here, Washington? Is this some ploy of Hall's?"

"No, well…okay, kind of. Look, I used to hate dragons. I saw them do horrible things, but Kristen changed that."

"Now you like them?"

"I like Kristen. She doesn't treat humans with any less respect than dragons. She treats everyone the same. I'd never seen that before—I'd never even heard of that before. I still have a few problems with what she does—protecting dragons is wrong in my book—but Kristen herself is a good person...or dragon. Whatever."

"I was there when you took Amythist Skyjewel to safety. I could have killed her if not for you."

"Believe me, I wanted her to die. But if you know anything about Kristen it's that she believes in justice for everyone. That means no executions on someone's front lawn. Besides, what was I supposed to do? Say no to her? She could merely use her aura to make me change my mind."

"Do you believe she'd do that?"

Jim let himself smile because it was an honest one. "No, I don't. But I respect her."

Constance sighed and looked at the field for a few moments before her gaze returned to him and bored into him like a falcon's. "You're right, of course. Hall is different than the rest because of how she was raised. Honestly, she's forced some of us to change our opinions on dragons and their place in the future. Her sympathy lends credence to the nature versus nurture argument. I won't lie to you more than I have to. We've had an eye on you for a while. Your connection to Hall means you could be a real asset."

"Asset for what?" he asked and attempted to sound ignorant but not too ignorant. It was an uncomfortably delicate place to walk.

"You know you're not alone in your dislike of living beneath the boot of dragon kind. There are others like you—many others. And I'm not only talking about kids yelling at each other over message boards."

"I knew it!" The Wonderkid deliberately injected a trace of excitement into his tone. "I guessed that you couldn't be working alone. You're too good for it to be a one-man—pardon—woman operation."

Truly, Jim was relieved. This was more like the script he expected for this meeting. The Kristen angle was interesting and he would have to use that—obviously ignoring it or denying it would be folly—but he'd hoped to play the part of the disgruntled cop who'd seen too much injustice to let it slide. It seemed she expected that of him as well.

"How can I help?" Jim asked.

"You're an interesting case, Mr. Washington. Having a member of our organization on Detroit SWAT would be valuable. After all, we wouldn't want any humans to get hurt unnecessarily, but I see more for you."

"I want to do as much as I can. I don't think we need to hurt Kristen, though. She knows how people struggle, but the other dragons need to stop treating us like cattle." It was easy to let his rage come through. He had been angry about what he'd seen dragons do to people for a very long time.

"I don't want to hurt Hall either, not unless we have to. Ideally, you could use your relationship with Kristen to win her over to our side. Our mission is not about hurting dragons at all. It's about equality. We don't want to make them live beneath our boot and only want them to stop doing that to us. If we have to go to that extreme, we will, but it would be better for everyone if the world saw this was about injustice. Hall on our side would not only give us a powerful asset but would help our optics."

Jim nodded slowly as if deep in thought. "It makes sense."

"It won't be easy. I can tell you that. I've tried myself multiple times and have not been successful. I think perhaps it's because we operate outside of the law."

"I think I can help with that," he cut in and hoped he sounded eager. "Kristen trusts me but you know that. I've been with her on raids to stop dragons before. I think if I brought this to her, she might listen to me."

"Very good," Constance said and nodded. "As soon as we saw you contact us, we came up with talking points for you to use on her. It's exactly what we tell everyone but we think it would be far better coming from you."

"Great. We have two innings and maybe overtime. Do you want to get started?"

The woman smiled and again reminded him of a snake. "We won't simply sit here and risk being seen. I think I can trust you given your history with dragons. I know you don't like them, but that doesn't mean I can trust Hall. We haven't sensed her nearby but I know she might be spying on you. If you really are interested in helping us, you'll have to pass a test."

"Anything to make the dragons respect us."

"Good," she said and promptly stood. "Your first mission is to keep up. We have to lose anyone who might follow us. If you make any attempt to contact anyone, we'll know you're not genuine so no funny business. You can let yourself fall up to three people behind me. If you get farther away than that, we'll assume you're waiting for someone. Got it?"

Jim nodded and followed her from the mezzanine. He tried not to grin. How hard would he be to tail? Constance had outfitted him in a Yankees cap.

His mood fell when he saw that was the first thing to go. As soon as they exited the mezzanine and stepped into the hall filled with people, a man snatched the cap off his head and gave him a Tigers one as well as a matching light windbreaker.

His guide didn't even slow. "Keep up."

The Wonderkid cursed inwardly as he put the items on and hurried after the assassin whom he might have once idolized if his life hadn't changed so radically.

What followed was the most convoluted walkabout he had ever undertaken. Constance first led him down a flight of steps, then into the stadium again. Jim—careful not to play his hand and betray the fact that members of his SWAT team were following him—located Drew, who easily kept pace. When the woman pushed through to force a group of drunk people to make way for each of them in turn, his team leader had to drop away.

From there, the Wonderkid was led inside, up another level, and past a corndog stand. As he attempted to navigate the thick crowds—despite the seventh inning stretch being over not every concession stand customer had been served—someone kicked a fridge filled with canned beer open.

"Free drinks!" a man in a Tigers hat shouted and two Bluejays fans started the stampede. Jim barely made it through the crush of people eager to empty the cooler.

Constance had paused to wait for him and had no doubt planned the distraction. *How many people are in this organization?* he wondered as he hurried after her.

From there, they turned to the expensive seats. His guide flashed two tickets to a security guard and pointed at Jim. When he reached the man, he let him through. It was clear that if anyone still managed to tail him, they wouldn't have tickets for this section and flashing a badge would only serve to blow his cover.

A ticket wouldn't have cost a ton of money, but it still begged the question of how many resources the group had if they could buy tickets for probably a few hundred bucks simply to avoid being followed.

Finally, the two exited that section on the ground floor. He knew that anyone who'd tailed him had obviously been lost, but his team had anticipated that and he immediately noticed Beanpole looking at a display of baseball cards. Even though Constance had gone through all the complicated evasions, she hadn't been able to find another exit from the stadium.

No matter how rich or well-connected someone was, anyone who wanted to see the Tigers still had to enter the stadium through the ground floor. For a moment, Jim had wondered if she had a helicopter to make their escape but of course, that wouldn't work with dragons as an enemy.

Still, they had her. Constance led him to an exit with Beanpole nonchalantly in pursuit. His height enabled him to keep his teammate effortlessly in sight and he even had a good cover story. One of the Tigers had emerged to sign autographs—no doubt against his Coach's wishes and also no doubt to the delight of the fans—and the tall spotter used the opportunity to gain ground on his quarry. He'd even managed to get one of the player's cards.

The woman didn't seem to realize that she was leading both men exactly where Jim needed the other man to go. Despite the extravagant measures to evade the others, they might actually have her.

The baseball player vanished into a hallway leading to the locker room, and Jim expected to move past the corridor and toward the exit. Unfortunately, it seemed that once again, he'd underestimated this meeting.

Constance led him directly into the hallway leading to the locker room and past a guard who nodded at her and said nothing at all.

The Wonderkid was allowed to pass so he did. He stole a backward glance to see the guard holding Beanpole as well as the fans at the end of the hall.

They had been thoroughly thwarted.

Still, he wore a wire. This wasn't over, especially since he transmitted everything he said and most of what Constance said provided that she was in range.

"We're almost there," she said as the crowd roared. The Tigers had scored and the noise made the game seem that much closer. He wracked his brain as to whether he'd seen anyone on the field when they'd cut through. If the Tigers had scored two runs and tied the game, it was virtually guaranteed that the halls of the stadium would be empty as every black-and-orange-blooded Detroiter would watch the game to make sure their team won. He merely couldn't be sure if that would work in his favor or against it.

"Are we close to implementing your plan?" he asked in the hope that he might glean something from the woman.

"Our plan has many parts and you're sure to be instrumental in it," Constance said as she led him past the door to the locker room and down another hall.

He followed but decided to press for more concrete details. "But what are you trying to do? How can I help?"

They were outside now and stood beneath two massive tiger heads holding baseballs in their mouths that, in turn, stood beneath the two massive tigers that prowled the top of the structure.

Absolutely no one was anywhere even close to them despite the stadium being filled to absolute capacity.

His gaze settled on a homeless man—the only other living soul—who stumbled toward him.

Jim thought it good that the space was empty. He was on the

wrong side of the stadium for Butters to be able to see him, but the lack of crowds meant he'd be easier to locate.

"You got some change sir?" the newcomer asked.

"No, sorry," he said almost by reflex, turned away from the man, and focused on Constance. It was a Detroiter's reflex to ignore the destitute when they were busy and a bad habit as it cost him dearly in that moment.

He sensed movement and spun as the homeless man drew an electrified baton from beneath the blankets he wore. Jim reacted instantly but the baton struck his hastily raised hands and his muscles seized.

Still, he was a trained cop and could overcome the stun attack and overpower his assailant.

That might have been true if Constance hadn't used that opportunity to kick him in the back of the knee.

The Wonderkid landed hard and her accomplice struck him again.

The last thing he saw was the woman standing over him, four massive tigers surrounding her like heralds of his own demise.

"Thanks for volunteering, Mr. Washington. We have no doubt you'll be a great help to us."

CHAPTER TWELVE

"**D**amn it, we need to move now!" Kristen roared as soon as Jim's audio feed went dead.

Brockton jumped, ready to obey her because of how much of her aura she had pumped into him.

Windlock shook his head. "We can't. Not until we have confirmation from the humans. Two dragons at this point would ruin everything."

"Then I'll go myself."

"Not if you value your friend's life."

She might have rushed off anyway but her phone rang. The display confirmed it was Drew and she answered quickly.

"Those motherfucking, piece of shit, lizard-fuck dinosaur-killers got Jim! They fucking got him!"

"Are you sure?" she asked, even though she had known it was true the minute the audio from the wire went dead.

"We stuck close but lost them when we couldn't enter the more expensive seating area. Beanpole had them in the end, but he lost them too. Goddammit. I think they're better connected than we fucking realized. No, Hernandez, I'm not fucking proud of my language. Shut your goddamn mouth!"

Well, that answered her as yet unspoken question as to whether the team had been reunited.

"Drew, I'll come in. We need to go after Jim."

"Negative, Steel Dragon. If we knew where he was, I'd be all for it, but we don't have a damn clue. If you take to the sky now, they'll know this was a play and they'll go deep into hiding."

Kristen looked at Windlock, who maintained a passive expression. It was obvious he agreed.

"What about the tracker and the mic?" the team leader asked, his voice suddenly hopeful.

"It's dead. I have no idea what that means other than that we can't track him."

"Goddammit. This means those dragon-killers have a cop as a hostage. Shit!" Drew roared. Kristen had never heard him so furious.

"Tell them to collect any video footage and return to base. We'll review it and go from there. We need to know if they knew about our device or if it was an accident that turned it off. For all we know, Jim might have ditched it," Windlock said.

"He will not betray us," she told him furiously.

"I intended to say to protect himself." The dragon held his hands up to protest his innocence.

"Windlock wants you guys here with the video footage but I think you should keep looking for Jim," she told Drew and really hoped he'd agree with her.

"No, he's right. Jim knew what he was getting into. He can take care of himself—he's the damn Wonderkid, after all—and besides, he's probably too valuable for them to kill him. A former-Marine cop with connections to the Steel Dragon? He'd be a perfect asset," he said and sounded dejected.

Kristen clenched her teeth, but she didn't know what else to do. It made her mad—no, it made her furious—but they were right. There simply wasn't anything they could do right now.

While they waited for the team to arrive with the footage, she went to the old gym in the vague hope that she might blow off some steam. It wasn't a good idea and by the time the others returned, she'd already destroyed the punching bag and two resistance machines.

"Damn, girl, you've been working out," Hernandez said. Kristen promised to replace the gear and the woman only laughed. "God knows I've blown shit up when I'm angry."

She nodded. It was good to have someone who understood. Windlock and Drew were both annoyingly professional. Kristen appreciated that they were already pouring over the video footage but was so pissed that they'd all suspected this might have been a trap and had still walked into it.

The exercise helped somewhat and her anger had dissipated slightly when Keith burst into the gym and told them Drew had found something.

They gathered in an office with a bank of computers.

"What do we have?" she said.

"Not much," the team leader said, "but we know where Jim went."

A screen displayed a frozen image from a camera at the front of Comerica Park. At first, she had difficulty identifying where it was and saw only a sidewalk and street.

"Is that a tiger tail?" Keith asked and pointed to an odd white shape that seemed to float in the frame.

Drew nodded. "This is the camera from the front, the only one we found with anything, and well, even this—"

"Play the clip," Kristen ordered.

Drew nodded and obliged her. In the footage, Constance led Jim to the front of the building. They seemed to be talking about something but of course, the camera didn't pick up audio.

Windlock pointed out that they had the audio for this point but it didn't reveal any clues.

A homeless man moved past Jim, then withdrew a stun stick and struck him with it. Constance kicked him in the back of the knee, her accomplice delivered another strike with his weapon, and the woman stood over him and said something.

"We think perhaps that weapon disabled our tech. The audio is garbled at that point," Windlock explained.

A van pulled up and Kristen managed a smile. Maybe they'd get another plate. Whether it was the same or different, it would be a clue.

But Jim's kidnappers didn't allow them that advantage.

The man dressed in rags shed the blankets he wore and climbed up so his face was directly in the camera. He mouthed the words, "Fuck you, fucking dragons," and sprayed the lens with paint.

"For fuck's sake!" Kristen roared. "What is the point of this?"

"The point is they obviously had a plan," the inspector said and sounded as cool as she was angry.

"Yeah, so they outsmarted us. How is that a good thing?" she demanded.

"They didn't outsmart us, though, not really," Brockton said. "They out-planned us, sure, and obviously had an escape route ready to go. They intended to evade us and leave us grasping at their tail."

"They even had access to the locker room." Beanpole sounded flabbergasted. She realized then that he really was a baseball fan. He hadn't acted when he'd attempted that autograph. Perhaps that meant Constance wouldn't have recognized him.

"Exactly!" Brockton exclaimed and sounded far too excited. "See, they out-planned us but that doesn't mean they're smarter. They merely had more time to work it out."

"How is that a good thing?" Drew asked.

Brockton settled his attention on the brawniest member of SWAT. "I'm getting to that. See, if they have plans, it means their plans can go awry. So far, both their attack on Dragon SWAT HQ and their kidnapping have been elaborate. My thought is that if we can manage to determine what they plan before they do it and throw a wrench in it, they might be screwed. They seem like the type of people who need every detail to go their way, which makes sense, given how they're trying to out-do dragons."

What he'd said had some merit, but it didn't seem like enough for Kristen. She told them all as much and Drew and Keith vowed to pour through the footage and the audio from Jim's wire to find any more clues they could.

She thanked them but realized she was still pissed. "First Dragon

SWAT and now Jim. Who else will these bastards hurt?" That only made her realize how worried she'd been about Stonequest and Heartsbane. She looked at Windlock, who obviously understood what she was thinking.

"Call us if you find anything else, even if you think it's nothing," the inspector said before the two dragons left to visit her injured friends.

When they reached the hospital, Windlock asked for the dragon surgeon who had operated on Heartsbane and Stonequest. Kristen knew the man probably had information about their injuries and even details about the bomb but she couldn't bring herself to care enough to talk to him.

No, that wasn't accurate. She did care but she trusted the other dragon enough to know that he would get all the information out of the doctor she would have been able to, plus more. Besides, she realized she had far more important reasons to come to the hospital.

She asked a nurse to show her to the Intensive Care Unit. At first, the woman gave her something of a run-around about how only family could visit but her Dragon SWAT badge plus the slightest flex of her aura were enough to convince the staff member that she should let the angry redhead through.

They proceeded to a room, where the nurse explained that the door would remain locked, no matter what Kristen did to her. It surprised her that the woman had obviously been aware of the dragon aura she had used on her but she simply nodded when told she was welcome to look through the window for as long as she wished.

Kristen hardly even heard her. Her gaze was locked on her friends inside the room.

Both were in beds with their upper bodies slightly elevated and were either asleep or unconscious. For some reason, that struck her especially hard. The last time she'd seen Stonequest, he'd been able to talk. For some reason, to see him resting humanized the dragon to her.

It was merely the whole effect, she decided.

She noted the bandages—Stonequest's on his chest, Heartsbane's practically everywhere. IVs were inserted into their arms and catheters protruded from under the sheets. Both were wired to a variety of sensors and resembled regular people who'd barely managed to survive a horrible car crash. She had never seen them—or any dragon, for that matter—look so frail. Their color was all wrong, and although she couldn't see their wounds, she couldn't help but think of them in the same bloody condition in which she'd last seen them. She told herself they were past the worst of their injuries. If they were in there resting, the doctors surely expected them to get better, but it was hard to see all the same.

It was all so frustrating. Since Kristen had become a cop, she'd felt her confidence—and later, dragon powers—had only grown. She had expected to reach a point where her people simply wouldn't get hurt because she would be able to protect them.

And now, Jim was missing. He'd given so much to her and she'd let him be snatched like a mouse taken by a hawk. Seeing Stonequest and Heartsbane only added to the feeling of not being able to help the people she cared about—her people.

That actually brought a tremulous smile to her mouth. *When did I start thinking about Stonequest this way?* She tried to pinpoint the moment and failed. *Or Heartsbane?* Now that was a funny thought. Her old sense of gallows humor—honed to a keen edge when working on Detroit SWAT—forced a laugh from her. The idea of Heartsbane's reaction to her pining for her on the other side of this window was simply too funny.

Although maybe it wasn't really that odd. After all, Stonequest had said that when she'd been falsely sent to prison, it was Heartsbane who had wanted to free her. Loyalty, friendship, or whatever it was that made people care so much about others that it physically ached was an interesting thing.

Kristen had always felt it. She'd gotten into fights for her brother

Brian too many times to count. With Detroit SWAT, she'd risked bullets for her team because the idea of them getting hurt was far worse than any pain a bullet could cause—and no one knew better than her how much the damn things could actually hurt.

She wondered if Stonequest felt this way about everyone on his team. Maybe that was why he'd been so adamant that she join Dragon SWAT. Perhaps he'd started to feel that ache of loyalty and desire to protect her, to make sure that if she was hurt, at least it would be on his watch so he could do something about it. She knew Stonequest treated his team like family and possibly more than family. He was committed to them, which made it hurt all the more that she had let him get shot.

It was possible that it was a dragon characteristic—this desire to protect others—but even the briefest thoughts about Drew made her realize that it wasn't.

He had treated her as someone he needed to protect and help, especially before she'd known she was a dragon. But really, even after she'd come into her powers, he'd continued to try to protect her. Why else had he worked so hard to make sure she could use her human form as successfully as she could?

Drew had recognized that he couldn't protect her in the same ways she could protect the rest of the team—he couldn't deflect bullets like she could, for one thing—so he'd found ways to make sure she could protect herself. It was almost the same thing her parents had done for. Her mom had said they'd taught her to stand so she could run, even if it meant away from them. Did Drew, Stonequest, and her mom all share that same desire?

In that moment, Kristen realized that she'd looked at dragon protectiveness the wrong way. She'd thought of it as the possessive nature of dragons, but everyone felt it, really. Whatever the differences between dragons and humans, there was a correlation between how much someone thought they could do to help another person and how much they felt that feeling and desire to care for another.

That's why her mom—and indeed, all parents—felt so strongly about helping their kids. There was no relationship with a more obvious power imbalance. Babies—even dragon babies like she had been—simply couldn't survive without the tender love and care of their parents. There was something to that. That was why teachers were willing to take bullets for kids and why firefighters were so willing to rush into a burning building.

Maybe that was why she had always felt such a desire to help others, even once she'd joined the world of dragons. Even in dragon society, she was powerful and could turn her skin to steel. She'd always felt a desire to protect those who needed it, and as her powers had grown, the number of people she'd felt obligated to protect grew as well.

She'd felt like she should have been able to do something to protect Heartsbane. Thanks to her training, she'd recognized that something was wrong with the bomb. If she'd only said something sooner, maybe her friend wouldn't be in this situation, fighting for her life in a way that she couldn't even begin to help.

All Kristen could do now was hope. That was all that was left. She was glad she had that at least, but it was hard to have nothing else. It had been a long time since she'd been reduced to that level.

The situation was also a reminder about how many people lived on nothing else. Refugees, cancer patients, and the survivors of wars they hadn't started all had that in common—hope. It was a desperate last wish, a desire to help those one couldn't otherwise help.

More than anything, she wanted to dismiss the feeling. Her nature drove her to do something, but there was nothing at the moment. Still, she couldn't stay there forever either. So, when Windlock texted her, she said goodbye to her friends, vowed to do her best to help them, and wished for them to get better.

CHAPTER THIRTEEN

Kristen had reached the main desk on the floor she was on when Windlock caught up to her.

"It's good you checked in on your people but we need to go."

"Did something change?" she asked as he followed her to the elevator.

"We have a destination," he said when they stopped to wait. "I'll tell you more once we have privacy."

"Good." She pushed the down arrow and her companion responded with a small smile before he pressed the up arrow instead.

She winced at her mistake. "Sorry. I guess I'm still used to going to the first floor of a building to leave. Even at Dragon SWAT HQ, I sometimes leave that way. And that has—had—a roof designed for takeoffs and landings."

An elevator door opened—and thankfully, indicated it was heading up—and the two stepped inside.

"There's no need to apologize," Windlock said kindly. "Your life experience with humans is one of the most fascinating and valuable things about you as far as I'm concerned. It changes one's perspective on being inside a building to think that the only way out is from the ground floor. It must be a constant state of dread for humans."

"I wouldn't say constant but as a cop, the ground floor is a place of concern. That's where people go in and out unless they're ninjas." Kristen chuckled.

"Or mages," he added. That stopped her laughter. It was a reminder that she had to be more creative in her assumptions. She had somehow been stuck on the idea that they were tracking humans, but she knew that at the very least, Constance had some mastery of magic. It wouldn't do to assume the perpetrators they were tracking would have the same limitations as a regular team of criminals.

The elevator dinged and they stepped onto the top floor of the hospital. Windlock located a stairwell labeled with a glowing, red, exit sign, as always. Kristen liked that at least they'd both looked for the same indicators to leave the hospital. Exit meant exit. It was merely that dragons went up and humans went down.

They took the stairs to the roof, stepped into the warm afternoon, and transformed into their dragon forms. It occurred to her that she felt like she was transforming out of her true form and into a kind of temporary one, while Windlock had to feel the opposite. He—as well as every other dragon on the earth besides her—possibly thought of his dragon body as his default body and the human shape as the false form.

It was also possible that dragons viewed both forms as equal parts of their identities. After all, a dragon's human face didn't change any more than their dragon features did. Both bodies were immutable. She realized it was possible that they actually did view both as equally valid.

The only thing all dragons seemed to have in common was that they viewed themselves as more powerful than humans. This was true in either form. As dragons, they were obviously god-like in the scope of their powers and in their human shape, they were as well, with even the weakest of them possessing superhuman speed and strength. Kristen realized she felt this way too, especially with her steel skin. Humans weren't less than her but they did need to be protected in a way that dragons didn't. Was that feeling the beginning of where the social inequality of the two species came from?

If it was, all that might be thrown out the window soon as humans actively tried to murder dragons.

They flew higher into the sky, above skyscrapers, and into the clouds. It was there, far away from anyone who could possibly be listening, that Windlock finally spoke.

"We have their target," he said but offered no further explanation at first.

Kristen craned her long dragon neck to look at the investigator. "Just like that?"

"There's a ball planned for tonight."

"Wonderful. Do you think the mages are throwing themselves a party?"

He chuckled. "Not at all. It's a ball for dragons."

"Oh." She was surprised as she hadn't heard anything about this. Normally, that kind of oversight didn't bother her but it surprised her all the same. "I guess you're more connected than me. I hadn't heard about that."

Windlock chuckled again. "I hadn't either. I assume it's simply part of being a cop. We never get invited to any of the fancy parties. Stonequest sometimes manages it as he's better at politics than most of us, but it's rare that I am included."

"Well, if cops aren't on the list, who do they invite?"

"This one's fairly exclusive, actually. It's only for the oldest and most powerful dragons in North America."

"So you're saying it's invitation-only?" she asked and recalled the last dragon party she attended when she'd brought her human team. They had probably amended the rules for their parties after that.

"Beyond that. Most dragons don't even know about it. They don't broadcast these things to most of dragon kind, let alone humanity."

"How did you find out about it then?" she asked, curious at how the rules of dragon society treated this particular dragon.

"Actually, I have you to thank. We followed up with Amythist Skyjewel after you saved her life at her mansion. She was grateful for the opportunity to talk and really does have a soft spot for mages.

Brockton buttered her up, so she let us know she had received an invitation."

"Are you saying she only received it today?" Kristen asked. It seemed very last-minute for the most powerful dragons on the continent.

"I asked Brockton to make a few calls. You might have noticed he's extremely good at getting humans and dragons to lower their defenses."

"It's something I noticed you don't try too hard to do."

"What's the human expression? Good cop, bad cop?"

"Yeah, I guess so." Kristen shifted her path to follow Windlock. He seemed to be heading somewhere downtown, but she couldn't even begin to guess where. It was still early so obviously, the ball wouldn't have started yet. "So, your guess is that our group of humans found out?"

"It's what makes the most sense," the investigator said. "I spoke to the surgeon as well as some healers who have worked on your team members. Stonequest should be up and walking perhaps tomorrow. Without a doubt, he won't be at full capacity yet, but we both know that won't stop him from getting into a fight. They think Heartsbane should be better the day after or maybe two more if they can manage to keep them there."

Kristen immediately relaxed. "I'm glad they'll be all right. When I saw them, they both looked so frail."

"It's always odd to see an injured dragon. We rely more on our powers than I think even we realize. But now that all the shrapnel has been removed, they should heal fine. Still, with wounds like that, it takes time and for a while, dragon powers are depleted. That is one reason why Emerald and Lumos cannot join us—they haven't recovered their full powers or strength. Aside from that, with the threat to dragon SWAT headquarters, they are needed there to at least back Timeflash up. Her strength isn't combat as much as it is clean-up."

"And you think our group of people know about their status?" she asked.

"I think it's virtually guaranteed. I wouldn't be surprised if they've pushed to get information from that hospital. It would be difficult to infiltrate, of course, but they've proven that they are well-connected and have resources to spare."

"But how would the people find out about the ball?"

"My guess is through mages. They probably have a good number working with them. Some surely know the mages who will work at the party. I think the existence of this ball is what spurred our killers to send the bomb when they did. In actual fact, dragon SWAT being injured instead of dead might make it an even better opportunity. More dead dragons raise alarms but injured ones—well, the powerful have a habit of looking the other way every chance they can."

"And you think these rich and powerful dragons will simply let us go in and frisk all their mages?"

"No, and we'll have to be more subtle than that, obviously."

"But how are we supposed to even make it past the door? I thought you said it was invitation-only?"

"It is, which is yet another reason why dragon SWAT cannot join us. The elite wouldn't stand for it, and even if they did, their presence would immediately raise warning flags. But I'm an investigator. There aren't many of us in the world, let alone this continent. They'll let me in if I arrive. It'd be bad manners not to. I might tell the Dragon Council next time I see them, which would be horribly embarrassing for anyone who cares about these things."

"What about me? I'm not an investigator."

"What kind of fancy party wouldn't allow people to bring a guest? If there are no new faces to show off how exclusive they are, what's the point in all this?"

"So you're saying I'll go as your plus one."

"Believe me, it'll be an improvement over my usual date to these affairs."

"Do you mean Brockton?"

"I have a feeling you'll look better in your formal gown than he does in his damn bright blue tuxedo."

Kristen snorted. "My formal gown? Yeah, obviously, I don't have one of those. How about we simply go in uniform? That might scare these assholes away and save the party."

"No, no. I'd much rather the assassins think they have an opportunity to kill us. If we don't catch them tonight, they'll merely bide their time and attack again, maybe after they've done a better job of eliminating SWAT. You'll need to dress the part."

"Well, like I said, I don't have anything that could be considered a formal gown. Hell, I don't think I have a bra that doesn't have sweat stains on it."

Windlock didn't seem surprised at that. "That's fine. It's also the reason why I felt I should ask. Your record doesn't indicate that you're the type anyway."

"Okay. Well then, why are we heading downtown? Isn't it too early to get to the ball? Plus, we're underdressed."

"We aren't going to the ball yet. First, I'll take you shopping."

CHAPTER FOURTEEN

The two dragons plunged past the skyscrapers and landed in front of a storefront in downtown Detroit. They transformed in a blink as people walked past and tried not to stare. Kristen marveled at how much faster she could transform than before. When she'd first begun to exercise her dragon powers, it had taken her almost a minute to change from dragon to human or visa-versa. Now, she could do it almost without thinking and in only a few seconds.

Windlock led her inside. She couldn't believe they had actually walked into Le Clothier. It held unrivaled status as the fanciest clothing store in Detroit. Real people didn't shop there, at least that was her impression. That wasn't to say humans didn't wear the clothes in this store, merely not regular humans.

Pop divas from Detroit's Motown past wore gowns from Le Clothier and hip-hop moguls wore their suits. Athletes from the Lions or the Tigers occasionally sported a tuxedo from Le Clothier—although often with sports commentators on the sports cable networks lambasting the person for wasting their money on such ostentation. Previously, she had thought it was too much—and honestly insulting—when a sports commentator went on a tirade about how an athlete wasted their money. After all, it was their money and simply because they were athletes didn't mean they didn't know how to spend it.

That's what she had thought until she saw the prices.

"Windlock…" Kristen hissed a horrified protest through her teeth. "This dress is thirty thousand dollars."

The dragon shrugged casually and looked down his nose at the garment. "Let's find something fresher. That was in style a year ago, which is why it's marked down. They'll sell it to a costume maker for a movie or something."

"Can't we—" She unfortunately managed to say nothing more as two tailors stepped forward and began to fawn over their new clients.

She might have called regular people shop-keepers or salesmen, but these two were so obviously committed to their craft that she couldn't help but think of them as couturiers.

"Darling, darling, darling," the woman said. "It has been too long." She spoke in slightly accented English—French perhaps, or maybe Italian? The word "cosmopolitan" popped into her head and stuck.

"You know I don't go in for this nonsense, Ell," Windlock replied brusquely.

"And yet here you are, Investigator, here you are!" The woman wore black pants, a black turtleneck with black buttons, and black heels that Kristen wouldn't have ever dared wear. Ell's hair was short, longer than a buzz but not by much. She was breathtakingly beautiful in an austere kind of way. The only color on her body came from the yellow measuring tape around her neck and a line of silvery pins with yellow balls on their end that were stuck into her shirt in a vertical line with the buttons.

The man was almost the complete opposite. His long hair was braided in what Kristen thought as a very feminine style, yet she had to admit it looked good on him. Instead of black, he wore a purple suit encrusted with sequins. His shoes looked like they cost more than her car. "Please, my love, let me take your overshirt," he said and extended a hand toward her.

"All I have beneath it is an undershirt and bra," she protested.

"Pay no attention to Vee," Ell proclaimed. "He is as harmless as a chai latte and as accommodating as a feather bed. We only wish to take your measurements. Come, darling, come!" She clapped and apparently expected her to strip without embarrassment.

"It's only—" She glanced hastily at Windlock. He had to understand that they'd been working. It wasn't like she was exactly fresh.

He winked at her and removed his coat and shirt. Although his undershirt was worn, neither Ell nor Vee seemed to care or even notice.

Kristen forced herself to relax. Their job was to make clothes for the fabulously rich so they'd probably seen all kinds of weird stuff.

Finally, she removed her shirt to reveal her slightly stained white tanktop. Neither of the hovering attendants even glanced at it. The woman simply measured her arm length, waist, bust, hips, inseam, plus a hundred more measurements she hadn't even known existed. She'd never been much of a dress girl and more of an athletic pants and sports bra kind of person.

"So tell me, my darlings, tell me. What is the event and more importantly, when are you expected to look as fabulous as we will make you look?" Ell asked.

"I hate to do this to you, Ell, but we're crashing an invitation-only dragon's ball tonight."

"Tonight? Ha!" Vee blurted.

"Hush, you little bitch, hush!" the woman chided. "That is more time than the investigator normally gives us. This won't be easy, though, not at all. That ball is hush-hush, you know. Only those in the know actually know anything, darling."

"Will that be a problem?" Kristen asked.

"More like a challenge," Vee replied. He also spoke in slightly accented English, but his was even harder to place than Ell's. Her choices ranged between Hungarian and Vietnamese, so she obviously didn't have a clue where he was from.

"It only means that we cannot make you something from scratch, my darling, and for that, I am truly sorry." The woman sounded heart-broken. "You will have to select one of these rags and we will attempt to make it worthy of your exquisite frame. Vee!" she snapped.

"Yes, my love?"

"Why did no one tell me that the Steel Dragon had such perfect breasts?"

Vee scoffed and continued to measure Windlock.

"How did you know about this ball?" Kristen asked.

"Windlock, your friend insults us," Ell whined.

"Are we under investigation?" Vee asked.

"Half the dragons at the party will wear Le Clothier," the investigator explained. "The other half will wish they did. Ell always knows everything there is to know about parties."

Vee showed him two suit jackets and he nodded at one.

Kristen nodded and let herself be measured and fawned over for a while. The two treated them like royalty. Ell brought her dress after dress, nodded and clucked in approval when she liked one and cursed when she was less than approving, regardless of how polite she tried to be.

"Rags, darling, all rags. Let me find you something more to your taste. I swear much of this should be burned but surely we can find something to satisfy your absolutely exquisite tastes."

Fortunately, it seemed the duo had a natural ability to know what she liked. She didn't know what she wanted other than the practical aspects. It had to cover her legs so she could strap a pistol to her thigh, and she wanted it fairly open on the top so she could move quickly if needed. Ell seemed to understand even better than she did herself. Each time Kristen said yes and no, the dresses began to follow a certain style that covered her legs, while most revealed her shoulders as well.

When the woman brought out one with a bodice encrusted with gorgeous beadwork, Kristen couldn't help but grin at it.

"Oh, thank God. Thank God, darling. I'm so happy we've found something that might actually suit you!" Ell gushed.

Kristen nodded. It was a beautiful gown, the color of Lake Superior, rich and blue and deep. The glass or jewels—or diamonds, although she didn't know—worked into the front made her think of ice floating in cold water. She wasn't really one for fashion but even she could see that the color would look great on her and contrast perfectly with her red hair.

Once she'd made her selection, Windlock chose a tuxedo with a vest and bowtie that matched the color of her dress.

"If she is your plus one, it will do to match," Vee said and nodded in approval.

"How do you two know so much about this party?" Kristen asked, glanced at Windlock, and flexed her aura to convey caution.

Vee noticed the glance between them "We would never say a thing, Lady Steel," he said—his obsequious veneer cracked to reveal terror hidden beneath. In an instant, though, his usual expression was restored and he continued to work. She didn't want to push it as he seemed fine again, but she found she no longer enjoyed the treatment they were given. It was almost a relief when Ell brought them each a glass of champagne, apologized, and vanished into the back room once she told them they'd need no more than an hour to get everything done.

"You can trust them," the investigator said after a moment and once they were alone. "They only mentioned the party because I mentioned it first. They're very good about that."

"How can you be sure?"

He shrugged. "You saw how Vee reacted. They know their place."

"Their place?" Kristen demanded and let her aura get a little away from her.

"They know we're dragons. I've been here before and it's not like people don't know your face, Lady Steel, especially people who know dragon culture."

"And that's enough to what? Keep them tame?"

Windlock frowned, apparently bewildered. "It's natural for someone to act that way around a being that can eat them or incinerate their entire livelihood."

"But that's horrible."

"They live very well because they know how to keep dragon business to themselves. I assure you, they're not a leak. If they were, dragon parties would be crashed more often all the time. They don't even tell other dragons about these parties. They know if they did, they'd lose their place and the trust they've earned. I don't see how these human assassins could have used them."

"Okay, I'll give you that, but don't you think it's problematic that you trust them only because they're afraid of being eaten?"

"That's not why I trust them. They are very well connected and understand dragon culture extremely well."

"And their place at the bottom of it."

Windlock smiled. Kristen thought she'd pissed him off but once again, he only seemed amused. "Here I was, thinking that of all people, Vee and Ell had it good, but I'm learning otherwise."

"How could you think living in fear is good?"

He indicated the area behind the counter with a quick glance and she understood his point. She'd let herself grow too loud.

"I always assumed all humans lived in fear. I honestly thought that was the natural condition, given how powerful dragons are and our less than illustrious past with mankind," he continued quietly.

"It's a little different to be concerned about getting caught up in the destruction of a dragon duel and having to face them every day, keep their secrets, and hope everyone likes the clothes they make."

"I see that now," Windlock said. Kristen could almost see him trying to internalize all this. It was yet another reminder of how different she was from the rest of dragon kind. She'd thought he would understand it as he worked with a mage and spent his time hunting dragons, but his job really was to protect dragons, not people. It seemed he'd given less thought to how people lived than Stonequest had.

Still, it was something that he at least tried to do, she decided and reminded herself humans were also quick to assume things and slow to accept change. She thought of Jim and his belief that all dragons were nothing but rabid killers until she'd proved otherwise by her actions. His change had come about because they worked together and he'd faced it every day. Perhaps he might never have adjusted his perceptions if not for that. The investigator might not wholly subscribe to what she believed was correct, but he was better than all the dragons they would meet tonight—the dragons whose lives they were supposed to save.

For a moment, she felt resentful that all this effort was simply to protect those who seemed to epitomize everything that was wrong with dragon-human relations. Practicality won through, however. They couldn't change if they were dead, for one thing, and she wasn't like Constance, who was willing to sacrifice lives—dragons, humans, and mages—to pursue her agenda.

Kristen forgot about that when Vee came out and gave Windlock a leather folder.

He nodded in thanks, accepted the folder, and opened it.

"Jesus, Windlock, that's a bill for over a hundred thousand dollars!"

"Hmm? Oh yeah, I guess it is." He retrieved a credit card, slipped it into the folder, and put it on the counter before he sat.

"I can't afford that. It's more than I make in a year."

"Don't worry about it. You're not expected to spend your own money on work. I have an expense account for such things. I won't send you a bill or anything." He chuckled and she had the feeling that maybe Brockton had once had a similar reaction.

"It might as well be a zillion dollars. I think that's more money than I've spent on all my clothes in my entire life."

"Dragons spend that much all the time."

"I was raised human, remember? Let me choose a different dress. The one I saw in the beginning was maybe a quarter of that price."

Windlock waved her protest aside. "That bill was for your dress and my suit. Yours was only about seventy K."

"Seventy thousand dollars is still way too much money."

"Not for the expense account. Besides, if you choose a different one, you'll make Ell feel bad. She's always proud to select something nice for a client."

"I only...it's so much money."

"You're really making a big deal over nothing," Windlock said firmly. "To put it in perspective, a dragon duel can cost millions in damages. Hell, seventy thousand isn't even a nice car. Plus, credit cards have a funny way of making numbers look big. That dress wouldn't cost more than a hundred gold coins or a small chest of silver."

"Do you even hear yourself? Gold coins? A chest of silver?" Kristen was flabbergasted.

"That's where dragons have historically held their wealth. We only use banks and credit and all that to make it more convenient for people. You saw Icebreeze's mansion. You know he could afford a dress like that."

"Yeah, I guess so. And I suppose it's good that at least Vee and Ell make good money."

"Correct. Trickle-down economics, right?"

Kristen didn't think she'd ever heard a better argument against trickle-down economics than that. How was wealth supposed to trickle down when one group of people could afford clothes that cost tens of thousands of dollars while people only a few blocks away went hungry? While it worked for Vee and Ell, they both obviously knew that if they pissed off the wealthy dragons—hell, if they poked them with a pin—their livelihood would be over.

"It's merely shocking to see you spend that much and not even flinch."

"It's only money," Windlock replied.

She shook her head and remained silent, although the words echoed in her head. Only money. It was only money. Maybe to dragons, those sums were only money, merely another chest of silver, another few gems, or pieces of gold, but to humans, that was more than most people spent on the down payment on their house. It was a college education and more than many would ever have in their bank accounts—even more than most people's retirement fund. For a dragon, it was an outfit for one night.

No, not only the dragons, she reminded herself. There was the human elite, that small but powerful echelon of society that thought nothing about spending money like it was water. They also knew that so many people lived on the breadline or were actually starving. Were they any better than the dragons who didn't have the same moral obligations to their own kind?

After a few more minutes, the duo emerged with the clothing. The two dragons retreated to dressing rooms, accompanied by Ell and Vee. Ell helped her dress, then wound a necklace around her neck that sparkled like the stars.

"Don't lose that one, darling," the woman said. "but with that dress and your breasts…" She sucked at her teeth and smiled.

Kristen had to admit that the fashion designer had done an amazing job. The dress fit her better than anything she'd worn before. The beadwork was amazing and the necklace complimented it perfectly. Between all the sparkles, she could understand why the attendant continued to compliment her chest. The fabric hung perfectly off her hips and yet didn't cling to her legs, which allowed her to easily hide a gun.

"Please tell me you like it, darling. It would be criminal to think I've dressed you in something you hate. We'd burn it, of course—burn it to ash—and get you something better."

"I love it." She at least felt honest saying that.

"Excellent, darling, excellent. Now, let us show Windlock. I would like to see his jaw hit the floor if you don't mind."

Kristen nodded and followed Ell out into the main room. The investigator looked great in his tuxedo, but everyone understood that she was the most beautiful person in Le Clothier, perhaps the most beautiful to come through in a while.

The dragon whistled appreciatively. "Do me a favor?" he asked.

"What?" Her tone was a little sharp as she hadn't appreciated the whistle.

"Turn to steel."

That was rather unusual for a catcall, so she obliged him.

The combined sharp intake of breath from all those present made her look in the mirror. Her steel skin gleamed like chrome while the gems on her neck and beads on her dress seemed more vital and vibrant. The hue of her skin reflected the blue of the dress and she smiled. She really did look like something out of this world and her transformed flesh tone was beyond striking. There was no disputing the fact that she'd make quite an impression. Still, there was one tweak necessary.

Kristen shook her head and changed her hair from steel to its natural red color.

Windlock smiled. Vee and Ell gasped audibly.

"Perfection, darling. Absolute perfection," the woman gushed.

"A goddess. We have dressed a goddess!" Vee added triumphantly.

"Thank you. I knew we could count on Le Clothier," Windlock said.

"Always, darling, always. Now, we have an appointment and you know how it is. We can't reveal these things too early. Clients don't like their dresses to be seen before they should be seen. That's simply how it is."

"No problem. Steel, do you want to wear that to the station and watch your human friends' faces when they see what real clothes look like? We need to go to Detroit SWAT next."

"God, no!" Kristen blanched at the thought of it. "I guess this is fine at a party…uh, I mean obviously, it's more than fine." Almost seventy thousand dollars more than fine, she thought but she didn't say it. "But I can't wear this to the station. The force would never let me live it down. I'll change into my uniform, thanks."

"But of course," Ell said and led her to the dressing room. "Although there is nothing wrong with turning heads," she added as she helped her out of the gown and gave her the Dragon SWAT uniform.

"No, I guess not, but my business is cracking heads, not turning them."

"And we're thankful to have you, Lady Steel," the woman said and her accent slipped into something any Detroiter would have been proud of. "It's an honor to have helped you get ready for whatever you plan to do. I and Vincent are big supporters. We're proud that you are from our city. I can't wait to tell everyone about all this."

"It's confidential," Kristen reminded her, shocked that the woman had maintained such a complete persona for so long that even Windlock appeared to have been fooled.

"I know, I know. By can't wait, I mean we won't tell a soul for years. But if you can change things, of course, maybe we won't have to wait for decades."

Kristen thanked Ell once more, then said farewell in the lobby. She looked at Vee—Vincent?—and wondered if he also played a role for the benefit of his dragon patrons. She felt a surge of confidence in the two tailors who were Le Clothier. If they could deceive so many dragons, maybe people really did have a chance at equality.

She also felt that the chances of Constance ferreting any information from them were slim. How frightening was a mage when one was expected to dress fire-breathing dragons?

CHAPTER FIFTEEN

The two dragons flew to the Detroit SWAT building to meet with the human contingent of their team. Hernandez noticed the dress bag right away but before she could demand that Kristen show it to her, Windlock asked about the status of the search.

Keith threw his hands up in frustration. "It isn't going great. The first time we see the guy who hurt Jim is in that video we showed you guys. We managed to track Constance from when she first entered the stadium, but it doesn't give us any clues."

Drew scowled with visible displeasure. "She enters with a ticket and goes directly to where Jim is waiting."

"There's no way they let the entire thing happen unmonitored, though," Butters said.

"Agreed," Beanpole added and for once, his mild manner had given way to irritation.

The two of them—Butters and Beanpole—seemed particularly annoyed, but she understood why. After all, these two were their sniper and lookout. It was their job to maintain perimeters and keep their people safe and they'd failed. They appeared to take that failure personally and no one could blame them for that.

"My guess is they had at least another five people scattered around the arena, maybe ten," Drew said. "I don't see how else they could have watched all the areas. Obviously, they hid in Tigers and Bluejays gear—in plain sight as it were."

"What about the audio from Officer Washington?" Windlock inquired. "Did you find any clues there?"

Again, Drew shook his head. "Nothing we don't already know. Constance must have known they were being watched—or assumed it, anyway—and everything she said was fairly nebulous. The only thing we're sure of is that they want you, Kristen."

She sighed. That meant Jim being in danger was all her fault.

"And what did you two turn up?" Hernandez asked and stared pointedly at the dress bag.

"There'll be a dragon ball tonight—extremely exclusive and by invitation only—on the roof of the Penobscot Building."

"Penobscot?" Butters asked. "It doesn't have a single roof—more like twenty."

"And the dragons will have every single one of them done up fancier than the last," Brockton exclaimed as he entered the room. "Penobscot? This will be great. Nothing gets the dragons going like Penobscot. Did you know the lobby was designed by dragons, too? Oh, and that roof! The very top will be the fanciest, of course, but the last party we went to there had different decadence at every level. My favorite was the—"

"Pixie brothel, yes. You say this any time we so much as fly past the building," Windlock said to silence him.

"How can they have a party there?" Drew asked. "That's an office building. People work there."

"Not tonight they won't. The building will be cleared long before the party begins. That's protocol, anyway, but given the recent string of dragon murders, I'm sure dragon security won't be lax. The only humans present will be the servants of the dragons attending and the catering staff." The investigator peered around the room and made his meaning clear despite not having to say anything.

"Man, this is bullshit!" Keith whined before anyone else could speak. "The last time we went to a dragon party, we went as guests. Now, we have to pretend to be butlers?"

"We've done worse things in the line of duty." Drew glared at his teammate as if willing him to shut up.

"This party will be a level above the one you attended, I can assure you of that. The last one was thrown in Kristen's honor—almost a nod to humans—but this one will be the opposite. The only reason we'll go is because of my rank, and it's not like I was actually invited."

"Do we have to be waiters, though?" Keith complained. "Is this because I didn't wear a tux last time?"

"I think humans will be better at discerning human villainy than I will, and I think that would work best if you are all undercover."

"Yeah, but—"

"That's enough, Keith," Drew said sharply.

The Rookie frowned but said nothing further.

"Does anyone else have problems with doing our job and saving lives?" the team leader asked.

Everyone shook their head except for Hernandez, who grinned. "I can't really tell what's in that bag of yours Kristen, but I see sparkles and have a feeling they're not for Windlock. I wouldn't miss seeing the Steel Dragon in a fancy gown for the world."

"Good. It's settled then. Until this evening, I want to keep looking for clues to help us to find Jim," Drew said. "We have no leads and…" He didn't have to finish. They all felt the weight of the reality that they'd let one of their own be taken. The team had been outsmarted, and the person most willing to sacrifice himself and risk his life was the one in danger because of it. It wasn't something pleasant to think about.

"We haven't turned up any leads either, but I'm reasonably certain that if these people attack tonight, we can use them to lead us to Officer Washington," Windlock said.

The team leader nodded. "It makes more sense than anything else we have, but what if they don't attack tonight?"

"Honestly?" the dragon responded. "I hope they don't. I'd prefer this to be a false alarm. This event is…well, calling it exclusive doesn't even begin to cover it. If these human assassins—or terrorists or whatever they are—decide to attack there, it means they're far more confident than I had previously assumed. I'd prefer this to be a red heron, but I don't think it is."

"Red herring," Keith corrected without thought.

Drew ignored the Rookie. "Okay, but why this event in particular?"

"Nothing else is scheduled in the next twenty-four hours," the investigator explained. "We checked on Stonequest and Heartsbane. They should be recovered soon, and our original assumption was that they attacked SWAT to give them an opportunity to strike at something larger. This is larger."

"What Windlock's trying to say is that occasions like these are often the biggest events of the year, let alone the week. This will probably be the most spectacular party to happen in North America this month," Brockton interjected.

"And you weren't invited?" Hernandez asked.

The mage laughed before Windlock could answer. "Good ol' Windlock is never invited to the nice ones. Believe it or not, dragons don't like an investigator snooping around their fancy parties, which are supposed to be private affairs. They honestly have all kinds of morally gray shit going on. The last thing they want is Windlock writing them up."

"Right, pixie brothels," Hernandez said and earned a grin from him.

"Like you would not believe." He winked at her.

"They'll have to let me in, though," the investigator said, "and I'll be able to pull some strings to get all of you undercover. After all, that's the point of my role. My bosses will be there, and they all know they can trust me."

"What he's trying to say is that they all know that despite him being a total wet blanket and complete buzzkill, he's committed to his job. They'll let him in to protect their own scaly hides," Brockton said.

"Larry, you do realize Kristen will be my plus one for this, correct?" Windlock asked.

All the pep and enthusiasm drained out of his assistant's face. "What? You mean I have to play penguin with the rest of these regular people?"

"I'm afraid so."

"This is a goddamn tragedy. It's offensive to my corpus. How am I supposed to simply serve trays of food at a party like this? You can't do this to me, Windlock! We never go to the nice parties."

"This is our only choice. And we can't exactly expect a world-famous dragon to go undercover while my mage bumps elbows with the rich. Maybe I can get you on the entertainment team."

"Oh, come on. That's even worse!" Brockton whined.

Windlock shot him a warning look and he subsided resentfully.

"If there's nothing else, meet on the first floor of the Penobscot in an hour. You need to wear all black, even down to your socks. Tame your hair, and make sure you look disinterested at all times."

"Will we meet there too?" Kristen asked.

"There will no doubt be a landing strip for us on the roof, but you mentioned the importance of first floors to human security, plus—"

"Plus, there is nothing like the entryway to that building for a dragon party," Brockton interjected. "You won't want to miss it. I swear."

Kristen nodded and hoped the dragon was right. It felt horrible to leave Jim hanging, but their best lead was the people who took him. And it made sense that they would attempt an attack. This party was the perfect target for the anti-dragon group of terrorists. If they were emboldened enough to strike at dragon SWAT HQ, they were probably ready for an assault of this magnitude.

The worst thing, though—the absolute worst—was that she didn't think they'd catch them by surprise. Constance had known who Jim was and everything about him. They'd intended to trick the assassin and her clandestine group but had failed. What if the dragon-killer expected them to be at the party? What if she'd finally run out of patience with Kristen and her growing allegiance to dragons—or if not allegiance, then at least commitment to the idea that dragons shouldn't be killed any more than humans should?

What if this whole thing was a trap not only for dragon high society but for her too? And if that was the case, what role did Jim have in this? Why take him at all?

She was wholeheartedly afraid of learning the answer to that question.

CHAPTER SIXTEEN

Jim awoke terrified. He was on a piece of canvas stretched taut between springs—a cot, he realized. A fucking cot. He was back in the Marines, about to be incinerated by dragon fire for doing nothing other than following orders.

He opened his eyes and sat quickly, ready to run and hide in the jungle. Somehow, he needed to live long enough to fight these monsters who could kill humans as easily as he could crush bugs.

His mind seemed to slowly click into motion, and he realized it had merely been a horrible fucking dream. The imagined jungle was, in fact, a pleasantly decorated room with a bed, a small desk, a curtain that could be opened with a plastic stick, and a TV. The absence of a kitchen and living room told him he was in a hotel and a little confused, he moved his hand to confirm the frame of the cot. That hadn't been a dream, then.

But if he was in a hotel, why wasn't he in the bed?

He looked around the room and his gaze settled on his answer. Constance Vigil smiled at him and the events of the last few hours came back in a flood.

"You were out hard," Constance said and passed him a glass of water and a small packet. "I know how shitty it can be to wake up from a jolt of electricity like that and you needed more than one."

"I didn't need shit," Jim retorted but speaking made his head pound and he winced. He took the water and checked that the Tylenol came in a sealed package, so he doubted it was poisoned or drugs. The water could have something in it, but he'd been unconscious while this woman apparently sat and watched him. They could have put anything they wanted in his system—hell, they could have killed him—and they hadn't. He tore the packet open, swallowed the two pills inside, and washed them down with the water.

"More," he demanded as a test to see exactly what the power play was and how he fitted into it. Was he being recruited in a bizarre way? Was he a prisoner? Constance's reaction would tell him everything he needed to know.

"You can get it yourself. This room is yours so help yourself from the sink."

That response wasn't exactly what he had expected—which really was one of two options. If she fetched it herself, it would indicate that she still wanted him to join and she'd pretend the shock stick had been some kind of initiation or personal protection or whatever. Or she'd deny him, thus cementing her position of power. To allow him to get it himself seemed an odd middle ground, he thought until he pushed to his feet.

His temple pounded a few times when he stood and at first, he didn't notice the weight around his ankle. As the sensation receded, he looked down, fully expecting to see he was shackled to the wall and that the woman was playing some kind of mind game. He did not expect to see a bomb.

But that, unfortunately, was the only thing it could be.

"Explosives?" Jim asked and looked from the metal anklet to Constance.

She nodded, her expression almost apologetic like a teacher who had wanted him to do better on a test but had to give the grade he'd earned. He didn't like the look or what it might suggest.

"This isn't the way I expected to be treated," he said and did his best to maintain a cool exterior despite the way his heart thudded. This was no worse than speaking in front of a crowd, he told himself —if he could forget the bomb, that is. He merely had to stay calm and not let her see how freaked he was. Unfortunately, if he fucked up, he'd blow up. Carefully, he sat again. Despite his mouth being bone-dry, he'd forgotten about wanting to get a cup of water.

"I do apologize, really." The woman smiled but it didn't reach her eyes. "I don't want to have to hurt a human."

"But you'll shoot a dragon cop?" He tried to goad her although he wasn't sure it was the best idea or what he'd gain from it.

"Dragons aren't people. I know they might sometimes act like they are when it's convenient, but they're not. They're inhuman—monsters. To call them fallen gods would be a kindness."

"No one knows more about the horrors they can do to people than me," Jim protested.

"I know." Constance held her hands up as if to emphasize her claim that there was nothing she could do. "Believe me, I know, and I also know what you've faced. We've read your reports and know what you saw. We know about your PTSD and given what you've been through, it's all the more impressive that you work in Detroit, a city with more than a few dragons."

"There are dragons everywhere," the Wonderkid responded and clenched his teeth to evidence restraint. "They build their mansions even in the most rural places. There's no escaping them and that's why we have to stand against them. It's why I wanted to join you."

"I must say I agree. And I hope that after tonight, you'll still be serious about joining our merry band of revolutionaries."

"What do you mean, after tonight?" Jim demanded.

"You're insurance, for now," Constance explained, her tone placating. "I don't want to hurt a human but currently, the ends justify the means. We all knew people would die in this revolution—potentially millions. It's not something pleasant to think about but it's better than the millions who have already died at the whim of dragons and the billions who live as unknowing slaves as we speak."

"So the dragons make slaves but you make explosive insurance policies?" He knew he should try to walk the anti-dragon line but it was damn hard to pretend you wanted to join a terrorist when they had secured a bomb to your leg.

"Only because I think you're our best means to stop Kristen Hall from interfering with us. We believe she's the only one—dragon or human—who might actually stop us, but we now have you to make sure that doesn't happen. If she screws our plans up, you lose a—" She glanced at the bomb, then at his face as if to measure his height. "Well, certainly a leg but maybe more."

"Great. So I'm simply supposed to sit tight and wait for you to kill the only dragon we can trust?"

"I know. Believe me, I do." The woman shrugged and retrieved the remote control. "But that's simply the way it is." She clicked the TV on. "We paid for all the cable packages so there are movies you can watch and we also ordered you room service. I didn't know what you liked so we got you a little of everything. There should be more than enough left for breakfast too."

"Oh, wow. Thanks so much." Jim knew he sounded caustically sarcastic, but he couldn't help himself. "You'll use my fucking leg as collateral to make Kristen do what you want but I'm supposed to be grateful because you ordered me a pizza and a burger? You're fucking crazy!"

"You're not supposed to do anything but stay where you are. We took the cord from the phone and your cellphone, obviously. The bomb is set to a proximity trigger. If you step outside the room, it blows up. If anyone else but me comes inside, it blows up. And, of course, if you try to take it off, you'll lose your hands in addition to your leg."

"This is not how you make allies," the Wonderkid said and tried to sound reasonable, but it was patently obvious that he was angry.

"I understand your frustration," Constance intoned politely. "And I realize that this probably has a very negative impact on our personal relationship, but we simply can't allow Kristen to intervene. If every-thing goes as planned, you'll go home tomorrow knowing you helped to make humans a little more free."

"And how do you know I won't try to blow you up like you did me?" he snapped. He regretted the words but nothing would affect her decision so he had nothing to lose, after all.

"If our plans come to fruition, a pissed-off cop will be the least of our problems. By the way, if I were you, I'd pay attention to the news channels, especially in a few hours and after dark. We've worked for years and we're finally on the verge of something great. You could very well go down in the history books as an instrumental part of what we'll accomplish tonight. I know you're frustrated, but once you see our plans, you'll realize how much good we're doing. Monsters will face the music tonight. For the first time in centuries, dragons will taste fear."

"Goddammit, I want to stand up to dragons too!" Jim roared when he finally lost any remnant of control he'd clung on to. "I want equality for humans. I want equal rights and real freedom. But killing dragons is not the way to do this! Killing dragons won't help humanity. It'll only piss them off and make them fly above our cities and incinerate people."

"This is the only thing the dragons have left us—the only way forward. We've groveled at their feet for so long, the only way to show humanity there's another way is to stand against them. Yes, people will get hurt and those monsters will kill innocents, but that is necessary if we are to reveal their true nature."

"You're talking about war!"

"Exactly!" Constance grinned wickedly, took a breath, and calmed herself. "That's exactly what I'm talking about. The only way to inspire the masses to fight is to let them see what dragons are truly capable of. We won't kill innocents and you're the only human life directly under threat tonight—well, the only human who hasn't sworn fealty to a dragon, anyway. All we'll do is show the dragons they're not invulnerable and that people—real human people—are strong enough to fight them. Once we do that, the dragons will start this war themselves."

"As soon as they start a war, it's over!" he yelled.

"No, it's not. I would have agreed with you a decade or even a year ago, but not anymore. A war will let my people come out into the open and defend humanity. We'll show the world what our weapons are capable of."

"But you'll lose."

The woman shook her head, although her eyes revealed that she knew it was a possibility. "We won't because we're not a monolithic group with a central structure. We're grassroots so you can't tear us all out."

Jim scowled. "Grassroots still burn."

"Even if we do, humanity will see we have weapons capable of hurting dragons. When that knowledge is out there, the paradigm will have shifted. Once people see dragons as a threat—one we can stand against—they'll respond to the branches of our organization that are focused on outreach. We'll give people the tools they need to protect themselves."

"You're not a community activist. This is murder. What's your plan —to arm every high-schooler with a gun to fight the dragons?"

"Our high-schoolers already are shooting each other," she retorted but remained cool. She'd had this argument before. "We live in a country dying from anxiety because the powerful have their boot— their claw, rather—at our throats. We're desperate people. If we gave people— even high-schoolers—the tools to stand against the powerful, we'd do it. I'd rather live in a world where the angry can turn their frustration against the monsters who truly enslave us than each other."

"Arming kids cannot change everything," Jim said and tried to make his tone reasonable.

"It might make the dragons fear us but no, it won't change the world. Nothing will change the world besides letting them all see—in high definition and on their own social media—what dragons are capable of. Once people see they are monsters, they'll come to us."

"You're crazy. People can't stand against them!"

"No. People can't. You're right. But militaries? Cops? If we arm our government and every other government that doesn't want to live in the palm of the dragons with the tools to say no, what happens then?"

He shook his head. "I've seen dragons fight."

"So have I."

"No. You've fought dragons. That's different. You're strong enough because of your magic, your team, and your beliefs. You're a person who can kill a dragon. But I've seen dragons who kill people by the dozen. If you do whatever you have planned to do tonight, it's their blood on your hands. All you'll do is start a third failed rebellion."

"What we'll do is start the first revolution," she countered and stood from the bed. "The last two rebellions failed because people tried to have others solve their problems. Yes, mages made dwarves and pixies to fight the dragons, but that was a mistake. We made a weapon that operated out of our hands and our control. This is different. A human revolution will have a chance—a real chance. We'll be the spark that will ignite the war for our freedom."

Jim sighed. "All you'll achieve is to ignite the dragon flame that burns everything."

"I hope, for both our sakes, you're wrong about that." She stepped out of the room and locked the door behind her.

The Wonderkid clenched his fists and dragged in a deep breath to calm himself before he stood to get the cup of water. He sat wearily on the bed and looked at the TV. Even though he knew nothing could happen yet, he began to flip through news channels. For the moment, he had nothing else he could do.

CHAPTER SEVENTEEN

Kristen hadn't been to the Penobscot building since she was a little girl, so genuine astonishment filled her face when she walked into the entryway to the almost hundred-year-old skyscraper.

Outside, it looked like business as usual. Security manned the door —mages as well as regular muscle—but that wasn't particularly unusual for an evening in downtown Detroit. Drew and the team were able to get in through the back once they'd provided the required credentials arranged by Windlock so Kristen felt confident when she entered the building.

The Detroit SWAT contingent had access, and security had been alerted to a possible incursion. They might be walking into another trap but this time, their eyes were wide open. Even the security force had been heavily vetted. If any were undercover agents working for Constance, they'd done so convincingly for decades and if that was the case, even the investigator had to admit they were all screwed.

She therefore felt at ease when she entered the building. If anything happened, they were alert and prepared to deal with it. This let her relax enough to enjoy what was most likely a once in a lifetime experience. The building had been decorated with sparkling ethereal garlands that rained gold and red sparks that evaporated moments before they reached their heads. Pixies flitted overhead to provide a decadent light show that somehow only enhanced the ornate entrance.

The building itself was elaborate. Within moments, they entered a massive and gaudy hall, the walls and ceiling decked in gold, red, and white tile that sparkled under the lights of the pixies. She had seen photos of this room and vaguely recalled visiting as a kid but being there now, it was obvious that it had always been a dragon stronghold. It seemed perfectly logical that an incredibly elaborate evening in honor of the continent's most powerful dragons would be hosted there.

The colors were garish and rich to represent the powers of gold and blood and the room was spacious and commanding. It dwarfed a human body but was strangely comforting to a being who could transform into a dragon at any moment.

Most of all, the painting at the end of the room served as a reminder of who had funded the structure and what their goals were. A massive map of the mitten-shape that made up most of Michigan was rendered in gold. A glowing figure was depicted at the center—a dragon flexing either their aura or perhaps a special ability only available to the most privileged of their kind. Connected to this were multiple ancient and esoteric symbols. At the bottom of the mural, people labored to harvest grain and pour molten metal. It was a depiction that could be read as a call to action, as a critique of the decadence that balanced on the backs of the hard work of others, but also as a hidden message. Dragons ruled there and no one should forget it.

Kristen thought it was the perfect painting for the entrance to a decadent dragon party for the most powerful beings on the continent. If she was being honest, though, it was also a good place to start a rebellion.

If there was any doubt in her mind that tonight would prove decisive to either start or prevent a war between human and dragon kind, it was washed away by that sight.

They entered an elevator and rode to the top floor of the building.

"What did you think?" Windlock asked.

"I was impressed with the care they took to make sure we weren't interrupted this evening," Kristen said. They'd talked about trying to downplay any investigation they were doing. He'd had to alert a few people to their presence so he could arrange for Drew and the team to work at the event but other than that, they planned to keep their real purpose very confidential. Their cover story was that they'd met on their last investigation, bumped into each other again, and Windlock had invited her out in an effort to impress her.

He nodded, obviously in agreement with her answer. "They do an excellent job to keep out those who don't need to be here," he said.

The truth of that was proven when they stepped from the elevator and were stopped by two more guards.

Thus far, the security members had been human, some magic and others not. These two were dragons in human form.

"Invitations?" one of them asked.

"I am Kristen Hall, Lady Steel, known as the Steel Dragon of Detroit," she said politely.

The guard obviously recognized her. She'd learned to be able to tell when someone was either a fan, the opposite, or simply a regular person who'd never heard of her, and this dragon was obviously the second.

"Sorry, ma'am. Entrance is by invitation only." His tone made his disapproval clear.

Kristen nodded. They'd talked about this beforehand too and she agreed that this was good. It meant they wouldn't let random people in without proper authorization, which was something she most assuredly did not have.

Windlock did, however. He flashed his badge at the other dragon, who nodded and stepped aside to let them pass. "Welcome, Investigator Windlock. Please try not to disturb the ambiance of the evening as you have in times past."

"How could I possibly?" he said and gestured to the party around them.

She immediately decided it was ultra-elaborate. The rooftop on which they now stood was canopied by more sparkling pixie magic.

Beautiful and sometimes sensual portraits of famous dragons floated around them. Elaborate tapestries depicted decisive moments in dragon history, often scenes from the first and second human rebellions. Ice sculptures shaped beasts of all kinds, men grappling with each other, and nude women. A massive table—utterly gorgeous and impossibly difficult to get there without magic—was covered with food the likes of which she had only ever heard of.

Bread and rolls had been baked to resemble gems, treasure chests, and weapons, and flaming bowls of dips enabled guests to ignite their treasure with imaginary dragon's flame. Racks of roasted chickens were surrounded by roasted ducks, quails, doves, and a few other birds she could only guess at. Three pigs and an entire cow spun slowly above magic fires that burned in golden braziers completely devoid of wood, charcoal, or any other fuel. Mages stood nearby, the perspiration on their brow either from concentration or the heat.

There was also a roast pig with a grinning pumpkin in place of its head. A chicken-headed octopus had sausages for tentacles, while a pig's head with an apple in its mouth and the body of a woman was made of fruit. Dozens of smaller and no less bizarre edible amalgamations of creatures were on display.

Innumerable varieties of finger foods floated for easy access. Each gravitated to a dragon after it received the slightest of glances.

All this, however, was simply window dressing compared to what rested at the very center of the roof. The largest cake imaginable had been placed beneath a towering scaffold of gleaming steel.

Her quick scrutiny confirmed ten tiers covered in fondant and it was absolutely breathtaking and as tall as she was. It looked like it had been carved from sandstone and primarily detailed dragons—in flight, perched on what she thought of as hordes of gold but dragons thought of as their hard-earned treasure, or battling with knights from times past. The only indication that this wasn't an ancient honorific artifact was that all the dragons were rendered in elaborate colored icing. While the people, treasure, and buildings in the background were shades of brown, tan, or yellow, the dragons were bright and vibrant in blues, purples, greens, and reds. The entire effect was awe-inspiring and remained so because, as one walked around the cake, a new scene was continually revealed.

Suddenly, Kristen's dress no longer seemed so decadent. The cake must have cost as much as the gown she wore and it would be ruined as soon as someone took a single mouthful.

Windlock kept his arm on hers and led her to the edge of the main ballroom. They looked down on all the other rooftops of Penobscot. There were perhaps twenty of them, and each seemed to have a theme of its own with different decorations, appetizers, and servants to match.

"We'll never search it all," she said, dumbfounded at the scale of it all.

"We'll taste a little from each corner," he said and elbowed her in the ribs to remind her that they would be more successful if they at least pretended that they intended to enjoy themselves.

"Champagne ma'am?" a butler asked and she turned to catch Drew's gaze. He gave her the faintest of smiles, probably the only expression acceptable to the dragons he served drinks to.

"Of course, and thank you." Kristen accepted the champagne and downed it. For the moment, she was able to enjoy the way it calmed the nerves that had begun to creep in.

"This way," Windlock said and gestured to a floating staircase that had appeared in front of them where they stood near the edge of the rooftop. Stairs was a generous term as it was merely four large tiles—each as wide as a step—that formed the start of a path. As he guided her down the steps, the tile behind them vanished and moved to float in front so they were gradually led to the next level. It would be a vertigo-inducing experience for anyone who couldn't simply transform into a dragon the moment they wished to.

"Check in," her companion said, and Kristen nodded.

She had an earpiece disguised as an earring. Fortunately, all the non-magic waitstaff were expected to wear earpieces so they were able to communicate without drawing unnecessary attention.

"Checking in," she said.

"I'm on drinks, particularly empties," Drew said.

"They like to be served by floating magic. That's where you need people like me," Brockton said.

"I'm working the coat check, which is dumb because these fire breathing-assholes don't need coats and yet they still bring them," Hernandez said acidly.

"I'm on breads," Butters said.

"Me too," Beanpole added.

"So you're telling me I'm the only person on this goddamn stakeout who has janitor duty?" Keith demanded. "Do you know what dragon puke looks like? Because now I do. I thought you guys had stomachs that could digest a horse. Why the hell is everyone throwing up so damn much?"

"Human stomachs have human limitations," Windlock replied and barely contained his laughter. "We can eat a horse as a dragon but not as a human. The thing is, if we change to dragon and back to a person, our body remembers what we ate so we're still full. That won't do with a menu like this."

"Then why not throw it in the Detroit River?" the man demanded.

"Environmentalists. Do you have any idea what dragon bile does to an ecosystem?"

"Yes, I do," Keith said. "It's doing it to half the damn trashcans here!"

"We're heading to one of the satellite rooms. Let us know if there's anywhere we need to be or anyone who looks out of place. We'll have to approach, not you humans," Kristen teased. Never was their discrepancy of power more apparent than when they worked in dragon society.

They took the last floating step and joined one of the satellite parties. It was immediately clear that these areas were simply an excuse to display more power. Two mages actively melted and refroze ice sculptures so that the figures depicted moved in extremely slow motion. It was an intriguing concept but seemed like a terrible waste of human potential. No one watched this performance as this roof was empty of guests. That aside, the sculptures moved so slowly there wasn't much to watch except the two mages who sweated as one worked at the ice with his fire while the other refroze the drips.

It was odd, but the two dragons turned away and pressed on.

On the next roof, incredibly lifelike sculptures drew her attention. The detail on the skin was so realistic that Kristen couldn't help but touch one.

She almost jumped off the roof when she poked actual skin instead of marble. "Ah! She's real! She's real? You're real," she exclaimed in a rush.

The woman didn't say anything and the only part of her that moved was her gaze. It flicked from her to the other dragons on that particular roof. The other guests also touched the statues to see if the people would break their perfect posture. While no one did anything overtly abusive, it was still extremely uncomfortable to watch dragons prod someone in the shoulder or brush their hair back, while the human simply stood frozen and lifeless.

Obviously, the area provided nothing of interest in terms of leads as these humans weren't hiding anything. They all wore nothing but paint.

As they walked to the next roof—again on floating tile steps that she realized were provided for them by a single mage—Kristen couldn't help but point out how uncomfortable the frozen people had made her.

"You mean the living art?" Windlock asked. "I must say, those were exceptionally good. At some parties, you can see them breathing but these were really like sculptures." He kept his voice low despite their relative privacy. They ascended floating steps now toward another rooftop.

"You like that you couldn't see them breathing?" She also kept her voice low—and her aura under control—but she couldn't help a frown.

"Excuse me?" he said asked, clearly confused.

"Do you think it's good for people to ignore their human biology for your amusement?" It was a struggle to keep her voice calm.

"It's part of the art form—like figure skating or a circus performer or something. They're good at what they do and have obviously put considerable time and effort into the craft and are well-compensated for it. There's no slavery here," he explained.

"Here?" Kristen asked, her voice like ice.

"The North American Dragon Council doesn't allow dragons to enslave humans. They didn't have to fight a war over it, either. Actually, they ended slavery in eighteen fifty-seven, so dragons have been slavery-free longer than humans have."

"To be clear, dragons were always free. It was the humans who were enslaved."

"That's what I meant," Windlock said but sounded slightly defensive. "But the North American Council has been consistent in their enforcement of that rule. Some dragons still break it, of course. It can be hard to follow up on every single dragon-human interaction, especially when dragons so often provide humans with all they need and all they could want but a paycheck."

"That's slavery," she said.

"Right. And it's rare. The Dragon Council takes it very seriously. It's not like other continents."

"Wait—what?" She stopped their walk on the floating steps.

"Not every continental Congress enforces an anti-slavery stance. Europe, Africa, and Australia all have those rules on the books, but Asia and South America don't. And Europe gets tricky the farther east one goes."

"It's legal for dragons to have slaves in Asia and South America?" She couldn't believe she only now discovered this.

Windlock shrugged almost apologetically. "It's often brought up at global meetings, but a number of the dragons find it simpler to have slaves somewhere in the world, especially with sex work. Many find it awkward to have to compete with a web camera for their concubine's attention. Asia has a stranglehold on brothels and some humans see it as an honorable profession."

"Says who? Their fucking dragon masters?" Kristen demanded. Part of her felt she was overreacting, but then she realized that she felt the same about human systems of slavery. It also reminded her that there were parallels—after all, humans had also committed some of the most unpardonable atrocities all on their own without dragon help or encouragement. Still, the sudden revelation was horrifying and it triggered an instinctive anger that she needed to try to quell if she didn't want to compromise their operation.

The investigator clenched his jaw, clearly uncomfortable. "Well, yes, I suppose so. I've never actually talked to any of the concubines. I see myself as a North American so don't support slavery, even if they do seem to be well treated."

"I cannot believe you're saying this shit right now. What's the slavery like in South America? Do they have kind masters too?" She pushed back the thought that there were numerous human trafficking rings based in South America—and elsewhere—that had no connection to dragons at all. She'd face that if and when she had to but for now, this triggered her inner conflict between her human and dragon self. While she loved being a dragon, she didn't want to accept the less palatable sides of that heritage.

"Your human government is as much to blame there as dragons are. The dollar has devalued many of the currencies in the region. Any number of people choose to work for food, lodging, and creature comforts rather than currency that might be worthless in a few years."

She was so angry she couldn't speak. Creature comforts? Windlock was all right with slavery because some of the slaves allegedly enjoyed creature comforts? How disassociated could someone be? She couldn't comprehend how someone could be that lacking in empathy. Kristen often felt bad when she used a drive-through because it wasn't customary to tip and she knew those people didn't make good money, but Windlock hadn't even considered what it was like to be enslaved.

"I simply…I can't believe you're defending slavery."

"I'm not defending it. I'm merely telling you the state of affairs. I think it would be better to not have it. It would certainly help with the way dragons are perceived by humans. Maybe we wouldn't have to face these assassins if our counterparts in South America and Asia took a more proactive approach."

Kristen shook her head, furious, livid, and fuming mad. She knew he was right and that she was, in effect, attacking the messenger. He'd not said he agreed with it and she didn't believe he'd bother to pretend. It was simply that he was there, was a dragon, and had made her confront something she hadn't known about at all. Her emotions distracted her and she stepped off the tile steps they'd walked on and immediately plummeted.

There was a time when that would have terrified her but now, it was liberating. She let the wind pull at her gown and her red hair before she transformed into a dragon and caught the air. Her fall arrested, she pumped her wings and flew up and around the Penobscot building. Other dragons were airborne as well, so she wasn't totally out of place. She used the opportunity to think.

Yet again, she'd been presented with a dark facet of dragon culture she'd been ignorant about and yet again, it had been presented in an offhand, second-thought kind of way. It was a reminder that dragons simply didn't think of people the way people thought of themselves. Humans would always be less, inferior, and a lower species. She knew that part of this was because of the power differential. It was simply hard to respect something when it was essentially defenseless. But at the same time, not all dragons kept slaves. Once again, a minority created the problem, and the majority did what they could which was, more often than not, ineffective.

Constance attempted to change that and prove that humans could have a place at the dragon's table. The purpose behind her actions was laudable if one looked no further than the surface.

The Steel Dragon still didn't approve of her methods, though. Going into people's homes—dragons or humans—and shooting them wasn't the way to change hearts and minds. And yet, with this new revelation, she wondered if a more subtle approach was even possible. Some dragons apparently believed that slavery was right or at least tolerable. How could they ever be convinced to change if not shown they must through violence? Then again, surely the Civil War provided the lesson that violence didn't always change attitudes, at least not right away, and that it demanded a terrible cost in lives. It often simply exacerbated the problem to include hate and greater discrimination.

It was frustrating that dragons continued to not fill her in on the state of the world because apparently, slavery—or indeed any inequality—was fine and normal and not a concern for them. At the same time, though, why was she so offended that the dragons were guilty of exactly what many humans perpetrated? Was it because she believed on some level that they were somehow better and so should know better? She recoiled at the thought and sighed heavily. Perhaps if Windlock had told her sooner, she would have had time to work through some of these feelings and come up with a larger plan on how to confront the dragons who viewed humans as little more than useful cattle. Perhaps if dragon attitudes changed, those humans who condoned the practice might change too.

But she didn't have that kind of time so instead, she convinced herself that they needed to find out what Constance was up to in order to make sure Jim was all right and that the rest of the team didn't get caught in the proverbial crossfire. In that moment, saving dragons had assumed secondary importance.

CHAPTER EIGHTEEN

Kristen landed on another of the satellite party roofs and gave it a quick scrutiny. This soon proved to be a poor choice given her mood as a group of pixies performed magic on the guest's bodies. Hedonistic grins were plastered on the dragons' faces and moans of pleasure issued from their mouths.

She transformed quickly, moved toward the edge—and shooed a pixie with glowing fingers away as she did so—and stepped out onto another set of floating tiles. As she climbed, she checked in with the team. "Any leads?"

"It's gotta be a bomb," Hernandez responded in immediately. "They've already demonstrated that they know how to make them, and what else could be used to fuck up a party full of dragons?"

"Have you seen any evidence in the coatroom?" she asked.

"No, of course not. There's nothing here but a pile of furs from dead and probably endangered or even extinct species. One woman had a rhino pelt cloak—I mean, why the fuck would anyone want that?"

"Anyone else?" Kristen asked as she approached the main ballroom, the largest roof in the center of the Penobscot.

"I had the building swept very thoroughly before the party began,"

Windlock said over the earpiece. "Given the bomb at dragon SWAT, we made it a high priority, but we didn't find anything. I can assure you that if there was something, Dragon SWAT Forensics would have found it."

"Still," Hernandez insisted obstinately, "it has to be that!"

Everyone else had to fight for airtime on the channel as they all protested more or less the same thing.

Butters might have summed it up best, though. "You always think it's a damn bomb."

"Yeah, well," the woman retorted once the chatter died down. "It usually is."

"Facts, Hernandez. We're talking facts," Drew reminded her, always cool-headed. "Have you seen any actual evidence of a bomb?"

"No, dammit," she grumbled. "But if it's all right with everyone, I'll leave the coatroom to poke around. This would be a dumb place for a bomb anyway."

"That's fine," Windlock said.

"Anyone else?" Kristen asked.

"Dragon barf continues to be gross," Keith stated gloomily.

"I haven't seen anyone armed and waiting in the wings or anything like that," the team leader said. "Although I've been busy with drinks so haven't been able to take a real good look. Anyone else?"

She had almost reached the roof and realized that the crowd was coming to meet her. Murmurs of "Steel Dragon" were audible and she knew it was about to become far more difficult for her to do any searching. Apparently, arriving uninvited had a way to make someone seem especially interesting, whether at human or dragon parties.

"I think I'm about to be MIA in this hunt. Everyone, use the next twenty minutes to really search. I'll work the crowd," Kristen said and would have happily traded places with any of them. She'd rather look for a bomb—hell, she'd rather wipe barf up—than pretend to enjoy talking to all these powerful and apparently slavery-complicit dragons. Unfortunately, this was the role she could play to help the team and their case, so she had to do it. Also, she hadn't seen dragon barf and had to admit, at least to herself, that it sounded worse.

She stepped onto the roof and was immediately surrounded by a circle of doting sycophants.

"Lady Steel, how fortunate we are to be able to steal you away from Investigator Windlock. He can be so dull, although of course, you seem to think otherwise. Tell me, how did you two meet?" a dragon in the form of a human woman asked her. She wore a red dress that Kristen thought was covered in sequins until she realized it was actually entirely encrusted with rubies.

"We met through work, actually."

"How delightfully macabre!" The woman giggled.

"Tell me, Lady Steel, do you have much of an investment portfolio? Detroit's industry is on the rebound and we'd love to take whatever gold you have and do something with it," said a man with a mustache who was obviously a dragon.

"Are you enjoying the party?" an androgynous dragon asked. In their human form, they wore a flamboyantly colored tuxedo with tails with an elaborate floral arrangement in the lapel.

Kristen tried to answer their questions with a smile, but it was difficult. She wasn't interested in any of this crap while her human team gathered intel without her.

"I'm checking the halls but there aren't any suspicious characters," Drew said. "If someone's planning an ambush, they have to already be undercover."

"Beanpole and I have checked the waitstaff," Butters interjected, "and I don't see any weapons. I know they're mages but this group is all about the guns, right? We'd have seen something, I'm sure."

"I stopped wiping barf up and found some naked painted people," Keith said. Kristen could practically hear his smile over the connection. "I don't see guns here either."

She giggled but had to quell it when she was joined by two dragon women in gowns even more beautiful than her own.

"So did you enjoy Ell and Vee at Le Clothier?" one of them asked. Kristen realized she'd tuned out. She couldn't do that again, not if she wanted to keep their eyes focused on her.

"I did. They were—"

"Eccentric, no?" the other woman said. At least it wasn't hard to keep people interested in her at this party. All she really had to do was keep smiling and pretend to be interested in their conversations.

The woman continued, "They dress us and act like their opinion matters! It is lucky they have such good taste or I think they would have come to an end long ago, no?"

She imagined the woman trying to eat Ell and choking to death and was thus able to make herself laugh.

"What about the catering plates?" Hernandez asked over the earpiece.

"Not happening," Drew replied. "Too small."

To test the theory, Kristen captured a platter with a lid floating past her. It was one of the only dishes capable of hiding even a grenade. Predictably, it held only oysters on ice.

"What about the food?" she said aloud.

"Oh, it is absolutely divine," a man in the crowd said. "I used a bread sword to chop off one of those chicken's tentacles. Such a delight, was it not?"

"Absolutely. I think I might have to help myself to more." She nodded, excused herself, and walked toward the food. Butters poked around furtively but it was already obvious he didn't need to. Most of the food was stripped clean. What platters remained were merely remnants of the feast and only the cake was untouched.

A cold hand of dread clutched at her insides.

She snatched a roll up so she could hide the fact that she was talk-ing. "Windlock," she said into her earpiece "When did the cake arrive —before or after the bomb check?"

"Hold up," he said. A long minute passed during which she spoke to those around her in a casual way. Yes, the salami was divine and yes, it truly was one of the best parties she'd ever been to. Finally, when her patience seemed worn to the very edge, Windlock responded. "It was sent in with the rest of the food, which means after the bomb sweep."

"I'll take a closer look."

CHAPTER NINETEEN

She knew she had very little time. Within moments, someone would approach with yet another inane question and she needed to reach the cake before that happened. It seemed sensible to try to use her aura to indicate that she was overwhelmed—not terribly difficult given the situation—and it did seem to dissuade anyone from accosting her for now.

Her instincts pushed her to run but she forced them down and instead, approached at a slow and steady pace and tried to look at it from an investigator's perspective. For starters, it was huge. It could easily hide a few people inside if they were willing to crouch. If there was a bomb in there, it certainly could be a big one. Plus, the intricate fondant icing meant no one would dare to touch it. Dragons were arrogant, self-absorbed creatures and the last thing any of them would want to do was smudge their likenesses on the masterpiece. Plus, even if someone did stick a finger in the icing, it would be easy enough to create a couple of inches of cake to complete the charade.

Now that she studied it without her initial amazement, it seemed obvious. It was too perfect, something designed and created to keep everyone at a respectful distance until the ceremonial moment when it was cut. That moment, she realized, would no doubt draw every dragon guest within range. Hopefully, she was wrong, but she had a cold conviction in her gut that she wasn't.

Kristen glanced around and saw an enormous pile of plates as well as a large serving knife on a nearby table. It wasn't time for cake yet— the more important guests had yet to arrive—but the human servants were ready for the dessert to be served.

She thought about all the bizarre questions she'd been asked and how disconnected from human society all these dragons were. What would they think if she cut the cake before the time? After all, she was seen as an ignorant human bumpkin by many so might as well use that for cover.

Furtively, she glanced around, saw no one, and reached for the knife.

A familiar voice stopped her in her tracks. "I wouldn't do that if I were you."

Constance stood directly behind her and she turned slowly to face the woman. The assassin had darkened her hair to make her more difficult to identify. The team had searched for blonde and it simply hadn't occurred to anyone that she might change her hair color. Once again, it appeared they'd been fooled. Her identity was obvious to Kristen, though.

"I've watched you since you arrived. You don't fit in any more than I do," the woman said.

"It's a bomb, isn't it?" she replied. Now was not the time to exchange political beliefs.

Constance took a step closer to her and proffered a floating champagne glass. She was dressed all in black like a caterer and that was obviously how she'd slipped in.

Kristen took the glass from the air and the assassin stepped closer to fill it. Once beside her, she seemed to relax. "Good, now we can talk,"

She scratched her ear and nudged the microphone in her earpiece with a previously agreed code. No one responded.

"I'm wearing a short-range radio jammer. You won't be able to talk to your team."

"What do you want?"

"Freedom and equality for all humanity." The woman spoke as if it was the most obvious thing in the world. "I thought it was something you wanted as well. Or have you changed? Has your time spent with dragons made you complicit with all this?" She gestured at one of the living, painted people frozen in place.

"I didn't know about any of this until tonight."

"That sounds like something a dragon would say," Constance countered. "Do you know there are places where dragons can abuse people however they like without paying them?"

That stung because she had so recently learned about slavery still being allowed. Still, this wasn't the way, she told herself. Calmly, she said, "Blowing people up isn't the way to change the world."

"What people? I see a gathering of rich monsters who think it's fine to eat a cake that lionizes how they've tortured people over millennia. Why do these…creatures, get to enjoy privileges no human can?"

"You won't change minds with an explosion."

"Not dragons' minds, no," Constance agreed. "But they've made their position on equality quite clear over the last ten thousand years, don't you think? They've had every opportunity to show us respect, and do they?"

"Some do."

"Yes, I know, and its dragons like that who we need on our side—dragons like you."

"I'm not on the side of murder," Kristen retorted.

"Oh? So you're on the side of the murderers, then? Can't you see that our rebellion would cost far fewer lives if it's not dragons versus people? If you join us, the whole world will see that this isn't about the species but about inequality. It's not about dragons but about justice."

"Look, I think… Well…I think your goals are noble enough…" She decided she needed to be honest. "But your methods are not. You can't use violence to make the world a better place. It simply doesn't work."

"You use violence. You killed Obscura and you killed Death," Constance responded quickly.

"You're right, but I did those things to stop violence, not to change the world. And killing both of them didn't make the world better or safer, not as a whole. I can't let this bomb go off either. The blood spilled here will only be used as an excuse to spill more blood. Can't you see that?" Kristen sighed. Much as she wanted to believe in this revolution of equality, she knew this wasn't the way. She stretched her hand toward the knife.

"Don't do that," the assassin warned and retrieved her phone.

"You won't change my mind, not as long as you're committed to this attack," she told her calmly.

"No, I guess not. I see that now. But that's okay because you changed my mind."

"What are you talking abou..." The question trailed off when Constance held the screen of her phone closer.

Her gasp was instinctive when she recognized Jim. He was in a room—a hotel room by the look of it—and paced constantly. Although apparently unhurt, he seemed agitated.

"Do you see his anklet?" her companion asked.

Kristen clenched her teeth and nodded.

"It's another bomb," the woman explained patiently. "It's linked to the one here and has the same timer—one switch, as it were. If you disable it here, it shunts the command to his anklet and he blows up instead. There's also a proximity alarm on the door and window. If he leaves the hotel room or anyone else comes in, it explodes. And, of course, if you tell the dragons about the bomb and they jump off the roof or whatever, I'll simply detonate it immediately. I actually prefer that option. We wouldn't kill as many as we hoped but it'll prove you're committed to people instead of dragons."

"How does this show that I changed your mind? This is crazy!" she protested.

"You said that sometimes, violence can be used to stop violence. The threat of your friend blowing up will stop your actions tonight. If you foil our plans, he dies. If you let it proceed, the bomb here goes off, the anklet pops off, and he can walk away."

"This isn't a fair choice!" Kristen was shaking with rage.

"You're right. It's not. You have to choose between a human friend of yours who has literally risked his life multiple times for you and a group of spiteful dragons who see human beings as nothing more than playthings. The choice seems obvious to me."

Constance handed her the phone, then turned to walk away.

"What is this?" She scowled and forced herself not to look at her friend on the screen.

The assassin turned once more to look at her. "The choice is yours."

CHAPTER TWENTY

Of course, she couldn't avert her gaze for too long and finally looked at Jim, who continued to pace with evident frustration. Finally, Kristen tore her gaze away and realized without any real surprise that Constance had vanished into the crowd. Strangely, she trusted the woman's words. Yes, she thought that killing these dragons was extreme. And yes, she thought that using Jim as a sacrificial pawn was horrible, but she didn't think she would have given her the choice of his salvation and lied about it. The assassin's goal seemed to be to sway her to their cause and lying to her wouldn't achieve that.

Hopefully, it meant they still had time.

"Windlock. Come in, Windlock," she said into her comm device as soon as she was able to hear the chatter of her team again.

"Where are you?" he asked.

"At the cake."

"Right. I have eyes on you." In the next moment, he stepped out of the crowd and beside her. The other dragons still kept their distance. They could no doubt still sense the anxiety coming through her aura which she made no attempt to hide.

"This video shows Jim with an explosive anklet around his leg. If we disarm the bomb, it blows Jim up," she narrated for the benefit of the team who only had an audio link.

"Butters, I want you over here," Windlock said. "I can see a glimpse out the window. Your sniper's eyes might give us a clue."

Kristen snatched the phone from him. She'd been focused on Jim's pacing and hadn't noticed that a corner of the curtain was open.

"Isn't that Lafayette Coney Island?" she said to Butters when he joined them.

"Are you asking me that because I'm fat?" the sniper quipped as he took the device and examined the window in the live footage. "Yeah, that's Lafayette all right, which means he's in a room in the Westin Book Cadillac. I'd say the tenth floor judging by the angle and fairly close to the southeast corner of the building. Not the corner room, obviously."

"How the hell are we supposed to reach him without blowing him sky high?" she asked everyone on the channel. "According to Constance, if anyone tries to enter the room, it's set to detonate automatically."

"So it's a choice between trying to disable a bomb strapped to Jim's leg and potentially save the Wonderkid's shiny ass or dig through a cake and try to disarm a bomb that's supposed to kill dragons. I gotta say, I choose the Wonderkid on this one," Hernandez said.

"It makes sense to me," Drew told the channel. "I'll come too, plus Butters, Keith for any tech we might see, and Hernandez, obviously. "Beanpole, you stay with Kristen, Windlock, and Brockton. They might need your eyes."

"Understood," the tall man said.

"We're on our way now. We'll let you know if we get him free and if we figure out any of the tech they're using," Drew said.

"All right, do we have ideas?" Kristen asked Windlock.

"My first instinct was to throw it off the side of the roof but if it's big enough to kill this many dragons, it could create a hole in the side of the building and bring the whole structure down. I think we can both agree that's unacceptable."

"Sure. So we need to disarm it or take it someplace where it can explode without hurting anyone," she said.

"No easy task in downtown Detroit," he replied with a frown.

"Why doesn't Constance simply blow it now?" Beanpole asked reasonably. "I can't see her but I'm sure she can see us."

"Yeah." She nodded. "There are already dozens of dragons on the roof and I assume they're all fairly important when it comes to rank."

"She doesn't want to throw a rock at the wasp's nest," Brockton said over the comms. "She wants to squash the queen." He sounded breathless, possibly from entertaining dragons with his magic skills. "The Council will arrive late as they always do. They like to be fashionably late so they make a grand entrance at events like this. You can't be the most powerful people on the continent and arrive early enough at a party to make small talk about the weather. Hell, I think that's where most of the power comes from. Those who can't be bothered with the rest of us make us idolize them. It's dumb, but there ya go."

"Brockton's probably right," Windlock agreed. "It makes sense that she wants to catch the Dragon Council in the blast. What surprises me most is that she's willing to sacrifice her plan for Jim. She really wants you on her side." He studied Kristen for a moment and although it wasn't necessarily suspicious, she didn't appreciate it.

Before she could speak, the sparks above the rooftop changed in color and intensity. A murmur rippled through the crowd and the dragons, together with the mages, pixies, and humans serving them, all took a few steps away from the door.

"What's that?" Kristen asked, but the sound of trumpets playing a fanfare drowned out her question as soon as she asked it.

Windlock grimaced. "Those horns announce the arrival of the Council members. We're almost out of time."

It was no relief to her that if the bomb blew the Council up, Jim would go free. She'd admittedly had a brief moment in which her friends had taken precedence, but common sense had reasserted itself. If the Council was killed today, the world at large would be thrown into a war that would make the rebellions of times past look like children playing capture the flag.

CHAPTER TWENTY-ONE

"We must have missed something." She took a deep breath and tried to focus. This couldn't come down to a choice between who would die. That might be how Constance wanted it, but it didn't mean it was the only choice. The assassin had planned a situation in which Kristen was forced to make a decision she'd regret either way. The woman obviously hoped she could force her to join them—or at least appear to support them—to protect her friend, but she simply couldn't do that.

"Maybe we should clear the roof," Beanpole said.

"Wait—wait, that's it! Constance said if we tried to do that, she'd detonate the bomb early. That means she has some kind of a remote for it. Whatever device she's using to set it off might be able to deactivate it as well, right? Hernandez, can you confirm?"

"Yeah, it makes sense to me." Her teammate's voice crackled with static, which she took as a good sign. It meant they were already close to the hotel that housed Jim. "I wouldn't make a bomb like this without a way to deactivate it. She's obviously a crazier bitch than me, but she did say if Jim's blows up, this one doesn't, so there has to be some kind of kill switch."

"Damn it! We need to find Constance again." Kristen wanted to punch herself for letting the mage escape but frustration served no purpose. They had to find her.

Unfortunately, that wouldn't be easy. While before, the party had been fairly spread out as guests mingled in loose groups across all the various roofs with their various forms of hedonism, the main roof of the Penobscot was now crowded with dragons.

Everyone seemed to jostle for position and tried to get as close as possible to the landing area where the Dragon Council would arrive. A huge, turquoise dragon landed to the fanfare of more trumpets and the crowd cheered as she took the shape of a human woman.

Kristen knew the assassin would be in there somewhere, plying the dragons with drinks while she kept a close eye on her targets. It was insane to think that the woman had a better idea of who these dragons were than she did, despite the fact that she was a dragon and Constance had sworn to kill them all.

She identified six new arrivals making slow loops in the night sky. The strike would doubtlessly come once they'd all landed and were close enough to the cake to be within optimum range. She was worried—given the size of the cake—that this might mean anywhere at all on the roof.

"Do we have any eyes yet?" Windlock asked as the second member of the Dragon Council landed while the horns played a different tune this time. Apparently, each member of the council had their own theme song. It would be funny if she wasn't at serious risk of being blown up with the seven of them.

"I have nothing. No one's looking for my tricks anymore so I'm trying to keep an eye out, but I don't see a damn thing. This woman's as slippery as they come," Brockton said.

"I see her." Beanpole's voice was calm, as always.

"Where?" Kristen demanded.

"On the opposite side of the crowd from you. She climbed up the tower, maybe ten feet, and is in a patch of shadow directly above the cake. It's a good vantage point. I should have thought of it sooner."

"I'm headed there now," she said and immediately realized it wasn't actually possible. The crowd was too thick and she couldn't cut across the main promenade. She had no doubt if she did something so overtly against Constance's wishes, they'd all be blown to pieces. "But it'll take a minute."

"Wait—wait she saw me," Beanpole said. "She knew I was watching her."

"What did she do?" Windlock asked.

"She smiled and climbed down and…she's walking toward the inside. She might have realized that we know she can deactivate the bomb. I'm moving in."

"Do not engage, Beanpole. Do you hear me? Do not engage!" Kristen said. "I'm on my way and we can take her together."

"I can't lose her," he said.

His tall frame moved away from the crowd and toward the door. She could see him but she couldn't reach him with so many dragons between them.

"Damn it, Beanpole. You can't take her! She has magic to augment her skills."

The man didn't respond and vanished inside in pursuit of Constance.

Kristen tried to hurry but the crowd and her dress and heels slowed her progress. In desperation, she kicked her heels off, ripped the skirt from the dress above the knee, and used her enhanced speed to close the distance to the doorway.

She pushed quite a few dragons out of her path and earned scowls in return. Fortunately, no one seemed inclined to make a scene, so she avoided further delays. When she stepped through the door into the Penobscot building, she caught a glimpse of Beanpole as he turned a corner. Without anyone to block her progress now, she raced down the hallway using her full powers.

The first gunshot cracked before she'd gone halfway down. By the time she rounded the corner, the fight was over.

Beanpole slumped against a wall with a bruised eye and bloody teeth from a busted lip, and he held his ribs with one hand. His other hand clung shakily to a pistol until Constance kicked it out of his hands.

"Your turn." He grinned and displayed his bloody teeth. While he sounded weak and possibly had a bruised rib, the fact that he was able to joke was a good sign. "She has a bulletproof vest so it might slow your dragon abilities."

It was both amazing and terrifying that the woman had managed to inflict so many wounds on Beanpole in such a short amount of time. Humans shouldn't be that fast. Only dragons could move like that.

"Don't worry, Beanpole. I've got this." Kristen appraised her adversary. The woman wasn't even breathing heavily and the outline of the vest was noticeable under her black server's clothes.

Constance cursed and moved forward like she intended to attack but stopped. "I don't want to fight you."

"It must be hard to fight people more powerful than you. I'm sure Beanpole felt the same way about facing a magic assassin."

"I hope he thought we should be on the same side," Constance retorted.

"You kidnapped our friend," was all Beanpole said in reply.

"I put his life in your hands," the assassin reminded Kristen.

"His life was not yours to place anywhere. That's what makes us different. If you ignore the law and hurt people to achieve your goals, you're no better than the dragons."

"We both know that's not true. They've been humankind's tormentors for thousands of years."

"So what? Are you trying to make up for all the atrocities in a single moment?" She took a step toward the other woman.

"The ends justify drastic means if it means freedom for humanity —true freedom. We don't even know what equality tastes like. Every civil rights movement has been a charade. Humans fought for the rights of women or blacks and were granted them. It's a small consolation given the way things work. At no point in history was the table leveled. The powerful—the truly powerful—were never forced to release their hold on the reins of humanity."

"Maybe not but lighting the entire saddle on fire will only burn the backs of the people carrying it. Give me the control for the bomb and we can work something out."

"I won't let you ruin this opportunity to bring justice to the world," Constance replied and clenched her fists.

That was it, then. She had to accept there was no middle ground to be had. They'd end this not with words or compromise but with combat. She thought of Jim, locked in a room with a bomb strapped to his leg, and decided the woman who had done such a thing deserved to be on the receiving end of the same type of violence she was so willing to dole out.

She drew a breath and raced into the attack.

CHAPTER TWENTY-TWO

Kristen vaulted into a flying kick that would have been impossible if she hadn't already ripped her insanely expensive dress. Constance caught her and spun her into a wall with sufficient force to crack the sheetrock.

The assassin held onto her leg and rocketed kicks at her crotch. Despite the mage's speed, they didn't hurt because she instinctively turned her skin to steel. The added weight meant the woman couldn't hold her leg up and had to release it.

Constance immediately realized she would lose if she faced a foe with steel skin and turned to run. Both combatants knew she didn't need to win this battle, only keep the detonator out of Kristen's hands. The Steel Dragon grasped her by the back of her collar, yanked her back, and lifted her above her head to hurl her into the ceiling.

The collision shattered a fluorescent light panel and rained sparks on the fighters but the assassin didn't fall straight into the dragon's waiting grasp.

Instead, a blast of wind came out of nowhere and pushed the woman slightly so she landed in front of her adversary instead.

The wind picked up and whipped at Kristen, but she was the Steel

Dragon. Of all the magic in the world, wind might have been the least effective.

She lunged forward and punched Constance in the chest with enough force that she sprawled and skidded a few feet.

"The last time we fought each other, you shot me in the leg to even the playing field. I've trained since then and this time, I'm defending my friend, not a dragon. You might as well give up."

The woman appeared to see the wisdom of this and held her hands up in surrender. Kristen straightened, half-shocked at how easy it had been, but cursed when her opponent drew a pistol with astonishing speed and fired.

The dragon dodged the first two shots, then surged forward.

Windlock and Brockton both shouted from farther down the hall.

Constance noticed them too and fired twice more to prevent the pair from approaching. They ducked out of sight behind the corner and Windlock cursed volubly.

"Stay back. I got this. These might be dragon bullets!" Kristen yelled over her shoulder before she pushed into a sprint.

The assassin had wasted no time and was already running down the hallway. It seemed for a moment that it was over as there was nowhere for her to go. Every door was shut, and the time it would take to open one would give her pursuer the scant seconds she'd need to catch up.

Her speed and miniscule head start were enough to enable her to shatter the window at the end of the hall and leap out into the night air.

Kristen cursed and covered the distance to the aperture in seconds, flung herself through, and looked down before a gust of wind whipped at her face. In previous encounters, she'd wondered if another mage had helped to manipulate the wind, but it seemed obvious now that the assassin had exercised her own wind powers to aid her escape.

The dragon transformed almost instantly and used her forward momentum to catch the wind beneath her wings and soar after her quarry.

Constance moved like a leaf in a tornado. Gusts buffeted her and pushed her from side to side as she tried to flee. The problem with wind, however, was that it didn't exist in or come from a vacuum. Her pursuer was able to catch some of the same gusts and given that they were farther away, they lacked the sharp force that jerked and pushed the woman. Kristen simply felt wind at her wings and used it to get closer.

For a moment, it seemed the plan was to reach the streets of Detroit but instead, an updraft carried the woman to one of the satellite parties on the top of the Penobscot building.

The Steel Dragon landed and changed to her human form so she could fit on the roof. Her adversary was ready for her and threw a punch hard enough to be felt through her steel skin.

She retaliated with even more force, but the assassin was ready and let the force of the blow hurl her off the building. Once again, the wind caught her and carried her to another satellite venue.

Kristen changed into her dragon form and launched off the edge as she reflexively breathed fire after the assassin. She managed to stop it, though, when she realized it might fry the detonator, which in turn would mean they wouldn't be able to deactivate the bomb. It wasn't the smartest thing she'd ever done, and she reminded herself to focus and not let her emotions take control.

Constance wasn't the only one to notice the fire, however. When the gout of flame lit the night, the pixies who'd provided the sparkling lights that illuminated the party joined the encounter.

It couldn't be called a battle as none of the short creatures seemed interested in actually fighting but suddenly, the air around her glowed with red and gold sparks.

This, in turn, alerted the dragons at the top of the main building. Many crowded close to the edge for a better view of the spectacle. Their excited and voluble response carried to where she took the shape of a human again and exchanged blows with the assassin on the rooftop of another of the satellite parties, this one filled with dozens of intricate ice sculptures.

Ultimately, it was a one-sided fight. Kristen had steel skin and

Constance didn't. In the glow of the red and gold sparks, the woman's face clearly said that she understood this too. She sweated noticeably, her mouth hung slightly agape, and a trace of fear shadowed her features.

In any of their previous confrontations, Kristen might have shown pity on her but this time, she couldn't. Not with Jim's life at stake. He was one of her people, not because she was a dragon and he was a human but because she cared about him the same way Stonequest or Drew cared about those who helped them. His life hung on the outcome of this fight and clarified things for her.

She pressed her attack while the guests at the party cheered for the Steel Dragon. They obviously thought it was some kind of exhibition and had no inclination to participate.

Kristen landed a few blows, knocked Constance's legs out from under her with a sweep kick, and delivered a powerful blow to her chest.

"You can't beat me," she said.

The woman drew her pistol and tried to aim it, but Kristen kicked it away and it skittered toward the edge of the roof. The dragon watched it for too long—hoping it would plummet off the edge—and her opponent used the opportunity to regain her feet.

"Come on, Constance. You're done."

"We've come too far to give up. We're so close," Constance said and darted away to hide behind an ice sculpture.

In response, she shattered it as if it were hollow. It was as thick as a man but with her dragon strength, it offered no resistance.

Her quarry ducked behind another ice sculpture, this one of a bear balancing on a ball.

She obliterated this one as easily. Shards of ice pinwheeled to catch and refract the light from the gold and red sparks that still illuminated their battle. The dragons on the rooftop cheered enthusiastically. It was very likely they thought it was fake as none of them seemed inclined to leave.

The Steel Dragon marched toward Constance, who continued to

bolt behind ice sculptures. This achieved nothing except to buy her a little time as the dragon destroyed statue after statue.

Finally, when there were no more to hide behind, Constance stopped and faced her squarely.

"It's not too late," Kristen said. "Give me the detonator, we stop both bombs, and demand a meeting with the Dragon Council. Show them you have restraint."

"I don't want to be eaten, thanks," the woman retorted and lunged into a swift attack, leading with an elbow.

She blocked the blow easily enough—flesh always lost to steel—but the momentum was enough to shift her balance slightly. That wouldn't have been a problem if the entire rooftop they fought on wasn't covered in broken ice.

Kristen moved, her foot settled on a piece of ice, and the weight of her steel body unbalanced her and she fell.

The crowd gasped. Obviously, they were rooting for her in this fight they thought was part of the evening's entertainment.

She found her feet—earning scattered applause—but Constance attacked. Blows pummeled the dragon's steel face, which did nothing but make it difficult to see, then the woman swept her legs again to force her to move her feet. Once more, she stepped on a piece of ice and sprawled heavily.

The dragons booed and she tried to shut out the distraction.

Kristen stood slowly and again, the assassin used the extra weight of her steel skin to topple her onto the icy surface.

When she pushed to her feet this time, she turned the steel to skin.

The crowd cheered at this and she resisted the urge to flash them a rude gesture. The watching dragons had begun to irritate her with their stupid assumptions that a life and death struggle was simply a choreographed scene for their entertainment.

Constance didn't waste her opportunity. She attacked with focused fury in a whirlwind of blows. The Steel Dragon was able to avoid some but many got through.

Thankfully, she was able to more than simply block and parry and gave as many as she received. At one point, the exchange was so furious that she wondered if the dragons could follow the action given that it was almost too fast for her to keep up with. She defended and retaliated more by reflex than anything else until the assassin delivered a powerful palm strike to her face. A crunch and instant pain told her that her nose was broken.

Her adversary backflipped off the building as soon she landed this blow—earning more boos from the dragons—and the wind caught her and took her toward the main area of the Penobscot building. The glint of steel in her hand confirmed that she'd retrieved her pistol.

Kristen knew her nose would heal with her dragon powers, so she allowed herself no time to wallow in the almost blinding pain.

Instead, she transformed into a dragon and streaked after her quarry.

Constance landed on a third rooftop and drew her pistol. The dragon changed into her human form before she landed to make a smaller target for her opponent and immediately surged into the attack.

"All I want is equality!" the assassin screamed. It was the first time that real desperation had colored her voice.

She ignored it, pushed for hand-to-hand range, and focused on pummeling her opponent's thighs and ribs—easy targets where the effect of blows could accumulate. The woman was weakening and rather than fight, she tried to fire a shot. Kristen dodged, caught Constance's wrist, and crushed it to force her to drop the gun. Before it landed, she kicked it with enough force to career it off the edge to plummet to the streets of Detroit below.

"No!" the assassin screamed, jerked her hand free, and clutched her wrist.

She seemed to understand that she had no chance outside. If she were to somehow defeat Kristen, the other dragons might join the fight. Rather than prolong the combat, she used her wind to fling herself through another window into a different hallway.

Kristen followed without hesitation. She landed on her feet and immediately broke into a run.

The dragon was hurt. Her nose was broken and she'd suffered a fair number of major blows when they'd fought among the ice sculptures, but the other fighter's condition was worse.

The pummeling inflicted on her thighs gave her a bad limp. She cradled her wrist, which definitely looked broken, and she darted glances over her shoulder as she stumbled down the hallway and away from her pursuer.

Distracted by her focus on the Steel Dragon, she didn't see Windlock and Brockton emerge at the end of the hall. Instead, she turned when they were already in position. The inspector was in his dragon form and filled most of the hall, and Brockton's robes seemed alive with power as he held a bevy of chairs, broken wood, and kitchen cutlery aloft with his magic.

Constance cursed and turned to run past Kristen, who saw the wisdom of Windlock's form.

The assassin was the last one to know the fight was over. When she approached, the Steel Dragon simply transformed into her larger body. She barely fit inside the cramped hallway but that was the point. The woman made it past a claw and a wing but Kristen leaned her body against her and pinned her to the wall. Constance struggled against her bulk but couldn't free herself. She was too weak and too injured, and the dragon was so much stronger.

It was over.

Beanpole approached. Despite his still slightly blood-smeared teeth, he seemed in better shape than either of the women. Windlock and Brockton held their position at the end of the hall as Beanpole slipped a pair of handcuffs on Constance.

Now that she was restrained, the inspector and his assistant approached. The dragon changed into his human form and it was evident from the way he carried himself that his guard wasn't down. The mage brought his arsenal of floating objects with him.

"The detonator," Kristen said to the assassin once she changed back to her human form.

Constance spat and moaned in pain.

She shook her head and dug inside the woman's pocket to retrieve an object with two buttons and a timer. A quick glance told her there were two hundred seconds on it.

"How do I turn the bombs off?" she demanded.

The assassin laughed.

"How?" She lifted her by her collar and thrust her into the wall behind her.

In response, the woman laughed even harder until she coughed up a mess of bloody phlegm. She tried to spit it in Kristen's face but she lacked the strength. The mess of red mucous simply dribbled down her chin.

"How stupid do you think we are? Do you think we didn't plan for this outcome?"

"What are you talking about?" Windlock asked.

"We knew our greatest threat was the Steel Dragon. Others wanted you neutralized, but I thought maybe here—at this place of decadence and inequality so vividly displayed—you might finally be convinced to join our side. I was wrong, but that doesn't mean I didn't listen."

"How. Do. We. Turn. The. Bomb. Off?" Kristen demanded.

"If you press the red button, it blows up, the anklet pops off your friend's leg, and he lives. On the other hand, if you press the blue button, you kill your friend but spare the party-goers. It's your choice. I told you. My preference is to let the clock run out and kill the dragons."

"Damn it!" she screamed.

Constance laughed weakly. "Why would we have brought a device that could stop our plans? Dragons have made their choices clear over millennia. There was nothing at this party that could have made us think differently. The only reason we were here at all was to try to convince you otherwise."

Windlock was able to accept this before she was. He clicked his radio on and contacted the other team.

"What's your status? We have the detonator but it's still a binary decision. Is your man free? Can we blow his bomb yet?"

"Yeah, I'm gonna need you to shut the fuck up unless you want me to blow him up. We're at the fucking door. Hold tight." Kristen could almost hear Hernandez sweating over the radio. "Asshole," the woman muttered.

"You have three minutes," the inspector said and the demolitions expert responded with a curse.

"What do we do now? Beanpole asked.

"At the very least, let's join the party and get a look at the cake. I wouldn't want Constance to miss the grand reveal."

The assassin only laughed as they pulled her to her feet and dragged her toward the party.

Kristen tried to count down in her head because every time she looked at the detonator, the number was lower than what she wanted it to be.

They burst onto the roof to cheers and applause. She tried to yell over the dragons but they were all determined to congratulate the victor of the exhibition they'd watched. Each time she tried to raise her voice, the guests responded with an enthusiastic chant in honor of the woman who had fought to save their lives as a phony champion. They lost themselves in revelry while the bomb that would kill them all lay silent at the center of it all.

CHAPTER TWENTY-THREE

"Asshole," Hernandez muttered.

"You have three minutes," Windlock said.

She responded with a string of curses into the radio before Drew took it away from her.

"We need to get in there and you're the only one with the skills for the job. If cursing a dragon will help, I will turn this radio back on. But if it won't, you need to focus."

"Let me fucking work, okay?" She tried not to sweat but they'd already wasted so much time.

The person working at the desk had been an absolute asshat and flatly refused to answer their questions about which rooms might have the view Butters described. Finally, Drew flashed his badge and told them the Penobscot was about to explode.

That had convinced the dick-weasel, but it had also caused low-key panic in the lobby. Everyone had rushed outside to look at the impressive building or better yet, record it with their smartphone. She had wanted to yell at all of them for not calling the damn cops but remembered she was the cops. Besides, even officers would probably have their work cut out for them when they tried to remove anyone from the scene of what promised to be the highlight of their lives.

Once Drew had made it quite clear that they were looking for a terrorist, the clerk had cracked like a walnut—which had also pissed Hernandez off as he hadn't asked for a warrant or anything else. He directed them to a room on the fifth floor that faced in the right direction and had been booked by a blonde woman. Apparently, she was the only blonde with a room on that side of the building, so that was at least a little encouraging.

The floor was low enough that Drew said it'd be faster to run. Hernandez wanted to protest, but Butters had nodded with his double chins and headed to the stairs, so she couldn't exactly complain about having to break a sweat.

Now, though, she wished she had. She had less than three minutes, was breathing heavily from the exertion, and her hands were both sweaty from the activity and shaking from her nerves.

"Constance said the door was triggered to blow. Do you have anything?" Keith asked.

"For fuck's sake, can you all shut up? I need to actually think about whether I can shut this thing down or not."

Everyone—wisely, for fucking once—listened to her.

There was a device on the outside of the door with some kind of transmitter. It was a guess—and maybe a bad one—but she didn't think the transmitter was the switch. She decided that it probably linked the two bombs together so if one went off, the other would deactivate, exactly like Constance had said. There was a possibility that it also had something to do with the door opening, but she didn't think so. The device was mounted directly beside the door and had a small metal panel that slipped between the frame.

Hernandez's first instinct was to simply disarm the entire array. She removed the front panel and found it would be impossible. The damn thing had a dead man's switch, which meant if she killed the whole thing, both bombs would likely detonate. The reality didn't surprise her much, though. She'd suspected something like this.

"These technomage assholes knew what they were doing when they did this." Hernandez wiped her brow and tried to focus.

If she couldn't disarm it, she had to find a way to not activate the switch connected to the door. Her next step, then, was to determine what the weird silver panel did. The wires leading to it obviously couldn't be cut as that would blow the damn bomb on the other side of the door, but the panel didn't seem to be a pressure plate. So what the fuck was it?"

"I need a paperclip," she said.

"You can't seriously disarm a bomb with a paperclip!" Butters protested.

"Shut your fat fucking mouth and give me a damn paperclip," she retorted sharply. She normally preferred to insult Butters with stuffing-your-face jokes as opposed to fat jokes—the difference was subtle but it meant something to her—but she was too stressed.

Drew held one out. He was a slave to paperwork, so it was hardly a surprise that he had one.

Hernandez took it and prodded cautiously at the steel plate. She would have used her regular tools but she was worried they'd apply too much pressure while a paperclip wouldn't have the strength to cause damage. She cursed when she dropped it.

Rather than fall, it simply hung there as if by magic and clung to the silver plate.

"It's a magnet." Keith beamed with pride at his observational skills.

She rolled her eyes. He was a great lay—better than most dudes and even some women—but God, he could be dumb.

"Of course it's a fucking magnet. Now give me a radio."

"Steel Dragon. Come in Steel Dragon," Drew said into the radio.

"Did I ask you to do that?" Hernandez hissed her irritation. "Give me the radio!"

Butters passed her his—they all noticed that Kristen didn't answer the call—and she immediately shattered it on the floor.

"What are you doing?" Drew demanded.

"Saving the Wonderkid's goddamn life, so please, try to calm the fuck down."

From the destroyed radio, she selected the copper wire—there wasn't much but it would hopefully be enough—and wound it around one of her own tiny steel tools. Carefully, she connected the copper wire to the radio's battery and earned a shock in the process, but she didn't care. She'd had reactions from chemicals in her work area that would liquify someone's lungs if they inhaled too deeply. A shock was nothing.

She manipulated the piece of steel—now wrapped in electrically charged wire—to touch the paperclip and picked it up to confirm that she'd made an electromagnet.

"Okay, here the fuck goes. I'll hold this at this switch and Drew, you kick the door open."

"Are you sure?"

"Nope," Hernandez replied. "I'd say sixty-forty we survive, but we have maybe a minute left. I'm fairly sure this is a magnetic sensor so the electromagnet should stop it from exploding when you remove the other part of the switch. If anyone else wants to not blow up, now would be your chance to move down the hall."

Butters and Keith shared a look but neither fled.

She scowled at the brave idiots but Drew grinned.

"I love the bravery, boys, but you might as well get against the wall. If this thing brains us, it'll be up to you two."

Both men nodded at the wisdom of this and pushed themselves against the same wall as the bomb, each a few doors down in opposite directions.

"Drew? If you don't mind."

The team leader nodded, took a deep breath, mumbled a prayer under his breath, and kicked the door in.

A scream from within was, thankfully, not followed by an explosion.

"Am I glad to see you guys," Washington sputtered. Hernandez could tell he'd been crying as there were tear streaks on his dark skin. "If you don't mind, I'd really appreciate you getting this thing off my ankle in the next forty-five seconds."

He was still alive and that reminded her that she had to keep panicking.

She raced over to him and grasped his ankle without even saying hello. He fell on the bed to give her a better look at the anklet, but it was already too late.

"I don't have time for this," she said.

"Yes, you do. Don't quit." Drew said.

"No, I don't." She stood slowly and realized her panic had faded. They would all die or they would let Jim die and run to safety. Of course, they were all too stupid and loyal to do that—herself included —so they would die.

"Come on, Hernandez, give it a shot," the team leader said, his tone encouraging.

"I've seen these things on the Internet. It's like a bomb-head's wet dream. The screws are custom, so I don't have the tools to get inside, but even if I did, it's spring-loaded. As soon as I crack it open…" She made two fists, then opened them to mime an explosion. "Boom."

"Well, there has to be a code or something. There's a timer, isn't there?" Washington pleaded.

"It's all inside. The timer is all that shows. Seriously. If I fuck with this thing, it will detonate. I might be able to work it out if I had a few hours but…" She shrugged

They could all read and there was no doubt that they only had thirty seconds.

"Steel Dragon. Come in Steel Dragon," Drew said over the radio.

This time, Kristen responded, although she was hard to hear. It was obvious she was in the thick of the party.

"The bomb is still on Jim's leg and still set to explode if the bomb inside the cake fails to detonate. We can't stop it or save him."

Hernandez loved that Drew said we and not her, even though it was totally her fucking fault.

"Kristen, you have to disarm the cake anyway!" Jim yelled over Drew. "You guys get out of here and let Kristen blow the anklet."

"We will not let you die," Drew said.

"I'll probably only lose a leg." Fucking Wonderkid. They all knew he would lose more than a leg but here he was, trying to be the hero. "The cake is more important. We have to protect civilians even if they are dragons. I'm a cop, I knew what I was signing up for. They didn't ask to risk their lives at a party."

"Jim, no," Kristen yelled over the radio. She yelled at the dragons to clear the roof but they all laughed.

Hernandez even heard some of them over the radio. "Be careful. The mage in that exhibition might come back. Let's hear it once more for the Steel Dragon."

The crowd cheered like drunken buffoons.

"You can't let them die. Some of them have to be innocent," Jim insisted.

The demolitions expert was shocked. She'd never liked dragons but Jim had hated them. When she first met him, he had acted as if every single dragon he'd ever met was personally out to get him and now, he was willing to sacrifice his life for a group of dragon strangers.

Hernandez hoped she never grew up that much.

"I will not let you die," Kristen said before the radio went dead. Hernandez wondered if any of the people on the street below were live-streaming the Penobscot and if so, did they have an angle that would show Jim's hotel room blow up?

Not that it mattered. They were probably all dead in about fifteen seconds.

CHAPTER TWENTY-FOUR

Kristen knew she didn't have time and was basically about to kill herself in spectacular fashion, but she wouldn't let Constance make this decision for her.

And that's what it amounted to. It was a fucked-up version of the trolley problem. The assassin had given her the choice to end one human life or end a large number of dragon lives. The trolley problem basically meant it headed down a track where it would run over five people but there was a switch that would let the operator make it run over only one person instead, but with humans and dragons. It was a false choice. The trolley problem assumed that one couldn't stop the damn trolley and—worse, in Kristen's mind—it never addressed the asshole who had tied the damn people to a track and left them in front of a train.

It was a false binary, and all it did was give power to the person demanding an answer to the question.

She certainly wouldn't answer. Instead of hemming and hawing about which switch to push, she dropped the remote and turned her dragon speed on. She raced to where Windlock, Brockton, and Beanpole held Constance.

"If you do nothing, the cake blows up," the assassin reminded her when she noticed that she had discarded the remote. "I'm glad you made the right choice."

Her smugness faded and was replaced by a look of horror when Kristen ripped the woman's bulletproof armor off and threw it on hastily over her dress.

"No! No, don't do this. You're too important and that bomb is filled with dragon parts. You'll be eviscerated."

Time seemed to slow as she raced toward the cake but she knew she still wouldn't have enough. From her belt, she heard Hernandez cursing about technomages—a term she immediately approved of in reference to their adversaries but also a term she knew she'd probably never get to use.

She had to end this and show that a dragon could protect both humans and people. It might cost her life, but it was a risk she had to take. No one else could do it.

As she sprinted forward, she transformed into her dragon form and hurled revelers aside with her steel tail and wings. There were dragons there who could beat her in combat, but they were all in human form. She was determined and moved with every ounce of strength and speed she had to barrel through the crowd and part them like the Red Sea.

The Steel Dragon grasped the cake in her front claws and launched herself skyward. She allowed herself one backward glance to where Beanpole, Windlock, and Brockton dragged Constance onto the roof. All four of them watched as she soared upward with the cake that would have killed them all—and still might if she didn't succeed.

Hard wingbeats thrust her higher with the power of desperation.

Time seemed to tick inexorably in her head but what choice did she have? She couldn't let Constance control this narrative. If she allowed the woman to force her to choose between which groups of people to kill, she'd be a killer always and forever. This way, the only person who might die was her. It wasn't a pleasant thought but it was the best she had.

She pumped her wings as powerfully as she could in an effort to get as high as possible above the party. While she had no idea how many explosives were in the cake, she knew that the higher she went, the safer they'd all be. She shifted it to her back claws as she counted down the final few seconds.

Her plan was desperate and she knew she would more than likely die. Oddly enough, she was more remorseful than angry. She had wanted to build a bridge between humans and dragons and she'd failed. A world she'd dreamed of in which her human parents would be safe would never be. She was more than willing to sacrifice herself for others and had grown up with her dad working as a cop for Detroit so knew firsthand what sacrifice really looked like. But if she was gone, she had no idea who would advocate for humans to the dragons or for dragons to the humans.

Kristen reached three in her internal count so she spun and hurled the cake as high into the air as possible with the momentum of her back legs. It careened away from her, but with her dragon senses, she could tell it was already slowing down. It wouldn't be far enough away, which meant she would be engulfed in the blast.

She proceeded with the last and most desperate part of her plan and transformed into her human body. Her clothes and the armor she'd taken from Constance rematerialized and she pulled the bullet-proof vest over her head. She tucked herself into a ball to make herself as small a target as possible and tried to cover her head, heart, and lungs with the protective material.

The bomb exploded a second or so sooner than she expected it to. A shockwave of force surged into her and catapulted her toward the ground much faster than gravity would have been able to do.

Still, if it had only been the shockwave from the bomb, she might have survived because she had a dragon's ability to heal. Concussions, bruises, and broken bones weren't the same thing for her that they were for regular humans.

But the bomb had been filled with dragon parts, shrapnel that was deadly to every living creature on earth, even one with steel skin. Chunks of what she knew on some level to be her own species shredded her. Her legs—completely bare since she'd removed the bottom half of the dress—burned with pain as countless slivers of dead dragon slashed viciously through unprotected skin. Her arms still clutched the bulletproof vest to her head and chest but also ignited with unimaginable pain. If she hadn't already clasped them around her as tightly as possible, they would have flinched and spasmed in agony.

The worst torment came from the shrapnel that managed to catch her in the abdomen. Every one of those felt like white-hot fire, a jagged blade intent only on inflicting cruelty to her midriff. It hurt so badly she wondered if her gut had been punctured. Her entire body screamed for it to end. Kristen remained silent and clenched her teeth.

She had survived the blast.

Now, she had to survive the fall.

Her awareness returned, spurred by her inner warning, and she called her dragon powers. She didn't have much time but she'd practiced and decreased the time it took for her to transform. All she needed to do was assume her dragon body and use her wings like a parachute. On some level, she was aware that at the speed with which she moved, her wings might break in their sockets, but much of how she flew in her dragon body was instinctual. If she could catch even a trace of wind and redirect her fall, she would survive.

Unfortunately, it appeared that she couldn't transform.

She called on her dragon powers, dug deeply into the font of strength she'd discovered not that long before, and found the paths it took through her body were blocked. There were simply too many pieces of shrapnel inside her. She began to disincorporate and the beginnings of the silvery glitter surrounded her as she fell, but her wounds were too grievous. Her body couldn't shed things when it changed and instead, it moved them around and adjusted their relative positions. Doing so would mean shifting a massive amount of razor-sharp slivers of dragon through her body, something it simply wouldn't allow her to do.

If that wasn't bad enough, the effort also caused her steel skin to fade into her regular flesh. Like a drunk trying to pound a couple of glasses of water much too late in the night to make a difference, the effort only caused her more pain and rejected this last attempt to save herself with unnecessary retribution.

Kristen tried to regain her steel form. Impact with the ground while in steel skin might still turn her organs into mush, but at least she wouldn't pop like a water balloon. Her body denied her even this small benefit. She was spent and it took everything she had simply to not pass out from the pain.

Without a doubt, she was well and truly fucked.

Somehow, she managed to rotate her body as the Penobscot raced past and she groaned inwardly. Impact with the top of the skyscraper might have saved her as she'd have less time to reach terminal velocity. Plus, there was the chance that she would plow through a couple of floors—shedding her momentum piece by piece—before she came to a stop. Now, however, she plunged toward nighttime Detroit and could only expect to strike the street or sidewalk.

Ridiculously, Kristen began to cry and her tears whipped behind her with the speed of her fall. In the next moment, dragon talons curled around her body and diverted her into a blindingly fast swoop across the ground.

She came close enough to the streets below that she saw people staring at her, many of them shooting video on their camera phones.

A cheer rose from the crowd—it seemed weird that sound might be one of the few things that still traveled faster than she did at this point—as the city saw their hero saved by a dragon.

She swung upward again and the sensation of changed momentum made her nauseous. Her rescuer continued to climb until she was once more on the roof at the party. The dragon who'd saved her set her down gently and she twisted slightly as he transformed into the human form of Windlock. That was the last thing she saw before she passed out from lack of blood.

CHAPTER TWENTY-FIVE

She drifted through the darkness of unconsciousness without dream or thought. Her only reality was the pain that gnawed the edges of her mind in a confusing demand for her to both wake and remain asleep. After a while, however, the pain diminished slightly and Kristen opened her eyes.

The first thing she saw was the night sky above her. Despite the fact that the lights of the Motor City washed out many of the stars, she could still make out a few of the glowing pinpricks of light. They reminded her of how fragile the earth was, how insignificant, and therefore how beautiful. Her hometown was tinier than every mote of light in the sky, yet it contained humans, animals, and dragons, all of whom had a right to be there. They had to find a way to share their world because the stars would forever remain out of reach, a tantalizing vision from thousands of lightyears away.

Her tunnel vision expanded to register a few glowing orbs of light. At first, she thought they were light bulbs, but the way they bobbed gently made her realize they were lights made by a mage or pixie. The party had been ruined, obviously, so the magic users had altered the quality of light to be more appropriate to what was currently in progress.

And as her vision settled and real awareness took hold, she realized those gathered so closely around her were a medical team.

Doctor Chakrabarti—the dragon surgeon who had attended Stonequest and Heartsbane—was there. His hands were bloody and his face grim but he wore no doctor's scrubs. A frilly shirt with rolled-up sleeves seemed out of place given his task and only his gloves confirmed his professionalism. He no doubt carried a pair in his pocket. For the briefest of moments, she felt anger toward the surgeon for being at the party rather than monitoring her friends in the hospital. When the man removed a piece of dragon talon as long as her finger from her gut, she decided it was preferable that he was there.

Three other mages stood beside him. Two of them were unfamiliar but the third was Brockton. As always, he harnessed his abilities to move objects without touching them. He held his hands near his forehead and drew a dragon scale the size of a quarter out of her leg. Her flesh squelched slightly as the foreign object came free and she almost passed out again, but she managed to stay calm and mumble her thanks.

"Ah, Lady Steel," Doctor Chakrabarti said. He sounded surprised to hear her voice but was professional enough that it didn't show in his demeanor. If anyone needed steady nerves, it was a surgeon. "We've extracted most of the larger pieces. Your liver was punctured and a kidney almost decimated, but both are in good enough shape that you should heal once we get the rest out of you."

"The rest?" she asked weakly.

He glanced over his shoulder and she craned her neck to where Windlock stood impassively. The dragon nodded. "She can take it."

The doctor turned to her again. "There were over a hundred pieces of…shrapnel, lodged in your flesh. Quite frankly, it's a miracle you're still alive. Based on the sheer number of them in that explosive, if you had not thought to protect yourself with that vest, a few pieces would have surely punctured your brain, lungs, and more than likely your heart. Facing the blast was also wise, as your spine was protected. You're a very lucky girl, Kristen Steel. You can still wiggle your toes, not something I thought you'd be able to do when I began my work."

"How long was I out?" Kristen asked.

"Almost an hour—enough time for us to remove most of the larger pieces but there are still dozens of smaller ones. I don't know how many, exactly, but we need to pull them out before your healing abilities return. While I'd prefer to do this in a sterile operating theatre, I don't want to move you as some of them could shift in flight. It's a good thing there's no chance of rain tonight. We'll be here a while."

"Thank you, Doctor. I guess I owe you my life," she murmured.

Doctor Chakrabarti laughed. "Well, then, consider us even. From what I can tell, you were over a hundred meters away from that bomb when it exploded. If it had detonated in the middle of the party, we'd all be dead." He shook his head, his expression a little sheepish. "Actually, I had been ogling the cake when you bulldozed through and knocked me over. I would've been deader than most if not for that."

"Well, thanks all the same."

He nodded and stood. "I need to stretch my legs and get some water but will be back soon. We're out of the woods but that doesn't mean it'll be easy going. I don't want you to move and the mages will keep working. I'm sure you understand certain…uh, obligations as an officer, but if you get upset at all or your consciousness level changes, they're all gone."

"If I yell or fall asleep, you'll get rid of them. Got it." Kristen tried to smile. She wondered if her own grin looked as phony as his. They both knew that "out of the woods" was a little presumptive.

Still, he moved away and Windlock approached.

The dragon knelt beside her and studied her with a serious expression. "You know, when you rushed out there with that bulletproof vest, I thought you intended to throw it over the top of the cake. It wouldn't have done a damn thing, obviously, even if it had been big enough. I thought you'd lost your damn mind. Instead, you picked the damn cake up and tried to fly it to the moon. If that wasn't the stupidest damn thing I've ever seen someone do, I don't know what is." He chuckled. "The thing is, though, it was also damn brave."

"That's our Kristen," Beanpole said as he moved behind Windlock and towered over him. His face was a mess of bruises from his fight with Constance. She wondered who looked worse, she or him.

"Wait, Brockton's working on me, so if you two are here, where's Constance?"

A stab of pain in her knee suggested that Brockton had startled and jerked while he attended to a wound. Windlock and Beanpole shared a grimace.

The mage spoke first. "I used magic to control her, but she had those cuffs on and...hell, I got sloppy. When you raced out there toward the cake, I think all our jaws hit the floor. I know mine sure did. I recovered after about half a second but when I turned, she had managed to remove one of the cuffs. You had broken her wrist and if not for that, I don't know if she could have."

"Are you saying this is my fault?" Kristen challenged, only half-joking.

"I'm saying I don't want to take full responsibility for how badly I fucked up, so yeah, I guess I'm trying to share the blame with everyone. There are ways to stop mages from using their abilities, but I hadn't exercised them on account of those handcuffs. That was all me. As soon as she was free, she blasted me with a flurry of broken glass from the door you shattered. I blocked it, but that was what she wanted. She used the opportunity to damn near vanish."

"And you didn't see where she went?" she asked Beanpole. The man was a master of observation. There were times when she thought he had eyes on all sides of his head because nothing seemed to escape him.

Except this time, apparently. "She ducked into a room in the hall. I followed but as soon as I went in, she hit me across the head."

"And you let her get away?" she asked Windlock.

"I checked Beanpole and found him alive but by then, my choice was to pursue her or try to save you from an unpleasant encounter with the streets of Detroit."

"I watched her in that room. She used magic. We couldn't have caught her," Beanpole said.

"We're sorry," Windlock said. "It was a rookie mistake."

Kristen nodded, disappointed as she'd thought they could finally get answers from Constance. If they'd taken her into custody, they could have learned something from her about both her organization and— she thought selfishly—the woman's role in her life. Strangely, she wasn't all that upset that the assassin had escaped.

She wanted to be furious with this woman who'd used her friend as a bargaining chip in her quest to destroy dozens of powerful dragons but there was something about the balance that had been struck—one human life versus all those dragons—that challenged it. It was unacceptable to threaten to blow people up, obviously. But at the same time, to think about one human life like that and to understand what one human could mean to someone who cared about them was something she couldn't help but admire. Except, of course, Constance didn't really care about individuals. If she did, she would never have used Jim that way. Her focus was entirely on her bigger picture.

Dragons didn't think about people as someone to care about either. Hell, in actual fact, people didn't think about people that way. There were exceptions, just as there were dragons who did care—or had begun to adjust their perceptions to work toward that. In general, though, everyone knew not to piss dragons off. If you so much as told a joke about them, it could cost you your life. That had been the way of things since written language had existed. It was still the way of things overall.

But Constance wanted to change that. She wanted to bring in a more just and equitable world. Kristen didn't agree with her methods and whole-heartedly believed violence would only instigate more violence, but the woman's vision had appeal. She couldn't help but share the fantasy of a more equal world—a world where dragons hesitated before killing people and in which not only humans knew the meaning of the word terror.

What she'd come to see, though, was that it wasn't an entirely one-sided situation. People like Drew and his team needed to care about the dragons before they were able to step in to save them. Yes, they'd looked at the impact the bomb would have had on humanity and that had been their driving motivation, but they could have turned their backs on the dragons.

If they still had the assassin in custody, they could perhaps have come to some kind of understanding. Maybe they could have built if not a bridge, then at least a path forward. It might have been complicated or difficult, but it could have been something positive. Now, the woman was free and doubtlessly already planning another act of terror. Still, they'd at least foiled this plan and avoided war for a while longer.

"What about the team?" Kristen asked Beanpole.

"Jim is fine. As soon as the bomb went off, the anklet bomb released."

"Constance told the truth about that, then," she murmured aloud. The looks on both Windlock and Beanpole's face told her they didn't share any of the questions she had about their adversary. They doubtlessly thought using Jim as a sacrificial pawn was a terrible thing and she was thankful they did. If the world needed anything, it was people with different opinions to work together.

"They've been on the damn radio the whole time. Finally, we had to tell them to shut up and turned the damn thing off. The last thing they said was something about a Coney Island? I gotta say, you inspire people in a way ol' Windlock doesn't," Brockton rambled as he continued to work on her wounds.

"They're fine," Beanpole reiterated. "Hernandez is freaking out about how fancy the anklet device is. Drew is trying to use past legal cases to make the dragons let them in here, and Keith, Butters, and Jim are arguing about hotdogs."

"Coney Islands," Kristen corrected him.

The tall man shrugged. "We're all happy you're okay."

"Indeed," Windlock said before he glanced at an approaching cadre of people. His face paled and he clenched his teeth. "Beanpole, if you'll excuse us."

Beanpole looked up and frowned in bemusement. He had no idea who they were and their presence meant nothing to him.

"Those are all members of the Dragon Council of North America," Windlock whispered urgently. "Get out of here."

The man ignored him and looked at Kristen instead. She nodded. "But first, help me sit."

"Lady Steel, Doctor Chakrabarti said not to do that," Brockton protested.

"I will not meet these dragons lying on my back. Now help me up."

Windlock nodded and the mage finally acquiesced. He told his colleagues to take a short break while Kristen's teammates helped her into a seated position.

It might have been a mistake, she realized when her limbs and abdomen protested mightily. Pain seared through her legs and reminded her that she'd never suffered like this before and that if she stupidly ignored the doctor's instructions, she might never suffer this way again.

And yet, if she was to build a bridge, she needed to be strong. She needed to face these dragons who ruled the world and do so from a position of something close to equality. Obviously, she couldn't do that while staring up at the sky.

After a few moments, the pain eased enough for her to understand that movement was not a viable option given her condition. Brockton used his magic to drift a few pillows from a nearby couch and positioned them behind her back so she didn't have to maintain her core while she sat.

She wondered briefly why the doctor hadn't moved her to the couch as it would have been more comfortable than the floor, but she realized almost as quickly that surgeons worked on flat surfaces, not comfortable sofas upholstered in ostrich skin.

"Now, if you'll excuse us, Beanpole," Kristen said to her friend.

He nodded, sent a glare at the approaching dragons, then retreated to the far side of the roof.

"You too, Brockton," Windlock told the mage.

"Ah, come on. They love me."

"They most certainly do not and besides, I do not want you to talk over Kristen's introduction to them."

Brockton grinned and complied. He didn't go as far as Beanpole, though, as he still had surgery to perform.

Five dragons strode purposely toward Kristen. The three men and two women exuded power and their auras were unlike anything she'd experienced in her time with dragon kind. They didn't tell her how to feel or take control of her but she knew that they could. It was like seeing a whale's tail protrude from the ocean before it splashed into the water or the tip of the iceberg. The little she could sense bespoke power that was deep and profound.

As they approached, Windlock knelt before them. For an awful moment, Kristen thought he would remain silent and leave her to flounder in the presence of these mighty dragons.

Fortunately, he laid her fears to rest but what he said merely revealed more of the Council's power. "May I present to you the head of the North American Dragon Council, Decimus Aurelius, a loyal servant of the Dragon Roman Empire almost two thousand years ago. He helped to found this country during colonial times and assisted the United States to establish themselves as an independent nation. In addition, he is one of the founder members of the North American Dragon Council. Hail, Lord Aurelius!"

"Hail!" the other members of the Dragon Council echoed.

Lord Aurelius chuckled. "It says something about progress that these days, I can be both a loyal servant of the Roman empire and one of the founders of the United States. I took considerable heat for that from the Europeans."

Kristen was shocked to hear this dragon greet her with a joke. It simply didn't seem possible. He was tall and held himself regally. His gray hair, smile lines around his eyes, and a wide grin could have given him a very lucrative career as an actor—or a politician—she thought. He wore a silver suit and a black tie that would have made her dress look shabby even before she'd torn it to shreds. Her brain struggled to process the sheer impossibility of the situation and decide how to respond to the dragon. He preempted her, though, and she actually gaped and was left utterly speechless when Decimus

Aurelius, a being more powerful than the president of the United States, dropped to one knee beside her.

He didn't kneel a long time, fortunately, and merely bowed his head for a few seconds before he stood again.

Part of her wanted to thank him but the other part seemed determined to protest that someone of his rank would kneel to her, so she played it safe and said nothing at all.

"Lady Steel, I and indeed, everyone on this roof," he said with a raised voice emphasized by his aura, "are alive because of the selfless heroism you exhibited today. We all owe you a debt."

Kristen—still speechless—only managed to nod before he turned away from her and pinned the rest of the crowd with his gaze. Many of the dragons still present nodded immediately but that didn't seem to be enough for him. He remained silent, his stare hard and compelling, and flexed his aura to show them he was serious. Soon, the entire gathering knelt as he had done. Finally, he turned his gaze on the other members of the Council. One by one, each of them nodded. They didn't kneel but she saw the looks in their eyes and felt the weight of their auras that conveyed clearly that they took this very seriously.

"Thank you, Lord Aurelius, truly."

"You don't have to thank us. A dragon debt is worth more than gold—especially a life-debt, which we all owe you now. If there is ever anything you need, you only have to ask, Lady Steel."

"Well, for starters, you can call me Kristen."

Lord Aurelius bowed graciously, "And you may call me Decimus. Please, Kristen." Her name sounded odd in his slightly accented English. She realized he must have spoken Latin fluently as well as various other languages he'd used in Europe. "Tell me what compelled you to be so willing to sacrifice yourself for us? We've never even met."

"Frankly, Decimus, I did it to prevent a war between humans and dragons. If those…" She struggled for a suitable word and recalled the name Hernandez had given them. "If those technomages had been successful, I'm sure dragon kind would have attacked humankind and the world would have been soaked in blood. I didn't want to die but losing one life is worth it if millions are saved."

Lord Aurelius—Decimus? Was she really supposed to think of the most powerful person on the continent on a first-name basis?—turned to address the crowd again. "This is the kind of dragon the world needs." Many of the guests nodded. "Your bravery is admirable and your views on human lives is commendable. It takes a keen mind to break through established ideas. When I helped found this country not by installing a new king but by helping to shape a democracy, dragons and people alike thought I was crazy, but I like to think that it worked out well." He chuckled. "You may have started something today—a path toward a future that no human or dragon had previously imagined. I will watch you, Kristen Steel, and if you ever need anything, remember that we are in your debt."

With that, the Dragon Council leader turned on his heel, strode to the edge of the Penobscot roof, and transformed into a resplendent silver dragon. While Kristen's form was the same color, he looked nothing like her. Her dragon body—especially in its steel form—made her think of chrome. It was bright, shiny, and not too detailed. Decimus, by comparison, looked like a finely worked piece of jewelry. Every scale was outlined in the faintest line of white light. His wings were larger than hers, although his body was smaller, which made him seem both more powerful and more delicate. It was like looking at a king in dragon form. As he launched into the night, she hoped she would have the opportunity to get to know this powerful dragon.

The other members of the Council nodded at Kristen as if to confirm once again, boosted by a flash of their auras, how seriously they took the oath they'd sworn. Silence hung over the rooftop as they stepped off the edge of the skyscraper and were swallowed by the night sky.

Once they were gone, Kristen collapsed into the pillows. It had taken considerable effort and determination for her to sit for that long. Her body was still on fire with pain and every part of her hurt.

The mages who'd worked on her knew this, obviously, as they rushed forward and resumed their task.

She knew they were helping her and that she wouldn't be able to heal until they had removed the dragon shrapnel. Still, it was hard to feel anything but annoyance when even the slightest touch stung and triggered more pain.

"How much of that crap is in me?" she asked and clenched her teeth.

"More than you want to know," Dr. Chakrabarti replied. Apparently, he'd had his break and now that she had been personally thanked by the Dragon Council, he wanted to make sure they wasted no more time. Unfortunately, no one had any idea how long that would take and she had to simply endure the process.

For the next ten minutes, Kristen forced herself to at least try to relax. It wasn't easy as every few seconds, she felt the equivalent of a wasp sting somewhere on her body when a mage yanked another piece of dragon out. She did manage to close her eyes, though, so that had to count for something.

"Once this is all out, will I begin to heal?" she asked Dr. Chakrabarti at one point.

"It will take time. These scales interfere with your natural systems, so once they are out, those systems have to reset, so to speak. I hope Dragon SWAT has a decent disability program. I think you will take much longer to heal than your two friends did."

She knew he was speaking about Stonequest and Heartsbane but her mind immediately went to her human friends. Aside from Beanpole, they didn't really need to heal so it wasn't a parallel that made sense. Still, they had helped her to prevent a war.

"Where are Drew and the others?" she asked Windlock.

"I was waiting for you to ask," he replied and spoke quickly into a radio.

A minute later, the SWAT team raced onto the roof.

"What the fuck happened here?" Hernandez yelled at the sparse crowd. "I was hoping to get leftover grub."

"Agreed," Butter huffed.

"Holy crap, Kristen, are you okay? You have to see this video of Windlock catching you before you met the pavement. Ten more feet and you would have destroyed this lady's phone, but she recorded the whole thing in high def. The video has already gone viral. It has over a million views and it's barely been an hour." Keith brandished his phone to show her.

"Good to see you're…alive," Drew said and examined her wounds.

"Thanks for saving my ass again," Jim said.

"No problem," she replied reflexively, even though it was definitely one hundred percent a problem to have her body riddled with shrapnel from another dragon. A dragon who—if the evidence proved correct—was more than likely related to her.

"Did you get her?" the Wonderkid asked.

Kristen clenched her teeth to bite back an acerbic response.

Brockton replied in his typically verbose fashion. "Kristen did. You should have seen it. They jumped from rooftop to rooftop and she battled in both her forms while the other woman used magic. It was epic! That technomage thought she could use ice against Kristen, but you can't box the steel dragon in. Oh, man, I should've recorded a video. It was too cool."

"If you beat her, where is she now?" Drew asked.

"That would be my bad," the mage confessed, his expression ashamed. "She escaped while I was supposed to watch her."

"I was also unable to stop her," Beanpole added. It sounded more convincing from him because his face was so bruised.

"Damn," Jim said. "I really hoped this would be the end of it. I was ready to blow up back there—thanks again, Hernandez, for not letting that happen—but I thought this would be it. We'd beat the damn technomages and stop a war."

"I'm not sure this will be something we can put an end to so easily," Kristen said. "This bomb would have killed most of the North American Dragon Council as well as dozens of powerful dragons, and the technomages didn't even have all their people here. They understand that they're fighting a long-term guerilla war and that any of their victories can be taken away by a foe who is much more powerful than they are. I think we'll have to continue to accept small victories and try to capture their leadership."

"Do you think they'd stop if we had a prisoner?" Drew asked.

Kristen shook her head—a huge mistake as the movement made her entire body scream in pain—and blinked tears away. "No, not at all. I think they are all committed to their cause and probably have contingencies in case someone is taken. Still, I keep thinking that if we can talk to Constance or someone else high up in the organization, we can get a list of demands. Maybe the Dragon Council can meet them halfway."

"You mean negotiate with the terrorists?" Windlock asked, obviously incredulous.

"I do," she said. "I don't agree with their methods but they're not the disease, merely a symptom. They see real injustice in the world and want more equality. Obviously, blowing people up is always deplorable, but this party was another reminder of how much dragons have and how little so many of the people actually control. Constance and the technomages have chosen to go about it all wrong because their actions will simply cause more bloodshed. I'm sure they see it as vengeance, but—and this is unfair to say—often, the victim has to forgive first. If we can understand their viewpoint, maybe we can do something to help them realize it."

"I thought their viewpoint was that killing dragons is good," Jim said.

How weird, she thought, that Windlock—a dragon who investigated dragon crimes—had come together with Jim—a man who had hated dragons with every fiber of his being less than a year before—to express confusion over her idea, but it made sense when she thought about it.

Jim and Windlock were both men who valued evidence. They saw the world through events and things that happened. Motives—other than self-defense—weren't particularly valuable to either of them. They both saw crimes committed and atrocities performed and wanted them stopped.

The others in the human SWAT team weren't like that. Butters,

Keith, Beanpole, and Hernandez especially saw things through their gut. They felt what was right and wrong, and she could tell that they grasped what she'd tried to say and understood what it felt like to be powerless and so lash out.

She was sure they would need everyone's perspective to thwart the technomages. Windlock and Jim, however, would have to accept that they'd need the mages too.

***

"Well, look what got caught on the dragon's claws."

Kristen rolled her eyes when Heartsbane walked into her room.

Once they'd removed most of the shrapnel, they'd relocated her to the hospital where Stonequest and Heartsbane had been treated. She hadn't possessed the energy to ask if either of the dragons were all right and had simply passed out and woken as her teammate strolled in. She wondered—not for the first time—if there were elements to a dragon's aura she still couldn't tap into. Had she been able to tell from her aura that she had woken or had she merely entered at a lucky moment?

"I thought I had it bad, but holy shit, they practically took an entire dragon out of you," the woman said.

"It's good to know you're feeling good enough to talk shit," she retorted. She didn't comment on her visitor's wounds, though. Obviously, the other dragon knew she still had a scar on her cheek. Normally, Kristen would have counted such a thing as a blessing, but given that Heartsbane's powers were about manipulation, she wondered if having her beautiful features marred would damage her effectiveness. She wanted to think things like beauty didn't matter to beings as powerful dragons but that was obviously naïve. Everyone at the party had been gorgeous and she had never seen a disheveled or unkempt dragon. And, of course, the scar might still heal so there was no point in mentioning it.

"I'm only happy I get to pay you back for saving my ass," Heartsbane said.

"Yeah, well, you and the Dragon Council."

"Wait—what?" her visitor demanded.

Kristen grinned as Stonequest walked in.

"You didn't hear?" he asked. He looked better and definitely stronger, although he was still pale. It seemed that getting shot in the chest slowed dragons as much as it did humans if you used the right bullets. "Kristen earned the respect of Lord Decimus Aurelius last night. Apparently, he knelt before her and promised her a life-debt."

"The Decimus Aurelius?" The woman's jaw seemed unable to close.

"No, a different one. Yes, that Aurelius."

"I...I can't... I've never even spoken to..." Heartsbane trailed off and her mouth appeared to stop moving now that her brain had basically ceased to function.

"We're proud of you," Stonequest told her. "And working with an investigator, no less. You should be proud of yourself."

Kristen shrugged, which hurt. "I think at this point, I'd rather have not been blown up than earn the honor."

He nodded, but she could tell from his aura that he didn't believe her. Her boss knew as well as she did that if it happened again, she would do the same thing.

The other dragon seemed to finally pull herself together and her mouth snapped shut, she stood straighter, and her aura fell away. "Lady Steel, I owe you a life-debt." Melissa Heartsbane—the most cantankerous individual she had ever met—dropped to one knee before her and swore an oath of allegiance.

"I...I don't know what to say," she said, both confused and a little uncomfortable.

"Say yes. Otherwise, it's a great dishonor," Stonequest said.

"I...yes, Heartsbane, thank you."

The dragon stood. "I'll protect your life with my own and do as you ask, but if I think it's a dumb fucking thing to do, I'll definitely let you know about it. So yeah, don't worry. You won't lose my peppy attitude."

Kristen smiled. It was a relief that Heartsbane was finally open about how much she respected her and also good to know it didn't mean their relationship would change substantially. After all, they were Dragon SWAT. Risking their lives for each other was part of the job description.

"She saved your life too, Stone." The woman directed a venomous glare at Stonequest.

"I know and I'm thankful, but I'd do the same for you—and you know that, right, Kristen?"

She nodded and again, triggered another wave of pain. *Note to self,* she thought, *give up on body language for the foreseeable future.*

"I won't swear allegiance to you because I'm still your boss, but… well, what do you think we should do next?" He raised an eyebrow.

Kristen hadn't had much time to think about anything. The night before had been a blur and she'd basically passed out as soon as she'd reached the hospital. On the other hand, she'd tried to decide on their best way forward since she discovered that Constance existed and that she had targeted dragons.

In her heart, she knew what they needed to do next if they wanted to prevent a war. They had to prove there were people who fought for both sides of the seemingly irreconcilable divide. Somehow, they had to prove to humans and dragons alike that justice existed for everyone and that neither the powerful dragons nor the humans who operated outside the law were above it. Perhaps most importantly, they had to prove that peace was a path into the future and if they decided to work together—actually work together, instead of merely continue to jostle for power—they could truly remake the world into something everyone could be proud of.

Her previous deliberations had revealed where it would start too. "Did you run an analysis on the shrapnel that came from my wounds?"

"Not yet," Stonequest said. "But we ran tests on what came from us. It's from the same dragon used to create the bullets—someone with a ninety percent match to your DNA."

"That's where we start, then," Kristen said. "We find this dragon, whoever they are."

"And if they're working with the technomages?" Heartsbane asked. The word had obviously stuck as it seemed everyone now used it.

"If that is the case, it's all the more reason to find out who they are and release them from whatever deals or bonds they have with Constance. We can show the world that either humans are powerful enough to exploit dragons or conversely, that dragons are willing to work with people to overthrow the world order as we know it. That will prove that people and dragons not only can work together but that we have to."

"It makes sense." Stonequest nodded. "But you know your healing powers haven't even kicked in yet. At this point, you'll be on your ass and out of commission for a month, maybe more. That might change, and it could be that Doctor Chakrabarti merely missed a piece of shrapnel. But until you start to heal, you're grounded."

"I understand," Kristen said and finally managed not to nod. "But please, keep me posted if you find anything." She didn't know if she hoped he found a lead super quickly before she healed or if she would have time to regain her full strength to help. It didn't really matter, she realized. It would happen when it happened.

"There is one more thing," she said quickly. "Heartsbane, I think I need to call in that debt."

"What? Now? Are you fucking serious?"

"I thought dragons took these things very seriously," she countered.

"They do." Stonequest glared at the other dragon.

"Yes, of course, Lady Steel," the woman said in a mock aristocratic accent. "What doth thou desire?"

"Would you mind calling my family a cab, getting them here, and picking up a couple of pizzas and beer for us?"

She had never seen the energy of an atomic bomb in human form before but she saw it now behind Heartsbane's eyes. After a long moment of silence, the woman nodded, took a deep breath, and stormed out the door. "I won't get that Detroit-style shit, though!" she hollered from down the hall. The sound of breaking glass suggested that the temperamental dragon had launched herself skyward through a window.

"Is there anything else?" Stonequest asked carefully.

"Nah, I'm fine." She closed her eyes and let herself relax. One day, she'd bring the world together—two worlds, both dragons and humans, would stand together to save the earth. What's more, she would do it with beer and pizza and the world would be better for it.

CHAPTER TWENTY-SIX

Amy Williams awoke with the kind of startled, heart-thudding response that told her immediately that something unexpected had happened. She had stayed awake until eleven thirty reading a thriller novel—fairly late for her, but she'd only collected the book from the Rangeley library that day and had been excited. They'd had to order it from one of the other Maine branches, which had meant a long wait.

She was twenty-three and back home after a fruitless search to find work in Philadelphia and Boston as neither city had offered anything that made staying there worth it. Thankfully, she had a good excuse not to stay up with her parents, who were watching their favorite show. It was basically a soap opera about dragons, but people didn't call them soap operas when they came on during primetime on extra cable channels and had actual naked people.

It wasn't like Amy was a virgin or her parents were prudes or anything—obviously not since they watched various dragons cheat on each other—but it was still uncomfortably weird to watch sexy shows or movies with them. The fortuitous arrival of the book at least saved an awkward discussion on this particular night.

They had retired hours before and although she'd been engrossed in her reading, she had apparently fallen asleep. The loud noise had yanked her into wakefulness and she lay for a moment with her eyes tightly closed as she tried to identify what it was.

It had sounded like someone crashed a truck into her parents' front porch, she decided, although the idea seemed a little far-fetched. Maybe it had simply been a dream.

Still, she wouldn't relax again until she'd at least checked, so she pulled the covers off—despite it being summer it was always chilly in Rangeley, Maine, at night— and pulled her slippers on. Then, unbelievably, a dragon tail pounded through the roof of her room.

Amy screamed and flung herself out of bed barely in time. The tail lifted again and widened the hole as it did so before it descended again in a powerful blow that converted her bed to splinters.

A bright light beamed from outside, as strong and red as sunrise, and Amy stared in shocked disbelief through the hole in the ceiling of her bedroom. She closed her eyes for a moment but when she refocused, there were definitely two dragons out there. A dark-blue beast with scales like armor plates seared its spiny green counterpart with flames. The green dragon retreated, unhurt but annoyed, until it collided with the house with a thud that could easily have been heard for miles and destroyed a chunk of the wall.

The entire building shook, and her bookshelf toppled slowly. She listened for the heavy impact with the floor—it held dozens of books —but instead, its weight simply destroyed the weakened floorboards and it plummeted into the living room. For some reason, seeing her books scattered carelessly below her upset her more than the damage to her room.

The green dragon stumbled a few feet but quickly recovered, shook itself like a wet dog, and whipped its tail behind it. The appendage created a fresh hole in the wall, but the creature paid no attention and lunged at its adversary.

The two opponents met in a flurry of claws and teeth and tails and careened into a maple tree her parents had planted when she was born. It snapped in half like kindling.

Now, smoke issued from the side of the building. The gout of flame had lit their almost hundred-year-old wood house on fire. Watching these two monsters battle was strangely hypnotic, though, and she might have stood there transfixed if not for the flames that licked up the side of the structure. The smoke seeped in and she realized for the first time that she hadn't seen her parents. Horrified, she imagined them unconscious and in danger of asphyxiation.

Amy ran to her door, flung it wide, and dashed down the hall, then the stairs. She screamed for her parents the entire time. The effort burned her throat and she struggled against the fumes that gradually filled the rooms around her. Her parents were on the far side from where the dragons had wreaked havoc so there was a chance they were still alive. They had to still be alive, she told herself, although it worried her that they hadn't reacted. Surely they couldn't have slept through the noise generated by the battle and the ensuing destruction?

Their room was to the right. To the left was the kitchen which was now filled with heat and smoke as the flames had spread rapidly along the exterior wall and found a way in.

Something started to shriek—like the world's largest tea kettle, she thought irritably—before the dark-blue dragon's flame licked the propane tank on the side of the house. In seconds, it burst from the pressure and the gas—exposed to the flame—ignited. The resultant explosion blew away half the house.

She huddled against the internal wall and her ears rang as she clutched her face and the back of her neck to protect herself from the explosion. Somehow, by a wild and impossible miracle, all the shrapnel from the blast missed her. Her mind couldn't even begin to calculate the odds of that happening, given that the wall to her left had been destroyed in a moment, but this wasn't the time to question good luck.

Reality clicked in once again and she raced through the living room—now a mess of wood, broken furniture, and kitchen gadgets. Before she could take the ten steps needed to cross the room, one of the dragons smashed into the roof.

Of course, she didn't know for a fact that it was a dragon. She couldn't see through the ceiling of the first floor other than where the hole in her floor was, and that was way on the other side. But if it wasn't one of the two beasts, it could only be a meteor—and honestly, how likely was that? The impact, however, brought part of the roof down on top of her.

Amy screamed and held her hands up to protect herself. She knew she would die, crushed by the roof erected by her great-great-grand-father…or was it her three greats? The brain went to funny places when faced with death.

Frozen in the certainty that this was the end, it took a long moment before she registered the fact that she was, in fact, still very much alive. She looked around, amazed that she could do so. A beam from the room had fallen but somehow come to rest about a foot above her head. Stunned, she gazed around her and realized that although the living room was practically destroyed, no significant debris had fallen in the space around her. A few kitchen gadgets and minor wreckage from when the propane tank had exploded littered the area but no shingles and no large fragments from the guest room that had collapsed into the living room. Something had saved her.

This seemed to be yet another instance of the weird string of good luck that had kept her safe thus far, but she didn't have time to wonder about such things.

The part of her parents' house with their room was still intact. Amy stumbled through the chaos, and as she stepped clear of the beam that had been suspended above her head, it shuddered and fell. Even from that height—maybe seven feet above the ground—it could have seriously hurt her. What was going on?

She reached her parents' room, grasped the knob, and recoiled from the searing heat it gave off. Close to panic now, she kicked the door. The hinges snapped and the wood careened across the room. Amy barely had time to register how far the door had catapulted from her blow when a blast of flame practically exploded from her parents' room, wound around her like a sheet of hot velvet, and engulfed her body in a quick burst of heat before it dissipated. She looked at her arms, certain she'd been horribly burned. To her surprise, there wasn't a mark on her. The flames must have swept past too swiftly to do damage.

She screamed into the roaring conflagration that used to be her parents' bedroom and shouted for them. "Mom! Dad!"

The far side of their room was on fire, the wall still standing but aflame although the window was broken. Amy could barely see anything through the blaze. The whole room was on fire and the bed collapsed, broken, and burning. The windows had all shattered from the heat.

A gust of wind blew through and briefly wafted the flames to one side. Charred lumps were all that remained to indicate that her parents had been in the bed. Tears streamed down her face, as much from her grief as from the smoke.

While her mind tried to assimilate the truth, her gaze drifted to the two dragons outside her parents' broken window who now fought each other in the wreckage of her dad's boat.

Her parents were dead.

They'd been slaughtered in their sleep by beings who couldn't even slow their fight to check on the humans they'd recklessly killed.

Amy had never met a dragon before. Rangeley was a tiny town with less than two thousand people, notable only in summer months for the lake where tourists could fish and maybe for the quilt store during the rest of the year. A dragon had come to enjoy the lakes— once. And apparently, they'd cared so little for the area they'd never returned. Her hometown was quiet, a welcome respite from the cities she had tried to explore. Dragons weren't supposed to be there. One of the best things about it was that it was simple and peaceful. The only dragons she knew spent their time trying to woo each other on the television.

Or kill each other.

Everyone knew dragons didn't exactly care for human lives. In the soaps, it was often a scandal when a dragon did care for a human but obviously, that was fiction. These two didn't care about the people they hurt or killed. They didn't care about anything but their stupid fight. Their callousness had killed her parents.

The thought of them doing that and not even noticing—like her mom and dad were little more than a biting fly to be swatted and tossed into a lake or maybe even less than a fly—infuriated Amy Williams.

She took a step toward them and the burning wall. As she moved, a sphere radiated from her body to push aside the smoke and the flames and encapsulate her within. She took another step forward as her fury flowed through her. It was hotter than the flames engulfing her parents' home.

Without conscious thought, she raised a hand and gestured at the wall in front of her. The flaming boards skittered into the night and struck the dragons in their path.

They stopped and turned as Amy walked through the hole she had created. While she had no idea how she had done it, she knew she had done it and not them.

She stepped from the house and her feet crunched a piece of glass from the broken window. It was only partially broken and caught her reflection mirrored in the flickering light of the blaze. Her hair was grimy with smoke and soot and her pajamas were dirty but somehow untorn after she'd negotiated the deathtrap the dragons had created from her parents' house. Her eyes, instead of an unremarkable brown, glowed scarlet, the color of blood.

One of the dragons hissed. The other inhaled and its nostrils and throat glowed as it readied itself to incinerate this woman who'd thrown a burning plank of wood—a reminder of its recklessness—from the destruction it had caused.

Amy raised her hands. "You killed my mom and dad," she said coldly.

The power coursed through her and transformed her fantasies of vengeance into reality.

CHAPTER TWENTY-SEVEN

Kristen Hall was still convalescing from the injuries she'd sustained from fighting the technomage assassin, Constance, and from the dragon bomb. It had been intended to kill dozens of dragons but in the end, she had been the only casualty.

Objectively, she was aware of this. She knew the incendiary device had been filled with shrapnel harvested from another dragon's body and had thus been able to tear through her steel skin like it had been tissue paper. Again, this was a fact her rational mind accepted. She knew these dragon pieces had penetrated her body and —despite having all been removed by a surgeon—were to blame for her especially slow recovery process. This too, seemed inarguable, given that she was healing faster than a human but much slower than a dragon.

While she'd made great progress over the last couple of days—as if her powers had begun to kick in and might have speeded up her healing—the rules were clear. She had been booked off work for an extended period because no one really had any idea how the healing process might have been compromised and so wouldn't take a chance. On a good day, she would most likely applaud their caution and concern for her wellbeing.

But knowing all this didn't mean she wasn't going out of her mind with boredom.

She also knew she shouldn't go into Dragon SWAT headquarters, given her condition, but this didn't stop her from stepping off the bus and walking into the Capital Square Building in downtown Detroit. Once there, she greeted the dragon in human form who manned the front door.

"Steel," he groused and used her dragon namesake taken from her abilities rather than the family name she'd always used with pride. "I can see from here you're not better yet. You're limping slightly and your face looks like shit."

"Oh, shut up, Grayclaw. You're only saying that because you've never seen me with makeup."

"I'm saying that because I can tell you're using it to cover bruises. What are you doing here?"

"I'm checking in." She shrugged. "Is that a problem?"

"Not for me." Some would call Grayclaw lazy, but she preferred to think of him as pragmatic. No one had told him not to let her in despite her being on leave, so he wouldn't stop her until someone did.

Kristen waltzed past him and into the elevator.

She headed to the fourth floor, but the elevator stopped at the third for someone else. The doors opened and Atramento stepped on. The mage's robe, together with his head and hand tattoos, immediately identified him to her but honestly, she could have identified him merely from his voice—or, rather, what he seemed to prefer to talk about.

"Lady Steel, your file has you out of the office for a minimum of another seventeen days. Has there been a miscalculation with your paperwork?" He had the ability to lift multiple objects and use them to do different things in tandem. It was the magic equivalent of being able to rub your belly and pat your head at the same time, multiplied by a hundred. And yet, all he did with these abilities was fill out multiple forms at once.

"Don't you ever get bored, Atramento?" Kristen grinned as she goaded the mage.

Atramento frowned. "The world is a dangerous, complex place. Boredom is proof that we're doing things right. I much prefer being bored and working for dragons than the alternative."

"What alternative?"

"The terror of true freedom," he said with an ice-cold smile.

"What does that mean?" she asked as they reached her floor and the doors opened.

He shook his head. "Nothing, Lady Steel. Nothing at all."

"Oh, come on, Jose. Don't bullshit me. You know you can be honest with me."

The technomage sighed and looked more like Jose Mendoza in that moment than his tattooed self. "I only mean I am thankful for my place here. You're a dragon, which means you can afford to get bored. Us mages…we're still people first. It's merely good to have a place to work with decent healthcare."

"You know I put people first, too," Kristen said.

"I know." He nodded. "That's the only reason I said anything at all, Lady Steel. Now, if you'll excuse me, I have more boring paperwork to file." He said it with such pride that she couldn't help but smile as she walked down the hall toward the workroom her team shared.

She pushed in to find Lumos, Emerald, and Timeflash going over something, but before she could tell what it was, Erin Timeflash turned to her and frowned.

"What are you doing here?" the woman said. Her voice edged toward sweet but it sounded forced.

"I wanted to come in and check on things." Kristen flashed the biggest smile she could.

"You're worse than Stonequest," Emerald said, folded his muscular arms, and shook his head.

"Oh, yeah, is he back?" she asked. Stonequest and Heartsbane, the other two dragons on her dragon SWAT team, had been severely hurt as well although he most likely only had a few days left before his return. Heartsbane would need a little longer but would probably also be back on duty before Kristen's allotted sick leave was up.

"No," the green dragon said flatly.

Lumos chuckled. "But he was here earlier asking to check in too." The old dragon shook his head, a grandfather amused at the energy of children.

"What did you tell him?"

"Nothing," Emerald said.

"Oh, come on. You have to give me more than that!" Kristen protested. "Constance almost killed three of us and she got away. Last time I checked, we still don't know much about the mages she works with or where they acquire all the dragon pieces. Plus, I have a sibling out there. Do you know if they are helping the technomages or are held captive—hell, or even dead by now?"

"We don't share that information with civilians," Emerald said. His green eyes twinkled—Kristen could tell he was enjoying this—but his jaw was hard.

"Oh, it's fine, Emerald, really," Erin said. She'd always been the softy on the team. "We haven't found any new information, but we haven't been running the hardest investigation."

"And why not?" she demanded.

"Because we've been focused on security," Lumos explained. "We've made the rounds and checked any meeting places with more than two dragons. We think Constance and the other technomages have chosen to lie low for a while. Either they're dumb and expended their resources on that bomb, or they're smart and they don't want to rush into a war when every dragon in the Midwest and most of the dragons in North America are still on edge from almost being blown up."

"Either way, we only have one thing to tell you," Emerald said.

"What's that?" Kristen asked and it was clear to everyone that her week of boredom fueled her curiosity.

"Go take a vacation!" His hard jaw finally cracked, and he laughed. Lumos did too and Erin smiled warmly.

"Seriously, though, Kristen, you've earned a rest," the woman said. "The Dragon Council has me positioned here until you, Stonequest, and Heartsbane are back, and between Emerald, Lumos, and I, we have centuries of security experience."

"I know, I know—really, I do. But I'm so bored and this is my case."

"Not right now it's not," Emerald said.

"Do you know what Melissa is doing?" Erin asked and used Heartsbane's first name, no doubt to remind her that they were all off duty right now.

"What?" she asked.

"She's at a three-day, all-inclusive spa. Maybe try that."

"You guys, come on. I know I can't fight yet, but I can help."

"What we need is the Steel Dragon back on the force. The best way for you to do that is to eat and sleep. Stressing over paperwork won't help," Lumos said.

"You know I don't care about paperwork," she complained.

"So how exactly would you help us, then?" the old dragon replied smoothly.

Kristen glared at him. He'd set that trap for her and she had walked right into it. "Okay, then. I can see I won't get anywhere with you three and that's fine. But promise me you'll let me know if anything happens."

They shared a look that told her their answer was a unanimous no.

"All right… I…okay, let me know when Stonequest and Heartsbane are back."

"That we can do," Erin said and shooed her out the door.

It was obvious she would achieve nothing there and she worried that if she stuck around too long, Atramento and Lumos might team up to get her to file paperwork. To avoid this, she headed to the roof.

She still wasn't a hundred percent—although her instinct said she was very close—but she felt good enough to fly and had done so for a while, although she hadn't actually put it to the test. Maybe she'd visit her brother Brian and play videogames to take her mind off being forced to stay home.

Their concern was understandable—and it made sense given that the long-term effects of the dragon weapons were largely unknown—but it was hard for her to sit still given that Constance was still out there. There was some consolation in the fact that after the bomb at the last party almost obliterated the majority of dragon high society in North America, the dragons were on high alert. She didn't think the assassin and her technomages would have as easy a time with any new plan they devised.

Aside from that, Stonequest and Heartsbane were also both at home while they recovered, so at least she wasn't the only one stuck on the sidelines. Still, it didn't help that she felt so much better than she had even three days before. Her mind was now diverted from suffering and free to rampage through all her frustrations.

She wandered out onto the roof and gazed across Detroit in late summer. The city continued its usual routines without her. That was good and she was relieved that there were no issues she needed to resolve, but it didn't do much for her boredom.

A dragon appeared in the distance and flew closer before it descended between the skyscrapers and approached Dragon SWAT HQ. Kristen knew she should leave but her curiosity immediately demanded to be sated.

She recognized it as Windlock and was a little disappointed at the impression he made. In dragon form, he was fairly drab. His scales were slate-gray and the horns that jutted from his head and the spikes that followed his spine were only slightly darker.

He landed on the roof and assumed his human form. Despite the warmth of the day, he still wore a trench coat and a black hat. He didn't smile when he saw her, but she couldn't take offense. The dragon hardly ever smiled.

"Investigator," she said, bowed respectfully, and felt goofy for doing so. "How are you?"

"I'm well, Lady Steel," Windlock said and bowed as well despite the two having worked together. "I'm surprised to see you here. Are you back on duty yet? The last I heard, Stone was still out."

"Yeah…er, no. That is, yes, Stonequest is still out, and no, I'm not back on duty yet."

He studied her for a long moment and finally narrowed his eyes before the corners of his mouth twitched with the faintest of smiles. For him, it was practically a guffaw of laughter. "Are you trying to make your dragon aura seem bored for my benefit or are you having a lousy time being on rest?"

Kristen smiled. "I confess, I'm guilty of boredom."

"Well, if it's any consolation, nothing's happened—at least in Detroit." Windlock raised an eyebrow and obviously waited for the inevitable questions.

"Then where have things happened?" she asked and snapped at the bait.

"Have you ever heard of Rangeley?" he asked.

"Is that in the upper peninsula or something?" she asked and tried to picture it on a map.

"Maine, actually," he said. "I was coming here to pick Brockton up to head that way. But seeing you here...well, there might be people involved and you definitely have an eye for humans that I don't. I could use your keen eyes and a compassionate heart, to be honest."

"Oh, yes, anything to get back to work," she replied immediately.

"I can have you assigned to me if you'd like, but I want to be clear —there'll be no fighting or anything like that. That's the only reason I'll take you at all."

"That's fine," Kristen said as her fingers traced the bruise on her face that was a constant reminder of her circumstances. Honestly, the bruises were slow to heal but they created the false impression that she was far weaker than she actually was. "I'm not a hundred percent yet anyway although I really don't feel as bad as I still look."

"Can you transform into your dragon form?"

She did so in a flash in the usual flurry of what looked like silver confetti.

"And you can fly?"

With a sigh, she nodded. "When the bomb detonated, I was in my human form so my wings didn't get hurt at all, and that bulletproof vest covered my face, chest, and shoulders. Honestly, flying is no problem." She didn't tell him that she had erred on the sign of caution and taken the bus over there.

"Walk with me," Windlock said and headed toward the door to the interior of the building. She changed into her human form and followed him.

"So here's what we know. Rangeley, Maine is a summer tourist town nestled between a number of lakes and has a population of less than two thousand. It's not exactly dragon territory."

"Okay."

"Two dragons were involved in a fight in the woods nearby. Apparently, they had a history."

"Had?"

The investigator nodded, understanding her question. "A mage called the Boston Dragon SWAT team and told them they were wreaking significant destruction on the town. By the time the team from Boston arrived, both dragons were dead. So yeah, their history has come to an end."

They exited the stairwell and moved toward Windlock's office.

"They killed each other?" Kristen asked.

"That's the conclusion the Boston team reached, but I don't think so, not based on the evidence."

"You think it was the technomages?"

"From the report I received, I think we can rule that out too. It doesn't sound like dragon bullets or a single bomb either."

"What do you think it was?"

Windlock did smile at that. "What kind of investigator would I be if I had an idea of what happened even before I saw the crime scene? All I know is that it sounds… What's the human term? Fishy. The situation sounds fishy to me. It might ultimately be nothing and could be that the Boston team didn't describe the bodies properly. But either way, I intend to investigate the scene with Brockton. Do you want to come along?"

"Absolutely," she said. "I mean, it would be an honor, sir."

He waved the courtesy away. "You saved my hide along with everyone else's on that roof. You don't have to use any of the formality on me."

They reached the office, where Larry Brockton was obscured by a thousand floating sheets of paper.

"Windlock!" the mage stammered, and every piece of paper hastily settled into messy, haphazard stacks on various surfaces. If she hadn't known Windlock and Brockton, she might have thought that he had thrown the dragon investigator's room into disarray, but the chaos was no different than it always was.

"Were you trying to organize again?" the dragon asked.

"Absolutely," Brockton said and grinned. "What would we do if we ever lost you, Windlock? You have evidence for a hundred cases in here, all buried in a thousand stacks. I see references to references and don't know what any of it means. If we could simply put it in order, maybe we could keep it that way."

"It is in order," Windlock said.

"This is not order." His assistant gestured to the leaning piles of files. "This is two steps from disaster."

"Which is better than one," his boss retorted and poked around in a few of them. He seemed to find what he was looking for about halfway down one, wedged his hand into the stack, and pulled out a little evidence baggy with something silver and sparkly inside.

Kristen didn't recognize the object—some kind of jewelry, maybe? —but Brockton seemed to. The mage frowned when he saw it.

"We have a case, then?"

Windlock nodded as he shoved the item into his pocket. "We do. Nothing conclusive yet, but I thought you'd want to come."

"Oh yeah? Do I have a choice in the matter?" his assistant asked, his characteristic jauntiness absent.

"It's in Rangeley, Maine. Isn't that close to where you're from?"

"Maine! Why didn't you say so? Let's go!" Whatever had bothered the man evaporated and he hurried ahead of them to the roof, where the dragons transformed and took to the skies with Brockton on his boss' back.

CHAPTER TWENTY-EIGHT

They reached Rangeley before nightfall—something only possible with the late sunsets of summer in the far north of the United States. Windlock had insisted that they'd fly slower than usual because of Kristen. Her wings didn't hurt—as she'd explained to the investigator, they hadn't been directly injured—but she'd definitely felt the exertion, probably due to lack of exercise.

Still, she hadn't been exhausted and the strength she usually had in her dragon form hadn't been noticeably affected. It might have been different if they'd flown at maximum speed, and she'd wisely chosen not to push too hard on her first time out and to rather use the air currents as much as possible. Her companion thrust through the air to forge through any resistance and she drafted in his wake like a migrating goose, a flying technique her team often used so she didn't feel it was cheating or a sign of weakness.

It had been an enjoyable flight. Once beyond Detroit, they'd flown over Lake Erie, then Lake Ontario. They passed over Niagara Falls, a sight she had seen before as a girl but not something she'd ever thought she'd see from above. One of the world's largest bodies of fresh water draining into another seen from that vantage point was truly memorable. From there, they'd soared over the vast tracts of forest that made up most of Vermont while Brockton had waxed philosophical about pine trees. He was able to make some kind of bubble of energy around himself to keep the wind off and it also somehow helped his voice to carry.

Kristen had thought they'd fly north of the lakes, though. She'd checked how to get to Rangeley on her phone before they left, and it was clear that a straight line would have put them over Canada. Windlock didn't want to do this, however.

"Canada is dwarf country. We're not supposed to go there without a reason."

"You mean like a warrant?" she asked.

"Not exactly. Warrants only work where your laws are valid and the Dragon Council's laws don't hold sway there, but we have an agreement. If a dragon strays into their territory, we offer to help catch them and pay for damages. It's better than having a hostile neighbor."

"What he means," Brockton said from the interior of his force bubble, which made her wonder if he'd extended it to carry the sound to her ears somehow, "is that the dwarves are tough little bastards. Strong as a dragon, and their skin is thicker than a rhino and about as flammable as rock. They're not fun to piss off. Oh, plus auras don't work on them."

"A fair assessment," Windlock agreed. "There is no reason to go there. Our target is in Rangeley, Maine, not Canada, so it's preferable to take the extra hour."

At some point, Kristen began to wonder if they had indeed flown into enemy airspace. They'd moved well beyond the forests of Vermont and entered Maine—not that this was at all clear from the air as forests didn't exactly respect political boundaries. The route the investigator had chosen now took them over the system of lakes that surrounded Rangeley and made it such a popular destination for summer tourists. In contrast to the almost idyllic scene, two dragons circled toward them from the tiny town.

Beyond them, the swathe of destruction caused by the dragons blighted the landscape. At the center of it all was the burned ruin of what had been a beautiful home less than twenty-four hours before.

"This is restricted air space!" one of the dragons shouted and flexed his aura to show them he was willing to defend the area by force if he had to. He was bronze with large thick scales, more like an ankylosaurus than most dragons were. "Turn back. If you're looking for Bangor, you have a way to go yet."

Kristen had expected an accent something like Brockton's, but he sounded more like he was from Boston. She filed that away under curious details.

"Who is your superior?" Windlock demanded and his aura made it clear that he thought he was the superior dragon.

"This case belongs to Garth Timbergust," the dragon replied. There was something in the way he said the name that made her think the bronze dragon and whoever was in charge weren't exactly old friends.

"Well, Timbergust should know to expect an investigator who is looking into this case on behalf of the North American Dragon Council. Are you telling me he didn't tell his officers about who you'd coordinate with?"

The other dragon—blueish-green like the color of the open sea and with spines that reminded her of an iguana—called out to his bronze teammate. "Captain Emberslight said to expect Investigator Windlock, but she didn't say there'd be two dragons and a mage." She noticed two things about this dragon. First, he said his captain's name as "Ember's light," and second, he seemed accustomed to try to cover for his more aggressive and volatile companion.

"I have brought additional help—something I would think Timbergust would recognize as prudent, given that he's the only member of dragon SWAT tasked with this rural area. Why are you here and where are you from?" Windlock didn't sound irritated, but he told everyone he was with his aura.

"We're from Boston, sir. Boston Dragon SWAT. Four of us came to help at Timbergust's request. I am officer Aquatos and this is officer Bronzeback. He is the best fighter we have on the force."

"And don't you forget it," Bronzeback all but hissed.

"Well, we're on the same side here so I don't see the relevance," the investigator replied dismissively. "This is Lady Kristen Steel of the Detroit SWAT—you've no doubt heard of her—and on my back is my personal mage, Larry Brockton."

"Of course, sir," Aquatos replied. "If you'll follow me."

Kristen noted that she'd never heard Windlock call Brockton that before. His personal mage. What did that mean, exactly?

Brockton seemed not to notice or, if he did, showed no reaction, which made her even more curious. Still, she tucked it away as something to ponder later. Aquatos and Bronzeback led them across the airspace over the tiny town and it soon became apparent that there was more than enough happening down below to keep them occupied for the evening.

They landed within a perimeter of tape that didn't quite surround everything that had been destroyed. It was centered on the burned, almost demolished house and encircled much of the surrounding property. The cordon included a maple tree stump that had been snapped in half and apparently cleared away and a boat that had been flattened, but it didn't surround a car that had been crushed on the street or a few blackened patches of grass, no doubt caused by dragon fire.

She didn't approve of the sloppy perimeter, but she could understand. Besides the two dragons in the air, there were three others, but none of them investigated what had happened to the house. Instead, they attempted to hold back the huge crowd of people who had converged on the crime scene.

"I thought this town had a population of less than two thousand," she muttered.

If that were the case, it looked like every single member of the town was there, but Kristen quickly recognized that only a few were clearly locals. A crowd of perhaps a few hundred people who wore mostly denim, plaid, and camo, held signs that basically demanded accountability for the damages wreaked by the dragons—*Reparations for the Williams!*, *Human tourism > dragon carnage*, and *Dragon-Free Rangeley* seemed the most popular.

Kristen thought that if this crowd wasn't from Rangeley itself, they were likely from the surrounding area and certainly from Maine.

The remainder, she realized with both amusement and disgust, were tourists. They didn't chant or join the protestors' demands about taking action and instead, milled around and took photos. Instead of denim, plaid, and camo, they wore khaki shorts, polo shirts, and merchandise bespeaking the beauty of Rangeley—no doubt only recently purchased in a nearby hotel gift shop.

To her shock, she saw a tourist—wearing stylish sunglasses despite the setting sun—sneak under the police tape to take a selfie of himself with one of the dead dragons. One of the SWAT members who worked the perimeter noticed him and moved with a burst of dragon speed to remove the selfie-snapper. While she was occupied with him, another few people used the opportunity to duck under the cordon to take pictures of their own.

In a word, it was chaos.

Unsure of what else to do, Kristen moved toward the two dragon bodies in the hope that her presence might spook the people enough to dissuade them from using their smartphones. The idea had merit, but it was doomed to failure. As soon as they saw an actual dragon— and the Steel Dragon, no less—they began to take pictures of her. She barely noticed the attention, though, completely distracted when she saw the carnage. No other word could really describe the two dead dragons, and her blood ran cold.

She didn't know exactly what Windlock had been told and she hadn't asked. He made good points about not jumping to conclusions without examining the evidence, and if he'd told her what he'd heard, she'd have already begun to form opinions. Even with him saying little, she had assumed that Constance and her band of killer techno-mages must have been responsible. She now saw that this was simply not the case.

There was no way that either of these dragons was killed by a single bullet to the chest or the head. Hell, there was no way either of them was killed with ten bullets.

Both were a bloody mess. They looked like they'd been shredded by a tornado, run over by a tank, then rolled downhill in a rockslide.

"What could do this?" Kristen asked aloud. She'd never seen a human body in such a condition, let alone the body of a dragon. It was beyond unthinkable that something could do this to them.

"Officially, we call this catastrophic massive damage," Windlock said. "That's not what killed them, exactly, but this is what happens when a dragon suffers enough damage to overwhelm their healing abilities."

"I thought you had to destroy a dragon's heart or brain to kill them."

"There are other ways. I read that in the first rebellion, a team of dwarves would sometimes drive a dragon into a castle and bring the entire structure down on top of them. That has a way of trumping healing powers," Brockton said as he slid off Windlock's back.

The mage raised his hands toward the dead dragons, and they began to glow. Immediately, one of the three members of Dragon SWAT who worked the perimeter strode toward them.

He was a burly man—a local dragon, given his baseball cap and bushy beard—and when he transformed, Kristen couldn't help but think of him as a forest dragon. His body was the green of pine needles and he had moss growing on him in places. His horns were large, brown, and curled like a ram's. He was beautiful, although the effect was diminished somewhat by the fact that he approached with evident anger, his nostrils smoking and smelling of pine.

Brockton—as intent as he was on the bodies before him—didn't notice at first, but the crowd certainly did. The protestors grew louder but the tourists drowned them out with oohs and ahs like they thought this was a performance they could later post on social media. In the appealing twilight of the early evening, their phones all flashed to better capture images of the forest dragon who marched toward the others, one steel and the other slate-gray.

The mage realized that a dragon was moving toward him a split second after the crowd did, yelped, and promptly hid behind Windlock's dragon body.

"Who the fuck are you?" the green dragon demanded. His aura proved that he was out of patience. Tired, exhausted, and overwhelmed were the sensations that emanated from him, the antithesis to his cool, green, mossy exterior.

"I am Investigator Windlock, here on behalf of the Dragon Council, and Garth Timbergust has been informed that I would be in attendance. Have you seen him? It doesn't seem he's done a good job of informing his inferiors."

"I am Garth Timbergust and I wasn't asking about you but about that damn mage. Did you return to finish the job, huh?" the dragon demanded. Kristen recognized the tone from when she was on Detroit's human SWAT force. He was in way over his head but wouldn't say so.

"I can assure you, Larry Brockton was in Detroit at the time of this incident and I have him fettered. He is no way responsible for this," Windlock said. "Now, I suggest we all take our human forms and stop yelling about an open investigation lest we risk alerting whoever is responsible for this to exactly what we know."

"You don't have any right to march in here and—"

"I have every right, but our difference of opinion is not important. This place is already a zoo and the last thing we need is an experienced dragon who has been responsible for this post for centuries to make it worse by starting a fight with an ally." Windlock didn't yell any more than Captain Hansen at Detroit SWAT did, but his voice grew icier as he spoke until his words seemed so brittle, she could almost imagine they might break.

Kristen thought she did an admirable job of restraining her grin during the tongue-lashing. She'd been through enough of those herself when she was on Detroit SWAT and had to admit, it was much nicer to see it from the outside.

The two dragons held each other's gaze for a moment. Timbergust's stout, dragon jaw was set, and he revealed no fear. He was bigger than Windlock, thicker, and broader at the shoulder—a pine tree compared to a city shrub. Then again, most dragons were bigger than the investigator, so a show of size didn't intimidate him in the slightest. He stared in response without flinching and showed neither fear nor anger in his aura, only steely, unblinking resolve.

Timbergust finally broke the impasse, not by looking away but by transforming into his human body.

Windlock immediately followed so Kristen did too.

This drew a disappointed sigh from the crowd. No doubt the tourists had hoped for a real story to tell their friends around the watercoolers when they returned to work.

"Shit, man, I'm sorry. Today's been an absolute nightmare, you know?" Timbergust said. "I knew these guys. Shit, Jadebite was one of my buddies. Orion wasn't a bad guy, not really. He liked a good scuffle, is all. That's why he lived out here. Neither one of them deserved to die at the hands of some...some..." His gaze briefly found Brockton, then slid away. "Business like this," he finished lamely.

"How about you get those two dragons out of the sky, station them on the perimeter, and tell me what you know."

"Yeah, sure. Emberslight!" the SWAT leader shouted to a slender woman with hair as red as Kristen's. "Go ahead and bring them down like you wanted to." He shook his head.

Kristen had begun to understand the dynamics at work. Timbergust was obviously local, but it seemed clear that no one else was. The rest of the team had come in from somewhere else—Boston, she assumed, given what Windlock had said before they'd left Detroit—and were apparently under Emberslight's command. Given how the forest dragon had reacted, this seemed to be the first time anything like this had ever happened in his sprawling rural jurisdiction.

"Jadebite and Orion were both small-time dragons," he explained. "Jadebite had a coal mine close to the power plant, which proved extremely lucrative. He made his money that way and hasn't had to work since. Given his aggressive tendencies, he liked to live in the woods. Orion didn't have as much money and he blamed Jadebite for it. He convinced the folks to put the power plant as close as it is to Jadebite's mine, which basically ensured the demand for coal, so he thought he should have a share. They would fight over it once or twice a decade."

"To be clear, are you working under the assumption that these two dragons killed each other?" Windlock asked.

"Fuck no!" Timbergust sent a furious glare at Brockton before he looked away quickly. "A mage did this," he stated coldly.

The investigator nodded.

"Anyway, they fought every ten years or so, like I said, especially when Orion was low on funds. It was never authorized but was always legal. They usually did it out in the woods and didn't bother anything but the trees. This time, they wandered into town and damaged a human house. I know it's not ideal, but it's happened before."

"Not ideal?" Kristen demanded. This was yet another example of how some dragons treated humans as expendable or as some kind of resource to be conserved when convenient and written off when lost. While she had learned that some were more sympathetic to humans, many still adhered to the old, established order.

"No, it's not fucking ideal. This crowd is a nightmare. The last time the two of them destroyed a house was in the winter damn near fifty years ago—a summer vacation home. I was able to get a team of humans to fix the damn thing before the owners even missed it."

"Well, that was kind of you," she said and tried to sound professional. Windlock stared intently at her, willing her not to say anything. She understood his position. Now was not the time to dissect human and dragon politics but it didn't mean it wasn't frustrating. While she had seen small but positive indications here and there that fueled her belief that change was possible, she had also witnessed a fair amount of injustice that was always skewed in favor of the dragons.

Somewhat naively, she had hoped that out there in the middle of nowhere, humans might get a fair shake since this was their territory, but that didn't seem to be the case. Still, the idea that human lives were seen as expendable even where most dragons didn't live pissed her off. Maybe it was simply boredom and frustration, but her patience seemed far less than usual.

"What happened to Jadebite and Orion?" Windlock asked.

"That's where things get screwy. Sometime after their duel moved onto the human property, they were killed. There were no eyewitnesses, of course, and no dragons until Boston Dragon SWAT arrived."

"And humans?" the investigator asked.

Timbergust shrugged and shook his head. "A few of them saw the battle. It was loud, of course, and they blasted fire at each other so woke up a few locals."

"What did they say?" Windlock asked.

Again, the other dragon shook his head. "This isn't in my report because it's unreliable, even for human testimony, but what a few of them say is that they saw a human step out of the burning building and annihilate the dragons. Apparently, they raised their hands and created a tornado or something. I don't know, though. Like I said, it's screwy. The only reason I said anything is because you asked and more than one person said the same thing."

"You don't believe them?" Windlock frowned.

"I don't know what to believe. It's been hundreds of years since a human killed a dragon, but all the evidence points to exactly that." Timbergust shook his head again as if physically denying the hypothesis might ensure it couldn't come true. "Emberslight and her team found traces of magic around the bodies. It's been a long time, but I know that in the past, there have been mages capable of that. There's one who crashed that party in Detroit, right? Maybe she came up here or something."

"That's an angle we're pursuing. Thank you for your testimony, Officer Timbergust. Now, if you'll excuse us, we'd like to take a look around. If you could make sure the perimeter is secure, that'd be great. If anyone from Boston SWAT gives you trouble, send them to me."

"You got it." He nodded and finally smiled. "Thanks for giving me back my beat," he said and wandered away, not realizing that the investigator hadn't given him his jurisdiction but had, in fact, taken it for himself.

Once he was gone, Windlock moved to look at the bodies more closely.

Kristen turned to Brockton. "It seems like a mage must have done this, right?"

Larry shrugged. "Once, that might have been the case but now, we're fettered so we can't," he replied.

"What do you mean?"

He pulled the sleeve of his robe up slightly and displayed a thin silver bracelet on his wrist. It looked familiar to her but for a moment, she couldn't place where she'd seen it before. Irritated, she forced herself to focus and her mind finally returned to the memory of when she'd had to stay in dragon prison. The bracelet looked like it was made of the same metal as the anklet she'd had to wear that had blocked her powers.

The man leaned in and lowered his voice. "All mages are forced into servitude to a dragon. I told you when we met that when my powers manifested, they gave me a choice to either join up or be eaten."

"Yeah, I remember, but you never explained that you had something like this on."

"Not all mages do. But if we're too powerful, the dragons clamp one of these onto our wrists which limits our potential. They can't have humans running around who might actually be a threat to a dragon, right?"

"Okay… So what you're saying is that if a mage did this, they'd have to be unfettered, right?"

He nodded. "Right, and we don't even call them mages. I like the term rogue mage and have worked enough of these cases with Windlock that he uses it too, but the official legal jargon is 'uncontrolled magic-user.' Mage is a status conferred on us by dragons."

"So what kind of uncontrolled magic-user would be unfettered?" Kristen asked.

"There are only two kinds, really. First, the people whose power has only recently manifested. That's how I started. In those cases, dragons find out and fetter us. Then there are people like Constance who have experience and haven't been taken under dragon control. They are truly dangerous."

"I don't understand. She has obviously used her powers for a long time."

"This may be a surprise, but Constance Vigil isn't all that strong as mages go. She has augmented speed and strength, obviously, and some control over wind—enough to make her capable of extended jumps—but that doesn't really make her a threat. She needs guns to kill dragons. It's impressive that she has never been caught, but with powers like that, she's not a real danger."

"You're saying that if a mage did this, they're more powerful than her?"

Brockton's eyes narrowed. "Much more powerful. We're talking hurricanes compared to a summer breeze. If a mage like that isn't fettered, the same thing always happens. Sometimes, they last a year or two or maybe even five, work on their powers and hone them, and try to control the magic in their blood. Eventually, though, they all end the same way."

"How's that?"

"Boom," he replied and mimed an explosion with his hands.

CHAPTER TWENTY-NINE

"Brockton, come take a look at this." Windlock gestured for Larry to join him and the mage complied. "I think I have all that can be found simply by looking at the bodies. I see considerable blunt-force trauma and some lacerations. My guess would be physical combat or somehow, these two encountered a hurricane. Can you confirm?"

"You got it, boss. It's been a while so I'm not sure what I'll actually be able to sense but might as well show the Steel Dragon how we work." Larry winked at Kristen and motioned for her to come closer.

He closed his eyes and extended his fingers. The faintest of breezes lifted his robe before the area fell still. The magic seemed to cast a chill over the assembled crowd as well, and she noticed that those who still lingered began to drift away. Maybe it was merely that with five dragons working the perimeter instead of three, it was far more difficult to get a selfie so there was less impetus to stay. She also noticed that many of the locals were very interested in whatever was happening at the demolished home.

Kristen banished these minor distractions and settled herself to watch the mage at work. Surprisingly, he opened his eyes again almost immediately.

"I did not expect that," he spluttered, his eyes wide with shock.

"What?" she asked, unable to stop herself from speaking the obvious question aloud.

"There's a ton of residual magic around this whole area. The house is practically glowing. It's no wonder Timbergust noticed it, honestly. I had a sense of something when we came in, but I thought there must have been other mages snooping around before we arrived."

"You saw Timbergust's reaction to you." Windlock nodded at him. "You're the first mage he's seen all day."

The man nodded like he understood but his brow wrinkled in confusion.

"What's wrong?" Kristen asked.

"There shouldn't be this much overt power present so long after the event. Magic doesn't come into being from nowhere. It has to flow in and out of things. That's why so many of us have the looped tattoos or the spirals shaved in our hair—it helps that flow. For this much to still remain in the air...I... Well, let's say there must have been one hell of a flood of power for there to be this much left." He closed his eyes again and looked around, still concerned. "The only way this amount is possible is that the person who cast this must have drawn on enormous reservoirs of power and hurled it willy-nilly."

"It doesn't sound like someone with training to me," Kristen said.

The mage shook his head. "No way. This seems like the work of someone untrained, but if so, it's one hell of a novice."

Windlock nodded like he wasn't surprised at these revelations. "Do you think you can show me anything from the event?"

"That's why you keep me around, isn't it?"

"It's certainly not for your charming personality."

Brockton rolled his eyes but he smiled, obviously comfortable with the banter.

He sat perhaps ten feet away from the two dead dragons, crossed his legs, and closed his eyes. First, his fingertips began to glow, then his arms, shoulders, and soon, his entire body was enveloped in a light-blue aura.

A mist formed in the air, faint enough to see through for maybe fifty feet but after that, Kristen couldn't see a thing. For a moment, she sighed and wondered if it would ruin his magic. She finally realized that it was the magic when the outline of a dragon barreled through the nebulous vapor, skidded through the yard, and careened into the front porch of the house that was now recreated in mist. When part of the dragon went under part of the porch, it vanished temporarily, then reappeared and swirled the faint blue trails in its wake.

Of course, the dragon wasn't actually there and only the shape of it was outlined. All she could see was the top of it or whatever part faced up. It tucked its legs under it and they vanished completely, and the mist stopped on the ridges and spines on its back.

Another dragon outline flew in and the first vaulted up and swung its tail through the roof. The dragons fought near the house for a few seconds—it was very difficult for her to tell their insubstantial versions apart—before one of them was hurled by the other into the wall of the almost spectral home.

The hazy magic didn't reveal much detail, but a massive crack appeared where the huge body had made impact. Suddenly, suggestions of detail were visible inside the house—a bedroom, maybe? It was hard to tell because barely a sliver of the interior could be seen, only the part exposed to the mist.

With an almost casual whip of its tail, the dragon proceeded to wreak further destruction on the already weakened structure.

A maple-tree outline broke in half as the combatants engaged once more and only a ragged stump remained

The misty façade of the house seemed to crumble, and Kristen realized it was on fire. No flames were visible, only their effects, but if the damage that slowly eroded the phantom-like veneer was any indication, the house blaze was substantial.

"We have survivors." Windlock pointed to a window where two people emerged and vanished into the night as their forms faded into nothing as soon as they stepped beyond the misty area the mage had created.

In the next moment, the building seemed to crumple.

"What was that?" Windlock asked.

"I can't really rewind this, you know?" Brockton said through clenched teeth.

Kristen focused on the vision and decided that a propane tank had exploded. It seemed to be what had done most of the damage to the property.

The two dragons were now locked in combat in another corner of the yard. Windlock watched them but she focused on the house and saw the roof collapse.

"What's that?" she asked and pointed to a sphere that seemed to form at the center of the wreckage. It was hard to tell exactly what it was because there was so much debris, but something about it seemed very odd. A giant ball had somehow stopped the roof from falling? It couldn't have been a piece of furniture because she could see the remains of the house now and there was nothing even remotely resembling that.

The mage merely grunted. He didn't seem to be able to do anything other than to display the events as they happened. She thought she might have imagined it or that it was perhaps a problem with the magic, but the sphere reappeared and this time, emerged from the side of the house closest to the dragons.

Some of the boards whipped ahead of the orb-like shape and struck the misty forms of the combatants.

"That's our mage," Larry said through clenched teeth.

"Can you get through the sphere?" Windlock asked and his tone verged on demanding.

"No…no way… It's too strong."

"You've cracked shields before," the investigator said.

"None like this."

Kristen assumed the dragons and the mage were talking—more like yelling at each other—because after a moment, the two dragons simply stood in what might have been astonishment. It was hard to tell with only their misty outlines.

Finally, one of the dragons apparently became enraged and it attempted to incinerate whoever was inside the sphere. Again, she couldn't see the flames, but she'd seen dragons inhale in preparation to release their fire and recognized the strike quite easily.

"Shit, here it comes." Brockton dripped with sweat and his teeth clenched again as if to ready himself to withstand an assault.

The nebulous mage made some kind of counterattack that careened the dragons away. They tumbled but weren't seriously injured and both found their feet almost instantly. Their battle forgotten, they reared, inflated their chests, and extended their long necks with open jaws aimed at the person inside the sphere.

She could only imagine what it must have been like for the dragons. Larry had used a shield to protect himself from the wind that was practically invisible. The massive creatures tried to incinerate the person at the same time, only for their target to shrug the flames off and remain standing. She wondered if a dragon could feel dread or if they merely took the human's survival as an insult to their own power.

Obviously, whoever was inside the sphere didn't like what they had tried to do and a moment after the massive jaws closed, the fire blasts expended, a bolt lanced out from the protective shield.

It struck one of the dragons and catapulted it farther than the first attack against them had. Another bolt followed and struck the second.

The two truly forgot their duel at this point and attacked in tandem with claw, tooth, and tail. They slashed and battered the orb in a combined effort to penetrate it, while blasts of energy tried to push them back.

The attacks continued until the hidden mage realized that the blasts didn't seem to be working and resorted to using parts of her burned house as projectiles against the attackers.

This seemed equally as ineffective, but the dragons swatted at these attacks with their tails as they continued to try to crack the barrier protecting their adversary. While it sparked and flared beneath their assault, they couldn't break it.

Instead, the mage discerned their weakness and began to bring in more objects to fight them with. Soon, trees and boulders rocketed through the mist to pummel them. For a while, they withstood this onslaught but eventually, one of the rocks connected powerfully with the skull of one of the dragons and it fell. Its misty version sprawled precisely on top of its dead body.

The other fought for a while longer with vicious attacks as it maneuvered around a growing stream of debris. The mage inside the sphere launched various objects like lethal missiles, all ripped from the landscape itself. Kristen finally understood the sheer devastation that defined the scene. Oddly, though, none of the debris littered the area and she frowned as she considered that. The scars remained but the actual weapons used seemed to have vanished.

The dragon tried once again to incinerate the mage, and this proved to be its downfall. It inhaled fiercely to gather air for its fiery blast and a tree trunk punched through its chest.

Its misty avatar fell on top of its body and lay still.

She knew enough of dragon anatomy to know that killing a dragon with a piece of wood—even a tree branch—should be basically impossible. While one could stab the membranes in their wings or maybe damage part of their tail, wood simply wasn't strong enough to penetrate dragon scale, the ribcage, and destroy the heart. That it had worked at all only proved how much damage the mage had inflicted first. For this to have killed it, there was no doubt that it had been completely exhausted and its healing power totally expended.

When the second dragon died, the mage finally dropped their shield. In the unnatural silence that followed, a woman gasped softly when the sphere vanished to reveal a young woman within. Kristen looked around quickly and made a mental note of the spectator's features. Could it be someone who knew the mage—perhaps her mother or an old friend? Someone had recognized her, though, which meant a possible lead.

Kristen squinted to focus on the faintest outline of a young woman, too roughly rendered by the mist to capture her features with any certainty. She looked at the destruction she had caused and screamed. There was obviously no sound but the anguish on the indistinct features of this misty version of her was clear.

As she shrieked her distress, trapped in silence, all the trees, boulders, and debris spun away from the misty area Brockton had created and presumably vanished into the woods or the lake, given that no one had reported a storm of boulders and branches in the area. The woman looked at her hands as if in shock before she collapsed to her knees and sobbed.

The mist vanished abruptly as if swallowed by an unseen vacuum.

"I'm sorry." Brockton wiped the sweat from his brow. "I couldn't maintain it any longer. That amount of magic…its… I can't."

"It's fine, kid. You did well." Windlock patted him on the back.

The mage smiled at the gesture, but Kristen found it haunting—like he was an obedient dog, she thought caustically, a little surprised by her reaction. Still, something within her seemed to have worked itself up into a tirade.

He had worked what a regular human would call a miracle, looked into the past, and received a pat on the back for it? What did he get when he stopped a murderer? A belly rub?

Kristen knew he spoke kindly of Windlock and that the two of them had a long-standing and very amicable working relationship. In this moment, however, with her senses and logic turned inside out by what she'd witnessed, it simply seemed like more evidence of the poorly balanced relationship people had with dragons. He shouldn't have to curry favor like a puppy, and mages shouldn't have to rely on being lucky with their dragon "owner" in order to continue a decent life.

Part of her instantly felt guilt about the inner snark while the other part protested that she was merely heartily sick of learning more and more about dragon culture, only to continuously find that it always struck the same notes. They would find this mage—she was committed to that—but the idea of doing it only so they could shackle her was too much for her to simply accept. Larry seemed to believe that it was also for the mage's own safety and she had no reason to doubt him. But was it really possibly for one's own power to destroy one or was it because there was no system in place to teach mages how to control and manage it?

The thought startled her into a momentary pause. Did Windlock believe that he was protecting Larry? Brockton's fetter had come as a shock to her because she'd never heard of anything like that. The truth seemed to challenge what she'd assumed about the working relationship between him and Windlock and the sense of friendship she'd assigned to them. It was hard to accept that the dragon she thought she knew was willing to effectively enslave a human—that was what fetters were for, after all—and that both of them seemed to have fooled her so completely. She was no longer sure what to believe.

With a sigh, she dragged her focus back to the case. She wanted to find this woman before she hurt herself or anyone else, but she didn't want to enslave her. She wanted something like equality, but if dragons could throw shackles on those who might oppose them, that could never happen. At the same time, she needed to find out more about the dangers of the power to themselves.

Wisely, she kept all this to herself. The first step was to find this mage. Once they'd done that, she would have to talk to Windlock and hopefully convince him to see things from her perspective. And she had to reconcile the investigator she thought she knew with the one she possibly did not. Dragons, she decided, could be complex—exactly like people.

CHAPTER THIRTY

K risten asked Windlock to step aside for a moment and he complied without question. Rather than start an existential argument about the place of mages, humans, and dragons in global politics, she told him about the woman who'd gasped when the figure inside the sphere had been revealed.

"You have a good eye. Do you mind following up?"

"Me? I know I used to be on a human force but that doesn't mean I did crowd control with civilians. I was on SWAT."

"It's a fair point." He nodded and his aura accentuated his agreement. "But you also have an excellent reputation with humans, something that is sorely needed at the moment. You'll have an easier time winning the trust of a human than any other dragon would, including myself."

"I don't need to win anyone's trust," she replied. "She's a grieving woman, probably pissed by losing someone she cares about. All you need to do to get through to her is to treat her with respect."

His eyebrows raised in obvious surprise. Clearly, he had picked up on the slight edge to her tone—or wasn't used to the idea of treating a human with respect for no reason other than it being the right thing to do. "I'll admit, when I enter these situations, I normally approach humans with…let's call it querulousness."

"You can learn to treat them with respect until they do something to lose that, you know."

"Of course I can, although let me remind you that I tend to respond in the same way to dragons when my focus is on a case." She nodded reluctantly because honesty compelled her to acknowledge the truth of that. "And I would love to learn more about it, but perhaps right now isn't the most opportune moment to address the issue of manners?" He glanced pointedly at the crowd to remind her of the need to locate the woman.

Kristen nodded. He had a point, of course. At that moment, finding answers for what had happened to the community of Rangeley, Maine, took priority. It wouldn't do for her to pursue what might be partially skewed assumptions when she could actually do something positive.

At least she had a place to start to improve human-dragon relations. As she walked toward the crowd of locals, she also reminded herself that Windlock had some idea of the need to address the relationship between humans and dragons as well. After all, he'd asked her to come on this mission and had given her the specific task to talk to the human woman. It took wisdom to realize when one's strengths weren't suited to a particular purpose. Perhaps he was more perceptive than she'd realized. His ideas about how humans, dragons, and mages should interact were possibly outdated, but he recognized that they needed to be modernized, which was more than she could say for most dragons.

With that adjustment in her priority list, she scanned the group of local protestors but without success. A few people still tried to take selfies, but unsurprisingly, the grieving woman wasn't among them either.

She almost told herself that she had gone home but as she turned, she noticed a shadowy figure beside the burned house. None of the other members of Boston Dragon SWAT had seen her, probably because she made no effort to approach the dead dragons and instead, stared longingly at the now blackened shell of a home.

Kristen could tell in the way the woman stared at the house that she used to live there. There was something about the way she looked past what was in front of her as if her focus was on something entirely different. She didn't see a missing wall but the photos that used to hang there. It wasn't a broken sofa but the place where she'd sat and watched television with her partner for decades.

Quietly, she walked toward the woman and considered how best to approach her. She didn't want to intrude on her moment, but she didn't want her to fall into despair either. She stopped beside her, but the stranger didn't notice and seemed lost in the past and her attempt to take the last memories she could from a home that, even if rebuilt, would never be the same.

"I know it doesn't seem like enough, not after what you've been through, but they will reimburse you for the damages. The Dragon Council will make sure reparations are made," Kristen said, not sure of what else to say. She felt that as an officer representing dragons, it was best to admit there was a fault and that it belonged to her kind.

It was only when she mentioned the Dragon Council that her companion reacted. She flinched and turned to look at her. Intently, she studied her uniform and paid special attention to the stylized dragon wings framing a five-pointed star that made up the Dragon SWAT badge before she looked her in the eye.

"Your kind wouldn't understand," she said sharply. "This is nothing to you. We all know that. It's hardly worth even a slap on the wrist."

"Ma'am, I assure you, I don't know what it's like to lose the home you grew up in, but I do know what it's like to grow up in a house with the people you love and I can only imagine how hard it must be for you to see all that turned to ash. I'm truly sorry, I really am, and will do everything I can to make this as right as I can."

"I don't believe that for a second. How could you possibly…" The woman trailed off as recognition flashed across her face. "You're the dragon who was raised by humans, right? The…uh, the steel one?"

"Yes, ma'am. I'm the Steel Dragon—not the cleverest of names, but there it is." She flashed her skin to steel, then returned it to its regular freckled form. "I wanted to check on you." Kristen didn't like lying and she told herself that what she'd said wasn't a lie or not a complete one, anyway. After all, she did need to check on her.

The woman shook her head and seemed to fight tears. "My…" She stopped and caught her breath before she began to cry. "My husband stayed in town with some friends. He had a tough time with all the smoke. It's kind of…what's the word? Ironic? If it wasn't for him smoking for so many damn years, he wouldn't be bugged by the COPD. Did he ever listen to me about that? Of course not, and yet now, he's stuck in a bed even though he made it out the window as soon as I did."

"So the two of you still lived here?" Kristen asked. What she really wanted to know was who the young woman was who'd stepped from her home and brutalized the two dragons. Her impulsive and often impatient nature pushed her to simply state the question, but she wasn't naïve enough to start grilling a woman who mourned the loss of everything she had possessed.

"Yeah, for forty-six years if you can believe it. My husband, John Williams and no, not the composer"—given the burned shell of her home, the joke fell flat—"grew up here. His father built it, actually."

"You can call me Kristen," she said.

"I'm Pat. Short for Patricia, but everyone calls me Pat or Mrs. Williams."

"Do you have people in the community who can help you and Mr. Williams?" she asked.

"Oh yes. Although I don't know how accommodating any of my girlfriends will be now that my fabric is all gone. I had the biggest collection of scraps in Maine, you know. Not that it…not that it matters now."

"I'm glad you only lost fabric," Kristen said. "Was there anyone else who escaped with you two?"

"No… No, no one else. Only me and my husband John—oh, but I already told you his name."

It didn't need a master detective to see that Mrs. Williams was lying about how many people lived in the house. She didn't push it, though. If she was trying to hide someone, she wouldn't simply spit it out.

For a moment, she wondered if perhaps her daughter or niece or whomever the young woman had been was perhaps involved with the technomages. After all, Constance and her followers had proven time and time again that they were more than capable of killing dragons, but she dismissed the idea fairly quickly. This didn't look like the work of the technomage assassins. While they were more than happy to attack in bold and even messy ways, the fight between the dragons had drawn too much attention. There was no way they could have planned this because the entire disaster hinged on the fact that two dragons inadvertently took their spontaneous fight beyond the uninhabited areas. No, whatever Pat attempted to hide, it was personal.

"Did you see the fire start?" Kristen asked and hated herself for the bland question, but she was enough of a cop to try to not lead a witness.

"No, but we knew it had to be those dragons, even before I saw that magical replay of the whole horrible thing. We felt the heat, first —and the smoke, of course. That's when we went out the window. This was a few seconds after the propane tank exploded. That's what woke us up, you know. We got out barely in time because the flames engulfed the room seconds later."

She nodded, a little frustrated. While she wanted more information, she didn't quite know how to get it. She'd never been trained in witness interrogation if that's what this was. Still, she had to try. "I know you've had a hard day, but do you know any reason why the dragons would have destroyed your home? Perhaps you have a relative who is a mage or something?"

Pat Williams froze like a blizzard. "Of course not. You may be from Detroit or Chicago or wherever, but the people of Rangeley don't go in for all this…tomfoolery."

"I'm sorry, ma'am. I didn't mean to insult you. I merely want to get to the bottom of what happened here."

"Two dragons burned my house and killed each other over

nothing of consequence. What else is there? I hope you can convince the Dragon Committee or whoever it is that pulls the strings to help John and I get back on our feet, but if they decide not to, we have friends in town who will help us, thank you very much." With that, she spun on her heel and marched away to her car.

Kristen shook her head. She was convinced Pat knew more. The woman might even know precisely who had killed the dragons, but she had failed to do exactly what Windlock had said—win her trust.

While she felt a little despondent, she also realized that perhaps it wasn't the right time. Pat was mad, grieving, and worried about her husband. It seemed a safe bet to assume she wouldn't try to leave town. That kind of extreme reaction was unlikely if her husband had trouble breathing and they had friends to support and take care of them.

Plus, she'd probably be more willing to talk to a dragon later, once she'd worked through the shock. She might be less than patient, given that her home had been destroyed by two of them, but it didn't mean she couldn't be reasoned with.

Absently, she watched the woman stride to her truck—an old Chevrolet that might have once been red—climb in, and drive away. She took note of the license plate as any cop worth their weight in donuts was trained to do, but it was the bumper sticker above the plate that was easier to remember. She couldn't help but think there couldn't be too many people with *I quilt for moose* bumper stickers on the back of their pickups.

CHAPTER THIRTY-ONE

Once Mrs. Williams had left, Kristen turned her attention to the blackened ruins of the house. Some of it was still standing—the only parts that had totally collapsed were where the dragons had crashed into the structure and where the propane tank had blown away a few walls, but that didn't mean it wasn't a wreck. Everything was either burnt or stained black with smoke. The kitchen was completely destroyed, obviously Ground Zero for the propane tank explosion. She hadn't thought they were prone to that, but dragon fire could very likely ignite them.

She worked through the living room and discovered a circle on the floor that was unburnt. It reminded her of a similar shape she'd seen during the misty recreation of the battle. The rogue mage had stood there, she decided. There wasn't any other explanation as there very obviously weren't any huge round pieces of unburnt or even undamaged furniture.

Cautiously, she peeked in the master bedroom, which was little more than a disaster scene. The interior of the outside wall was twisted and burnt, and she assumed it must have caught a direct blast of dragon's fire. The flames had spread and consumed almost everything inside. A bow-tie patterned with American flags lay near the bed, its edges singed, and a romance novel was blackened by smoke but seemed to have escaped the flames. A few feet away, a pair of sensible heels were burned to a crisp. The room had very clearly been shared by Mrs. Williams and her husband so that, at least, seemed to be the truth.

Kristen left the room once she noted that the wall that had been blown out by the mage, then explored the rest of the house in search of clues. The stairs were, unfortunately, impassable as those sections that weren't crushed were burned. Still, the second floor was mostly intact, so she stopped at the base of the stairs, crouched, and vaulted up with a surge of her dragon strength. Thankfully, she managed without even a twinge, which she took as a positive sign that her healing had definitely improved.

She landed precariously on the edge of the upstairs hallway and moved quickly to the two rooms.

One of them was a ruin, the roof collapsed and most of the floor sagging toward the ground level. There was no way Kristen could get inside without causing even more to collapse, and she didn't want to drop the rest of this building on her head. But she didn't think she needed to investigate this room more closely. As close as she could tell from the ruins, it seemed barely lived in like a guest room. It contained none of the knick-knacks and personal items that would fill a person's bedroom.

The other room was interesting, however. It appeared to be where one of the dragon tails had pounded through the roof, but there was still much to be gleaned within. It was obviously a woman's room, as the burnt bureau was filled with the remains of bras, panties, and cute socks. The chest of drawers had obviously been broken before the fire and had spilled their contents all over the bedroom. What remained of the closet contained a pile of incinerated clothes, although she managed to retrieve remnants of one or two she thought were reasonably trendy. They were certainly not the clothes of an older woman or even of someone who'd spent their entire time in Rangeley, not unless they'd been a master of online shopping.

Kristen poked around but didn't really find anything unusual.

Between the destroyed books, clothes, and shoes—both sensible and stylish, from what she could see—she found nothing that screamed "dragon slayer." There were no odd items that might have been mage robes and no enchanted swords—Kristen still didn't know if those existed, but she hadn't known mages could kill dragons until quite recently either—and no guns.

From the few remaining pieces of book covers, she was able to deduce that most of what had been on the shelves were fantasy novels, not occult tomes or scrolls in dead languages. Of course, paper burned all too easily so it wasn't impossible that they might have been incinerated beyond recognition. Her instincts, however, told her that the occupant had been an ordinary young woman and it was improbable that she'd collected anything even remotely like that.

Unfortunately, given the extent of the damage, all she could really tell from the room was that whoever had slept there had probably lived there and that she was normal. The only odd thing was that Pat Williams had made a point of saying that no one lived there, even though someone obviously had. It seemed logical to think it was the woman's daughter, but why lie for her? Did Pat know that the girl had killed the dragons? She had seen the tableau Brockton had summoned —her reaction was what had called attention to her—but did she only guess as to the identity of the mage or did she actually know who she was?

A bit more snooping revealed the younger woman's smartphone still plugged in next to her bed. Much could be learned from such a device but unfortunately, the fire had melted the cord and scorched the device. It wouldn't turn on, which wasn't much of a surprise. Still, someone clever enough and with skill in that area might get some information off it, even if it was damaged.

What it did highlight, however, was that the girl was without a phone. That meant—if she was anything like she had been before she was a dragon—she'd have a difficult time skipping town with no maps, no car services, and no simple portal to buy airplane tickets. She hoped the girl being without her phone would buy them a little time to find her. With a sigh, she took out an evidence bag and dropped the device inside.

It didn't appear that she'd find anything else of value, so she leapt up onto the roof and dropped the two floors to land outside the house. To a human, it would have seemed an impossible feat of strength, but when she alighted beside Windlock, he barely noticed. She grinned. The jump had been another test, a way to gauge her level of healing, and while there was a small twinge or two this time, it didn't feel like anything to be concerned about.

He stood with another dragon—not Timbergust but one from Boston in his human form. The investigator's quick glance at her suggested that he intended to ask what she'd found, but his companion spoke first.

"Why did you waste your time in there while we dealt with the stupid humans trying to snap selfies?" he demanded. His human form was extremely muscular, so much so that he virtually had no neck. Kristen would have guessed steroids, but she wasn't sure if dragons could use them.

"I examined the scene of the crime," she said and tried not to sound annoyed at the beef-headed dragon, although she failed miserably.

He scoffed. "Do you think the mage who killed those two was a resident of this house?"

"It's one possibility I wanted to follow up on," she replied slowly as if explaining a new concept to a child.

"For fuck's sake, the stories are true. The Steel Dragon really is no smarter than the average human. There is no way a normal human could have done this shit."

"I never mentioned a normal—"

"Well, that little magic show your pet mage conjured was impressive, but I still think that's all it was—a show. Mages haven't been this powerful for centuries. Every dragon knows that." He sneered nastily and she had to restrain the urge to punch him. "Hell, they made pixies to be able to do this kind of shit and even they can't. It was a dragon—one with weirder powers than yours, for sure, and able to use them in human form—but a dragon." He folded his arms and nodded as if to indicate that the case was closed in his opinion.

Kristen had heard enough. He represented everything that was wrong with dragon culture and made a mockery of the dragons who weren't so narrow-minded. His assumptions were not only derogatory to humans and mages but were legitimately dangerous to dragons as well. She took a deep breath, ready to tell this oaf exactly what she thought of him, but Windlock cut her off.

"If you think she wasted time, I'd appreciate it if you produced some actual clues, Officer Bronzeback," the investigator chided caustically.

"There aren't any clues in there." She was surprised she hadn't recognized Bronzeback by his aggressive and arrogant tone.

"I'll be the judge of that. Now, if you'll excuse us, I'd like to debrief my partner."

The dragon's eyes widened as he looked from Kristen to Windlock, then back to her. "I'm...uh, my apologies Investigator—that is, Investigators. I thought you were here on some kind of publicity tour or something. I didn't realize you were an investigator as well." Bronzeback bowed awkwardly—it was difficult for Kristen not to smile at his discomfort, but she managed—and he hurried away to shoo more tourists from the crime scene.

"That's funny," she said, looked at Windlock, and let herself smile. "I didn't realize I was your partner either."

"Isn't that what you're doing right now?" he replied. "This case is already a jurisdictional headache, what with Boston's Dragon SWAT involved. I don't have the patience for them to wonder what the chain of command is. I'll call you whatever the hell I have to if it helps you to do your job and find out what happened here."

"Well, thanks, partner." She nodded at him.

"Don't make too much of it either, Lady Steel. When this is all over, you'll go back to Detroit to take care of drunk dragons with the rest of your team."

"Thank you, sir. It's an honor to know you're familiar with the work of Detroit Dragon SWAT."

Windlock laughed at her joke. "I simply don't want delusions of grandeur to stop the investigation, but for now, let's operate like you are my partner. At the very least, it'll make Bronzeback shut up."

"Going back to facing unruly dragons in Detroit is definitely worth that." She was more than happy to work above her station. This was the first time she had partnered with a dragon who had actively—albeit temporarily—promoted her and given her authority without her having to bitch about it first. Stonequest had brought her onto dragon SWAT and for that, she was grateful, but he'd also become confused fairly quickly when she'd wanted to conduct actual investigations. It was gratifying to have someone listen to her.

"All right, Steel, get your aura under control or the crowd will start singing 'Kumbaya.' What did you find in there?"

"Right, sir. Sorry, sir." Kristen clamped down on her aura. "The woman I talked to—one Pat Williams—lived in this house with her husband. He is John Williams and no, not the composer—" Kristen smiled but like her, Windlock didn't laugh at the joke so she continued. "And at least one other person also lived here. The odd thing is that the woman said it was only her and her husband. She lied to a cop and a dragon—a brave thing to do when you think about it—and my guess is she did it to protect whoever lived in that upstairs bedroom. I believe it was her daughter. She definitely seemed younger from what I could see when I looked through what was left of her belongings—and in Brockton's reenactment—and like I said, it takes guts to lie to either a dragon or a cop. I don't think she would have done it for a random tenant as she didn't seem like the lying type."

"Do you think this younger woman was a mage?" he asked.

"Uh—not sure?" She shrugged. "Firstly, I'm not too familiar with mages. I didn't see any robes or anything like the mages at Dragon SWAT HQ in Detroit wear, but I don't think she was a technomage either. There was no evidence of a gun or other weapons, for starters, and although most of her clothes were burned, they didn't seem like the all-black style Constance is so fond of. That said, I can't imagine a rogue mage or whatever you called them going toe to toe with two dragons. Is that even possible? I know I saw what apparently happened, but I've never heard of anything like that."

Windlock grimaced. "I've heard of that kind of power but not since the last human rebellion. In that war, there were a few mages powerful enough to tackle multiple dragons at once, but they were rare. Plus, those with that level of power took a long time to get there. They had to hone their skills, which was a good thing for dragon kind, really. Otherwise, the rebellion would have gone completely differently."

"Yeah, what great news for us dragons," she said and made no attempt to hide her biting sarcasm. Of course, she immediately regretted it but decided not to voice it. Bronzeback seemed to have stirred up her frustrations again.

He noticed her discomfort but was a professional, so he continued despite the growing look of disapproval on her face. "Today, any mage with something even approaching that kind of potential is cuffed."

"Like Larry," Kristen said bitterly.

"Yes, like Larry," he agreed.

"And you're okay with that?" she asked.

"It's the way of things."

"I don't know if you've ever had your powers stripped, but I have. I went to prison and had to wear one of those cuffs. It was horrible to be denied part of what you are—to be denied part of who you are. And I was there because dragons thought that I had done something wrong. I understand that he has access to some of his powers, but how much is he being denied?"

"I can't say for certain. Brockton has worn a cuff since I took him under my wing."

She shook her head distastefully. "It doesn't seem fair, is all. Dragons don't lose their powers despite being the greatest threat to humans, mages, and each other, but mages are routinely denied their abilities despite having done no wrong."

"I understand your frustration, but it really is for the best. You need to remain open to the fact that every situation has multiple points of view. In this instance, that symbol of slavery as you seem to think of it is what currently protects him. Brockton is fairly powerful. If he had refused to wear the dampening cuff, he'd have almost surely been executed."

"You mean if he hadn't agreed to submit."

Windlock shrugged but at least he didn't argue. Still, she wasn't quite sure what to make of that. To her, it was very simple—either it was right and fair, or it wasn't. Her patience currently didn't seem to extend to gray areas.

"Quite frankly, I'm glad I found Brockton so early," he continued. "I've had to defend him to quite a few dragons over the years because they aren't fond of personal mages. Too many lives were lost in the wars for them to trust magic like Larry's. I trust Larry Brockton and I have for years, and since I'm an investigator, I have some weight I can throw around to keep him safe. The reality, though, is that there are quite a few dragons out there who'd rather he simply ceased breathing."

Kristen nodded although she felt more confused and angrier than ever before. Maybe her enforced downtime had been less beneficial than it should have as it seemed to have allowed her mind to dwell on the problems rather than work to address them. Right now, while she could understand the logic in his reasoning, his response simply felt like more hypocrisy.

It was an established fact that dragons held all the cards in the world. Somewhat hypocritically because she hated to even think of war and its cost, she wondered if mages had actually been successful in one of their wars—or at least had succeeded in stopping the dragons from systematically dampening their powers—the world might be a more balanced place.

After all, mages were human. If they could stand up to dragons, the powerful beings might have to respect regular people and no longer regard them as nothing more than collateral damage. Of course, most dragons didn't see it that way. They didn't want balance and wanted all the weight to be on their side of the scale.

Then again, Constance was no better. She was determined to force a war to achieve her vision, no matter what the cost. It seemed that between the dragons on one side and the technomages on the other, regular humans were completely downtrodden, disregarded, or merely expendable pawns in the various power games. So really, they were the ones who needed a protector and an advocate—together with mages like Brockton who were trapped by their own abilities.

She sighed. All this thinking and reasoning and questioning was exhausting, and she wished she could turn her mind off completely.

"Did you see any magical things in the young woman's room?"

Work was what she needed, she decided, something positive to capture her errant thoughts and into which she could direct all the impatient energy. She seized on the question with renewed focus. "No. I don't think so, anyway, but I honestly don't really know what to look for. Most of it was burned, so there might have been things that are no longer recognizable."

Windlock nodded and called Larry to join them. The mage obliged and stepped beside them.

"What's going on, boss?" Brockton asked.

"Steel has reason to believe that the mage might have lived in this house and could be the daughter of the homeowners. Do you mind taking a peek to see if she had any idea of what she was?"

"That's why I'm here, right?" He smiled. If the investigator mistreated him, the mage certainly did a good job of hiding his discomfort at their arrangement. Once again, the odd surge of guilt rippled through her. Was she simply affixing her own negative interpretations to their working relationship? Did they, in fact, have the strong bond she had always believed they had? It was a reminder to not jump to conclusions she might later regret.

Windlock transformed into his dragon form and Brockton scampered up his tail, onto his back, and climbed up his neck. He stepped from the dragon's head into the second-floor bedroom. As frustrated as she was with dragon culture, she had to admit that these two treated each other almost as equals. She had never seen a dragon allow a human—mage or otherwise—to use them as a ladder.

"There is nothing overtly magical in here—or more like nothing magical at all. Of course, it's all charred but I sense no enchanted artifacts or books about magic. Even after a fire, they would still retain some kind of magical residue. Hell, I've been to garage sales with more magic items than there probably were in this room. It's about as plain-Jane as can be."

"So she's not the mage?" Kristen asked, a little disappointed.

"I wouldn't go that far." He sniffed and moved his hand a little, and his fingertips glowed blue. "There's a lingering sense of magic here. It's not nearly as strong as that outside but it makes sense as there was a hurricane of damage out there and this room is a fair distance away."

"It's related?" Windlock asked.

"Oh yeah," Larry said. "It's definitely the same magic I felt outside in the yard around the dead dragons."

"How sure are you it's the same?" his boss pressed.

"Gee, I don't know, you old windbag. How often do you confuse a dragon's aura with another's?"

The investigator chuckled at that before he turned to her. "We can be sure that whoever attacked those mages outside lived in this room then. Good work, Kristen. Brockton, nice work. I owe you a cup of coffee."

"Cheap bastard. I want a latte, or I quit."

Windlock seemed to not even register the joke and his expression remained concerned. "We need to find this girl, whoever she is. I think it's reasonable to assume her powers have newly manifested since we didn't find any evidence of training materials or tools of augmentation, but that doesn't mean she's not a threat. If she truly is an untrained rogue mage and what we're looking at is only her raw power, we need to stop her before she loses control and kills again."

"Do you think she might target us or the Boston team?" she asked.

"Honestly? With this kind of power, I'm more concerned about her wiping the town of Rangeley off the face of the Earth."

CHAPTER THIRTY-TWO

"Uh-oh. It looks like we have company," Kristen said and stared across the yard toward the perimeter. Two news vans had arrived, and each had an antenna towering from the back of their van. She grimaced when she identified one as an affiliate of one of the liberal news companies and the other as one of the conservative ones. It essentially meant the entire event was about to be evening news on everyone's television.

"Most people haven't ever seen one dead dragon, let alone two," Brockton mumbled after he climbed down Windlock's neck and stood beside them once more.

"They're fairly far away," the investigator said.

His companions shared a look. Dragons could be so oblivious.

"It's called a zoom lens, you old windbag. They'll be able to get a shot of this and there's no way we can stop it," Larry said. "We can safely say there's about to be two dead dragons all over the evening news."

"That means Constance Vigil will hear about it," Kristen said and her hackles rose. This was already complicated enough. The last thing they needed was the assassin and her technomages to arrive.

"I imagine everyone will hear about this if they have this zoo-oom lens you talk about," Windlock said and mispronounced the word, although that might have been deliberate. He didn't sound terribly concerned, though.

"Right, but if Constance hears that two dragons died of mysterious causes and there are a number of dragons out here investigating, she'll come knocking. She'll assume this is either a weapon or a mage, right? If you two know about all this, she probably does as well."

"It's a safe bet." Concern grew on the other dragon's face like a wildfire.

"She'll try to recruit the mage and use her in her war. That's what she's pushed to achieve with me this whole time, but it might actually work on this girl since she lost her home to dragons. We can't let that happen, but those media crews will make that tricky."

"Right. Cover story time," Windlock said decisively. "We've concluded our investigation. The two dragons fought—play up the old grudge angle, people like that stuff—and one of them killed the other and succumbed to his own wounds before he could heal."

"That happens?" she asked skeptically. It sounded very suspicious to her.

"It's not unheard of," he said. "Go with one of them having a wound on their heart that was bleeding into their lungs. There was a case about a decade ago where that happened. It made a fair number of dragons paranoid for a while about sustaining too many chest wounds. It'll play in the dragon community, and people won't know what to think of it."

"Okay. Fine, I guess it makes sense. If we're lucky, the technomages didn't kill those dragons. Otherwise, Constance will see right through it."

"Obviously, you won't bring her up," Windlock said.

"Right. Obviously I won't—wait, me?" Kristen was incredulous. "Why me?"

"Because you're the darling of the human media." He gestured to the camera crews. "When you were discovered, it was global news. No doubt those reporters would kill for an interview with Detroit's Lost

Steel Dragon or whatever the headlines were. Use that to get them off the case."

She looked at the two vans and realized she didn't have much time. One of the camera operators was already climbing onto the roof of their van to get a better angle on the bodies. She strode toward them, not thrilled to be on media duty but not completely terrified either. When she'd first manifested her powers, she'd done a few press conferences—Captain Hansen had insisted on it—so this was uncomfortable but not alien territory.

"Ma'am, ma'am!" One of the reporters was already yelling at her and recognition slid over the woman's face. "Kristen Hall—what brings the Steel Dragon to Rangeley?"

Kristen kept moving so that when the camera operators framed her, the background would be the pine trees of the area, not the burned home or dead dragon corpses.

"We're here because two dragons died in a duel. We were investigating foul play to determine if another dragon was involved and catch them to make sure they pay for the destruction here."

"And do you think you'll catch them?" the other reporter asked, a man with a thick mustache.

"I guess you don't watch the Detroit news." She flashed a grin at the camera.

The tourists—drawn to the camera crews like moths to a flame—chuckled at that.

"So you think a third dragon was involved?" the female reporter asked.

She shook her head. "No, we don't. It looks like this is a long-standing feud that turned deadly. One dragon killed the other, but his heart was punctured and bled into his lung. We've ruled it double homicide currently, but of course, if anything else comes up, we'd appreciate you bringing that evidence forward."

The female reporter wilted. She'd obviously hoped for an ongoing case.

"Really, I'm relieved," Kristen said. "This means I get to explore Rangeley."

"What does a city girl like you think of a town like Rangely?" the mustachioed reporter asked.

"I liked it more before the dragons arrived," she replied and earned chuckles from the news crews.

"Is there anything you want to do while you're here?" the woman asked.

"I could do with a few restaurant recommendations. Do you know anywhere that serves entire cows?" Another laugh followed and she smiled inwardly with satisfaction. She'd given them their soundbites. Now, it was time to end this on a more somber note.

"I hate to ask you to move on, but this is still a crime scene and the dragons need to remove the dead. It's a sad day for everyone involved. Two dragons died needlessly and they hurt the community in doing so."

"Of course, Ms. Hall. Perhaps we could ask a few questions about your time in Detroit?"

She agreed and answered a few more questions. It was a little awkward but all in all, she felt like she did well enough. They asked her about her involvement in the bomb that had almost blown up one of Detroit's most famous buildings and she answered as honestly as she could without saying anything about Constance. It was common knowledge, at this point, that someone had tried to obliterate the dragons. Hundreds of people had caught the event on their smartphones, but this was the first time a dragon had spoken publicly about it.

After a few minutes, the reporters changed the subject and attempted to dig further into her past, but she was able to remind them that this was a sad day for dragons and asked them once more to leave. They obliged her and left without protest, chatting to each other about which clips they'd use for their different outlets.

"Thanks for your time," one of the reporters said. "I'm not sure if this will play nationally, but everyone in Maine will be wicked excited to have the Steel Dragon here."

Kristen nodded and looked once more at the protestors. They

were still upset at the two dragons who'd come in and trashed their town.

Very definitely, she didn't want to talk to them. They were angry and stirred themselves into a ferment as they worked one another up to greater rage. Still, she felt a responsibility to approach them. After all, she was a dragon raised by people. She knew what it felt like to live in a world where lives could be lost at the whims of beings so much more powerful but also what dragons could do to help.

"Hello, everyone," she said, approached the group, and raised her hand in a friendly greeting but also to show she wasn't armed. "You may not know me, but I'm Kristen Hall. Many folks call me the Steel Dragon."

"We know who you are. You're the dragon raised by a human. A traitor!" someone from the back of the crowd yelled. No one else echoed the insult, though, which she counted as a good sign.

She extended her aura subtly to make this group calm a little. While she didn't want to take their emotions away—they were valid, after all—she did want them to take a second to breathe. "I understand you may feel that way, but I assure you, I've always been committed to people first. Ask my mom in Dearborn, Michigan. If she caught me showing favorites to anyone because of whatever group they were born into, she'd rip me a new one."

That drew scattered laughter which was at least a small margin of progress. Obviously, this was a much tougher crowd than the reporters had been, but that made sense. Her presence would give the reporters the evening news' highlights. These people hadn't gained anything from her being there.

"Ma'am, I get that you're upstanding an' all that, but someone's home was destroyed. The Williams were good people."

"And it could have been any of us," a man wearing plaid interjected and cut off the woman who'd spoken first.

"Their home will be rebuilt, I assure you," Kristen said. "In fact, that's why I wanted to talk to you. I want to make it clear that I will make sure the Dragon Council will make reparations to the family."

"Haven't you been a dragon for, like, a year? How you gonna push them around?" the plaid-wearing man asked.

"Well, it's longer than that, but you saw that the news wanted to talk to me. If the Dragon Council won't play ball, I'll make a stink on every news channel that will hear me."

That finally earned her a few nods.

"I understand that this has really struck the community." She tried to maintain her momentum before someone stirred them up again. "But there's no point in compounding this tragedy by bringing in even more news crews. The last thing we want is the Dragon Council to be embarrassed over all this. What's best is if we all head home and let me contact who I can about getting this all straightened out."

"You're only saying that," the woman who'd spoken first said.

"Ma'am, I promise you, if they don't fix this, I will be on the frontlines of whatever civil disobedience you think is best. But before we do that, let me at least make the attempt. Think of this as a chance to not only build a house for the Williams family but a bridge between humans and dragons."

That mollified the crowd enough to persuade them to disperse. Kristen was slightly concerned that she'd overstepped her bounds and not because she wouldn't go through with it. Her reservations came from the certainty that if the Dragon Council refused to do this for these people, she'd fight them tooth and claw. It was only right when faced with such a loss.

Still, they were content enough to leave and hopefully go home and get some sleep. She watched them go, grateful that the situation was defused. Larry came up to her and slapped a hand on her shoulder.

"You did good. Were you in debate or something in high school? You're good with a crowd."

She shook her head, "Please don't ever tell anyone that. I'd be fine with never having to do public speaking again—like ever!"

CHAPTER THIRTY-THREE

A knock on the door at the top of the stairs startled Amy Williams so badly that the coffee cup she'd held in shaking hands hurtled up and shattered against the ceiling.

"Amy? Can I come down?"

Of course you can come down. It's your house. She bit the words back because she understood why Jennifer had asked. Her friend was probably terrified and not without reason, given that she'd already trashed the room with her weird powers. She was scared too.

"Yeah…" she managed, and her voice sounded ridiculously weak. She'd never been so frightened in her entire life. It was strange to be more scared of herself than she was of the dragons that had destroyed her parents' house.

The other girl came down the stairs with a plate of food—a fried bologna sandwich with extra tomatoes, no lettuce, a pile of potato chips, and a pickle. It had been their favorite meal since they were eight-year-old best friends.

"Are you doing okay?" Jennifer asked. It was obvious from her tone of voice that she didn't think she was doing okay. Again, she couldn't blame her. The room was a wreck. Any time she'd been startled— which was often when one was concerned that dragons would kill you if your own powers didn't blow you up first—she'd inadvertently flung something across the room. She had already trashed Jennifer's dad's collection of records, an alarm clock, a box of chipped china that her friend's mom had kept in the basement for parties, and most of the windows.

"I don't know, Jen. I only…I can't get a handle on things, you know?"

"Sure," the girl said, although her face was pale. Of course she didn't know. Who could? How could one relate to suddenly manifesting powers strong enough to kill not one, but two dragons?

"I can't stop thinking about my parents. They were in their room when they…that is the fire…" Amy tried to push the thoughts from her mind, but they wouldn't leave. She'd come back to Rangeley because of her parents. Many young people left home because they didn't have a good relationship with their folks, but that wasn't her. She'd left to see if she could make something of herself. When she'd failed to amount to anything special, it had been a relief to return to Rangeley and move in with them. She loved them and now, they were gone.

The bed she was seated on began to shake before it rose off the floor.

"Amy, calm down," Jennifer implored.

She focused hard because she knew she could control these powers if she did that. Finally, her fists clenched at her sides and she forced the bed down, but as soon as she relaxed, the coffee table where Jennifer had placed the sandwich launched upward and shattered against the ceiling. The pieces clattered around them, while the bologna sandwich remained stuck above.

"Amy—please listen to me. There's something I need to tell you. Your mom is all right."

"Please don't lie to me, Jennifer, okay? I can't stand to believe that and lose her again when I find out it's not true."

"No! I'm serious." Her friend smiled, and she knew her well enough to recognize her most honest face. "Take a deep breath, okay? I finally managed to contact her. She just got here."

Amy dared to feel hope again, which made all the furniture in the basement shake alarmingly.

"Girl, you have to calm down."

She nodded and wiped her tears. "Okay. You're right."

Jennifer gave her a minute, then called up the stairs. "All right, Mrs. Williams. Come on down."

The door at the top of the steps cracked open and her mom's face was framed in the opening. A wave of relief washed over her and again, the furniture shook and shuddered. It was a good thing her friend had given her a warning. If she hadn't had that, she might have demolished the entire room once and for all.

"Oh, sweetie," her mom said as she rushed down the stairs, pulled her against her chest, and hugged her like she had when she was seven years old. Amy let herself cry, and when she did, she again heard things move around her, but Pat didn't seem to notice. She merely held her daughter and whispered how much she loved her in her ear.

Amy loved Jennifer, but there was nothing like a mom's love, even to a grown woman.

"Oh, Amy, I'm so glad you're all right."

"You too, Mom." She sniffed after she'd taken a few breaths and managed to stop all the stuff in the room from floating. At least she hadn't broken anything that time. She drew another deep breath. "How are you all right?"

"Your father and I broke the window and got out. He wanted to run in again to get you despite the smoke. He yelled at me about how he smoked that pipe all these years to get ready for something like this —you know your father—but then…well, we saw you step from the building."

She nodded. "You saw me kill those dragons."

"I saw my little girl lose control. That's what I saw."

"Seriously, Amy. It's like when you hit that ball in softball and broke my nose." Jennifer smiled.

"And I'm still sorry about that."

"Oh, come on. We all know it was an accident," her mom said. "Exactly like this was. It wasn't your fault."

"But it was, Mom! I'm the only one who can do this…this stuff!" She held her hand out and pointed at a box across the room. It levitated a few feet off the ground and when she choked out a sob, the box fell.

"No sweetie, you're not. You're a mage. Your powers came in a moment of stress. There are others like you."

"I've never heard of a mage killing a dragon," Jennifer said.

Pat clenched her jaw and looked from one to the other. She made her mind up and turned to Jennifer. "Jenny, sweetie. I am so thankful you went to our house and brought Amy here. It was quick thinking on your part and I wasn't able to do it, what with having to get her dad to safety. You gave us quite a fright because I didn't know where she was, but it also gave me the time I needed. Right now, though, I need you to go upstairs."

"What are you talking about, Mrs. Williams?"

"Jenny, please. We have to protect Amy right now. That's what's important. We both know she didn't intend to do this, but there's a team of dragons out there who probably think very differently. We need to be smart. That's why I couldn't try to find her last night. I was worried someone might be watching me and I'd lead them to her."

"Are you saying I'm in danger, Mom?"

"What I'm saying is that Jennifer, you need to go upstairs so I can talk to my daughter alone. If you hear what we talk about, the dragons might try to get it out of you. Those lizards were there, sniffing around the mess they left of our home. We need to be careful."

The other girl paled, nodded, and went upstairs without protest.

"Mom, what's going on?"

"I want you to take three deep breaths, okay? What I'm about to say will be scary and the last thing we want is for you to trash Jennifer's parents' house, okay?"

Amy nodded and took three deep breaths.

"Sweetheart, I know you didn't mean to, but to dragons, intent doesn't really matter. To them, it looks like you killed two dragons and got away with it. They've brought in a whole team of cops or investigators or whatever they are. They haven't left this to Timber-gust, which means they're taking it seriously."

"Timbergust?"

"Our local dragon officer, sweetie. You'll need to start paying attention to these kinds of things."

"Are you saying they'll send me to jail? Because maybe they should. I killed those two dragons. I thought you and dad were dead, but now that you're okay…I messed up."

"You didn't mess up, Amy, you did what you could to protect us. We're lucky to have a daughter who is so strong." Her mom hugged her, and Amy took another couple of deep breaths—fortunately, because what her mom said next truly terrified her.

"But, Amy, you need to understand that they don't send mages like you to jail. They take vengeance."

"But I didn't mean to do it."

"I know, sweetie, I know, but they won't see it that way. They even brought in the Steel Dragon, who they normally use to hunt other lizards. It's obvious that they won't let you simply walk away from this."

She was horrified. "I didn't even know that a human could kill a dragon. I was angry and scared, and they attacked me, so I lashed out with…these powers. I didn't know what was happening. It was like the entire forest had attacked them."

"I know, sweetheart. We saw the whole thing. Those dragons attacked you and you hit them with the full force of your newborn powers. You really did throw the whole forest at them—and boulders and even a car!"

"But I thought dragons could heal?"

Her mom shrugged. "They have a limit. You pushed them to it, and when it was over, you threw everything into the woods. That's when your father took a bad turn and I had to get him to safety. You were out cold."

"Why didn't you go back?"

"I did, but you'd already left. I wanted to rush out and start searching but of course, the whole town was abuzz by then. We were obviously the center of attention, and you know how nosy people can be in a small town. I decided to simply tell everyone you'd gone to try your luck in the city again—maybe that you'd had a call for an interview or something—while I searched quietly. Thankfully, when Jenny put two and two together and realized you thought we were dead, she managed to find us."

"But I can go with you now, right?"

"No, sweetheart, that's not a good idea because your father and I will be their primary witnesses. If you stay with us, they might find you and this will all be over. They have a mage with them, and he seems to be adept at discerning magic."

"How do you know all this?"

"When I was young...I spent some time in Canada."

It took her a good minute to even begin to process what that was supposed to mean. "Do you mean with the dwarves?"

Her mother nodded. "That's right, sweetie. They have a very... pragmatic view of dragons. While they don't hate them, they don't live in fear like we do here either. I would've stayed there but I met your father and well...you came along and suddenly, living in a community of humans seemed more important."

Suddenly, the pieces clicked into place for her. "Do you think we should go to Canada?"

Pat nodded, but there were tears in her eyes. "I think you should go to Canada. Your father...he's okay, but his lungs aren't doing great after all that smoke. Plus, if I'm here, I might be able to buy you the time you need to get across the border."

"You want me to be a fugitive?"

"No, Amy, that's the last thing I want, but you already are a fugitive. If you stay here, they'll find you. If you go to Canada, there's a chance they won't want to follow. And...well, like I said, dwarves are a pragmatic people. They won't view your...powers the same way dragons will. They might be able to help you."

"But Mom, dragons can fly. Can't they follow me?"

"I don't think they'll think of Canada, at least not right away. I made some calls last night. I know someone from my time there who will protect you. His name is Alp and he's a good guy. If you can reach him, he'll be able to help you more than I can."

"Alp is a dwarf?"

Her mom nodded.

Amy swallowed. This was insane—absolutely insane. She had returned to Rangeley because she had thought Philadelphia was too crazy and Boston was too mean. Suddenly, she was a mage hunted by dragons and who needed to get to Canada so dwarves could protect her? On top of all that, there was the weight on her shoulders of two dead dragons. She had already felt guilty about killing them, but now that she knew her parents had survived, the guilt was only worse.

Still, what choice did she have? She couldn't stay there, that much was obvious. If there were dragons looking for her, she had to get away. And these dwarves could teach her something about her being a mage. The thought was still alien to her but what other explanation was there?

Finally, she wiped a few tears she hadn't realized were running down her face and nodded at her mother. "Will I ever be able to come home again?"

For the first time since she'd come down the stairs, Pat Williams sagged. "I don't know, sweetie. This might be… I'm so glad you came home and spent the last few months with us. It's been wonderful having you home again. You know you'll always be our special little girl. If everything goes okay, maybe Dad and I can visit one day, although John never did like Alp." Pat laughed, the sound a little pained, and Amy smiled. After all these years, she had discovered there were stories her mom hadn't told her—many stories, apparently. "But if we can't…you know we love you, right?"

She nodded. It was the safest response as she didn't have the strength to form words and keep herself from shaking the house.

When they embraced, her mom stuck her hand out and put the keys to her old red Chevrolet in her hands.

"Beula has a full tank, which should get you there. I have cash in the glovebox, both US and Canadian dollars. It should be enough to get you food or whatever else you need before you meet Alp in Thetford Mines."

"Thetford Mines?"

Pat nodded. "It's in Quebec, about two and a half hours from here. I already printed directions out and put them in Beula. Take Sixteen all the way to Lustis, then hop on twenty-seven and head north. Don't drive so fast that you'll wreck, but there's no point in following the speed limits either."

Oddly, her mom telling her to speed made all this sink home. The woman stopped at stop signs in the middle of the night when no one else was around. She didn't think she'd ever seen her so much as jaywalk. Now, she told her daughter to flee across an international border with a fistful of cash?

"The directions will take you to the La Face De Boeuf."

"La Face day what?"

"It's a restaurant near the mineral and mining museum. Alp will be there. He wouldn't shut up about it, actually. When you get there, you'll be safe."

Amy nodded, trying not to replace the when in her mother's statement with an if.

"I love you, Mom. Will I have time to say goodbye to Dad?"

Her mom shook her head and wiped back tears. "He doesn't understand any of this, sweetie. He could barely understand what happened with your magic and the dragons. He'll know you're safe, and that's enough. You have to go, and you have to go now. The Steel Dragon will try to catch you, I'm sure of it, and I don't know if anyone can stop her."

Amy nodded. It hurt like hell, but she'd go without saying goodbye to her dad.

She walked out of the basement, slid into her mom's car, and prepared to flee for her life.

CHAPTER THIRTY-FOUR

It was late, and the Detroit investigators had finally left the crime scene to find food when Larry and Kristen had demanded it. Windlock had seemed like he could keep going forever—she couldn't help but wonder if he'd snuck away in his dragon form and eaten a moose or something while she'd investigated the house—but when he ordered, she gave up the notion of a secret meal.

While they waited for their food—she had thought she was ridiculous ordering the rotisserie ribeye, but Windlock had ordered a basket of seafood and a whole chicken—she called the local human police department with the license plate number. At first, the officer who answered didn't seem to have any idea who Kristen was talking about.

"It was on an old red, Chevrolet," she explained. "A bumper sticker of *I quilt for moose* was on the back."

Another voice said something on the other end of the line.

"Oh sure, yeah. That's Pat Williams' truck. You know, I would never have remembered that. The woman don't speed—like, ever. I must've given every person in town a ticket at least once, but not Pat. Is she all right?"

"Is this the same Pat Williams who lived in the house that was burned down in the dragon fight?"

"Yes, Lady Steel," the officer answered, his voice shaky. He'd done well talking to her despite the fact that she'd introduced herself as a dragon investigator, but when she'd mentioned dragons for the second time, it seemed to affect him. "I only want to do whatever I can to help, ma'am—that is, my lady. We never had no dragons cause trouble in town before. Even those two normally kept all their business in the woods. Anything you need, all you got to do is ask."

"I want you to put out a BOLO for the car. Statewide."

"Yes, ma'am. No problem, ma'am." The man cleared his throat. "Uh…ma'am? What's a BOLO?"

Kristen tried not to chuckle over the phone. At least it wasn't only the local dragon law enforcement that was decidedly small-town in scope. The human police department seemed fairly casual as well. "Be on the lookout for that car, is all."

"You got it, ma'am! Be on the lookout. We do that all the time. Do you want us to detain Pat if we see her?" He sounded hesitant to do this, but as far as Kristen could tell, he still seemed willing.

"No, that won't be necessary. And actually, I have reason to believe that Pat won't be driving. I merely want to know if anyone sees that car anywhere. If they do, you call this number right away and don't engage. The driver might be dangerous."

"You think a dragon stole the truck, ma'am?" He sounded horrified.

"Not exactly, Officer, but I can't say more. This is an open investigation conducted by dragon investigators on behalf of the Dragon Council. We'd appreciate your cooperation, and please advise the state authorities of that BOLO but do not engage. The last thing we want is for a human to be hurt over this."

"Yes, ma'am. Anything else, ma'am?"

"That'll be it." Kristen hung up.

Windlock nodded at her and a smile teased at the corners of his lips. "That was good detective work, talking to the mother and getting the identification number of the truck."

"The license plate," Brockton corrected.

The dragon waved the correction away. "I'm pleased you agreed to come along. Cases like this can be difficult and humans have entire systems that dragons simply don't know about. The idea of every one of your vehicles having a unique code. Brilliant."

"Thanks, Windlock," she said and leaned back as their server brought them their food. Her ribeye looked amazing, and the mage's bowl of pasta certainly looked ample and good enough, but her jaw dropped when Windlock began to all but inhale his food with gusto.

Kristen began to cut into her meat with her fork and knife, while the other two simply used their hands. "I only wish I could have found more," she said after she'd taken her first mouthful and savored the tender beef. "I'm positive Mrs. Williams knew more but I wasn't able to coax much out of her. If it really is her daughter—and my gut says it is—she'll be our best lead."

"Do you really think a human mother would be a good lead?" Windlock asked.

"What do you mean by that?" she asked.

"Not anything specific. I simply mean that humans have a familial bond we dragons lack. Would your mother be a good lead in a case like this?"

"How would Mrs. Hall react to her daughter killing dragons?" Larry smiled. After all, she had killed dragons.

"My mom would do anything to protect us. She always was like that—my dad too. They were mama and papa bear, fierce to anyone who was mean to us, but my dad was also a cop. If he and my mom thought we'd broken a law? Well, I don't know. One time, Brian stole a pack of batteries from a grocery store and my mom dragged him back there by his ear and made him personally apologize to every single teller in the whole store. I don't know if she'd let us be fugitives."

"Do you think most mothers are like that?"

"Most moms are the mama-bear variety," Brockton interjected. "My mother would have lied to a cop's face if it meant keeping us out of trouble, no questions asked. Man, this one time, I had hopped a fence and gone swimming in a pool after hours and the cops arrived. My mom had already busted me, though, and she dumped a bottle of water on my head so they wouldn't be suspicious of my wet hair."

In the time it took Larry to tell that story, Windlock had already finished half a chicken. "What steps do you think Pat would take, Kristen?" the investigator asked. "We obviously can't expect her to dump water on her daughter's head, but what do you think she will attempt specifically?"

"It's hard to say but probably the same thing any mom would do," she mumbled around a mouthful of food.

"No, Kristen, you misunderstand me. My work is mostly with dragons, and our relationship with our parents is often quite different than the relationship you have with your parents. For example, it's not uncommon to break another dragon's eggs or steal them and raise them as one's own. Both actions would be considered horrible to mammals but to dragons, they're considered practical solutions. How a dragon would react in this situation is irrelevant. What I want to know is how a human mother would respond to this. Let's assume this is her mother. She's already demonstrated that she's willing to lie to a police officer—a powerful police officer I might add—and that she's hiding her daughter from an investigation into murder. What other steps might such a mother take?"

Kristen thought for a moment as she chewed. "Well, honestly, I think most moms—maybe even my mom—would try to protect their daughter, and that might mean trying to hide them. I'd guess that if anyone knows where that girl is—if she is her daughter—it's her mother. If she doesn't know, she's probably working even harder to find her than we are."

"Yeah, it makes sense to me, but the thing is that this girl is a mage," Brockton said. "There really isn't anywhere that can hide magic effectively."

"Okay, I don't mean to be rude but you haven't found her yet," she pointed out.

"Yeah, that's true enough, but that crime scene is twenty-four hours old. She's probably still recovering. Hell, she might be unconscious somewhere for all we know. Once she uses her power, I'll be able to locate her."

"Really?" she asked, a little dubious.

Larry nodded and ate another shrimp. "Yeah, if she's an untrained rogue mage—and I really do believe all the evidence points to exactly that—she'll let more magic slip. That's one of the reasons Constance has been so hard to find. She's well trained and doesn't use her magic much of the time as far as I can tell. Or she uses such a small amount that it's below my ability to detect with this, uh…" He glanced at Windlock and jiggled the silver bracelet on his wrist.

"What does it feel like to sense someone else's magic?" Kristen asked.

"From what I can tell, it's like dragons sensing each other's auras. Sometimes, I can sense dragon auras, especially those who have odd powers. That dragon—Timeflash? She lights up like a streetlamp, for example. You and Windlock not so much. I think it's because mages and dragons are actually more closely related than most of us think."

"Do you think mages were descended from dragons or something?" She couldn't help how her brain seized on a potentially new and intriguing possibility.

Larry shook his head. "No, no, nothing like that. Magic can manifest in almost anyone, remember? I don't have a history of magic users in my family tree, yet I have abilities. What I think—and Windlock will disagree here as soon as he stops cramming his face—is that maybe dragons are a type of mage."

Kristen nodded vaguely—the idea was beyond anything she'd ever considered—but Brockton didn't slow. He continued to talk, pleased to have an audience while his boss's mouth was full. "See, there's no evolutionary history for dragons, right? Like…they have six limbs— four legs and two wings. There's nothing else on the planet like that. No centaurs or whatever, if you see my meaning."

"Not really but—"

"I think that's because dragons—or maybe the first dragon anyway —was a mage who had this transformative ability because of course, dragons are magic. There's no other way something that big could fly without jet propulsion, no other way you could breathe endless amounts of fire, and hell, no way you could turn to steel if not for some kind of magic. I think it makes sense that dragons are merely another being on the magic spectrum—like a pixie or a dwarf or a mage but obviously way more powerful."

"And less prone to believe baseless conspiracy theories, too," Windlock said. He'd cleared his plate and dabbed surprisingly daintily at the corners of his mouth with a napkin. "Brockton's been over all this before. The problem is that it's a theory that relies on a lack of evidence so it can't be substantiated one way or the other."

"There's not no evidence," the mage complained, although he grinned. He clearly enjoyed arguing. "There's merely no fossil evidence."

"Sure, fine." Windlock held a hand up in a truce gesture. "But is any of this relevant to the case at hand? Do you think, for example, that this mage can turn into a dragon?"

"Well…no…"

"Then let's focus on the matter at hand. Kristen asked about your ability to track her. If this young woman uses her powers in town, you'll discern her, correct?"

Larry nodded. Kristen was sure he would've talked his theory to death, but she also knew that he was an experienced professional and the case would take precedence. They had a case to solve and they'd solve it faster if they all knew what their fellow teammates were capable of.

"So yeah," Brockton continued, "if this mage does anything more than lift a plate, I'll be able to detect the pulse and that'll give me a sense of direction."

"What if it's another mage?" she asked.

"It's like dragons' auras—I'm sure I mentioned this earlier. I'm familiar enough with hers that I won't confuse them."

"Crazy theories aside, he's right about that," Windlock said.

"Well, what if she doesn't use her powers?" Kristen asked.

The man shook his head. "Okay, that's not gonna happen. Of course, it's possible, I guess. But you saw the raw power she had.

There's no way she can keep it clamped for long, and if she does manage to contain it inside, well..." He once again mimed an explosion with his hands. "She'll feel it build up in her like an antacid tablet and will be compelled to release that pressure. When she does, I'll have my lead."

"You seem confident," she noted.

He gave her a half-cocked grin. "Detecting magic is kind of my thing."

She nodded while she tried to put herself in the mother's place. What would she do if her daughter was suddenly a powerful mage with magic seeping from her? "Maybe the mom will encourage her to run."

"Run where?" Windlock asked although something in his tone made her think it was a rhetorical question. It seemed an odd response, but she decided now wasn't the time to explore it too deeply.

"Well, she'd need to get away from dragons, obviously, as well as any other mages so she can avoid detection, right?" the investigator said.

"Yes, it makes sense to me." Larry nodded.

Kristen pounded the table in frustration. "Yeah, but that doesn't help us at all. Dragons are everywhere. Even out in Noplace, Maine, we have dragons. There's nowhere a human could escape a dragon. They rule everything. No offense, Windlock."

Larry looked at the other dragon and raised an eyebrow.

"Who wants dessert?" the investigator asked.

"I understand it's need to know but doesn't this qualify as need to know?" the mage asked.

"Okay," she said firmly. "Now, you two have to tell me whatever the fuck you're talking about."

The mage grinned—this was no doubt his intention—while Windlock clenched his jaw for a moment before he nodded at Brockton.

"Dragons don't quite rule everything," Larry said. "There were two human rebellions, remember?"

"Yeah, sure, but the mages who led those rebellions lost both of them." Kristen tried to quell her frustration. Everyone knew that.

"The mages lost, but there were winners too," he continued. "After the first rebellion, the dwarves—having been created by the mages—were given Canada to rule themselves if they would stay out of dragon territory."

"And you think she might try to make it to Canada?" she asked, suddenly very thankful she'd put the BOLO out.

"If you think she needs to run…" Windlock replied and shrugged.

"I don't know how far she'd have to actually go." Larry leaned forward conspiratorially. "This is all classified, of course—and for once, I actually agree with this being need to know or whatever—but…well, there's something of an 'underground railway' for mages that runs into northern Canada."

"How do you know?" Kristen asked.

"They tried to contact him, didn't they, Brockton?" Windlock said.

The mage nodded. "That they did. They contacted me after my powers first surfaced. I have no idea how they found out. Maybe one of them saw me do something in my shop or something, but I got a call asking if I wanted to go."

"And you said no?"

"Well, at this point, I hadn't heard from the dragons yet, so I declined. I assumed I could simply continue to work at the store, only I wouldn't have to hurt my back when I swept. Before too long, the dragons contacted me and said join up or be eaten. That's when I thought it might be best to go with the dwarven railroad but of course, by then, it was much more complicated. I might've been caught by dragons. It was good Windlock found me and convinced me to stay. I've worked for him in exchange for seafood baskets and protection ever since." He smiled at his dragon boss.

"Would it have been that bad to run?" She frowned as she considered his options and wondered what she might have decided if she'd been in his shoes. "You would have left dragon territory. What's wrong with that?"

Windlock shook his head. "It's known the dwarves have managed to hide a few mages up in the north, where few dragons go—"

"They don't like it because there aren't enough humans," Larry interjected. "They prefer to be around big human populations. It's more interesting and provides better servant possibilities." He winked.

"But there's a difference between a few mages hiding up north and an underground railroad funneling potential mages away. The North American Council's policy is to stop fleeing mages."

"Why?" Kristen asked.

"Because dragons feel like they must control all mages or they risk another mage-dragon war," Brockton said with a shrug. "It almost sounds altruistic until you remember that they also use us to take their notes." He made a pen float up and sign the check for the food to prove his point.

"What happens to mages who are caught running?" she asked with real dread that she already knew the answer.

"They're killed," Windlock said without a smile.

"That's fucking horrible." She was unable to keep the scowl off her face or the fury out of her aura.

"Hey now, you're right, it's messed up, but it's not Windlock's fault. I could've run and would probably have been caught and killed, but there were already a number of dragons who wanted to kill me even if I didn't run," the mage explained. "Do you have any idea what it's like? To have a dragon appear out of nowhere and argue for your life after three other dragons threatened to take it?"

"It doesn't sound fun," she admitted.

"That's the truth, right there." Larry grinned. "But that was what Windlock did for me. He argued for my life even though the powers that be definitely wanted it taken. Even now, he's all right. Yeah, I have to wear this bracelet, but so does every mage who can do anything more than lift a piece of paper. That's not his fault. Plus, he pays for dinners out of his pocket." He winked at his boss yet again, who rolled his eyes.

"You're right, I guess," Kristen said and nodded in understanding.

That black-and-white voice within tried to protest, but she pushed it aside because she caught something of what he tried to explain.

"All our hands are tied in one way or another by centuries of dragon law and dragon rulership," Windlock said. "Yes, I admit, dragons have the best of that deal, but it doesn't mean we have complete freedom either—and I don't only mean having to make reparations if humans are hurt. If I were to try to walk away from this job or send Brockton to Canada, I would have to answer for that."

"Fair enough. I guess, when you think about it, patriarchy is like the human equivalent of dragon rule," she said, a little surprised by the thought. "It sounds like it benefits men the most, but there are men who suffer from it, and many women reinforce it as well."

"Yeah." Brockton nodded. "I sometimes wonder what would happen to dragon society if all the mages stopped doing magic for them. Civil disobedience, wizard-style."

Windlock chuckled at the idea. "Most of us don't know how to cook our own food, let alone clean up after ourselves. If you all did that, dragon society would fall apart in three days."

"Is that necessarily a bad thing?" she asked, perhaps not completely rhetorically.

"You mean if the established social order the entire world has functioned under for centuries simply collapsed?" The investigator's tone left her in no doubt as to what his answer to that was.

She shrugged. "I guess that, to me, it seems like this whole mess will collapse sooner or later."

"You don't sound particularly sorry about the idea of that," Windlock challenged.

Kristen only shrugged again and tried to hide a devilish smirk. She did not want a war, but if dragon control of the world simply dissolved? That didn't sound so bad.

She was pulled from her anarchic fantasy when her phone rang and picked it up quickly.

"Who is it?" Larry mouthed silently.

"Local police," she replied and answered the call.

"Lady Steel, ma'am?" She recognized the voice as the man she'd spoken to earlier.

"What do you have, officer?"

"Someone picked that plate up."

"That's great! Could you give me the address for where it was seen?"

"Uh…er… Well see, the thing about that is—"

"Where was the truck seen?"

"It was crossing into Canada."

"It was seen going into Canada?" Kristen was shocked. Yes, they'd thought that was a possibility, but none of them had expected the mage to already be on the move.

"Yes, ma'am. The driver was a twenty-something female. It crossed where twenty-seven turns into QC one-six-one."

"Wait, she crossed? You didn't stop her?" Kristen asked.

"Uh…yes, ma'am. I mean, no ma'am. We didn't stop her, ma'am. You said it was a BOLO or whatever and that she was dangerous and not to apprehend."

She dragged in a deep breath. He was right, of course, but she might have given different instructions if she'd realized the mage intended to head for the border so quickly. "Okay, thank you." She hung up and related what she'd learned to her companions.

"That has to be the mage, don't you think?" Brockton said.

Windlock didn't answer and simply looked at her.

"I agree. I don't see why the mom would leave town, and the idea of her giving the truck to someone else to send us on a wild goose chase is a little much." Kristen pushed from the table and the other two stood and followed her out of the restaurant.

In the parking lot, much to her dismay, Timbergust and the four members of Boston SWAT walked across the asphalt toward the restaurant.

"Do you have any leads?" Emberslight—the Boston team's leader —asked.

"A few possibilities but nothing concrete yet," she answered before

Windlock could say anything. Fortunately, the investigator didn't contradict her and merely gave a non-committal shrug.

"Are you sure about that?" Bronzeback sneered. "I saw you move quickly after that phone call."

"That's enough, Bronzeback," Emberslight snapped, and her subordinate fell quiet. Kristen noticed that Timbergust now watched her more closely than he had before. "We have the bodies bagged, and they're being sent back to their estates," Emberslight told them. "We have a team of human and mage guards on high alert."

"Let us know if we can help," Timbergust added. He still looked shaken. Obviously, the dragon had totally lost control of the situation.

"We will," Windlock replied.

The Boston team leader led the other dragons into the restaurant.

"Why didn't you want to tell them?" the investigator demanded as soon as the door had closed behind the dragons. He simultaneously made his aura seem disinterested so if the others tried to sense them, they wouldn't think he was particularly agitated.

"Sorry, but I don't really know them and wanted to know what you think they'll do if they catch this woman—the mage."

"She's a fleeing mage," he said dispassionately.

"Who already killed two dragons." Larry's voice throat caught in his throat. "Even Windlock couldn't argue a mage's life out of something like that."

"That's what I was worried about," Kristen said and frowned. "Windlock, I want to try something and I'm sure you'll say it's not a good idea or whatever, but… Well, I think it's worth a shot."

"Why do I already not like the sound of this?" he asked.

"How about we don't tell the other dragons and see if we can get her to come in peacefully with us?"

"They'd never go for that," Brockton interjected.

"They might if we bring her back with that bracelet Windlock has in his pocket wrapped around her wrist."

The other dragon grimaced, then reached in his pocket and removed the bracelet she had seen him put there while in his office.

He tossed it and caught it a few times. "That's a huge breach of protocol," he said finally.

"Protocol being to hunt this woman down like a rabid dog and kill her?" She growled her obvious disapproval.

"I didn't say I was opposed to the idea," he retorted, "only that it's a breach of protocol. But...well... I don't know."

Larry seized the opportunity to add his encouragement. "Her powers have only now manifested. She probably didn't even mean to kill those dragons."

Windlock nodded.

"Plus," Kristen added hastily, "I might be able to talk to her. I know what it's like to be a regular human and suddenly have these crazy powers and be thrust into a whole new life. I think we can do this. Larry can track her magic, you can help deal with dwarves in Canada, and I can talk to the mage. It's worth a shot."

The investigator remained silent for a long moment, his face drawn in thought before he finally nodded. "This might all blow up in our face, of course. Protocol exists for a reason, but...morally, I think you're right. However—" Windlock tossed the bracelet to her and she caught it without thinking. "This won't work unless you bring her in. We'll back you up, of course, but I think you're right in that you'll have to take point on this."

"I understand," she agreed but with real reluctance. She didn't like the feeling of the bracelet in her hand. It was strangely heavy, and she found she couldn't turn the part of her hand that touched it into steel. Aside from that, it was discomforting to realize that her indignant rejection of what still seemed akin to slavery had been somehow fuzzed by reality. While part of her protested what might be considered compromising her moral high ground, the facts left her with a difficult choice. Even she was forced to acknowledge that shackling the woman was better than killing her.

"You also understand that if this goes south, we'll have to eliminate her before she blows something up, don't you?"

"I thought you said dwarves were tough when it came to fire?" she asked.

"There are people in Canada too. If she can't be brought in, she could kill more than two dragons."

Kristen nodded. She didn't like it, but she understood what he was saying. "If it comes to that, I'll make sure she doesn't hurt anyone."

Windlock held her gaze for a minute, finally saw what he liked, and nodded. "Let me check in with the other dragons and tell them we'll follow those possible leads you mentioned."

He entered the restaurant, exchanged a few words with Emberslight and Timbergust, and emerged moments later.

"Are we good?" Larry asked.

"They agreed but they had to, of course. I outrank them. Although there was something in Timbergust's aura… I think he knows this is all getting away from him and he's worried he'll lose his post. We'll need to be careful."

"Sure," Kristen agreed.

The two dragons transformed and Brockton climbed onto Windlock's back. They took to the air, but rather than heading north over the forest toward the place at the Canadian border where the mage had crossed, the investigator led them south toward the crime scene.

"We can't let them know we're heading to the border," he explained.

She nodded politely at first—although she thought he was simply being paranoid. When she glanced at the parking lot where they'd transformed, however, Bronzeback and Timbergust both stood outside and watched them.

While she didn't know if they were suspicious, simply curious, or what, she could tell that they were less than trusting. She couldn't decide if they didn't trust her, Windlock, or Larry, but it was obvious now that she'd made the right call. If she didn't reach this mage before the other dragons did, she knew it wouldn't be pretty for anyone. They had to save this girl before anyone else was hurt.

CHAPTER THIRTY-FIVE

The new warehouse wasn't as good as the last one, Constance Vigil had remarked when they'd first moved in, but it had grown on her. It was near the old boatyard in Detroit and still held a few old boats that had been abandoned and left to rot decades before. They'd patched the roof when they'd arrived but not moved the boats. Nor did she intend to. For whatever reason, she rather liked them.

Once they'd checked the perimeter, they'd set to work manufacturing more dragon weapons. Their bullets had come a long way since the early versions. They'd learned that the best way to make them was to carve them out of an entire tooth, claw, or bone. It involved considerable carving, but her cell of mages was adept at the work.

What was more exciting was that they'd discovered they could use what was left from carving the bullets to make bombs. True, Kristen had ruined their attempt to blow up the Dragon Council's party, but the bomb had struck the Steel Dragon and proven that it was effective even against dragons with unusual strengths.

There were members of her cell who were annoyed that she had "let" her bulletproof armor be taken by the Steel Dragon, who had used it to protect herself from the bomb and save her life, but she still counted the event as a victory. After all, they'd confirmed that there was a use for the leftover dragon pieces and had struck fear into the hearts of dragon kind. It wasn't bad for a night's work.

They'd moved twice since then and hopefully, would be there long enough to harvest their source once more before they moved on. Constance preferred to occupy new hideouts with as large a supply of raw materials on hand as possible. Idle hands were the devil's plaything, as the expression went, and that was doubly true for mages determined to destroy dragon kind.

As it was, they had almost run out of materials to work with, and some of her team had already become restless.

"It's almost grown back what we need," Vindication said, one of her more trusted mages.

Constance shook her head and didn't bother to look up from the bullet she worked on. "If we harvest early, the bullets might be too small. We'll waste a whole week of growth."

"I don't see how it's a waste. Letting it keep all its teeth seems like the waste to me."

"I said no, Vindication. I want more high-caliber rounds. We have what we need for handguns. I want to show these dragons they're never safe. I want to strike without being seen."

"Fine," he huffed. For such a big man, he really could pout. "I'll only take some scales then. It doesn't need those, not in the fluid we keep it suspended in."

"We'll harvest the scales on the regular schedule, Vindication. If we take too many, we might cause its regenerative properties to slow or even stop. Then, we'd no longer have a goose that lays golden eggs."

He scowled. "There's a solution for that too. Our sources say the Steel Dragon left Detroit. Now would be a good time to attack another target."

"It's still too close to the party. The whole city will be on high alert. Wait—wait, turn that up!" She pointed to a television playing a cable news channel.

One of the mages fetched the remote and turned up the news story.

"—making sure that the Dragon Council pays its due after a dragon duel became double murder."

The camera cut from a peppy reporter to the corpses of two dead dragons.

"I thought we were supposed to keep a low profile," Vindication joked. "Is that your work or is someone from one of the other cells stealing your thunder?"

"Be quiet and let me listen," Constance said and listened as the reporter talked about a ruined house and a small town coming together and blah, blah, blah.

"So, was it you?"

"No, it wasn't me. I've been here, you dolt. I don't think it was one of the other cells either, though. We don't have anyone in Maine." She glanced at their map of the United States. Cities with cells were marked in red and indeed, exactly as she remembered, there was nothing at all in Maine. There weren't any cities big enough.

"They did it to each other, though, right?" one of the other mages asked, a new recruit. Constance was glad for the extra muscle but some of them were so much less observant that she needed them to be.

"Did you see those bodies?" she demanded and fixed the man with a hard look. "Those dragons both died because their healing powers were overloaded. It looks like someone brought a building down on their heads. That wasn't done by a dragon. They go for the heart or the neck. Something else did this."

"Do you think we should try to get those bodies?" Vindication licked his lips in anticipation.

Constance held her hand up and barely managed to not blast him with a gust of icy wind to make him shut up.

The Steel Dragon was on the TV now. The technomage leader cursed under her breath while Kristen talked to the reporter about how the dragons had killed each other and how the Dragon Council would pay for the damages. It had been a surprise to see her there, but now that she saw the woman was at the location of another dead dragon, she wasn't surprised. It seemed that when she wasn't the one killing dragons like Death or Obscura, she stopped them from being killed. How could one person simultaneously serve the mage's cause and thwart it so effectively?

"Do you think we should eliminate the Steel Dragon?" Vindication asked when the news clip ended. "She might make an easier target without the rest of Detroit SWAT around."

She wished she had an easy answer to that question. Again and again, Kristen had stood in the way of her realizing her plans. It wasn't a stretch to say that without her, a war between dragons and mages would have already started. Her existence was antithetical to her goals and yet, she couldn't bring herself to order her execution. She was the only dragon who stood up to the others. She really was a champion of people. Constance still wanted her to join them, to fight for the liberation of humans from the yoke of dragon oppression. It was a pipedream, maybe, but a dream all the same.

It also didn't help that she still felt responsible for the girl. That kind of thing tended to happen when you cradled a newborn infant in your arms.

"No, we won't kill the Steel Dragon. We don't have the resources for a mission like that."

"You're biased—"

"She knows about us in a way most dragons don't. We won't surprise her like we can others."

"So you'll simply let her waltz around up there?"

Constance shook her head. "We won't do that either. She may one day be an ally, but you're right, we need to treat her like a threat—for now. And that means we can't let her secure whoever this killer of dragons is before we do."

"You mean..." Vindication grinned.

"Pack up," she told her team. "We're going on a trip."

Smiles touched the faces of all the technomages. None of them particularly minded harvest and construction—as they called their home-base chores—but there was nothing quite like being out on the hunt.

"You two stay behind and move our golden goose in a few days," she told two of her team. "Everyone else, I want to be out of here within the hour."

"I understand that you think we can still sway the Steel Dragon, but that doesn't mean we should leave dragon bullets behind, right?" Vindication said. For him, that practically counted as polite.

She clenched her jaw. While she didn't want to kill the Steel Dragon, if she got in their way again, what choice did she have? If Kristen—she reminded herself it was better to think of her as the Steel Dragon—continued to stop them, the technomages would grow restless and begin to question their leader's commitment to the cause. After all, she'd taught them to judge everyone's actions and to look for those who would help or hurt them everywhere. She wasn't above their judgment.

"Yes. Yes, bring the new rounds."

There was no way to know whether they'd need to use them or not, but she'd be damned if the Steel Dragon ruined her plans again.

CHAPTER THIRTY-SIX

Once they had covered a few miles south of town, Windlock led Kristen higher and higher to avoid detection. At what he called cruising altitude, they turned north to Canada. She pumped her wings powerfully to test their limits before she slowed to fly alongside her partner. With the long flight ahead and possibly combat—although she obviously hoped it didn't come to that—she wanted to determine what she was capable of. While she could sense that her powers weren't completely restored, her healing had certainly progressed noticeably over the last few days. Hopefully, that would continue.

"So what's the plan?" Larry asked from his boss' back. He had raised a sphere of magic to protect him from the wind and the cold.

"She's obviously powerful and a clear threat to dragons, so I don't think we should start a fight," the investigator said.

"I second that," Kristen agreed, thankful that he would let her apprehend this woman peacefully if possible.

"I think our best bet is to take her by surprise. Brockton can contain her magic—"

"Yeah, right!"

"Or at least keep it directed away from us," Windlock continued.

"Then Lady Steel can block the road with her steel skin, and I'll scoop the car up and take her into the air. She won't know how to levitate herself yet so hopefully, once she's airborne, she'll stop any attempts to attack."

"It sounds solid," Larry said.

"I don't think that's a good plan." She made an attempt to phrase it kindly, although she believed it was a terrible plan. "I think it would be better to talk to her first instead of trying to snatch her. We should win her trust and convince her to come with us willingly. If she sees us as a threat, she's far more likely to attack us."

"That's why we need to surprise her. She can't see us as a threat if she can't see us coming at all," the other dragon replied.

"And if Larry can't contain her? What if she ends up hurting herself?" she protested.

"That's a risk we have to take." Windlock's tone was firm. "I understand that she's a victim in this, but we can't give her any chance to attack us. She killed two dragons. That's not easy to do, not even for a dragon. The longer she's on the run—scared and probably not thinking clearly because of human fight or flight hormones—the higher the chance she hurts innocent bystanders, be they dragon, human, or dwarf."

"So let's talk to her and get her calm," she argued.

"I agree with Kristen. We should talk to her and hopefully bring her to a place where she can control her powers," Larry said.

"Thank you," she said but the mage continued to talk.

"But I also agree with Windlock. The longer she goes uncuffed, the more dangerous she becomes, to herself, to us, and to anyone near her. We need to bring her into custody, get her powers under control, then talk to her. Believe me, Kristen. I don't want her to die and making sure she has a cuff on is the best way to ensure that."

"I'm simply not sure—"

"Let's vote on it," the investigator said.

She glanced at Larry, who nodded, and she knew how the vote would go. It was basically a power move from Windlock to give a human a vote he knew would go his way. It was both empowering to humankind and disempowering to her. And clever, she acknowledged, which left her resentful—not only that she'd been outmaneuvered but because he'd done it so easily.

"I vote we talk to her first," she said.

"And I vote we surprise her, cuff her, and prove we're friends once it's safe," the other dragon said.

"I vote with Windlock." Brockton's choice came as no surprise.

"Fine," she agreed, although she still didn't like the plan. She tried to think of another way she could dissuade them, but the mage spoke suddenly and there was no time to argue any further.

"I sensed her!"

"Where?" Windlock asked.

"Ahead. Follow the highway."

They'd crossed the Canadian border—not that the forest below seemed to care—and continued north for a short distance when they located her. The red Chevrolet raced along the side of a lake. The body of water looked narrow from this height, but Kristen was familiar enough with the dragon perspective to know it was actually quite wide.

"Here we go," the investigator said and dropped from their altitude to move above the truck.

Kristen surged ahead.

She felt a pulse of something like a dragon aura and realized it was Larry's magic. He'd cast one of his protective spheres around the truck, and the girl hadn't seemed to notice.

This might actually work, she thought as she landed on the highway a couple of miles ahead of the vehicle.

If her companion could get it airborne, the mage might decide not to fight.

The other dragon dove suddenly and with the speed and deftness of an eagle, hooked his claws through the roof of the vehicle. A flash of light from inside the cab was probably a blast of magic from the mage, but Larry's spell held. Windlock pumped his wings and lifted it off the road.

Kristen held her breath, unable to fully comprehend that it seemed to be working. Brockton had contained the girl and the investigator had been able to sneak close enough without her noticing.

Windlock lifted the truck five feet, then ten, and she allowed herself a smile of relief.

Another flash erupted inside the cab but this one was not contained by Larry's shield. It blew through it and into the night sky like a bolt of lightning that seemed to be made of pure force. The dragon barely moved his head out of the way in time, but he kept his claws latched in the metal and tried to go higher.

The mage obviously didn't know she'd disabled Larry's shield around her, only that despite her attempt to wound the dragon above her, she was still rising. Understandably, given the circumstances, she reacted violently. Kristen gaped in equal parts terror and awe as the woman spun her hands in a circle and released a ring of force that severed the top of the truck from the bottom like it was made of Styrofoam.

Windlock continued to pump his wings to lift the vehicle and suddenly rocketed up from the unanticipated change in mass with nothing but the roof of the cab in his claws.

The vehicle fell the ten feet to the ground, bounced mightily, and landed on its wheels. It skidded and slewed wildly for a moment before it straightened and continued to race forward without a top.

Kristen realized she had a choice. She could turn her dragon body to steel and simply block the road. The mage might be able to lash out with some kind of force and strike her, but she didn't seem to have the control yet to simply move her. Plus, when she was in her steel form, she weighed tons. If she did that, the woman would definitely collide with her. She could be hurt and perhaps killed, but she'd most likely be stopped unless Larry had totally misjudged her skill with magic.

The other alternative was to simply step aside. She could let her go, spare her life, and try to bring her in again using a different approach.

She had only seconds to decide and chose neither. Instead, she turned into her human form—but kept her steel skin because she wasn't a complete fool—and held her hands above her head to show the woman driving the vehicle that she meant her no harm.

Come on, come on. See that I'm different than them. She pushed her aura at the girl in an effort to calm her. *See that I mean you no harm and that I don't want to hurt you. I only want you to be safe.*

Unfortunately, the woman had one more trick up her sleeve. Moments before the seemingly inevitable impact, she swerved sharply. The tires skidded before she regained control and accelerated past.

It all happened so fast that Kristen instinctively flung herself to the side of the road. She landed, rolled, and pushed up as the taillights vanished around a turn.

"Come on, Lady Steel. It's time for plan B," Windlock said as he circled overhead and descended to alight beside her.

Kristen nodded. Both their plans had failed. They wouldn't surprise the mage again and it didn't seem like they had a chance to befriend her either.

Still, she had to be stopped. She only hoped the woman wouldn't be hurt in the process.

CHAPTER THIRTY-SEVEN

Amy had no idea what the hell had happened. Obviously, dragons had attacked her, but it didn't exactly encourage confidence that the simple truth of that was the only part she really understood.

Her mind tried to piece it all together and she recalled that she'd been driving fast when one of them had grasped the roof. She hadn't tried to use whatever powers she apparently possessed. It seemed safe to assume they were magic. Her mom had said she was a mage, which meant what she'd done was magic. It had been purely instinctual, however, and not a deliberate choice. She'd wished the dragon would go away and her powers had listened.

Not at first, though, she realized and let her thoughts explore the vague memory.

Something had blocked her—a sphere of the same kind of force she had used to hurt the dragons she'd thought had killed her parents. Thankfully, her mom and dad were still alive, although this made the death of the dragons even more troubling and stirred a definite surge of guilt. The moral implications weren't important right now, she reminded herself as she eased up on the gas pedal to take a turn.

She checked her mirror. The dragon who'd transformed into a

woman in the road had made no effort to follow. Why wasn't she chasing her? Amy knew they could catch her if they wanted to. That was obvious. She'd driven as fast as she could from the moment her mom had told her to flee and they had still caught up. There weren't speed limits in the air, so they had nothing to hold them back.

The car tires screeched, and she jerked the wheel but overcompensated and the back of the vehicle began to slide out. *Please stay on the road.* The thought had barely formed when her powers obeyed her.

The same thing had happened when she'd almost collided with the woman dragon—the Steel Dragon, her mom had said. She'd lost control and tried to regain it, and something besides her driving skills had saved her. A force—her magic, she tried to tell herself—had reached out from inside her and applied pressure to the back of the vehicle to align it. Once it stopped its skid, the tires caught, and the truck surged forward.

Amy laughed. It was fucking insane, but she laughed. A dragon had ripped the roof of her truck off, a mage had tried to trap her in a bubble, she'd almost run over a dragon, and she now steered her truck with her mind. It was crazy. She knew these things existed. Everyone knew dragons and mages existed, but that it was happening to her was unbelievable.

A road sign indicated that Marsboro was coming up soon. She had checked the map before she left and remembered the city because she'd thought it sounded like a cigarette company. It was a fair distance from Thetford Mines and she cursed. She still had miles to go before she reached her destination. Once she did make it there, she'd have to find a dwarf, convince him that she was who she said she was, and accept his help to hide from a group of pissed-off dragons. It didn't sound easy, especially given the dragons already in pursuit.

But what was their intention? Amy had assumed they'd try to kill her. She hadn't been surprised to be lifted by the one dragon. After all, she'd proven that fire wouldn't work on her, so they had to use other means. But why hadn't they struck? The Steel Dragon could have transformed into her dragon body and become steel. If she'd done that, it was very unlikely that she could have survived the collision.

She could use these new powers reflexively, but the idea of saving herself from a car crash sounded impossible.

Surely the Steel Dragon could have made that same assumption. It stood to reason that she was far more familiar with magic than Amy was.

And there was what she'd done. She'd held her hands up—not in front of her but above her head, the same way a cop would ask a criminal to hold their hands to show they wouldn't try to hurt them. Had she been trying to tell her something? Could she be certain she was an enemy?

A major realization intruded to end that particular series of questions. She had bigger problems than a dragon who might not want to murder her, namely any other dragons who might. Her mom had mentioned Timbergust. Would he feel differently? If he decided to hunt her, he'd probably find her far easier than the Steel Dragon had.

After all, the roof of her truck had been ripped off. Her current pursuers had seen the vehicle when it was still intact but now that it was a makeshift convertible classic truck, it didn't exactly blend in.

Amy drove for a few more minutes and checked her mirror repeatedly. Fortunately, it was attached to the top of the windshield. Any higher and it would be gone. Despite her caution, she didn't see the dragons approach and she didn't feel any of the magic bubbles try to trap her either. It seemed like she had an opportunity and she decided to take it. When she reached Marsboro, she drove through it and exited near the last gas station on the outskirts of the city. She didn't have any idea if the dragons were still in pursuit but she felt like they were breathing down her neck.

As calmly as she could, she drove behind a little grocery store, parked beside a dumpster, and slid out.

She rifled through the glovebox for the maps and cash. "Thanks, Mom," she mumbled, took the keys with her, and hoped she could return them to her mother one day. The bag of clothes and sundries her mom had packed for her wasn't too heavy, thank goodness, and she slung it over her shoulder.

After another furtive look around her—including a scan of the skies above—she wandered casually to the gas station.

An eighteen-wheeler filling up caught her attention. Amy nodded as the driver clambered in and she hurried to the edge of the parking lot, where she stood and hooked her thumb toward the on-ramp.

The trucker pulled up and rolled his window down. "You looking for a ride, eh?"

"Yes, sir. I need to reach Thetford Mines," she replied and tried to sound polite.

"Thetford Mines, eh? It's your lucky day. I'm headed to Quebec City. Thetford Mines is on my way. Hop in."

"Thank you, sir." She climbed into the cab and they continued north.

CHAPTER THIRTY-EIGHT

"What happened to the plan?" Windlock demanded, still in dragon form. He didn't yell but he had the voice of someone who was used to being obeyed and hadn't been in a situation where failure seemed to be the result of the fact that someone didn't respond as expected. It was a voice Kristen knew all too well and didn't like.

"The plan was for me to land and force her to stop. She didn't stop." She tried not to sound defensive.

"The plan was for you to stay in dragon form with your steel skin activated. If she had been confronted by a steel dragon instead of a human, she'd have had to stop." His tone was biting.

"Or she might have driven into me!"

"We both know you would have been fine. I've seen many regular dragons shrug off being struck by a car, even if it was one of the old heavy American ones, and you're the Steel Dragon. You would have crumpled that vehicle like a can of soda pop," Larry exclaimed from Windlock's back. He wiped his nose and she realized it was bleeding.

"You're right, the truck would have been destroyed and she would probably have died. Are you okay, by the way?" she added. She hadn't seen him get hit but it was possible.

"Yeah, I'm fine. This happens sometimes when a mage goes head-to-head with another one. If they overpower our powers, it often sends a shock through the body. It only gave me a nosebleed because I was able to deflect most of her energy. She really is strong, though."

Windlock shook his head and his aura radiated disappointment. "Yet another reason why we need to catch this mage," he explained slowly. "I agree, alive is preferable, and our plan gave her two chances to come in willingly, but she's murdered two dragons. If she won't surrender voluntarily, we need to bring her in by force. If it has to be lethal, it has to be lethal."

"She didn't murder those dragons. She acted in self-defense."

"They didn't kill anyone, yet she still used lethal force," he pointed out.

"That doesn't matter. They all but obliterated her house and attempted to incinerate her. If someone tries to shoot you and you return fire and kill them, that doesn't mean it wasn't self-defense. Practically any lawyer could make her case into a win. I agree she needs to be brought in but if we kill her, we deny her justice, which she is entitled to."

Brockton chose that moment to have a coughing fit and turn away from her, but not before she saw the corners of his mouth turn up in a smile. He was, apparently, stifling a laugh.

Kristen looked at him for a moment. "What is it, Larry?"

"Oh, nothing. Nothing at all.

She looked at Windlock. "What? What dragon rules am I missing now?"

The investigator at least had the decency to look uncomfortable—not exactly an easy thing in the body of a fire-breathing dragon.

"There's no such thing as a valid killing of a dragon by a human on the basis of self-defense," the mage said ruefully. "If a human kills a dragon, they're hunted and generally killed. Any human that powerful is a threat to all dragon kind and is treated as such. They would've killed me too if I'd done what Amy had done."

"You can't be serious." She recoiled instinctively from the idea.

"Do you think I'd joke about this?" Larry's voice was strained.

"We're supposed to pursue justice, not vengeance."

"I agree," Windlock said.

"So this whole chase is nonsense, then? She's killed, so when we catch her, you'll simply kill her?" Kristen transformed into her dragon form. She couldn't help herself. Had Windlock lied to her this whole time? She'd thought that he worked with her, but what if he had manipulated her like Shadowstorm had done? A growled protest emerged at the thought. She didn't want to fight him, but if he told her their intention was to kill this rogue mage, she couldn't allow that either.

"I want to bring her in alive. Really, I do," the investigator said and his aura radiated calm. He didn't want to fight her either. "But we have to hurry. Eventually, the other dragon SWAT team will get a lead on the mage and go after her. All they have to do is ask the local police force, and they'll tell them exactly what they told you. I'm only frustrated because we could have captured her already. If you'd stayed in your dragon form, she might have stopped."

"And she might have kept driving and killed herself."

"You're correct, and that was a risk I thought we all understood," he said slowly. "I understand that you don't want her to die, but we can't play this safe and take our time. When the other dragon team realizes that she fled, they will come after her and I promise you, they won't hunt to capture."

CHAPTER THIRTY-NINE

Once in the air, they found the abandoned truck easily enough. Kristen would have probably missed it—parked as it was behind a grocery store—but Larry was able to sense it.

"There she blows," he said, pointed toward the vehicle, and made it glow with his magic. "She's learned a thing or two about subtlety—and by that I mean she didn't obliterate that entire stretch of highway like she could have—but she's still left an insane amount of magical residue behind."

They landed and poked around but it was immediately obvious that the woman wasn't there. Even without the roof missing, there was nowhere to hide, and the glove box was open and looked like it had been looted.

"I'll go in and see if the grocery store has camera footage from this area," Kristen said.

Windlock looked at Larry and the mage waved the suggestion away. "Nah, that'll take too long. This is still fresh. I should be able to discover something about what happened."

"Sure," she said as the mage sat on the pavement near the dumpster, crossed his legs, and closed his eyes. Once again, a mist descended and through it, she saw the now familiar figure of the young mage wander toward the gas station.

"Follow her," Larry said, his voice strained.

The two dragons did so and sprinted from behind the store toward a gas station. The misty wraith version of the mage looked around and moved to the access ramp to the freeway before she stepped from the misty area Brockton had created and vanished.

The mist dissipated, and a moment later, the mage joined them. He was breathless but not drenched in sweat like he had been when he'd recreated the scene of the fight that had killed two dragons. One of his nostrils had resumed bleeding, though. She realized then that there was some kind of price to using magic. Maybe it wasn't anything more than the energy an athlete expended while exercising but still, him recreating the scene had been enough to start his nose bleeding again.

"She went that way, huh?" he asked and wiped his nose on his sleeve when he saw that she stared at him. "Sorry about that. The clot came loose."

"I don't understand." Windlock had taken his human form and his eyebrows were furrowed. "She's walking down the highway?"

This time, it was Kristen and Larry who shared a look and a grin.

"She's probably hitching," she said.

"It makes sense," Larry agreed. "A young woman wouldn't have a hard time finding a ride from someone."

"You humans." Windlock chuckled. "You go through the effort of registering every one of your vehicles so you know exactly who is driving each of them, but then you lend the vehicles to each other or give each other rides. What is the point of registering the vehicles in the first place?"

The mage laughed but she ignored him while she checked a map on her phone. "Do you think she'd go to Quebec City?" she asked. "It's the biggest city in the direction she's heading and this road goes there."

"Maybe," the investigator said. "But there are probably a few dragons there, so maybe not."

"I thought this was dwarf country." She looked at him in confusion.

"It is, but that doesn't mean there aren't dragons here too. Which is lucky for us, really, otherwise us flying overhead might draw a few more eyes than we'd like."

"Is she in danger?" she asked.

"The dragons here won't move against her or anything, but I don't think this dwarven railroad will be stationed near them either."

"Do you mind if I see that map?" Larry asked.

Kristen handed them the phone.

His eyes widened as soon as he saw the screen. "Thetford Mines. That's where she's going. I'd bet my pinky toe."

"What makes you so sure?" Windlock asked.

"When they tried to get me out of the States, that was the destination," he said.

"You never told me that," his boss countered.

The mage shrugged. "When we first met and that information was still somewhat relevant, I thought you would eat me if I didn't listen to you. What kind of a person would I be if I had revealed the whereabouts of a group of people who wanted to help people like me at the first opportunity?"

"I'm merely…impressed, is all." Windlock muttered. "I didn't know you had any secrets after all these years."

"Don't be mad, you old windbag. I trust you. I told you that's where she's going, didn't I?"

"You did."

"Which means you'll need to keep the location a secret as well," Kristen said. "We can't have Investigator Windlock spilling the beans about these people's only escape."

The dragon looked perplexed. For a moment, he said nothing but he finally nodded. "That's fair, I think. If she's headed there, we need to intercept before she arrives. I was serious about what I said earlier. Boston SWAT and Timbergust will come after us, I have no doubt. Timbergust has something to prove and Emberslight is too competent to let us and the mage vanish without her knowing about it."

"Are you considering a roadblock?" Larry asked.

Windlock nodded. "I have a contact in the Mounties. If we tell him we have a mage who killed two dragons, he'll cooperate. Even though this is dwarf country, no one wants to openly harbor fugitives from the Dragon Council. It's not good politics."

They waited for him to talk to his Mountie. After a few minutes, they decided on a roadblock north of Saint-Joseph-de-Coleraine. It was something of a gamble as whoever was driving the rogue mage might have taken a different path, but it seemed like the most logical choice. They took to the air and followed the highway north.

The team soared over the truck Amy was in without being alerted to her presence. Now that she had been given a ride, she could relax and her magic remained dormant until she called on it again.

CHAPTER FORTY

The investigators arrived at the location outside Saint-Joseph-de-Coleraine and made their way to the roadblock. The officer who met them—the Mountie Windlock knew—had a thin, crisp, mustache and the faintest of French accents. Despite facing two dragons and a mage, he didn't so much as flinch.

"Investigator, I would say this is a pleasure, but it never is with you," the man said.

"Antoine." Windlock nodded at the man in his red uniform, odd black pants, and brown hat. "Did you get us uniforms?"

"I did, and you may wear them as long as you hold yourself to a higher standard than usual." He glanced at Brockton. "For you, I do not have a hat. You have lost the honor."

"Yeah, whatever," Larry grumbled. There was obviously a story there, but now wasn't the time for it. Kristen and Windlock went into a nearby gas station to change.

She didn't like the idea of impersonating someone from another force, but she agreed with Windlock that this was probably the best way to bring the mage in without frightening her too much. She imagined it would be a novel thing to see Mounties stop them, but two people in civilian clothing might be odd. That was the hope, anyway.

Once dressed, they returned to the roadblock. The two Mounties Antoine had selected for duty fulfilled their responsibilities professionally but waved most of the drivers through enthusiastically. They occasionally stopped someone and checked their documents, but even these were conducted with a level of cordiality that wasn't normally present in interactions between American cops and the civilians they policed. Maybe it was that everyone in the United States carried weapons. Or possibly, it was the threat of dragons. Who knew?

Either way, all of it was a farce. Larry said he'd experienced the mage's powers enough times that he'd be able to sense her coming unless she'd mastered the ability to dampen her powers. He assured them that was unlikely and his teammates had no reason to question it. Kristen still hadn't mastered her aura and so knew that controlling the energy that emitted from one's body wasn't exactly second nature. This mage was probably still focused on not being eaten or blowing things up. Again, that was the hope.

It didn't take long for the truck to arrive.

It was about a quarter-mile out when the mage said, "I have something. That big one—Labatt's blue truck, I think."

"I thought you'd give us more notice than that," Windlock said and moved into position on the driver's side of the truck. Kristen moved to the passenger window. They had agreed it would be best if she confronted the mage as she'd have the best chance to convince her to come willingly.

"I thought I would have had more notice," Brockton replied. "She shouldn't have any control yet but it's almost like she's learned how to clamp it down."

"Are you sure it's her?" she asked and tried to remain calm.

He nodded. "Again, you can't confuse them. That'd be like you thinking Stonequest was Windlock."

She smiled at the idea. The two dragons' auras couldn't feel more different.

The eighteen-wheeler rolled to a stop and the driver rolled his window down.

"License and registration, please," Windlock said and sounded efficiently bored.

"Sure thing. What's this about, eh?" the man asked. "We got a runaway dragon or something?"

"Nothing so dramatic," he responded. "Merely a routine stop." He took the driver's documents and turned to look at them, pretending that he needed to see them better.

Kristen moved to the other window.

"I don't see her ID here," the investigator said languidly to the driver.

"Who her? This is Amy Williams. She's here for a little sightseeing. You got your passport, Amy?"

So her name was Amy and she could only be Pat Williams' daughter. Kristen smiled inwardly. She didn't need to be able to feel auras to tell that the girl was frightened. Her gaze darted nervously as her hands fidgeted at her pockets. Finally, she dug in her bag and pulled out a passport, but she hesitated before she leaned over the driver to hand it to Windlock. Even though the man didn't seem to have any idea that this was anything but a routine stop, the girl seemed to sense that the roadblock was there for her.

Kristen knocked gently on the window and Amy flinched, startled by the sound. She smiled when the young woman turned to her.

This was her first time seeing her face and in it, she saw a kindred spirit. Not that the fugitive looked like her. The Steel Dragon was, by most accounts, stunningly beautiful as most dragons were. Amy was pretty but in an understated way. She had straight brown hair that hung to just above her neck and big brown eyes that currently brimmed with fear. It wasn't her appearance Kristen related to, though. It was the look in the girl's eyes.

She recognized the same feeling she'd felt when she'd first turned to steel—fear of her own body and of a power she'd never asked for and yet didn't want to lose. Like her, the girl had never asked to be made special and now that she had been, was afraid of what it might make her into. Without a doubt, she saw herself in Amy's eyes and she wanted to help.

"Hey there, miss. Is everything all right?"

The young woman nodded far too quickly. Kristen wondered if she'd ever been pulled over by a cop before. If she had, she probably would have known it was better to stay calm.

"Everything's fine," she said curtly.

"Are you sure there's nothing I can help you with? If you have problems, the Mounties' job is to help solve them."

Amy nodded and her eyes welled with tears. "I…I don't know if you can."

"I can, really."

In the next moment, the young mage's eyes widened. "Not with that." The fear in her voice was gone, replaced by rage.

Kristen turned as Timbergust and Aquatos landed on her side of the truck. On the other side, Emberslight and the other dragon from Boston touched down—Crimson, she thought they'd called him.

"We have this under control!" Windlock shouted at the newcomers.

Predictably, they ignored him. Bronzeback landed in front of the semi-truck. He was massive in his dragon form—bigger than Kristen and probably bigger than most—and his bronze scales seemed to be connected with nothing but shadow. It was terrifying to Kristen, who knew exactly who and what he was. But to poor Amy, who'd already been intimidated by a redheaded woman dressed as a Mountie, it was too much.

She began to shake.

"Hey, it'll be okay," she said and tried to use her aura to calm the woman, but she felt something slap it away. The girl had been learning, apparently.

"You need to back the hell off," Windlock shouted. "We have this under control."

"You may be willing to handle a killer with kid gloves, but that's not how Boston SWAT handles murderers around here," Bronzeback retorted aggressively from his position in front of the truck.

"We appreciate your help, Investigator, but we'll take it from here," Timbergust said. "Stand aside." He growled and used his aura to tell Kristen he would fight if they had to.

She clenched her jaw. "Miss Amy? I want you to stay calm while I get rid of these assholes, okay?"

The young woman nodded but it was very apparent that she didn't have much time left before she lost it.

Kristen turned to Timbergust—a full-sized green forest dragon— took a step toward him, and turned to steel. She knew that if she assumed her steel dragon form, she'd be able to beat him in a minute. He was obviously out of shape and she had defeated other dragons in combat, but she didn't want to further spook Amy. The poor girl was already frightened enough. Another dragon battle might set her off and that was the last thing they needed.

It was too late for that, though. "You're not a Mountie," the mage shouted. "You're the Steel Dragon."

What followed could only be described as an explosion but not from some kind of combustible or heat or anything like that. Magic energy simply ripped the entire vehicle apart. Pieces of steel tore free and hurtled toward the dragons who now surrounded the vehicle.

A pallet of beer pounded into Kristen before she had time to act and she sprawled flat on her ass. It landed on her chest—not landed, as that implied gravity was at work—but was forced there and pinned her arms above her head. She had the strength to lift it, but it had her in an awkward position and seemed to force her to stay down.

She looked out from where she was held immobile and realized that the big pieces of metal had rocketed into the other dragons. The engine had hammered into Bronzeback, who tried to get it off him with his tail.

The girl's using her powers to drive these pieces into us, she realized. That seemed like her powers had increased in control, which wasn't a good sign.

Kristen half-transformed into a dragon and grew large enough to push the pallet off her, then returned to her human form and stood slowly.

The eighteen-wheeler had been completely obliterated and all that remained were its tires and the seats. Everything else had either been thrown into the dragons who'd tried to stop Amy or used to crush the police cars that had formed the roadblock. One of the official vehicles was on fire and she assumed a piece of shrapnel must have pierced a gas line. No one moved except the driver, who gaped stupidly as if to grasp the truth that the rest of his vehicle was no more. The seat he was in lowered slowly to the ground, and he darted to his feet and raced into the woods.

The young mage stood where the truck had been, her brown hair blowing in a wind that touched nothing else. She didn't look like she wanted to run. Not at all.

CHAPTER FORTY-ONE

Amy didn't understand how she'd disassembled the truck but she slowly began to understand how she'd used its pieces to stop the dragons. Since she'd lashed out with her powers and killed the first two dragons, every minute that hadn't been spent worrying had been devoted to testing her powers. She now knew she had two main types—a kind of telekinesis that let her lift things and move them around and what she thought of as a force shield power. The telekinesis was much stronger and seemed to obey her every whim.

She reached out with this part of her abilities and found all the scraps of the eighteen-wheeler, as well as some of the damaged police cars. Everything gathered together weighed tons but it wasn't any more difficult for her to lift than toy blocks were for a child. And, like a child, she would learn control with practice.

Her next step was to bring all the pieces together to form four floating walls around her.

"I don't want to hurt any—" she called but before she could finish, one of the dragons breathed fire at the amalgamation of scrap metal and heated it enough to meld it into a solid piece of metal. If that had struck her, she'd be dead. How could the dragon do that to her? She hadn't attacked anyone. All she'd done was knock them back.

She heard her assailant breathe in for another blast of fire—a sound she already knew intimately—and she decided she'd had enough. Grimly, she took the piece of metal he had fused and flung it at him. It struck him in the chest, but she sensed she could do more. Rather than simply strike him, she wound it around him like it was a piece of aluminum foil wrapping a taco. Once he was completely trapped, she lifted him and dropped him so his head now faced away from her. She didn't want him to release another attack.

"She trapped Crimson," an aquamarine dragon yelled.

"He's not hurt," Amy said.

"You don't know that," the dragon retorted and lunged forward. This one knew she could stop its fire, so it attacked her with its claws. Every time it struck at her, she threw a piece of metal up to block its talons. It attacked again and again, faster and faster, but she continued to deflect the attack. The dragon, driven into a frenzy, roared and snapped at her with its teeth. Didn't it realize it could swallow her whole?

Without a doubt, she needed to make sure that didn't happen. The most logical way to prevent it was to take the door from a police car and thrust it into the dragon's jaws to wedge them open. It fell back and struggled to get the metal out of its mouth.

"Let me get away," Amy said. "I don't want to hurt anyone."

"You killed two dragons," a dark-green dragon yelled. Amy recognized him. She'd seen Timbergust fly over Rangeley before.

"I didn't mean to. They destroyed my parents' house. I tried to defend myself."

He lunged at her in response and she reacted immediately. She'd crushed the pieces together so she had three solid shields to use against the dragons and now hurled one of her walls of metal at him. The force knocked him back.

The other two dragons attacked at the same time. One was orange and more controlled in her strikes, while the other was the big mean bronze one who'd landed in front of the eighteen-wheeler. She blocked attack after attack with her metal shields. "Please, let me go," she pleaded at intervals.

After a moment, Timbergust returned to the fight, and the orangish dragon stopped attacking. That was when Amy started to feel hot and glanced down. The asphalt below her glowed the same color as the orange dragon's eyes and radiated heat.

She realized then that they would stop at nothing to hurt her. Calmly, with her last three pieces of metal ready, she waited for the dragons to attack. The bronze one and Timbergust moved together and she drove her shields into them. The force of impact was enough to stun them for a moment. While they were dazed, she used the metal she'd hit them with to wrap them like she'd done with her first attacker.

The orange dragon was still focused on melting the surface beneath her feet, so the mage did the same to her. Timbergust and the orange one were easy enough, but the bronze dragon almost destroyed his bindings. She picked up a cop car and rested it on top of him and that seemed to do that trick.

A moment of silence followed during which all the dragons struggled at their restraints. The blueish-green one still hadn't removed the car door from its mouth. Amy glanced at the Mountie who'd checked the truck driver's ID. There was something odd about him but he didn't attack her so she ignored him.

She approached Timbergust, who struggled to free himself from the metal in which he was encased.

"I didn't mean to hurt them. I was only defending myself and it got out of hand."

"Murderer!" he roared and blasted her with fire.

The fire got close enough for her to feel the heat from it, then it parted, deflected from her by the magic sphere of energy she'd used to protect herself before.

She shook her head. "All I want is peace and you try to kill me."

"You're a killer."

"Am I?" she demanded, furious now. "Because if that's all I am to you, I might as well kill." Her magic sensed her frustration and tightened on the four restrained dragons. All of them squirmed until they began to run out of air. She saw Timbergust's dragon eyes begin to bulge and a vein ruptured in one of them to wash it with red. "I could kill you right now—all of you—without even breaking a sweat," she said. "Is that what you want? Do you want me to be a killer?"

"No!" Amy blinked and turned to the red-headed Mountie. The Steel Dragon, she told herself. "I want to help you."

The mage choked out a laugh and when she did, she tightened the restraints she'd created around the dragons. Timbergust attempted to suck in a ragged breath with little success.

"I wish you hadn't lied to me," Amy said.

"Me too," the Steel Dragon said. "I'm Kristen, by the way."

"Amy," she replied. "But don't think I'm like you. I'm not. I don't kill for no reason. I don't take vengeance on people simply because I can. I never wanted to hurt those dragons. I never wanted to hurt anyone. I simply tried to help my parents."

"I know. I know you did. And if you come with me, I'll make sure you and them both stay safe."

"I wish I could believe you, but all I know about you right now is that you're a liar." She was crying now and hated the hot tears that streaked down her face.

"You're right, I shouldn't have done that. But I do want to help you. I know what it's like to gain these kinds of powers so suddenly. Please, let me help you."

"I don't need any help," Amy replied, and with a flick of her wrist, her magical abilities careened Kristen into the woods.

"This is the last time I say this nicely. Don't follow me."

Now, all she needed was a way to escape. She looked around and realized there was nothing but the floating scrap metal from the truck she'd used to stop the dragons. At first, a rush of despondency swept over her but an idea trailed in its wake.

She ripped the hood off a cop car with her mind—it was easier than tearing paper—and brought it closer. Carefully, she stepped onto it and made it elevate a few feet.

The motion made her wobble and she fell and landed on her butt on the car hood. Now, she tried to use her powers to anchor herself to the floating piece of metal and grinned when it was successful. She felt like it was a floor now and that she wouldn't fall.

Amy eased it forward, away from the wreckage and past the roadblock. She tried to go faster and sighed with relief when her powers understood her. They kept her firmly anchored to the piece of metal while she increased speed.

She released the dragons once she was about a quarter-mile away and pushed her power to accelerate to almost breakneck speed. Jubilant, she urged her makeshift magic carpet even faster until soon, she hurtled over the cars on the road below her. She uttered a whoop as she spun the hood upside down. Her powers kept her firmly anchored and she didn't slow at all.

Her stress melted away as she flew toward Thetford Mines. This was amazing—a totally surreal but wonderfully satisfying outcome she'd never imagined. Not only could she lift things but she could fly. She felt strong now that she'd faced the dragons and won, but better than that, she felt in control. Without a doubt, she could have killed them, but she hadn't. She didn't want to kill them. Even if they treated her like a murderer, they hadn't actually hurt her yet. And her powers hadn't made her kill them. She was strong, in control, and she was free.

When the excitement of the battle and her flight settled, she considered her options. She could fly all night if she wanted to, maybe keep going, outpace the dragons, and fly forever until she reached… what? The north pole?

How would that work, exactly, and how would she eat? Would she turn to petty theft to feed herself? Or become a fugitive who did magic so she could eat? No, she couldn't run forever. Even if she could, that wasn't a decent life for her. She wanted to see her parents again—or at the very least, get them a message that she was all right.

Plans had already been made that would enable her to do that. She had to reach Thetford Mines and get help before the dragons caught up to her. While she'd slowed them, she knew there were limits to her powers—there had to be—and she didn't want to find out what those were in a fight. No, she needed to find Alp, the dwarf her mom had told her about, and make a future for herself that didn't involve her living on the hood of a car for the rest of her life.

CHAPTER FORTY-TWO

Kristen couldn't believe how swift and decisive the fight had been. Amy had disabled five dragons in seconds. Honestly, to call it a fight was an understatement. It might well have been appropriately called a slaughter if anyone had been hurt or killed.

She suddenly realized that the dragons were the only ones accounted for. "Larry!" she called.

"I'm all right," the mage replied and stepped from behind a pine tree. "I sensed her warming up and took cover but it was close. Windbag? Did someone puncture your sails?"

"I'm fine." Windlock came out from behind a police car. "Although I think she might have sensed I was a dragon."

"Don't talk to your superiors that way," Bronzeback hissed at Brockton from his metal cocoon beneath a police car.

"And to think I was about to set you free," Kristen scolded the big dragon. "Now, I guess we'll debrief first."

The Detroit investigative team walked a dozen or so paces away from the other dragons who all still struggled to free themselves. Aquatos had got the car door out of his mouth, at least, and attempted to peel the metal cases off the other dragons.

"Is what she did normal?" Kristen asked. "Can most mages do that if they're uncuffed or whatever?"

Larry threw his head back and laughed. She had the sense he was still high on adrenaline. "No way! Even without a cuff, there's no way I could use a semi-truck to stop five damn dragons from attacking me. That was unbelievable. I would've tried to contain her with my force, but that would've been like opening an umbrella in a hurricane."

"So she's the strongest mage you've ever seen?"

He nodded enthusiastically, "Oh yeah! She's crazy. What she did to that truck was impressive on its own, but what she did to the dragons was wild. I can't imagine being able to do such a thing. She's a damn inspiration—I mean...uh..." Brockton trailed off and looked at his boss.

The investigator merely grimaced.

"Windlock? She's not the strongest you've seen?" Kristen asked.

He sighed. "I've seen that kind of power before but it's been a long time. Not since the last mage war."

"Mages used to be that powerful?"

"Not many, but some, yes."

"What happened to them?"

Windlock shook his head. "They were hunted mercilessly. Those who manifested that kind of power had to be destroyed—that was the stance of the dragons, at least. It took a considerable number of dragons to defeat each one. Honestly, losing only two dragons to a mage of that power would be considered a success. When news of what she did here gets out, the Dragon Council won't stop with the dragons we have here."

"They still feel that way even though the last war was centuries ago?"

The investigator nodded. "Since then, anytime a mage even approaching that kind of ability appears...well, we make sure they don't fully come into their powers."

"Do you think the dragons would come into Canada to pursue her?"

"I can't say." He grimaced again, obviously alarmed. "It's not official policy for them not to come here, exactly like there's no official policy that dwarves will harbor mages. In the past, dragons have captured the mages who have killed dragons. A few have made it here, but none like her and no one who had already killed dragons."

"If dragons come here, the dwarves might strike back," Larry said.

"We can't let that happen." His boss assumed a grim expression.

"We can't let any of this happen," Kristen said. "We can't let history repeat itself. I don't want Amy killed, but we can't let her be pushed into a corner either. She didn't kill any dragons this time, which I think proves she doesn't see herself as an enemy of dragons, but if that changes, there could be many more bodies lying cold when this is over." She didn't say that the body she was most worried about was Amy's because truthfully, it didn't matter. The girl had proven herself to be a force of true power. If the dragons killed her—and she knew they could kill her because there were hundreds of them in North America alone, after all—she had no doubt that the young mage would take more than a few with her.

That wasn't acceptable, but given where they were now, it was totally unacceptable. If a dragon killed a mage in dwarf country—or worse, killed a dwarf—a war could be ignited. That, in turn, would provide Constance and her team of technomages with the perfect opportunity to take advantage of the situation and douse everything with proverbial gasoline.

They had to move, Kristen knew that, but there was something she had to do first.

She walked over to Timbergust, who was still wrapped up like a Christmas present.

"I hope you're happy," she said. "We had the situation under control until you and these goons arrived."

"Under control?" He sneered. "You were talking to a killer. How the hell do you think that counts as control?"

"You don't get it, do you?" Kristen laughed. How could these dragons be so dense? There she was in her human form—with steel skin, yes—but human-shaped and walking around free. The dragons had all been thoroughly beaten like they were nothing but yapping dogs. "You can't beat her and she demonstrated that very clearly. She knows how to block fire and she knows how to stop you from striking her. We're in this whole goddamn situation because two dragons put her in danger. We won't solve this with more violence."

Kristen stepped toward him, took hold of the metal that encased him, and bent it with her bare hands enough for him to be able to squeeze out.

Timbergust—obviously not thankful—thrashed angrily as soon as he had the space to do so and shook himself free. "Well, at least you're not a traitor to dragon kind," he sneered. "Aquatos, help me with Bronzeback."

"My allegiance is to peace, that's it," she hollered as Aquatos and Timbergust wrestled to move the car Amy had placed on top of their teammate and began to unpeel him. Their human forms weren't as strong as hers—steel skin had many advantages—but in their dragon forms, their claws weren't quite dexterous enough to free Bronzeback quickly. The dragon whined and complained as they struggled to release him.

Kristen shook her head—she knew full well that neither of the dragons would ask for help—and went to free Emberslight. "The point is to not pit dragons against mages. It's for us to live as peacefully as we can. This is a world we all need to share. There's more than enough for everyone if we're willing to give each other a little space."

"And you gave Obscura space?" Bronzeback roared. Timbergust and Aquatos had finally liberated him. "And Shadowstorm? Did you give them space, or did you kill them?"

"They were both threats to peace."

"You mean they were threats to humans." The Boston dragon's aura was red-hot with rage.

"Both of them wanted to subvert the Dragon Council. Shadowstorm tried to throw Detroit into chaos so he could rule over the ashes. Obscura was willing to burn the whole city to get her vengeance. Both failed because they advocated violence. As long as dragons and humans fight, we won't be successful."

"She's not human," Timbergust bellowed in fury.

"Easy, Timbergust," Emberslight said now that she was free.

"No! She can't have it both ways." Sparks and spittle spattered from his mouth as he spoke. "She says this is about human and dragon peace, but this mage isn't a human. Humans can't kill dragons. She's an abomination, a monster, and a killer. I can respect peace with humans and I've maintained peace in the northeast corner of the United States for decades. This rogue mage is the threat to peace, not me. We have to stop her."

"Treating her like that is what got us into this mess," Kristen retorted. "We were so close to getting her to come with us willingly." She held up the silver bracelet that Windlock had given her. "In one more minute, I could have had this on her and this would have all been over. Now, instead of us returning to Rangeley, you've sent her even farther north. She's angry and won't trust me because of you."

"I don't care!" Timbergust screamed. "I don't care about her. She's a goddamn killer. She murdered dragons in my district and she needs to die. You think you'll put a cuff on her and those dragons will what? Come back from the dead? You're fucking crazy. We're out of here." He launched skyward and headed north.

Bronzeback spat a ball of fire at Kristen's feet that burned a hole in the pavement before he took flight and followed Timbergust.

"You told my team the Steel Dragon is an investigator and she's not," Emberslight said and sounded disappointed.

"Maybe not officially, but she's more than proven herself," Wind-lock replied placidly.

"All we have is officially," the Boston team leader said. "You broke protocol by coming here without telling us. I have to follow protocol, and that says we need to apprehend her—or kill her if she won't cooperate."

"If that's what you think is best." The investigator's expression remained inscrutable.

"It doesn't really matter what I think. What matters is that we follow precedent, and Timbergust is right. She's a killer. The Dragon Council's stance on this is clear."

He only nodded as she took to the air. She spun one circle above them as Aquatos and Crimson joined her.

"Emberslight," Windlock called.

"Yeah?"

"Be careful, okay?"

"You too, Windlock," she replied and swung north.

Kristen rushed over to the investigator and transformed into a dragon as she did so. It was hard to rip her gaze from the five dragons on their way to kill Amy—to kill her without even a semblance of a fair trial—but her teammate had yet to transform.

"Let's go, Windlock. What's the problem?"

He merely watched them vanish into the night sky.

"Windlock, come on. If they catch up to her, they won't hold back. I know you said mages are normally taken in but they will slaughter her. She must have limits."

"That's a big if, though, don't you think?" He raised an eyebrow.

"I know she was fast, but—wait, what do you mean?"

The investigator shrugged. "I'll admit, I think I underestimated her. She's obviously smart and knows how to handle herself. The hitchhiking move was clever."

"Hitchhiking ain't exactly unusual, you old windbag," Larry joked.

"Still. She's proven herself to be resourceful and coolheaded. Also, she's shown a remarkable level of control over her powers. I think…I think I was wrong. I don't believe we'll be able to catch her."

"We have to try," Kristen pleaded.

Windlock shook his head. "She won't let anyone catch her, not after what happened here. Her skills are such that she'll be able to avoid capture. It was clever of her to use that piece of metal as a vehicle. I don't think Dragon SWAT will catch her either."

"You can't know that." Her frustration mounted. How could they let them continue the hunt?

"But let's say…you're right. Let's say they catch up to her. Which side do you think will win? Five dragons or young Miss Amy Williams?" He allowed himself a small smile.

She couldn't help but snort and return a grin. "Okay, if that was her restraining herself, then yeah, I guess my money would be on Amy."

"Exactly. It's not a bet I would take," he agreed.

Larry chuckled. "But seriously, I'll put ten to one on Amy. If one of you bets a hundred bucks and somehow, those dragons do succeed, you win a thousand bucks."

"I won't give you a hundred dollars." His boss frowned.

"But still, I think we owe it to her to stop them. We need to show Amy that not all dragons are the same." Kristen paced, eager to get back into the air but also cognizant of the fact that if she went alone, there was no way she'd be able to slow five SWAT-trained dragons, let alone stop them.

"I don't think that would be wise," Windlock countered. "You did a good job talking to her and I don't want that work undone. If you arrive with those five, especially with Timbergust and Bronzeback, what'll she think?"

"That I'm trying to stop them."

"Is that what you'd think?" Larry asked and his tone made it clear that it was a rhetorical question. "Because I think if it was me in her position, I'd be all like, 'oh, that nice dragon changed her mind and now, she'll eat me like all these other dragons she's flying around with.' But what do I know? I'm only a mage who was in almost an identical situation."

"So what? We're supposed to sit around here and wait for Amy to kill them? I admit, part of me thinks that sounds fair after the bullshit they tried to pull on her, but I don't want her to kill five dragons either." Her tail twitched with building impatience. She wanted to go, not stand around in discussion.

Windlock, though, was as cool as she had ever seen him. He drew a slip of paper out of his pocket and held it up for her to see.

"What will you do, memo them to death?" Kristen asked.

"This is the contact I have in the dwarf underground."

"Wait a—what?" Larry seemed shocked.

"Come on, Larry. You withheld information from me. Is it so surprising that I did the same?"

"I guess not," the mage replied. "And call me Brockton. It's weird when you use my first name."

Windlock ignored him. "This is the information for a dwarf named Alp. He's sympathetic to mages, but…well, I'd say he's pragmatic. He's helped me divert a few would-be fugitives into gainful employment."

"Alp? I remember him," Larry said.

The investigator raised an eyebrow as if that wasn't at all surprising. "I think that Amy's mother sent her to meet someone from the underground. It's the only thing that makes sense. For that matter, it could be Alp himself. Even if it's not, he'll have heard about her by now."

"And you didn't tell us this before?" Kristen was shocked. They'd been on a wild goose chase when they could have simply called the guy on the phone.

"It's not a phone number. He says he's never trusted dragons to have his contact information."

"Then what is it?" she asked before a gust of wind appeared to snatch the piece of paper out of Windlock's hand. For a moment, she panicked until it landed between Larry's fingers and she realized the mage had used his magic powers to snatch the note.

"What is this, Windlock? Gibberish? Le Face De Beouf?"

"It's French, you ignoramus."

She couldn't help but laugh. Larry's pronunciation sounded nothing like French.

He surprised her, though, when he translated it. "Yeah, I know, you old dinosaur, but it means the Beef Face. Or the face of beef, I guess. It's not exactly an address."

"It's the name of a restaurant in Thetford Mines. That's where Alp and his people often hang out. He told me to go there if I ever needed him."

"Well, what are we waiting for?" Brockton said with a grin. "Let's go meet this cow-face!"

Windlock transformed and his assistant climbed onto his back. They took to the air and started north. Despite the older dragon's cool demeanor, Kristen noticed he flew even faster than he had before. That told her clearly that she wasn't the only one who could feel the sense of dread building. Honestly, she didn't know if it was a good thing or a bad thing that he shared the presentiment.

It certainly didn't feel good.

CHAPTER FORTY-THREE

Amy followed the road for about a mile, then abandoned it. It was the most obvious way to navigate from the air, so she assumed the dragons would use it to follow her. She knew she had to go roughly north, so she headed that way. Ahead, a glow above the treetops indicated a town, so she used that as a point to focus on. She didn't think it was Thetford Mines but couldn't be sure. Unfortunately, she'd destroyed her map when she'd dismantled the eighteen-wheeler.

The memory brought a smile. She had torn the truck to pieces rather than simply dismantling it and she was sorry—especially for the driver whose livelihood it had been—but she hadn't hurt anyone. It was a victory for her that she hadn't hurt any people or the dragons. Whatever these powers were, she could control them. She had to.

A blast of flame in the night sky made her glance hastily over her shoulder. The dragons were in pursuit, then. She wasn't surprised. What mattered now was that she remained calm. If she could get to Thetford Mines without them catching up to her, maybe the dwarves could find somewhere safe for her to hide. She hadn't actually thought that was possible until now but after escaping five—no six, or maybe seven—dragons, she thought there was a chance. If she could hold her powers and not let others see her, that was the key.

At the thought that she needed to decrease her visibility, she descended until she flew over the tops of pine trees. It wouldn't do for the dragons to look toward her and see a glint reflected from the metal she rode on or have her block a star or something stupid and know she'd left the highway.

A few more furtive glances indicated that her pursuers hadn't followed her away from the road. If they had, they didn't breathe any fire again, which would at least have been a warning for her. It wasn't much of a consolation, she realized, but it would have to do. She maintained her present route toward the city, very aware that if the dragons still followed the road, that was where they'd go.

Which meant she couldn't continue her journey to Thetford Mines on the hood of a car. There was simply no way to disguise who she was or what she'd been doing. She needed to be discreet and to be able to blend in, if only for a few seconds. It seemed obvious that these dragons wouldn't give up. She didn't think even the nicer one—the Steel Dragon—would stop. Given the reality of that, she needed to find somewhere to hide.

The trees began to thin as she neared the town. A billboard announced that it was, in fact, Thetford Mines, and Amy couldn't believe her luck. Her changed route had avoided the other town— Black Lake? Black Pond?—and brought her directly to her destination.

If she was lucky, the other dragons would search for her at the other stop along the way. While she couldn't be sure of that, it did seem logical so she might actually reach a place of safety before they found her. But, she reminded herself, not if she careened high above the city. She needed to be less visible and so searched the streets below her for what looked like a safe place to stop. A souvenir shop tucked into a corner seemed promising and she dropped behind it and left the car hood leaned up against the back of the store. Positioned thus, it would be harder to see from the air.

She walked into the store, waved a greeting at the shopkeeper, and located the sweaters.

A quick sift through the racks provided a t-shirt with a grizzly bear on it and a grey hoodie with the Canadian maple leaf on the front in dark red. She bought both and asked the attendant to use the bathroom. Once inside, she removed her shirt, put the grizzly on, and pulled the hoodie on over it. It wasn't the best disguise but better than wearing what her pursuers would instantly recognize.

She left the shop and returned to the street. Hitchhiking might be her best option, she thought and kicked at the dirt. A wild idea entered her head and she scooped a little of the dust and rubbed it gently into the sleeves of the hoodie. It was a small detail but if the clothes looked worn, they'd look less like a disguise. What she really needed was a hat, she realized and wondered why she hadn't thought of it earlier. She was about to return to the shop—they had plaid ones with the ear flaps—when she noticed a BMX and skateboard shop across the street.

Amy smiled. She hadn't ridden a skateboard in years, not since she was seventeen and still in high school, but she'd been fairly good when she had. In fact, skateboarding was the closest thing to flying she'd done before. There was nothing like dropping into a halfpipe and shooting up the other side.

She checked the wad of cash in her pocket. Sadly, there wasn't all that much left—she'd given all the US dollars to the man who'd given her a ride, anticipating that things might not end well—but enough to get a skateboard, she was sure. She had wanted to conserve her money, but she was already where she needed to be so she deemed it worth it. Plus, this would let her cover more ground than simply walking, especially if she could use her magic to augment her speed.

Being in a skate shop was a little like being a kid again for her. The last time she'd been in one, it had been to ask her mom for a Christmas present. Pat Williams hadn't been thrilled about the idea of her daughter squandering her future skateboarding instead of studying. Now, her future depended on having a good board—or so she told herself.

The wall of decks brought a wave of nostalgia but time was tight and she forced herself to focus. After a few minutes, she selected a board with a kickass-looking bearded dude on it, complete with glowing eyes and a battle-ax. Amy had always wanted to get a board that was so cool she wouldn't want to do a boardslide on it and scratch it. All it had taken was manifesting magic powers, accidentally killing two dragons, and becoming a fugitive to realize that dream. She laughed and wondered if she was so tired that she was almost delirious. Now wasn't a time to laugh and yet she couldn't help herself.

"Good choice, my canuck," the shopkeeper said, a young man with a beanie pulled down to his bloodshot eyes.

She almost asked what canuck meant before she remembered that, duh, she was in Canada and it must have been the guy calling her dude or whatever.

"Thanks, dude," she responded, suddenly unsure if she should have said that but he didn't seem to notice.

"Do you need trucks, bearings, and wheels with this?"

Amy smiled. "Yeah. Give me a pair of Thunder trucks, the smoothest bearings you have, and those yellow fire wheels."

"Yes, yes, yes!" the guy said and hurriedly assembled her board. While he worked, she chose a baseball cap with the image of a bear skateboarding on a salmon and a pair of skateboarding shoes because why not? If she reached the dwarves and they needed money, another fifty bucks wouldn't matter. If they threw her to the dragons, she might as well be comfortable and trendy too.

A few minutes later, the assistant had finished the board. "Cash or card?"

Amy proffered the cash and he nodded. "Very nice, my canuck." He counted her change—enough for a burger and not much more—and she left.

In front of the store, she dropped the board and moved with it a few times to get her legs back, but it was like riding a bike. In a few minutes, she was comfortable enough to bust an ollie, then a kickflip.

A shout from inside drew her attention and the store assistant gave her a huge thumbs-up.

She grinned and decided to really show him something. When

she'd gained sufficient speed, she ollied and this time, gave herself a tiny magic boost. Unfortunately, it was slightly more than she'd planned and she actually cleared a car. She landed smoothly—loving the feel of the board—and set off. A quick glance over her shoulder confirmed that her audience was suitably impressed.

Now, all she had to do was find Le Face de Boeuf.

As she cruised down the street, she had a momentary regret that she hadn't bought a helmet but decided her destination now took precedence. She thought she remembered it being off 112, so if she could only find that, she could locate it easily. With at least five dragons hunting her, she wondered if a little more speed might be in order.

It seemed her powers remained poised to do her bidding. She'd barely thought about moving faster when they augmented her speed. She grinned. It was like being on one of the electric scooters that had been all over Boston and Philadelphia, except instead of paying by the minute and using electricity, it was magic-powered.

Amy also discovered she could anchor herself to the board too. The former skater in her told her that was cheating, but the person who didn't want to wipe out was totally okay with it.

She pushed herself to greater speed around the town as she adjusted to her new form of transportation and searched for the restaurant. Her attention on her quest, she ran into a pothole and ollied reflexively. The board came with her and in a second, she was in flight. Her grin was spontaneous and jubilant, but she reminded herself to not draw too much attention and turned the flying ollie into a boardslide down the back of a park bench.

"You kids!" a short man with a huge beard yelled. His beanie looked like it had been knitted by hand out of the brightest yarn in all Canada.

"Sorry!" she said as she cruised into motion again. Before long, another man appeared and stopped to watch her. He was short, much like the other man, with a beard so long it almost touched his knees. A tie-dye hoodie and a pair of bright blue shorts seemed out of place in the chilly air. His face was unusual too, she thought as she tried not to stare and failed horribly. He had thick bushy eyebrows and a huge brow, almost like a gorilla. His nose looked like it was carved of stone and his eyes glittered like gems.

"Let's see a trick, human!" the man said, and she realized that, duh, these were dwarves.

Amy obliged him, ollied up to the edge of a planter, and did a grind on her trucks before she hopped off again.

He whooped and she decided she liked dwarves. Thetford Mines seemed to be about half-dwarf. All of them had big, thick beards, which made her wonder if their women grew facial hair like the men. They also all seemed to wear bright clothing. While the humans dressed more or less like Americans—with more maple leaves instead of stars and stripes, obviously—they still mostly wore jeans, shirts, and jackets. The dwarves, on the other hand, appeared to be at war with the rainbow itself. They also seemed to be fans of piercings. Many of their ears, eyebrows, and noses sported bright pieces of carved rock that went in one side and came out the other.

She wondered if it was a defense mechanism against the cold, gray, winter months. Maine could be miserable in winter. The snow was pretty at first but eventually, it was plain dreary. Maybe the dwarves dressed brightly as a way to fight the grays of winter.

It was a theory she immediately realized she could soon ask the dwarves about because she finally located Le Face de Beouf.

Her first impression was rather underwhelming, she had to admit. The restaurant itself looked pleasant enough and fairly dwarf-like. The front was paneled in wood and framed by two brick pillars. Two giant cow heads made it look like something out of the medieval days. The problem was that it was located smack dab in the middle of a strip mall. This resembled any other outdoor shopping center set back from the street and behind a sprawling parking lot. She didn't know if she was more disappointed in Canadians or dwarves for using such bland American architecture.

Still, there were no dragons overhead, which meant she had made it. This was where her mom had said to go, the place where the dwarf

Alp would be able to take her under his protection and where she could finally stop running.

Amy had thought it might have been more of a fortress, but maybe that proved a lack of imagination on her part. Surely there were tunnels beneath it or a hidden magic shield or something.

She skated onto the sidewalk, hopped off her board, and kicked the tail of it so it popped into her hands before she walked inside. The gentle *ding* of a bell attached to the door heralded her entry. She had hoped for some kind of enchanted door knocker or something but accepted that she would simply have to get over all that.

After a deep breath—both of relief and trepidation—she looked around and realized that every person inside Le Face de Beouf was a dwarf.

Almost every table had a group of the short, bearded folk eating huge slabs of beef or entire chickens. Tankards of ale littered every table and steaming piles of vegetables as well as dark brown loaves of bread were crammed into every available space. One table in the middle was completely cleared of food, and two dwarves in skirts—kilts, maybe, although she really had no clue about dwarf gender—looked like they had danced along to a trio of musicians. The instruments themselves were appealing—a big drum made of a hollowed-out log, a flute of some kind that looked like it was made of gold, and an old violin. Only the violinist still played, however, and the other two had stopped with the dancers.

It looked like an extremely welcoming place, and Amy immediately felt like she wanted to spend the night here, eating, drinking and making merry. Her enthusiasm faded slightly when she focused on a dwarf who stood in front of her, his arms folded across his chest and an expression on his face that while not unwelcoming was also not particularly encouraging.

"Hi," she said, not sure what else to say because it looked like he had something on his mind.

"Greetings, traveler," the dwarf replied.

"How did you know I was a traveler?" she asked. Could this be

Alp? Had he waited for her to arrive this whole time? She felt a weight begin to lift from her shoulders.

"I knew you were a traveler because this isn't an establishment for people like you. The locals all know that already," he said and his face colored in what might have been embarrassment.

"Like me?" Her heart dropped. Did they know she was a mage and were ready to ostracize her? If that were the case, she might as well walk out and wait for the dragons. She knew she had an incredible amount of power but she was so incredibly tired and the smell of the food reminded her she hadn't eaten anything for hours. She hadn't even bought a protein bar back at the convenience store. The idea of sitting there and eating steak and listening to music while Alp told her everything would be fine was a fantasy that had built in her head since she opened the door.

The dwarf cleared his throat and held a hand up to indicate height. "Not to be discourteous, you understand, but you're a little…uh, tall."

Before she could say anything, he smiled and took her arm to turn her toward the door. "Now, don't get us wrong. Hospitality is very important to us, and while you're visiting Thetford Mines, you'll find that we love our visitors, human and dwarf alike. We merely need a space of our own, is all. The humans have one too, and I daresay their steaks are even better than ours."

"Don't lie to the girl, Trook," another dwarf yelled.

Trook smiled. "Okay, so maybe the steaks here are the best. There is a lovely little venue for humans down the way, though. I'd be happy to give you directions if you want to ride or take you there myself. Now, if your heart is set on dwarf-seared steak, give us the name of your hotel and we'll send a meal over. How's that? Now come along, come a—"

"No," Amy said and braced herself so he couldn't push her out the door.

"We really don't mean to be rude but we need a break from humans sometimes, is all. It's nothing personal—"

"No, you don't understand. I can't be turned away from here. It's my last hope—my only hope."

"Is something wrong, sweetheart?" a dwarf with steel-blue eyes and a jade nose ring said to her.

Between him and her sat a human woman who wore all black. She watched the exchange from behind a tankard of ale.

"Please. It's either this or dragon chow," Amy pleaded.

"I understand that it can feel that way, but you're in Canada now," Trook said. "If you ask for asylum, you can stay here. Dragons don't care about regular humans."

"Then why does she get to be here?" she asked and pointed to the woman in black.

"She's not exactly regular…but she's our guest and her privacy is her own. Now, I'll ask nicely once more—"

There didn't seem to be anything she could say to change his mind so she decided it was time to show these dwarves rather than try to explain. She raised her skateboard, which made the dwarf fall silent, then released it.

Trook startled and obviously expected it to fall on his head but it merely floated above him instead. "I don't know what I am." She tried to keep her voice from cracking but didn't do a particularly good job of it. "But I know I need help. I don't think I'm a regular person, either."

"No kidding, you're not regular," he retorted and a smile grew on his face. "You invented a damn flying hoverboard."

That drew a chuckle from a number of the dwarves. Amy reddened with embarrassment, but she realized she didn't need to feel that way. Their rich laughter seemed to break the tension and everyone returned to their meal, jokes, and relaxed enjoyment. The musicians struck up again and after a moment, the drummer elbowed the violinist to join them. He'd been the last to stop playing and apparently the last to realize it was time to make merry again. The dancers resumed their shuffle on the table.

The dwarf with the blue eyes and the jade nose ring approached her.

"What did you say your name was?" the dwarf asked.

"I didn't. It's…uh, Amy. Amy Williams."

"Nice to meet you, uh, Amy," he teased. "If you'd led with that, we could have brought you food way quicker. I'm Alp. You're Patricia's girl, right?"

"Yes, sir," she said and her voice broke and tears came unbidden to trickle from her eyes.

"Oh, hey, it's all right. I know I'm no looker but I'm not that bad."

She smiled and wiped her cheeks. "No, no. But I'm so relieved to be here. There are dragons chasing me and…well, I want somewhere I can be safe. Do I need to get into a cellar or something?" Her weary brain seemed determined to offer no assistance and she hadn't realized how exhausted she was.

Alp waved that away. "A cellar? Before you eat? Don't be crazy. Come sit with me and we'll talk about what to do next. I'm sure we can find you a job here somewhere, far, far away from dragons. Once everything calms, we'll let your mom know you're safe. It won't be a glamorous life but it'll be a proud one, and you'll always be welcome here."

"It's a good offer," a woman said from behind.

Amy turned and her gaze settled on the human woman in black. "Excuse me?"

"I said it's a good offer. You should consider it. The dwarves are excellent hosts, and they know how to make mages feel welcome. If Alp says he'll give you a proud life, that's what you'll have. Well, as proud as any humans' life can be while dragons rule the world."

"I'm sorry…who are you?" she asked.

"Constance. Constance Vigil. I'm a mage like you."

"Oh." She'd never met a mage before. She'd expected robes, though, and said as much.

The woman chuckled. "Robes are the uniform of the oppressed."

"Can we get food in her before you start with the whole recruitment speech?" Alp asked.

"Of course." Constance smiled and gestured for her to sit at her table.

Alp joined them and waved at a server for beer and food. "Like she said, this is Constance. She's a…a freedom fighter, you could say. It's not the kind of work I recommend, but she's always been good to dwarves and mages alike and respects our wishes. If you want to get rid of her, say so and she's out." Alp raised an eyebrow at the woman.

Amy had the sense that only his sense of hospitality allowed the woman to stay. Still, there was something interesting about Constance Vigil.

"No, she doesn't have to go. What did you mean when you said freedom fighter?" she asked.

"I fight for the only freedom that matters—the freedom to be what you are, whether it's human, dwarf, dragon, or mage. I fight for equality and a world that's not ruled by one group while the rest are enslaved."

"We're not enslaved, Constance," Alp protested.

"As long as you stay in the frozen north, no, you're not," she replied smoothly. "Although, of course, the dragons don't always respect those boundaries, do they?"

He frowned. That was true, then, although Amy already knew it given that dragons were pursuing her.

"What exactly are you proposing?" the girl asked.

"Nothing, yet. First, listen to Alp's offer. I'm sure he can set you up as a lumberjack or an ice fisherman or something. If it sounds good, take it. But if, after hearing him, you're still curious about what I have to offer, I'd be more than happy to tell you how with your help, we can remake the world into a better place. A world where humans don't live in fear of dragons."

She nodded as she listened to Alp talk about hideouts, new identities, and the communities she could live in and she tried to take it all in. The details, at this point, seemed overwhelming given her tired brain and body, and she couldn't help real curiosity about what Constance had to say every time she glanced out the window and wondered if the dragons had arrived yet.

CHAPTER FORTY-FOUR

"So, is there anything I need to keep in mind about dwarves?" Kristen asked her two companions. They'd landed a few blocks away from La Face De Beouf and approached the restaurant.

"They're a feisty people, make no doubt about it," Windlock said. "That's why I wanted us to approach on foot. If a dwarf sees a couple of dragons flying overhead, they'll assume the worse."

"Do you mean they'll be scared?" She felt clarity was important as she needed to know even vaguely what to expect.

Larry chuckled. "You have never met one, huh? Dwarves don't do scared. You have to remember that they were created by mages in the first dragon war."

"You're saying they have a chip on their shoulder?"

Windlock nodded. "That's a good way to think about them. They were made for war and for all we know, they might have been able to win it, but they quit. They refused to continue fighting the dragons on behalf of the mages who made them."

"Why?" She'd never thought about that intriguing truth before, not that she knew much about that almost forgotten history.

He shrugged. "No one knows exactly. The dwarves say it was because they realized they were committing murder, but that doesn't exactly check out because in the centuries since, they have killed more than a few dragons who wander into their territory and make too big a scene."

"And the Dragon Council allows that?" It seemed contrary to everything she knew.

"The Dragon Council is, first and foremost, interested in staying in power." Windlock rubbed his chin. "They don't really care if a few dragons die. Would your president go to war over the death of a single person?"

"I suppose not," Kristen admitted. "Although I don't know. I think it's possible it could happen."

"I suppose it would be for dragon kind too," he agreed. "If someone from the Dragon Council was killed by dwarves, for example, it might be enough to anger the rest of them, but historically, the only dragons who tango with dwarves are those like the two killed in Rangeley. Fools with nothing to lose on a grudge mission."

"What would happen if, say—and this is purely hypothetical here—but what if a dragon investigator were killed by dwarves while investigating a runaway mage responsible for the deaths of two said dragons?" Larry made his tone sound like it was a joke but she wanted to know the answer to the question.

"My plan is to not engage the dwarves. It seems like we beat the other dragons here so hopefully, we can all reach an agreement before they arrive."

"And that should be possible, right?" Kristen wondered more and more about the insanity of this plan. The dragons she'd met weren't exactly known for their ability to compromise. Far from it. In fact, she would say virtually every dragon she'd ever met—even the ones she liked—were used to having their way, period. Of course, the certainty of this was cemented by the fact that she was exactly like that. While she might have different priorities, the obstinacy—or was it arrogance?—persisted. Even she had to admit that she wanted her own way and believed it was the right way. In that, she was no different than the other dragons she so often resented.

"I think so. The dragons and dwarves came to an agreement

during the first mage war, after all, and that was with mages causing everyone headaches. This is minor compared to that."

"How did they come to an agreement, though?" she asked.

"Do you want to know what I think?" Larry waggled his eyebrows.

"Would you stop talking if we said no?" Windlock raised an eyebrow in challenge.

"Of course not." The mage winked at her. "I think the dragons made them a better offer. It's possible that the mages could have won that first rebellion if they'd offered the dwarves a proper continent. Hell, even Australia probably would have done it. But they didn't—at least, the few historical records we have don't say they did. When a cunning dragon came along and offered them the great frozen North, I think they saw it as a deal. They're a pragmatic people, dwarves, and good eaters too. You should see the steaks they—"

"This isn't the time for dwarven chit-chat." Windlock gestured to the restaurant. They were close enough to identify the distinctive façade from the other shops in the strip mall—not a challenge given the two giant cow-head statues on the front. "What's important is that their skin is incredibly tough, more like hide than skin. It takes far more than you'd think to scratch a dwarf. In fact, I've seen dragons chip a tooth on them before."

Kristen couldn't help but laugh at the idea.

"They're not indestructible or anything like that but they are sturdy and strong too. I'd venture that one of them could beat your steel human form in a melee."

"Is that right?" she asked. Her steel-covered, dragon-power augmented human form had the edge in any fight she'd had against a humanoid. Dwarves had to be extremely tough to be stronger than a dragon. Then again, they didn't have any other form to switch to like dragons did if the fighting escalated.

"I'd put even money on it," Larry said. "It depends on the dwarf but yeah, some of them are damn tough. Plus, they have a low center of gravity and all."

"Anything else?" she asked and filed that interesting fact away. It seemed like something that might prove very useful.

"Yeah. Don't blow fire at them. They're extremely resistant to heat but they still hate our fire breath," Windlock told her.

Brockton nodded emphatically. "I read that during the first mage war, dragons had been beaten to death simply for singeing a dwarf's beard. Apparently, it's the first part of them to be damaged by fire and the one they take the most pride in. Of course, with the lack of real historical records, it's simply rumor. Aside from that, I feel it doesn't make sense to take pride in your most fragile part, but I guess many men care about the size of their—"

"Enough, Larry," the investigator said sharply.

"I'm only saying they're sensitive, is all." The mage laughed.

Kristen clenched her jaw. "Are we going in there to parlay or fight?"

The investigator shook his head. "It's hard to say before we get there. Like I said, I've worked with Alp before. If it was only him, I think we'd be fine, but this is a whole community of dwarves."

"That's a ton of hard heads," Larry said.

His boss grunted disapproval. "Brockton? Seriously?"

"Last one. Sorry. I know they don't like that. No thick-skin jokes either on account of them not having them."

"Are you done?"

"Yes, sir. Sorry, sir. I will be entirely professional from here on out."

As they drew closer, Kristen was able to make out individuals through the big windows of the restaurant.

They really were fascinating people with large beards, brightly colored clothes, and many unusual piercings, and everyone seemed to be having a fine evening. A few even danced on a table accompanied by a trio of musicians. It seemed unlikely that Amy could be inside. They seemed entirely focused on enjoying the food, drink, and entertainment, not like they harbored a fugitive and alleged murderer.

More than alleged, she reminded herself. Amy had killed and that truth wasn't in question. The only real issue was whether she'd done it in self-defense or not, although to dragons, that apparently didn't matter.

She almost felt bad for interrupting their evening but the thought vanished when she saw Amy Williams.

The young mage was seated in a booth with a blue-eyed dwarf. His legs dangled, not even close to reaching the floor. But the woman who sat opposite the girl was more shocking than any dwarf could have been.

It was Constance Vigil, the technomage who'd systematically killed dragons in Detroit.

Worse, the woman saw her. Their gazes locked and Kristen scowled instinctively in anger. Her adversary's eyes narrowed in recognition of a threat and she moved a hand to her ear and touched something. She realized that the assassin used a radio to talk to someone.

"Down!" she yelled and in a burst of dragon speed, threw herself into Windlock and knocked him to the ground. It was a good thing she had practiced turning to steel so many times because if she hadn't had the extra mass her steel skin granted her, he might have managed to stay on his feet. A half-second later, a bullet whistled through the space he'd occupied and passed harmlessly, unbloodied thanks to her quick and effective action.

"Move!" she snapped and half-crawled, half-dragged the investigator toward the restaurant as more gunfire erupted.

"Not today, you tricky bastards!" Larry yelled into the night and threw a shield up between the dragons and the rooftop farther down the strip mall where the gunshots seemed to come from.

She allowed herself a moment of amazement. Not that Brockton had stopped bullets—her steel skin did that all the time—but that he had made a shield to protect the two dragons instead of himself.

"Get over here, you crazy bastard!" Windlock bellowed, pushed into a crouch, and moved toward La Face De Beouf. "Get behind your shield."

"It won't matter much," the mage said and clenched his teeth grimly. Sweat had already formed on his brow. "I can't hold this long anyway. Stopping bullets isn't really my thing. I'm more of an investigate crimes when there's no chance of being shot at kind of guy, honestly."

"I'm on it." Kristen's words turned into a roar as she transformed into her steel dragon form, lunged toward the restaurant so she could stay behind the shield, and inadvertently made the dwarves inside panic. She pumped her wings and soared over the building.

Her wide arc forced the gunmen to abandon their focus on Windlock if they wanted to track her with their weapons. She flew away from the mall and noticed immediately that she didn't hear more shots. That told her the technomages used dragon-killing rounds. Otherwise, they would have taken potshots in an effort to keep her at bay. That they conserved their rounds meant the ammunition was dangerous.

It provided an opportunity for her. She circled the building before she angled toward the parking lot. Someone fired at her, but she tucked her wings and the shot missed. She landed running and destroyed a few light poles with her tail before she vaulted into the night sky again.

This time, she made a curved approach from darkness. One of the gunmen saw her but not soon enough. He'd expected her to stay near her dragon allies so wasn't ready for her sudden appearance from the opposite direction.

She elevated slightly before she could fly into the back of the strip mall and immediately washed the roof with fire.

The gunmen flung themselves off, which was what she had expected. She had not expected them to slow their falls, however.

The six technomages descended as if they moved through molasses rather than air. The first to land fired at Windlock, but his shot was deflected by Larry's shield. The other five used the covering fire to move between the dragon and the restaurant and found a position about halfway between the investigator and the dwarf stronghold.

Kristen hesitated as she considered her options hastily. These people were murderers. They'd killed dragons and had shown that they didn't care about human casualties. If it was only them, she would have had no qualms with incinerating them. After all, they'd fired on her a few seconds before, tried to blow her up, and actually shot her more than once. The fact that they ran from her fire proved they were far more vulnerable than dwarves were, apparently, which provided enormous temptation.

But they currently stood directly in front of the big glass windows of the restaurant. What would the patrons think if a dragon engulfed five people in flame while they were having dinner? Probably nothing good if they didn't like a dragon's ability to breathe fire.

She still wrestled with her dilemma a few moments later when Constance stepped out of the building and raised both arms in the universal sign of truce. Amy came with her.

Her decision had been made for her. It might have been distasteful to burn a group of people who had fired sniper rifles at her but would perhaps be considered understandable. However, she couldn't imagine any good coming from her breathing fire on a woman who had been having dinner with the dwarves. She landed on top of the restaurant so the two cow heads were beneath her and looked at the assassin.

"What do you want?" the Steel Dragon demanded of the woman who had both tried to kill her and had claimed to think of herself as her mother.

"The same thing we've always wanted," Constance responded, her voice loud enough for all the parties to hear—the dwarves inside, the technomages guarding her with their weapons, Kristen and her team, and most importantly, Amy Williams. "We want equality between humans, mages, and dragons. We don't want this young woman to be hunted for defending herself."

"Neither do we," Kristen told her coldly from her perch atop the building.

"Says the dragon hunting her." The woman scoffed. "We were in the middle of making Amy an offer if you must know—an offer to be treated with the respect someone of her talents deserves. If you have a problem with that…well, we made sure to bring a good supply of dragon bullets this time."

One of the technomages cocked his assault rifle. It was a pointless action given that the weapons could fire multiple rounds automatically, but they made their point—fuck with us and we'll shoot.

"And you're not holding a gun to Amy's head like you are to the dragons?" she demanded.

"Constance has been nothing but kind," the girl said tremulously.

"Of course we have," the woman all but purred. "My team could have killed your mage but none of them did so. Speaking of which, Mr. Brockton, that shield spell you're casting could be very useful in our organization. If you tire of serving as the lapdog of a lapdog, you are welcome to join us. We're always looking for people with your experience."

"Oh, it sounds wonderful!" the mage retorted and barely restrained his anger. "So, do I drink the Kool-Aid and start dressing like a goth before or after you turn me against the man I owe my life to? I've worked with dragons for years to bring dragons to justice. What the hell are you doing? Taking potshots at the way the world works? You disgust me. I'd never work with you. Not even if you did win your stupid rebellion."

"Not if, when," Constance corrected. "We will triumph, of this, we have no doubt. Victory always comes to those on the side of justice. Your refusal is noted but we will not hold that against you when the war finally does come. As long as you don't turn your powers against us and use them to defend the dragons who have enslaved this world, you will be spared, even if you refuse to join the right side."

"Mother fucking Teresa over here," Larry muttered.

"Constance, you can forget about all this. We're not here to hurt Amy but that doesn't mean we'll let you use her like a weapon either," Kristen stated with grim determination.

"What is she talking about?" the girl asked her apparent benefactor. "You didn't say anything about me using my powers."

"You might as well give her the whole pitch," she said, turned into her steel-skinned human form, and vaulted calmly off the building. The weight damaged the pavement where she landed beside the two women. The technomages all aimed their guns at her, but she didn't flinch. While she knew their dragon rounds could pierce her steel skin as easily as they could tissue paper, the situation demanded that she show no fear in front of these terrorists.

"I have no intention of using you," Constance told Amy. "You'd be a valuable ally in our group—a full member. And you'll be safe from dragons there. The Steel Dragon might try to tell you stories about us, but even she'll admit that they can't find us. I live in the same city as her and yet she's never been able to track me. If you come with us, we'll teach you how to use your powers in such a way that you stay safe from the dragons. The dwarves can keep you safe from the fire-breathing lizards too, but only by locating you far, far away from them."

"What she means, Amy," Kristen said quietly and addressed the rogue mage directly, "is that she'll keep you safe until it's time to assassinate random dragons."

"Wait. Assassinate? You didn't say anything about that." The girl frowned. "Is that true?"

The assassin's smile remained firmly in place. "Not the statement about random dragons, no. We only kill dragons who have hurt humans. It only seems random to other dragons because they don't care about the people whose lives they've destroyed. They regard people as ants. The idea of us claiming justice for their murders simply doesn't mean anything to them."

"That's not true," the Steel Dragon said.

"But is it true that you kill dragons?" Amy pressed.

Constance nodded. She didn't seem at all uncomfortable admitting it. "Yes. We do kill dragons. As often as we can, I might add. We are preparing for a war against dragon kind and would, in fact, have already started that war if not for the interference of the Steel Dragon herself. If you join us—and again, Amy, it's your choice—we would ask you to stand in the front lines of that war. You could help lead our members in battles that would forever free mankind from the oppressive yoke—no, the claws and teeth—of dragon kind. Join us and be a hero."

"Heroes don't assassinate," Kristen said.

"We don't assassinate." The technomage hissed annoyance, her rigid calm ruffled for the first time. "It's not assassination if it delivers justice."

"Delivers justice? Is that what you call it when you place a bomb made of dead dragons inside a cake and set it to explode at a party?" She glared at Constance.

"That party was filled with the most privileged, hedonistic, and cruel dragons in North America. We did our research. The only dragon there who didn't deserve to have their crimes repaid was you," the woman replied sharply.

"And what about the human police officer you kidnapped? Was he somehow responsible for the deaths of innocent lives? Is that why you strapped a bomb to his leg and tried to make me choose between blowing either my friend up or a group of partygoers?"

"You never chose to save Washington," the assassin said petulantly, "and no one died."

"Yeah, because I saved them and not because you grew a conscience. You do know, don't you, that if the bomb on the rooftop had exploded, the mages would have died too?"

"Again, do your research." Her adversary made no attempt to hide her disgust. "All the mages at that party were dragon sycophants—the kind of people who are more than willing to hide the crimes of the masters simply to keep their place and beg near the table."

"You'll notice that she didn't deny trying to blow up a party or kidnapping a cop?" Kristen said to Amy.

"Is…is that true?" Amy asked.

Constance nodded gently as if to reassure a child after a nightmare. "It is but we have been desperate. You saw what dragons can do. They burned your house without even noticing and they do things exactly like that to people. Every. Single. Day. They are ruthless leaders and slave owners who hide behind their abilities. We have to end their reign of terror—we must. I can admit that a bomb was crass, but if you join us and stand against them, we won't have to resort to such methods."

"I can't believe you'd make me do things like blow people up." The girl was horrified. She'd turned pale and now regarded the other woman with open disdain.

"Then come with me." Kristen extended a hand to her. "I won't make you do anything."

Amy shook her head and didn't reply but it was clear what she was thinking. It was plain on her face. She couldn't get past the fact that Kristen was a dragon and that dragons were what got her into this mess in the first place.

"I know what it's like to feel what you're feeling," she said.

The girl's expression evidenced disbelief.

"Really, I do." She dropped her steel skin. "I thought I was a normal person until one day, I unlocked hidden powers that suddenly changed everything for me."

"What, you woke up one day and saw you were special?" the rogue mage asked. "Did you think your parents were dead and that you would die?"

She shook her head. "No, I never feared for my parents' life until a dragon tried to kill them. My powers woke when I tried to protect my friend Jonesy. He was simply a regular cop—hell, he was a shitty cop and kind of racist, and he had a horrible mouth on him. Every other word was fuck, you know? He swore so much I still think of him every time I hear the F-bomb."

"What—what happened to him?"

"I saved him from a rocket. Can you believe that? I thought I would explode but somehow, I saved Jonesy from that, only for him to get shot and die in my arms. It was…it was the worst day of my life, and not only because I lost a friend. It was the worst day of my life because that was when I realized what I was and that all the dreams I ever had no longer mattered, you know?"

Amy nodded and wiped a tear.

"I wanted to be a beat cop, like my dad, and to spend the next thirty years walking the streets of a neighborhood in Detroit. I didn't even care which neighborhood as long as I could get to know the people, lock some up, and get others out of trouble. I wanted to help the world by making little differences in people's lives, exactly like my dad."

The girl snorted a laugh and wiped tears away. "Are you saying I can't be a magazine editor anymore?"

"No." Kristen shook her head. "No, you can't. A dragon can't be a beat cop and a mage can't be a magazine editor. We've been given too much and can't squander it."

"So don't," Constance interjected. "Don't squander your gift. With your power, we could remake the world into a truly just place. We could make a world where dragons are afraid to kill people because they'll be forced to fear justice. Together, we can forge a world where someone who defends herself doesn't have to go on the run to keep her life."

"All you have to do is become a killer," Kristen finished for the assassin, determined that the girl should hear the full reality. She gestured around her. "What they did here is the perfect example. She claims they made no effort to hurt Brockton, but if not for his shield, he'd probably have died when they fired at Windlock. Look, I don't have all the answers and I don't have plans for you like Constance does, but I promise that I can help you discover your place in the world and keep you safe while we do it."

Amy nodded, looked from her to Constance, then back at her. She wiped her face and looked at the dwarves as well. It wasn't an easy decision—a life of solitude, a soldier, or a dragon cop, none of which sounded remotely like what the girl had wanted to do. Kristen had joined SWAT barely out of the academy and before she'd been ready and then dragon SWAT, but at least those were still more or less police work. This young woman was forced to choose something completely different.

But it looked like she had reached a conclusion. She drew a deep breath and glanced at Constance as if to speak. The words remained unspoken as flames lit the sky and the five dragons who had pursued her arrived.

CHAPTER FORTY-FIVE

Timbergust and his companions landed and immediately surrounded everyone else. Kristen wasn't even slightly surprised that none of them transformed into their human shapes. They weren't there to make peace, after all, but to enforce dragon justice on a scared girl.

She was about to tell them to back off when Constance laughed. It wasn't a gentle chuckle or quick guffaw either but a full-throated, deep-bellied sound. She threw her head back and laughed for a long moment before she finally stopped and wiped tears from her eyes. "It looks like we have a three-way tug of war now," she said and motioned to her technomages. They turned their guns on the newcomers.

The dragons didn't flinch, which made the woman's grin wider. Kristen stifled a grimace. *Boston SWAT doesn't know about the dragon rounds,* she realized. Or if they did, they didn't realize that the people who now aimed guns at them used bullets that could kill dragons as easily as any normal bullet killed a human.

She swallowed. This wouldn't end well if it came to violence, and she knew the assassin enough to know that she'd love the opportunity to kill a few members of a dragon SWAT force. After all, she'd sent a bomb to Detroit SWAT.

Quickly, she appraised her opponents and acknowledged that this would be tough. She, Larry, and Windlock—not exactly a battle mage or a battle dragon—stood against two formidable adversaries. On one hand, the team of technomages was trained to fight dragons and armed with weapons that could kill them. On the other, a team of five pissed-off dragons showed little inclination for diplomacy and were all both skilled and battle-hardened. She wouldn't put her money on her group, that was for sure.

Things became even more complicated when the doors to Le Face De Beouf swung open and a dozen dwarves marched out into the parking lot and stood behind Amy.

"Ye needs to learn to count, eh?" one of the dwarves said to Constance. "The ways I see it, this here's a four-way tug of war." He had a curious accent like something out of the Middle Ages mixed with the polite speech of a Canadian.

Another dwarf cleared his throat. "My name's Alp, just so you know the name of the dwarf who's about to kick all yer teeth down yer throats. This young woman came to us for help and we offered her our hospitality. Now I know that might not mean much to a group of dragons or your black-clad friends with their fancy pea-shooters, Constance, but it means a great deal to us."

He glared at those assembled and rested his hand on an ax that had apparently been hidden in the restaurant. All the dwarves had weapons—broadswords, axes, and long pikes with odd tips. All the blades looked unusual and not like steel. She had a feeling these weapons might very well puncture dragon skin as well as a bullet made of dragon could.

Alp continued in his calm but very deliberate tone. "Amy, I understand our offer might not be the one ye wish. There are better lives than ice-fishing, eh? But it's yours to choose. You tell us what you want to do and we'll make that happen, even if it's not with us. But no one— and I mean no one—will take you anywhere against your will. You got that, you fire-spitting lizards and wannabe wizards?" His steel-blue eyes settled on Kristen. "And I don't know what the hell you are either, other than that a minute ago you were shinier than an uncut diamond."

"I'm here to help," she said and tried to sound calm.

"Maybe ye is, maybe ye isn't. I'll leave that for Amy to determine, but I ain't letting you take her as you're standing with another dragon and the only shackled mage I can see."

A moment passed where no one seemed to breathe.

While she felt she should do something, she was uncertain as to what that should be. She was still in human form so she didn't want to start a fight, not yet and not when there was still a chance to resolve this peacefully. She looked into Amy's eyes and hoped she could win the woman's trust. Her dragon reflexes demanded that she flex her aura and use it to bring the girl to her side, but the human part of her —the part she'd always been—told her this was not an option.

Her aura might well be her greatest weakness in this situation. Even if it worked on the mage—and it might—it would forever undermine Amy's faith in her. She couldn't allow that and wanted her to see that she was a dragon with a human heart, a cop who believed in justice for all. If she won her over, it would have to be the human way.

"Amy," she said at last and broke the silence. "I know that what you did was in self-defense. Any human court would respect that and as crazy as it sounds, I think I'm actually the most human person here."

Amy smiled and responded with a tentative and uncertain nod. She obviously didn't know what to think about dwarves, techno-mages, or dragons either.

"I know you didn't murder anyone, and I know that when these dragons attacked, you didn't kill them even though you could have."

The girl nodded again, which made her smile because it proved she had been right. She could have killed Timbergust and Boston Dragon SWAT, but she hadn't. Despite barely learning how to control the unimaginably powerful magic at her fingertips, she had shown restraint.

"You're a good person, Amy. If you weren't, you would have killed them." She pointed at the other dragons. "Come with me. I'll get you to safety and together, we can find the best way for you to use your powers for the good of everyone—humans, dragons, mages, dwarves, everyone. If that's the future you want, it can be yours."

Constance snorted and didn't give the young mage a chance to reply. She pointed at Dragon SWAT. "Do you think they will let you go unpunished for killing one of their kind?"

Kristen honestly wanted to eat Constance in that moment. Windlock stood in front of Timbergust, still in human form, and glared at the dragons to will them not to attack. At the same time, the assassin tried to goad them into a fight. "Trust me, Amy," she said and made an effort to not yell the words even though she was seriously pissed-off.

"Who should you trust—another dragon?" The technomage pointed at the Steel Dragon. "Or a group of mages like you—people who are fighting the very dragons who have hunted you?"

"I'm not merely any dragon, Amy. I'm the Steel Dragon. Have you heard of me?"

The girl nodded. "Yeah, I…uh, I saw a made-for-TV movie about you, actually."

Great, she thought, now people were making crappy movies about her without her knowing, but that was neither here nor there. "Then I hope you know that I've always fought for humans and dragons alike. I've killed dragons because they threatened my city and I've stopped… people." She could have said Constance and her sycophants but thought it maybe wasn't the best time to land a barb like that. "I've stopped people who have threatened dragons and other people too. I care about justice—actual justice, as crazy as that may sound. I want to make the world better for everyone, not only people, not only mages, and definitely not only dragons. If all I cared about was dragons, Constance would have killed me already. I can promise you that."

Amy looked quickly at the technomage, who nodded, although begrudgingly. "That much is so. I won't lie about our work or hers. The Steel Dragon doesn't only fight for dragon kind. In fact, I've offered her a position with us fighting for true equality. A position that's still available, Kristen."

"I didn't take it then and I won't take it now," she replied. "We're too different, Constance. You think human lives are part of an equation and I'm not willing to sacrifice them."

"Fair enough," the woman agreed. "If you joined my organization, Steel Dragon, I would not give you control. The same goes for you, Amy. Despite your power, I would expect you to argue for any decisions you want made, as I do all my members. But, Kristen, if you're not willing to join me because you wouldn't be in command, how can you serve the dragons when you're so obviously not the one in charge, now are you?" While that was not at all what her opponent had claimed—and Kristen almost protested the inaccuracy—the last words were directed at Timbergust. She was also familiar enough with Constance's magic to recognize that the gust of wind that blew in the forest dragon's face had come from her.

"No, she's not," Timbergust said and stepped past Windlock's human form. Apparently, he'd waited long enough. He'd probably only needed time to decide who he would attack first, Kristen or the technomages.

"I'm in charge of this investigation by the authority of the Dragon Council," Windlock said and sounded exasperated.

"When you broke protocol, you messed that up," Emberslight said. She didn't sound too happy about it, though.

"All that is clear is that you—a rogue mage—killed two dragons in my jurisdiction," Timbergust said and his voice became significantly louder.

"We're no longer in your jurisdiction," Kristen pointed out.

"The law is clear!" the green dragon bellowed and his voice rose to a full-blown roar, complete with smoking dragon nostrils. "She killed in my turf. It is my duty to bring her in, dead or alive, before she kills anyone else. And I suggest you come willingly, you sick little mage, or we'll be forced to investigate the source of your power and how you knew to come here. I reckon your mother may know a thing or two."

"Don't threaten her," Constance said coolly.

"Or what? You'll shoot me and hope you get me in the eyes so I can't incinerate you? I have no qualms with you dwarves. Step back, give us the murderer, and we'll be on our way. Any damages to your restaurant will be repaid, you have my word."

Alp hefted his ax. "You can go fuck yourself, eh?"

Perhaps there could have been something more politic to say, and if there was, it might have bought them a few minutes. Unfortunately, the dwarf had gone for shocking and thus forced everyone's hand.

Timbergust—none too keen on the insult—shrieked a challenge. Windlock transformed and the dwarves moved forward to attack.

In other words, all hell broke loose.

CHAPTER FORTY-SIX

Flames welled in Timbergust's throat, but before they could erupt from his mouth and engulf Amy, Kristen, Constance, and the dwarves, the technomages opened fire on the forest dragon. Apparently, the time for conserving bullets was past and at least ten shots caught the dragon in the chest. They were obviously all dragon rounds. In a moment, his torso was transformed from a rich moss-green to a mess of blood and bone.

He was dead, that much was obvious.

His four dragon teammates recognized the threat and took to the air. Windlock followed at their heels and commanded them to stop their attack before they ruined everything.

It was too late for that, unfortunately. The dwarves formed up around Amy, who looked terrified. More gunshots followed when the technomages fired at the approaching dragons. Three of them pulled off their attack, but Bronzeback—probably more accustomed to being impervious to bullets than anyone else—continued to fly toward his quarry. He opened his mouth wide enough that his throat was visible and there was little doubt that he intended to burn them all. The aggressive dragon had apparently lost all patience and didn't care who was caught in his attack.

Kristen transformed into her dragon shape, complete with steel skin to protect her from the flames. Bronzeback, however, wasn't aiming at her. Despite the disagreements, he was a dragon loyalist. He wouldn't attack her, not when there were mages to kill.

Instead, he flew over Kristen, held his fire while he did so, and unleashed his breath at Amy.

It didn't do a damn thing. The dwarves had surrounded her and stacked themselves into some kind of gymnastics pyramid. The flames struck their leathery hides and bounced off as if they were made of stone.

They grinned at each other as the fire-breathing dragon exhausted his reserve of flame and took to the sky. Kristen wondered if they'd expected to be more burned. They probably didn't know the girl could block flames with her powers.

Not that she looked like she had much left in her. She held her hands up in an attempt to protect the dwarves but she shook visibly, probably on the verge of complete exhaustion.

Bronzeback circled above and prepared to swoop into another assault. If he was smart—and he was at least smart enough to know how to fight—he wouldn't try fire again but would instead knock the dwarves into Amy and maybe crush her in the process. They were strong, obviously, but they couldn't be strong enough to stop a dragon that size with metal scales. It seemed he knew what he was doing and didn't advance at the same angle but from the side, which forced them to rebuild their pyramid—a task it appeared they didn't have time for.

Constance cursed at the dragon and ran from the dwarves. She must have reached the same conclusion as Kristen. Her technomages fired at Bronzeback, but either they missed or his bronze plates were stronger than anticipated as he merely hurtled closer, apparently unscathed.

The large dragon spread his wings seconds before two light poles ripped out of the parking lot. Each was close to twenty feet tall with a decorative lamp at their tip. The first floated in place while the second rocketed toward him, punctured his wing, and whipped him violently to alter his trajectory. It pinned him to the side of one of the shops in the strip mall like a bug struck by the windshield of a moving car. The other pole followed and speared his other wing.

He flapped his wings but the membranes tore and he screamed in pain. His effort hadn't brought liberty and he remained stuck there like a bug. He had no time to suffer, though, as Constance's technomages saw an opportunity and took it.

Apparently, Bronzeback's movement had been all that prevented the shooters from killing him. Now that he was trapped, a hail of bullets struck him in the face and chest to end his life as quickly as they had Timbergust's.

Of course, that was enough to drive the other dragons into a rage. The three of them separated and swooped in a coordinated assault to strafe the technomages, who fired at them as they raced into cover. One of the mages had already made it inside a building, though, Kristen realized when the asphalt at her feet exploded. The idiot used the opportunity to fire at her.

She sprinted behind an SUV in the far corner of the parking lot. While it seemed unnatural to hunker there, she knew from experience that steel skin wouldn't protect her against dragon bullets.

What followed could only be described as chaos. The dragons seemed to simply want to burn everyone to ashes. They attacked the technomages, the dwarves, and even Windlock with reckless enthusiasm. The technomages were more focused in their rebuttal, but they made no effort to spare the investigator despite him not attacking any of them.

The dwarves focused on little more than defending Amy, but that kept them busy. Emberslight picked a car up and dropped it on them. Four of them darted beneath it and amazingly, caught the vehicle by its wheels and flung it at the dragon. They didn't have anything like the accuracy she did but they made it clear that they would not be crushed.

Kristen only had eyes for Amy, though. The young mage rubbed her face and one of her nostrils was bleeding. She'd clearly over-extended herself and wouldn't last much longer out there. In the current battle, she was probably already more of a liability than an asset.

The dwarves must have known this as six of them ushered her inside while the others remained to guard the door against the chaos in the parking lot outside Le Face De Beouf.

She had to follow them indoors. This fight was about Amy and would end when the girl was no longer a threat. To the dragons, this meant she had to die. To the technomages, she would have to join them, but that wouldn't happen as long as there were dragons to kill. She didn't know what that meant to the dwarves, but she did know that if they tried to take her to safety, the fighting in the parking lot wouldn't stop until either all the dragons or all the mages were dead. Kristen—as little as she cared for either side—didn't want a slaughter.

Despite the obstacles, then, she had to get to Amy. Grimly, she considered those obstacles—heavily armed assassins, a trio of enraged dragons, and a half-dozen dwarves. The odds weren't good, but she reminded herself that she'd faced worse.

Kristen took a deep breath and waited for a pause in the madness. She quickly realized that there were simply too many players for that to happen and instead, simply made a break for it.

She darted out from behind the SUV and lunged toward the restaurant. It seemed logical that if she took to the air, the technomages would have an easier time shooting at her.

What seemed like a good plan lasted only until a dragon dive-bombed and raked her steel back with their claws. Thankfully, her protection blocked the hot-fire pain that should have come from the attack and she glanced up as Emberslight flew away.

"You're not serving the Dragon Council's interests," she shouted and her talons glowed hot. Kristen had never seen that before and realized that her adversary must have used her powers to super-heat her claws.

In response, she ripped the wheel off a truck and hurled it like a frisbee. The other dragon incinerated it long before it could reach her, but it bought her a few seconds and another leap forward, and that was what she needed for the moment.

She sprinted toward the wall of six dwarves who guarded the entrance to the restaurant. After she saw them fling a car like it was an oversized pillow, she didn't exactly think she could simply knock them out of the way. She needed to think about how she could get past them, but that wasn't her biggest priority.

It was the six assault rifles aimed at her face.

Kristen had faced death many times. Hell, she'd literally killed a dragon assassin named Death, so she wasn't exactly one to fear her own demise. In that moment, however, she saw no way to survive. The six weapons were spread out enough that she couldn't eliminate them with a single sweep of fire, nor could any other dragon. She thought her life would flash before her eyes, given that this was most likely her final moment.

Instead, she thought of her mother, father, and brother at her funeral, standing in front of a gravestone engraved with *Died in Canada*. It was a stupid, bizarre picture, and hardly fitting for her last thought on earth, yet it was surprisingly vivid. She even wondered what kind of flowers her mom would bring and decided she'd probably choose blooms from the garden.

The moment faded into reality once again and she startled when all six technomages lifted their guns a few inches so none of them were trained on her any longer.

"Move!" Larry shouted, his voice strained. Somehow, he had forced them to aim their weapons elsewhere when she needed it most.

She didn't need to be told twice. Without hesitation, she barreled forward and drew a little closer to the dwarves who guarded the door.

Foolishly, she chose to look at the field of battle to confirm that no other surprises might hinder her progress.

Windlock was high above and fought tooth and claw with Aquatos. Both dragons snapped and scratched at one another's wings in relentless attempts to knock their opponent from their great height.

The other two dragons had separated. Emberslight seemed to make one of the technomage's guns glow red-hot, which forced him to drop it. This, however, left her open to Constance, who used a magically powered gust of wind to rocket herself toward her target and whip her across the jaw with some kind of glove. It drew blood where it struck the dragon, but not enough to slow her. She swung her tail and catapulted her attacker through the front window of an automotive store. The woman launched from impact directly into motion and yelled orders to her mages to try to eliminate her opponent.

Crimson—the third surviving member of Boston's Dragon SWAT division—attempted to attack Larry. It was rather like watching a lion try to eat a mouse and the dragon obviously had the advantage. If he landed on his target—even by accident—it would all be over.

The mage moved deftly around the parking lot and remained in constant motion as he slid over and under cars, darted behind them, and occasionally flicked license plates or pieces of trash in the dragon's face. He seemed fine and she had to assume he would continue to be. He knew his limits. The best way she could help her teammates was to talk to Amy and end this fight.

The delay had cost her, though, and she turned to the dwarves too late. Aquatos had curtailed his battle with Windlock and reached them first. The investigator was now engaged with Crimson, apparently less sure of his mage's fighting prowess than she had been.

Aquatos lunged at the dwarves, who scattered like bowling pins when the massive dragon drove into them. But, also like bowling pins, they didn't stay down long. Instead, they rolled and tumbled toward their assailant. The dragon tried to shatter the door with his jaws but one of the dwarves caught him in the chin with a hammer and he shook his head as if to clear the ringing in his head from the blow.

He snapped at the dwarf but came up short. Two others had him by the tail and he simply couldn't move forward. He whirled to attack them and another took hold of one of his front legs. Furious, he managed to shake this one free and hurled him over the parking lot to connect with the front of a red sedan. The car alarm shrieked for a second and promptly died.

A fourth dwarf tried to climb the dragon's back but he wasn't fast enough. Crimson knocked him loose with his wings and snatched him in his claw. When he proceeded to pound his captive into the asphalt again and again, Kristen decided she'd had enough.

She lunged and was able to thrust the dragon off-balance. Aquatos fell and before he could right himself, the dwarves who had him by the tail yanked as one and swung him about one hundred and eighty degrees before they released him. He careened across the parking lot while he flailed in an attempt to find purchase on the asphalt.

Gunshots rang out and the dragon hissed and took to the sky. He had evidently grasped the fact that although the dwarves were tougher, the mages were the more lethal opponents.

"Thanks, eh?" one of the dwarves said to Kristen.

"I need to get inside," she replied.

"Yeah, we realized that, what with the running over here," another said.

"You won't wreck our place, will ya?" a third asked.

"No, sir…er, ma'am?" She noticed this dwarf had very long eyelashes and—despite having an impressive mustache and a short beard—also wore lipstick. "I only want to talk to Amy. If she'll make a decision, we can end this fighting. That's all I want."

"Aye, all right then," the first dwarf said.

She gave him a grateful smile and entered Le Face De Beouf.

CHAPTER FORTY-SEVEN

"Amy!" Kristen called as soon as she was inside.

The mage was in the back of the restaurant near a door to the kitchen. She turned to face her, although reluctance seemed to define the movement. Her hair was a mess and one of her nostrils was ringed with blood. She looked so incredibly tired.

Between the two women stood six dwarves who looked as fresh as daisies. Or maybe cactus was a better comparison, she thought as they looked tough.

"Look, I don't want to fight," she said and changed to her regular human form. She'd already shifted from dragon to steel human, but she understood that a shining silver person didn't exactly make the best conversation partner. "I want to help."

The girl simply stared at her. She was in shock, obviously, was wrung out and tired, and had probably never been in a fight before. Kristen glanced out the window to where the battle still raged. How bizarre it was to see it muffled behind the glass like it was wraparound film instead of a battle she had been in only a few minutes before.

"How will ye do that?" a dwarf asked. His jade nose ring and blue eyes identified him as Alp.

"Come with me," Kristen said.

He shook his head. "Constance is right in that regard. Those dragons outside will never let a mage this strong live. She's a threat to the dragon paradigm. They'll do whatever they have to do to eliminate her. We've never had to hide a mage of this power before."

"But you can?" Amy asked. She took deep breaths and some of the color had returned to her face. Smart girl, Kristen thought. She had probably recognized that she was going into shock.

"Aye. We can send ye someplace where you can be free of the dragons. It'll be far from here but ye'll be safe. Ye may have to move a time or two over the next two years, but I gave ye my word. We'll keep ye safe."

"But at what cost, Amy?" she asked. "If you go with them—and you can—you'll never see your home again and you'll never see your family. You'll be alone."

"Not alone," Alp admonished. "We ain't going to send ye to some igloo in the middle of the tundra. There'll be dwarves there and maybe a human or two as well, but the dragon's right about the rest. If ye come with us, it'll be goodbye to your family, your home, and your country. You'll be a Canadian from here on out."

"Is that the life you want, always running?" Kristen asked.

The girl looked at the dwarves as if to confirm this.

"Aye, there's a chance ye'll always be running. Two more dragons are dead out there. I know ye didn't kill either but...well, dragons don't always like to parse the details in these kinds of fights," Alp said. "If ye come with us, ye'll always be a rogue mage. Always. They might not always hunt ye, but ye'll have to live like they are. It's the only way. If they come for ye, we'll help you fight them—although we might not need to, not with powers like you have." He chuckled darkly and his expression conveyed that the dwarves were more than capable of holding their own.

"Do you think it's better to fight like Constance said?" Amy asked.

"No. Absolutely not," Kristen replied quickly. "I think it would be better to run than to join Constance. She wants a war that will devastate the world. I know dragons have too much power, but her path is not the way forward."

"I don't know," one of the dwarves muttered. "It seems like she may know a thing or two about killing dragons."

"Humans have enough tech now to be truly deadly to dragons," she admitted. "If it came to war, the dragons would massacre billions, of that I have no doubt, but the humans would fight back. And with Constance's weapons, they might truly be able to slay every last dragon or at least enough to drive the remaining few into hiding. But at what cost? The entire world would be devastated by a war of that magnitude. Nuclear weapons might be used. Whole cities would burn. It's a nightmare scenario that we cannot let happen."

Amy nodded. "I don't want vengeance. Those dragons who destroyed my home...they didn't actually kill my parents, although I didn't know it at the time. And I didn't want to kill them. I only wanted... I wanted them to take responsibility."

Kristen nodded. "I know. I really do. We live in an unjust world but it's better than it was a century ago. We don't need to tear the entire thing down to start again. I think we can bring change to the system and continue to improve things for most people."

"Maybe for you, but you're a dragon," the girl pointed out.

"What do you suggest?" Alp asked.

The Steel Dragon had given this considerable thought. She'd pondered it from every angle as they'd flown to the town and considered what it was like to realize one's incredible powers and not have anyone to help. Her thoughts had included Larry and Windlock's relationship as well as Atramento, the mage and glorified paper-pusher who managed all the paperwork at Dragon SWAT. She tried to take all this into account while she searched for a solution that would keep the mage safe yet also allow her to change the world. And, while her conscience had protested volubly and she'd needed to consider the implications very carefully, she thought she had a solution.

Those gathered regarded her with varying degrees of curiosity and suspicion, and she realized that they waited for her to respond. After a deep breath, she slid her hand into her pocket, withdrew the silver bracelet Windlock had given her, and held it out.

"Wear this and become my personal mage. Dragon law is weird. Yes, much of it is corrupt, but there is still law. If you become my mage, other dragons will have to respect you or risk dueling with me, something most of them don't like to do." She flashed her steel skin briefly to make her point.

"I don't know," Amy said and regarded the bracelet dubiously.

"You could still be attacked. No one can offer you a future where that's not a possibility but this way, you'd have the law on your side. You could return to the US, visit your family, and live a—well, not a normal life, but something more normal than being an ice fisherman. If you become my mage, you could use your powers for good."

"And all she's asking you to do is wear that slave chain," the mustachioed dwarf said.

The girl frowned. "Is that true?"

"It's true that the mages who wear these are treated as possessions by dragons," she admitted and clenched her teeth to display her disapproval. "But if the other dragons see it, they'll know they're safe. They won't attack and if they do, I'll stop them."

"They'll know they're safe because that bracelet will take away most of your power." Alp's voice was like ice. "You'll still be able to use some, of course. Like a bird with clipped wings, you'll still be able to flutter around but that'll be it. And don't try to attack a dragon again, not even in self-defense. Those bracelets won't allow that. You'll be a slave, Amy—a pampered one, maybe, but a slave all the same."

"How dare you," Kristen retorted hotly.

"Here we go with the dragon arrogance," the dwarf replied.

"Nonsense," she snapped. "You know who I am, yes? The Steel Dragon."

"Aye, we get the news," he admitted.

"Then can you explain how anything you've heard makes you think I'll treat anyone like a slave?"

He frowned but made no effort to answer the question.

"Do you know what my mom would do to me if I ever became that pigheaded? She wouldn't care that I'm a dragon. She would murder me!"

"I thought ye didn't have a mom."

"My human mom, the woman you'll have to meet if you want to come with me," she said to Amy.

The dwarf finally smiled. "You give us her number and tell her to call us if she ever needs helping spanking you, and I'll agree you can be trusted," the dwarf said and nodded at Amy.

Kristen didn't even hesitate. She wrote her parents' phone number down on a napkin and gave it to him. "There. Insurance. Now, Amy, come on. What do you think?"

"I don't know. I…I mean, these powers are frightening but they're mine. I don't want to lose them."

She nodded. This had occurred to her as a likely response, which made what she did next all the easier.

Without hesitation, she turned her hands to steel and ripped the silver bracelet into pieces. A spark of blue energy flared briefly before the dampening power of the bracelet vanished.

The dwarves gasped.

The young mage smiled. "Do you promise me that I'll actually meet your mom?"

Kristen groaned. "Yes, sure, but you'll have to meet my brother and dad too."

"Is that a problem?"

"Oh yeah." She nodded.

"Speaking of problems," Alp said. "there's still the issue of the dragons outside."

She turned to them. Beyond the window, the parking lot now resembled a war zone. The cars that remained were either charred by fire or crushed and battered from being struck by a dragon's body. Most had already been hurled away.

Yet the dragons continued to fight the dwarves and technomages, who retaliated with equal resolution.

"I'll take care of them if this is really what you want," she said to the girl. "If you really want to go, don't let me force you to stay. I'm sure these dwarves have a way out. You can take it while I run inter-ference."

Amy furrowed her brow in thought and Kristen strode to the door. Every step was heavier than the last. She wanted the mage to join her. Hell, she'd even take her to her folks, but Amy had to choose. She had to want this. Otherwise, it would never work. It was okay and even inevitable if she was scared, but she had to choose all the same.

She raised her hand to open the glass door. Her heart hammered in her throat, a physical response to the tension, when Amy finally agreed.

"Okay. I'll be the Steel Dragon's mage."

Kristen turned and grinned at her. "No, you'll be the Steel Dragon's friend." She held her hand out and the girl approached and shook it. The two women smiled as the battle raged on the other side of the panes of glass.

"But first, I need to stop them from burning this place down."

CHAPTER FORTY-EIGHT

It was crazy, but Kristen was ready to take on the dragons and the technomages by herself if that was what it took to prove to Amy she was serious about protecting her. She hoped the dwarves who had stayed outside would help her and that Windlock might come to her aid, but even if they didn't, she was ready. By this point, she was heartily fed up with the handful of dragons who acted like they ruled the world. In Canada—a country not beholden to them but governed by a completely different species of people, she had hoped they might display a little more political sensitivity, but that didn't seem very likely to happen.

They left her with little choice but to force the issue.

She faced the door, turned her skin to steel, and prepared herself to transform into a dragon when a skateboard rolled in front of her.

Amy grinned. "I can't let a friend go out there alone."

"Are you sure about that?" She raised an eyebrow.

"What's the worst thing they can do—eat me?"

Kristen snorted a laugh. "If you're really lucky, they'll cook you first."

Ah, gallows humor. How she loved it. That the girl could joke about her own demise boded well for their friendship.

"You convinced me to work with you without fighting so maybe we can convince them of that if we go out there together."

"It's worth a try," she agreed.

The two young women who were anything but human stepped outside.

The battle showed no signs of slowing. The dragons kept to the air and took turns to attempt to incinerate the technomages or the dwarves. The latter were too flame-resistant and the former were too good with their weapons.

Aquatos swooped in for an attack on the mages but one of them shot him in the wing joint and the dragon tumbled.

If Emberslight hadn't begun to heat the ground the technomages stood on, they would have killed the wounded dragon then and there. He moved away hastily to take cover, now denied his ability to fly.

Kristen used the temporary retreat to transform into a dragon and deliver her loudest roar. All eyes turned to her and the fighting ceased temporarily. She knew she had to speak quickly and persuasively, though. It would only take one bullet from the technomages to end her speech before it began.

"It's done," she said decisively. "Amy Williams is no longer a fugitive. She has agreed to work with me as a mage, which means she's under my protection. If anyone wants to hurt her, they have to come through the Steel Dragon first." She thought that about summed it up but to make her point to both the technomages and the dragons, she exhaled a massive inferno of flame at the sky. The dragons would hopefully see she was fresh and ready for a fight, while the mages would know she knew her way around guns and had the fire to melt their weapons.

"Damn it, Kristen, we almost had them," Constance shouted. "Two more of their damn strafes and they'd be done, but you had to come and ruin us again. Amy, come with us."

"I don't want to kill these dragons," the mage replied quietly.

"The world will burn. Can't you fucking see that?" The assassin was livid. "If you would only join us, we could at least decide which way the fires would spread."

"I don't want to fan any flames," she said.

"This is naïve. You're being a fucking child right now." Kristen didn't think she'd ever heard the woman so angry. The leader of the technomages continued with something close to desperation in her tone. "Lady Steel—Kristen—I implore you to rethink this. With you and Amy working with us, there wouldn't have to be a war."

"I won't kill dragons," she replied. "And I don't want to kill you either. But if you target me again or fire any more of those bullets at those dragons, I might not have a choice."

"Goddammit!" Constance screamed, but she gestured for her technomages to retreat. They obeyed, although one of them—a man with broad shoulders and a five o'clock shadow, didn't look too happy about the order. Still, they complied and the technomages vanished into the woods behind the strip mall.

The Steel Dragon shook her head. She wouldn't join Constance, not on her vendetta to destroy dragon lives to start a war, but damn, she really did wish there was some way they could work together. The assassin was right in that the idea of a revolution that put humans, mages, and dragons on an equal footing was a beautiful dream. While she could applaud the notion, she didn't believe that her and Amy joining technomages who were willing to harvest dragon body parts was the way to achieve that goal.

Still, it was a small victory that the woman had agreed this fight was over. She had thought she could outmaneuver the shooters, but a single well-placed bullet could have killed her. It would have been a damn hard fight too but with Constance gone, the battle was over.

Unfortunately, the other dragons didn't agree.

"Four dragons are dead because of that mage," Emberslight screamed as she landed violently and proceeded to shred the asphalt of the parking lot with her talons.

"The evidence suggests that the first two died when she defended herself. However, I assure you I will look into their deaths and make sure that Amy didn't act maliciously and that she won't do it again."

"I really didn't mean to, ma'am. If there's anything I can do—" Amy tried to say but the dragon roared in fury to silence her.

"Four dragons are dead. Not two. Timbergust was a fool, but he only tried to do his job—a job you have forsaken, Steel Dragon."

Kristen had no idea why she was so enraged. Yes, two dragons had died, but Timbergust had fallen into the madness of vengeance and Bronzeback… Well, honestly, she wouldn't be surprised to find that he was the kind of dragon who enjoyed killing people. Not that it was a reason for him to die, but he'd essentially brought it on himself.

"Bronzeback attacked Amy. He didn't deserve to die, but he intended to incinerate her." Kristen tried to keep her voice calm in the hope that it would extend to her opponent.

Emberslight seemed beyond even the desire to control herself. "So he wasn't perfect. So what? You should have seen what he was like before he met me. He'd come so far. Yes, he killed people—many people." She uttered a ragged laugh that seemed to indicate that the dragon had become unhinged, although there seemed to be no apparent reason for this. "But he was getting better. And he was so sweet when he wanted to be. He didn't deserve this."

The truth clicked in. They'd been lovers. She cursed inwardly as she had hoped to reason with Emberslight. The leader of Boston's Dragon SWAT had seemed like a person who took her job and her duty seriously but now, it appeared that any chance of discussion was gone.

She had never been in love, so she could only imagine what Emberslight felt, but she knew it must be hard for a dragon. They'd probably thought they had decades ahead of them or even centuries

"Emberslight, I'm sorry, I really am, but more death is not the solution here. None of this would have happened if human beings had actual rights when it comes to dragons. Of course Amy fled for her life. She had no other choice."

"And what about the humans who did this to my wing?" Aquatos hissed and shook the appendage to show her that it was in tatters. The bullet had struck a joint and when he had fallen from the sky, the wind had shredded it. The dragon bullets stopped a dragon's healing ability, but this also meant that its wings became more fragile as a dragon's inherent magic was needed to make the wings work at all. "You let them go like this was nothing."

"They killed Timbergust and Bronzeback," Crimson said. The rookie officer's voice was shakier, but he seemed no less furious than the other two.

"Killing Amy won't change any of that," Kristen said.

"It'll be a start," Emberslight said. "But if we must go through you, fine. So be it. You killed one of us—one of our team."

"I did not," she retorted.

"She did." Emberlight raised a claw and pointed it at Amy. "And if she did, you did. That's how it works in dragon law. And since you took one of ours, we challenge you to a duel."

"We?" Kristen asked. "You mean the three of you? Fine."

Crimson and Aquatos approached to stand beside their leader. Aquatos nodded. "You've wronged us, Steel Dragon. We will make this right."

"Can you believe this, Windlock?" She turned to the other dragon and fully expected to see him grin and join her, or better yet, reprimand the three dragons for attacking a fellow officer. Instead, he looked nervous. "Windlock?"

"Kristen, I'm sorry, but this is their right. No dragon in the world would believe Bronzeback would have died without Amy performing magic against him."

"That's bullshit and you know it!" she shouted. "Those mages could've shot him. They would have."

"They only did because she pinned him to the wall," Emberslight said. "We heard about your little technomages in Detroit. Everyone's heard about them. Don't you think we practiced fighting bullets? Bronzeback only died when she intervened. His death is as much on her hands as it is theirs."

"And the three of you intend to fight me?" Kristen demanded, incredulous.

"You fought us with a mage, dwarves, and those technomages. One on three is far fairer than that," Crimson said.

"You mean two on three," Kristen said and nodded at Windlock.

The investigator shook his head. "I'm sorry, Kristen. I cannot join you in this battle. Blood feuds are old rules. They date back long before jurisdiction or even the role of an investigator. They have a right to a duel to avenge their fallen brother."

"But you said I was an investigator. Doesn't that mean you can fight with me?" she asked and tried not to let fear creep into her voice or her aura. One on three would not be an easy fight.

"Investigators don't get to call on kin in duels. We're given great power and leeway from the Dragon Council, and that's the downside. I'm sorry. I can't help you with this."

"Are you ready?" Emberslight growled.

"How am I supposed to beat the three of them while you watch?"

"You never should have agreed to this."

"I didn't."

"You said 'fine.' That's enough. This fight is yours, Lady Steel." Windlock looked disappointed and Kristen had to admit that the feeling was mutual. She was supposed to face three dragons while he simply sat there? While she was strong, she wasn't this strong and aside from that, had never fought three at the same time before. She'd battled two once, and it hadn't been easy. These three were trained in tactics and combat so it wouldn't simply be a free-for-all. She knew full well they'd use their strengths against her. Thankfully, she seemed to have regained most of her powers, although she couldn't be sure of that. Even at full strength, the multi-opponent combat would test her to the limit of her abilities and powers. What would happen if some or all of them failed her under extreme circumstances?

"You're a coward, Windlock," she grumbled.

"I'm tired of this dithering!" Emberslight's claws began to glow but she didn't attack. It must have been one of the rules that she didn't know.

Windlock blanched, not at Emberslight's words but at Kristen's. She hadn't meant for him to hear her but now that he had, she couldn't simply leave it at that. "You uphold a system you know is unjust. You support dragon laws you know aren't good for people."

"Not all of them," he said and held his dragon claws up. Between his thumb and forefinger dangled a tiny silver chain. For a moment, she didn't know what the hell the chain was supposed to represent and was too furious at him to think straight. He continued to stare at her, a message in his gaze, and she finally recognized it as one of the bands that were used to control a mage's power.

She turned when Larry strode up, a grim smile of determination on his face. The sleeves of his robe were rolled up and she saw that indeed, his wrist was free of the chain. "I owe you for that, Kristen, really I do. You convinced the old Windbag that I don't need to be cuffed anymore and I'm grateful. But if you don't mind not letting me die in the next five minutes, that would be great."

"Doesn't dragon law prevent you from helping me in a duel?" Kristen asked. She was thankful—beyond thankful, actually. She was impressed and amazed that he was willing to face dragons with her, but she was also a realist. The last thing she wanted was to somehow manage to defeat these dragons with his help, only for the Dragon Council to rule that he'd acted out of order and sentence him to death or some other nonsensical punishment reserved only for humans.

"Are you kidding? These rules are too old to even mention humans. In fact, back in the day—and by day I mean centuries ago— dragon duels would consist of two dragons throwing entire armies of people at each other. Only when the armies had done some damage would the dragons come in. I can help you as much as I damn well want."

"Another freed mage. How fitting." Aquatos growled disdainfully.

"If he can, so can I, right?" Amy said and rolled forward on her skateboard.

It was odd to see her stand so straight and roll like something out of a movie. She realized that if the girl stuck around, she'd have to get used to things like that.

"If you insist, but Amy, I know you're tired. You don't have to do this," Kristen said.

"The best thing about these powers is that I can do something about bullies like them," the girl retorted. "I won't waste my first opportunity to stand up to dragons just because I had a little nose-bleed. I'll have time to recover, even if it is only a little."

"All right, then." She nodded decisively. "Three against three."

"Then we begin." Emberslight's eyes began to glow even brighter.

"Wait, wait, wait, wait!" Larry threw his arms up to stop the dragons from attacking. "The challenged claims the right to choose the location."

"A mage can claim no such thing!" Aquatos roared in protest. The three dragons were clearly impatient. It was a good thing they'd formally challenged her because if they hadn't, they'd be fighting already. Then again, if they hadn't, Windlock would be a part of this fight too. The pros and cons seemed equally matched but what was more important was the fact that since they had, they were apparently constrained to follow a few rules.

"The challenged claims the right to choose the location," she said with a smile.

Emberslight roared in frustration. "Fine. That is your right, but it must be within ten minutes' flight from here—or were you not familiar with that particular rule? Choose where you wish to die."

"If I may suggest a place?" one of the dwarves said and stepped forward. "Take this to the old asbestos mine and don't burn our city."

"That's where we fight," Kristen said.

"Fine," Emberslight agreed before she and Crimson lifted Aquatos between them and the three dragons took to the air. "Ten minutes. If you three aren't there in that time, we burn this city down."

CHAPTER FORTY-NINE

As soon as the dragons were at a safe range, the dwarves rushed forward and to Kristen's shock, began to remove their clothes.

"What are you doing?" she demanded as they surrounded the two human mages.

"We ain't got much time, so hold still and put this on," one of them said, removed his breastplate, and gave it to Larry.

"No way will this fit," he protested but the dwarf ignored him and strapped it on. Strangely, it did fit, and it took a moment before she realized the dwarf's torso was about the same size as a human's. It was their arms and legs that made them shorter.

"It's gonna take you five minutes to get there," the dwarf explained as he tightened the breastplate around the mage. "And you can't be late. We can't have them burning our town down now, can we? We'll get ya outfitted and sent over quick-like."

Three minutes later, the two mages looked like poorly dressed renaissance fair attendees in thick boots as well as gloves and odd hats. Both garments were knit and brightly colored, but the dwarves explained that they were fire-resistant and together, the armor created an aura of magic that should protect them from fire.

In addition to his boots, gloves, and hat, Brockton wore a breastplate with the face of a cow chiseled into it, while Amy had a leather vest on that looked even harder than the shiny piece of metal over her colleague's chest. Each mage had also been given a staff. Larry's had a tangle of silver wire at its tip while Amy's had a huge red gemstone.

"Not so bad, eh?" one of the dwarves said. "Those'll help ye defend yourselves. And augment your power too but be damn careful about that as they don't increase power, only let you use more at once. It'll drain ya faster than a bathtub, it will."

"What about me?" Kristen asked.

The dwarves all looked at each other and laughed.

"What's so funny?"

"We ain't got nothing that can protect the Steel Dragon better than her own powers."

Kristen supposed that was a comfort but she was still jealous of the two mage's brightly colored hats.

"What can you tell us about this mine?" Windlock asked.

"You'll see it when ya get there," one of the dwarves said and sounded apologetic. "I didn't mention it because it'll give you some advantage but because we can't have you wrecking our town."

"Still," another said, "there are a few tunnels. I reckon the mages could use those for cover if they needed to."

She nodded. They were out of time. Both mages climbed onto her back—she insisted that Amy conserve her strength for the battle—and Windlock flew behind them to watch the proceedings.

Her mind raced throughout the short journey. A dragon battle between her, Windlock, and the mages would have been better, but this would have to do. It meant much to her that he had freed Larry. She still wished he could join her in this fight, but if doing so meant it would cost him his place as a dragon investigator, she didn't know if that was worth it.

He was a kind, sensible dragon in a position of extreme power and she regretted how easily she'd jumped to conclusions and written him off as simply another self-centered dragon, even if it hadn't been whole-hearted. Not only that but if he were to be ousted, the chances of someone more reasonable and friendly to humankind taking his position were basically nonexistent. If her aim was justice delivered over the entire world, she had to admit that Windlock was probably a greater force for good than she was.

After all, she was merely a Detroit SWAT dragon. She busted heads and stopped assholes from being assholes, which was exactly what she intended to do at this mine. Windlock had arranged this entire investigation. If he hadn't done so, she had little doubt that Amy would already be dead.

She swallowed as she realized the implications. In the same way that her beliefs pitted her constantly against the technomages who treated people with so little regard, this fight wasn't only about her, Bronzeback, or even Amy. It was about standing up to the dragon establishment by confronting the people who defended laws and rules that were unjust. In this situation, the people were dragons. With the bomb, the people had been the technomages, but the principle remained exactly the same. The responsibility felt a little daunting when she realized she couldn't lose. To do so would be to give the dragon law establishment a huge victory. They'd march over her body, claim Amy's life, and force the status quo back to where it was.

Which might have been okay if only a lack of bloodshed mattered and if she subscribed to the dangerous belief that the ends justified the means. But as long as the status quo remained, Constance would continue to agitate to start a war. In standing against the three dragons, she could actually defeat the technomage as well, at least in part. This was her first major step in a fight for justice and to prevent a world war from happening. She'd lost sight of that in Rangeley when her frustrations had driven logic and clear thinking from her mind. Her fight was against injustice, not dragons or mages themselves.

Fortunately, she didn't have time to dwell on the fact or its repercussions as they arrived at the mine.

Kristen immediately understood why the dwarves had sent them there. There was nothing to destroy. The mine—or what was left of it —was little more than a giant pit. Huge steps were cut into the sides of it, each large enough for a dump truck to drive on. Presumably, they'd been carved almost a century before when the mine had still been active.

Here and there, scrubby trees and wind-battered plants grew. Dark holes were visible in random places, probably the entrances to tunnels that wound who knew how deep into the earth below this open part of the mine. At the center of this giant, desolate, abandoned amphitheater was a pool of water that she could tell was ice-cold merely by looking at it.

Above the mine, turning slow circles in the air, were Crimson and Emberslight.

She had no opportunity to look for Aquatos as the two dragons attacked as soon as the new arrivals entered the airspace above the mine.

Crimson exhaled a massive blast of fire that she might have been able to bat away with her steel wings if not for the two humans on her back. To avoid it, she dove toward the shelves of earth below her.

"We can take a little heat," Larry reminded her and raised his voice over the wind.

"There's no point in them knowing that yet," she replied and accelerated the descent. They'd all agreed that their best strategy would be to split up. As long as the mages were on her back, they presented a single target. They needed to get off and defend themselves as best they could. She hoped their armor would help, but she didn't see how it could possibly stand against the onslaught of three dragons.

Where is Aquatos? One of the shafts, perhaps? That would be bad as it was where Amy and Larry planned to go.

Kristen swooped low and her companions jumped not a second too soon. Claws raked her back and if not for her steel skin, she had no doubt she'd be out of the fight.

She swooped up and used the ax-blade at the end of her tail to strike her attacker's face. He pursued her and released dragon flame as he flew. She wondered if there was perhaps more to the dragon's name than his color. He seemed to have an endless supply of fire.

Thankfully, an unexpected distraction drew him from his focused attack. He veered away as a cloud of dust whipped from the ground to create a cloud between the Steel Dragon and her pursuer. Apparently, there were flecks of something inflammatory the dust as it ignited in a blinding flash that forced him to pull off.

"All right!" Larry shouted. "It feels good to be free again."

It seemed Emberslight didn't like the idea of a free mage any more than Kristen liked the idea of a cuffed one. In response to Brockton's jubilation, she turned to surge toward the mage. Her eyes began to glow, brighter and brighter and laser-focused on his breastplate.

She's trying to melt it, she realized but the dragon's attempt proved futile. Whatever the dwarves had done to the armor seemed to work particularly well against her powers and Larry didn't even seem to notice. He constantly hurled small stones at Crimson's face in an effort to keep the dragon distracted. It was admirably brave but also dangerous. Brockton wasn't a battle mage and had done nothing more than forensics for the last decade. This fight wouldn't end well for him if it lasted for any length of time.

Kristen turned and swooped low over the lake in the middle of the mine. Both dragons were distracted. If she could get behind one of them, she might be able to strike one hard enough to knock them unconscious.

Amy must have had the same idea as a boulder seemed to rip itself out of the ground and hurtled toward Emberslight. The dragon saw the attack and tried to change direction but apparently, a dragon had far more momentum than a magically levitating boulder. The young mage was able to adjust and drive the boulder into her target's face.

Kristen suppressed a whoop of triumph as the dragon—temporarily stunned—plummeted. If they could get her inside one of the tunnels and collapse it, she'd be out of the fight. She didn't want to kill the dragons—after all, their job was to stop murderers. While she understood that they were furious about the death of Bronzeback, if she could defeat them and restrain them so they couldn't fight back, Windlock had assured her that it would fulfill the terms of a duel and she would be victorious by dragon law. Not only would Emberslight have to admit defeat, but none of them would be able to challenge her in the future.

All she had to do now was reach Emberslight, she thought as she pumped her wings to gain more speed over the lake. If she stopped the leader, the other dragon might be reluctant to continue.

In her excitement, she'd forgotten there were actually two other dragons.

She was reminded of this when Aquatos surged from the water and grasped her with all four of his legs. Although she tried to break free, his long, sinuous, snakelike tail wound around her neck and together, they plunged into the frigid lake.

Obviously, anyone who was still alive didn't know what death felt like but being forced into the water felt as close to having the life sucked from her as anything ever had. It wasn't freezing but that only made things worse. If it had been ice, she wouldn't have been surprised because her enemy would not have been able to ambush her.

Instinct clicked in and she clawed at her attacker in the crystal-clear water while the aquatic dragon kicked and scratched at her. Nothing in her experience could have prepared her for this encounter and the dilemma she faced. While she remained steel, Aquatos's claws couldn't hurt her, but if she didn't transform to skin, she'd continue to sink.

For a brief, desperate moment, she thought she might somehow outlast the other dragon, but his gills and webbed claws brought sudden clarity to the relevance of his name and she immediately understood that he intended to drown her.

Kristen thrashed in the cold water and attempted to strike the injured dragon with her tail, but she wasn't able to reach him. He was too fast and too accustomed to fighting underwater. Rather than retaliate, he simply remained above her and blocked any attempt at escape by using his claws and teeth to force her to stay in her steel form.

Her lungs—massive though they were in her dragon form—began to burn. She couldn't last much longer and briefly considered turning into a human. The idea didn't last as she realized Aquatos would simply devour her. The only way to avoid that would be to remain in her steel skin, which wouldn't stop her from sinking.

Frantic, she dropped her steel skin. Immediately, she felt more buoyant and kicked toward the surface as she pumped her tail furiously. Unfortunately, this was what Aquatos had waited for.

He attacked and savaged her neck with his teeth. When she flung him away with her tail, he kicked at her gut with his hindlegs and drew blood that clouded the clear, cold water. Kristen tried to fight back, but she simply couldn't land a strike. She wasn't used to fighting underwater—hell, compared to Aquatos, she wasn't used to fighting as a dragon. Not only that, it seemed her resilience and staying power weren't at peak either and she realized that perhaps her healing wasn't as complete as she'd thought. Her blows were weak and ineffective and her vision began to collapse when she ran out of air.

Again, the primitive urge for survival pushed through and she thrust through the water with her adversary's jaws locked onto her neck. The two of them burst from the frigid lake and floated in midair above the water, dripping wet. She thrashed and tried to free herself from his claws. Now that she had air, she was able to do so and before he could lunge to take hold of her again, she used her tail to strike him across the back of the head, which effectively curtailed his strike.

No sooner did she do so than both dragons rocketed into the air.

Kristen glanced down at Amy, who pointed the staff the dwarves had given her at them, her eyes glowing red, before they were so high that the action on the ground was blurred and indistinct. Abruptly, the young mage's powers withdrew and the two combatants plunged immediately when gravity took hold.

Thankfully, as a dragon, she didn't fall and was able to glide. Aquatos, however, had no such advantage as his wing was in tatters. He plummeted and flapped the appendages desperately, but the broken one caught no air and the other only sent him into a spin.

He landed head-first and lay unmoving.

The Steel Dragon dove and sliced her tail into the wall of earth above him, loosened the soil into an avalanche, and buried everything but his head.

One was down but there wasn't time to celebrate. Kristen scowled when she noticed that Larry stood with his arms outstretched and a glowing shield of energy between him and Crimson. Amy was behind him and the girl held her head and wiped the blood from her nose. Whatever energy fueled her magic was almost gone. That she'd managed thus far was a testimony to the incredible power she possessed but she couldn't push herself any further or she'd risk... blowing up? That was what Larry had said would happen if she recalled correctly. It was something Kristen couldn't allow, not after everything the two mages had done to help her.

"Get into one of the tunnels!" she roared as she pumped her wings and hurled herself into Crimson.

She struck with the force of a bomb detonating and bulldozed the dragon into one of the sides of the mine.

Larry reacted quickly and used his powers to lift Amy off her feet and float her toward a tunnel. Emberslight moved to intervene, obviously determined not to let them reach safety. Kristen hadn't noticed her—she'd been distracted by Crimson's attempt to incinerate her friends—but the Boston leader had been close and had waited for a moment exactly like this. She swooped behind the two mages, which drew a curse from the Steel Dragon. She might have been able to trap Crimson if she had another few seconds, but she couldn't let Emberslight hurt her allies.

With a roar of fury, she spun after the threat to her friends. The dragon seemed to make a similar calculation—either attack her enemy's ally or play defense—and she made the same choice. She turned in midair and brought her claws up for a vicious strike.

Pain blossomed in her chest. She hadn't put her steel skin up, not because she hadn't thought to but because it made her too slow. Now, she paid for it with her blood.

Emberslight grinned at the wound and redoubled her efforts.

Kristen tried to hang on but her opponent was obviously a strong fighter. Her blows were quick and powerful and her defense impenetrable. When she realized she couldn't defend herself from the onslaught of attacks and keep herself aloft, she landed. Fortunately, this meant she could put her steel skin in place, which she did a moment before Crimson barreled into her back.

Now that she was wrapped in steel once more, she was better able to withstand the combined onslaught. Her confidence increased as well as she was certain the two dragons would have difficulty penetrating her metal shell without the explosive force of a high-caliber bullet behind their dragon claws.

Emberslight struck her with her red-hot claws and unbelievably, they split her steel like a hot knife through butter. Their heat was so intense that they seared the flesh beneath as well.

The pain was indescribable and dragged a reflexive scream from her throat.

"I offer you a surrender," her adversary bellowed. "It would be a shame to lose a dragon such as yourself over a mage. Surrender the two to us and we'll call this duel a draw."

"I would never give my friends to murderers," she retorted.

"But you would give your life for humans?" Crimson said from behind her as he lunged.

Kristen turned to parry the attack but she immediately realized she shouldn't have done so. He could knock her over but he couldn't do much else. By turning, she had exposed her flank to Emberslight, who happily took advantage of the opening.

Once more, hot fire ripped into her as the dragon raked her side.

"They will die no matter what you do," she said. "You fight against the inevitable."

"I fight for justice," she roared and whipped her tail into Emberslight's face.

The blow caught the dragon low on her forehead and the ax-blade sliced her scales and blood poured into one eye.

The Boston SWAT leader backed away and tried to stem the blood. Rather than pursue her, Kristen targeted Crimson.

She turned her full power on the dragon. He was smaller and while he was aggressive, he hadn't demonstrated the discipline and combat skills that came with advanced training. His lack of experience proved crucial and she was able to pummel him with her steel body and batter him significantly to bruise bones and pulverize muscle.

He was winded, she could tell. While she had to finish him, she wouldn't kill him. She was better than that and besides, he hadn't killed anyone. It wouldn't be fair to hold him responsible for trying to do his job, even if he obeyed corrupt laws, but that didn't mean she would let him go free either.

"Now, Amy!" she yelled and looked over Crimson's shoulder.

The dragon followed her gaze and lunged toward the hole into which she had looked. He inhaled to fill it with flame and in that moment, she bulldozed into the back of him and forced him into the hole.

The earth rumbled and the tunnel collapsed on top of him.

Two had been effectively trapped, which would make things a little easier.

Kristen turned to where Amy stood at the entrance of another tunnel. Her concern for the young mage wasn't misplaced as it seemed causing an earthquake large enough to trap a dragon had drained the last of her strength. She collapsed into Larry's arms and he dragged her into the tunnel, then threw a shield up to protect the opening. He checked her pulse and nodded. Both mages were out of the fight, but they were all right.

"This ends with your death, do you understand that?" Emberslight said. She'd taken to the air, having wiped the blood from her eye and apparently cauterized the wound with one of her glowing claws.

"Why? Why can't mages have some of the dignity that dragons have so much of?" she demanded as she took flight as well.

"Because they're less than us! Why should a wolf spare the deer? Why should the spider spare the fly?" Emberslight roared and released a blast of fire.

She retaliated with one of her own and the two flames met above the center of the mine to push and jostle each other as the two dragons struggled for dominance.

Kristen lasted longer, but only barely. It wasn't much of a win, not with Emberslight's powers.

The other dragon understood this as well. She didn't seem perturbed that she'd lost the power struggle and instead, focused on using her own unique powers to bring her the advantage.

When one of her wings began to burn, Kristen realized that Emberslight used her ability to heat objects from afar on her.

She tried to flap away, to get clear and stop the pain, but it seemed impossible. Every time she moved, her adversary simply moved her gaze to follow her. When she thought of eyes, an odd idea crept in. One of them had been covered in blood, which she'd wiped somewhat messily, but despite the fact that she flew above a pool of water, she hadn't cleaned it. Did that mean something or was it merely a dumb coincidence?

It wasn't much to risk an attack on, but she was out of options. She couldn't fight Emberslight in her steel form. The dragon was too fast and her powers seemed almost tailored to work against hers. She couldn't fight her in her regular dragon body either, though. The Bostonian was too fast, too powerful, and too experienced.

But she'd remained dry throughout. If she couldn't use her strengths to beat this dragon, maybe she could use her opponent's weaknesses. Every dragon had to have at least one weakness. Her steel skin made her impervious to bullets and resistant to dragon claws and bites, but she was particularly vulnerable to electricity, magnets, and of course—as heavy as she was—drowning. What kind of weakness would a dragon have if their power enabled them to heat things?

Kristen couldn't think of a better idea to try than a frigid lake. Maybe, if she submerged her attacker in the water, it would drain her powers enough for her to disable her. It was a crazy idea and all the more dangerous since she could barely swim as a dragon, but what choice did she have?

The fact was that she had to try something so she surged toward Emberslight and tried to ignore the burning pain in her wing.

The other dragon simply flew higher. She was faster, at least when they traveled vertically. The problem was that the Steel Dragon was too heavy. No matter how hard she pumped her wings, her foe was able to outpace her. The red dragon flew higher and higher and easily remained focused on her wing, which grew hotter and hotter.

Eventually, Kristen could no longer endure it. She dropped her steel skin to gain speed and—hopefully—stop the burning. Her decision worked on the first point and failed horribly on the second. Immediately, she moved much faster as her wings continued to pump and needed to do less work to carry her mass. Unfortunately, the pain intensified. While the steel was conductive, her flesh was more vulnerable to heat and she felt it like a thousand ant bites in the joint.

She cried out in pain and exhaled a massive flame, not because she'd wanted to but because she hadn't been able to do anything else.

By some stroke of luck, it worked. The fire broke Emberslight's focus and the pain began to dissipate like a finger burned on a frying pan and dunked in a cup of orange juice.

Encouraged, she streaked forward and maintained the flames as long as she could. When she ran out, she blew smoke. As she raced toward her adversary, she twisted, twirled, and spun through the smoky screen to get closer to the other dragon and her bizarre power.

Emberslight let her come. She knew that because when she impacted into the Bostonian, she'd already heated her claws. The red dragon dug them into her attacker's dragon hide and they rent the scales and skin to tear the muscle like it was nothing more than chicken breast.

Kristen resisted the urge to kick her opponent away and instead, bit her neck and turned her skin to steel. She'd hoped that when she did so, the steel would have forced Emberslight's claws out. Perversely, the dragon clung even more tightly to the wounds she'd already inflicted. She didn't withdraw her claws but forced them in deeper, although the hardened skin didn't tear so easily. Instead of the burning hot claws ripping free, they remained dug deep into her flesh.

She clawed at Emberslight as well but didn't have the right angle. All she could do was hold on. Thankfully, that was all she needed to do because gravity took hold and their meteoric rise slowed until they reversed direction.

Despite the somewhat unnerving sense of plunging to her doom, she didn't try to fight it. This was her plan, after all, suicidal though it might be. She had hoped to fall and had achieved what she'd set out to do. She tucked her wings and tried to point her nose to the pool of frigid water at the center of the exposed mine. It wasn't an easy task, given that the two dragons spun head over heels, locked in a deadly embrace.

Emberslight wasn't as comfortable with their rapidly accelerating descent. She tried to flap her wings and stop them, but the Steel Dragon was simply too heavy. The red dragon could lift cars but with her steel skin, Kristen weighed closer to a train's diesel freight engine than a sedan.

Their velocity increased with each passing second. The red dragon's aura shifted from rage to panic. She did not want to hit the ground, although she'd most likely be fine if she fell from this height. Dragons were strong, resilient creatures with healing abilities, but that didn't mean she could withstand something as massive as the heavy steel form that might well crush her on impact. Kristen knew she wouldn't die, while her adversary struggled to avoid being crushed.

Good, she thought as Emberslight tried to yank herself free. *Let her fear being crushed instead of the water.* Of course, it could also indicate that the Bostonian simply wasn't concerned about the lake, which was a troubling thought.

The ground rushed closer and Emberslight finally withdrew her claws and released the Steel Dragon. She spread her wings and tried to flee but she'd miscalculated. Kristen still had her jaws sunk into the back of her neck and when she tried to fly away, she wouldn't release her. She maintained her hold on the dragon's neck and was rewarded when one of the Bostonian's wings snapped from the weight of trying to carry both of them.

She tried to flash her aura at the other dragon to tell her to calm and surrender. With only one wing, there was no way she could defeat the Steel Dragon, but she seemed beyond reason. She flapped with the other one and inch by inch, she pulled them away from the water.

The two dragons collided into the side of the mine with a thump that would register on Richter scales all over Canada. One of Kristen's wrists snapped like kindling and something echoed it in her chest. She hoped it was only a broken or cracked rib.

Emberslight didn't fare much better. She'd landed on the damaged wing and now writhed in pain. Still, she looked at her foe and her eyes glowed. Once again, heat blossomed, this time in her face, and it became hard to breathe.

She lunged forward and barreled into her opponent, hoping to thrust her into the water, but the other dragon held her ground, even against her massive bulk.

"We can stop," she said, not sure if a draw was a possible outcome, although she certainly hoped it was.

"I'll stop when you're dead!" Emberslight roared, then stood on her hind legs and inhaled to release a blast of fire. Kristen put her wings in front of her to protect herself, but she feared this might be the end. Already, the heat from the red dragon was excruciating. Her fire would doubtlessly be hotter, which meant her steel skin would likely melt.

The irate dragon flapped her one good wing and pulled herself higher. Her chest was full and ready to release searing hot dragon flame.

Incongruously, given the heightened tension that came with looking death in the face, a skateboard rolled out of one of the mine tunnels and raced down the hill toward Emberslight.

Kristen would have ignored it—after all, a skateboard compared to a dragon was hardly worth noticing—but something about it demanded her attention. It struck a rock and gained height, spun in a complex maneuver, and landed smoothly to roll directly toward the red dragon. She understood then that Amy was controlling it and also that she would only have one opportunity.

She stepped forward and stationed herself squarely in the middle of Emberslight's blast. The dragon responded by taking the smallest of steps backward. It had no advantage except to position her better for a blast, but the action meant that the skateboard rolled neatly beneath her foot as it settled.

The weight snapped the wood easily, but the metal trucks and wheels proved more durable. When the dragon put more weight on them, she slipped. Instinctively, she flapped her wings to steady herself but of course, one of her wings no longer worked. Her efforts served only to unbalance her even more and she toppled into the frigid water.

Immediately, a great blast of steam rocketed from the lake. It rose dramatically as the surface bubbled and it climbed further until it was high enough to slow and spread into a mushroom cloud of steam.

The water boiled but as the dragon thrashed and kicked, she mixed and churned the deeper layers until the simmering ceased. Emberslight only had so much thermal mass. As hot as she was, she couldn't compare to a frigid Canadian lake.

While she struggled, the water she threw into the air from her heat condensed into a cloud and it began to rain.

Still, the dragon didn't cease her frantic efforts, even though she made no progress at all. She didn't move toward the shore and in fact, did nothing except sink.

Emberslight gulped air before she screamed, "Help!" and sank beneath the surface.

"It's over!" Windlock shouted.

Kristen—despite fighting this dragon seconds before and the fact that she'd been told this was a fight to the death—didn't hesitate for a second. By the time the investigator had finished his statement, she had transformed into her human body and dove into the lake.

She had been prepared for the water to be freezing cold and was pleasantly surprised to find that it was much closer to a warm bath. To think that Emberslight had possessed that much energy was almost unimaginable.

But she had more important priorities than astonishment at another dragon's powers. Quickly, she paddled to where she'd last seen her opponent, took a breath, and dove below the warm water.

Emberslight was barely below the surface and sinking slowly. Her eyes were still open but her movements had become jerky and lethargic. She was running out of air and probably hadn't even known to take a proper breath before she went under. Obviously, this was one dragon who never messed with water. And why should she? With a dragon like Aquatos on her team, she would have been able to leave any aquatic activities to him.

Kristen swam toward her and flexed her aura at the dragon. *Be calm, I'm here to help.* She tried to broadcast what was a fairly familiar emotion for her to create as it was often necessary when working with humans. She swam closer and closer to Emberslight, whose struggles had almost completely stopped.

Cautiously—because there was no way to be sure that her erstwhile adversary had understood her aura and believed her—she swam into position beside her head and caught hold of one of her horns and her chin. She looked into her eyes and willed her to understand that Kristen would save her, but not like this—not wouldn't but couldn't save her like this.

Finally, Emberslight nodded in comprehension. She transformed into her human body in a cloud of sparks that were immediately extinguished by the water.

Kristen moved behind her and took her in a rescue hold—one arm wrapped under both of the other woman's with her head on her shoulder—and swam powerfully to the surface.

She burst into the air—the Canadian summer night now felt chilly after the warm water—and gasped for breath. Emberslight proved she was alive but less dramatically. She sputtered, coughed water, and tried to pull herself up on her rescuer.

Fortunately, she was familiar enough with handling people to be able to deal with the terrified dragon. She pulled her to shore, where Larry waited for her. He caught Emberslight by her lapels and she popped out of the water. For a moment, Kristen thought he possessed some measure of strength she wasn't aware of before she realized that he'd simply used magic to haul her out.

Wearily, she climbed out of the pool, sat beside Emberslight, and tried to catch her breath.

Windlock circled in his dragon form, landed, and transformed into a human.

"You did it, Kristen. You won this duel. Legally, Amy is under your protection."

"Great," she managed to respond between gasps of air. "Does this mean I can take a nap?"

She remained conscious long enough for him to nod before she passed out beside the dragon who'd tried to kill her.

CHAPTER FIFTY

Kristen opened her eyes in Le Face De Beouf. She would only ever be able to describe it as a Snow-White moment because she woke on a table with dwarves all around her.

"Huzzah! The Steel Dragon ends her slumber," Alp called and the restaurant roared with whoops and cheers.

A dwarf helped her from a table and asked if she'd like to sit at a booth. It was another surreal moment. These seemed to be more and more common in her life, though, so she took this one stride and nodded.

He grinned and led her to one in the back of the restaurant where Windlock, Larry, and Amy were seated around half-finished plates of food.

"Lady Steel, you're awake." Brockton grinned and stood quickly. He was in his regular robes with no more dwarf boots, breastplate, or gloves, although it looked like he had argued to keep the staff with its twining silver wire and the brightly colored hat. She liked the pom-pom on top.

"Nice to see you up, Kristen." Windlock smiled warmly and stood so she could sit in the middle rather than at the end. She appreciated the gesture as it let her see the entire restaurant and also out into the desolate parking lot. It was far preferable to have eyes on everything given how she'd been on the receiving end of more than one surprise attack.

"Hi, Kristen," Amy said and smiled broadly.

Kristen smiled in response. The girl had kept her leather vest but returned the rest of her borrowed armor. She wore a baseball cap with the image of a grizzly bear skateboarding on a salmon. Not only that, but she'd also left her staff resting near the edge of the booth. Apparently, the mages liked the devices.

"Thanks for saving me back there. The skateboard was a stroke of genius," she said.

"Oh, that wasn't me," Amy said and laughed. "I've never had a board that nice. I wouldn't have thought to send it out there and let it get crushed. Plus, I was completely unconscious at that point."

"Then who?"

"Guilty!" Larry beamed.

"I didn't know you had that kind of range," she said.

"That's because I didn't. But now..." He raised his wrist. No bracelet adorned it so he was still unfettered. "There are some real perks to being a free mage."

"And to working with one," she said warmly.

"And to acquiring one of your own to protect," Windlock added and lifted his glass. "Or was it two?" The investigator darted a look at Brockton and looked both guilty and nervous.

Larry looked abashed. "Aw, don't be that way, you old bag of wind. In a fight, I'll always want to side with the Steel Dragon, especially if it's against bullshit dragons who lost their minds like those from Boston SWAT. But that doesn't mean I'm gonna ditch you."

Kristen hadn't thought she'd ever compare a dragon to a sad puppy, but Windlock's expression reminded her of nothing more in that moment.

"I've kind of grown fond of you over the years," the mage added.

"I feel the same way," the investigator said.

"Plus there's the fact that you would be absolutely lost without me. Can you even imagine old Windlock here bumbling about a crime scene on his own? Amy could have made it all the way to Nova Scotia without you catching her. You wouldn't last a day without me."

"I don't know about all that," his boss harrumphed but his smile was broad.

"If it comes down to it, I'd appreciate being freed again for a fight like this, but if we gotta do this in the meantime, I'm happy to be your mage." Brockton held his wrist out for the dragon to put the dampening cuff on it.

Windlock nodded, retrieved the cuff, and held it between two fingers while he stared at the light from the restaurant reflected on its silver surface. He moved it toward the mage, then apparently thought better of it. His fingers changed to dragon scales and he crushed it in his hand. It emitted a tiny burst of magic as if to protest its destruction before it became nothing but a sliver of silver.

"Did you get the shakes or something, old man?" Larry asked although he grinned from ear to ear.

"There's been enough of that," the investigator said, almost as if he spoke only to himself. "Brockton—no, Larry—I've known you for years. You've never been anything but the best partner a dragon could ask for. I trust you with my life, and after watching what you did to help Kristen, I'd be a fool to leave you cuffed. You could help me far more if you are free than if you're not."

"I thought mages had to be shackled?" Brockton said.

"To hell with the rules on this one." Windlock smiled. "That is if Kristen and Amy can keep the secret?"

The girl laughed.

Kristen smiled. "You know I won't put one of those things on Amy. Of course I'll keep your secret. Personally, I'm glad to see more dragons finally coming around to seeing humans as beings worthy of respect and friendship."

"The friendship one I think I knew, but you're right about the respect. Larry, I should have shown you far more of it much sooner."

The mage waved the apology away. "You always pay for my lunch. I know that's because you're barely worthy of my magnanimous friendship and that you're only trying to prove yourself deserving of the greatness that is Larry Brockton, world-class mage."

"Whatever you say, Larry." Windlock smiled.

After that, the conversation was mostly about the battle and Kristen's victory. The dwarves were all impressed that a dragon and two mages had defeated three dragons, and all thought her broken wrist and bruised ribs were fair prices given the magnitude of the triumph. She disagreed at first, but as the hearty dwarf food filled her belly and her dragon powers used the nourishment to mend her bones, she thought maybe they were right. It occurred to her that while her healing had increased in pace, her body hadn't fully overcome the debilitating effects of the dragon-based bomb. Thankfully, it had progressed to the point where she had fought three dragons and won but it had been a close call. She had sensed that she hadn't battled at peak so maybe a little more time off was called for. The unexpected combat, although necessary, might have set her back and it would be foolish to comprise the progress she had made.

More importantly, though, the battle meant she had struck a blow for not only Amy's freedom but for humankind as a whole. The young mage—whether Kristen liked it or not—had killed two dragons in self-defense and would now walk free. Windlock had assured her of that. Although many dragons might—hell, would most definitely—hold a grudge, they couldn't do anything about it, not if they wanted to respect the rules of their own kind. She still wanted to tear those rules down and build a more equitable system, but it felt extremely satisfying in the short term to use the rules that had been designed to protect dragons to protect a mage—one who deserved protection, unlike Constance.

She asked what had happened to the two buried dragons and the investigator explained that while the dwarves had transported Amy and Kristen to the restaurant, he and Brockton had excavated them, woken them, explained in simple terms that they'd lost, and sent them on their way. They hadn't been in any condition to protest and even if they had legally been allowed to fight, they weren't able to physically. Neither Aquatos nor Emberslight had healed enough to fly, so they left in their human forms on Crimson's back, their auras reeking of disgrace.

Once their meal was finished, they thanked the dwarves and headed into the parking lot. Kristen had asked the dwarves if she should try to send Timeflash to fix everything and restore it to the way it had been, but they wouldn't have any of it. Apparently, they rather liked working with stone and laying asphalt counted as stonework to them.

There was the issue of the wrecked cars, but Windlock assured them that the Dragon Council would cover the damages, and this seemed to mollify the community. They said they'd rather have the cash for the humans and dwarves in their community to get new vehicles than magic repairs that probably wouldn't work on internal combustion engines anyway.

Once that was settled, the two dragons transformed.

Windlock cleared his throat as Larry climbed onto his back. "I'll head to the Dragon Council. No doubt the Boston Team will report this whole escapade—as is their right and their duty—but I want to make sure all facets of these events are correctly reported."

Kristen nodded. "Do you think it'll be all right? I mean, you didn't tell them that we intended to pursue our target to Canada. Didn't that break protocol?"

He shrugged. "It did, but I'll take the blame for that decision. I asked you to come in on this investigation because I respect your insights. In fact, without those insights, there's no way we would have brought this to a close with so few casualties. I'll make it clear that the intel was yours but the decision was mine. You have nothing to worry about."

She was momentarily stunned into silence. Had he really said that there hadn't been many casualties on this mission despite the fact that four dragons were killed? Detroit had gone into a frenzy of paranoia when dragons were assassinated one by one. She couldn't imagine what losing four within forty-eight hours would have done to the community of dragons in the Motor City. Windlock saying there hadn't been many casualties could only mean he referenced the fact that no human, mage, or dwarf lives were lost. It was a welcome viewpoint, in her perspective.

"Do you think I need to come?" she asked.

Windlock shook his head firmly. "Absolutely not. I'll handle this. The Dragon Council will already be…let's say upset at what happened here. If you arrived with your…er, bombastic style of arguing, I'm not sure it'd be helpful."

"What he's trying to say is that he needs you far enough away to let this blow over," Larry translated.

"And that's fine with me," she replied.

The investigator nodded and leapt into the air. He pumped his wings to gain height, made a few circles above the parking lot, and headed south toward the United States and out of dwarf country.

"Where will we go?" Amy asked.

"Well, for starters, I don't want you to think you have to do what I say. I want us to be equals, Amy, and I'm not saying that because I know you can rip a forest up and pummel me," Kristen said.

"Hey, it's no problem. I'm your mage and you're my dragon. You saved me from those dragons. As far as I'm concerned, you're the boss."

Kristen smiled. "I'm glad to hear it. In that case, if it's all right with you, I thought we'd go past Rangeley first and check on your folks. Your mom was worried about you—worried enough to lie to a dragon, which can't be easy."

"She didn't!" the girl exclaimed in horror.

"She did. Not that I blame her. Dragons are scary and she did what she had to do to protect you from them."

"I suppose so." The young mage took a deep breath and climbed onto her back.

It took a moment for her to settle with her legs astride in a secure position directly in front of her wings. "Are you ready?"

"Sure. If I slip, I'll use my powers to hold on tight."

"Right, of course." She took flight with extra care to make the transition as smooth as possible. Some pushing resulted when Amy needed to keep herself anchored firmly on her back, but after a few miles of flight, the girl relaxed and the sensation faded.

"So what happens after Rangeley?" her passenger asked. "For some reason, I can't imagine the Steel Dragon staying around for the quilting group and foregoing her job in Detroit."

"No, not really. Actually, I hoped you'd come to the Motor City with me. You have to see it. I grew up there, of course, and know all the best places. Have you ever had Detroit-style pizza?"

The girl laughed at her enthusiasm. "Is that deep dish or something?"

"Ew. Of course not. Detroit pizza has cheese in the crust and is cooked on top of a steel pan so it's crispy. Cut into squares...ugh, I can't begin to describe it. You'll have to taste it for yourself. My team will want to meet you too."

Amy was quiet for a moment before she said, "Since I'll be working for a dragon, does that mean some of my expenses will be covered? I don't want to be rude but I had just bought that skateboard."

She laughed. "Yeah, we can get it replaced. Oh, shit. I guess if you come to work for me, you'll need a salary too."

"Uh...yeah, that is normally how these things work."

"Don't worry. I know the perfect mage to resolve all this. The man loves paperwork. He has tattoos to help him do it faster."

"You're the boss," the girl quipped as they soared over the forest in a southerly direction toward home.

Kristen couldn't help but think that her world had become a little larger. Amy represented the first member of a coalition of people who might undo the mess human-dragon relations had become. And with the young mage at her side, she felt they might be able to show the world that they were a force worth respecting.

CHAPTER FIFTY-ONE

Kristen Hall loved the feeling of the wind beneath her wings. Her body thrummed with a sense of freedom, life, and power.

Apparently, Amy Williams liked it too and held on with only her knees. Her arms were probably outstretched—she couldn't feel the girl's hands clasped anywhere—and she would no doubt have a grin on her face. She couldn't see her, of course, since the mage was on her back while she was flying, but her aura communicated sheer happiness.

"Better than first-class, huh?" the Steel Dragon said.

"I'll say!" her passenger responded enthusiastically. She was braver than she had first appeared. When they'd first met, she'd been scared and meek despite her unimaginably powerful telekinetic powers. Not that anyone could blame her as she'd been hunted by dragons at the time.

The girl on her back felt like a different person—a woman, not a girl, she thought despite the fact they were both young.

"I flew when I tried to escape the dragons," Amy said and it seemed that talking about the events of only two days before no longer bothered her. "On the car hood, obviously, so it wasn't like this. My powers let me fly but…I don't know, it's kind of like being on an electric scooter compared to being on a skateboard, you know?"

"Uh…not really, but I think I maybe understand. Dragons use wings to fly, while you merely blasted yourself through the air. Does this feel more natural?"

"Much more." Amy laughed. "I guess when I was on my makeshift magic carpet, I blocked the wind somehow because I hardly felt it. It wasn't anything like this. I can even feel it between my fingers."

"Yeah, speaking of which, do you mind holding on? I'm not exactly the best flyer." They were close to Detroit, and the last thing she wanted to do was drop her new mage and splat her against the side of a skyscraper. Although given Amy's power, the building might be in more danger than the woman. She couldn't be sure but also had no inclination to try it.

"I can catch myself, remember? Plus, I'm using my powers to stay anchored to you."

"Right." Kristen nodded and decided to test those powers. She tucked her wings and dove toward the Capital Square Building, the headquarters for Dragon SWAT. Sure enough, despite the fact that her speed increased rapidly, the girl remained firmly stuck to her back. A yip of joy as they plummeted toward the roof of the building clearly showed that rather than any nervousness, she actually loved the experience.

The dragon spread her silvery wings, diminished her speed, and settled with her four legs on the roof of the building. Before she could even kneel to let Amy off, the mage simply jumped and slowed herself with her magic before she landed smoothly.

Apparently, she couldn't use her telekinetic powers on herself but she could use them on anything else, including her shoes, which meant she could basically fly. Kristen never thought she'd be jealous of someone's powers—there wasn't another dragon on the planet who could turn their skin to steel—but she couldn't help wondering what it would be like to fly in her human form.

"Once you get me a new skateboard, you'll have to let me drop off your back into a pool or something."

"It's not exactly a priority right now," she said and tried to remain serious. Was this what it had been like for all the senior officers who had tried to train her? She'd never been one for protocol either, although for Amy, this didn't seem to be about rules or regulation. The girl was simply a former adrenaline junkie turned office worker who had come into magic powers less than a week before. Of course she was ready to relive her glory days. And tempting though it was to give her the opportunity to do so, she knew they wouldn't have the time. Not with the pressure building between human and dragon culture.

It was fortunate that their last confrontation had taken place in Canada. If it got out that dragons had battled humans and died in the process…well, she didn't want to think about what could and probably would happen.

"Come on, Amy. Let's meet the team." Before she could lead the mage inside, another dragon landed on the roof and this one also carried a mage on his back.

"Well, if it isn't my two favorite ladies of law enforcement. Here I was, thinking we wouldn't see you for a few weeks or so but you're back in the saddle already."

"Brockton, off my back, please."

"Right, boss." Larry Brockton grinned and climbed off Investigator Windlock's back.

"Investigator," Kristen blurted, suddenly anxious. "I didn't expect to see you so soon. How did your meeting with the Dragon Council go?" It took everything in her power not to look at her mage, who had been the subject of that meeting. The young woman had killed two dragons with her powers and another two had died from human-made weapons while pursuing her. If history was any indication, Amy should be dead already.

"I made a few compromises." Windlock began slowly.

"By that, he means no one will be happy about it," Larry interjected, obviously unable to help himself.

"They weren't happy about us taking Amy in like we did," the investigator clarified.

"You mean alive?" Kristen growled. She would have liked to avoid saying such things in front of the girl, but she couldn't help herself. The issue had nagged at her constantly over the last few days and her nervousness had been exacerbated by a very real sense of protectiveness that had slowly assumed an aggressive edge. She simply could not accept a policy that enforced the death penalty even if people had acted in self-defense, no matter where it originated or who it was applied to.

Windlock understood her anger and also felt it from her aura, and he held his hands up in a placatory gesture. "I don't agree with the policy, Kristen," he reminded her calmly. "You helped me to see how flawed it is, but the reality is that most dragons still do. They weren't happy, but when I explained that you took her on as your mage, some of them felt better about it."

"Because the old bag of wind reminded them that you saved their scaly butts at that party here in Detroit," Brockton said with a grin.

"Indeed." The Investigator nodded. "Which means I might also have inadvertently used up some of your favors, but I can't be sure. The end result, however, is that those who feel they owe you their life were willing to give her a chance as long as you took responsibility."

"And those who didn't?" she inquired pointedly, her tone clipped. Part of her knew she was being unreasonable. She reminded herself firmly that he had, after all, approached the council on her behalf to make sure the reports that had been submitted by the other dragons were fair and accurate.

"Well, I pointed out that she was your mage—"

"I don't like that either, by the way. My mage. Like she's a possession," Kristen snapped. She regretted it immediately, of course, but was so damn irritated and had stewed on the matter long enough to have worked herself up about it. But, while she needed a way to vent that, she shouldn't take it out on someone who'd proven to be a good friend.

Windlock sighed and she could tell he tried not to roll his eyes. She knew he felt like she did—and the guilt over her snark made her irritation worse—but it was so frustrating to hear the repercussions of dragon culture voiced by the people she thought of her closest allies even though she knew they had no choice.

"I can't believe I'm the one saying this, Kristen, but let the man speak," Brockton said.

She clenched her teeth and nodded.

"When I pointed out that she's now technically yours, the dragons who don't support you saw that this could work in their favor."

"How's that?" Amy asked.

"Well, Kristen will be legally responsible for any of your actions as a mage. Which ostensibly means that she'll be responsible for anything you do."

The girl shrugged. "So? The last thing I want to do is hurt anyone. I'm with Kristen on this. The way to a better world is not through battling dragons. I don't want to pick a fight with anyone."

"That's good to hear," Windlock said and uttered something that might have been a snort-laugh before he smiled. "But what I referred to was the implication of collateral damage. You'll be financially responsible for her as well, Kristen. That means damages."

"Collateral? What's he talking about?" Amy turned to the Steel Dragon, who groaned when she realized a negative consequence she hadn't considered.

"What he means is that normally, when dragons or mages cause damage, the Dragon Council makes someone pay for it. Those dragons who destroyed your parents' home both had estates, and even though they're dead, their estates have to pay for it. If you break anything, I'll be charged."

"Oh, uh…how big is your estate?" the girl asked with a crooked grin.

Kristen snorted. "I live in a one-bedroom apartment and fly to work to save money on gas. My parents live in a house in the suburbs. I think the most valuable thing they own is a couch. So, uh…please don't break anything expensive, okay?"

"No problem." Amy forced a smile.

"There are clauses about all this, of course," Windlock added. "Let's get you both to the Paper Dungeon to start working on the paperwork and make all this official."

"The Paper Dungeon?" she asked Kristen as the investigator led them down to the third floor.

"Trust me, it's even worse than it sounds," she told her but didn't answer any further questions. Maybe it was kind of mean but she really wanted to see how she reacted when she saw it.

The mage didn't disappoint her. The elevator door opened to let them off, but her mouth opened almost as wide.

In front of them stood a dozen desks covered in forms, inkwells, and quills made of feathers in various stages of decay. As crazy as that was, the real impact of the Paper Dungeon lay in the fact that mages filled out all the paperwork for every dragon action in the Midwest using only telekinetic powers. Quills dipped themselves in ink before they completed documents that then rolled themselves up and deposited themselves near hot wax and a stamp. Coffee cups, snacks, and post-it notes of gossip floated about as well, adding to the sense of chaos.

In the middle of it all stood a man in a blue robe decorated with elaborate black embroidery. The blue sleeves of the garment ended at hands tattooed with swirls as elaborate as the embroidery. His head and face were also tattooed.

"Amy, this is Atramento, our head mage," Kristen said as the man joined them.

He took one look at Amy's bare wrist and sucked his teeth in disapproval. "I'd ask why you're here but it's obvious. Is she yours or Windlock's?"

"Is that really necessary?" she asked. "Can't she be an independent contractor or something?"

Atramento stared for a moment before his breath caught. "Really necessary? You truly don't realize how much of your education you missed out on by not spending the time you should have with me in the Paper Dungeon. Really necessary? What a question!" He shook his head and began to wiggle his fingers in arcane gestures.

"Where are you from?" Amy asked, no doubt noticing his accent.

"He's from Detroit like me," Kristen said. "And your real name's Jose Mendoza, not Atramento."

The mage scowled but when he replied, his accent was less pronounced than it had been. "I studied abroad. That was a big part of my life." Rather than elaborate further, he held his hands out and papers began to stack up as if some invisible intern put them in place one by one.

Kristen was tempted to tease him further, but when she noticed the growing pile of paperwork in his hands, she didn't dare.

"You'll need to provide me with proof of citizenship, proof of residence, and blood type."

"Blood type?" Amy asked, dumbfounded.

"It's all in the forms, dear," Atramento said and one rocketed from the stack and landed in her hands.

"She doesn't have a place of residence yet," Kristen said.

He sighed but she knew the mage enough to hear the pleasure in it. Silently beckoned, another stack of papers appeared from the maelstrom that was the Paper Dungeon. "This is a temporary residence form. Fill that out with your master's address and reference it in the form. If there were any collateral damages during her acquisition, we'll need to deal with those now as well."

"Those have been taken care of by my account," Windlock said.

Atramento frowned as part of the pile left his hands to return to wherever it had come from.

"But from here on out, any damages will be on Lady Steel," the investigator added.

"Excellent." The mage smiled and sent a form into Kristen's hands for her to complete.

She made the mistake of trying to read it. "Damages to be paid in gold, heifers, or equivalent value?"

"Currency or food. It's plain enough, don't you think?" He whisked the form away from her as soon as she'd affixed her signature to it.

She would only ever be able to describe what followed as a literal whirlwind of paperwork. It was a good thing Windlock was there, as he and Brockton were able to explain some of the finer points of the contracts to the two women and let them gloss over the rest. Atramento didn't seem too happy that they didn't read every word of every form but he didn't protest. She felt she could trust Windlock and that she didn't have much choice. It was either trust him or die of starvation and a broken wrist from signing so much.

"Are there any damages that need to be remediated on behalf of the mage?" Atramento asked.

"I already took care of your parents' house," Windlock replied.

Amy piped up with a smile. "My skateboard broke and I'll need a new one. Trucks, bearings, and wheels too."

Kristen hadn't realized how much Atramento had controlled with his telekinetic powers of bureaucracy until the statement made him pause. All the papers they'd looked at, signed, and completed stopped in midair as he turned to appraise her.

"Your…skateboard?"

"Yeah, it's…uh, like a tiny, flat wooden car without an engine. You ride on top of it. Mine was trashed by a dragon."

Atramento darted a look at Windlock through the room of frozen papers and pens, who nodded. It was a good thing the papers were between Atramento and Larry because he proved how different from the master of the Paper Dungeon he was. He laughed so hard he wheezed and tears streamed down his cheeks.

"I suppose we can always fill out an itemized form… I don't think we have a section for…skateboards."

"A gift card to a skate shop is totally fine, too, by the way," Amy said cheerfully. "If you're worried I'll spend your doubloons or whatever on something less valuable than a new skateboard."

"Less valuable?" Atramento muttered before he went back to his work and all the documents resumed their motion.

Not much else slowed the process until the very end. They were all seated at the table, the two women's fingers stained with ink and their wrists aching, when Atremento used his powers to bring forth a dark-brown envelope sealed with red wax. He deposited it in Kristen's hands.

"Everything is filed and you are ready to present her with her…

uh…" Despite being the mage who most enthusiastically embraced dragons' rules, he didn't clarify what he meant. He merely jiggled the silver bracelet on his wrist.

She took the envelope and opened it. Inside was a bracelet almost identical to the one on the head mage's wrist. She took it out and marveled that something that looked so light and flimsy could limit magic so completely. From experience, she knew that if she put the bracelet on, she'd no longer be able to take her dragon form. It would limit Amy, although not completely.

"Do we have to?" The girl moaned.

"Indeed. None of this is official until you attach the bracelet. In fact, I have another couple of forms to fill out to prove that you accepted it and demonstrated that you know how to clasp it and thus…shackle the mage." Atremento was smiling at the prospect of more paperwork but he shuddered when he mentioned the shackle.

"All right then," Kristen said. "Let's do this." To Amy, she mouthed the words "For now." She had no intention to leave it on her but it was obvious that it had to be done to ensure that the girl had her legal protection until they could find a way around it.

With deep inner reluctance, she took the bracelet and wound it around the young mage's wrist. Amy smiled and it seemed the power of the bracelet had no effect on her until the clasp snapped shut.

As soon as the tiny snick was heard, the girl sagged. She looked like someone had placed a fifty-pound sack of grain on her shoulders or a plant that had suddenly dried up. It was as if most of the vitality that gave her life had been drawn out of her to leave only a residual flutter, barely enough to keep her alive.

"I'd use my powers to throw you at a window for this, but I don't think I can," Amy mumbled.

"Indeed not," Atramento confirmed. "The primary purpose of the cuff is to make it impossible for you to use magic against your dragon master. Your powers are limited too, of course, but you'll get used to the feeling before too long."

"He's right about that," Larry said. For once, there was no humor in his voice. "If you wear that too long, you'll forget what you're really capable of."

Kristen noticed that Windlock's mage kept his sleeves extended as far down his hands as he could. He didn't want to reveal that the investigator had removed his cuff. Despite the master of the Paper Dungeon being a mage and not a dragon, he seemed more loyal to the dragon hierarchy of power than most people, either human or dragon. Which made Kristen wonder.

"Who put your cuff on, Atramento?" she asked.

His face tightened. "I'd rather not say. It's a rather complex situation."

"Tell her," Windlock said.

He seemed to struggle internally before he acquiesced to the command. "At first, it was merely a mid-level bureaucrat who worked for the Dragon Council, but he was killed in a duel over missing paperwork. By then, the Dragon Council had realized who really managed their office. I was made a Master of Papers in a ceremony performed by the Council itself on behalf of all dragon kind."

"You mean..." Amy's voice caught. She took a deep breath and continued. "You mean you can't do anything against any dragon in North America?"

Atramento nodded stiffly before he replied. "Neither can you unless the Steel Dragon orders it."

"That seems harsh," the girl said.

"It is an honor. Now, if there's nothing else. I have paperwork to file on your behalf." He pushed himself from his seat and retreated into the maze of shelves and flying paper that was his kingdom.

"I'm sorry. I didn't mean to make him mad," Amy said. "It's only...I feel this awful weight on me. I can't imagine how long he's lived with it."

Kristen shrugged and bit back the response she would like to have made. She didn't think it was because both Atramento and Amy—mages she knew personally. The entire practice sickened her and not because it was dragons controlling humans. She would feel the same about any injustice, no matter who the perpetrators and the victims were.

Her recent adventure with Windlock and Brockton had shown her, however, that things weren't always black or white. She'd promised herself on the journey from Rangeley that she would try to temper her responses and learn as much as she could about a situation before she made hasty judgments. It required ongoing effort. She had already overreacted earlier, so obviously, there was a fair amount of work still required.

This particular situation, however, seemed utterly irreconcilable, no matter how anyone looked at it. How could people imprison others in their own bodies because of a few bad actors? It seemed inhumane, unnecessary, and—if she felt patriotic—un-American. How could they deny so many people their freedom? It was also troubling what people endured when confronted with power beyond their ability to resist.

She vowed to deal with it later—both the cuff and the system at large—but she was no longer the naïve girl she'd once been. Yes, she had some hard learning ahead but she knew better than to remove the device in dragon SWAT headquarters, especially if putting it on in the first place was what afforded the mage protection.

Fortunately, she didn't have to explain her reasoning to the girl yet. As they strolled to the elevators, Stonequest came down the stairs.

He pushed the door open without looking up. His broad shoulders and tall frame sagged and he shook his head, looking tired and worn.

"Stonequest! Hey, are you all right?" she asked quickly.

If her boss was surprised to see her, he didn't show it. Instead, he looked at her, raised a heavy eyebrow, and said simply, "You're back."

"Yeah. I arrived earlier and filed the paperwork for my new...uh, mage. This is Amy Williams."

"Hi," the dragon said. He didn't look surprised to see her, nor did he seem surprised that Kristen had introduced him to a mage. She had vaguely thought that might be significant.

"You don't look so hot, Stone. Shouldn't you still be on leave?" she asked.

"Shouldn't you also be on leave instead of out there disrupting dragon society?" Stonequest replied in a voice that was barely more civil than a growl.

She didn't know exactly what he was talking about but winced as a pang of cold dread stabbed into her gut. Worry and gloom radiated from her boss. He must have held it in, but now that he saw her, he'd released the hold he'd had over it. His aura churned the emotions out like waves during a thunderstorm on Lake Michigan.

"What exactly do you mean?" Kristen asked. She tried to force a smile and only managed to make herself feel even more awkward. "Has something happened?"

He merely shook his head and turned his back to her, then gestured for her to follow him up the stairs. "You might as well bring the whole gang. This isn't an order, Investigator Windlock, but I have a feeling you'll want to see this as well."

CHAPTER FIFTY-TWO

They walked up two flights of stairs to the fifth floor, then into the gym. Kristen couldn't help but smile when she saw her Dragon SWAT team assembled. They all stood in a rough semicircle and looked as strong and tough as ever. John Emeraldeyes was there and his green eyes sparkled, his face framed by dark dreadlocks. Lumos stood beside him and twirled his elaborate mustache. Erin Timeflash was the only one of the team who gave the newcomers a smile. The other two looked far too worried.

"Are you guys all right?" Kristen asked.

"Fuck no," Heartsbane said and looked out from behind Erin.

Seeing her made Kristen's heart drop. Her face was still a mess and the memories surged painfully. The last time she had seen her teammate outside a hospital was in this very room. She'd opened a box that had been an explosive made with dragon pieces. Her injuries had been extensive, and she'd been hospitalized, as had Stonequest after he'd been shot trying to get her to safety. Heartsbane did not look like she was ready to check out of the hospital yet, let alone report for duty.

"What's going on, you guys?" Kristen asked and noticed for the first time that the entire team was gathered around a TV, of all things. That alone was weird. There were TVs in the gym, of course. She had never seen one that didn't have TV, but her team was far more focused on their form and training maneuvers to watch. They didn't even watch sports when they worked out, yet they'd formed a rough semicircle around the screen and their gazes darted to it continually. They barely seemed to notice that she'd arrived with the investigator and a brand-new mage.

"Do you have any idea how much trouble you caused?" Stonequest asked and looked first at Kristen and then at Windlock. That was also strange. The investigator far outranked Stonequest, and the SWAT leader was a dragon who went by the book. She didn't think she had ever seen him address a superior that way. Hell, he practically bit her head off every time she did it and questioning orders was like second nature for the Steel Dragon.

"If you're talking about us saving Amy's life, you're out of your mind if you think I'll apologize—" she began before Windlock silenced her with a look that clearly told her to shut up and let him handle it.

"Stonequest, I should have told you I had requisitioned one of your officers, but you were out of commission so I took Steel. That's well within my right as an investigator."

"It's not about her going but about what you did."

"Everything we did was handled according to proper procedures. I had seniority on that case and filed the appropriate paperwork with the Dragon Council to clarify any decisions I made that might have seemed inappropriate to anyone not involved. Is this about something the Boston Team said?"

"No. They didn't say anything."

"Then what exactly is this about?" Windlock demanded. "Kristen handled herself very well. No lives were lost because of her actions, and I think we might very well have prevented a war. She displayed exceptional insight and…" Windlock trailed off when Stonequest held up a hand to signal to him to stop talking.

It impressed Kristen that the investigator listened. Many a superior officer would have steamrolled an underling who dared such a gesture while they were speaking. Her dad—a career police officer—

had many stories about bosses messing up cases simply because they wouldn't listen. It seemed Windlock wasn't one of those.

"I'm not saying she didn't handle herself well. The Steel Dragon always has done her very best and more than the job demands."

Despite Stonequest's tired face and the lackluster delivery of the compliment, it still filled her with a warm glow to know the dragon thought of her that way. Lately, she'd worked more with Windlock, but Stonequest was the first dragon to actually treat her as an equal rather than a curiosity—or worse, something to be manipulated as a tool to hurt mankind. But if he felt that way about her and didn't doubt her actions, what the hell was this all about? Ever forthright, she asked him.

He gestured to the TV. Emerald nodded and pointed at the screen with the remote control—which reminded her of her mom for the briefest of moments because he didn't really need to point it. It was a habit of people who'd been around before televisions had remote control and a reminder that all the dragons in this room were at least a century old.

Emerald then proved himself more capable than her mother Marty because he manipulated a digital video recording menu without difficulty and pressed play as Stonequest began to speak.

"This is a recording, obviously, but parts of it are playing over and over on most major news networks right now."

It was footage of the battle in Canada, and judging by the quality of the video, it had to have either been a news crew or a very dedicated amateur. Kristen watched herself battle the three dragons from Boston SWAT above the asbestos mine near the city of Thetford Mines in Canada in stunning high definition.

"I don't understand. Windlock, you said this was a sanctioned duel and that we were following rules. Is it because the mages intervened that it's a problem?"

"No. Dragons have always been able to use their mages and humans to help them in a duel. Stonequest, what's the problem?"

"Watch."

Before the fight between the dragons reached its dramatic conclusion, the new network cut to the two news anchors, who discussed how the battle started and what the repercussions were. Below them, in the lower-left quarter of the screen, an inset played the battle at the dwarven restaurant where she'd finally managed to talk to Amy.

She watched as Timbergust's chest erupted beneath a barrage of dragon bullets and the quality of the recording captured the moment in vivid and gory detail. The camera cut to where Bronzeback was impaled by two telephone poles before he too was killed by a storm of dragon bullets. Even in the small viewing area in the corner of the screen, the footage made it as plain as day that the dragon had died from gunshot wounds. An argument could possibly be made that Bronzeback had been the victim of a magic attack, but Timbergust's death was unquestionably caused by gunfire.

"Show her again, please," Stonequest said and Emerald obliged.

He paused the video, then rewound it to the point where Timbergust was killed. It was painfully clear what had killed him and Kristen swallowed. The entire planet—every human, dragon, dwarf, and pixie —knew that guns couldn't hurt dragons. Perhaps, if one fired again and again, you might hurt it, but their bodies didn't react like a human's did.

Until now.

On the screen was incontrovertible evidence that humans could now kill dragons.

"But…I… Okay, they were talking during this part. Maybe people didn't notice," Kristen said and felt foolish even as she spoke.

Stonequest shook his head, his expression grim. "We recorded this a few hours ago because it was the first time any of us had seen it. Since then, the news team that recorded it has released the footage to every major news channel. From what we have ascertained, it was a woman out of Maine."

"She followed us?" Kristen asked and he clenched his teeth so hard she hoped he wouldn't crack a tooth. "I should have known that sneaky reporter was too damn accommodating. Bitch."

"Regardless, she shared it," Timeflash said. "And apparently angered the corporate structure at her company when she did so, but she felt she had to. There's an interview with her but what matters is that every channel has dissected this footage. Most of the cable news networks are focused on the dragon battle part on account of the…uh, fireworks, you could say, but some of the smaller outfits have already zeroed in on what happened to Timbergust."

"Can we get them to stop?" Kristen asked weakly.

"The word is out," Stonequest said with finality. "Everything I've done to try to keep this under wraps for the last few months has all been undone. The world might not know it yet, but they will very soon. Within twenty-four hours, everyone will be aware that someone has guns capable of killing dragons."

CHAPTER FIFTY-THREE

"But what does that really mean?" Kristen asked a little desperately. "People used to kill dragons in medieval times, right? Two wars were fought in which people killed dragons. How bad can this be?"

"This is way worse," Heartsbane interjected. "The last time dragons fought people, there weren't nukes or weapons like these. Good job, Kristen. You might have started the apocalypse."

Stonequest silenced her with a gesture. "It's not the Steel Dragon's fault." He shook his head. "Kristen had an idea of what these techno-mages were long before anyone else did. If we had put more resources behind this, maybe we could have stopped them before they arrived there."

"You didn't call them in, did you?" Heartsbane snarled.

"Melissa!" Timeflash said and earned a scowl from her teammate. She was not a fan of her first name, and Erin knew it.

"We had no idea," Windlock said. "In fact, I had thought we had done a good job of laying a false trail, as we were concerned that the mage might draw the technomage's attention."

"I have a name, you know," Amy said, her tone both polite and sharp.

"Yeah, we know all about you," Emerald replied, his voice a low rumble. "The mage who killed two dragons without even trying. You'd better stay away from social media. There are pages and pages of fan sites all about you."

"And as many wishing you were dead," Heartsbane added.

No one snapped at her, which Kristen took to mean that it must be true.

"I know you didn't intend this, Kristen," Stonequest continued, "but I also want you to see the repercussions of your actions."

"And how would you have wanted me to do this differently? Maybe I could have let them slaughter Amy? Of course, the problem with that is she was way more powerful than those dragons so she would have killed more of them. Not only that, Windlock was with me the entire time. I didn't do anything without his approval."

"She's right," the investigator said and seized the opportunity to redirect the conversation. "Lady Steel was entirely by the book during the operation. There's no point in rehashing the past. It could have gone better, sure. We could have all sat down and sang together. But it could have gone worse as well. I'm not sure if you saw how close we were to igniting tensions between dragons and dwarves again. We did the best under difficult circumstances. I made sure the Dragon Council understood this. What matters now is managing the fallout. What are we looking at?"

"You mean you don't know?" Lumos asked. "I thought you came from a meeting with the Dragon Council. Surely they told an investigator more than they told us."

Windlock shook his head. "I've been airborne and out of communication for the last eight hours. This story broke after I had already left. Stonequest, do you have anything?"

The dragon SWAT nodded and looked like the weight of the world was on his shoulders. "The Full Dragon Council is convening."

"Truly?" the investigator sputtered. Kristen didn't think she'd ever seen him look that surprised before. She recalled that he had been with her when Amy had taken an eighteen-wheeler apart with her mind and used it like playdough to incapacitate five other dragons. If he was this affected, the news must be of tremendous importance.

Stonequest merely nodded as if he didn't have the words to do it justice.

"Oh, wow..." Windlock said, rubbed his head, and sat on the padded floor with Heartsbane. He looked at the footage on the TV once more, then back to the floor as he shook his head. His expression revealed that he was deeply disturbed.

"What's the big deal?" Amy asked into the silence that followed.

"Yeah, I thought the Dragon Council met all the time?" Kristen added. She was confused by the severity of Windlock's reaction and Stonequest's demeanor.

Lumos smiled at her and clicked his tongue. "You are such a capable officer and fighter that I often forget how much you don't know about dragon culture. There is so much for you to learn, but it seems like you're always whisked from one calamity to another."

"Tell me about it," she muttered, which served the dual purpose of telling them all how she felt and also to convince Stonequest to explain why it was of such import.

"The regional councils meet all the time. The North American Council, for example, is almost always working on something. But a Full Dragon Council meeting is another thing entirely. Normally, when the different councils want to coordinate policy—say the price of beef or gold or perhaps a crime that crossed from North to South America—they send a delegate. A full council meeting means all the councils from every region around the world will come together in one place."

"I still don't see the big deal," Amy said. "It sounds like a UN summit. Those happen all the time."

"These very much do not happen all the time," Windlock added. "The last time a full council meeting was called was the onset of your second world war."

"So one hasn't happened in more than seventy years?" Kristen asked, a little shocked.

"Indeed not." The color had begun to return to the investigator's face. "It's only convened when there is great need, which is generally in times of massive change and disruption. Humans engaging in world wars prompt full council meetings. The Mage Wars precipitated full council meetings too, of course. That a meeting was called so soon after the coverage reached the news indicates that the council members are taking this very seriously indeed." The last words seemed to drain him of his strength and he stared at the mat once more.

"Is this why you were so desperate to keep any information about the dragon bullets secret?" she asked her boss.

He nodded.

"I still don't quite follow here. What will this Full Dragon Council do?" Amy asked and fiddled with her new silver bracelet as if it irritated her skin. "Won't they simply pass an international treaty or whatever like the Paris Accord? Get everyone to stop making these bullets the same way humans made it illegal to use certain kinds of mines and defined war crimes and stuff?"

"The Dragon Council doesn't pass laws that apply to humanity." Lumos sounded somber.

"Which means what?" Kristen demanded and her pulse began to race. "Will the Council vote to go to war then?"

"They won't call it that," Emerald said.

"Then what? They'll call for the mass extinction of humanity?" Kristen was pissed-off now, and all her fears and frustrations seemed to coalesce into this new target. At the same time, she was immensely frustrated by the team's reaction. How could they all be so despondent when they were closer to a world-ending war than they'd ever been before?

"They won't start with that," Stonequest said. "That would be extreme, even for them. My guess is that they'd start with eliminating the human population of North America, given that's where the dragons were killed. Hopefully, they won't draw the dwarves into it, but it happened in Canada so it might be unavoidable. If the weapons appear in other places…" His shrug was one of pained regret.

"Then we need to go to this council meeting and tell them not to do that!" she shouted at the depressed dragons. "We can't simply accept the end of everyone I know. This is crazy! All we need to do is stop Constance. Most of mankind doesn't want to kill dragons. They only want a good job and a decent house. We can't go to war over the death of two dragons."

"There's no way they'll listen to you," Stonequest told her firmly. "You're too young and you've lived as a human longer than you've lived as a dragon."

"That's stupid. Me living as a human is why they should listen to me."

"Stonequest is right. Even if you are a steel dragon—and a tenacious and irritating one—they still won't listen. Age means too much to them." Lumos smiled warmly at her. She loved him like a grandfather, but he was the oldest one among them and it rankled to think that maybe he implied that even he wouldn't listen to her, despite them being friends.

"It's not like it matters if they'd listen to you or not," Emerald added. "No one knows where they'll meet. All Stonequest knows is that the meeting will be soon."

"No one knows?" Kristen said in disbelief. Every UN meeting venue was always known months in advance.

"Of course not," her boss pointed out. "Think about it. They will gather to discuss an enemy capable of killing dragons with handguns and bombs. This is literally the greatest threat they've ever faced. Before, their enemies had to create other beings simply to stand against them, but there's no way a dragon can convince a gun not to shoot them in exchange for freedom or a parcel of land. Now, their enemies would simply have to blow up this one meeting place and end them all at once. No mage in history had that kind of power. I doubt even Amy does."

The girl shook her head, her expression somber. "I could barely handle five. I can't imagine more than that."

That earned her a long look from the dragons on SWAT. Kristen saw Heartsbane mouth "Five?" to Emerald, who nodded and shook his head as if to say he'd heard it but didn't believe it.

"The fact is that they won't take any chances with the location," Stonequest said with finality. "Too much is at stake."

"But there's has to be something we can do," Kristen said.

"If you can think of something that doesn't interfere with our work, by all means, let me know. But right now, I can't imagine what you could do."

"So we're supposed to sit on our hands while they decide the fate of the world?"

"No. You are supposed to sit on your hands. The Dragon Council agreed with me that you're probably the technomage's number one target outside the actual council members. You're to stay here at the SWAT base with your mage."

"What will the rest of you do?"

"Every SWAT dragon has been recalled to active duty, effective immediately. We're all on full alert for any possible indication of another attack," Stonequest said and his posture finally straightened. "I received the order and it applies to everyone here. Even you, Heartsbane. They want the skies patrolled so these mages don't try anything before they can decide what to do about it."

"But that's asinine," Kristen protested. "The technomages won't simply be out on the streets where you can see them."

"And they won't take potshots at dragons a mile up either. This is a show of force so everyone—human, mage and dragon—knows we're taking this seriously. Furthermore, it's an order directly from the top for all of SWAT, exactly like your order to stay at HQ came straight from the director of SWAT. Deal with it. The rest of you, let's go."

"Yes, sir," Kristen said, but Stonequest had already turned his back on her and moved toward the roof. She thought the orders foolhardy but mostly because she wished she could trade places with him. She'd rather be in the skies and at-risk than know he was, while she was supposed to remain in safety and hide behind a desk.

CHAPTER FIFTY-FOUR

Kristen clenched and unclenched her fists as she watched others in the team leave the training area and head to the roof. She made no attempt to mask the frustration in her aura and was absolutely furious. The orders were nothing more than bureaucrats making decisions for the benefit of the elite.

"Hey, it's not a big deal," Amy said with a weak smile. "Maybe the dragons and the technomages will make friends and all hang out while we're trapped here. Either that or…you know, they'll blow each other to pieces."

"That's not funny," she snapped and immediately shook her head. This was not the mage's fault. Hell, it wasn't even Stonequest's fault. The blame belonged to a system that valued obedience and the status quo more than it valued individualism and justice. The frustrating part was that it was hard to be pissed at it, given that it couldn't look her in the eye or debate itself. She had to content herself with the idea that she would be able to say, "I told you so," when everything inevitably went to shit.

"Will you tell her or do you want me to tell her?" Kristen glanced at Larry Brockton, who practically bounced from foot to foot and glanced from her to Windlock. "Because I think it would make more sense if you told her, what with you being a dragon and everything. But if you simply stand there smirking, I can go ahead and tell her because I really, really, think someone ought to."

"What is he talking about?" Amy asked the investigator. That finally made Kristen smile. It was nice to see someone who was even more direct and less politically correct than she was. There were times when she didn't think that was possible.

"I intended to wait for a more opportune moment but Brockton's right, I suppose," Windlock said.

"A more opportune moment for what?" Kristen asked.

"Let's continue this conversation in my office," he said.

They all agreed and followed him to his office. As usual, it was a mess of stacks of paper and manila folders crammed with different documents, all arranged in teetering piles. Windlock gestured at Brockton with a sigh and the mage sprang into action. He wiggled his fingers and the papers and folders picked themselves up and began to swirl in a cyclone of notes. It was hard to follow exactly what was happening inside the tornado, but it seemed that some papers stuffed themselves into other folders, which then stacked themselves in a filing cabinet. A minute later, all that was left were three piles for Kristen, Amy, and Brockton to sit on.

Larry released a contented sigh. "You know, when I was cuffed, I could have done that, but it would have taken me ten times as long and damn near tired me out. I have to thank you once more for setting me free, Windlock."

"As long as you put it all back when we're done in here."

"Given that I have full access to my magic, that won't be a problem."

"How did you do that?" Amy asked with both glee and jealousy in her eyes.

"That impressed you?" Kristen asked, shocked at how excited the girl was. "You took an entire forest and used it to clobber two dragons to death. Why are you worked up over putting papers away?"

"I don't have that kind of control. While I'm all right with controlling one thing at a time—"

"You mean like a skateboard," she cut in, unable to help herself.

The young mage smiled and stuck her tongue out. "Exactly! Which, by the way, I have yet to be compensated for. Just saying, your mage can't get around as well without her own set of wheels."

"So you're saying you can throw a forest around but not an office?" Kristen asked.

"Oh, I could throw it around fine. But putting everything away?"

"And filing by date," Larry added.

"I can't do that," Amy exclaimed honestly.

"Aw, give yourself time. I saw you take that truck apart. You're a natural. Keep practicing and soon, you'll be able to put things together."

"Even with this bracelet on?" the girl asked and lifted the dainty bracelet to hold it like it was made of lead rather than silver.

Kristen looked at Windlock. "I can take that off her, right? You took it off Brockton."

He set his jaw. "Let's not get ahead of ourselves. I'm an investigator, you're a grunt for Dragon SWAT. As long as you're in this position, first and foremost, you need to follow orders."

She glared at him. Did he really tell her not to free Amy after he'd already liberated Larry?

"Now, hold up. Don't get your aura all out of whack," he continued. "There's nothing you can do to change the way things will turn out while you're stuck in the SWAT base, but... Well, I've seen you in action. You're a vector for change. I'm sure of it. Everywhere you go, you alter things. And not little victories either. You stopped Boston SWAT from starting a war with those dwarves, and you proved the danger of the technomages to some of the most powerful dragons in North America.

"Maybe it's luck, or your unique perspective, or merely something about who you are as a dragon and a human being. But I believe in your ability to do something here too."

"Thanks for the pep talk, Windlock, but what does this have to with me being—"

The investigator held a hand up to silence her and she obliged him, although not without rolling her eyes.

"Furthermore, you've convinced me that this coming war will be devastating to everyone. I've seen what those bullets and explosives can do to dragons. And those were basically the home-made version." He chuckled darkly. "What if the human military gets hold of this tech? They could develop armaments capable of wiping dragons out with even greater ease."

"It's not all about dragons, you know," Kristen said.

"I know. Really, I do. I already thought I valued human life more than the average dragon, but you've made me realize how precious every human life is. Plus, I know none of you were born then, but I remember the Mage Wars, too. Entire human cities were burned to the ground to root out a few rebels. Mercy was not a good word in those days, and I have no reason to think that will have changed now that dragons are even more concerned with human power than before.

"The Mage Wars were dark times for both species, but this looming war feels even worse. At least with the Mage Wars, it was primarily mages versus dragons. Regular humans stayed out of it. But with Constance and these weapons of hers, she'll make every American think it's their constitutional right to have the firepower to kill a dragon."

"Is she wrong?" Amy asked.

Kristen couldn't help but smirk at her. She was from rural America, after all. Obviously, she knew her way around a gun.

"I don't think humans should live in the shadows of dragons any longer. I don't think it's good for either species," Windlock said. "But I also don't think the way to eliminate that shadow is to shoot dragons out of the air."

"Well, what can we do?" she asked.

He shrugged and let a wry smile tug at the corners of his mouth. "To use the modern parlance, I don't have a fucking clue."

Larry laughed uproariously. "So you have paid attention to the way people talk these days."

The investigator continued to smile and shrugged. "I really don't have any ideas. My next step would be to continue the investigation into the technomage group and hope I could find some of their cells. Perhaps that could maybe defuse the situation before it exploded but honestly, I don't have any idea where I'd begin. Here in Detroit, I guess, but beyond that? I don't know how to think like a human to be able to even guess where they'd hide. Plus, I'm not confident that stopping a cell will be enough now that the genie is out of the bottle. If these weapons are made available to people—especially Americans, who know how to use guns—dragon dominance might be over."

"So you have nothing?" Kristen asked, a little dumbfounded and mostly frustrated.

Windlock nodded. "In this case, I'm actually counting on your tendency to always go to the next right thing and come up with a better answer than I have."

"While I'm stuck here in SWAT HQ? It might be tricky. Constance won't target this building again, especially if I'm the only dragon here."

"Then why stay here?" he asked.

"Because I was ordered to. Something you pointed out."

"Dragon SWAT ordered you to stay here," Windlock said and slid his hand into his pocket. He withdrew an object in his closed fist, then uncurled his fingers. In his palm lay a seven-pointed silver star with the slitted eye of a dragon in the center. It was the same badge that he wore on his trenchcoat, the badge of an investigator. "However, investigators are not part of that chain of command."

"Are you…but… You can't be serious," Kristen managed to stammer.

"I am," he said. "It's yours if you want it. The seven points reference the seven traditional seats on a Dragon Council. The eye in the center means nothing escapes our vision. The Council didn't want to at first, but I convinced them to approve it if you want it. And there's no obligation. You can return it any time you want to resign. Being an investigator is a solitary existence. You won't be able to rely on other dragons in the same way. I wasn't able to help you in that duel if you remember."

"Oh, come on, you old windbag. It's not that bad. You have me," Brockton said.

He smiled warmly at his mage before turning to Kristen again. "You'll of course still be able to have friends and it won't affect how you interact with humans or mages at all but…well, it will change your place in dragon society. It's long been the policy of the Dragon Council to not force the responsibility on those who don't want it. The choice is yours."

She had no idea what to say. Part of her knew she had to take it and that this was the chance to prove herself to dragon and human society and to make things right, but the other part was terrified. Before, when she'd made mistakes—as she had many times—someone had always been there to pick up the pieces. Be it a simple reprimand or disciplinary action, someone had been there to tell her she was out of line. From what she'd seen with Windlock, that wouldn't be the case. He didn't seem to answer to anyone other than the Dragon Council.

"So what kind of responsibility are we talking here?" Amy asked as if she'd read Kristen's thoughts. "What?" she continued when everyone looked at her in astonishment. "If I'm the Steel Dragon's mage, I want to know exactly what her job requirements are."

"Smart mage you got there," Larry quipped.

Kristen looked at Windlock and waited for him to answer.

"With that badge, you can question almost anyone in dragon society."

"What do you mean by almost?" she asked.

"Well, Dragon Council members are excluded of course. That means the North American Council members who appointed you as well as the council members from other regions."

"Who investigates them?" Amy asked.

"No one," he said flatly. Kristen couldn't tell if he meant no one should or that no one ever had, so she waited for him to clarify. "They are beyond reproach. Well, that's not technically true. You could investigate one if you wanted to, but you'd need prior permission from a majority of another council. There are a few other bigwig dragons like that. For example, if you wanted to investigate me, you'd need permission as I'm a fellow investigator."

"Okay. That seems reasonable enough. I suppose. So you're telling me I need a warrant for the big ones but any other dragon is fair game?"

"Basically, yes." Windlock nodded. "But I'm not only talking about dragons. My last job was to investigate Amy, who I suspected to be a mage. Investigators can investigate all parts of dragon culture. That means dragons and humans who work with dragons. We could investigate dwarves or pixies too. Or mages." He raised an eyebrow and Kristen did not fail to understand him. She'd have the authority to investigate Constance Vigil and her technomages on her own terms. That was worth gold to her.

"Are there perks?" Amy asked.

He chuckled. "An office anywhere you want it plus a better stipend, but I must say the best perk to me is that if you call for assistance, dragons will listen. That badge carries the weight of the Dragon Council of North America. That's no small thing. If you ask a SWAT team for help, you'll get it unless they're in the middle of something bigger. Even then, they'll normally get me help. Stonequest was always willing to share you when I asked.

"Most importantly," he continued and held the badge out to her, "you won't be part of SWAT anymore. You won't be part of the chain of command. You'll be free to take action."

"What action?" Kristen asked, overwhelmed by what she was offered. This was crazier than when she'd graduated from the police academy and immediately been placed on SWAT. It was crazier than when Stonequest had made her part of dragon SWAT. All of the previous indescribable moments seemed to fade into ordinariness against an opportunity so enormous she hardly knew what to do with it.

Windlock merely smiled his wry grin once more and shrugged like he'd rehearsed the gesture. "I really can't say. If I knew how to tackle these technomages, I would. The problem is that this is a modern threat and none of us are modern dragons. I didn't expect you to bring humans in to help stop the mage terror attack at that rooftop party. That was a stroke of brilliance—and in hindsight, completely obvious—and I would never have thought of it. I wouldn't have thought you'd adopt Amy as your personal mage, not after she'd killed two dragons."

"In self-defense," she reminded him.

"You're right," Windlock agreed. "You are absolutely right, and yet that line of reasoning didn't even occur to me. Hell, I would never have considered using a bulletproof vest to protect myself from a bomb, let alone carry it into the air."

Larry chuckled. "To be fair, Windlock, I don't think anyone would have thought of doing that."

"Okay, we seriously have to sit to swap stories in the near future," Amy stated, her eyes wide.

Windlock continued. "Everything I have seen of you demonstrates that your instincts are superb. You have exceptional moral fiber and are more than capable in a fight. In fact, your only shortcoming seems to be an inability to follow orders you don't agree with—which for an investigator, is actually a boon."

"I can't believe this is happening. Honestly…I-I don't know what to say." It irritated her that she actually stammered the words, but there seemed a slight disconnect between them and her brain.

"Say yes," Larry said with a grin.

"I trust your instincts, Kristen," the investigator said, "and it's my job to not trust people. I think you can trust your instincts as well."

"What about you?" Kristen asked.

"Oh, I'll follow your lead—this time. Don't think this is my way of getting rid of you or anything like that. I'll be along to advise and help you, but you've more than proven yourself capable of making the right calls. We don't have time for you to check in with me on every decision you make. Plus, if you work as an intern or something along those lines, I'd have to explain your actions to the Dragon Council when this is all over. Given that I don't understand said actions half the time, I'd rather you do that yourself." His eyes twinkled. Apparently, that counted as a joke for him.

"I don't know. I mean…I want to say yes but I worry that other dragons will resent me for it."

"Aw, who cares about them?" Amy asked.

"Yeah!" Larry interjected. "Besides, what's the worst that could happen? Massive global war and the possible extinction of the human and maybe even the dragon race?"

Kristen laughed, shook her head, and took the pin from the other dragon's outstretched hand.

"All right, then," Windlock said and nodded as she tried and failed to pin it on her uniform.

"Do you mind?" she said and handed it to him again.

The old dragon chuckled. "Are you giving it back already?" he asked as he pinned it in place with a practiced hand. She wondered how many dragons he'd honored in this way in his centuries and centuries of life.

He adjusted it, leaned back in his chair, and appraised her. "It looks good on you."

She smiled and thanked him. To her, it felt heavy—not only from the metal but from the responsibility that came with it. Windlock had said she would have freedom with the pin to do as she wished, but she knew better. Her mission was clear. She had to prevent a global war. The seven-pointed dragon eye was a reminder to herself that this was the mission she'd been given in life. She couldn't squander this opportunity, not with the fate of the human race hanging in the balance.

CHAPTER FIFTY-FIVE

Constance reached their temporary base moments before she saw the story on the news. They couldn't fly like dragons could, and she didn't like major highways, so the trip to a warehouse in Detroit from Canada had been a long one.

Her team was exhausted but proud. They'd killed two dragons, one all on their own and another when they seized the opportunity the mage had created. It felt good to know they were an accomplished task force.

The satisfaction of victory felt even better when she turned the television on and saw the battle replay again and again on the screen. The first few stories had focused on the dragon battle, but before long, other channels began to report on the two dragons who had—to quote Constance's favorite line—"obviously been slaughtered by some kind of modified firearm in the hands of a human."

Slaughter was exactly what she wanted people to think of when they thought of dragons. This story would be the first chop into the massive tree trunk that was the dragon power structure. It had already been dealt and there was no going back now.

She allowed her team to watch the news for a few hours when they first returned. They laughed when the dragons died and marveled at

Kristen's power. For the first time, they all saw why the Steel Dragon would have made such a powerful ally. She knew how to fight dragons and many in the group wished she could be convinced to. Maybe if—no. She shook her head. Now was not the time to think of Kristen Hall. It was time to move forward with their years of planning.

More than anything else, Constance hated dragons. She hated how they wantonly killed humans, how they hoarded treasure, and how their culture existed on the backs of human culture like a clutch of leeches on an Olympic swimmer. But that didn't mean she didn't respect them. She knew they were cunning, smart and powerful. It would be the epitome of stupidity to think the dragons would take the deaths of two of their kind at the hands of a small band of humans sitting down.

While the others watched the news, she began to make calls.

It was a misconception to think that a sleeper cell like hers could exist in a vacuum. One simply couldn't hide in a hole and hope to overthrow the status quo. To be effective, one needed contacts. She knew that and had some in the most powerful human organization in the world—the United States Military.

It hadn't been easy to develop these relationships, but she had found a way. After all, the military needed to buy their weapons somewhere, as did she. A little patience was really all it had taken to create a solid network. She simply made sure that at the end of each trade show she attended, she was invited to the next one. Over the years, she'd made her way into more and more exclusive weapons offerings until she located some of the people who always asked the same questions. Each of them was wise enough to see that humans could not let the proverbial sleeping dragon lie.

This group included people like General John Andrews of the US Army.

He was stationed in Fort Drum, New York, and had been in charge of the base for half a decade. Constance had met the general many times, and he was one of the people in the US military who shared her distrust of dragons. He liked single malt whiskey, didn't like to eat pork—but also didn't like to admit that in front of other members of the military—couldn't stand golf, and was a Mets fan. General Andrews didn't realize that she knew all these things about him, but she had made it a point to learn them because that was how someone like her was able to manipulate people like him.

"Constance," the general said after he'd answered his phone on the first ring. "I was waiting for you to call after your recent performance. You do know the last number you left me is dead."

"Not all of us are protected by a US base, General. I have to keep moving if I don't want our mutual enemies to barbeque me like a pork chop."

He grunted but didn't respond to the comment. "You've made quite a splash, Constance. Every major media channel has realized what you and your team did. You might be the first normal people in the world to kill a dragon."

"You flatter me, General," she said coyly. He knew a little about her —one couldn't build contacts and remain completely anonymous, after all—but he didn't know she was a mage. As far as he was aware, she was a weapons dealer with a healthy respect for the second amendment who viewed dragons as the greatest threat to humanity.

Andrews didn't much like mages and viewed them in a similar light as dragons in that they were stronger than regular people. He tolerated them as a necessary evil and was aware that she had a few on her team, although she'd been careful not to reveal that every one of her fighters had magic. She didn't share his bias, obviously, not with her magic powers, but she saw his point. There would be no equality until everyone on earth was on an equal footing. People needed to be able to defend themselves against all attackers and with lethal force if necessary. "But I didn't call you for praise, sir."

"Of course not, Constance. Let's get to it. We have good intelligence indicating that the Full Dragon Council will convene sometime soon."

"I'm sorry, sir—did you say the full council? As in the leaders of the entire dragon society?"

"That's what our sources say, and it fits with their history. The whole world is watching people kill dragons on loop right now. They'll try to get in front of this one way or another. They can't afford to stay quiet and for once, the damn lizards want to be united."

"Do you have any idea where this meeting will be?" Constance asked, practically salivating at the prospect of every dragon leader in the world being together in one building.

"Supposedly, it'll meet somewhere in Northern Canada."

"Do you know more than that? Northern Canada is a big place."

She could almost hear Andrews scowl over the phone. "I can't even tell you a state. Those damn dwarves—well, you know what I think of them. You'd think they'd be loyal to people since people made them, but it doesn't seem that way. I'd tolerate the short little bastards if they were actually neutral, but they always seem to side with the damn dragons."

Constance didn't bother to mention that she had a different perspective of the dwarves. When she'd gone to Canada, they had let her speak to Amy Williams in an attempt to woo the mage to her side. They hadn't given that opportunity to dragon SWAT although, in the end, they had let Kristen take the mage. She thought they could handle themselves fine. It wasn't worth trying to explain their politics to the general. What she needed was someone who was willing to take decisive action. Presenting the dwarves as a complex, multifaceted people wouldn't achieve that.

"Do you think the dwarves know where this meeting is?" she asked and played off his biases.

"You're damn straight I do! Those dragons know they can't plan a meeting in our homeland without us finding out about it. Our surveillance is too damn good but in the great white north? There's not much we can do there. What grinds my gears is that I'm sure the dwarves must already know the location but have they shared that intelligence with their allegedly closest ally? Not at all."

"I wish I knew the location," she said.

"Tell me about it," he agreed. "It's the chance of a generation. Sources show that they haven't met together since the invention of the atomic bomb. Can you imagine if we attacked their little meeting with only one of those puppies? Dragon or not, there's no way they could survive that. And all the better that it's in Northern Canada—less risk of casualties."

Constance liked the general because he spoke about the missed opportunity to kill dozens of power-hungry dragons with the same longing in his voice as a fisherman might use to describe the biggest fish he ever caught, only to have it slip off his hook.

Except that they still had a chance to snare all the dragons.

"I don't know, Andrews. A few platoons of soldiers armed with dragon bullets would probably make a wonderful mess of things up there. A nuke might do the job more completely, but soldiers armed with weapons would drive home the point that dragons are no longer indestructible more effectively."

"Which is precisely why they've kept the meeting place secret, of course," he grumbled.

"Well, if you hear anything, let me know. You and I both agree that the second amendment provides for well-regulated militias, and my people are ready to work with you and the army against this threat."

She made it sound like her people would work under the authority of the army, as that was what military people expected. While she never told an outright lie, she also never went so far as to tell General Andrews or any of her other contacts in the military that her people would follow orders. After all, wasn't that what the second amendment was all about? Armed people needed to exist outside the chain of command in case the government became corrupt and moved against the people. The only problem was the government had been complicit with abuse from the all-powerful dragons from its onset.

"Believe me, you'll know when I know. Not everyone is on board with a strike against those damn lizards. Not a preemptive one, anyway. The idiots don't realize that if we wait for them to attack us first, it's already over. If I hear anything, I'll let you and your team know first thing."

"Okay. Thank you, General." Constance didn't bother to tell General Andrews that she planned to mobilize multiple cells across the country so that when the spark met the dynamite, they'd all be ready. It was better if he thought of her people as good ol' boys, gun aficionados, hunters, and small-town folk who believed in private property above all else. She'd far rather he undervalued them on those grounds than know he was working with a highly skilled and well-trained network of magic assassins. That was much better, in her view.

"In the meantime, I want you to expect a shipment from me," she said.

"You know it's not my birthday. I still haven't used the last gift you gave me." On his last birthday, she had provided him with a revolver filled with six dragon bullets. He'd doubted their veracity until he'd used one on a piece of dead dragon hide. That had impressed him but despite the available footage—he wasn't a man who simply accepted everything the media touted as fact—he still hadn't fully grasped how capable the weapons were of hurting living dragons.

"I hate to say it, Andrews, but this gift will make my last offering look downright stingy."

"Is that right?"

"Be on the lookout for a case or two of the same quality pieces I gave you last time. And don't be jealous when some of my other contacts get something similar. You know I'm not exclusive with you and the boys at Fort Drum."

She heard something spray out of the general's mouth and the man coughed. He'd probably sipped whiskey while she'd dropped that bombshell on him.

"I'm sorry. Did you say cases? With an 'S?' As in you have cases of those?"

"That is indeed what I said, General Andrews."

"Well, how in the hell did you manage that? It seems like just the other month you were all proud of those six little bullets. Now, we're talking about thousands of them? And you're dumping 'em off? How the hell can you afford that kind of material? We tried using the body of a dead dragon, and there was hardly enough to make one case, let alone multiple, and of course, we couldn't get anything to stay together. What's your secret?"

"Exactly that, sir, a secret. We live in America, after all, the land of free business. If I told you my secrets, wouldn't that amount to socialism?"

"If it did I guess I might be voting socialist," he muttered before he cleared his throat and addressed her in a more formal tone. "And you're sure they'll work as advertised? It wouldn't do for me to send my men and women in only to find out you filled these cases with duds."

"Andrews, please—you offend me!" The almost purring tone balanced the playful rebuke. "I can hear your TV in the background. You're watching the same footage I am. The proof is right there. Yes, the bullets work and soon, your confidence in my efforts will be justi-fied. You'll be one of the people responsible for saving and liberating the human race."

"Hmm…" Andrews intoned thoughtfully. The assassin could prac-tically see him lean back in his chair and take a sip of his whiskey. She knew that the idea of John Andrews liberating the human race thrilled the man. He'd told her once at a Brazilian steakhouse that he joined the military because he wanted fame. He wanted to be known as one of the great generals in history, one of the men who made the hard choices and to whom even pacifists and liberals looked with begrudging respect. Men like Lincoln and FDR, although he had never been one for public speaking, so a run at the presidency had never really been an option for him.

"You've already achieved so much, John," she said and gambled with his first name. Normally, she didn't use it unless he was drunk—but maybe he was, albeit slightly. "You're a general at one of the most well-respected bases in the country. You saw action in Iraq in the nineties and earned your medals. By all accounts, you could rest on your laurels. I know this is asking a lot, but I'm scared, John. I really am."

"There's no reason to be scared," the general said, gears no doubt turning in his mind. He had also expressed to her that he didn't like his posting at the base. While he would never complain to anyone in his official chain of command, of course, he felt he was in a dead-end posting at the end of his career. Everyone knew he was close to retirement and warfare wasn't what it used to be. It made sense for him to stay on the base, even though he wanted more. "Those who made history were never scared."

"I'm sure they were," Constance said, "but they didn't let fear stop them. They weighed the consequences and acted in the name of freedom."

"You're damn straight," Andrews said. She heard him swallow the contents of his glass. "These weapons might give us the edge we need to win the final war to free humanity from the dragons. I think…well, I think that's the only way for the history books to look at this time without shame. They need to see that when given the opportunity, we acted. We didn't sit around and we forged history itself by breaking the chains those damn lizards have put on us for centuries."

"I knew I sent them to the right man," she said warmly. "And use that speech for your troops. It gave me chills."

"Yeah, that's a good idea." Paper rustled in the background. He wasn't a great orator, but if he believed in the speech he was making, he was passably good. She had made sure he liked many of his speeches over the years they'd known each other.

The leader of the technomage group wasn't so naïve that she thought of someone as accomplished and experienced as Andrews as a pawn. He was an ally, nothing more and nothing less. But she wasn't above pulling strings either. She knew he craved fame, so was it wrong of her to present his current situation to him in that light? She didn't think so. It was the smallest smudging of the truth in a grand scheme that would free humanity. It was nothing she had any reason to feel guilty about.

"So if you find anything, you'll let me know?"

"Of course," the general replied. "And we look forward to receiving the shipment."

"I can't wait to see it in action."

"We'll be ready. We've been ready for this for years."

They said their goodbyes and she hung up.

The assassin took a deep breath to calm herself. Not knowing where the Dragon Council meeting would be was a blow. She'd fostered relationships with men like General Andrews precisely for situations like this. Still hopeful, she made a few more calls but no one knew anything more, which really was too bad. While her hope had been a confirmed location, she also wasn't surprised at the outcome of her efforts.

Dragons were powerful, obviously, but they were also cunning. They understood the threat to themselves better than humans did and by now, they knew what the future would bring. Constance—knowing dragons to be the bloodthirsty killers they were—knew it was only a matter of time before they struck at humanity. A preemptive strike was inevitable. Unfortunately, it was also the only way humanity would be galvanized to throw off their oppressors, so it had to happen in order to achieve her goals. Timing would therefore be crucial. When it happened, she had to be ready. Humanity needed to see the brutal cruelty of dragons met by her own people.

Still, there was nothing to be done now but make sure they were as prepared as possible.

Constance returned to the members of her cell. They were still celebrating the footage of them killing the dragons. She gave them a smile and turned the TV off.

"It's time to up the production of our bullets. The long game is over. I want as much ammunition as we can possibly make and I want it within a week. There's no saying when this conflict will break, but it'll more than likely be soon. I want as big a harvest as possible."

"Are you saying we can finally kill the damn monster?" Vindication asked. He had never liked keeping their subject around. Not that she blamed him. It was a little creepy to live, work, and sleep in whatever interim base they occupied with nothing for company but a giant dragon kept in a vat of chemicals and hooked up to electrodes.

She turned to the dragon. The goo they kept it submerged in aided its healing powers, but it still was a sorry sight. Its scales were pale and poorly formed from never seeing the sun and always being submerged. Recently, its fingertips had been torn away, as had many of its teeth. Its wings had long since stopped trying to form properly, so they were tattered ribbons, a parody of their true destiny.

Vindication hated fishing the membrane from the dragon's wings out of the tank. The material was basically worthless but if not removed, it would jam the filters. The dragon's eyes had been cut out too. Actually, they looked like they were due for another removal as they were rolled back and milky. The dragon was far more docile when it couldn't see, so part of their harvest was to remove its eyes.

"He's been far too good to us for us to simply slaughter him," Constance said and smiled faintly at the creature. She'd cared for it since it had hatched from the same clutch of eggs as the Steel Dragon herself. For the first time, she wondered vaguely what he would look like in his human form. He'd never been taught that he could be a human, but he hadn't been taught much of anything. Mostly, he was kept unconscious through drugs.

Constance examined him through the glass that supported the fluid he rested in. "Okay, we haven't harvested ribs in a long time. Take as much as you can from both sides but leave three or four—enough to support his chest. Also, take finger bones and one of the forearm bones on each hand as well. Those should grow back fairly quickly if we leave flesh there. Then go ahead and take his legs and tail. Those will give us the most ammunition and he's proven himself more than capable of growing that all back."

"Aren't you worried we'll kill it?" one of the mages asked.

"I don't want that to happen. Start with its tail and ribs and continue to monitor his vitals. If anything becomes erratic, take a break and try again after a few minutes. He—it—will be fine."

She nodded and fought back a single tear. It was easier to do the work if she thought of the dragon as what it was—an it like a mushroom, an apple tree, or a wonderful organic creation that would grow and grow as long as they tended to its needs. Once they started calling it things like he and him, it became more complicated, especially when she started to think of the similarities between him—it—and its sister. Both had the same ax-tipped tails, for example. She made those comparisons more often since she'd fought the Steel Dragon.

No matter, Constance told herself and turned away from the impending harvest. She wasn't a butcher or a blacksmith but a battle master.

While her team hurried to the tasks assigned to them, she moved to her battle map hung on a far wall of the warehouse where she—despite its distance—could still hear the sounds of the power tools needed to harvest the dragon.

The map was of the United States with a pin to highlight the rough location of every dragon they had intel on, along with those of the dragon centers of power—SWAT buildings, dragon courthouses, a few of the communal retreats and estates, and others. It represented decades of research and tens of thousands of man-hours, and yet it still wasn't enough.

Constance retrieved a silver-headed pin and rammed it home into Detroit. Kristen, the Steel Dragon, was no doubt there by now. If anyone could unravel her carefully laid plans, it would be her. But what would that look like? Surely she wouldn't allow her and her mages to kill dragons indiscriminately. The girl had proven that time and time again and yet, what would she think if the dragons attacked? The last time they'd met, the Steel Dragon had let them go so she could fight dragons. Had her opinion changed now that she knew how far the persecution of mages went?

There was no way to know. Kristen was simply too clever and too unpredictable. She was the most powerful piece on the board and one of the hardest to anticipate, and yet she had to find answers or risk losing everything.

What will you do? Will you side with your blood or your family? Because the time has come to choose.

CHAPTER FIFTY-SIX

Before Kristen could decide what to do with her newfound power, a knock at Windlock's door pulled her from her thoughts.

"Come in," the other dragon hollered while she slapped her hand to the seven-pointed silver badge on her uniform.

It was still unreal to think that she had been granted this kind of power. She wasn't hiding it, exactly, but she also didn't want Stonequest to simply see it. It seemed only good manners to say something, and she at least owed him an explanation of how she got it before he reached all kinds of conclusions on his own.

"Hey, Kristen, I thought I might find you in here." He sounded a little sheepish.

"What can we do for you, Officer Stonequest?" Windlock said, his grin carefully hidden. He didn't do a great job at controlling his aura though, and the dragon SWAT leader raised an eyebrow at him. When the investigator didn't respond, he turned his attention to his erstwhile teammate.

"I think I was a little rash in grounding you. My boss definitely wants you kept out of harm's way, but I don't think you staying at HQ is the best way to achieve that. They've attacked here before."

"What were you thinking?" she asked. The badge felt heavy beneath her hand and reminded her that she no longer had to obey him. She knew this, yet it was hard to go against conditioning she'd fought so hard to internalize.

"I thought you could fly patrols with Emerald. You two work well together and we all know we can use every hand we have. You're more than capable."

Kristen said nothing, unsure of how to tell Stonequest that her status had changed. Windlock remained silent and left her to it but that made sense. He'd said he didn't want to speak on her behalf anymore. In a way, this was her first test. But, while he made no effort to join the exchange, his aura made it very clear that he thought something was fishy.

The dragon SWAT leader didn't seem to pick up on it, though, so maybe he was distracted. He continued without so much as a glance at the investigator. "Some of the elder dragons are leaving town and heading to more remote places. It seems they already understand the implications of that footage—although yeah, of course they do. Detroit Dragons were picked off by these mages before all this went public."

He shook his head and looked like he carried considerable weight on his shoulders. "They want SWAT to cover their exodus and I can't say that I blame them. If those damn technomages manage to kill any more dragons, the entire situation will explode. Many of the younger dragons are ready to start this war already, with or without permission from the Dragon Council. I could use people who know how to defuse a situation."

She looked from Stonequest to Windlock. The investigator merely smiled knowingly, which echoed his aura perfectly. He said nothing, though, and obviously wanted to see how she would handle this. She didn't like him to simply sit there with a smile on his face, but she had to admit that she respected what he was doing. If she wasn't able to stand up to Stonequest—a dragon she knew and liked—how would she ever stand up to the Dragon Council? How would she be able to investigate rogue dragons if she couldn't refuse those she knew?

Kristen stood, squared her shoulders, and faced Stonequest. "I'm sorry. I'd love to help and protecting lives is always my priority, but I can't. Not with bodyguard duty."

"You can't?" For a moment, his fatigue gave way to surprise and amusement. "Saying you can't is not an option. You're part of Dragon SWAT. That means you—"

His gaze alighted on the badge and he fell silent.

"I can't because I'm no longer part of Dragon SWAT."

"Wha— When did this happen? Why didn't you tell me?" Stonequest demanded.

"Calm down. It only happened a few minutes ago," Brockton said quickly.

"Windlock has honored me with this position. I don't think the best way to use it is to be seen protecting the very people who might go to war."

He stood in silence, shocked into confusion and his mouth agape. After a moment, the corners of his mouth twitched into the faintest of smiles. He looked from Kristen to Windlock.

"Are you taking my best asset?" he said.

"You could say that, I suppose," Windlock replied.

"Why?" Stonequest asked abruptly, which diminished the warmth that had washed over her when he'd called her his best asset.

"Because Kristen's talents are best suited for things other than patrols," the investigator said. "And because if anyone has even a remote chance of cleaning this mess up, it's probably someone with a foot in both worlds. And because we both know how good she is and don't know what to do with her." He chuckled at that.

Larry and Amy both smiled.

"She'll work under you, though?" the other dragon asked.

Windlock actually laughed. "No, no, no, of course not! We don't do internships. It might color the new investigator too much. I gave her the badge and plan to let her loose. Of course, I'll follow and provide advice if requested, but Kristen has already proven herself to be ingenious and adaptive."

"It's only…well, it seems a little fast."

"Dragons have been advanced to the role of an investigator with far less experience than Kristen Hall. For that matter, every dragon who's ever held the position in the entire history of investigators has had less experience than her when it comes to maneuvering through human culture and society—which I think, given our current threat, will be of the utmost importance."

"I mean…yeah, that makes sense, I guess," Stonequest didn't sound like he believed it but his aura seemed to have warmed to the idea somewhat. "Kristen, is this what you want?"

"It is." She nodded. "Come on, Stonequest. After all those headaches I caused you by not following orders, are you really surprised? At least this way, the only person responsible for covering my butt is me."

"I wouldn't go that far," Windlock said quickly. "Although you two have a professional history and Kristen has only held this job for about one hundred and eighty seconds, I do expect you to give Investigator Hall whatever support she requires to get her job done. I don't want you to second-guess her simply because you know her. You've always done an admirable job of following my orders—as is required of you—and I expect nothing different when it comes to our new investigator, especially given the urgent nature of her job."

"What job?" Stonequest asked.

Kristen couldn't help but smile at the question. The dragon SWAT leader could have asked any number of things about why she was promoted or given excuses about how his team was defending dragons or anything else, but he hadn't. Instead, he'd looked at the threat dire enough to make Windlock promote her.

"I think Investigator Hall is our best chance to stop these rogue technomages. She has proven herself capable of handling them in combat and is also able to think like them. I've followed their trail as long as they've been active and have come up with nothing. On my first job with the Steel Dragon, she managed to lure them out. If anyone can bring them to justice, it's her."

"Well, all right then," Stonequest said and glanced at the badge again. "If you need our help to take the fight to the technomages, I'll provide it. I don't think I can call off protection runs in the middle of one, but Emerald is here and the others will be back soon. How do we catch these mages?"

While the two men had been talking, she had been thinking. She didn't blame Stonequest for his surprise at her promotion but she also couldn't afford to dwell on it like he could. She had been given this role so she could act. It wasn't a political move because she had grown up like a human or because she was a woman. There were other female investigators and apparently, the dragon world wasn't as gendered as the human one. The appointment had been made because Windlock thought she could prevent a war from consuming the planet.

It was more than a little pressure, but Kristen felt she could handle it. She straightened, made sure her aura radiated confidence, and addressed her two former bosses.

"It's far more than merely catching these mages," Kristen began. "We don't need to only put an end to this group of terrorists. We need to stop a war from happening. It might be simple enough to stop Constance—and we should, of course—but that can't be our focus. We need to think bigger and prevent her from putting anything larger in motion."

The two dragons nodded and she swallowed. It was a sobering thought for her. This was huge, bigger than anything she had ever tackled before. She couldn't even imagine where to begin unraveling the mess, but she believed there had to be a way. For now, she had that smidgeon of hope.

Windlock cleared his throat. "So…what will you do next?" His eyes gleamed. He must have known about the promotion for days—or at least for hours, as that was how long it had been since he talked to the Dragon Council. He probably thought she was already formulating plans and designing sting operations. She was—after a fashion—but was still very much at the beginning of that whole process. Still, she knew she couldn't do it alone.

"First things first," she said briskly. "This war threatens humans and dragons alike. It'll take humans and dragons working together to put an end to it. We need to join our forces. I'll call the human police in and bring them here. Working side by side is the best way to bring both our people together." She assumed that with all their talents in one place, they could maybe solve the case once and for all. It certainly seemed a better method to her than multiple agencies—Dragon SWAT, Detroit SWAT, multiple investigators—all working toward the same goals without coordination.

"Now wait a minute," Stonequest sputtered. "I'm all for working with humans and frankly, as soon as I saw that badge on your chest, I had a feeling there would be far more of that in my future. But you want to bring them here? People don't come here."

"I'm a person," Amy said with a smile.

He rolled his eyes. "Based on the footage I saw, you are the most powerful mage to emerge in a century. You're about as human as I am. Kristen, she's a mage. Dragons have worked side by side with mages for a long time. That's very different than working with regular humans."

She thought he might have handled the suggestion better if Windlock hadn't chuckled openly at his frustration the entire time.

"What? You can't be afraid of them," the investigator said. "Is it that you're worried they'll embarrass you or are you scared you'll shake one of their hands and accidentally crush them?"

"Wait, is that something I need to worry about?" Amy asked.

"No, of course not!" Stonequest sputtered. "It's only…it's not done. And Windlock, stop laughing. You're acting like a hatchling."

"Perhaps you're right," Kristen replied sweetly. "Perhaps bringing humans into the dragon sanctuary is a dangerous idea. I mean, Keith does like taking pictures on his phone. He might accidentally share some of the mysterious inner workings of Dragon SWAT HQ. He might reveal the power of the bureaucracy."

"You know it's nothing like that. We've worked with your Detroit team before. It's not like I don't trust them," Stonequest admitted.

"Well, if you'd prefer that we work there, we can do that. I merely thought working here made sense since dragon SWAT has better equipment or more resources than your human equivalent."

"We're not equiva—you know what? Never mind. I'm only... This is all happening so fast."

"We need to move fast if we intend to stop the worst war this world has ever seen," Windlock said. "Investigator Hall has the authority to do this and I, for one, am already excited to see what humans and dragons actually working together will achieve. This is exactly the kind of thinking that made me choose Kristen for this role in the first place."

"What'll it be, Stonequest?" Kristen asked. "Will you do it my way? Or do I order Lumos and Timeflash to help me anyway? I bet Emerald would go for it too."

"No, no. You don't need to be so dramatic. I only...I'm not used to working this way, is all. I've been in command here for...well, decades. Being bossed around by the fricking Steel Dragon has kind of thrown me out of my element."

"Hey, she's your boss, now. Show some respect!" Amy said and some of the papers they were seated on fluttered at their edges with a small blast of her magic.

"I'm sorry, I didn't mean to offend. Of course we'll help you, Kristen. You know I trust you with my life. The fact is most of the dragons in this city owe you their life. I needed to get some of that off my chest, is all. I'll be professional from here on out. Bring the humans here. You're right, that makes the most sense."

Kristen smiled and nodded at him. "Thanks for seeing things my way, Officer. Dismissed."

Stonequest grimaced. He could tell from her aura she was mostly joking but still, he had to accept that this was the way of things now.

"Heartsbane hasn't left yet either. We were going to fly patrols together. I'll go upstairs and let her know about your promotion and what our next moves will be. Maybe if I'm lucky, she'll burn me to a cinder on the spot and save me some grief."

She chuckled as he walked out and pulled out her phone.

"Is this my office?" She raised an eyebrow.

"Don't get ahead of yourself. I got you one next door."

Kristen nodded and excused herself, although Amy came with her.

"What's the plan, boss?" the young mage asked and grinned. She'd really enjoyed watching Stonequest's reaction to the power shift.

"I thought you would meet these guys over beer and pizza but it looks like you won't have the benefit of thinking they're the way they are because they're drunk and off duty." She dialed a number.

"Do you want me to step out?"

"You can if you want to but if you're serious about working with me as a mage, I want you to be about as attached as my hand. If you need the bathroom, go for it. Otherwise, stay with me so I don't have to catch you up on anything."

The girl nodded as Kristen brought her phone up to her ear.

It rang twice before Drew picked up. "Well, look who it is. Ms. Hollywood herself. Me and the crew have been watching your little highlights reel on TV. Hernandez wants you to know—" A scuffling sound followed as Drew put his hand to the speaker of the phone. She could hear him talking to Hernandez. "Yeah, I know. I'm telling her!"

More scuffling ensued before he returned to the call. Apparently, he'd won. "Hernandez wants you to know that you're a real bitch for not bringing us along."

Kristen couldn't help but laugh at that. If Hernandez only knew who she was talking to. She had actually called a dragon investigator a bitch. But maybe that was what was so great about the woman. She didn't care who she was talking to.

"Well that's good news actually," she replied.

"Really?" Drew asked. "How so? Do tell."

"Well, as you can imagine, there's been considerable blowback about the whole world seeing a dragon get shot on TV. To cut a long story short, they made me an investigator."

"You have to be kidding me, Hall. That's great!" The irritating shuffling sound resumed as he took the phone away from his face and bellowed at whoever was near him "They made her an investigator!" She thought she could hear Butters and Keith cheer alongside Hernandez.

"Yeah, which means I get to boss around whoever I like."

"Is that right? Who are you bossing around today?"

"You won't believe this, but it's Detroit SWAT. I want you and the gang at Dragon SWAT HQ as soon as possible."

"Are you serious?" he asked.

"We need to stop Constance, Drew. and you're the best team for the job. I'm sure of it. What do you think of that?"

"Honestly?"

"Of course."

"Well, honestly? It sounds like Dragon SWAT doesn't drug test as much as we do because from the sound of things, you've been smoking dragon crack."

Keith and Hernandez laughed.

Kristen allowed herself to chuckle too. It might be the last time she had the opportunity for some time. "No fooling, Drew. I need you here. I'll speak to Windlock now and he can help me with all the paperwork or whatever to square it with the captain. But seriously, this is urgent. We need to move now because I have a feeling the tech-nomages are already a few steps ahead of us."

"We're already on our way, ma'am. And Kristen, congratulations again. I can't think of a dragon—or a person—I'd rather take orders from than you."

"Save the ass-kissing for after we prevent World War Three. Get the team here."

"Yes, ma'am!"

CHAPTER FIFTY-SEVEN

Kristen had never been in the auditorium before. It was on the second floor of the basement of the Capital Square Building and was a reasonably classy area, she thought as she tried to focus on the lamp fixtures and beige carpet between the rows and rows of folding seats.

Don't think about those. Of course, it wasn't the chairs that bothered her but the people who filled them. She had expected to have a larger force attend than usual, but she hadn't expected anything like this.

Hundreds—maybe a thousand—people filled the seats while she orbited the room and tried to think about what to say.

She knew their goal, of course. It was the same goal she'd had since she realized the threat that Constance posed, but she'd never had resources like this. She'd never had anyone on board but herself.

Well, that wasn't exactly true. Even from the onset, her human SWAT team had always been on board. They sat in the front row now. Keith played on his phone while Beanpole sat beside him, watched the podium, and waited politely for the briefing to begin. Washington was next to Beanpole with his arms folded, clearly uncomfortable to be in the presence of so many dragons, but he was there all the same.

Behind him sat Hernandez, who smirked wickedly at her old

teammate while she munched on popcorn. The woman must have brought it with her, and although it seemed entirely out of place, she had it all the same and didn't seem fazed. She stuck her tongue out, then stuck a kernel to it when she saw Kristen looking at her. Next to her in the aisle seat was Butters. He smiled pleasantly as he did what she tried not to do—look at all the people in the room.

Perhaps the most out of place were those seated behind her old SWAT team. Drew and Windlock must have made the situation very clear to Captain Hansen, as it looked like she'd sent every available officer from Detroit to help Kristen with her plan. There were beat cops who had worked with her dad when they were younger and detectives who'd handled all of SWAT's non-dragon cases. Even other SWAT teams were present, although she mostly recognized them from the airsoft arena.

Surrounding these seemingly regular humans were all the members of dragon SWAT. They were in human form, of course, but it was still unmistakable that they were dragons. They pretended to chat amongst themselves and ignore the human police inside their stronghold, but she could feel their aura. It was no doubt what made the human police so jittery.

Heartsbane, Emerald, Timeflash, and Lumos sat directly behind the human officers. They seemed amused to see their old rookie giving the orders, with the exception of Heartsbane. The scowl on her face said she wanted to murder Kristen and anyone else who told her she had to remain seated, but her aura said something different. It said she was proud of her. She knew the dragon had a level of control over her aura beyond almost any other dragon. Without a doubt, she was the only person aware that Heartsbane was actually proud of her. She probably radiated disgust to everyone else.

It wasn't only dragons, though. All the mages from the Paper Dungeon were crammed into the auditorium as well. They passed notes to each other without bothering to be discreet about it. One of them wrote something on a post-it, folded it into an airplane or paper crane or another origami figure, and sent it across the room to a fellow mage.

Windlock was there too, of course. He stood in the very back with Larry Brockton. The investigator had a self-satisfied look on his face which she tried to keep telling herself was because of the presentation she was about to give.

It's not a presentation. She looked at the stage at the front of the auditorium. *This is only a briefing. I can* do *briefings.*

The truth was that she hated public speaking. All her failed attempts at making speeches went through her head. When she'd first become the Steel Dragon, the news had been obsessed with her and while she'd coped and even seemed to excel at being in the public eye, any mass gathering only served to remind her that it had made her a target. She'd thought she might have conquered her anxiety when she'd gone to present at the hospital, but that only earned her a sniper bullet made of dragon parts through her shoulder. If anything, that had exacerbated her innate anxiety over being at the center of attention. More recently, she'd done okay with two reporters in Maine—or she thought she had but apparently, one of them hadn't bought her story and tailed her, recorded her, and shown the world the danger that humans now posed to dragons and perhaps sparked World War Three.

On top of that tight little ball of anxiety, Kristen also had to consider that her words today would determine not only these people's lives but those of the entire planet. If she messed this up, the future of both species could go up in dragon flame, bullets, and atomic blasts.

No pressure, she told herself, took a deep breath, and totally failed to calm herself.

Drew came into the room and strode down the sloped floor and past the rows of chairs like he owned the place despite only having now been invited in. He came up to her, looking serious until he was directly in front of her with his back to the crowd so no one could see his face except her, and he broke out a grin.

"You look like you'd rather fight a dragon than get on that stage," he said.

Kristen couldn't help but guffaw. "Is it that obvious? Me and public speaking don't mesh. If I'm lucky, someone will shoot me with one of the bullets I'm trying to confiscate. If I'm unlucky, the world will literally end."

"Don't be so melodramatic. There's nothing we could do to end the world," Drew said.

"Are you serious, Drew? We are literally talking about a war between humans and dragons. We're talking fire breath versus fighter jets armed with dragon bullets, but if the dragons do too well, there's always atomic bombs to worry about."

"Atomic bombs can't end the world, Kristen," he said and put a reassuring hand on her shoulder. "Cockroaches will survive as well those weird tubeworm things near ocean vents or whatever."

"Have you watched more nature documentaries or something?"

Drew smiled broadly. "Things get boring without you around, Kristen Hall, Steel Dragon. You have nothing to worry about, though."

"I really do, Drew."

He shook his head. "No, you don't. You're right. If we don't stop this from happening it might very well be the end of everything we love. It might be that the mages already have a crazy plan and that we only have twenty-four hours left to live—"

"You're really not helping," she cut in.

Drew held up a hand, "Let me finish, okay?"

Kristen shrugged. He couldn't make it worse, right?

"My point is, yes, the world's in danger, but there's nowhere I would rather be than right here, working with the Steel Dragon herself. You're the only person who might be able to find a way out of this mess that doesn't involve all of us fighting over the last can of beans."

She smiled sardonically. "Sure, Drew, I know you feel that way, but you've saved my ass and I've saved yours. We're friends. Most of these people here don't know me."

"They know of you. Every cop in Detroit is always pounding us for stories about the Steel Dragon. They all know that although your skin is made of steel, your heart is made of gold."

"Come on, Drew, that's a little cheesy." She chuckled. "Did Butters tell you that one?"

He turned to the sniper, who put his hand to his heart and winked, which made it even more obvious that he was the one who'd given his team leader that particular line.

"The point is that I've watched you grow—we've all watched you grow. Hell, it's damn hard not to with the media being such a sucker for you. You came in headstrong but damn if that stubbornness didn't save my ass again and again. All these people know you—either directly or by reputation—and know you'll do your best to solve this and won't compromise lives to do so."

"How can you say that?" she demanded and tears came to her eyes unbidden. She turned her back on the crowd so no one had to watch the Steel Dragon cry. "Jonesy died because of me."

Drew took her by the shoulders. "Jonesy died because he was a bad cop."

"What?" The words shocked her because he had never said anything like that about anyone.

He shrugged. "He was. He was hungover half the time and drunk the other half. He was racist and didn't do a good job of leaving that bullshit at home. He swore—"

"So does Hernandez."

"Not in front of civilians." Drew shook his head. "I'm sorry Jonesy died on your watch, but that would have happened one way or the other. Kristen, you took a rocket for that man. Not a bullet, but a goddamn rocket! What more could you have done?"

"I don't know. If I had only known more—"

"You do know more, Kristen. Think of everything you know now that you didn't know then. Hell, has anyone tried to attack Detroit since they discovered what you are? You even scared Shadowstorm into hiding inside the recycling plant instead of risking an all-out battle! You're a hero, Kristen Hall, and we all know that if you lead us, we can do this."

Kristen nodded and wiped the last few tears from her eyes. "You're right. I can do this."

"Damn straight you can!" Drew clapped her on the shoulder a little too forcefully. "And if you don't…well, we're all fucked. So who really cares anyway?"

Her eyes widened but she couldn't help but laugh. Ah…the humor of those who knew they were about to face their own death. Gallows humor was precious to human SWAT in a way it wasn't to the dragons Kristen had worked with more recently.

"Great, we're all fucked anyway. Words to live by, I guess," she said, surprised that those were his last words and even more surprised that they'd worked.

After a deep breath, she walked onto the stage and stood behind the podium. The crowd continued to talk, which wasn't too encouraging. Still, it gave her a moment to steel herself, then switched on the lapel mike she wore.

Feedback briefly blared and most of the crowd turned to look at her.

"Shut the fuck up," both Hernandez and Heartsbane yelled loudly. They caught each other's eyes after the outburst and seemed to appraise one another. Now that was a relationship Kristen did not want to see develop, so she took a deep breath and began to talk.

"Hello, everyone. My name's Kristen Hall."

She paused maybe too long, so Keith yelled, "Are you an alcoholic?"

The humans laughed at that but the dragons didn't. If they had been in their dragon forms, they'd doubtlessly be twitching their tails in frustration.

"I'd say I'm the Steel Dragon or Lady Steel or tell you my credentials, but you all know me. I'm a cop, exactly like the rest of you. The main difference between me and any of you is that I've been yelled at by both Stonequest and Captain Hansen."

That drew a few laughs, which did calm her somewhat.

"You also probably already know that the reason I get in trouble so damn much is that I refuse to defend dragon lives over human lives or visa versa. I believe we need to share this world. We can't continue to pretend we're two separate cultures. We've been mixed together forever and it's time to acknowledge that. Our enemies hope we won't realize that until it's too late."

She looked across the room to see somber faces. "I don't use the word enemy lightly either. We're all cops, so we all know the power and importance of words like alleged, and suspected, but we are not dealing with alleged or suspected criminals here. We are dealing with murderers. This job will be different than anything else we've ever done because if the enemy isn't stopped, it will mean war is certain, not merely possible."

Kristen paused to let those words sink in. It appeared to be an unpleasant process, but she also saw many people nod. They knew what was coming because they were all detectives and enforcers of the peace. If anyone knew the dangers of new kinds of powerful firearms in the hands of the unstable, it was them.

"Make no mistake, it will be a brutal, bloody war. Human cities will be torched. Dragons will be cut down by bullets made from dragon parts."

"That's disgusting!" a dragon yelled.

"Oh, I agree," she said calmly, determined not to allow herself to be derailed now. "But that's not the half of it. These enemies—techno-mages, we call them—have acted in a limited capacity, which means there are limits to their weapon production capabilities. Even if they have built up a cache they think is big enough to win a war, they will not hesitate to harvest more dead dragons on the field of battle and use them to kill even more of their kind."

"Humans are monsters," another dragon bellowed in protest.

"And how long before dragons start to think about the first two human rebellions?" she demanded in response. "How long until the dragons decide they miss eating meat? You dragons have all read the history books that aren't available to regular humans. You know as well as anyone what you ate to survive in those wars. I'm not so naïve to think it would be different."

She paused to let the weight of that sink in. You could hear a pin drop in the room before she continued. "It's a nightmare scenario. What's worse is that the Full Dragon Council will meet soon and if nothing changes, that might well be what they elect to do—unless someone can change their mind first."

Kristen smiled at her friends, dragon and human alike.

"This was never my dream as a little girl. I never thought I'd be in this room with all of you, human and dragon both, the bravest police in the Midwest. All I ever wanted to do was be a cop, but so many of you believed in me and helped me and gave me a leg up that I became something more. I know some of you might say that I brought all of these people from two different species together, but that's not true.

"You came together to help, and that gives me hope. It ought to give all of you hope," she said, "because this kind of cooperation doesn't usually happen. It's never happened, not in all of our centuries together, but it can.

"These two species—the one that raised me and the one I am—can work together and defend peace for all. The trust and bond that everyone in this room must have for each other if we are to succeed can spread. When we are successful, the world will look at this cramped auditorium and say this is the kind of thing that made it possible for both groups to stand side by side. This whole meeting is a symbol of hope for a better future."

The crowd applauded and she let them. They clapped for a dream that Constance and her technomages worked so hard to rip apart and that the Dragon Council itself was afraid of. The noise finally died down and she continued.

"Unfortunately, symbols aren't enough by themselves. Not when war is looming so near at hand. We must stop the terrorist cells before they can take more action. To do that, we need to find out where they're hiding, root them out, stop their dragon bullet production, and end this threat once and for all. Maybe if we can show the Council that humans and dragons working together will make dragons safer than a human-dragon war ever would, they will elect to pursue a path other than war."

Kristen looked around the room. "You're all professionals. We all have teams and bosses."

"Not you," said Brockton, grinning like a fool.

"My point is that we all know we need to find these technomages, so get onto it. You don't need me to micromanage. Everyone in this room is now assigned to my anti-mage terrorist task force, effective immediately. Everything else is on hold until they're brought to justice. If you're not working, know that the technomages are. So you're all dismissed and will proceed under the direction of your commanding officers. Let's get to work."

CHAPTER FIFTY-EIGHT

The applause following Kristen's speech was as long as necessary and no longer. She smiled and decided that even if she had been nervous, she had got what she needed to say across. Every human would get the details from Drew's files. Every dragon and mage would get them from Stonequest. She had already spoken to a few teams about cross-overs, but she had full confidence that people would work to find answers and bring her the leads they found.

Kristen couldn't help but smile as Jim Washington approached her from the seats. It was exactly like the Wonderkid to have a lead moments after the investigation began.

"What do you have for me, Wonderkid?" she asked and let herself grin as he responded with a look that seemed to ask how she knew.

"Well, I don't have any new evidence but something's kind of kicked around my head. Now that we're all hands on deck, I thought I might as well share it."

"Sure. What do you have?"

"Well, honestly, I think it's weird that a group of technomage terrorists are still in control of the dragon bullets."

She nodded and tried not to laugh. "Yeah, you're right, but weird has basically been my job description since I found out I was a dragon.

What aspect of magic users making dragon bullets to wage a more successful war than those that involved dwarves or pixies are you talking about?"

Jim smiled. "Fair enough, fair enough. I guess I've gotten used to all this crazy shit too. What I'm wondering about is their money."

"Their money?"

"Sure. Most groups like this—terrorist cells, gangs, cartels, and those kinds of assholes—have some source of funding. Many cartels sell drugs, for example, while some kidnap people and ransom them. But as far as we can tell, Constance and her folks don't have anything like that. We've never busted a drug-dealing mage, and she's never made any demands beyond war, right?"

Kristen rubbed her chin and tried to think if Constance had ever demanded anything other than to overthrow the dragons' grip on society. "I think… I think you might have something there."

"Right? Plus, they're making high-quality rounds. Think about it. We've fought against them a few times now, and no one has ever reported a jammed weapon, a dud bullet, or anything like that. Their facilities have to be reasonably professional to get that kind of consistency. And then there's the elephant in the closet."

"You mean the dragon," she said with a frown.

Jim nodded. "Yeah, I do. I had a chance to look at some of Dragon SWAT's data before this meeting started. They've recovered bullets from more than one of these crime scenes that have over a ninety percent match to your DNA, Kristen."

"Don't remind me."

"I wish I didn't have to, kid." He sounded far older than he was for a moment. "But it's like you said. We don't have that kind of luxury anymore."

"You're right, of course. Go on," she told him.

"Right. Well, at first, I assumed these mages harvested their materials from the dragons they killed, but the DNA testing seems to show otherwise. They must have an individual restrained or complicit or something."

Kristen nodded at the idea, as disgusting and macabre as it was.

"They're probably using their healing power to continue to…" She let the sentence trail away because she didn't want to say the word aloud. The very thought of them harvesting a living being to make weapons was repulsive.

"Exactly." Jim looked disgusted at the idea. "Which means they have a dragon they need to keep fed, healthy, and restrained, not to mention move occasionally if they remain mobile—which, let's face it, most terrorist cells do. An operation like that, plus building weapons? It can't be cheap."

"Okay, funding…that's a great place to look at. I'll get some of our desk jockeys on it," she said, ready to get to work.

"Hold up. I have one more thought for you. Who else might benefit from the bullets?"

It didn't take her long to follow his train of thought. "You're thinking about the military."

"Bingo," he said and his jaw clenched. "We saw hell over there. Dragons aren't supposed to participate in human wars, but that doesn't mean they don't. I'm not the only one with an ax to grind against dragons. And even if there isn't a personal grudge involved, from a tactical position, dragons are a nightmare. There are many folks in the military who think the US has maintained global military dominance since World War II, but that doesn't extend to dragons. These bullets would let us lead the world in military might. There are those who won't ignore that."

"I have to say, Jim, I don't like how much sense you make," Kristen said after she drew a deep breath. "Do you want to infiltrate a base or something crazy?"

The Wonderkid smiled. "No, nothing like that. Not yet anyway."

She hated that she couldn't tell if he was joking.

"I want to check in with my old military contacts and connections," he continued. "I'll run things through the grapevine and see if I can get any news. If there are officers high up involved in manufacturing dragon bullets, they're bound to have told at least a few people down the chain. If that's the case, I might be able to find out. But don't get me wrong. Part of me hopes I come up with nothing at all."

Kristen nodded. "Me too. If you're right and there are parts of the military that have their hands on these bullets, it's a significant problem. If the US military gets hold of them, I don't see how we could prevent a war. That's too big a threat for the Dragon Council to let it go. They'd authorize a preemptive strike, which of course would earn retaliation from the military…" She shuddered at the thought.

In two strikes, it could all be over and Constance would win. The world, however, would burn.

"Jim, I have to say it makes sense. You might be right and if you are, you need to be damn careful. You've already stuck your neck out a little too far more than once. Don't get it chopped off this time."

"Believe me, that is not my intention."

"All right, then. Let me know as soon as you find anything out. If I'm not here, tell Drew."

"You got it, Steel Dragon." The Wonderkid winked and headed off to get to work.

Once he'd left, she watched the rest of the auditorium come together. Many people had already left, but a fair number of the joint human and dragon teams were still in discussion about how they would go about things.

Kristen moved through the auditorium and listened to snippets of conversation.

"Hell no, we won't be bait for you guys. You don't even know what it takes to kill a human."

"We do too."

"That's the problem."

Another conversation a few paces away presented an entirely different perspective.

"You want to ride us? Forget it. I don't care how much time it will save."

She saw scowls from humans and felt flashes of anger from dragon auras. Arguments flared between senior officers and junior officers took sides with their bosses.

But no one threw a punch and no one resorted to profanity or name-calling.

The humans and dragons didn't work together perfectly, but they worked together. There was friction and tempers manifested, but that was to be expected. They were in a room with hundreds of people who all thought they were the one who knew what justice really meant, and she had forced them all to reconsider what their definition of the word was. Until now, few individuals from either species ever considered what justice looked like for the other. Now, they all struggled to not only define it but enforce it. Given what they were going through, she thought they did admirable work.

On the other hand, they also all knew the price of failing to work together. War was not justice and police weren't soldiers. If war came to this continent and spread to the world, it meant every police officer in this room had failed at their job's primary function—to keep the peace.

As Kristen made her way through the auditorium, she saw more and more groups break away. Everyone seemed purposeful and no doubt headed to offices or coffeeshops or already out to walk beats that might yield information of value.

She couldn't wait to join them, to follow the leads of a thousand of the brightest minds in law enforcement, but first, she had a mission of her own to tackle. A highly functional team was the key to successful law enforcement. She had to make sure hers worked at the highest possible level.

Larry Brockton stood alone and waited for Windlock to finish a conversation with another dragon.

"Hey, Larry. I need your help with something."

"Given that you're the boss of everyone in this whole building, I think I'll go ahead and simply say yeah, you got it. Whatever you need."

"Great. Let's take a walk, though. This is something I need you to do in…uh…" Kristen glanced around. It was as she expected. People couldn't help but watch her. After all, she was the Steel Dragon and now their boss. She radiated energy and controlled the space, and as long as she was around, people would pay attention to her.

She led the mage up the stairs to her new office. They closed the door and she sat behind her desk—a weird feeling. The chair wasn't particularly nice, and the desk—while made of wood and in decent shape—didn't feel particularly special. Despite that, there was something very right about sitting at her own desk—the desk of an investigator.

"What you need, boss?" he asked and seemed to be at a loss. She didn't think he was used to seeing an investigator's office so clean and knew she only had to give it time. While she'd yet to work a case, her first one promised to be a doozy.

"I want that cuff off of Amy," she said, perhaps too bluntly. "It hinders her magic and it seems to make her feel like crap. I saw her wince and stagger when it was first locked on. I had one of those damn things on me when I was sent to prison and it was horrible. I understand that hers isn't quite as restrictive, but still. I almost died when I didn't have access to my powers. If she is restricted like that—especially if and when we go up against Constance or God forbid, we have to stop a dragon from burning a city to the ground—she'll fail. Hell, she might die and take me with her. I won't have her life or this mission risked because of dragon paranoia."

"Will you take it off her?" The mage rubbed his wrist where his own magic-inhibiting bracelet had been until recently. He didn't sound particularly flustered at the idea, but he was Larry Brockton, after all. She had seen him ride into battle on Windlock's back and not complain about anything but the wind.

"I want to, but I'm concerned about how the dragons will react. I realize Windlock took your cuff off, but you've been a staple in dragon culture for years. Many people know you and everyone knows Windlock. It's odd, but you two have kind of earned it."

"You're worried that if you take it off, the dragons who don't like the Steel Dragon raised by humans might take offense?"

Kristen sighed. "If it was only that, I wouldn't be so concerned, but Amy's safety is my priority. While it was in self-defense and that has been made clear, there's still no question that she killed two dragons. That's not the kind of thing everyone will simply forget. If she's not cuffed, I'm worried dragons will simply wait for an excuse to snap at her."

"She could defend herself, though," Larry said and barely hid a grin. He knew better than anyone how powerful Amy really was. Kristen had a fairly good idea based on what she'd seen, but he was an experienced mage. He knew exactly how much power she needed to do the things she did.

"If she did that, we'd have a war on our team. It's not an option."

"Okay, so you want to take the bracelet off but you don't want anyone to know? How exactly do I help with that?"

She smiled. "There are times when I'm very thankful you worked with an investigator for so long because you pick things up so quickly. That's exactly what I want. So, can it be done? I doubt I could put any old silver bracelet on her and expect it to trick all the dragons and mages into thinking she's not a threat, right?"

Brockton took a deep breath and leaned back in his chair. "I... that's interesting. You know, I've never really considered all this but you're right about that. There's a spell on the cuffs. Any mage can read it on another mage and many dragons can too. In fact, I'd wager that most dragons will try to read hers on account of her being new and so powerful."

"So the cuff gives off an aura?"

"Yeah." He nodded. "You can think of it like that. It doesn't change like a dragon's or a mage's aura does, though. It's more like a stamp or something. It's there and most dragons and all mages can read it."

"Okay. Is there a way to fake that spell?" Kristen asked and leaned over her desk. "Is there a way to make a bracelet look like it functions as expected to keep a mage's power level in check but doesn't actually do anything?"

Larry's eyebrows raised in obvious surprise. "I hadn't really thought of that before." He chuckled. "I'm a cop—or a dragon one anyway. I'm not the kind of person who goes around breaking the rules, so it never occurred to me, but..."

"But?"

"But yeah. I believe it ought to be possible. It's a different spell than the one that stops the power, which is always the same and very powerful. The one you're talking about—the identification component of the bracelet—is more complex, but I don't see why it would be particularly high-powered. It's probably something I can achieve on my own."

"So you'll do it?"

The mage chuckled. "It's not like I'll be in trouble, right, Investigator?"

"We both heard Windlock say he gave me the job so I could explain all this to the Dragon Council myself. There's no way I'd let you get in trouble for following one of my crazy orders."

He nodded. "Yeah, of course I'll try. Actually, I'm intrigued by the idea and the challenge of it."

"Excellent. If Windlock needs you for something dire, help him of course, but if you can work on this and get me a solution as soon as possible, that would be great."

"Yes, ma'am." He darted from his chair and saluted as a knock sounded at the door.

Stonequest waited for her response. Since his original shock at learning that Kristen had been promoted to an investigator, he'd become one of her staunchest supporters. It was great to see him take her so seriously, even though it wasn't really a choice. He had tried to hide the existence of the dragon bullets from dragon kind, the mages, and humans too. She'd sometimes been frustrated by this decision, but he'd understood better than anyone what would happen if their existence became common knowledge. His worst nightmares were now on the verge of reality if the combined team's efforts failed.

"What can I do for you Stonequest?" she asked with a small smile. How completely their situations had changed was quite amusing despite the seriousness of the situation.

"We have a possible lead," Stonequest said, his tone all business although his aura betrayed his excitement.

"Already? That's great! How?"

"The Wonderkid turned something up."

She beamed. The fact that Jim had found something was great, of course, but it was the fact that he'd gone to the dragon SWAT leader to relay the information that truly inspired her. If he of all people could work with dragons, a bridge could truly be built between the two species. The challenge would be building it before Constance tried to burn the foundations.

"Washington said an officer from the supply division at Fort Drum reported an unusual incident."

"And can we trust this guy?" she asked.

"Jim seemed to think so. He said he was an old friend and was afraid after he'd seen the footage of the dragons on TV."

"Go on."

"Apparently, he has an incoming shipment of something—he's not sure what—that has no verified sender. He did his job correctly and filed a report with the base MPs, who put it out to other law enforcement for assistance to track the origin."

"It doesn't sound like anything concrete," Kristen said, a little disappointed.

"That's what I thought at first too, but Washington pointed out the timing and I think that might be all we'll have to go on. It's not like Constance will write 'dragon ammunition' on the side of weapons and post them on social media."

"Fair enough. So that's what you think it is? Dragon bullets?"

Stonequest looked like he wanted to shrug and dismiss the idea as pure paranoia, but something in him—the cop, no doubt—wouldn't allow him to make the familiar unconcerned gesture. Instead, he nodded grimly.

"The way I see it, this is either nothing—drugs or something stupid —or it's the worst possible scenario. We might find out it's a bust, but if this is a shipment of weapons to a US military base, we're basically already at war. The Dragon Council will not tolerate it, and if Constance chose her target right—and we'd be fools to think she didn't find the perfect person—they won't wait for the dragons to attack. Your military has a preference for preemptive strikes."

"All right. Then we mobilize. We'll treat this as our first operation but can't drop every lead we have. I want people to continue the search for Constance here in the city and follow anything else we have, but I'll have a list of who I want with us in ten minutes. We'll leave in twenty. Tell Windlock he'll be in charge of HQ until we get back and let's all hope to hell this is a wild goose chase, even though my gut tells me it's not."

Stonequest nodded. "I wish you were being paranoid, but I think this might be it. We need to douse the spark that might set the world on fire."

CHAPTER FIFTY-NINE

Twenty minutes later, Kristen stood on the roof of the Capital Square Building with the team she'd asked for.

Emerald, Heartsbane, and Stonequest would be the dragons on the team and Drew, Washington, and Amy would be the humans. The dragons were chosen in case they encountered trouble, Drew for his cool head and as a capable tactical fighter, and Washingon for his military experience. Amy was in case they encountered mages and they needed to fight magic with magic.

"All right, it'll be a long flight, so get comfortable and let's do this," she said, already in her dragon form. Everyone nodded and Amy used her magic to lift herself onto her boss' back. Thankfully, she was learning to use what abilities the cuff allowed her to their maximum advantage.

Stonequest lowered a shoulder for Drew to climb on. Emerald let Washington ride on him. It came as no surprise that Heartsbane was the first to take flight. She'd never liked humans and no one had expected her to offer to let one of them ride her.

The flight took hours given that from Detroit to northern New York wasn't exactly a short distance. While they flew, they talked tactics and theories and Amy provided a bubble around the human passengers so they didn't get cold from the wind and could actually hear each other.

What struck Kristen most on the journey was the beauty of the lakes below them. They soared across Lake Erie—once renowned for being so polluted it would often catch alight—but both its cleaner condition and the late hour of the day made it look beautiful. Gentle rolling waves hosted schools of freshwater fish and the occasional fishing boat dotted the seemingly endless stretch of water.

How can something look so peaceful while the world is so close to going to hell?

The question became even more pronounced when they flew over Niagara falls. There, tourists from all over the world gathered to gawk at a natural wonder. People snapped pictures of the dragons flying overhead and would no doubt post them to social media later, only concerned about the appropriate hashtag. It was both wonderful and terrible that her job could keep so many people oblivious to the dangers in the world.

If they did their job right, everyone would spend another night in comfortable oblivion. It was a weird goal to work toward, but Kristen infinitely preferred it to the other option in which world peace was shattered and every single person was thrown into the chaos of war. At least, when the world was at peace, they had some semblance of control over their lives. War did not give people control of anything. It would only take what little they had.

An hour later, they hovered above Fort Drum. From the air, it was obvious that the base was laid out in a huge oval. The northern half contained the barracks and training areas for combat, the military police, and other units. A small mall, a grocery store, and a fast-food outlet were positioned on the west side. The base headquarters took precedence in the center of the oval.

Even from the air, the southern half looked much older. People moved about there uncertainly and Kristen assumed those were new recruits awaiting allocation to a proper unit. There also appeared to be offices on the southside, as well as old equipment and warehouses. She could tell from the architecture that the northern section of Fort

Drum saw far more practical use. The brick and concrete buildings looked both newer and in a better state of repair. The south wasn't derelict or anything like that, but the paint didn't look quite as fresh and there were more wooden buildings than concrete. In fact, there didn't appear to be any brick at all.

"Should we land at the south and walk in?" Emerald asked.

Kristen considered his suggestion. It would be the polite thing to do and would give the soldiers time to form up as the dragons walked through their base. Unfortunately, they didn't have time for niceties.

"No, follow my lead. I have a feeling we'll need to talk to someone from headquarters."

She whooped as she tucked her wings and plunged toward the base. Amy screamed with joy from her back—she really was more of a thrill-seeker than her boss had realized when she'd tried to track her. The other dragons followed and remained in tight formation as they plummeted and only slowed at the last second when they spread their wings, made one last cursory loop, and landed in a diamond formation facing the headquarters building.

While she wasn't surprised at the reaction of the soldiers, she was impressed.

As the dragons tucked into formation, close to a hundred soldiers ran into position. They'd fortified the entrance and stationed troops in the trees across the street from the building. While they surrounded the dragons to make it clear access was not permitted, no one actually raised a weapon to aim at them. Whether that was a begrudging sign of respect or simply policy because it was known that regular bullets couldn't do much damage to dragons, Kristen didn't know, but she took it as a good sign either way. If these soldiers already had the dragon rounds, some of them would no doubt aim them, no matter how well trained they were.

A moment of silence followed while the mage, Jim, and Drew climbed off the dragons and the soldiers held their positions. A sergeant with a mustache and a hard face that looked like it had seen combat stepped forward.

"To what do we owe the honor of this unannounced visit?" he demanded, his tone civil but sharp.

"We're not here to hurt anyone. My name is Kristen Hall, otherwise known as the Steel Dragon," she said as she approached the sergeant and transformed into her human form as she moved. She pointed to her dragon investigator badge and he calmed visibly.

"Pardon our response, ma'am," he said, chagrined. "The rumor is your kind will hold the first full council meeting in decades. Normally, those don't go well for people, and well…being a base so close to Canada, we've drilled for ages for this kind of possibility."

"Rest assured, Sergeant…"

"Smith, ma'am. Sergeant Ulysses J Smith."

"Rest assured, Sergeant Smith, the last thing I want to do is hurt any of your men and women. As you can see, I brought a small group to aid me in my investigation. We merely want answers to a few questions, nothing more."

He appraised her team and nodded. The four dragons had taken their human shape and appeared much less formidable—merely like seven people visiting a base that held hundreds. The tension eased now that they seemed less threatening. Kristen wanted them to continue to feel that way, even if it wasn't technically true.

"Who can I direct you too, ma'am?"

"Who is in charge of your supplies?" Washington asked.

"If you have questions about our supplies, I'd direct you to Major Dunning. I'll show you to his office," the sergeant said and brushed his mustache with his finger and thumb. He turned to the soldiers. "Back to it, men. Some of you dragged ass getting into position, which means you need five miles as a reminder not to do that. Not yesterday, now!"

The troop broke ranks as Kristen and her team followed Sergeant Smith to Major Dunning's office.

"Here he is, ma'am. He has access to all our emergency comms so if you need anything, he'll be able to get it for you." The sergeant's subtext was clear. *I may be going outside and this guy might seem nice, but he can press a hidden red button and this whole base will be up your ass faster than you can sneeze.*

The Wonderkid knocked and an older man answered, "Come in, come in!"

It was immediately clear that Dunning had been there a while. The walls of his office were covered in photos of him meeting various political figures over the years. His bookshelves were crammed with books that had a layer of dust on them that hadn't appeared overnight.

"Jim, how are you?" he said, stood quickly, and shook the man's hand warmly.

"I'm good, Major. I'm not in the service anymore but working as a cop."

"Yeah, you mentioned that when you called. That's what brings you here, right?" Everything about Major Dunning radiated calm. He was a thin black man in his late forties or maybe early fifties with tight, curly hair that was now more gray than black. His spectacles didn't look like they'd last long in a combat scenario. Kristen couldn't help but like him.

"Well, like I said on the phone, we don't know exactly what we're looking for, at least from the outside. But we're concerned that illegal arms will reach the military. I appreciate you letting me know that you noticed something."

She knew that Jim had called Dunning, and yet the way he had phrased the last statement made it sound like the man had called him. That was the power of the Wonderkid, though. He was great with people.

"Of course, I don't know what's in there, but I saw a shipment that seemed designed to basically be invisible. It came in late, no one needed to sign for it, and it was unloaded into a warehouse without anyone to help, that kind of thing."

"You still have them eyes, huh?" Jim said with a laugh.

The major smiled. "Oh yes, that's why they don't want to move me out of this office—thank goodness for that, of course. I don't miss these kinds of things. I thought that was why General Andrews kept me here anyway, but when I reported this to him, he wasn't exactly thrilled about it. He said something along the lines of who did I think would order a shipment like this but him. I tried to tell him I could square the paperwork so the soldiers wouldn't know but the big brass would, and he got all bent out shape. But that's fine. Who wants to be bossed around by Major Supplies? That's what the troops call me."

The Wonderkid looked like he was about to ask more about General Andrews but Kristen flashed her aura at him to make him feel like he should remain silent. She wasn't subtle about it all, so he looked at her and raised an eyebrow. Her response was to give him a look that told him to simply let the man talk.

The opportunity to perhaps apprehend a person—especially a general—was important to her, but first and foremost, they had to stop the guns. After all, the old axiom was true. Guns didn't kill people but people with guns did. She needed to stop the weapons.

Major Dunning seemed to also be more interested in the shipping itself than in further complaints about his boss. If there was something nefarious afoot with his commanding officer, he didn't seem particularly concerned about it.

He opened his desk and removed some documentation, which he handed to her.

She glanced at it and noted the time and the instructions to leave without signatures. "And when is it supposed to come in?"

"That one? It should come in later tonight."

"Wait—what do you mean, that one?" she asked.

"Another shipment like that already arrived," he said with a smile like these were all pieces of some fun little mystery instead of the possibly the catalyst that would set the world ablaze. "Honestly, if there hadn't been two of these, I probably wouldn't have thought to say anything to Jim. The other one came in a few days ago. I tried to track it but couldn't find it anywhere in the warehouse. Then Andrews gave me his glib answer and I thought maybe it was something personal and he'd had it delivered here to qualify for a military discount or something. He wouldn't be the first CO to use his position like that and probably wouldn't be the last, but then this one showed up. Well, when Jim called me, this all came to mind."

"The loads are the same?" Washington asked.

"They both come late at night and are simply dropped off without signature or any help unloading, but the shipment that's coming tonight looks like it'll be much larger," Dunnings said, removed his glasses, and polished them.

"And you never found the first order?" Kristen asked.

"No, and I'll be honest with you, it's begun to drive me crazy. What do you think it is anyway? Drugs? I don't want to speak ill of any of our men and women, but everyone—even soldiers—has vices."

She shook her head. "Something worse than drugs." Her instinctive caution made her hesitant to tell him more. He seemed trustworthy enough and had even questioned this General Andrews—although he'd also simply left it there—but might not quite understand the meaning of a secret. Obviously, he respected classified information—one had to be able to do that if they were in charge of supplies—but he appeared to have a need for transparency that might be a disadvantage.

Dunning didn't press, fortunately, and simply nodded. His eyes widened behind his freshly polished spectacles and he leaned back in his chair. "I suppose you would like me to take you where the shipment is?"

"Don't you mean where it's supposed to be?" Stonequest said. He was the only other dragon who had pushed into the small office.

"Yes, I suppose so, but I thought with you being dragons, maybe you could...I don't know, smell it or something."

The two dragons looked at each other and laughed. She smiled at the kindly man. If this was an act, he was a master of deception but she didn't think so. In fact, it began to seem that her reservations had been groundless and perhaps they could trust Major Dunning after all.

Their entire team followed him through the headquarters building and out the back to a transport truck. Kristen and Washington sat in the front with the major while everyone else piled in the back. Dunning drove them south to the older buildings positioned around the huge oval that made up the base. It almost felt like driving back through time.

After ten minutes of comfortable silence, they arrived at a warehouse.

The team disembarked and entered. Their guide took them to a place where scuffed flooring suggested that a crate had been there, although it was now empty.

"Huh, exactly like you said. Nothing," Stonequest said, obviously not impressed.

"No, not nothing," Drew said. "Something was there. That area's not as dusty as everywhere else around it."

"Exactly!" Dunning looked like he had seen a ghost. "When I came and checked here last, there was nothing unusual. Now, though, it looks like this spot has been swept or something. I…this is very peculiar. I've never seen anyone bother with that in a warehouse before." He removed his spectacles and polished them once more as if doing so might make the missing crate appear.

"You said earlier that whoever received this shipment had already moved it," Drew said and again assumed the role of detective. "This seems to indicate that they didn't want any trace evidence left behind."

"Which means we don't know what the hell was in there and have no way to find out." Stonequest growled with the frustration they all felt.

"We know that whoever arranged this took some extraordinary precautions," Washington said. "It would have been far simpler to try to fit this in with a larger shipment, but that would have risked discovery. This way makes it more obvious that it's something odd if it's discovered, but balances that by making it far less likely to be discovered by accident."

"Do you think this is what we came here to find?" Kristen asked Washington.

"I can't say. It could be nothing but it does seem like the best lead we have unless Windlock has something for us."

Kristen shook her head. She hadn't heard from the investigator.

"There's nothing to be done, then." Heartsbane sounded furious like her time had been wasted.

Jim, Drew, and Kristen all looked at each other and smiled.

She spoke first. "Come on, Heartsbane. The major said another shipment was planned for tonight and it's even bigger than the first. Have you never been on a stakeout before?"

"A stakeout? You mean where we hide in the bushes and drink bad coffee and wait for nothing to happen? That's mage work," the dragon huffed.

"Not anymore it's not. I want to know what is in those crates and I want to stop that shipment before anyone can get their hands on it."

Dunning grinned. "Now this is how a discrepancy in supply paperwork should be handled."

CHAPTER SIXTY

While most of the team readied themselves for the stakeout, Kristen and Jim flew to the Military Police building. On the way, she realized this was the first one she would be on with Drew that didn't involve snacks. Butters must have been in charge of those because they'd been almost a ritual.

"Do you think these guys are complicit or what?" her companion asked when they landed out front.

"Nothing like that." She actually laughed at the idea. Her dad was a cop and she was essentially hard-wired to trust police in any form. She knew—intellectually—that there were problems with that thought and that corrupt officers existed on every force, human or dragon, military or civilian. Still, she couldn't help but give police the benefit of the doubt.

She flashed her badge at the two MPs guarding the door, who saluted smartly and let her past. Another led down a hallway to the office of the XO.

"Lt. Colonel Barnes, Ninety-first Military Police Battalion," he said and proffered his hand to shake hers. If she hadn't been a dragon, her knuckles might well have been crushed. The only thing harder than the man's handshake was the expression on his face. He was younger than she thought the rank suggested but perhaps his short-cropped red hair made him seem younger than he was. Still, he looked as disgruntled as any old-timer she had ever seen.

"Hello. I'm Kristen Hall, the Steel Dragon and investigator."

"Yes, ma'am, I am aware," Lt. Colonel Barnes snapped and barely let her finish before he spoke. "Now, what exactly can I do for you today? And may I point out that nothing I do will be against protocol—for example, landing in the middle of Fort Drum without following the proper chain of command is something I would not have allowed."

"Well, Lt. Colonel, that's exactly why we're here. It seems someone has delivered late-night packages to your base—without the proper paperwork, I might add. We're here to see what that is."

The officer's unreadable demeanor was such that she might not have noticed his reaction to her mentioning the late-night delivery, but she could read his aura like any other's. He was surprised that she knew about the delivery and disgusted, either with her or with the problem shipment. None of this reflected his face, however. The only expression he seemed capable of was being perpetually pissed-off.

"Do you know something about that?" Kristen asked, which surprised Jim, who turned to raise an eyebrow at her. Honestly, it was a risk. Barnes knew about it as Dunning had reported it, but he might also be in on it, which meant he might call the latest shipment off. Or—if her suspicions were true—he was a true hard-ass who loved the rules and someone had asked him to bend them for this.

For a moment, the Lt. Colonel somehow appeared to look even more pissed-off before his features finally softened slightly. While it didn't make him even close to agreeable, it tempered his overall disapproval somewhat.

"I...uh, I already took that up with my boss, Colonel Fox, and he said not to worry about it. He didn't fill out the proper forms to officially enable me to not worry about it, but chain of command is chain of command."

"And what if I told you that your Colonel Fox and perhaps even General Andrews have been compromised by an enemy of the United States people?" Kristen asked.

Barnes didn't react to this in the way she thought he might—again, she read his aura, not his face—which made her think he had already entertained the idea.

"I would say it's not my place to entertain conspiracy theories about my superiors…ma'am." It sounded like a canned response to her, maybe one he had been given by the man he'd asked about the matter.

"We're here to investigate that shipment and another that's supposed to arrive tonight," she told the military man. She wanted to tell him more but again, how could she be sure she could trust him? Even with her ability to read his emotional state, she wasn't sure. Still, she had to give him something. "We suspect the missing supplies and the shipment arriving tonight involve terrorists, but we have yet to confirm that."

Barnes stiffened visibly at that. It was the first body language he'd actually displayed, which indicated that her words had definitely made an impression.

Kristen wanted to trust him. He seemed cut from the same cloth as Dunning—a man who took the rules of the land more seriously than the people who claimed to enforce them—but even if he was, it didn't guarantee his support. Hard men like him might be glad to have dragon bullets. Clearly, folks at Drum knew a war might be brewing and a soldier like Barnes might be relieved to finally have the arsenal he would need to carry out his orders.

For a moment, no one said anything, then the military man spoke. "You're not telling me everything."

"No, I am not, Lt. Colonel Barnes. I am a dragon investigator, and what I do is confidential. But I can assure you that I act in the interests of the people and dragons of this country. If you've heard of me, you know my reputation. I don't take sides."

"I already have people withholding intel from me and demanding that I take risks, but at least they're part of my chain of command. That's part of my job. If you think you can come in here and walk all over the protocols of the US military, you need a reality check, Lady Steel." At least he'd used the proper honorific for a dragon, she thought before she realized that perhaps he'd said that rather than address her as Investigator because he didn't want to recognize the rank. Technically, humans were supposed to help dragon investigators too.

"All I'm asking is for you to help stop that shipment," Kristen said. "You know it's illegal. I know it's illegal. Your superiors know it's illegal. Let's see who clucks the loudest if we cause trouble in the henhouse," she said.

"I'm not doing a thing, ma'am. Not for 'suspected terrorism.' That bullshit is what got us into the Iraq War."

"You understand that I can go ahead and stop the shipment with or without your help, right? That I have three more dragons with me and a mage."

"Ma'am, there is nothing I understand more than a show of force. I recognized you and your people as soon as you entered the airspace over my base. But I also recognize that you wouldn't be in here if you didn't need me. We both know your job would be much harder if the MPs actively did their job to stop incursions into this base at say around oh-one hundred hours tomorrow morning. Is that why you're here? To make sure I stop you? Do you want to incinerate my men and women or something?"

"No! Of course not. I told you, I only want to stop this delivery from reaching its destination. What do you want?"

Barnes wrinkled his brow and sat. Clearly, no one had asked him that question in a very long time. He looked around him as if his office might be bugged and this last cursory check might finally be what cleared it. "I want the real information. Real intel. What is actually going on? What the hell do you think is in those shipments? Because I don't think it's drugs. So what? Bombs? Some kind of dragon bombs maybe?"

While he had talked, Kristen had barely focused on his words. Instead, she'd concentrated on his aura as she tried to determine his true loyalties and now thought she finally understood. When he spoke of the law or rules, something in his aura shifted. Rules and the law seemed to be the ideal he treasured the most. He was stressed because people he'd looked to as men worthy of carrying this banner—the banner of the rule of law—now seemed to shirk their responsibilities or at the very least, didn't allow him to do his.

That was enough for her. Drew had a very similar aura to Barnes. She loved people who, like her father, believed in the rule of law for everyone. Even the poorest had rights, and even the most powerful— even the president, or the Dragon Council—should follow the laws that protected those rights.

She decided to be honest. It was what she would have done with Drew. "We think a terrorist cell is shipping cases of bullets made from dragon pieces. Our suspicion is that both shipments are filled with those bullets and that someone at Fort Drum has a connection to these terrorists."

"Like on the goddamn cable news channels." Barnes leaned back. "It's true, then? There really are bullets that can kill dragons?"

"Oh yeah. That footage you've seen is real. I was there," she replied.

The officer clenched and unclenched his jaw a few times, a frown on his hard features. Kristen had the sense that this was his equivalent of pacing the room. He didn't seem likely to become emotional.

"You know, with the rumors that dragons might decide to wipe humans out, those supplies sound like something I might like to have around."

She nodded. "I don't blame you for thinking that, but you have to consider the broader implications if those bullets are widely distributed and become commonplace. The Dragon Council has ruled by sheer will for centuries. If people suddenly start killing dragons, they won't have any choice but to go to war."

"I don't know..." Barnes took a deep breath. "You're saying we shouldn't have these weapons because if we do, the dragons will attack? If all it takes is us showing a little spine for them to get all bent out of shape, it sounds like a good reason to fight them."

"I understand wanting to be as strong as them. I really do. I was always afraid of dragons on some level—I think all people are—and when I became one, it was an amazing feeling because I didn't have to live in fear anymore."

"But can't these guns give that feeling to people?" he asked.

"Yes, they could, but not like this—not as an illegal shipment to the most powerful military in the world. If these guns suddenly appear in soldiers' hands, it won't do anything to make dragons trust people. They know this tech exists but they don't know who has it. If they did, I think we would have already seen retaliation. We need to stop the terrorists and bring them to justice. Then and only then can we have a real conversation with the dragons about what this new power looks like."

"And I'm supposed to simply believe you? What assurance do I have that you're not simply trying to hamstring people and that you really want to bring them to justice?"

"In our hearts, we're the same. We're cops. This is what I do. If all of this was official and the president was in discussion with the Dragon Council about our military's new capabilities, I don't know that I'd be here having this discussion with you. But stopping an illegal shipment of arms from reaching a hothead gun-nut? That's something I need to do. It's not only my job but it's part of who I am."

Barnes held her gaze for a long time before he finally nodded.

"Maybe I'm finally taking after my mom instead of my dad, but... you seem like a kindred spirit. My people will stand by tonight to assist yours in any way they can."

CHAPTER SIXTY-ONE

The team had made a point of departing the base very visibly to create the impression that they had left. Barnes had directed them to a little-used entry point and had waited to let them in after nightfall and led them personally to where they had previously agreed would be the best location for their stakeout. To the best of their knowledge, no change had been implemented to the delivery schedule, which indicated that whoever was involved had simply assumed they posed no threat and things could proceed as arranged.

It was late—or early, depending on one's perspective at a little after one in the morning. The shipment should have come in at around twelve thirty, which made everyone jittery. The dragon and human SWAT team leaders shared command of the operation—both had far more experience than Kristen with these kinds of missions so she didn't mind delegating the responsibility, but even they were nervous.

Drew and Washington were on another warehouse overlooking the door to the one where the shipment was supposed to arrive. Both were armed with sniper rifles but she couldn't help but wonder if it would have been smart to bring Butters. He was the best shot on the force and she'd have felt far more confident with him on board.

"Movement!" Jim said, then sighed audibly through his radio. "Only an owl."

Stonequest, Emerald, Heartsbane, Kristen, and Amy were all on the ground, hidden behind trees and in brush near the warehouse, where they waited with growing impatience. It clearly indicated how anxious everyone was that when Jim mentioned movement, the team shuffled in place as if readying themselves to attack.

"Kristen, what's our plan?" Stonequest asked and sounded tense. She thought it was odd that the dragons—beings who had lived for centuries—were the impatient ones. It seemed logical that they would be masters of patience but he seemed to have moved past his earlier agreement to make the final decision once they knew what they faced.

"I hate to jump the gun on this, but I think Stonequest might be right," Drew said. "Something's up. You can't plan an operation like this and clear out any witnesses, only to be an hour late. Maybe our arrival spooked someone? I don't know, but I have a bad feeling."

"Okay, I'll call Barnes and—" Her phone vibrated in her pocket.

It was Barnes. They'd agreed it would probably be best if his people weren't involved in the actual stakeout. Whoever had planned this seemed to have extensive working knowledge of how Fort Drum was run. If a number of MPs suddenly began to scout a random location instead of doing their regular rounds, it might raise red flags.

The officer had said he'd only shared the mission with people he trusted, but she knew how that went. You trusted your people, and they trusted their people, and soon, everyone knew. It wasn't inconceivable that someone had got wind of their sting.

Or maybe Barnes had seen something, she reminded herself and pushed the negative thoughts aside. She answered, excited to be doing anything besides listen to owls.

"Investigator, I might have something," the man began without preamble. Kristen had to admit, she respected anyone who didn't waste time. "One of my people called in something that looked odd. A truck arrived on base loaded with supplies but it wasn't a regular shipment."

"How do you know?"

"It's not one of the usual vehicles, plus it's damn near two in the morning. On top of that, my MP said it was a new driver."

"Do we have any idea where it's going?" Kristen asked.

"Not really. Based on the order I saw, I thought it would head to where you are, but it doesn't seem to be doing that. Maybe they suspect something or that whole paper trail was merely a red herring."

"Dammit. So we've lost them?" Kristen was so frustrated she wanted to incinerate the woods around her but that, of course, would literally blow their cover.

"Not so fast. I put an MP on a motorcycle to tail them. We don't know where they're headed but we know where they're going if you see my meaning."

"Perfect! Good job, Barnes. Call me if there's anything else but I think we'll locate them and pursue." She hung up and filled her team in via the radio.

"It sounds like our truck," Stonequest said.

"But we can't be certain," Drew countered. "We should split up and make sure this isn't a diversion."

"You can't be serious," Washington complained.

"Drew's right," she said. "I need some of you to stay here. Stonequest, Heartsbane, Washington, keep this area secure. We'll call if we need you."

"Oh, this is bullshit!" Heartsbane and Washington shouted over each other despite being in totally different hiding places.

"Emerald, Drew, Amy, let's go."

Drew clambered down from his position on the roof and hurried to Emerald, who had already assumed his green dragon form.

Kristen stepped out onto the field and transformed. By the time she was done, Amy floated down to land on her back. The Steel Dragon smiled. They were becoming very good at anticipating each other's actions. That might prove essential in a very short space of time.

They became airborne as quickly as they could and pushed to gain altitude with every ounce of strength they had. If anyone saw them, their cover would be blown and the shipment would no doubt be rescheduled for another night when dragons were unlikely to make unexpected appearances.

It didn't seem like anyone was close enough to have seen them take to the skies, though.

As they pumped their wings and headed north, they examined the base below them. It was close to two am so even on a military base, traffic was light. It didn't take too much effort to identify a truck driving with a motorcycle tailing it about a quarter of a mile behind.

"That has to be our target," Emerald said. "I only saw one other truck and nothing was following it. Are you ready?"

"Oh yeah," Kristen said and tucked her wings to descend a little and follow the vehicle.

Rather than head to the warehouses where the team had waited in ambush and where the order had appeared to direct the shipment, the vehicle now drove toward the munitions storage depot. Even at night, it was an impressive sight. The base had numbers of bunkers where they stored ammunition for all their weapons. Dunning had mentioned them at some point and told them it was where they kept all their tank shells, mortar rounds, artillery, grenades, and ammunition. Basically, anything that could detonate or be exploded was all stored there. The concrete bunkers were huge, partly buried by dirt on either side and heavily locked down. Kristen didn't really see how anyone other than the higher-ups could have access to them. She told herself not to jump to conclusions but ideas of who was orchestrating this with Constance had definitely begun to form.

Her suspicion that the higher-ranking officers on the base were involved was further strengthened when the truck drew up the gated entrance at the bunker area. It didn't even come to a complete stop before someone waved it through. She couldn't imagine how someone could—at two am, no less—check identification and paperwork while a vehicle was rolling. It made far more sense that the soldiers on duty had been told what to expect and how to behave and reminded not to ask any questions.

The truck drove down the lane between the bunkers before it

finally stopped at one near the end of a row. The driver killed the engine—probably because of the noise—and turned the lights off.

"It's now or never, Lady Steel. What do you want us to do?" Emerald asked.

Kristen took a deep breath. The gravity of the situation weighed heavily on her. If she was wrong, she was about to interrupt a totally legitimate arms shipment. Furthermore, given the secrecy around it, there was a good chance that if the contents of the boxes weren't dragon bullets, they were some other kind of proprietary military tech. If she revealed what that was, the military would be all over her for stealing national secrets.

It put her in an unenviable position, but she couldn't afford to risk not doing anything.

"Amy," she said to the mage on her back. "Radio the other team and fill them in. We'll make contact and might need backup soon."

The girl did as her boss asked before she patted her on the back twice—their signal that she was prepared.

"Is everyone ready?" Kristen asked.

"If you're asking if I'm ready to dive into battle with people wielding weapons that can't only kill people but dragons too, and that some of these people might be magic users, the answer is hell no," Drew said. "But if you're asking if it's time to stop these assholes, then let's do this."

"That's good enough for me," she responded as she and Emerald rocketed earthward.

CHAPTER SIXTY-TWO

The two dragons landed at exactly the same moment with Kristen on the driver's side of the truck and Emerald on the passenger's side. As soon as their feet touched down, Drew and Amy scrambled off in opposite directions and both moved away from the vehicle. It wouldn't do for the squishy humans to be caught by a bullet meant for a dragon.

Then, as they'd planned, the dragon teammates transformed into their human bodies. This would limit their capabilities somewhat—no flight, no tails or claws, and no fire breath—but if the technomages were inside, it only made sense. Dragons were larger targets than humans, after all, and the mages literally planned a war against dragon kind. Somehow, she didn't think they would be intimidated by dragons the way most people were.

Plus, they both had superhuman strength and speed in their human bodies in addition to body armor. It might not stop bullets but then again, it might, and it was better than nothing. Even as the Steel Dragon, she was vulnerable to the dragon bullets. This was the smarter way to fight, she knew that, but it still made her incredibly nervous.

Drew didn't seem to have any inhibitions, though, and why should he? He was used to fighting in his human form. He already had his gun raised and aimed at the passenger window of the vehicle.

That was enough to snap Kristen into action. She readied a pistol and Emerald did the same. Amy raised her hands and a few rocks began to float. The girl had practiced her skills and despite her bracelet, she could throw pebbles at almost the speed of bullets.

"Come out of the vehicle with your hands up!" Kristen shouted and tried to recall the last time she'd given such a pedestrian order to a hostile. These days, it was all, "don't try to incinerate anyone," or "keep your magic under control." There was something satisfying about a simple, "hands up and get out of the vehicle."

Or so she thought until the rear door was flung open and two people wearing robes began to spray everything around them with bullets from their machine pistols.

She fell prone—and thanked her lucky stars that Drew had trained her—but that seemed to be exactly what their attackers wanted. Immediately, the driver started the engine and floored the accelerator.

"The two in the back were wearing robes!" she shouted.

"So were the two in the front," Drew yelled in response and fired his pistol. He delivered a succession of shots at the passenger windows and the wheels of the truck, but with no success.

"Then these are our guys," Emerald said and raced after the vehicle.

Kristen pushed to her feet and shuddered when she realized how close she'd come to being removed from the battle forever. A bullet had lodged into the soil about a foot from her head. It was the off-white of a dragon round.

She wasted no more time. "Emerald, no!" she shouted and sprinted after her teammate, using her dragon speed to close the distance between them.

He raced toward the back of the truck—and probably enjoyed the pursuit since he hadn't bothered to run at his full speed yet—but the two mages were ready for him.

They lowered their machine pistols and actually took aim—she didn't think she'd ever seen anyone wielding the crazy, rapid-fire handguns actually aim before, whether in real life or the movies.

Kristen leaped with every ounce of strength she had and bulldozed into his back to thrust him off his feet.

The mages opened fire and the air above the two dragons was suddenly filled with a fusillade of deadly fire.

"What the hell was that?" Emerald demanded and scrambled to his feet.

Kristen slammed the bullet that had narrowly missed her before into his hand. "Did you forget what we're up against?"

He looked at it and his dark skin went ashen. "Oh, fuck me. I…I never thought they'd use these rounds in weapons like that."

"They filled a bomb with this, remember? Obviously, they have a stable source, a huge stockpile, or both."

"Right. I'm sorry about that." He shook his head. "And Kristen…"

"Yeah?"

"Thanks. You saved my damn life."

"Don't mention it," she said, then paused. "Actually, on second thought, please keep it in mind and save my ass the next chance you get."

"What now?" Drew asked, caught up to them, and stopped to catch his breath. Amy floated over effortlessly, although she looked shaken after the gunfire.

Kristen was already calling Barnes. He picked up with a, "What the fuck was that?"

"We met our delivery guys. They were packing," she replied.

"No shit! I heard the shots. What's going on? Are they down?"

"No, not even close. They fired at us and are driving off now. We had to let them go."

"Where are they headed?"

She turned at a loud crash as the vehicle barreled through the gate that secured the bunker area. Apparently, they either hadn't wanted to wait for the guard or he'd decided that people shooting at dragons was beyond the level of discretion that was expected of him.

"Well, they destroyed the gate so they could leave the munitions depot, and I don't have a clue where they'll go next."

"All right. I already called in every MP I have on duty and they're on the move. I'll send them that way. We'll catch these bastards and finally get answers!" Barnes sounded more excited and nothing at all like the stony soldier they'd met with earlier.

"Great. That sounds good."

"Investigator," he said before she could hang up.

"What do you need?"

"The Fort's security is my job, but if there's anything you can do to help, that would be greatly appreciated."

"Oh, don't worry about that, Barnes. I'm merely happy you want to cooperate. These assholes tried to hurt my men. For their sake, I hope you catch them first."

"Right, then. We're on the same page. But remember, we have questions."

"I won't get carried away. See you soon." Kristen hung up and tossed Amy her phone. "Let's go!" she ordered and took the form of the Steel Dragon once more. The mage climbed on her back and with Drew on Emerald, they took to the skies to catch the assholes who were willing to use body parts to kill.

CHAPTER SIXTY-THREE

The problem with a getaway vehicle being a truck was that it had very definite limitations. Despite the driver obviously driving as fast as he dared, it hadn't covered any significant distance before the dragons located it once more. They didn't engage, though. If it was merely a matter of dragons versus bullets, they were at a standoff, but unfortunately for the mages, she had made friends.

"Amy, call Barnes and keep the line open. I want you to update him on where that truck is at all times."

"You got it, Kristen. But if you're trying to predict where they'll be, I'd say forget it. I don't think they really know."

Sure enough, the vehicle swerved erratically down a road and seemed to have no particular destination in mind. Kristen could almost hear the driver and his passenger arguing about what to do next.

Amy did a good job of telling Barnes where they were and he, in turn, directed his MPs efficiently and coordinated their approach. Kristen had worked enough roadblocks to see that the man knew what he was doing. The truck was able to continue, but any of the roads it might want to turn down were being blocked one by one and the flashing lights of the military were very visible. The trick to an effective roadblock was to let the criminals see it so as to force them to realize they had nowhere to go.

The vehicle swerved down one of the few roads Barnes hadn't sent MPs to and Kristen thought it might have a chance to escape. She soon realized this was part of the officer's plan as well as yet another roadblock blocked the end of the twisting road the driver had chosen.

The driver seemed to realize this and instead of following the road, he pulled off into a field. For a moment, she thought he would try to lead them in an off-road chase but apparently, he realized how foolish this was, given that they were pursued by not only police cars but also motorcycles, military vehicles, and flying dragons.

The truck pulled to a stop in the middle of a field surrounded by the old buildings that defined the southern part of Fort Bend. Every single one was a wood structure.

Military police vehicles of different makes and models drove into the field and formed a perimeter around their quarry, although they kept their distance. Kristen had told Amy to make sure their commanding officer knew to remind his people how dangerous the hostiles were.

The Steel Dragon landed and changed into human form. She was impressed that Barnes was already there to meet her.

"I guess these are our assholes," he said and grinned. Apparently, all the hard-nosed Lt. Colonel needed to be cheered up was a good old high-speed chase through the early hours of the morning with a couple of potentially lethal hostiles.

"Yeah, it looks like it," she agreed. "But I don't know why they haven't left the truck. I'm not entirely sure what I expected but it definitely wasn't for them to simply sit there."

"Are you saying you're bummed we're not being shot at?" Drew asked.

"No, I'm only curious. Sitting tight while the noose tightens around them doesn't seem like a bright idea and I'm sure that's not all they're doing. They have to be planning something."

"Tell it like it is. There's no need to dance around it. What the fuck is going on?" the military man demanded.

"Honestly, I don't know so let's proceed with caution. I don't think we want to rush in yet. Let's see if we can get them to come to us."

"No problem." Barnes retrieved a megaphone and switched it on. He grimaced and moved it away from his face after a blast of feedback, then held it up. "All right, step slowly out of the vehicle."

The driver and passenger side doors both opened and raised hands extended through each.

"That's good…real good," he said encouragingly. "Now, keep those fingers in the air and take a few steps away from the vehicle. We'll say five steps. That's how many men have guns aimed at each of you right now, by the way. Five men. Five steps. Got it?"

The men each took the required number of steps. Unlike the two in the back, they both wore regular clothes. The jumpsuits looked vaguely like some kind of company uniform, no doubt an attempt at a disguise, and Kristen narrowed her eyes. She was sure Drew had said they had worn robes, but perhaps they had changed and hidden them somewhere in the vehicle.

"All right. I'm loving how we're all complying and no one's getting a bullet through them. That's real nice," Barnes said. "Now, I want you both on your knees and your hands behind your head with your fingers interlaced."

Again, the men complied without complaint. Kristen began to get a bad feeling. She'd never had criminals comply so easily but couldn't determine what their end game might be.

Cautiously, she reached out with her aura and suddenly realized why they were so calm. The other two members of their little delivery team were gone and she couldn't sense their auras in the back of the vehicle. She cursed herself for not noticing that sooner.

"All right, men, arrest them," Barnes told his team and Kristen didn't tell them to stop. Instead, she told Emerald and Amy to remain alert for a trap. For all they knew, the drivers might simply be regular folk. Maybe the mages stayed in the back—or had somehow escaped from there. But where had they gone now?

She hadn't seen anyone jump from the rear of the vehicle, nor had any of the dozens of MPs who had been in pursuit. How did two people—dressed in robes and armed with machine pistols, no less—manage to vanish in the middle of a military base?

CHAPTER SIXTY-FOUR

Now that the two men from the front of the vehicle were restrained, Kristen had a decision to make—to investigate the vehicle or to leave it and try to find the two missing mages. She decided she had to stay laser-focused on the weapons, although it did leave a hollow pit in her stomach to make that choice.

"Emerald, I want you in the air. Two of these guys are missing. Keep an eye out for anything unusual and be careful. If you hear or see anything, do not attack. Do you understand me? These people have dragon-killing rounds. I don't want you to engage."

"No problem," Emerald said and took to the air. Whether he meant no problem, he wouldn't engage or no problem, these mages didn't stand a chance against him, she wasn't totally certain. She would merely have to hope the dragon would heed her orders.

Her orders. It was still a strange thought.

"Amy, I'll examine the back of the truck. Please put a shield over me in case this is all a trap."

"You got it, boss." The young mage nodded and raised her hands, which began to glow with blue energy.

"All right, here goes nothing," Kristen said with a nod to Drew and Barnes.

She approached cautiously, only to find that she was right. There was nothing at all in the vehicle. Startled, she stared, shook her head and glanced into the darkness of the night, and finally looked at the empty truck again. There was still nothing there.

It meant that they either tried to pick something up rather than deliver it—she honestly doubted that—or whatever they had hauled was small enough that the two mages took it with them when they left. But why use a truck at all? Maybe it had been something bulky and the mages used their powers to move it invisibly somehow. None of it made any sense, no matter how her brain tried to rationalize it.

Kristen shook her head. It wasn't worth her time to attempt to come up with a hypothesis before she had all the evidence. And surely more evidence could be gleaned from the delivery vehicles. Why else had these two men spent so much time trying to keep it away from her and the MPs? If there was nothing, they would have pulled over way sooner.

Kristen examined the seemingly empty interior once more. Scrape marks were visible on the floor from something heavy being hauled around, but that wasn't exactly definitive evidence. The back of a truck wasn't a forest floor and there wasn't any way to tell if the marks were fresh or not.

She startled and almost whirled into a defensive stance when Amy said, "Boss, I think something's weird."

"What is it?"

"I can't say exactly…but…something about the vehicle doesn't feel right." She peered into the back of the truck and squinted as if to focus on something, but her effort brought no result. Kristen felt exactly the same way—that she was missing something right in front of her.

"Do you think it could be a spell?" she asked the young mage. She couldn't feel anything at all but she had skipped the time she was supposed to spend in the Paper Dungeon and gone directly to patrol work. While she'd been relieved at the time, the downside was that she was unfamiliar with magic and mages. If Amy could sense something she couldn't, it wouldn't surprise her.

"I think it might be, but I can't tell…" The girl held her wrist up and shook the bracelet. "I feel like I'm trying to see something through a t-shirt, you know? Like I can sense that something's right there but there's a shirt over my eyes and I can't quite make it out."

"Does the bracelet interfere that much?" Kristen asked.

"Yeah. I can feel it damping most of my magic but I don't know if taking it off would help. I'm working more from intuition than real training anyway. Larry could probably discern what's going on but all I can do is guess. Even with my full powers, I might not be able to do more than that. I'm sorry." Amy's shoulders slumped.

"It's okay, don't beat yourself up over it," she told the girl. "I want to take that damned bracelet off of you too, but I don't want you to get in trouble. As long as you wear it, everyone knows you're with me. I don't want any dragon to get the wrong idea."

Stonequest and Heartsbane landed before she could continue. "What's the situation?" he asked before he had finished transforming into his human form.

Kristen filled them in, then ordered them to help Emerald with his efforts to find a clue of some kind. She knew it was risky to have them airborne, but if there really was a crate of dragon bullets somewhere on the base, they would have to take risks.

That was one nice thing about working with dragons as opposed to people. It didn't bother her as much to put a dragon in harm's way because they were so damned hard to kill. Of course, Constance worked hard to change that reality but still, she deemed it worth the risk and knew her dragon teammates would feel the same way.

No sooner did Stonequest and Heartsbane depart than another vehicle pulled up and a general stepped out. She could tell not only from his uniform but from how all the MPs recoiled from the man's scowl.

"That's General Andrews," Barnes whispered to her as his superior approached. "And Colonel Fox, my boss." The two had a small team of guards with them as if their lives might come under threat at any moment.

"General, Colonel, you'll be happy to know we've apprehended two men who were on our base unauthorized," the MP began.

The general didn't grace him with a response. He left the beratement to Colonel Fox. "Goddammit, Barnes, an allegedly unauthorized truck is why you have every MP in this base driving around like madmen at two in the goddamn morning? What the hell is wrong with you? What on earth makes you think it's appropriate to cause a ruckus of this magnitude at this hour without so much as telling me what the hell you planned?"

"I'm sorry, sir. I tried to bring this to your attention but—"

"Don't attempt to drag the Colonel's good name down," General Andrews interjected, his voice like ice. "You took unauthorized action when you called this circus and with an enemy no less." He glared at Kristen when he said the word enemy.

If this wasn't the guy who was planning to start the third dragon-human war, she would turn into a dragon and eat one of the tires from the truck.

"There'll be discipline for these actions. You understand that, right?" Colonel Fox demanded.

"Sir, I merely followed protocol. This vehicle wasn't on the arrivals schedule. The shipment paperwork looks valid, but there are no records of it in the base registry."

"And is that how you think the military works, son?" General Andrews asked. "You think that every little thing that happens is supposed to be accounted for and available in public records? It didn't occur to you that maybe—just maybe—what was going on tonight was above your paygrade?"

"General, are you saying that you knew about this truck?" Kristen asked.

The base commander glared at her for a moment and his eyes flinched when he saw her investigator badge. "Some deliveries are classified, isn't that right, Barnes?"

"Yes, sir. It is, sir, and I realize I was taking a risk. But sir, those men shot at us with machine pistols when they were confronted. Those are not the actions of law-abiding soldiers or citizens. When they turned to violence, it became clear to me that the investigator's suspicions were true."

"And what suspicions are those?" General Andrews asked.

The MP seemed conflicted for a moment. He obviously didn't trust his superior officer but he'd been asked a direct question. His face froze for a moment before it seemed his military training won. "Sir, the investigator has reason to believe there are illegal weapons being shipped to this base by a terrorist organization that will attempt to start a conflict between the US military and the dragons. When the passengers in the truck fired at the dragons, it confirmed my suspicions."

"Confirmed your suspicions, huh?" Colonel Fox asked. "Tell me something, Barnes. Have you found any weapons on these two delivery men?"

Barnes forwarded the question to his MPs, who confirmed that the prisoners had no weapons and that the truck didn't seem to have any in it either.

"No, sir," the MP said and readily took responsibility for their failure to locate the cargo.

"Did these two men fire at you in this field when you apprehended them?"

"Sir, earlier—"

"The colonel did not ask about earlier. The colonel asked you about what happened here. Were the men armed or unarmed?" General Andrews asked.

"They were unarmed, sir." Barnes stiffened, his posture at attention.

"And did you see these two perpetrators who fired shots on my base?"

"No, sir." All emotion had gone from his voice. He had retreated into the military attitude he'd been in when Kristen first met him.

"Tell me, what did the dragons say these perpetrators looked like?" Colonel Fox demanded. There was no kindness in the way he said it.

"The investigator told me there were two of them wearing robes and armed with machine pistols."

"Were they male or female?" Fox snapped.

"She did not say, sir."

"Skin color?"

"She did not say, sir."

"So we're supposed to believe that two wizards jumped out of that truck, armed not with staffs or spells or whatever it is mages use to serve the dragons but instead, armed with guns?"

"Sir, the nature of this investigation is centered around firearms, so I don't think it's that—"

"We're supposed to believe," Colonel Fox continued and cut the man off without apology, "that they saw these wizards but couldn't tell if they were male or female, or black or white?"

"You should believe it because that's what happened," Kristen said.

"Of course, ma'am," Fox said, his tone sarcastically pleasant. "Of course, and we do. I have no trouble believing this."

She tried to give the man the benefit of the doubt but her ability to read his aura made it damn hard. It was obvious that he hated her—not only hated but loathed her. Whether it was because she was a dragon or for some other reason, she couldn't be sure.

But it didn't matter, not really. These two men could bark and yell and do whatever they wanted, but they would not stop her from preventing this war. She was about to say as much when Amy spoke from beside the truck.

"Hey, boss? You might want to check this out."

Kristen nodded—happy to have the distraction—and moved toward the vehicle. As she did so, she felt General Andrew's aura shift from one of assuredness to one of desperation.

"Do we really need to waste our time out here? Investigator Hall, come to my office. Let's have coffee and determine how Fort Drum can best help you in your investigation."

Even without her ability to read auras, it was painfully apparent that he tried to keep her away from the truck.

But why? It was empty and no one had found a thing. Why would her going near it bother him?

"What did you find, Amy?" Kristen said and left Andrews rooted to the spot. His aura began to heat like a volcano ready to explode.

CHAPTER SIXTY-FIVE

When Kristen reached the truck, Amy sat outside the rear door, her eyes closed in concentration, with a slight blue glow emanating from her. The first pinpricks of perspiration began to form on her forehead. Whatever the novice mage was doing, it looked like more effort for her than fighting dragons had been.

"Hey, Amy, what's going on? Do we have a clue? Because I could really fucking use a clue right now."

"We have…something," the girl said and gritted her teeth. For a moment longer, she simply sat there, her body rigid and hands clasped tightly before she opened her eyes and exhaled a ragged breath.

"What kind of something did you find?" she asked.

"A magic something, I'm certain of that," Amy said. "There's definitely a spell on it and maybe more than one. I can't really tell. I'm still new to this and whoever did this has far more power than I currently have access to." Whether she meant to or not, her free hand found the bracelet on her wrist and she fidgeted with it absent-mindedly.

"Can you tell me anything else?" Kristen asked.

"I can tell you that I don't have enough raw magic available to do anything more than sense it right now. It was cast by someone with more skill than I have. Maybe if Larry were here he could do something about it. I don't really know."

"I thought he said you were more powerful than he was," she whispered, not eager to reveal to General Andrews how powerful the mage working with her was.

"I'm still new at this and he's way more skilled than me. Larry said magic is kind of like anything—there are two ways to force something. You can use a pick to open a lock or a sledgehammer. I don't have the power to sledgehammer it with this bracelet on and I don't know how long it will take me to learn the lockpick method. Years?" The girl sounded so apologetic it was almost cute.

Except it wasn't cute that she was shackled and now hampered this investigation due to dragon customs and superstitions. It was tragic, actually, that they inadvertently prevented the one person who could possibly save them with her magic from exercising it on their behalf. Without realizing it, they had become their own worst enemy. It gave Constance the platform she needed to pursue her ruthless objectives. If they could only change that single rule, it would remove the moral high ground the technomages used as the foundation for their cause and give them time to change the rest.

Frustration surged once again. While she found the system abhorrent, she knew it wouldn't change overnight. At the same time, both dragons and humans would perish before they could even begin the process if Constance wasn't stopped. Someone had to take the first step.

"Tell me what you need," Kristen said.

"I don't know." Amy threw her hands up in exasperation. "It's like you're asking me to crack a nut. I don't have the tools I need, but if I could put my boots on..." She looked at the bracelet but didn't say anything.

She respected the mage for not demanding that the fetter be removed but also knew that the thin band of silver was what stood in their way. More than anything, she wanted to solve this case and find out what kind of spell had been cast. Maybe the other two mages had been illusions? She couldn't even begin to guess. The limits and possibilities of magic were not something she knew much about. But to lay Amy open to attack from other dragons? She didn't know if it was worth it.

General Andrews recognized her indecisiveness and strode toward her. "Clearly, we've had a misunderstanding," he said, all fake smiles and nods. "I don't know why we need to get worked up over an empty vehicle. I agree that if there's been an illegal shipment, we need to track it. Barnes doesn't have access to the same information I do, so how about we go back to my office, have that coffee, and see what we can turn up?"

That did it for Kristen. The man had gone from a barely camouflaged tiger to a house cat as soon as they'd approached the truck. There was no reason to do that unless he had something to hide.

Emerald swooped overhead and landed smoothly before he transformed into his human form. "There's nothing out there, Kristen. I didn't sense any magic or see any other..." His voice trailed off as he looked from Kristen to Amy and finally, the general. "Is everything all right?"

"Yes. I was speaking to Amy. General Andrews, can you tell Emerald exactly what you thought was going on while I help Amy with her bracelet?"

The other dragon moved to intercept the general, but not before he gave Kristen a hard look. "Are you sure about that?" It was obvious from his tone that he didn't approve of her removing the fetter.

"I'm sure," she replied, her voice like steel.

He merely nodded. She outranked him now and that seemed to be enough to silence his protest. The general, though, had other ideas.

"Isn't that a violation of protocol?" he demanded when Kristen began to disconnect the clasp on the bracelet. "I thought registered mages had to wear one of those things."

"You sure do seem to know a lot about mages," Emerald said and deliberately remained between the two women and the general.

"I don't see why this has become such a big deal," Andrews said and his tone now shifted to politician. "If you have a mage running around, maybe she left the magic residue or whatever it is."

"It's not residue," Amy said as the fetter came free. "It's a spell."

The young mage took a deep breath and it felt like all the air in the field rushed toward her for a moment and the grass actually bent her direction. She smiled.

"Better?" Kristen asked.

"Oh, you have no idea how much better." The girl grinned. "Oh, I guess you do. You were in jail, right?"

"Jail?" General Andrews sputtered. "You're a criminal accusing this base of illegal activity? I will be forced to report this up the chain of command if it continues."

"She was fully exonerated and this is the time when you shut up," Emerald said.

Kristen helped the man to do exactly that by ignoring him when she focused on Amy. It wasn't a difficult task, given what followed.

The first thing the girl did was float off the ground. Apparently, she'd become so adept at levitating her shoes with her in them that she could do so without conscious thought. Next, her fingertips began to glow before golden sparks erupted and left trails that extended all the way to her fingers, like bottle rockets whose sparks never seemed to run out.

These glinting tendrils poked and prodded at the truck. The exploration started tenderly at first but her limited skill soon became apparent when she began to batter the vehicle with the sparking tentacles. She shattered a window, then knocked a dent into the side of the truck.

General Andrews earned some of Kristen's respect as he didn't flinch when she did this but stood taller. It was, she thought, merely more evidence that he had worked with mages.

These vibrant lines of magic brought no apparent result and Amy dismissed the sparks, pointed at the truck, and simply lifted it. She spun it idly like a child examining a particularly fine rock before skipping it across a pond.

When that had no effect, she set it down and it rocked on its suspension.

"The spell isn't on the outside," Amy said and pointed at the back doors. They both jerked off their hinges and careened away. Almost as an afterthought, she stopped them and plunged them into the field like grave markers of the vehicle she was about to disassemble.

"Do you see anything?" Kristen asked.

"Oh yeah, I got it," the mage replied and released a blast of sparks into the back of the truck.

A little beyond where the drag marks had ended, the sparks from her hands encountered something, although nothing was visible. It was like the power had rebounded off an invisible wall.

"There it is," Amy muttered, and delivered another surge of power into the shield. This one was more like a kinetic force than sparks. It collided with the unseen barrier with such an impact that it knocked the entire vehicle forward. Still, the spell didn't crack.

"Are you sure this is safe?" Barnes shouted.

"Not at all," the mage replied before she inhaled deeply and whirled her hands. A wind picked up where there had been none.

"All right, cool. I only wanted to check if we would all blow up, is all," the man said. He looked serious but he didn't step away. A vortex appeared between the girl's hands and spun faster and faster. It began to suck in leaves and debris and she grinned, then hurled it against the barrier. The projectiles streaked like razor blades to slice at it.

At first, they seemed to have no effect, but slowly, leaf by leaf, something began to appear in the back of the vehicle.

"That's working!" Kristen shouted over the roar of the wind. "Keep it up!"

"Oh yeah," Amy said. She smiled, then gritted her teeth and focused. She'd turned her baseball cap backward at some point, but it was a good look.

The vortex whirled with ever-increasing speed. It drew in more and more debris, brought all the leaves, sticks, and twigs into violent motion, and flung them at the shield as if a tornado had decided to make this particular vehicle its only target.

For Kristen, it was odd to watch—like finding out her brain had lied to her about something. It was as if an invisible sheet had simply been tossed into the vehicle and Amy obliterated it piecemeal. The mage reached some kind of tipping point and suddenly, with the sound of a hundred sheets being shredded, the spell was gone and the contents were laid bare.

"There we go!" The girl sounded pleased with herself and also out of breath.

The Steel Dragon clapped her on the back and scrambled into the truck to look at the crates.

"Now wait a second," Andrews protested immediately. "If you intend to interfere with a shipment coming to a government base, at the very least, we need to see some kind of warrant or something."

"I'm confused, General," she said and glanced at him while her fingers worked the edges of the crate and tried to find purchase on the nailed-down lid. "Is this an empty vehicle you know nothing about or is this a legitimate shipment you claim is protected by the government?"

"I— Either way, you don't have the right to open that!"

"Is that right? We'll have to let the courts decide, I suppose."

"There will be hell to pay for this, dragon, mark my words."

"I'd walk through fire to protect the people of this planet. If I'm in the wrong on this, so be it, but I don't think I am." Kristen finally located the crack she'd looked for and applied with her dragon strength, but it wasn't quite enough. Despite its very real power, it didn't make fingers into a crowbar.

"You can still stop. We can chalk this up to a misunderstanding," the general protested, his gaze focused on her fingers.

His intense stare was good because it meant he saw them transform into steel. Now made of metal, it took hardly any effort for her to pry the lid off the crate.

Despite having suspected what was in there from the moment they left the Motor City, she could not help but gasp when she saw the contents.

Inside were ammo cases of different sizes. She opened one that was full of dragon bullets.

She opened another to find more dragon bullets of a slightly different make.

Kristen took a step back. There had to be hundreds inside the truck, maybe even thousands. Enough, she acknowledged, to start a war. Hell, there was enough in there to kill every dragon in North America if the shooters were properly trained.

She fixed her attention on Andrews. "I think it's about time we had that little chat in your office as you suggested."

CHAPTER SIXTY-SIX

"This is preposterous," General Andrews said and barely managed to hold himself in check. "You come to my base, make wild accusations, and you…you use magic to plant fake evidence."

"That's weak," Emerald said. He still stood in front of the man and showed no inclination to move. "Even for a human."

"That's exactly what I'm talking about," the officer retorted. The quiver in his voice was gone and he'd replaced it with rage. "You dragons come in here, make a mess of things, then have the audacity to blame us for a shipment we didn't even know about."

Barnes cleared his throat. "There were records, sir. Records that you said earlier you knew—"

"Were you her accomplice on this, Lieutenant?" Colonel Fox cut him off. "Did you alter those records?"

"You both know I can tell when you're lying, correct?" Kristen said. "Dragon magic."

"It doesn't take magic to tell you two are lying," Stonequest said and—to her shock—he fell asleep.

She looked up quickly and realized he wasn't the only one. All the MPs who had stood near the two occupants of the truck were now asleep. She wasn't surprised at all when the driver wiggled his fingers and light glowed from inside his handcuffs before they snicked open.

"You take the Steel Bitch and I'll get the green one," the mage who'd opened the cuffs said.

His companion nodded and his hands began to glow.

Kristen turned her skin to steel as a blast from the passenger struck her in the chest. It felt like a bowling ball had rocketed into her ribs at forty miles an hour and would have no doubt cracked a bone if not for her abilities.

Emerald was ready and parried his first attack. The driver launched some kind of a spinning disk at him, but the dragon moved quickly, dropped to land on his back, and kicked the flat edge of the disk. It careened ineffectually into the night sky.

His action might have saved his life too. He'd no sooner fallen when gunshots were fired from the nearest building. The soil beyond her teammate exploded in three places. Each bullet would have caught him if he'd have been only a second later.

"Down! Stay down," she said and threw herself onto the grass as more shots rang out.

"Do you think they're using dragon bullets?" Emerald said as he wriggled toward the truck to use it as cover.

"I'd bet on it!" She followed him and crawled toward the vehicle.

Her progress was unaccountably halted by something that had latched onto her leg. It felt like a python had taken hold and constricted tighter with each moment. A second one caught her other leg and she glanced at the mages. The passenger held his hands extended and a long and writhing tentacle made of some substance blacker than ink crept from each fingertip. Two of them had already grasped her ankles and the others attempted to bind her as well like the semi-intelligent yet seemingly mindless arms of an octopus.

Kristen rolled, sat, and struck one of the weird appendages with a steel fist. She hit it hard enough to break the tip off. Once she'd severed it from the rest of the tentacle that connected it to the mage, the inky blackness seemed to lose its power.

Unfortunately, there were seven more and she had put herself in range by her altered position.

Two latched onto the arm that had punched the one binding her ankle. Another caught her other arm before she could react. The rest aimed at her torso and wound around her in both directions like the world's creepiest hug.

She had damaged one of them so she knew she could break the magic with force, but she didn't have enough strength in her human form. While she could transform and shatter them all effortlessly, common sense warned her that it was what the mage wanted.

If she transformed into her dragon form, she'd be the biggest target on the field. That aside, the gunmen wouldn't have to hit her with a lethal shot to disable her. If any dragon bullet was lodged inside her body, it would cripple her powers. It was a lose-lose situation and her adversary no doubt knew this. Constance's team had practiced for a war with dragons for years so it was hardly surprising that they had tactics to fight them.

The mage, however, hadn't expected to battle its own kind.

Amy stepped forward—or floated, really, as her feet dangled a few inches above the ground. Her entire body glowed with the warm yellow light of the sun despite it being the middle of the night. Gradually, the glow seemed to dim until it issued only from her hands but that light was far brighter than her body had been.

With a scream that would have made any powerlifter proud and perhaps envious, she seared the mage who attempted to bind Kristen's body with a blast of what appeared to be pure sunlight. It caught him squarely in the chest and instantly dissipated the tentacles like a house fire had been dumped over an inkwell.

He fell back and landed on his ass but found his feet in a moment. Apparently, the blast had affected his magic far more than it had affected him.

"Go help Emerald!" Amy shouted at Kristen. "I can handle this asshole."

Her adversary seemed to have also practiced his villainy as he threw his head back and laughed. "An untrained neophyte like you has no chance against me. Your dragon friends are as good as dead, but there's still time for you to join our cause. Constance could turn you into a goddess, girl."

"All women are goddesses," she sneered and delivered another concentrated beam of light.

He was ready for this one, though, and countered with a hundred threads of the black magic he'd used to bind the dragon.

The two forms of magic collided with the violent sound of a pair of semi-trucks meeting head-on. Red and blue sparks erupted where the powers touched. Kristen knew she had to help Emerald but she'd never seen a magic battle like this before.

It was unreal.

The mage was obviously more practiced and each of his ink threads darted at Amy in complicated loops and whirls. Her raw power, however, seemed to do quite well for itself. Every time one of the threads touched her arms, the tendril would start to swell. Before any of them could become as thick as those that had bound the dragon's legs, the girl surged her magic and forced her adversary to focus more on defense so the tiny threads simply fell away.

"Lady Steel...a little help!" Emerald was on the ground and when she turned to look at him, the other mage now used the same type of tentacles to bind him. Six had already wound around his body, and one of them tightened around his neck. "Anytime...would be great..."

Kristen snatched the tentacle with her steel fist and yanked hard. It didn't break, so she chopped it with her other hand. That provided enough force to sever the magic, but she immediately understood that she couldn't beat this magic like that. She was too slow. In the time it had taken her to sever one, the mage had reached Emerald with two more, one of which already slithered to his neck.

She needed magic and she didn't have it...but she did have a gun.

Mage or not, no one much liked to be on the receiving end of bullets.

Quickly, she drew her weapon, aimed at their enemy's face—he was closer than the targets she practiced with on the shooting range—and squeezed the trigger.

The bullet flew true. She knew this because about a foot out from the space between his eyes, the bullet evaporated in a shower of silver sparks.

He laughed. "Did you think we came to a military base without being able to protect ourselves from bullets?" He didn't sound quite as villainous as his companion but she was suitably spooked all the same.

Kristen didn't let herself get flustered. While he could obviously stop a bullet, could he stop an entire clip? At this range, a clip would hurt even a dragon fairly severely.

With no other ideas, she tested her hypothesis with four more shots at his face.

None got through, so she aimed three at his chest.

When none hit him, she emptied everything else she had at the mage, who didn't even react to her after the first shot. He was too busy crushing the air out of Emerald. The clever bastard knew that dragons could heal from stab wounds and the like but needed air as much as every other creature on earth did.

Kristen was about to attack when a spray of bullets pushed her back. She cursed when she realized it was covering fire from the reinforcements on the nearby building. Apparently, they'd waited for her to expend her rounds before they tried to eliminate her.

She took a step back to avoid giving them an easy shot and made the mistake of looking around.

The battlefield was a grim place. Almost all of Barnes' MPs were asleep, and those who weren't obeyed Colonel Fox, who ordered them to not break cover. Stonequest, Drew, and the Wonderkid had vanished, but she had no time to try to locate them on the field. She wondered vaguely how the sleeping spell worked as it seemed to have the ability to target some and ignore others and even to work less effectively on certain individuals. At least the members of her team had somehow managed to escape it. Perhaps having the mages occupied with fighting had diminished it somewhat. It was something she made a note of to discuss with Larry later.

General Andrews hadn't actually loaded a weapon with dragon bullets but he looked like he would if he could.

Amy fought the mage, but both her arms were now wound in the black tendrils of energy, while the light she hurled at her opponent with was noticeably dimmer.

The Steel Dragon cringed when she realized she had brought all these people there and they were about to die. Worse, it would give the Dragon Council all the reason they needed to start a war.

For a pain-filled moment, she didn't know what hurt more—the idea that the cops she respected would die in a barrage of gunfire or magic or that her family would soon live in a world known only for dragon fire and atomic blasts.

No, what hurt most was knowing that all this was her fault and there wasn't a damn thing she could do to stop it.

CHAPTER SIXTY-SEVEN

Kristen was about to transform into a dragon—being a bigger target be damned—when Heartsbane appeared out of the night sky and literally landed on the mage's head.

While his shielding was such that he could block a few bullets while he kept Emerald restrained, the entire weight of a dragon overwhelmed it.

He barely had time to scream before she shattered his magical armor and ground him beneath her like an insect under a boot.

Gunfire retaliated immediately from the nearby building and the dragon hissed at it while she transformed into her human form and took cover.

Her tactic had been entirely successful and the mage she'd landed on was indeed crushed.

The distraction only lasted seconds and Kristen grabbed Emerald and dragged him behind the truck while the two mages in the building rained bullets on them. The report of the weapons made her think that her opponents still used the Uzi-style machine pistols. Those were great for spray and pray violence, but not especially accurate at the range they currently fired from. The two reached cover without being hit and she joined Heartsbane, who was also unharmed.

Part of her brain registered that the two technomages who had vanished from the back of the vehicle had probably snuck away at some point to join their comrade in the ambush. Either that or they lurked nearby, waiting for the perfect moment to join the battle to greatest effect. It was a worry but there wasn't anything she could do about it until they acted, so she pushed it aside and tried to focus on solutions for their current predicament.

The blackness of the night sky was swallowed by a vivid flare of light as Stonequest rocketed from a great height and swept the building the mages had selected as their sniper location with a blast of fire. She stared in bemusement for a moment, as the last time she'd seen him, the dragon had been asleep. The logical answer was that when the mages engaged in the battle, he had been able to shake the sleeping spell off thanks to his dragon abilities—although she had no idea why he'd been susceptible to it in the first place.

While the others had drawn all the attention, he must have crept away and launched into flight, then returned to wreak havoc.

To the mages' credit, they actually tried to return fire as one half of the top floor of the building they were in caught fire. Thanks to the speed of his assault, they were hardly more effective against the dragon's fiery assault they had been against the human-sized targets below them.

Their difficulty was compounded by the fact that Drew and Jim were on Stonequest's back and laid down covering fire that kept the mages' heads down as the dragon virtually skimmed them before he elevated once more.

As he ascended sharply, the mages scrambled into position once more. Before they could fire at the dragon overhead, however, the SWAT teammates responded with a concerted barrage that drew curses and curtailed the enemy's efforts as Stonequest turned for another attack.

The flames were intense enough to vividly illuminate the scene as the mages tried to run from the approaching dragon. Apparently, they'd trained to fight against giant, flying, superpowered lizards but not when their adversaries attacked with armed humans on their back. It was yet another reminder of why humans and dragons should be allies, not enemies. They were more effective working together than they were apart.

When Stonequest ignited the other half of the building, Kristen was given a graphic reminder of why humans and dragons should not go to war. In a second, the entire roof area was on fire, a burning crown that had erupted from two simple exhalations from the dragon.

All gunfire from that direction had ceased. Obviously, the mages were more concerned with not burning to death than they were with completing a mission in which they'd failed to properly anticipate the unexpected interference.

The dragon banked for a third strike, but he flew over the building without an attack, either with fire or with his talons. His aura and his body language indicated that the targets were no longer there.

He tucked his wings, turned sharply, and circled the building while he and his two riders checked the windows as they raced past them for any sign of their quarry.

No shots were fired, and the dragon landed. Drew and Jim disembarked, reloaded their pistols, and aimed at the building to cover Stonequest while he transformed into his human form.

"Those were slick moves," Kristen murmured to Heartsbane where they held their position behind the truck.

"Yeah. for a horse. I can't believe Stonequest lets those two monkeys ride him like a pony."

A flash of light drew their attention to the battle between Amy and the other mage.

Through some unspoken agreement, the two combatants had progressed from the types of magic used in their original attacks against each other. Instead of tendrils of dark energy, the technomage now hurled tiny balls of energy at the girl. They weren't much bigger than marbles but when they struck, they exploded in flashes.

She dodged these with deft twists and spins and looked terrifying as she did so. Her telekinetic powers couldn't be used on her own body and when she flew, she could only move her clothes so it looked like the mage fought a skateboarder punk scarecrow. She evidenced impressive control as she yanked her own shoes and hoodie to haul herself around with uncanny motion as her enemy tried to catch her with his tiny spheres.

Amy seemed to grasp the concept of these projectiles on some level as she attempted to replicate them. She couldn't make them as small as the technomage could, however.

Instead of a marble, she formed a glowing orb the size of a basketball in her hand. It glowed like a miniature sun before she hurled it at her opponent.

The ball of energy exploded with enough force to crack the mage's armor and catapult him across the field. He landed and tumbled but found his feet immediately, recast his defensive spell, and lobbed more balls at his foe.

A few of them actually struck home and burned holes in her clothes, but the vast majority simply popped harmlessly against another sphere of energy she grew slowly in front of her.

It was already larger than a basketball and continued to expand beyond the size of a beachball, then one of the balls trendy offices let people sit on—bigger than a person, larger than two people, and finally, as large as a car. As it grew, Amy yelled like a shotput thrower from the Olympics going for the world record. It began to vibrate and it soon became abundantly clear that the young mage wouldn't be able to control it much longer.

Kristen made sure she was under cover and that her skin was steel.

The mage ceased his continuous barrage of magic and fled.

The girl simply released the orb of energy and it rocketed after him and outpaced his sprint so easily that it wasn't far-fetched to imagine it could outrace even a dragon.

At the last second, the target spun and tried to stop it with a web of the black tentacles he had used earlier. The energy projectile burned through these like they were nothing more than strands of cotton and struck the mage squarely in the chest.

A flash of light seared and surrounded him before his skin and flesh seemed to vanish and leave only a skeleton. In seconds, that too turned to ash.

Amy gasped for air and Kristen ran to catch her before she collapsed. Despite bleeding from one nostril, the mage was smiling, obviously proud of winning her first magic duel.

She didn't pass out, fortunately, and Kristen dragged her to Heartsbane and Emerald.

The group looked at one another where they hunkered behind cover but before anyone could speak, the top floor of the building Stonequest had sprayed with fire caved in.

Sparks exploded from where the windows had once been to illuminate the action below.

Drew and Jim were outside, guarding doors on two sides of the building. A moment later, Stonequest ran out.

"There's too much smoke," he said. Despite breathing fire, dragons still needed oxygen like any living being.

"I have movement!" Drew said and moved toward a door. Jim followed.

"Stay with me!" Stonequest shouted at the two humans and they immediately complied. All of them knew the danger of facing these mages alone but safety also meant they lost the advantage they could have gained by splitting up as a combined search took longer. The three teammates circled the building but found nothing.

Kristen couldn't imagine that the enemy had let themselves be incinerated. She'd seen magic users fly and had recently seen them turn the crates invisible. They were dauntingly capable and it was safer to assume they were somewhere nearby.

Everyone—or at least everyone who was still awake—gaped as the wooden building, now almost completely engulfed in flames, began to collapse in sections with showers of sparks and smoke.

Even that sound wasn't enough to wake some of the MPs, but that might be for the best. Her friends were safe, two of the mages were dead, and the others were hopefully licking their wounds, and she turned her attention to General Andrews.

She walked toward him, convinced that he'd known exactly what was in the truck. He'd acted suspiciously and even contradicted himself, first swearing there was nothing in the vehicle and then saying it was confidential. But, still, she couldn't be sure. Yes, he was in charge of the base and that, together with his attitude and reactions, made him the prime suspect, but it was possible that the entire operation was put together by an officer below him. It still left her with the necessity to determine who the culprits were—there had to be more than one—so she could act on informed and confirmed information.

The nagging voice in her head reminded her of his attempt to persuade them to have coffee instead of investigating the illegal shipment. No, he wasn't blameless, she decided firmly. Andrews had to have something to do with this. If he wasn't the sole actor, he had to at least be a member of the conspiracy.

Her hard, unflinching gaze met and held his. "I think it's about time we had that cup of coffee you offered," she said with a mirthless smile.

CHAPTER SIXTY-EIGHT

"I don't think we need to go all the way to my office," the general said. His voice approached a whining, wheedling tone, no doubt kept in check only because of years in the military.

"Then we do this here. Tell me how you met Constance Vigil and why she gave you these bullets," Kristen replied, her voice as hard as her steel skin.

He blanched at the mention of the technomage's name—as good as a confession to her—but he tried to continue to push the lie. "I don't know who this…this Constance is or what the hell you're accusing me of, but I need to see a goddamn warrant if you think for a half a second I'll cooperate with you."

"One of your own soldiers admitted there was an illegal shipment coming here, a fact you've attempted to obscure. It's obvious you're in on this. My only question is how deep. Did you know about the technomages and their terrorist attacks in Detroit?"

"Terrorism?" Andrews puffed himself up as he said the word. "You dare accuse a general of the United States Army of terrorism? How dare you! This merely proves that you…you lizards can't be trusted. You're vermin. All of you. Look at the damage you've done to my base."

"We did that damage stopping four mages who used lethal force—and who disabled your MPs with their hands cuffed." She had begun to lose her patience. The man was a terrible liar and his aura didn't help. He knew he wasn't being honest but the emotions she sensed the most were rage and anger. Both burned inside him like white-hot fires.

"Putting my MPs to sleep is hardly as bad as wrecking a building. In fact, now that I think of it, that building was historical. You assholes burned down a national treasure."

"What is wrong with you?" Kristen demanded harshly. "Your people were attacked and this is what you care about? We should work together from here on. Tell me what you know and we can focus on the real problem. We'll even fill out paperwork to make you look like you cooperated if you're scared of punishment." It wasn't exactly true but if he confessed and provided details, she would be sure to note that. Of course, only after her paragraphs detailing the general bullshit.

"You dare to threaten me? I represent the United States of America! Who do you represent? A cabal of power-hungry, gold-obsessed dragons who don't want anything more than the eternal enslavement of mankind?"

"I represent everyone." Her words were uttered like a rock that the wind of his tirade blew against and couldn't move. "I am trying to stop a group of terrorists from starting a world war that will hurt everyone. People. Dragons. Mages. Dwarves. Dogs. Cats. Shit, a war like this could hurt the fucking Kirkland's warbler, for fuck's sake. I am not here because I don't like you or don't trust you. I am here because I followed a line of clues that led me to that trove of illegal weapons." She pointed so he might better understand. It didn't seem to help.

"If you think you can pull this communist kumbaya bullshit, I have another think for you—" Andrews replied and launched into another predictable tirade in which he insulted her patriotism, her gender, her parents, and the shithole city she crawled out of.

Kristen only half-listened to it. None of it addressed what was actually happening. All of it was bullshit meant to distract from the crates of weapons that were literally made from the body parts of her species.

As he spoke, she couldn't help but prod his aura. It was so filled with hate it was almost hard to believe. His was like a great bonfire of anger and hatred, while most people's was like a torch. She wanted him to see what he was doing but how could he when he couldn't even think beyond his rage?

Her senses were still wrapped around General Andrews' aura when she cut him off with a question. "Why are you so angry?"

For a moment, he said nothing. The man stared at her while a vein near his temple throbbed and his face reddened significantly.

"Tell me," she said gently and didn't realize she was using her aura against him until it was too late.

Like a hot-air balloon punctured by a katana, he deflated and fell to his knees, and the high color in his face faded somewhat as he breathed deeply. "Because—because it's only a matter of time before you fucking dragons kill again."

Kristen hadn't intended to force him to speak. In fact, she'd resisted far stronger pushes to use her aura before but apparently, the honest question combined with the general's rage was enough to crack the façade the man had hidden behind.

"It'll be okay. We'll stop the dragons from hurting more people. That's why we're here." She tried to pull her aura back because she didn't want to push Andrews any farther than she already had. In fact, she already felt like she'd overstepped the boundaries of her abilities where she felt comfortable. She hadn't meant to crack the man, but he'd been under so much pressure that it had only taken the smallest of chips.

"You're here to ruin everything we've worked for!" the general screamed as tears ran down his red face.

"Who is we?" she asked. While she didn't want to take advantage of this man in this state, she had to have answers. Lives were at stake—billions of lives.

"You already know, you fucking bitch! Constance made those bullets, the same mage who should have put a fucking bullet in your brain when she had the chance." The words flowed freely now like a dam had been broken and the utterances had only needed time for gravity to drag them out of him. "She gave us the first shipment so we could protect ourselves in case more of you fucking monsters arrived." Spittle sprayed from his mouth as he spoke.

"Where's that shipment?" Kristen asked.

"In the second bunker from the end," Andrews told her coldly. He seemed to be regaining some control of himself.

"I'm on it," Emerald said, transformed into a dragon, and flew away. He'd obviously already recovered from almost being strangled.

"If the shipment was to protect yourselves, what was this one for?" she asked.

"You'll have to eat me, you fucking lizard," the officer replied. "You won't get an answer out of me, so you might as well transform into a fucking lizard, cook me with your fucking napalm breath, and eat me. I'm not telling you a fucking thing. You'll get a bullet in your chest from your sister like all the rest of your fucking kind."

Before, she had felt bad and still did on some level. She didn't want to use this power against humans, but Andrews was talking about starting the very war she wanted to stop and he had mentioned her sister?

"What do you mean? I don't have a sister," she said as her rage built like a storm cloud inside her. It was a strange thing, rage. While she tried to control herself and not hurt this man despite him being complicit in a war that would kill billions, as soon as he'd mentioned the family she suspected was embroiled in Constance's schemes, the anger surged within her and grew from a storm to a tempest to a hurricane in mere moments.

Kristen let her aura push at the general, swirl around him like a cyclone, get inside him, and strip away the phony face he used to lie to his superiors, his soldiers, and every other human being he'd sworn to keep safe. She asked only one question. "Why now?"

He was incapable of resisting her aura now. She could hardly control it because she was so mad at him, so he stood no chance at all.

Unsurprisingly, he cracked like glass beneath excess pressure. "The war is about to start," he yelled. She opened her mouth to ask him for more but apparently, he was now more than willing to oblige without prompting. "Do you think you can stop Constance? She's a genius, a brilliant warrior and a hero to humanity. You're merely a fucking reptile. I spoke to her yesterday. We were all to be ready by midnight tomorrow." Andrews grinned savagely.

"It's a good thing we stopped you, then," she replied.

His laugh was strange given that his mind had effectively been forced open. It sounded empty, hollow, and terrifying. "Do you think Constance relies only on me and my men? Can you honestly believe she's so short-sighted?" He fell into his dark laughter like he no longer cared about the failure of his part of the plan.

Kristen's mind raced. She had assumed that the war would most likely be started by the Dragon Council at their meeting but no one knew when or where that meeting was scheduled, only "soon" and "somewhere remote." It had been deliberately kept secret to reduce the threat of an attack. Even Stonequest and Windlock didn't know the details.

But if Constance had given an Army general—Army generals, if Andrews could be believed, and Kristen found that in his current state, she very much believed him—a specific date for the war to kick off, she had to have planned something to spark it.

She turned to Stonequest and Drew and it was immediately apparent that both dragon and man reached the same calculation.

"She's planning something big," Drew said.

"Did you see that crate?" Stonequest asked rhetorically. "This is bigger than big. She wanted this base and who knows how many others to be ready for war tomorrow."

"But how can she know when the war will start?" Heartsbane asked.

"Because she'll start it," Kristen said.

The dragon SWAT leader nodded grimly.

Kristen continued. "I would be willing to bet—given her history of showing her power—that she'll choose a massive demonstration of these weapons, which will give the Dragon Council no choice but to begin the war."

"Do you have any ideas what that could be?" Drew asked. "If we know the place, we could stop it before it starts."

Stonequest shook his head. "There are too many viable locations they could choose to even hazard a guess. They could target any of the Dragon SWAT headquarters buildings. There's the one in Detroit, obviously, plus one in Boston, New York, DC, Miami, Los Angeles... even more than that. Plus, there is any number of estates out there. If she attacked one that had a fair number of dragons on it, the Council would retaliate."

"Can you tell which ones of those have the most dragons?" the human SWAT leader asked. "Let's say the top three."

Again, the dragon shook his head. "Not with everyone moving around so much. Most dragons don't carry ID or phones. It's not like we can simply run them through a database. Plus...well, I hate to say this, but Constance had consistently shown she has better intel on where dragons are than we do."

"We need to find her," Kristen said. It was the only solution. "And fast."

"How the hell are we supposed to do that with two dead mages?" Heartsbane asked.

"Well, sorry for saving your butts," Amy interjected.

The dragon half-smiled at the mage. "I killed one too, remember?"

"Who the hell would know where she is?" Kristen asked, but no one had an answer.

She looked at Andrews. He seemed to have gained control of himself and now sat on the ground, seething. When she looked at Colonel Fox, he seemed both horrified and furious with her actions.

Before she could say anything to him, however, Barnes came over.

"I can't believe you were right about all this, ma'am," he said. Some of his formality had returned now that they were no longer in a firefight.

"I wish I wasn't," she responded.

The man nodded and she was sure he understood. Serving on the military police couldn't be easy. Being expected to police soldiers—the people who were supposed to keep their country safe—wouldn't make him any friends. Now, he had to apprehend his bosses too. Barnes didn't seem to mind that, though.

"Not to worry, ma'am. I'll place them both into custody until they can be tried. I'm not quite sure what they'll be charged with yet, but… something appropriate. Conspiracy to end the world might not be an official charge but it damn well should be."

"History will validate our actions," Fox snapped at his lieutenant.

The MP stared at him for a long moment before he said thoughtfully, "You know, General Andrews and Colonel Fox always taught me to be thorough."

"Shut your mouth, Lieutenant," his superior retorted but looked scared. "That's an order."

"It's an invalid order, sir, what with you being a terrorist and all," Barnes said crisply and turned his attention to Kristen. "But like I said. They were always thorough. I'd be a little surprised if they already told you everything. I can't imagine either one of them letting that shipment travel for any length of time without knowing about it. It's too dangerous."

"History will judge your words, Barnes!" Fox hissed in fury. "History and God himself."

The man jerked a thumb at his boss. "I'm only saying that if I worked with a terrorist cell, I'd want some kind of dirt on them in case they tried to double-cross me. I'd want information about them I could use in a pinch to get myself out of a bind. Their whereabouts, a list of names—something that would be suitable insurance."

Andrews scowled when Barnes said the word "whereabouts," something Kristen noticed and which seemed to prove the MP correct.

She turned to Fox first. "Tell me where their base is."

"I don't know anything," he blurted. "General Andrews handled those kinds of details."

"I know the phrase is no honor among thieves, but maybe we should change it to no loyalty among terrorists." Heartsbane sneered.

"General Andrews," Kristen said and forced herself to stay calm. "I will ask you only once. Do you know the whereabouts of the technomage base that made these bullets?"

"No," he said and spat in her face.

Her expression coldly calm, she wiped the spittle from her face. "Don't say I didn't warn you. Now, General Andrews, tell me where the technomage base is."

Despite her enormous reluctance, she didn't have time for what she liked or what was nice. She needed information and she needed it now, and the urgency reminded her that perhaps not everything was as black and white as she believed. This wasn't the first time that circumstances had pushed her to make a decision based on which was the lesser of two evils depending on what was at stake. It was something she'd have to work through and come to terms with but for now, she flexed her aura to force Andrews to tell her.

He resisted mightily for a while. She realized that when he'd last cracked, he had wanted to say certain things—perhaps his way to be heard and to justify his transgressions. The knowledge of Constance and her base was his trump card. If he told her the rest but not this, he could still tell himself he won. In reality, it meant that she hadn't really battled his will and had merely guided him down a path he'd already considered.

This was different. Andrew's will resisted like a wall and she assailed it with an aura like a sledgehammer.

He stared at her, fully aware of what she was doing but unable to fight her in any way besides clenching his fists and remaining single-minded. "No."

His effort wasn't sufficient, however. She was trying to save the planet and he only tried to save himself. It was inconceivable that he should be allowed this triumph while others died literally by the billions.

"Fuck!" the man finally screamed. "There is a war coming! Do you even know what that means, you mewling child?"

Kristen continued to push at his aura. He hadn't cracked yet and simply attempted to talk to dissuade her and make her change her mind. The words gave him power and shored up his failing resistance. "Those bullets are humanity's only chance of survival. This is us against them. Can't you see that? Can't you see your mother and father will die if you stop us?"

"If we don't stop Constance, no one will be able to save my parents," Kristen said and sighed. Her inner struggle against what she'd always believed was inherently wrong made her task so much more difficult. The person she was rebelled against the thought that she could use her powers to force compliance and the conflict generated an inordinate degree of strain. Still, she had to do it. They had to know. "Tell me where the technomage base is."

Finally, General Andrews snapped. He collapsed and stared into the night sky, his eyes focused on something behind the stars. "It's on a ranch," he mumbled.

"What ranch?"

"Deephealth. It's called Deephealth Ranch. It's in Wayne County in Michigan."

From there, he gibbered incoherently and continued to stare at nothing. She was disturbed by what she'd done to him. Her conscience shrieked that she had reduced a grown man to an incoherent pile, barely cogent. Hopefully, he'd recover with time and she fervently hoped that would be the case. She couldn't bear the thought that she might have destroyed him permanently.

Unfortunately, she had to know one more thing.

"You said something about my sister. What were you talking about?"

"It was something Constance said. Your sister is key to all this. The…the secret ingredient." Andrews started to laugh and cry after that and his brain seemed fried.

Kristen took a few steps away from the man she'd broken. Was this who she was now? She looked at him in horror. It seemed like it would have been more humane to simply kill him than break his mind.

"Jesus, Kristen… I didn't know you could do that," Amy said and made no attempt to hide the disgust in her voice.

"I… Neither did I," she responded shakily.

"Don't beat yourself up too much about it," Stonequest said, his face an unreadable poker-mask. "This happens sometimes when a hostile won't cooperate. You did the right thing. It's distasteful to leave a human like this, but no one would argue that this wasn't necessary. He'll recover—"

"Who the fuck cares if he doesn't?" Heartsbane countered. "The dude was an asshole. We are fulfilling a responsibility to not only dragons but humans as well, thanks to you, Steel Dragon. Who cares if we hurt the people on the wrong side of our fight?"

Kristen wanted to say that she did but held the words back. There was time to worry about this later when there wasn't a war to prevent. Right now, there was work to do, and she didn't want to think about what else she might have to do to protect the planet from its own inhabitants.

CHAPTER SIXTY-NINE

There was nothing left for the team to do at Fort Drum but take the bullets. They loaded them—including the earlier shipment Emerald had located—on an enormous canvas cloth that Heartsbane and Emerald took the corners of to lift it into the sky. Kristen had little doubt that they'd confiscated all the ammunition. When Colonel Fox had seen what she had done to General Andrews, he'd become very cooperative. She was relieved that he didn't dig in against her, but she'd used fear as a motivator and as much as she hated it, she had to confess that it could be very effective.

"All right, Lady Steel, is there anything else?" Stonequest said, looking at the other dragons already wheeling about in the sky.

"No. I think that's it. Go ahead and get Drew and Jim back to base. I'll carry Amy."

He nodded and his gaze lingered on her for a moment as if he tried to understand something about her. Finally, he shrugged and took flight.

She was about to transform when Barnes came up.

"I'm sorry to delay you," Barnes said, "but do you have a second?"

It was an odd request after such a crazy night. They'd upended the entire power structure at the base in a single event and now, the man was concerned that he wasted her time?

"Of course. What do you need?" she replied. They could never have been successful without the Lieutenant Colonel so she would certainly give him a few minutes.

He looked at her for a moment, and she realized that maybe he didn't actually want to say anything. Maybe he wanted something from her.

It was fair enough, she thought. "I'm sorry about dropping all this crap in your lap. It must be a nightmare to arrest your own boss and process the paperwork for illegal weapons. If you have any trouble, please contact me. I don't want you to jeopardize your career over this."

The man was already waving his hand for her to stop. "It's fine, really. Stop apologizing. I don't mind. You could say this is a dream come true, in a way. I think many MPs who wonder how high up the ladder we'd be able to stop someone. It's damn scary to stop a general, but I'm glad we did it. This is what the job's about—no one breaks the law, especially not so they can start a war with our own soldiers. Shoot, if I play my cards right, I might get a medal out of this. It's only…" He trailed off.

"Only what?" Kristen prodded. She could give the man a minute but they also had intel on where Constance's base was. The urgency of the situation meant that they couldn't spend more time there than what was required.

"I guess I'm worried that Andrews and this Constance woman might be right. What if a war is inevitable?"

"My people will do everything in their power to stop anything from—"

"I know, I know," Barnes said and cut her off. She might have protested if he didn't sound so damn concerned. "But if it all goes to shit anyway, I guess I'm worried that we might have given up our only chance to defend ourselves. I'm no fool. If the Dragon Council decides to go to war, there's no way they'll overlook military bases and especially not one where those weapons were found. We'd be attacked within the first week of the war, if not the first day. That ammunition might have been the only thing we had to save soldier's lives."

"You don't need to worry about that," Amy said.

The man turned to her, a look of faint surprise on his face.

"If Kristen says she'll do something, she'll do it. She found out I was a mage at basically the same time I did and after I had killed two dragons. The Steel Dragon stopped at nothing to bring me in safely. She risked her life, her job—everything. Now, she has a thousand people behind her, all working on this problem. If she says she'll stop this war from happening, she will."

Barnes smiled at that. "A thousand and one now, I guess."

Kristen could sense his aura enough to know she could have left it at that. The man felt better and he would make sure Andrews and Fox saw justice, but something Amy had said didn't sit right with her.

"I guess…that's kind of my biggest fear," she confessed to the lieutenant and her mage.

"What is? That you'll make a promise to someone for something ridiculous one day when the war is over—like you'll get them a hotdog or something, but you won't find any and you'll burn three states to buy one?" The girl smiled.

The jokes didn't lighten her mood, though.

"No. That I'll stop at nothing to prevent this war. What I did—" She took a deep breath. She had to be able to talk about this and for some reason, it seemed right to do it there in that moment. "What I did to Andrews was harsh. I crossed a line and learned something about me that I didn't want to know. I always thought I didn't have much aura power but now I see that I simply haven't flexed that muscle. I broke that man like an egg and I don't know if he can be fixed. What I do know is that I can't help him and I don't want to leave a trail of broken people in my wake. I'm afraid I would if it meant stopping everyone on the planet from attacking each other."

Barnes frowned at her. "Lady Steel, with all due respect, I don't think you quite know what you're talking about. You didn't break that man. General Andrews was broken long ago."

Kristen startled at that. "How do you mean?"

"Now that all this has come out, it makes everything so much clearer. He'd drummed up hate toward dragons for months, ran drills on how to fight them, and talked constantly about how they hate mankind. I realize that you cracked his shell but the inside of that man was rotten with hate."

"Still… I think I went too far."

The man shrugged. "I think you did what you unfortunately had to do. It was hard to watch and I'm sure it was hard to do, but it was the right thing. You have a tool at your disposal and you used it to help. If Andrews is the sacrifice who prevents humans and dragons from finally turning on each other, I think it's a fair price."

She nodded, albeit reluctantly. Something about what he said made sense and coming from a military man, it was hardly surprising. The military couldn't afford to be idealistic in the same way the police could. Cops were expected to bring those who opposed them—namely, criminals—in to face justice, while the military was expected to stop its foes, period. It was naïve to think otherwise, yet something about it still rankled.

"Do you believe that the ends justify the means? That I can do anything as long as it stops others from killing each other?" She wasn't sure exactly what had caused her to blurt that. Maybe it was post-combat fatigue, being up all night, or merely Barnes' straightforward demeanor. Whatever the reason, she had said it.

"No, I don't think the ends always justify the means. That's why we have war crimes, right? There are some things that can be considered too far under any circumstances."

"Then how am I supposed to know what's too far? There are no rules like that among dragons. I have all this power and it seems to grow constantly. I don't want to use it. If I start to focus too much on my goals, I could lose track of what I'm doing now. Terrible actions done for the right reasons are still terrible actions."

Barnes nodded at this, frowned slightly, and looked impressed. "I agree. I really do. Power corrupts. Not to side with General Andrews, but the power dragons command has corrupted many of them. It's a huge issue everywhere."

"Then what do I do to make sure I don't abuse my own power?" she asked.

"Keep asking that question, I think," he said and scratched his chin thoughtfully. "I think that's the only way to go about it. As long as you ask yourself what you're doing with your power and as long as you constantly check your actions against your motives, I think you're the best we can hope for. If a person still asks themselves whether they are misusing their power, they are probably already doing their best to not abuse it."

Kristen nodded and managed a weak smile. It was something to keep in mind, she decided.

"Well, don't let me keep you any longer, Investigator." Barnes saluted. "You have a war to prevent, after all."

She nodded at the man, transformed and let Amy levitate onto her back, and pumped her wings to lift herself into the lightening sky. The sun was at their backs and the land below them had barely begun to stir to greet a new day.

Ahead of them, the rest of her team were merely silhouettes.

"You know…" the mage said tentatively and sounded nervous, "I kind of feel the same way as you do. About your power—or mine, rather."

"Amy, you've done nothing to harm anyone since we've met—"

"I know. Believe me, I know. But I killed those dragons and I still feel horrible about it."

"That wasn't your fault."

"Maybe not," the girl countered. "But I still did it."

"You didn't have control then like you do now."

"No, Kristen, but thanks to you, I have access to the same power now that I did then. That's kind of my point. We're both…hell, I don't know how else to say this, but we're both insanely fucking powerful. You're like a superhuman when you're in your weak form, and a goddamn steel dragon when you really want to kick ass. I have powers that make most comic book heroes look like wimps. Together, we're really fucking powerful."

She couldn't help but laugh at the blunt crassness but nor could she argue.

Amy continued. "So, if shit gets bad out there, I think we need to look out for each other."

"We will. That's what it means to me that you're my mage. I don't own you or anything, but if anyone else tries to hurt you..." She growled as the dragon possessiveness rose within her.

"No, Kristen, that's not what I'm talking about. I know you have my back. You've made that very clear and I'm thankful, but I think we can help each other to not...you know...not go too far. We were both raised in the human world and thought we were normal far longer than most of these dragons and mages did. We can't lose that part of us. When we face Constance, I don't want to hold back. She told me she wanted this war, which is crazy. We have to stop her, but when it's all done, I hope you and I can sit down, look each other in the eye, and at the very least, tell each other where we messed up."

"We can do that." Kristen nodded and seized the offer like a life raft in a freezing ocean.

For the rest of the flight, she felt lighter. She didn't feel better about what she had done to the general but it was good to know that someone would hold her accountable. She promised to do the same for Amy. It was the right thing to do, even if it wouldn't be easy.

A few hours later, they settled on the roof of the dragon SWAT headquarters building. Through some quirk of wind currents, they barely managed to beat the other dragons and waited to greet Stonequest, Emerald, and Heartsbane as they landed and deposited the crates of dragon bullets on the roof.

"All right, Investigator," the dragon SWAT leader asked, "what next?"

"I want those dragon bullets destroyed. Every. Single. One," she replied.

"I can do that, Lady Steel," Atramento said. He'd appeared beside them while she'd been focused on her teammates.

"Are you sure?" she asked the boss of the Paper Dungeon.

"Hell yeah," he said with a grin and dropped his fake accent for a moment to allow his real voice—that of a Detroiter—to come through.

A number of mages exited from the door to the building. They levered the crates open with pry bars and used their powers to lift the bullets out of the cases like a swarm of bees ready to find a new nest. Atramento issued orders in Latin or another language she didn't know, and the mages directed the bullets down to the third floor to begin the process of destroying them.

It felt good to know that each one of those could have killed a dragon but never would. At the same time, it reminded her forcefully that this was what Constance had sent to one base and there were quite likely many more out there exactly like these.

"All right, boss, what now?" Drew asked with a grin.

"Did any of you punks Google Deephealth Ranch on the flight over?" Kristen raised an eyebrow.

Jim held his phone up. The screen displayed a route to the countryside that followed streets as they obviously didn't make apps for dragon flight. "We were merely checking if it was pizza time yet or if we still had a war to stop."

"When do we head out?" Stonequest asked.

"As soon as we can get dragon SWAT and Detroit SWAT here," Kristen said with a grin. "I'm not saying it's a competition, but I am saying everyone better hurry the hell up because the loser will buy drinks when this shit's all over."

Stonequest nodded and pulsed his aura to tell the other dragons there was something urgent, while Drew pressed the button on his radio.

A minute later, both teams were assembled.

The three dragons already there were joined by Timeflash and Lumos.

It seemed the humans might have won the race except Hernandez was late. Drew and Jim stood at attention while Keith, Butters, and Beanpole arrived, each with a duffel bag that was no doubt stuffed to the seams with guns and ammunition.

"It looks like we win," Stonequest said with a roguish wink.

"Only because none of you assholes know how to help a fucking lady," Hernandez said, kicked the door to the roof open, and struggled through with four duffle bags. Two were slung over each shoulder.

"Do you plan to hit up a spa?" Heartsbane sneered.

"I wanted to bring enough explosives to blow up any smart-talking dragons if you really want to know," the woman retorted smartly.

"Fair enough." The dragon was obviously impressed by the human's fiery temper.

"You're fucking right it's fair enough, Jesus." Hernandez dropped her bags beside her teammates.

"Humans win," Kristen said.

"How so?" Stonequest demanded as Windlock ran out onto the roof with Larry.

"Sorry I'm late. It's been a long time since I've been called to action like that," the dragon investigator said.

"All right," Kristen said and looked at the two teams that were now one. "We'll head to what we have reason to believe is Constance's base of operations. I doubt this is the only one as our inability to locate it means the team has to keep moving. Still, Andrews was able to pinpoint it, and that tells me that this could be a kind of headquarters that operates like a long-term safe house or something. It might turn out to be another damn wild goose chase, but we'll take every precaution in case it's not.

"We'd be fools to think they won't have aura detectors as part of their perimeter defenses, which means we'll have to set down far away and let the humans take point on this one. Drew, can you handle that?"

"Do we really have time for rhetorical questions?" he responded with a grin.

"Good man. I want Larry and Amy with you as well. They're mages, which means they won't have anything that can trigger blaring alarms. Once you get in there and use as much advantage as you can from the element of surprise, call in the big guns."

"If we need the big guns," Hernandez said and raised an eyebrow in a challenge at the dragons.

Everyone laughed, which thankfully bled a little of the tension from the air.

Heartsbane seemed ready to bring it back, though. "I hope you don't, sweetheart, but if your firecrackers aren't quite up to snuff, don't be afraid to ask for help."

CHAPTER SEVENTY

Barely twenty minutes later, Kristen scowled and shifted irritably on yet another stakeout.

She was decidedly more on edge this time, mainly due to the fact that while immobile, her thoughts were allowed to range at will through all the possible things that could go wrong. A part of her knew she had to send the humans in and that they might, in fact, stand a better chance against the mages. This reasoning was based on the very real truth that the technomages had trained for years to kill dragons and with a war looming, this would be their focus, not humans. While she didn't doubt this, a growing dread curled in her stomach as Drew, Amy, and the team moved farther and farther away.

A burst of static yanked her into action and she scrambled to answer her radio.

"We've reached the perimeter of a group of buildings."

"Tell her it stinks," Keith whispered loudly into the radio.

"It stinks, Kristen," the team leader confirmed. "And…well, how sure are you that this is the right place?"

"There's no way Andrews was lying," she said and shuddered as she recalled the state she'd left the man in. "And given the way our source guarded the intel, I don't think it would be false. He must have had reason to believe it. Why? What makes you think that we're at the wrong location?"

"Well…it doesn't really look like a secret base. It looks like a pig farm."

"And smells like one," Keith added.

"A pig farm?" Kristen was both surprised and confused. She'd expected Constance to hide out in an abandoned warehouse and that the ranch part of the name was a historical reference to what it used to be. She had assumed this was an old factory and hadn't even thought to clarify with Jim's Google search.

Out of the corner of her eye, she saw Heartsbane lick her lips. "There's nothing like fresh pig. That is one thing humans and dragons definitely have in common—we can all agree that pigs are damn tasty."

"Kristen, I think it's time we faced the ugly reality we've all wanted to avoid," Stonequest said.

"What do you mean?"

"Well, it's easy to pretend that they obtained the parts for these bullets from the dragons they killed—and they might, to some degree —because that's the comfortable explanation. This location says otherwise, however, we have to accept the reality that they have a living source. I know we'd rather not and I've been as guilty of avoiding it as anyone, but I don't think we can do that any longer."

It was something she'd considered as well, and it reminded her of what Andrews had said about her sister. Even in his compliant state, she hadn't wanted to dig deeper—in all honesty, she was afraid he might tell her the truth and hadn't been sure she could control herself when she heard it. Still, this was no time to be squeamish. He was right. They'd all tried to circumvent it as long as possible because the truth was so unpalatable. "Go on."

"Well, this entire situation points to the fact that the source is a living dragon—either a captive or someone helping them willingly."

"That's fucked," Heartsbane said.

"None of us wanted to take the idea seriously but he's right. It makes sense," Lumos said. "We dragons need to eat a huge amount so a pig farm is the perfect cover. There is sufficient food, and things will come and go so it'd be easy to hide stuff here—much easier than in an abandoned warehouse in the middle of nowhere."

Kristen relayed all this to Drew.

"Okay, that makes sense I guess," the team leader responded, "but if we run in and give some poor old farmer a heart attack all because a few dragons wanted pork chops, I'll never forgive you or your bacon fetish."

"Bacon is a perfectly acceptable pizza topping," she joked before she took a deep breath and allowed the gravity of the situation to seize them all once more in preparation for the combat that was likely to come. "Let's hope the intel's good, though. Are you ready to go in?"

"Yeah, we're moving in toward the buildings now."

A tense minute followed before Drew spoke again. "We have nothing."

"Nothing?" she asked with a frown.

"Yeah, but in a weird way. This place is big and we can hear the pigs. There ought to be people moving about outside and working on a farm of this size, so where are they?"

"They don't need farmhands if one mage can do all their chores with magic," Larry said.

It made sense to her. "We need to operate under that assumption."

"All right, where to, boss?" Drew asked. "We have a farmhouse, two smaller barns that we can hear pigs in, and another bigger barn that looks like it's seen better days."

Kristen thought for a moment. "To get a dragon in, they'd have to do it through somewhere big. Try the big barn."

"You got it." The Detroit team leader left the radio on so they could hear the footsteps as they approached.

A creak must have been from the doors opening, then someone—Kristen thought it was Keith—muttered, "Holy shit."

"Kristen, this has to be the place," Drew said crisply, "unless this farmer uses magic runes to protect his old barn from rats."

"What do you see?"

"We have a hayloft, a few old farm implements on the walls, a rusted tractor, fresh hay on the ground, and did I mention the magic runes crawling the walls?"

"Larry?" she asked.

"Yeah, I'm checking now. We have typical detection stuff, a few defensive ones—all keyed to dragons, probably so they don't inadvertently blast delivery people—and there it is." A rustling sound suggested that fabric was rubbed on wood. "All right, that should do it. I wiped out any reference to dragons. I'll remove the others, but you can move in without triggering any alarms right now."

Unfortunately, it seemed the detection spells had already fulfilled their purpose.

A shout echoed in the barn, followed quickly by what was most likely a blast of magical energy.

"Hit the deck!" Drew yelled and muted thuds indicated that the team had complied.

Living bodies, Kristen told herself again and again as she barked orders to the dragons to transform and join the fight. That meant her team was fine. It seemed they'd already lost their element of surprise so it was pointless to try to creep in.

CHAPTER SEVENTY-ONE

Drew often missed the times when he'd worked with Kristen. Even before she'd become a dragon, she'd been a charismatic, idealistic cop, his favorite kind of person. Once she'd become a dragon—or realized she was one, he supposed—it had been an honor to work with her. Time after time, it had been a real pleasure to go into a fight with her and come out on the other side.

Now was not one of those times.

He and his SWAT team, together with the two mages, had barely managed to avoid their heads being blown off. And not figuratively either like when a bullet went through a man, but literally. The resident mages lobbed glowing spheres of energy at them that seemed to explode everything they touched. They'd already struck the old rusty tractor that had been in one corner of the barn and it had become almost like a bowl of soup in the microwave.

There was no way he would let that happen to his people.

"Split up, take cover, and try to attack them from different angles," he ordered, but his team was already moving into position. They'd been in enough high-stakes fights to know what to do, even if this one was against magic-hurling mages rather than gunmen.

Larry and Amy didn't seem to have the same instincts. She stood in the doorway with her hands up to protect herself, the perfect example of a girl in a firefight who was way out of her league.

The team leader responded without hesitation. He raced forward and leapt toward her as a bolt of energy sizzled on a direct path to the undefended mage. She might have been a rookie, but he had seen what she could do at Fort Drum. They couldn't lose her. He was far more expendable.

All this went through his mind as he careened with his arms outstretched to intercept the blast the mage had hurled.

The expected impact never came. Instead, when he sprawled directly in front of her, he noticed an almost invisible blue shimmer that absorbed the blast of energy like the surface of a pool assimilated a bucket of water.

Amy knelt quickly beside him. "Are you all right?"

Drew pushed to his knees, brushed the hay off his body, and tried not to look as sheepish as he felt. "Sorry. I thought you were wide open."

"No, I'm fine," she said and retaliated with a few attacks of her own at their attackers. "I hoped to draw their fire. That works better when it looks like I'm not shielded."

He nodded and scrambled to his feet. Inside her energy barrier, it was like watching a crappy action movie with bad computer-generated effects.

The mages stood in front of the doors to what was most likely a workshop, except behind the old wooden door he had seen when they'd entered, sliding double doors of burnished stainless steel were visible. The defenders fired an ongoing fusillade at the young mage. From behind her, Keith, Jim, and Hernandez answered the blasts of energy with good old-fashioned lead.

Their adversaries blocked the bullets with a shield similar to Amy's, but it seemed to take all their attention. Neither of them noticed Larry, Butters, and Beanpole sneak into the hayloft until it was almost too late.

As soon as the sniper reached his preferred position, he aimed his rifle at them. It was almost comically large in the close confines of the barn and after a single shot, one of the mages staggered from the strike. The bullet hadn't caught him but the force of it seemed to have shattered his shield.

He fired magic blasts in response, but Larry deflected these up and away from the hay they were seated on. The energy seared holes in the roof of the barn and he checked hastily to make sure no sparks had drifted to smolder unnoticed.

Drew took aim at the mage whose attention was on his allies in the hayloft. He shot him in the arm, which earned a curse from his target, and the enemy retreated hastily.

They delivered some kind of concussive wave that threw the hay in the barn into the air to obscure them as they withdrew inside the little workshop that obviously concealed something far more technologically advanced.

"Is everyone good?" Drew called quickly.

All responses were positive.

"All right, then. Let's blow those doors open. Hernandez, if you'd do the honors?"

The woman grinned. "I thought you'd never ask."

She stepped up to the doors and began to affix shaped charges to them.

"And Hernandez, I'd rather you didn't bring the entire damn barn down on top of us."

"What do you think I am? An amateur?" she huffed, but she also removed a few of the charges. After a minute of quiet work, she stood and nodded at the team leader.

"All right, Butters and Beanpole, down from there. I want everyone behind Amy and Larry with shields up."

"Don't be such a chicken," the demolitions expert complained.

"I, for one, think that if we have magic protection, we might as well use it," Butters said as he returned to the barn floor and moved to stand behind Amy's shield. She'd changed the shimmering blue shield from a sphere to a wall of force, the better to protect them all.

Drew nodded at Hernandez for her to proceed.

"Fire in the hole!" she said and detonated the explosives.

An enormous bang was immediately followed by a wild flurry of hay and smoke. Larry swept it out of their line of sight with magic, and Drew could see that Hernandez had quite efficiently blown the shit out of the doors. One of them was still in its track but the other was a twisted scrap of metal.

"What the hell was that?" Kristen demanded over the radio.

"Hernandez," he said and the Steel Dragon merely laughed.

The team approached with their weapons ready.

It turned out the doors actually were an elevator. Drew peered over the edge and looked a long way down into darkness. If he was more prone to poetic language, he might have even called it an abyss, but he was a cop, not a fucking poet, so he turned his flashlight on and tried to make sense of what he looked at.

The shaft went down about forty feet before it reached the roof of an elevator carriage. The cable that had carried it down was still intact, as was the panel with the controls, but some component he couldn't see must have been damaged as the controls were unresponsive. Fortunately, he located a small ladder running down the side of the shaft. From the looks of it, he assumed it was for maintenance and little else. He couldn't imagine that people could have used it to take anything up or down.

"I guess there's no second floor to the barn, but I'm not exactly thrilled about going down there," Butters said ponderously. "I'm not sure that ladder will be able to handle a man of my stature."

"Dude, those are steel rungs. What did you eat for breakfast—lead?" Keith grinned.

"I'll have you know he did not," Beanpole said. "But I don't think I've ever heard of a five-egg omelet until I went to eat with this guy."

"Butters, if you're too big to climb down, stay at the top. You can be the cork to this shaft if anyone tries to escape," Jim said.

Drew was glad to allow his team to let off a little steam. Everyone being calm and thinking positively could be the difference between life and death. And, of course, Butters had set himself up with his "man of my stature" statement.

"I think Butters is right," he said. "I'm not sure if those rungs can hold him." He pointed at a few chips and blackened areas near the top of the ladder, obviously blast damage from Hernandez's bomb. "We'll need to take this carefully. Butters, there's rope in my duffel. I left it maybe thirty yards outside the barn. Let's get that and secure it before you go down. Everyone else, hold this position until we get back."

The two men hurried out to retrieve the bag and exited the barn as the dragons arrived.

"What's our status?" Kristen asked.

"We have two hostiles—mages. I guess I should clarify—on the run down there. The element of surprise is over."

"Okay, we'll take point on this, then," she said.

"Investigator, with respect, I don't think that's a good idea," he replied.

She smiled at the forced formality. "Why's that?"

"We found an elevator shaft that goes down about forty feet. It would be the perfect choke-point. If there's a bomb at the bottom of that, it'd be a great way to eliminate a dragon. I don't think it makes sense to risk any of you this early in the operation."

Her expression hardened as if she didn't like what he had said, but she nodded all the same. "We'll keep an eye out up here. Let us know when you want us down there. We'll look for another way in until you give us the all-clear."

"I can stay here too," Butters said as the two men returned to the barn.

"Are you all right, big man?"

The sniper tried to nod but he looked pale. "I'm not great in small spaces."

Drew was shocked. He'd had no idea his teammate was claustrophobic. "Is that right?"

"Look, I'm a big man, no doubt about that, right?"

"Those tunnels won't be so tight you can't get around, Butters. We're looking for a dragon."

"I know. Really, I do, but that's also one of the reasons I became a sniper. I like being able to see the whole field of combat. If I have eyes on everyone, I feel like I can keep everyone safe. Down there will be all twisting halls and closed tunnels." He shuddered.

"You did all right when we saved Kristen from that maze with Obscura."

Butters shook his head. "That was a warehouse. I knew we could get out. If something goes wrong down there…" He swallowed.

"I understand, Butters, I do, but your eyes keeping everyone safe is why we need you. We'll stick together, all right?"

He agreed because he was too good a cop not to.

When they returned to the others, Amy immediately confronted Drew with the same argument he had used with Kristen.

"If we go down one at a time, I should go first. I can shield myself against their magical attacks. It doesn't make sense to risk all your lives when I don't have to risk mine."

"Don't forget that they have guns. I know you can make that snazzy shield, but these technomages know how to shoot. Do you think you can stop bullets?"

She shrugged. "Maybe a few but you're right. I can't hold gunfire off for long. But it's still longer than any of you can. I'll be careful."

"I think you're too valuable an asset—" He tried to argue but she shook her head. There was something in her eyes that brokered no argument.

"What's the point of having assets if we don't use them? Let me do this and let me do it now. We're wasting time as it is."

"Fair enough, I guess. Go ahead, but take it slow and be careful."

The young mage nodded before she jumped down the elevator shaft and plummeted forty feet into the darkness.

CHAPTER SEVENTY-TWO

I t was nothing short of amazing how having magic powers had given Amy her old thirst for adrenaline back. A month before, she wouldn't have jumped from a twenty-foot cliff into Lake Michigan. Now, she plunged into a dark elevator shaft that fell forty feet into darkness, where deadly mages might be waiting at the bottom. Yes, her heart pounded and yes, she had the giddy, scared-shitless feeling in her chest, but she felt alive—the most alive she'd felt since she stopped skateboarding and moved away from her parents.

She held her clothes with her telekinetic magic abilities to make sure she stayed that way and landed on the top of the elevator as silently as she could. Skateboard tricks as a teen had taught her good control over her feet so she thought she did all right.

Still, she wasn't a fool. She threw as much energy as she could into her shield as she opened the hatch to the top of the elevator, fully expecting to take a blast of magic in the chest.

When the attack failed to materialize, she took a moment to confirm that no one was in the elevator to greet her.

Amy stepped into the space where the hatch door had been and floated into the carriage. Instead of a matching set of burnished steel doors like the pair that had been at the top of the shaft, an open hallway beckoned to her. A piece of steel wedged the doors open. That had to be what had prevented the elevator from returning to the top of the shaft.

She stepped carefully under the metal bar and removed it. The hallway ahead appeared fairly pedestrian with concrete walls, fluorescent lights, and a button to summon the elevator behind her.

"The elevator should work now," she said into her radio and sure enough, the doors closed, summoned to the surface by her team.

For the moment, she was on her own.

This super-sub-basement was obviously not a part of the original barn and could only have been added in recent years. The construction was modern but simple and concrete walls restrained the tons of dirt overhead. The hallway continued for perhaps fifty feet before it ended at another set of double doors. There was no panel beside these, though, and she didn't think it was another elevator.

Amy hesitated. Part of her knew she should wait for the others to join her, but no mages had attacked her, despite the fact that the two they'd been fighting had escaped. That meant they weren't guarding the entrance to their hideout, which plainly suggested that they were doing something else. Her reasoning said this was something they didn't think they needed much time for since neither of them had stayed behind to slow the invaders.

Urgency won out over caution and she hurried down the hallway. She reached the steel doors at the end and found them unlocked. Cautiously, she pushed one open and peeked into a cavernous room.

The space seemed to bristle with the signs of concerted activity. While she wasn't quite sure what it all meant, she was still reasonably certain that she'd found some kind of planning and control room. A massive whiteboard with notes, maps, and other materials dominated a wall. A few computers were positioned on different tables, tethered to the wall with orange extension cords that were taped to the concrete floor in places. Two long workbenches—as big as school cafeteria tables but taller—were both covered in assorted tools for what she assumed was shaping dragon bullets. She also recognized a few reload presses, mainly because she'd grown up in rural Maine and one or two of the locals used them.

There was no doubt in her mind that they'd found the location where Constance—or at least some of her team—manufactured their bullets. There were even pieces of partly completed dragon bullets on the workbenches.

Her gaze scrutinized the room and finally settled on the two mages. They were huddled over a device in a corner, and sparks of magic flickered faintly as they worked. It spoke to the size of the room that she hadn't noticed them and they hadn't turned to her when she'd opened the door.

Now that she had seen them, she was immediately overwhelmed by the power that radiated from where they were but also registered that it couldn't be the energy from the two mages. She'd battled them —albeit briefly—and they hadn't possessed anything even close to this degree. It could only be the device that contained it.

When she focused in an effort to understand what it was, she realized the power was getting stronger.

The magic energy in that corner of the room was building rapidly. It made her think of a bonfire. If properly built, a single match could ignite kindling, then branches, and entire tree trunks. It seemed to her like these mages attempted to provide the spark.

Amy also realized that she would have to snuff it out before it accomplished its purpose.

She fired a blast of magic which they blocked. It seemed they'd maintained an almost invisible shield like she had, but the defense barely stopped her attack and in fact, her power had been enough to rip a hole in their barrier.

One of the mages cursed but they continued their frantic task.

Dread stabbed painfully in her gut. Whatever they were doing, it was apparently more important than a mage trying to attack them.

If she hadn't been so stressed about the possible results of their single-mindedness, she might have been offended to be so easily disregarded.

A little out of her depth and uncertain as to what she should do, she released three more energy missiles at the mages. Two of them went wide but the third burned one of her target's arms and knocked him off his feet.

"Come on—its charged!" Rather than sounding frightened, the mage who hadn't been hit sounded almost excited. He caught his companion by a sleeve of his robe and pulled him to his feet and down another hallway.

Amy gave chase and raced across the room toward the hallway down which they'd vanished, but she slowed when she approached the device.

It still gained power as far as she could see, although she wasn't sure exactly what she was looking at. If her perception was accurate, the mages had sparked the bonfire inside the machine and it was now able to build its own energy.

She hesitated for only the briefest of moments before she stepped closer to examine it. Given that it was apparently more important than defending their own lives, she would have to treat it with the same gravitas the mages had.

It was made of a series of tubes that all seemed to be connected to a central chamber. Whatever it was, the energy in the central chamber —that continued to expand alarmingly—seemed to have only one purpose. There were no prizes for guessing that it was to blow the whole damn farm to smithereens.

Of course, she had to at least try to do something. Her first thought was to yank out one of the tubes connected to the central chamber—if she could deny it whatever feedback loop that powered it, perhaps it might run itself out. As soon as she made the attempt, a jolt of energy surged up her arm.

The force was enough to hurl her onto her ass. When she looked at her hands, the veins on the one that had touched the machine had turned black all the way to her elbow.

Amy grimaced. "Larry, I think we have a problem," she said into the radio.

"Yeah, you ran off."

"And it's a good thing I did too. I'm looking at some kind of a...

honestly, I don't know. Some kind of magical device. It's throwing off a ton of energy and I think it might be a bomb."

"Tell me what you see. I'll be there in maybe two minutes. Hernandez must have damaged the elevator as it's a slow ride."

"Um…okay. It's made of metal, and—"

"What kind of metal?"

"It looks like copper, I think."

"Okay, what else?"

"It has all these tubes going into a central area. I can feel energy growing in there—a ton of energy."

"It sounds like an amplification device. Regular people worked out that copper could carry electricity after watching mage devices—"

"This is no time for a history lesson, Larry!" She cut him off and decided she'd apologize for the sharpness in her tone later.

"Right, well, if you can remove a couple of those tubes, it should bleed itself out. It might get kind of hot in there, but you'll be all right."

"I tried that."

"And?"

"And it did some weird freaky shit to my arm. It made my veins go black."

"Don't touch it!" he yelled so loudly into the radio that he managed to produce feedback. "How far did your veins turn?"

"To my elbow."

"Oh, thank God. If that shit gets to your heart, you're a zombie. It's…it's not pretty and there's no coming back from that. That's dark, dark magic. I might be able to disarm it but it would take a couple of hours."

"Yeah, we definitely don't have a couple of hours. It's starting to vibrate."

"Amy, you need to get out of there. Do you hear me? The magic has reached its peak. It'll keep vibrating until it finds a crack in that copper."

"And then what happens?"

"Given that I can feel the energy from up here now? I'd say it'll vaporize everything down there with you and maybe make a sinkhole out of this whole damn farm. Get. Out. Of. There. Now!"

"I can't do that and you know it," Amy said.

"Don't be stupid."

"I'm not. You're in the elevator, right? If I don't stop this thing, you're all dead."

"No, Amy, we'll be all right. I can make a shield so get the hell out of—"

Larry's voice was silenced when she tossed the radio aside.

He didn't know how to stop it, not with all his mastery over magic.

Unfortunately, it meant that brute force was the only option.

Amy wrapped a shield around herself and working quickly, unwrapped it until it was like a sheet of force. The easiest thing to do with shields was to cast them around herself and other people near her. Even the wall was kind of tricky and making another sphere trickier still.

Her forehead creased in concentration, she twisted it, bent it, and shaped it until it cocooned the device. Once she put it in place, the magic seemed to curl in on itself. It was a familiar shape, a sphere of protection, although it wasn't used to being around a device instead of a living thing she cared about.

She concentrated and forced it to grow smaller and smaller while the copper tubes rattled and shook with ever-increasing fury.

Finally, she managed to shrink the sphere as small as she could—the size of a beachball—so it completely enveloped the magic bomb.

After a deep breath, she began to push her power into it.

Both common sense and instinct made her focus on strengthening the shield she'd made. She thickened it, made it denser, and weaved threads around it until it wasn't a sphere in front of her but a series of concentric spheres bound together with threads of magic. All of it was held in place by the sheer force of her will.

The young mage was sweating now and one of her nostrils had begun to bleed at some point, but she couldn't relax. Even now, with all her power brought to bear to contain this machine in front of her, she could feel some of its energy bleeding through.

It was strong—possibly stronger than her—yet she was the only one who might be able to stop it.

Amy focused on her breathing as she tried to further strengthen her shields, but she seemed to have reached an impasse. She used every ounce of power she had—the same power that had effortlessly killed two dragons by dropping a forest on them—and it still might not be enough.

She realized that she couldn't hold this level of power for much longer. If the device didn't detonate soon, she might pass out from the exertion of expending all this energy.

"Come on, you bastard!" she shouted at it. "Show me what you got!"

As if the magic powering it could understand her, it responded.

It exploded and ruptured her spheres one by one until the force traveled through her tendrils of energy and struck her.

The last thing she saw was her own shoes, the only things left where she had been. The force of the blast had hurled her across the room.

The young mage had time to realize that she'd failed and that all her friends would die before her head struck the workbench and she was knocked unconscious.

CHAPTER SEVENTY-THREE

"Tell me that was a good explosion," Drew said to Larry as the elevator finally came to rest at the bottom of its shaft. The blast had rattled the elevator, the shaft, and the walls of the earth all around them. He had a feeling it would be read on Richter scales the world over.

The mage shrugged. "We're still alive, right? That's good enough for me."

The team leader could see that for the lie that it was. Larry was worried about Amy. The foolish girl had rushed off by herself and Drew hoped she was all right. She reminded him of Kristen.

"Let's move!" he ordered his team. They'd all barely managed to cram inside the elevator. He didn't want to take a guess at how lucky it was that they'd all come out of it alive.

The team raced down the hallway to a pair of double doors.

Drew and Jim each kicked one open as the others poured into the room. Despite surroundings that he thought would have been more at home in a science fiction film than a farm in rural Michigan, his team quickly and efficiently secured the room.

They ignored the table of bizarre implements, the strange charts and diagrams, and the smoldering mess of copper tubes in a corner, and made sure there weren't any immediate threats. He couldn't check on Amy, not before they knew the room was safe.

Larry ran to her, though. He knelt and muttered an incantation while the team leader checked the weird copper device. It was the only thing in the room that seemed hostile and his team had all given him the all-clear. Drew radioed the dragons and told them it was as secure as it could be.

He turned his attention to the remnants of the bomb. A circular scorch mark as wide as a large table surrounded the device. Just outside the scorch mark were Amy's shoes.

"Is she all right?" he asked. Apparently, the mage had been at point-blank range when the blast detonated.

In response, Amy fluttered her eyelids open. "I'm better now. Are you guys all right? I thought the bomb went off."

"It did!" Larry Brockton sounded beside himself with excitement. "You contained it, Amy. That was amazing."

"Then why do I feel like shit?" she asked and rubbed her head.

"The last remnants of power traveled through your connection to your shield and blew you out of your shoes and across the room."

"Radical," she said, but she didn't sound like she meant it.

Drew radioed Kristen and the others.

He approached the young mage and helped her to her feet. She was wobbly and her nose was bloody. "Kristen should be down here in a minute. Stay put and wait here for her, all right?"

Amy looked like she was about to protest before a wave of dizziness swamped her and she was forced to sit. "Okay."

"Jim, Keith, you two stay with her and keep this room secure. Everyone else, you're with me. Brockton, do you mind providing us with a little cover?"

"That's why I'm here," the mage said.

Butters, Beanpole, Hernandez, and Drew formed up around Larry and a sphere of shimmering blue energy surrounded them.

It wasn't hard to determine where the two mages they had been fighting went. Other than the door they came in through, there was only one other entrance to the room.

Beanpole kicked it open and moved clear while Butters, Drew, and Hernandez all stood ready to fire at anyone who might be waiting in ambush. They looked down yet another hallway.

"Proceed with caution," Drew ordered. "Beanpole, you and I are in the front with Brockton in the middle—keep that shield up, Brockton, even if one of us gets hit—and Hernandez and Butters follow. Butters, our rear should be secure, so I want you to one side. Don't be afraid to give me a shave with a bullet if it means you can eliminate one of these magic assholes. No offense Brockton."

"None taken. I do use magic to wipe my ass."

All eyes turned to the mage.

"What? A little humor to lighten the mood?"

"Don't drop that shield while you're working on your comedy," the team leader said and they started down the hallway.

They progressed about fifty yards before the hallway ended in a T.

"Butters, Beanpole, I want you with me. Hernandez, Brockton, you two go left. Hernandez, I give you full permission to blow any hostiles to tiny little pieces."

"You got it, sir!" she said and fiddled with a row of grenades at her waist.

She and the mage turned into the left passage and Drew shuddered as Brockton's shield passed over them and left them exposed.

"Wait up!"

Drew turned as Amy half-jogged down the hallway. She had a wad of paper crammed up her nose but it was already mostly soaked with blood.

"What the hell are you doing here?" he demanded.

"I feel way better. I don't have much magic left, but..." She held her hand up and a shimmering blue sheet appeared about the size of a handkerchief. "I have enough to block a blast or two."

"I don't think that's smart," he said.

"Boss, with respect, we don't have much defense against magic. And by much, I mean not a damn shred," Butters said. "If we're to keep moving down this tiny damn passage and the mage wants to help, I say let her."

Beanpole nodded. "Anything she can do is better than nothing."

"Okay, I'll let it go," Drew agreed begrudgingly, "but only because it might be safer for you to be with us. But I need you to keep your own safety in mind as well as the team's. It seems like this place is mostly deserted. I expected more hostiles than two mages, which means we have another fight ahead of us in the near future. I want you to be there."

She nodded. "You're right and I will."

They moved on with her in the lead despite a half-hearted protest from Drew. She held her wisp of a shield in front of them and moved it randomly as they progressed.

"I couldn't do this before," she muttered. "I'll have to talk to Larry about it."

The members of SWAT were far more focused on securing the hallway. They found nothing, though, until they reached the end of the hallway and a man-sized hole in the ceiling with another ladder leading into it.

Drew shined his light at a closed trapdoor.

"Damn it. That's an escape route, I'll bet. Those mages are probably long gone."

"We ought to make sure, though," Beanpole said and grasped a rung on the ladder.

"This might be another trap," Amy said and stepped quickly beside him. "I should go first."

He looked like he was about to argue but decided against it—knowing Beanpole he probably considered it rude—and let her go first.

They climbed through the tunnel to the surface and their words echoed in the confined space.

"If there are more of these jerks up there, I'll cover you while you deal with them, okay?" Amy said to Beanpole. Drew could hear both determination and fear in her voice and didn't blame her on either count. Both of those emotions currently battled for supremacy in his own chest, as they did on most missions. He quelled his fear with a deep breath as he had thousands of times before.

They reached the top and popped the hatch.

"Nothing!" the mage shouted down the tunnel and sounded disappointed.

Drew—having noted her perhaps less than perfect attention to detail—scaled the ladder and exited as well.

Her shield fluttered around them—it was already bigger than a handkerchief and more like a towel now—and Beanpole held his gun ready, but neither defense was required as the room they'd entered was empty.

"What is this place?" she asked.

"Some kind of outbuilding," Beanpole ventured.

Drew could see the barn through the open door. The floor was concrete. "I think this was possibly a garage," he said and pointed to an oil slick on the surface. "They must have kept vehicles here. I bet they waited for the dragons to go inside the barn, then used them to escape. Damn it, we should have thought of that."

At the time, having the dragons there to help fight what they'd believed would be a significant number of adversaries had seemed like a priority. Yet again, they'd been outmaneuvered by Constance and her technomages.

He didn't have any time to sulk, though, as his radio crackled and Brockton spoke.

"We found something…" Even over the crappy radio connection, it was easy to hear the pain in Larry's voice. He sounded like he had seen something that had broken his heart.

"What's wrong?" Drew asked, immediately concerned for the safety of his team. "Is everyone all right?"

"No…everyone is not all right."

"I'm fine, Drew," Hernandez said over the radio. She understood his concerns after working with him for so many years. "But we found something and…you guys need to get down here. You too, Kristen, and bring the dragons. I don't think anyone will want to see this, but I think the dragons need to."

CHAPTER SEVENTY-FOUR

Kristen rode the elevator while relief and anxiety fought for control of her aura.

"I know how you feel," Heartsbane said.

She looked at the other dragon, shocked that she revealed any kind of compassion, but reminded herself that it made sense, given her power. Heartsbane had incredible control over her aura. She was even able to make different people feel different things at the same time. It therefore came as no surprise that she could read Kristen's like a book.

Still, it felt out of character for the blonde woman to show any kindness.

"Oh yeah?" Kristen raised an eyebrow.

"Yeah. Equal parts relieved they didn't fuck this up and anxious about whatever the hell is so serious it has them pissing themselves."

At that, she couldn't help but chuckle. Heartsbane had the right of it. While it was great that the humans and mages had cleared the area —she still couldn't believe she thought of them as humans and wondered vaguely if it meant she'd finally accepted her identity as a dragon—but it had been almost worse than being in battle. At least when she fought an opponent, she knew the outcome of the battle rested on her shoulders. When others fought for her, she had no such reassurances.

The elevator finally came to a stop and the doors opened. Drew waited for her, his eyes grim.

"What's wrong?" she asked.

This was a man who'd seen family members shoot each other over nothing and had watched a city turn on itself at the prodding of a dragon. What could be so bad that it made him look like he'd seen a ghost?

"You need to see this. It's bad." He shook his head and led them down the hallway in front of them.

They walked in silence and reached a large room. It was some kind of a control center, obviously, and judging by the scorch marks in one corner, also the place where Amy had stopped the magic bomb from collapsing the entire complex.

Kristen scrutinized the area—pieces of dragon on workbenches, tools for turning the body parts into bullets, plus charts, maps, and some kind of plan—but her gaze settled on her friends. None of them would look at her. Not Keith, nor Jim, nor Butters, and both mages looked nauseous. Even Hernandez stared at the ground and fidgeted with a grenade. If she was too freaked out to talk shit, it meant that whatever it was, it was truly awful.

"It's..." Drew seemed to reconsider before he shook his head and his already grim expression tightened. "It's through here. To the left."

She nodded and led the dragons through a door close to where the blast had been and into another hallway.

Immediately, the stench of whatever had bothered everyone so much swept over her. It was powerful and unpleasant like old, festering wounds mixed with stale stable scents. It reminded her of when she was a kid and her dad had taken her to the circus. Instead of going to the show, he'd taken her to the back of a tent and shown her an elephant. It was knee-deep in its own shit and had open weeping wounds from where it had been chained around its neck and legs.

Kristen had been horrified—she'd thought they were going to the circus—but Frank Hall had only wanted her to see why the Detroit

PD was about to be all over the news for taking clowns and acrobats to jail. At the time, she had been furious with her father but as she'd grown, she had come to understand what his intention had been. Right now, the smell reminded her of cruelty and she wasn't the only one.

Heartsbane's aura—normally so controlled—pounded against hers. "I don't think I'm going to like this." The dragon growled and her tone emphasized her anger.

The group reached a T in the hallway and turned right. They followed it for a short distance, then pushed through another pair of wide doors.

The massive room they entered was about halfway filled by its sole occupant, a dragon—or what was left of one anyway.

It was suspended in a giant glass vat of some kind filled with mostly transparent slime. A massive respirator on its face appeared to be about the only comfort the creature had been allowed. Despite being in a glorified aquarium, it had chains on its neck—three separate cuffs—as well as on all four of its arms and legs, its tail, and another that connected to a cruel-looking piercing through the ridge that ran down its back.

Most of the spines had obviously been cut off. Kristen recognized the marks of pruning shears from her mother's garden. Its claws were all gone too so its fingers all ended in bloody stumps, and what should have been wings were useless tatters. More than half its scales were missing. The skin beneath was either the fresh pink of scar tissue or the whitish-green of infected sores filled with pus. It had no teeth to speak of—or so she thought until she took a few steps closer to the giant vat and saw that the dragon had a few off-white nubs in its mouth. The teeth were growing back. Her bile rose as her mind wondered how many times the captive's teeth had been ripped out. Had one been in the bullet she had taken in the shoulder?

"I guess we know where Constance has sourced the dragon parts for her bullets," Emerald said darkly.

No one else said a thing. It was almost too much to comprehend how such cruelty could be inflicted on any intelligent being. She struggled to comprehend this, knowing that the tortured wraith of a dragon before them was as smart as anyone—human, mage, or dragon—they had ever spoken to. That such cruelty was inflicted so someone could attempt to start a war was the very definition of atrocity.

It couldn't go on any longer.

Kristen blinked her tears away and stepped forward. She felt like she could have remained locked in that place for years, trying to process the horrors that had been inflicted on this captive creature but she couldn't. Her next step was obvious. She had to help it.

Slowly, she approached the glass with a hand raised in greeting and tried to smile through her tears. "Hi. My name is Kristen Hall. I'm a dragon like you. We'll get you free, okay? Hold on a few more minutes." She put her hand on the glass.

The dragon either couldn't hear or couldn't understand, for as soon as she touched the glass, it lurched back in its tank. The chains held it so immobile that it couldn't even slosh any of the slime it lived in over the top of the tank. It made pathetic mewling noises as it struggled weakly against its bonds and reminded her of a runty kitten that had yet to open its eyes. Hardly a fair comparison for the world's most powerful being, but nothing seemed more tragically apt.

She removed her hand from the glass and stepped away, and after a few seconds, the dragon seemed to tire itself and stopped thrashing.

"It's been like this since Larry and Hernandez first came in here," Drew said. "If anyone gets too close, it tries to flee." His voice was heavy with guilt. "I...I was worried about it hurting itself, so I had everyone retreat to the other room. Hernandez wanted to try to crack the glass, but I ordered her to leave it. I...I'm so sorry."

He didn't weep but two tears rolled down his cheeks, one from each eye, and he made no effort to wipe them. They all witnessed the same horror and there was no shame in feeling awful about cruelty.

"I've looked at the tank," Hernandez said. Kristen hadn't seen her come into the room as most of her focus had been on the dragon. "I think if I put a few charges on the bottom, it'll crack the glass. There are drains on the floor in here."

She looked down and nodded for the woman to proceed. Shock

had robbed her of spatial awareness, and she hadn't even noticed that the floor was comprised of grates.

The demolitions expert worked quickly and laid a few tiny charges. Once she had finished, she detonated them and shattered the glass to allow the goo to stream out and into the drains.

Whatever it was, it was the source of the smell. While it was obviously filled with dragon's filth, it also smelled of chemicals. No doubt it was packed with whatever medicines might aid a dragon—not to ease its suffering but to keep it productive. It poured down the huge drains and sprinklers suddenly activated in the ceiling.

The technomages had installed some kind of spill cleanup system. It was disgusting to Kristen that a living being would be cared for in the same way an apartment block was, but the water helped with the smell and let everyone hide their tears in plain sight so for the moment, she was thankful.

She stepped over the broken glass and toward the dragon. "Hey there, I'm going to break these chains, okay?"

The dragon flinched at her voice and opened and closed milky eyes that tried to focus on her.

It pulled back as she approached, but it couldn't go very far with the chains. She took one of those that cuffed the poor creature's wrist and pulled. When it didn't break, she turned to steel and it snapped in her fingers.

The dragon clearly didn't understand that she tried to help it and lashed out with its newly granted freedom to strike her in the chest. She tumbled back and made no effort to stand strong against the pathetic captive. It didn't understand what she was doing for it, which could only mean it hadn't been freed in a long time.

"Hey, be calm, okay?" she said and flashed her aura. It blinked its milky eyes a few times at this, possibly sensing a kindred spirit.

"Heartsbane, can you try to keep him calm? I'll change into my dragon form and snap these chains where they connect to the wall and floor. I don't want him to start thrashing and whip them around."

Her teammate nodded and a wave of calm washed over her. Heartsbane could have focused her aura only on the dragon, but she could no doubt sense how everyone was feeling and gave them all a dose of her aura. It was amazing that she could experience the same horrors as the others and yet could still use her aura to help in this way.

Kristen took a few steps back and transformed into her steel dragon form. There was barely enough room for her in the room. The tank took up about half the space and she now filled the other half. Despite the close quarters, none of the other human-formed dragons retreated.

She used the ax-blade on her tail to slice deftly through the chains that bound the dragon's neck.

The prisoner—not knowing what to do with even this modicum of freedom—let its long neck sag and its head clunked on the floor. It didn't look hurt, though, but relieved.

Encouraged, she didn't waste a moment. The tiny measure of freedom plus Heartsbane's aura gave her the time she needed.

Her tail broke the rest of its bonds easily—first on its front legs, then its back limbs, and finally, its tail. She was afraid of jerking the spike that went through its spine, so rather than snap that one, she stood as tall as she could, flapped her wings a little to keep her torso upright, and blasted the mounting with fire. It melted and she caught the drops of molten steel on her tail before they could hurt the dragon's exposed skin. Molten steel did little to her steel scales.

It was done. She'd freed it. Kristen settled onto all four legs, tucked her wings behind her, and wound her tail around her legs to take up as little space as possible.

The dragon stood—trembling on all four limbs as it did so—and turned its milky eyes toward her. One of them was slightly clearer than the other and it focused its slitted pupil squarely on her.

"Hoo yoo?" the dragon said in an oddly sing-song voice.

It took her a moment to realize what it had asked.

"I'm Kristen Hall. The Steel Dragon."

"You like me?"

"Yes. I'm a dragon too," she said and wondered how alike they really were. Was this the sister General Andrews had mentioned? Was this the source of the dragon bullets that gave their lab-techs a ninety percent DNA match to her? Was this why her dad's sister had snuck out a tiny, redheaded baby from a dragon biotech lab so many years before—because she knew the horrors of what awaited her if she stayed? Was this what she was supposed to have been? Rage grew steadily inside her unlike anything she'd ever experienced before. It glowed hotter and hotter like the core of a nuclear reactor that had started meltdown.

"Please! Please, no hurt," the dragon said and misinterpreted her rage for anger directed toward it.

"No, I'm not mad at you, only what's been done to you," she tried to explain, but the dragon shied away. It had made no effort to leave the footprint of the tank, despite now being free.

"Please, please—no hurt." The terrified creature trembled.

"Do you have a name?" she asked as she tried and failed to regain control of her aura. She could feel Heartsbane trying and failing to work on her rage too.

"She-bitch! Others call me she-bitch."

"Those bastards didn't even give her a name," Stonequest said.

"She was only supplies to them," Emerald said through gritted teeth.

"Please. Please, no hurt," the creature protested.

"We won't hurt you," Kristen said but her voice didn't sound nearly as calm as she wanted. "We'll take you out of here."

"Out of home?" the dragon asked. "Nothing out of home. Home only place."

The weight of the statement struck her. Had this dragon never left this tank in this cave?

"Where Mama-Constance?" the dragon asked and sounded frightened.

"They must have fed her enough to keep her alive and healing while they stripped her for parts like she was a goddamn apple tree," Stonequest said. His fists were clenched and flecks of dust formed around him like he wanted to transform into a dragon.

"Constance is not your mother," Kristen said. To think that she'd let the woman live so many times. If she had known what she was doing—what she thought was acceptable to fuel her war—she would have eaten the damn mage.

Lumos stepped forward. "Okay, I see everyone's upset and I understand why, but you're not helping her."

Kristen clenched her teeth. Somehow, Lumos was actually calm. She didn't know how but it was in his aura as plain as day.

"Kristen, transform to human so I can have space to take my dragon form, all right? Then, I need you all to leave," the old dragon said.

She complied, although it was difficult. As livid as she was, she wanted to be in her dragon form to exact vengeance, even though they didn't know where Constance was.

Lumos transformed. "Hi there, sweetie. My name is Lumos, and we'll go to see the sunshine, all right?"

"Sun…shine?" the dragon asked and it was obvious that she understood neither word.

In response, he began to glow. "That's right, sweetie. Sunshine." To the others, he said in a lower tone, "I've helped captured dragons like her before. Humans would try to take them—this was thousands of years ago, mind you—but she'll be all right. Won't you, sweetie?"

"All right?"

"I got this. The rest of you"—Lumos turned to them and his eyes burned with the furious intensity of the sun—"go deal with the bitch who did this."

Kristen nodded. "We will, I swear it."

CHAPTER SEVENTY-FIVE

The walk along the hallway toward the first room was a hard one.

Heartsbane didn't make it. "I'm sick of this shit. These fucking humans! They do this to us, to each other, and to animals. I say we burn them all."

"That's out of line, Heartsbane," Stonequest said, his voice like granite.

"For fuck's sake. Did you see what they were doing to that poor girl?"

"And we're trying to stop them," the team leader shouted. Kristen had never heard him so angry. "So take a goddamn minute to calm and get yourself under control."

Heartsbane's eyes flashed, transformed into the eyes of a dragon for a moment, then turned human again. "I need some fucking air."

"There's an access tunnel down that hall," Hernandez said and pointed.

"Thanks." The dragon practically spat the words.

"If you burn anything around here, I'll take you down myself. Do you understand?" Stonequest growled.

"Yes, I fucking understand, now shut the fuck up before I stop giving a shit." With that, she stormed down the hallway, climbed a ladder, and vanished.

Kristen was both impressed and appalled. Impressed that Heartsbane could be so furious and still able to use her aura to help calm the wounded dragon and appalled that she wanted to use the condition of the captive to justify attacking humans. Then again, she doubted that any of them were thinking very clearly and reminded herself that she'd needed her teammate's help to control her own rage. Still, she hoped it was simply a response to what they had witnessed and not an underlying truth about her attitude toward humans.

Before she had time to ask Stonequest how serious her teammate really was—she wasn't sure she really wanted to know anyway—Keith and Jim met them at the door to the control center.

"We have some things to report that might help us stop the people who did that," the Wonderkid said and nodded toward the chamber of horrors they had come from. It really said something that even he seemed appalled by what they'd seen. He used to hate dragons. Now, he saw them as what they were—living beings, albeit powerful and flawed ones, but living, thinking, feeling creatures all the same.

"We were lucky, really," Keith said and immediately grimaced. He looked uncomfortable for bringing up anything positive given what they'd all witnessed.

But they couldn't simply stay angry and disgusted. They had to do as Lumos said and stop the monsters who did this.

"How so, Keith?" Kristen asked.

"Those two mages must have counted on that bomb to destroy this entire room. There's considerable evidence here that we can use."

She let herself feel a smidgeon of hope. "What kind of evidence?"

The Rookie's grimace shifted into a grin. "We found records of dragon bullet shipments to half a dozen places."

"That's terrifying but yes, it's good."

"For one thing, it seems Constance and a small team remain constantly on the move but call in here regularly, but entirely at random so they don't set an identifiable pattern of movement. They must have any number of temporary bases, and if they are producing these weapons while on the move, it stands to reason that they must have…well, another…uh, source readily available—perhaps one they move with them. We also found references to other cells with their own supplies. I think it means there might be more of these dragons trapped elsewhere," he finished and his positivity was swallowed by evident disgust.

Any hope she had felt was swamped by a flood of anger. "Where are these other cells?"

"We have some leads but nothing like an address," Jim interjected quickly. "But Kristen, that's not the most urgent thing we found."

"What could possibly be more urgent than freeing more of—" She was about to say her siblings but the possibility that these dragons were all related to her infuriated her to a point where she could hardly think. It brought home the fact that she'd been raised by humans only because her adoptive dad's sister had been brave enough to steal her away from a future like this, while her flesh and blood had endured unimaginable suffering. She took a deep breath and finished with, "These dragons."

"Look at these." Jim led them to the whiteboard. It was covered with lists and diagrams and surrounded by maps that displayed movement routes, printed spreadsheets of timing schedules, and supply lists. Everything was dated and seemed to converge in one place. The maps were mostly of Michigan and Canada.

"Two things stand out about all this," he explained as she tried to process what she was seeing. "One, there are references and plans here for far more than only two mages and Constance. I think this base must have housed many more than those we saw, and none of them are here. It means they are out there, either with Constance or at some other base."

"Okay, that makes sense," she agreed. "What's the second?"

"That would be my discovery." Keith pointed to a map that to her didn't look like anything more than a clearing in a forest. There were probably thousands like it in the piney woods of northern Canada. "Do you see those GPS coordinates? They match an old hotel built deep in northern Yukon territory. I checked it on the Internet. Apparently, it was built with the money from gold and whale blubber, but the gold ran out and the whales grew wise. It was thought to be abandoned but all these maps seem to say that Constance and her friends are headed there."

"It's in the middle of a mountain range, cold, and remote—in other words, the perfect place for a meeting in which all the attendees can keep themselves warm and are capable of flight." The Wonderkid looked pleased with the discovery.

Kristen nodded. This was why General Andrews had received his shipment and why Constance had warned him to be ready. It also answered the question as to why this base was empty and why they had attempted to blow the whole compound despite their source of bullets still being inside. The technomage wasn't guessing when the Council would declare war. She intended to launch the first strike, eliminate the attendees, and begin the war herself. The bomb Amy had thwarted was simply insurance against discovery. The treasure trove of information was too valuable to risk leaving it available for discovery and the bomb was a failsafe—a way to destroy all the evidence, including the dragon. It also suggested, if Constance was willing to obliterate the source of the bullets, that she had others and wasn't averse to sacrificing one.

It was logical that they would have destroyed their base and especially since all indications were that the woman intended to start the damn war herself. She wouldn't allow anything to get in the way of that.

"She can't be serious about this," Stonequest said, having come to the same conclusion as she had about what their adversary planned. "The Dragon Council will have security—considerable security—and the Councils themselves are made up of some of the most powerful dragons on earth. They won't be destroyed so easily."

"Stonequest," she said, turned to him, and looked him in the eye. "That's precisely the kind of thinking that has caused most of these problems. Dragons believe they are untouchable and beyond human ability to hurt. Constance's entire war is predicated on the idea that she can convince people that it's false before she can convince the dragons. But no matter who she persuades, the fact is that humans now have the ability to hurt and even kill dragons."

"Still, this is another level. It's totally beyond anything she's previously attempted."

She poked him gently in one of the places where he was struck by a dragon bullet when he'd tried to save Heartsbane after a dragon bomb had detonated in her face. He winced as it was still tender and clenched his jaw. She'd made a point.

"We know better than this," Kristen said. "We know humans can hurt us and even kill dragons. Obviously, dragons can hurt people too, but you're not all invulnerable. You all have a weakness."

"We know we do," Emerald said. "Each other. The only way people can hurt us is by using the dragon body parts against us."

"No." She shook her head. "Well, yes, that too, but I'm talking about your hubris. Too many—practically all—dragons believe they are untouchable. That might well be the Council's undoing because Constance knows how strong they are and she has still made them her target."

"She must have made a miscalculation," Stonequest said. "Even for her, this is wildly ambitious."

"Must she have? Did she make a miscalculation when she started killing dragons in their own homes? What about when she sent a bomb to SWAT headquarters? Or when she tried to detonate another bomb in downtown Detroit and almost killed the North American Dragon Council? We've seen her fail before, yes, like when she tried to recruit Amy, but we've never seen her take wildly unjustified risks. Constance is a careful, cautious planner. She's not reckless. If she made a plan to annihilate the Council, she believes it has a good chance of succeeding."

"So because she plans it, that means it will work?" Stonequest shook his head and clearly didn't believe any of it.

"Do you really doubt this woman's assessment of her foe?" Windlock asked. He'd been quiet since they'd come down, no doubt appalled by the condition of the dragon, but he sounded frustrated now. "Stonequest, you're a good cop but you worked to keep this covered up for a long time. I think those instincts are betraying you right now."

"I'm not trying to keep it quiet anymore—"

"Only because the Steel Dragon convinced you not to. I made her an investigator exactly for moments like these. She had instincts about people and these technomages that you and I lacked. I also find it hard to believe that anyone could be so arrogant as to attack a meeting of the Full Dragon Council, but would you have believed someone if they'd told you of a dragon captured in a vat beneath the surface of the earth that was periodically harvested?"

"That's different."

"It shows cunning and commitment that we are not used to thinking humans capable of possessing. We can't underestimate Constance, not with the world at stake. I think we should continue to follow Kristen on this. She's already uncovered so much. Let her uncover the rest while we still can."

"Thank you, Windlock," she said and didn't give Stonequest the opportunity to respond in the hope that his silence would allow him to save face. It seemed to work as he simply nodded and took a few steps back to stand beside Keith, Jim, and Emerald, a physical admission that she was still the leader.

Kristen nodded her thanks at him but looked at Windlock. "Is there any way you can reach the Dragon Council and warn them? You've been an investigator for a long time. Surely there's a channel you have access to?"

He shook his head and smiled grimly as he did so. "These dragons existed long before cell phones. They have no back channels to speak of. There was a time when they had mages to perform long-distance communication, but two wars saw an end to that."

"Well..." She took a deep breath. "I guess that means we have our marching orders." She snatched the piece of paper with the GPS coordinates off the wall. "We'll leave Lumos to take care of the hurt dragon until we can send more help and find a way to get it—her—out. As for the rest of you, take the elevator to ground level. I hope you packed your winter coats because we're going north."

CHAPTER SEVENTY-SIX

Constance's perimeter defenses didn't pick up the signature of the two mages but she saw them all the same. She'd mastered the ability to control wind with her magic long before so could detect the artificial currents the two mages used to fly across the great expanse of northern Canada to arrive at their new—and decidedly temporary—base of operations.

She had been there for two days already with the other five members of her cell. It was the perfect location, a small cabin on a neighboring mountain to the one that housed the abandoned hotel where the Dragon Council would hold their meeting. They'd found the interior to be dusty and without electricity, although the propane tank for heating was still mostly full. It must have been a rarely used vacation home or something and hadn't had visitors in a while—and likely wouldn't anytime soon, not with the snow falling thicker and thicker.

Across the valley between the two mountains, the dragon's hotel was visible. It had also been abandoned for quite some time, not that one would think that by looking at it. The dragons had sent servants ahead, who had used their God-given magic powers to clean their masters' meeting place like they were nothing more than slaves.

While she had little real respect for the mages who served the dragons, she didn't blame them for their weakness. Had she been anyone else, she might have submitted as well. And irrespective of how she felt about them, she would free them from the yoke of their oppressors. She did wonder if the mages had any sense of what was coming, however. It seemed absolute folly to hold a secret meeting with such little discretion. Yes, the location was remote, which was an advantage. She had made sure not to turn on any lights when their cabin's windows weren't magically shielded so no one would have any idea they were there, but could the dragons still be so arrogant?

Smoke billowed from the chimneys of the old hotel, and lights gleamed in all the windows. The servants had even cleared much of the snow. Any passersby would undoubtedly take notice of an abandoned establishment that now showed every sign of occupation.

Constance peered at the other mountain through a telescope. Seeing the silhouettes in the windows made her giddy with excitement. She could tell by their posture alone that they were all self-important, arrogant dragons. They had no idea she was so close and watched their every move.

Her time to act had finally arrived. After all the years of preparation, humanity was finally about to break free of its chains.

Or die trying.

She had weighed that outcome and deemed it appropriate. Failure was always a potential outcome of a revolution. Death, for many, was a certainty. It was worth it for the chance to win freedom for humans and nothing mattered more than that. Plus, by her calculations, it wasn't exactly a long shot. She had studied her prey for years and learned everything about them, all while she'd waited for an opportunity like this. The proverbial cannons were loaded and the pieces were all in place. Of course, something could still go wrong, but she had thought of every eventuality.

While she continued her surveillance on the old hotel, she wondered what had caused these two mages to flee, but it was more an intellectual curiosity than a source of concern. She'd anticipated this like she anticipated every other possibility and had left a bomb that one of the mages would have been able to charge. No one could have deactivated it, not even her and especially not in the time it would take to blow.

Constance greeted the two mages without ceremony. "Why are you here?"

"The farm was attacked," Resolution said, the more senior of the duo.

"By who?" she demanded

"I can't really say, ma'am. There were mages as well as armed humans. We set the bomb and escaped, but I don't think it went off."

"How could it not go off? Did you charge it?"

"We did, but you said it should have been strong enough to blow that entire farm away."

"That didn't happen," the junior mage said.

She wondered if this could be the work of another cell from their organization, perhaps someone looking to weaken her position before she cemented herself as the leader of the movement. In-fighting like that wasn't unknown, but it had been a few years since anyone had been so brazen about it and given her recent successes, she would be very surprised. Any other cell—no matter how ambitious—would have realized that any attack on her at this point in the game would hamper the overall progress of their forces. Plus, it wasn't like any of them knew her exact location any more than she knew theirs. The organization operated on a policy of paranoia and privacy, one that was critical when facing dragons.

"Were there any dragons present?" Constance asked, suspicious that it might be something else.

"No, ma'am," Resolution said. "And I'm sure of that. None of the aural alarms tripped, so no dragons. We checked the skies when we made our escape and didn't see any nearby either."

She nodded as she took her phone out and pulled up a collection of known associates of the one dragon most likely to use humans to help her—Kristen. She held her phone up and flipped through pictures of the human SWAT team and Amy.

"That's them, ma'am," the junior officer said and sounded relieved.

"Dammit!" She cursed and her magic flared to inadvertently shatter one of the cabin's windows.

"Let me guess—your little pet managed to follow at your heels yet again?" Vindication all but purred. She respected the man in a fight but he could be annoying at times like this.

"Quiet. Now's not the time to gloat, not when everything we built might burn. Are you sure the location didn't explode?" she asked Resolution. It was a stupid question but she had to be certain.

"They had a mage with them. A free mage," he said and sounded shaken. "She was extremely strong. We faced her in a battle on the surface and she followed us down. We barely managed to get the device charged before she caught up to us. I think—given the raw power at her command—she might have disarmed the bomb."

"That's impossible," she protested. The mage must have contained the blast somehow or thrown the device somewhere else or… It didn't matter. What did matter was that they'd left bullets there and a captive lab-dragon. Her blood froze for a moment when she recalled all the plans they'd laid. "Did you leave the intel intact for our enemies?"

The two mages looked at each other before they both nodded. "We did," Resolution admitted. "We barely got the bomb charged and didn't think the mage could have stopped it. We thought it would all be vaporized—"

"But it wasn't," Vindication said and pushed into the debriefing. "Constance, we must assume your little friend has all our plans and operational information. The Steel Dragon must know precisely where we are and what our objective is. They're probably already on their way north, no doubt expecting to meet you and talk you out of all this, as that seems to be all the two of you ever do."

"We can't let this interfere with the mission," Constance said, ignored the truth of his words, and vowed to herself to not make any of those mistakes—mistakes of kindness—again. "We need to speed up the op. There's no time to wait until nightfall. We have to move now. Otherwise, the Steel Dragon will take away our only opportunity."

"But the dragons might still be on guard," one of her other mages protested.

"I know." She fumed. Her frustration was such that she wanted to light Resolution and the other one—in her rage, his name escaped her —on fire, but she wouldn't. A leader had to be fair, not hard-handed.

She knew from personal experience precisely how frustrating going up against Kristen could be. After all, she had lost to her more than once. She couldn't fault these two for failing to beat a dragon who a more experienced and more powerful mage like herself had failed to defeat.

Still, she could punish the two of them—no doubt the other mages would approve—but she wouldn't. Instead, she would use them as something positive, minor though it was.

"Get some food and some rest, then prepare to move. Since you're here and our timetable is moved up, you'll join our strike force. With luck, we can wipe out the Council before Kristen and her people ever get close."

CHAPTER SEVENTY-SEVEN

Hours later, Kristen and virtually every person she'd ever trusted her life to were close to the secret location of the Full Dragon Council's meeting. The only one who had stayed behind was Lumos. He was good in a fight and his experience gave him an edge in many situations, but Kristen couldn't abandon the dragon they'd discovered, especially since she was her sister.

"Yo, Kristen, are you all right?" Amy shouted from her back. "You have smoke coming out of your nostrils."

"I'm fine but I don't want to be late."

"Do you really think a group of monkeys can beat us here?" Heartsbane asked.

"I'm sure Constance and her mages have some form of fast travel. I've seen her use the wind to make her fly. Plus, they might not have needed those two mages to spring this plan," she responded and tried to sound confident. Of course, she knew she failed because of her aura.

"We'll be all right," Emerald said. He and Stonequest had the human SWAT team on their backs. "I can see the hotel where the Council's supposed to be. We made it."

"I'm not so sure about that, junior," Windlock said as a wing of a dozen dragons swept toward them.

Kristen had to admit she was impressed. She was used to flying with her fellow officers, but they never did much with in-flight formations. Stonequest might take the brunt of the wind for them, but that was about it. Watching these twelve dragons was like watching organic fighter jets.

They flew in two six-member triangles slightly offset so if the first formation missed a target, the second could swoop in and finish them off. The first group banked toward her and her rag-tag team of dragons—some of them loaded with humans wrapped in parkas and insulated coats and who clutched duffel bags filled with weapons—and they didn't even bend their wings to do so. It was like each team of six dragons flew with one mind.

"Follow us to the ground and explain yourselves," the leader of the formation that now flanked them ordered. He spoke in a gruff voice, and his face—even in his dragon body—was a mess of scars. Two eyes as red as hot coals looked at her from the mess of scar tissue.

"We're here to help. We have reason to believe that the Dragon Council meeting will be attacked," Kristen replied.

"The only threat we've identified in our secure, top-secret location is six dragons flying in what civilians might call a formation loaded with armed humans and a couple of mages."

"We're not here to hurt the Council and are only here to help keep them safe," she reiterated, impressed that the scarred dragon had already identified the mages and guessed at the contents of the duffel bags.

"What you need to do is land," he said, his voice harder than before.

"We're worried about an attack by those technomages armed with dragon explosives and projectiles. They might already be here!" she shouted.

"They aren't. We would have noticed them. You tripped our aural sensors and we found you and even identified your two mages. Now land, or we force you out of the sky. If it makes you feel any better, we'll put you down on a mountaintop so we can all see the hotel you're not supposed to know about."

Kristen knew that time was of the essence. Even if the mages who had escaped from the base hadn't made it there yet, they could have used cellphones to warn Constance. Which meant she knew she and her technomages had to attack as soon as possible.

But there was nothing to be gained by trying to circumvent these dragons. They were obviously well-drilled and they outnumbered their small force by two to one. If they fought to get past, she had to acknowledge the possibility that at the very least, her human friends might lose their lives. These dragons would be better as allies than antagonists, so—with real reluctance—she ordered her team to follow the other formation of six dragons to the ground. The scarred one—and obviously the leader—landed beside them.

They settled on a mountaintop amidst black rocks and a few tiny, stunted pine trees that protruded from the snow that looked like it hadn't been touched by human, dragon, or any other living creature for decades. She knew it was simply a fresh fall and someone—like Constance—could have been there only days before. Still, she couldn't shake the feeling of isolation in the frozen mountains of the far North. It was incredible to think that the mage had somehow determined where the meeting would be.

"Sir, there are mages who intend to attack. We recently found a trove of evidence that points directly to this location and—"

"Ma'am, I need you to calm down," the dragon said and made no effort to assume his human form like she and her dragons had. "We know damn well about those mages. Everyone does. That's why this meeting is happening. You claiming to have intelligence only makes me wonder how you got it. I told the damn Council our intel wasn't as secure as they thought it was, and it stands to reason that this mage has a dragon working with her. Now, tell me why the hell we shouldn't incinerate your little humans and scramble another dozen of my guards here to eliminate you all."

"Because she's Kristen Hall, the Steel Dragon," Windlock said and stepped forward.

The scarred dragon furrowed his brow and looked at the investigator for a moment. "Is that old Windlock over there?"

"Indeed, Emberwing. Long time no see. Now please, you've no doubt heard of the Steel Dragon. She was the one who fought so valiantly against those mages, but you may not have heard that the North American Dragon Council promoted her to the rank of investigator."

Kristen took her badge out and showed it to Emberwing. His scarred faced calmed somewhat at the badge and Windlock's tone.

"I guess if the Dragon Council promoted you and Windlock vouches for you, the least I can do is hear you out. Still, it's a pity you didn't destroy these mages when you had a chance to in the dwarf village."

As usual, Kristen's frustration pushed her to vent in scathing style. She wanted to point out that the only reason she hadn't was because a team of misinformed, bigoted dragons had been too obsessed with revenge to give her the opportunity, but there was nothing to be gained from that particular argument.

"We're here because we raided the base of one of these mage cells and found maps of this location. We think Constance—she's the leader of these assholes—will use this meeting to start the war. What better way to show humans they're not as helpless as they thought and piss off all dragon kind in one strike?" Her gaze only left the hotel on the next mountain to scan the other peaks nearby. She saw nothing but trees—dark against the snow—and a few shadowed cabins and gritted her teeth. That was more than enough cover for Constance and her mages.

Emberwing only chuckled in reply. "Twelve of the finest dragon warriors in the entire world stand before you. Together, we have centuries of experience fighting mage, man, dragon, beast, and anything else the earth has thought to throw at our society. The only warriors who could challenge the twelve of us are stationed at our security base. Together, we are three dozen of the best-trained, fiercest warriors the world has ever seen. We know the nature of the threat—bullets that can shred us like bread. And yet my warriors think only of facing a worthy foe."

To emphasize his statement, the eleven warriors behind him all shouted, "Hoo-waa!" in unison. Coming from a dozen dragon throats, it was a truly fearsome sound.

"The Council is secure. There's nothing a small band of humans can do to get past the guard force. Even if they're armed with magic and weapons the likes of which might actually scratch our tough hides, they will perish if they stand against us."

She nodded and tried to keep her aura under control and her voice something other than an angry shout. "I am relieved to know that a team as experienced as yours is here, but you cannot underestimate these humans. Every time a dragon has underestimated Constance and her team, a dragon dies."

"No one dies today," Emberwing stated as if it were a fact as inarguable as the presence of snow on the mountain.

"I know you want to think that, but we know what we're up against, dammit." She clenched her teeth and took a deep breath. While she hadn't meant to curse in the dragon's face, it was hard to argue all this crap again when literally, every second mattered. "You cannot anticipate what they'll do. No one can. They had maps and plans of this area. They might very well know more about the hotel than you do."

"One can only hope they do. We've refitted the hotel in ways a human will fail to anticipate. If they are familiar with the old hotel, their ignorance will betray them."

"Pardon me, Investigator Steel, but perhaps I can offer a solution?" Windlock said and stepped forward.

"We are not in need of a solution, old friend. I assure you, this location is secure." Emberwing nodded as if to punctuate his statement.

"Certainly," the investigator agreed amicably. "But even with all your forces, it couldn't hurt to add the Steel Dragon's forces to the mix. We could fly our own formation—under your command of course—or we could integrate with your other teams or even serve as scouts or simple security. We'd all rest better and I assure you, we wouldn't be in the way."

Kristen tried to smile pleasantly. She was beyond relieved that Windlock had stepped in as she knew she wouldn't have been able to ingratiate herself with Emberwing the way he had.

The dragon commander stroked his scarred face with a claw and nodded. After a moment of consideration, he cleared his throat. "I suppose we cannot have too many guards—and who knows? Perhaps your team will learn something." He chuckled at his own joke. "But you must promise me to not get in the way. When we order something, you obey. You may be investigators, but this is my—"

He didn't get to complete his sentence because at that moment, the top half of a nearby mountain exploded.

CHAPTER SEVENTY-EIGHT

Kristen had been looking at the hotel—the only building that had been illuminated in the dark mountain range—when the mountain beside it exploded.

"Tell me that the Council is actually in that hotel and it wasn't some kind of decoy," she said when the roar of the explosion no longer echoed in the mountains.

Emberwing was pale—only his scars kept their color—when he turned to her. "That was our security site. We were on patrol but the other two wings were stationed there to be near the council meeting."

One of the other dragons transformed into human shape and called their base on a radio.

There was no response beyond static. "There's nothing, sir," he mumbled.

"I know there's nothing!" Emberwing roared, but that seemed to be all he was capable of. He continued to stare at the peak that was now a little over half its size. The top had been obliterated completely and the ruins of Emberwing's base were nothing but ash and debris.

"Someone must have survived…" the dragon commander managed to say after a moment. His voice sounded dry like he hadn't drunk any water in days. She realized he was going into shock.

The dragon with the radio tried again and again with no response.

"They would have used dragon shrapnel," she said. "Your team is dead—or so close to it that it won't matter if we don't stop Constance."

"What would you have me do?" Emberwing said, almost to himself.

"Are you asking me for advice, old friend?" Windlock asked in an attempt to pull him out of his own mind as it swirled in the abyss.

"Yes... Yes, Windlock—Investigator Windlock, what... What can we do?"

"Are you really asking for my advice, old friend? There was a time you tried not to take what was offered and it cost you dearly."

This seemed to shake the old dragon out of the pit of despair he'd fallen into. He touched the scars on his face in what must have been an old habit, then looked once more at the investigator. Some of the color had returned to his face.

"Yes. Tell me what you'd do if you lost two-thirds of the world's strongest and bravest warriors in one strike. Tell me what those of us on this mountaintop could possibly do against a foe as clever and as strong as the one we now face."

"Simple. Do what I did. Put her in command," Windlock said and pointed at Kristen. "Then follow her orders like your life bloody well depends on it, because it does."

Emberwing was shaken far enough from his stupor that he was able to turn and glare at her for a moment. Between his expression and his aura, she could practically read his mind—*this young upstart must think she's hot shit, coming in here acting like she owns the place.* He broke the glare only to look at his friend. Windlock merely smiled his wry smile.

Finally, the other dragon sighed. "New times and new ways of doing things, I suppose." He reached out a clawed talon to Kristen. She transformed into her dragon form and took it.

They shook and he studied her as they did so. "All right, same question," he said and seemed to recognize something he actually liked in her. "What would you have me do?"

"Before we go, we need to know what your backup plans were in case something like this happened."

"We never expected anything like this, but in the event of an attack, the plan was to evacuate the mansion and clear the area of any potential snipers before the members of the councils took to the air."

"How would they evacuate and remain under cover?" Kristen asked. She knew they had to go and not waste more time but there was no point in rushing in, only to find an empty hotel. Her team sensed her urgency, though. Even as she spoke to Emberwing, the dragons transformed into their dragon bodies and the SWAT team climbed on their backs, now with assault-style rifles at the ready.

"There is a secret passage through the mountain. It's a long, straight passage that eventually meets up with a few abandoned gold mines. It will allow the different councils different points of egress."

"That's good." Kristen nodded. "How is this tunnel secured?"

"We have a dragon and a mage on duty there," Emberwing said.

"Make sure the evacuation is going as planned." She didn't dare voice her fears that there would be no evacuation. There was a possibility that the Dragon Councils were already dead and the warriors didn't know it yet.

The dragon on Emberwing's team with the radio tried and failed to raise the protective detail on the radio.

She didn't have to wait for him to tell her he had failed.

"Your guards have been eliminated."

"That's impossible—" Emberwing started to argue before she cut him off.

"We will not use that word again today. Anything you think is impossible is now a threat, do you understand?"

"Er...yes, ma'am."

"Take us there. Now!" Kristen leapt skyward and wheeled toward the hotel.

Emberwing and his dragons—despite obviously being unprepared for the kind of guerilla terrorist tactics that Constance and her tech-nomages were so fond of—still seemed capable enough. Despite the fact that she'd been airborne first, the wing commander quickly outpaced her.

They followed him for a long couple of minutes—waiting all the while for gunshots to batter the flying dragons—and he led them down to what looked like a small cave.

They landed near an opening to a mineshaft. It was framed with old timber and there were no footprints in the snow around it.

He sighed with relief. "It looks like this escape path is still untouched."

"Don't be so sure," Stonequest said. "We've seen these mages use their powers to hide their tracks in snow before."

"We're wasting time," Kristen said, took her human form, and led the others into the tunnel at a brisk pace.

After another painfully long couple of minutes, they learned what had happened to the mage and dragon who guarded the tunnel.

The teams emerged from the narrow mine shaft into a passage wide enough for even the largest of dragons to walk through. The walls were made of the stone of the mountain and cut in smooth, even lines. It sloped up, no doubt toward the mansion. Farther down, her dragon sight noticed the faintest hints of light that suggested more of the escape mines that Emberwing had mentioned. Still, she had no doubts that Constance and her technomages were down there.

Sprawled in the middle of the tunnel was a dragon corpse riddled with bullet holes.

"Oh, Talon," Emberwing said and shook his head.

"Cassandra's here too, sir," one of Emberwing's dragons said and gestured to the cindered remnants of a dead mage, little more than a skeleton and a few charred pieces of a robe.

"Does anyone have any idea where Constance and her goddamn mages went?" Kristen demanded.

"Are there any more escape tunnels higher up in the passage than this one?" Windlock asked Emberwing.

The scarred dragon shook his head.

"Then, if we're lucky, maybe we'll come up behind them and

surprise them," she said with feigned cheerfulness. It was a foolish thing to say but sometimes, a leader's duty was to inspire others.

In reality, Kristen didn't see how they could possibly sneak up on Constance. Ahead of them stretched a long open tunnel. It was beautifully made as if some ancient, massive creature had dug it out and sanded all the edges, but to her combat-ready brain, it only meant there was no cover. They wouldn't be able to sneak up on their quarry any more than the members of the Council would be able to hide. The expression "like shooting fish in a barrel" came to mind.

There was no time to lose, though, so she gestured for them to start up the tunnel.

"Shouldn't we transform into our dragon forms? There's enough room in here for us and we'll be able to incinerate the bastards. Even if they're tangling with the Council, our flames will cook human flesh far sooner than it will cook a fellow dragon," Emberwing said and although he spoke in a hushed voice, it still somehow managed to echo in the confined space.

"I don't want any dragon to transform under any circumstances. These mages have fought us for years—they know how to avoid being burned—and if we take our dragon form, we'll make a huge target for their guns. Remember, if only a shard of those bullets is lodged in your flesh, it severely limits your ability to heal."

She considered telling Emberwing to retreat. Her team all had bulletproof vests, human, dragon, and mage alike. His team didn't. That meant if the mages opened fire, they'd be shredded like her mom's azalea bushes in a hailstorm. Unfortunately, she couldn't simply order them to leave. She could be sending them into sniper fire for all she knew and besides, they knew the risk and were still there to work security. She needed warriors like that at a time like this.

As they made their way up the passage, Kristen's vision easily pierced the darkness. Now that they were farther from the mine shaft, there was next to no light. In all honesty, she didn't like what she saw.

"Emberwing, did you construct this tunnel expressly for this meeting? Can you tell me anything about it?"

He grunted, an obviously negative sound that she had not hoped for. "This tunnel's been here for a long time—decades, probably. My team had scouted out a dozen of these kinds of locales all over the world. Remote, secure…" He shook his head at the word before he refocused. "Supposedly secure locations. We chose this one because of the tunnel. No one was supposed to know about it, but this magic bitch of yours must have."

"Is there anything about it we can use to our advantage?"

"I hate to say it, but I don't think so. We came out of the last place that could even vaguely count as cover. The stone is hard too so we can't hope to burrow into it unless you have a dragon with abilities different than those on my team."

One of Emberwing's warriors spoke. "Stonepush could—"

"Stonepush is dead, son. So are we if we mess this up."

Kristen didn't bother to correct Emberwing. He was right. As dire as it sounded, that was the short of it.

"Humans, how are you doing?" Kristen asked.

"I gotta say, I've never held hands on a mission like this before," Keith replied. "But I'm not gonna lie, it's not terrible."

"That's easy for you to say. You're holding the pretty girl's hand," Butters retorted.

She had paired humans and dragons beforehand and could think of any number of situations where dragons might need human assistance or visa versa. A dark tunnel had not been in those plans, but she was pleased to see that the pairs still worked together, even if Butters held hands with Emerald.

"Hernandez, do you have a plan to give you all some eyes?"

"You fucking know it," the woman replied. "I have flares primed and ready. As soon as the shit hits the fan, I'll light this place up and give us more than enough to annihilate these mages. Did you ever see a human out-fight a dragon?" The last question was directed at Heartsbane, who was partnered with the demolitions expert. Both women were so gruff and ornery that she had been shocked to see them gravitate toward each other. Then again, birds of a feather and all that.

"I'd be more than happy to watch you hurt these petty mages with your little firecrackers," Heartsbane responded. They weren't holding hands but Heartsbane did help to carry a duffel that was no doubt crammed with explosives.

Gunfire erupted—violently loud in the tunnel—and for a moment, Kristen thought all her worst fears had come to pass. The mages had already killed the Council and had merely waited to ambush the Steel Dragon. A moment later, her brain registered that there had been no cries of pain and she realized that they still had time.

Not much—maybe ten seconds—but some was better than none.

"It looks like the shit has hit the fan!" Hernandez sounded enthusiastically ready for combat.

"Light the way," Kristen ordered as they sprinted up the tunnel, ready to engage and hoping they weren't too late.

CHAPTER SEVENTY-NINE

Crystal loved combat but she hated this.

She'd spent her entire life honing her skills. In human form, she was a black belt in seven forms of martial arts. In her dragon form, she was considered one of the most dangerous duelists in the world.

Emberwing had joked that it was time to put her skills to the test and she had accepted this job because of it. He'd told her that the Dragon Council was paranoid and wanted pedigreed warriors to defend them, and she fit the bill.

They'd all been ready to fight should the unthinkable happen and the safety of the Full Dragon Council come under threat. Somewhere in the back of her mind, she'd expected a conventional battle in which the combatants used their skill, abilities, and powers in a large-scale version of a duel between enemies. In all honesty, though, she'd prepared herself for a few days of utter boredom and routine because an attack was improbable.

She was therefore not prepared for what had happened.

In the blink of an eye, twenty-two fellow warriors—some of whom she had known for years—were gone. This wasn't a fight but a slaughter, not combat but murder.

Her instinct was to race out and show whoever did this what a true warrior was capable of, but that wasn't the task Emberwing had given her. She and Brownscale were the only two guards in the hotel itself. If anything happened, it was their job to get everyone into the tunnel and out of their respective smaller escape tunnels.

"Brownscale, lead them down into the tunnel. I'll take the rear," Crystal shouted as soon as the ringing in her ears had stopped.

He raced to their exit door and they began to shepherd the Dragon Council into the secret tunnel.

They made it a few hundred yards before gunshots rang out, blood blossomed on her teammate's chest, and Brownscale fell dead.

"Don't transform!" Crystal shouted to the Dragon Council and adrenaline made her ignore the strangeness of her ordering the most powerful and esteemed dragons in the world about. "We don't want to present larger targets for their weapons. I repeat—don't transform."

What they were supposed to do, she didn't know. Their escape plan was compromised and Emberwing had been very clear that they shouldn't let the dragons fly. The last thing they wanted was to give these mages targets to shoot out of the night sky.

It turned out it was far more difficult to make a group of powerful, bossy dragons sit on their hands than her commander had made it seem.

"What do you say, Dragonshire—shall we show these rapscallions what we're made of?" one of the dragons from the European Council asked another.

"Indeed." Dragonshire looked as if he'd been wounded. He bled from the shoulder and wore the curious dragon expression of half-grin, half-rage. It was that of a combatant who knew their enemy would pay.

"You should retreat. Let me hold them back!" Crystal yelled, but neither of the dragons obeyed.

They raced deeper into the passage and took their dragon forms.

———

The light from Hernandez's flare illuminated the scene in time to show everyone exactly what Constance and her technomages were capable of when armed with their dragon bullets.

Two dragons sprinted down the tunnel toward the invaders. The one in the front roared and a great gout of fire poured into the wide hallway and completely filled the space.

His targets, however, were unaffected and shielded themselves magically from the fire as easily as a child might protect themselves from a light drizzle with an umbrella.

When he stopped breathing flame, two of the mages opened fire and killed both before the two dragons could follow up the initial attack.

"Now—get them now!" Kristen shouted and raced forward toward the enemy while her teammate launched flares overhead. Her brain was already in combat mode. She didn't lament those two dead dragons—not now and not until this was all over—and instead, she saw them how she knew Constance would see them. The enormous bodies provided substantial cover.

The dragons joined her in her sprint while the humans laid down covering fire. One of the mages fell, shot between the eyes by Butters, no doubt.

Constance shouted orders and her mages seemed to vanish into the two dead dragon corpses. Kristen wasn't surprised to find that they were willing to hide in the still-warm body of a dragon. After what they had done to the creature trapped beneath the earth, nothing would surprise them.

From their hiding place inside the corpse, the technomages delivered a concerted barrage at her. A bullet took her in the chest, then another. She almost didn't notice—her bulletproof vest transformed the lethal bullets into nothing more than bruises—but when a third exploded inches in front of her, she stopped her mad race toward their enemy.

"Did you forget you don't have a vest on your face?" Amy shouted. She'd made them stop to buy her a skateboard and she used it now to roll up the slanted tunnel and come to a stop beside her boss.

"I saw her—Constance," Kristen replied. "I've let her go so many times."

"And she could have killed you so many times," Windlock said. "Don't let her now." He had come up the tunnel with Larry. Now, both mages worked together to create a barrier between them and their enemy.

It had been her plan to use the mages this way and yet, seeing her adversary so close had almost cost her the caution she'd worked so hard to instill in her team during their flight.

"Did you get a count?" she asked her force.

"I counted eight of the bastards—seven now!" Emberwing roared. "We'll take them. They can't even hit us."

"No, Emberwing!" she yelled, but he'd already sent two of his warriors toward the enemy.

They were gunned down efficiently and unceremoniously.

The mages—empowered by this victory—continued to fire at the others but their bullets only struck Amy and Larry's combined shield.

"How…how did they hit them so quickly?" Emberwing was flabbergasted and he gestured at the others who remained unscathed.

"We have mages covering us right here."

"More like right now." Larry grunted. He was already sweating, and blood streamed from one of his nostrils. It was obvious that he wouldn't be able to hold his part of the shield much longer.

Which meant that all Emberwing's dragons were about to become much more vulnerable.

"Emberwing!" Kristen shouted over the relentless fusillade. "I need you and your team to turn back and fly around from the other side. You're too vulnerable here and your people can't shoot."

"We won't leave simply because there's a little danger," he protested. One of his warriors, no doubt encouraged by this sentiment, raced forward. She was fast—much faster than Kristen was in her human form—and insanely agile. With flips and leaps, she closed the gap between her and the mages and seemed to be able to evade the bullets fired at her.

She made it halfway across the field between the opposing forces and in another blink, she reached the dead dragons. She grasped one of the mages by their robe and hauled them up and out of their cover.

That was when Constance put a bullet through the dragon's skull.

She crumpled, but Butters shot the mage she'd held. Drew, Jim, Keith, and Beanpole launched their own combined volley at Constance, but she dodged it like they threw paper airplanes instead of bullets.

"You can't help here," Kristen told Emberwing. "And if you don't go, the Council doesn't have a chance."

Invoking the Dragon Council gave him pause. She took advantage of it and yelled at him through the gunfire.

"Get to the hotel and get the Council airborne and out of here."

"The mages might shoot them out of the air!" Emberwing protested.

"They might, but I don't think so. Constance seems to have her entire force engaged here. We need to keep the Council from coming down here—you need to keep them from coming down here. I'd bet there's a bomb that could eliminate the whole damn Council if the technomages get inside. Get them out of here and close in on this position. We'll keep her distracted." She didn't add what she was thinking—*if we're still alive.*

Emberwing nodded, obviously not one to leave a fight, but also—if his scars were any indication—one who knew the advantages of living to fight another day.

"My team, with me." His dragons obeyed. They turned, raced down the passage, and rapidly vanished into the gloom, powered as they were by their dragon speed. "But save some for us," he said to Kristen as he left.

That was good. She didn't want to bust out the gallows humor yet, but she couldn't help but think that all that would be left was pieces.

"What's the plan, Lady Steel?" Stonequest asked.

"We hold this position and keep them occupied while Emberwing goes around and evacuates the Dragon Council."

"I don't think that's the best plan," Windlock said and gestured to

Larry. Both of his nostrils were bleeding now and he was down on one knee. He simply didn't have the power Amy had.

"SWAT, increase covering fire on the mages. I want them to shoot less than we do."

"We've tried," Drew told her. "But we've already used most of the ammunition we had for automatic weapons. We still have rounds for our handguns but—"

"They must have brought every damn bullet they had," Butters added. "We won't win a shootout. As things stand, we can't shoot past their cover and ours is tired."

Kristen knew their assessment was correct. Constance had spared no expense on this operation. She'd not only abandoned a base but tried to scuttle it and had no doubt brought every piece of weaponry she had to this battle. This was it for the mage—her Big Bang and her last chance to start a war.

At another blast of gunfire, Larry stumbled and fell back.

Windlock raced to him. The mage's eyes fluttered open. He was all right but his powers were overwhelmed.

"They will simply chew through this," Amy warned as she expanded her shield to cover the space her teammate had taken care of.

Indeed, Constance's mages began to fire at the wall of magic as casually as if they were on a shooting range with more bullets to be purchased if they ever ran out.

This definitely wouldn't work. Amy's shield would fail and when it did, they would all be dead. Bulletproof vests could only protect so much, and if any of the dragons had a bullet lodged in a limb, they'd be as good as dead.

"What's the plan?" Drew demanded.

Kristen didn't know. They couldn't stay where they were and would be shredded if they didn't.

"We retreat and join Emberwing and try to rout them from behind," Stonequest suggested. "The Council...the Council should be able to defend themselves for a few minutes." He sounded like he'd rather die than go through with his plan but what other choice was there?

They couldn't approach the mages, not with them shielding themselves and using the dragon as cover. Retreat was the only option, but it wasn't a real choice. If they did so, the Dragon Council would suffer catastrophic losses and those who survived would no doubt vote for war.

If any survived.

Hell, maybe war was a forgone conclusion at this point.

As long as Constance was alive, the Dragon Council would move to stop her. The only way to avoid the inevitable was to stop the tech-nomages now. They had to kill her or bring her in.

Which meant they had to risk everything.

"Hey, Drew, I think I have an idea!" Kristen yelled.

"What kind of an idea?" he asked. He'd detected the glee in her voice and interpreted it as recklessness in the face of insurmountable odds—basically her signature.

"Nothing crazier than usual."

Drew grinned at her. "You heard her, people! I need everyone ready. The Steel Dragon is about to do something dumber and more desperate than any of us would ever dare. Be ready!"

"You all get behind me. Amy, focus your shields."

The dragons braced themselves and the humans cheered as they moved into position.

She transformed into her dragon body.

CHAPTER EIGHTY

The half-formed plan worked as well as she had expected. Now that she was a massive steel dragon, the mages focused every source of firepower they had on her.

"My chest and head," she muttered to Amy. She kept her legs tucked close to her body and fought every instinct she had not to let her tail twitch out from behind her.

The young mage obliged and narrowed her shield until it was a smallish sphere around Kristen's head and chest.

The Steel Dragon slunk toward them and kept her arms tucked into her body as she moved—if she was struck in a leg, this whole attempt would probably end poorly.

Rather than risk her limbs, she gave her enemies another option.

She spread her wings. They almost filled the entire hallway and provided a huge target. Unable to help themselves, the technomages attacked her with their combined force.

Her ploy proved successful and the enemy didn't concentrate their fire on her chest or head like they should have. Instead, those who attempted lethal shots were rebuffed by the shield Amy generated, while those who took the easier shot at the wings were rewarded with the membrane shredding.

It hurt to have holes ripped in her wings, but the membrane was too thin for the bullets to remain lodged in it. She bounded forward before the mages realized this.

She halved the distance between them—hoping all the while that her team of humans and dragons approached as well—and executed the final part of her arguably suicidal plan.

Kristen roared and exhaled a huge blast of fire that completely filled the stone passage.

"Barbeque those bitches!" Hernandez shouted while the human SWAT team cheered.

The mages scrambled to huddle together on top of the dragon corpse and tried to shield themselves from the blast.

Their layered shield was clearly visible and she burned it away layer by layer like an onion dropped in a deep fat fryer at a carnival.

She had desperately wanted to turn one of them into ash, but she didn't have that little victory. The mage on point's nose began to bleed, though, and she decided to count that as a consolation.

"Their shields are gone," Larry said quickly. He'd recovered enough to sense their magic, at least.

Kristen flicked her tail forward and launched two of its spikes as she did so. One went wide but the other caught the lead mage in the chest. He crumpled, dead before he fell.

"Shish-Kabob!" Keith shouted.

The mages opened fire again and she took her human form and let the bullets career overhead.

"You missed me." She grinned. It was a stupid thing to say but nevertheless made her feel good.

Windlock hauled her back as the other dragons advanced.

Her shoulders were bruised and bloody. When she'd taken her human form, her shredded wings had transferred their wounds to her back, a sick reminder that she was still injured despite being in a different form.

She looked up to see that the mages no longer hid inside the dragon's corpse now that she had burnt it to a crisp. They had wisely retreated to the far side.

"We need to push forward," Kristen said. "We can't afford to give them time to recover."

"What, no snack break?" Butters said as he took another shot and cursed when he missed.

"If we make it through this—"

"Yeah, yeah, the pizza's on you," the sniper said.

She grinned at him as Windlock pulled her to her feet. Her back hurt considerably but the wounds had all been to her wings, which had no direct correlation in her human body. Despite the pain, she could still fight.

"I thought more about Coney Islands."

"Not this again!" Jim shouted and rushed past her.

Even Beanpole seemed to outpace her. "Did you need to check your phone or something?" the quiet, well-spoken man asked. It was basically the most trash she had ever heard him talk, and it worked.

Kristen raced forward to join the fray.

"The mages are still between us and the Council Members," Stonequest told his dragons. "We can't let them get away—not now and not ever!"

The thought of Constance escaping gave her a fresh surge of adrenaline. She raced past her human allies and leapt over the charred dragon to find that her quarry and her four remaining mages were now atop the corpse of the second one.

"Now! We take them now!" On top of a dead dragon was about as good a position as anyone could have in this cursed tunnel, but the mages were outnumbered. She and her team could defeat them.

The members of Dragon SWAT raced up to the dead Council member and attacked the mages. It didn't prove to be easy.

The enemy obviously knew they couldn't hope to stand against the dragons in close combat. As Stonequest and his team approached, the technomages leapt or flew or whatever else they could do to evade them and fired continuously as they bounced around the tunnel, powered by magic.

It was like trying to swat heavily armed magic flies.

Drew and his team had all switched to handguns, which proved to be slightly more effective than the assault-style rifles were in close quarters.

The mages lunged and withdrew, darted near a dragon to fire a shot, and vaulted off again only to land in front of a human. In the chaos, Timeflash was shot in the leg and fell, screaming in pain.

Keith managed to graze one of the mages in the shoulder but this only earned his opponent's wrath. A blast of ice froze the Rookie to the wall.

Butters hung back and attempted to use his vantage point on the top of the dragon Kristen had burned. Unfortunately, he succeeded only in falling through the charred flesh and was soon stuck inside the dead dragon's ribcage like it was a macabre prison.

Windlock hung back and directed the two dragons' mages to use their shields where they could. Most of that work was done by Amy, while Larry did his best to anticipate magic attacks and call them out.

Hernandez lobbed a grenade but the mage she'd aimed at was somehow able to use her magic to pluck the pin from the air and shove it back into the device. She then rocketed it into Emerald's face and pulled the pin once more.

The blast knocked the dragon over, bloodied his face, and blinded him. Although the grenade had been made of metal—not dragon parts —it had still shredded his eyes and he was effectively out of the fight.

Constance darted through the battle, daring Kristen to catch her. She was impossibly fast and every time it seemed like a dragon was about to take advantage of a mage, she was there to unbalance them, to throw sand in their face, and to keep the fight alive.

But when Emerald and Timeflash were disabled, the technomage leader seemed to deem the battle over.

She moved to stand on top of the dead dragon and beckoned Kristen to fight her while their allies fought to the death all around them.

The Steel Dragon obliged her and rushed forward in human form to engage her enemy. The mage was more than ready for her.

They locked in combat and their fists and feet moved faster than a normal human would be able to track. Constance had trained her entire life for this. She augmented her speed and strength with magic as well and was a powerful, formidable foe. The fact that she'd killed before without remorse made her that much more intimidating.

To counter this magic-fueled fighter, Kristen had her own years of athleticism, plus hours and hours spent in grueling combat with Drew, Stonequest, and even Shadowstorm—the evil dragon who'd first taken her into dragon society. She combined this training with her own dragon-augmented speed and strength.

Both held grudges against the other and fought for what they believed in.

Kristen couldn't help but grin as her first blows hammered into her opponent's forearms. This wouldn't be easy.

"Even you must be able to see that you've gone too far," she said between punches.

The woman dodged a jab and drove her leg up and into Kristen's chest faster than she would have thought possible with any other opponent.

She stumbled back and looked at the mage, whose face was a haughty glare illuminated in the harsh light of the flares. "Too far? I would think that of all our missions, this is the one you could most appreciate."

"You've gone off the deep end," she continued and launched into another rapid attack. Constance blocked her fist but not the other arm's elbow, which caught her across the jaw and spun her away.

The assassin had obviously taken the blow's momentum and transformed it into her own escape. She bounded back almost immediately, looking like something out of a kung-fu movie, and landed. The hard strike to her jaw seemed to have not made any impression at all.

"Hardly! This is what we've waited for—an opportunity to attack the dragons most responsible for the suffering of mankind. You also see the flaws with the status quo. I know you do! The monsters at the top of this tunnel are those responsible for it."

"You can't bring change through murder," she retorted, then braced herself as Constance jumped, kicked off the back wall like an Olympic swimmer, and launched herself into her stomach.

She turned to steel before her adversary made impact, yet the force —no doubt magically augmented—was still enough to fold her in half and she fell with the mage on top of her.

The woman had her arms pinned now, one bicep beneath each knee. "What would you have me do?" she demanded, her fist lost in a swirling maelstrom of some kind of energy that crackled like lightning before she punched Kristen in the face. The blow itself didn't hurt her steel skin but the energy surged through it and triggered the muscles in her face and neck to spasm painfully.

"What would you have me do?" Constance demanded again before she struck her once more in the face. Rather than waiting for an answer, she delivered a third blow. "Should I try to sue the dragons for years of genocidal clandestine warfare against humanity?" The electrifying punch descended again. "Should I write a letter to my representative in Congress and ask them to demand reparations for the gold dragons made slaves mine and refine?" The next punch was enough to cause her steel skin to flicker and turn off. "Should I go to their courts since they don't recognize ours as having any legal sway over them and present my case while they laugh?" One final punch was hard enough to break Kristen's nose.

"Did you try any of that?" she sputtered, still on her back while blood ran freely from her nose and down her throat and made her gag. "What have you done but kill?"

"You're naïve. A child in a woman's body. I guess the dragons and I agree on something." She tried to punch her again but Kristen bucked her hip and used the momentum to roll her over so she was now on top.

"All you and the dragons have in common is your willingness to spill blood," Kristen said, her point accentuated by the blood pouring from her bloody nose onto her enemy.

"Let me get this straight," the assassin said, tried to push her off, and failed. "The dragons spill blood, yet they should be given every chance to redeem themselves despite the fact that they never have."

She was about to punch Constance—she thought she could break her nose in the same way as the woman had broken hers—but a gust of wind caught her and hurled her into the ceiling.

Kristen struck the roof and fell. She managed to restore her steel skin before she collided with her adversary, but the mage was wily and stepped aside at the last moment. The Steel Dragon landed heavily on the dragon's corpse and broke through the skin to sink into the enormous body.

"There are dragons who care about people," she screamed and her voice rose to a shrill shriek as she tried to extricate herself from the horrible gore of the bullet-ridden corpse. She was too heavy and couldn't climb out in her steel skin. Worse, her attempts snapped the bones so she couldn't find leverage.

"And there are people who care about puppies. Does that mean they want to give them the rights of humankind?" Constance noticed that she had turned her steel skin off, seized her by the lapels, and yanked her free.

Kristen punched the assassin in the neck—once, twice, and three times, but the woman didn't drop her. Instead, she tightened her grasp and shook her like a ragdoll. "What do you want, Steel Dragon? What are you fighting for? Have you ever paused to consider why you work so hard to prevent the utopia we've worked so hard to bring about?"

In a blink, the mage's hands moved from the dragon's lapels to her neck so she had to answer through a choked windpipe. "All I want is to share this world."

Constance laughed ruefully and flung her to the ceiling of the tunnel. She struck it hard enough to dislodge a few pieces of rock before she fell again. Before she could get her breath back, her adversary kicked her in the chest and she careened into the back wall and loosened more rock. As if this wasn't enough, the assassin then kicked the debris that had fallen from the ceiling at her.

She tried to activate her steel skin but she was too tired. Instead, she watched with her teeth clenched while her eyes tried to squeeze shut as the rubble streaked toward her.

It didn't connect and stopped inches from her face, then boomeranged back to Constance.

The technomage dodged it with an effortless backflip but she looked around and tried to determine who had thwarted her attack.

Kristen tried to catch her breath and only focused on her breathing and turning her body to steel. She knew where the intervention had come from.

Her adversary seemed to give up on her mysterious assailant and turned back to her with murder in her eyes.

That was the moment Amy had waited for. She rocketed up the side of the tunnel on her skateboard, then launched off it, using her magic to propel the board toward Constance's neck.

The woman brought her arms up in time to block the attack and the skateboard shattered, but not before it bloodied her forearms.

"Another fucking board?" the novice mage shouted in disbelief.

The enemy vaulted toward her, launched by the small flex of her muscles. Again, she obviously used her magic to propel herself forward.

Amy knew she was outclassed and didn't try to engage in a direct battle. Instead, she began to throw anything that wasn't stuck to the wall or floor at the other mage.

"How can you act like you're a defender of regular people when you have powers like this?" the girl yelled while stone, discarded bullet casings, and even pieces of the dead dragon rocketed toward Constance.

"You have power exactly like them," Amy continued and flung piece after piece of debris. The assassin flicked each one away like stone and metal were nothing but slow-moving insects. "I don't buy for a second that all this is pure altruistic bullshit. If it were, you'd fight with civil disobedience or whatever other normal shit normal people have to fight oppressors. You're nothing but a dragon in human's clothing."

"I am nothing like them!" the woman shrieked and closed the distance between them with an uppercut that caught Amy on the chin and catapulted her away.

"Nah, you're right. Dragons have better peripherals." The girl smirked as she pushed to her feet.

Constance turned in time to catch a steel foot in her face. The force of the blow pounded her into the wall and stone cracked on impact.

Kristen walked toward her, no longer hurried. "Face it, Constance, you're done."

The assassin looked around and scowled at the scene. One of her mages was dead from a bullet to the head and another was either dead or unconscious. Two remained alive but both were captured, one by a ring of humans, each with a gun pointed to the mage's head and the other by the dragons, who held the mage in vice-like grips.

Wearily, the woman pushed to her feet and coughed up blood as she did so, but she didn't surrender or quit or try to run. She simply looked at her adversary with bloody teeth. "Don't you get it? The dragons underestimate us because they think about people instead of a person."

"It seems to me like you forgot about a person back there," Kristen said and gestured to Amy before their combat resumed. Even now, with who knew what kind of internal injuries, the mage fought back with unbelievable vigor.

She caught the steel blows when she could and dodged the ones she needed to but only attacked when she had a clear opportunity.

A powerful blow caught Kristen in the sternum and forced her back a few paces. "People are weak," the assassin continued as if she needed to justify herself in this final encounter. "When we group together, we make dumb choices, choose bad leaders, and let fear drive our decisions. But there's no way to anticipate a single person's actions. As long as dragons treat us like cattle, that's what we'll be. But when people and dragons see that one person is all it takes to break the shackles of our servitude, then and only then will mankind rise up against our false masters."

"You're wrong," she said, lurched forward, and caught the woman in the groin with a knee. The mage stumbled and before she could straighten, Kristen hit her in the back of the head with an elbow. She threw every ounce of force she had into the blow—it would have crushed a regular human's skull like a melon—and it hurt Constance, but not much. She fell but caught herself in a pushup. Kristen kicked her in the ribs, rolled her over, and placed a foot on top of her chest so she couldn't wiggle away.

"The reason we're beating you is because we're a team," she explained as the captive punched at her leg. "We're stronger—men, women, dragons, mages, whatever—when we work together. If we would all sit and listen to each other, we could live in a better world."

The woman stopped struggling and an expression crossed her face that seemed entirely out of place. It looked like…acceptance. Kristen took her foot off the other woman's chest and reached her hand out to help her up.

Constance headbutted her hard enough for her to see spots despite her steel skin.

She stumbled back while the mage darted to her feet. Her forehead had split from the blow and bled openly, but she didn't seem to mind.

"I think I finally understand what you're talking about," she said and spat some of the blood. "I even have a word for the world you want to live in."

"What's that?" Kristen asked and lunged forward.

"A fairytale." The assassin vaulted over her head, planted her feet on her shoulder, and launched off her. The force thrust the dragon into the stone floor and a tooth chipped.

That's a new and awful form of pain, she thought as she pushed to her feet and raced up the tunnel after her adversary.

Constance was fast and Kristen was tired and unsure if she could catch her. Confident in the success of her team, though, she transformed into a dragon.

"Fool!" the assassin shouted, sliding to a stop to face the Steel Dragon. "I'm far more lethal against this body than your human one."

She had no intention of engaging in a melee, though. Instead, she exhaled flame at the mage, who dodged in a series of flips and spins. The dragon had seen it before, though, and in fact, she'd anticipated the response. She flicked her tail, once, twice, thrice and each time, flung barbs at her enemy. The first went through the woman's foot and pinned her to the ground. The next trapped her forearm when it drilled through and into the wall, and the third narrowly missed her head.

Constance screamed in pain as Kristen approached her. "You're done, Constance. It's over."

"You might have won this fight but you're out of your mind if you think that I'll submit myself to the dragon justice system."

"Spoken like someone who knows they're guilty," she countered.

"When the revolution comes, I only hope you see that you alone can stand against these dragons," the mage said. She stretched her hand across her body to the arm that was pinned, tapped a jewel on a bracelet she wore, and vanished.

CHAPTER EIGHTY-ONE

"No!" Kristen screamed and blasted the tunnel with an inferno of fire. Nothing burned as only rock stretched ahead of her. No hidden figures, no hidden tunnels, and nothing but stone, now superheated.

"She's gone, Kristen," Larry said and limped toward her. Apparently, he'd been shot in the leg at some point but she had had no idea when. "There are invisibility spells but none that can be paired with invulnerability. Plus, she's never used one before. It looks like a teleportation spell to me and is probably linked to another gem at a safe house somewhere. My bet is she's gone to lick her wounds. Sorry about that. I had hoped to bring her in too."

"She won't," Kristen said and assumed her human form. Both bodies were hurt, but her tattered dragon wings hurt far more than the broken nose, chipped tooth, and scrapes and bruises in her human body.

"You beat her, Steel. Don't sweat it," Heartsbane said.

"No way. She'll go after the Council. Right now. By herself. She practically told me as much."

Stonequest came up and shook his head. "Kristen, that would be suicide, even for her. Emberwing must have reached them by now and it's not like he'll let anyone get the jump on him again. Now that his warriors are on alert—"

"How many of them died when they were down here? Three?" she demanded. While she didn't want to be morbid, she was also furious that people were underestimating Constance again. It was as the leader of the technomages had said. Dragons couldn't help but underestimate an individual person when in reality, individual people were the only way things got done.

"Okay, sure," Stonequest said and looked pissed that she'd used the dead dragons to make a point. "But there's the Council as well. It's not like they're helpless. They might not be warriors like Emberwing's team was, but they have those positions because they're the most cunning and powerful dragons alive."

"How long have they had those positions?" Kristen demanded.

"What? I don't know." He looked even more annoyed and his gaze darted constantly to Emerald, whose eyes had yet to heal, and to Timeflash, who still clutched her wounded leg. She understood his concern—they were her teammates too—but there would be far more dragons hurt soon or even worse. She was sure of it.

"Decades," Windlock answered. "Why?"

"That proves my point. They have those positions because dragons are complacent. That's exactly what Constance is counting on. I'm sure she knows everything there is to know about them. Every one of them she can kill is a victory. These are dragons who have been seen as untouchable for decades. Even killing a handful will prove they're not as strong as humans and dragons think."

"You make good points," the investigator admitted but didn't sound happy about it.

"I know I do, which means we need to move—now. She'll be in that hotel somewhere, I'm sure of it."

Stonequest cleared his throat "You can't be sure—"

"It makes sense, Stone. Go. We'll be all right," Emerald said.

"Amy, Larry, you need to stay here and keep those mages contained. Will that be a problem?"

"Not with these," Larry said and revealed three of the magic-dampening cuffs.

"Good. And if you three try anything," she said to the mages. "They will kill you." She gestured to the human SWAT team. "Drew, I won't lie. We could use backup, but I need to know these mages are secured and Larry and Amy don't exactly have that kind of experience."

"We'll get the cuffs on them, post guards, and make sure no one comes this way. Right now, I want Jim and Keith to go with you. Butters, Beanpole, Hernandez, and I will stay here with Amy, Larry, and the two hurt dragons."

"That sounds good, except we need to move. Jim, Keith, stay with us."

Kristen looked at Stonequest, Heartsbane, and Windlock. They all nodded, understood that this was on them despite facing a foe who knew more about how to kill dragons than any other species.

Still, there was nothing to be done about it. She turned her dragon speed on and raced up the tunnel with the three other dragons hot on her heels. They outpaced Jim and Keith by a factor of ten. The two men could be heard only starting their run up the tunnel by the time the dragons reached the hotel.

They burst through a door at the top of the tunnel and into a moderately sized room lined with sacks of rice, beans, and flour. A pantry, she thought as she burst out of it and stopped short as two dragon guards in a large kitchen spun to face them.

"Halt! Stop right there," the woman shouted.

"It's all right, Crystal, that's the Steel Dragon. She sent us around." The other guard smiled. "Did you finish off those chumps? I must say, that's good news."

"Hardly," Kristen said. "Where's the Council? Take us there."

"Emberwing gave us orders to guard this passage. We can't abandon our post—" the guard named Crystal tried to argue but she cut her short.

"There are two mages on guard in there, one of which is insanely powerful, plus well-trained and well-armed humans. That way is safe. We need to make sure that Constance can't carry out her final attack."

"Final attack? What are you talking about? No one got past us," the woman protested. She was armed with a spear and looked like she wanted to use it to bar their path, but the other guard marched past her and beckoned for them to follow. With a sigh, his companion let them through.

"We took the mages into custody but Constance escaped," Kristen told the two as they walked.

"How?" Crystal asked.

"A teleportation gem. The Steel Dragon thinks the egress gem must be somewhere inside the hotel," Windlock explained.

"But that would be suicide," the woman exclaimed.

"It very well might be, but she won't go down without taking as many of these dragons with her as she can," Kristen said.

"Where are the members of the Dragon Council evacuating from? One location or multiple?" Windlock asked the guards.

"Evacuating?" Crystal sounded confused.

"We haven't had any trouble whatsoever since we arrived," the other guard explained. "Your team did an excellent job containing the mages in the tunnel. Emberwing has the rest of the Council under guard. We were to sound the alarm if anyone but you came out of there."

"Constance probably planned this," Kristen said and quickened her pace to draconic speeds once more.

"It makes sense. By only attacking one place, if it failed, there was a better chance the rest of the dragons would gather in another location," Windlock said.

"Are you seriously considering the idea that a single human, even a mage, can kill more than fifty dragons?" Stonequest asked. "They were tough but not that tough."

"Their bomb at our security base caught us off guard, but Emberwing is cunning. He won't let that happen again," the other guard said. Kristen didn't have the time nor the brain space to ask him his name.

"Neither of our forces was their target," she said and increased the pace. "Them failing to kill all of us only proves that they're committed to their mission. Their room is upstairs?" she asked as the two guards began to lead them up a beautiful staircase in the hotel's main lobby.

"Yes, ma'am," Crystal said. "The big doors at the top of the stairs. The ballroom."

Kristen paused for the briefest of moments and considered the best way to use everyone.

"Okay, you two stay here. That tunnel should be secure, but I wouldn't be surprised to see someone try to force their way in. We'll find Emberwing."

Before the guards could reply, she raced up the stairs.

As she reached the door at the top, Emberwing appeared ahead of her. Even though he was in human form, the scars on his face made him easily recognizable. A dragon must have done it as any other wound would have been fully restored by his healing abilities.

"You beat them." He sounded both relieved and triumphant. It was a bummer to dispel both illusions.

"Not the one who matters. How are the evacuations going?" she demanded.

"Evacuations? We haven't had any reason to begin that. The Council has yet to deliberate."

"That doesn't matter right now," she snapped at the warrior.

"It does to them, but from a security standpoint, it didn't make sense either. We encountered a tiny force there. It stands to reason there'll be more stationed around the mountain to fire at any dragons who flee," Emberwing explained, his chin stiff with evident disapproval.

"Did anyone shoot at you?" Heartsbane sneered.

"No, but that doesn't mean—"

"You need to get the Council out of here. Now!" Kristen barely managed to stop herself from yelling.

"I—"

"You asked for my advice, old friend," Windlock said prosaically. "I gave it to you. Listen to the woman!"

Emberwing nodded and returned to the ballroom. Kristen had

never been so relieved to hear so much yelling or the sound of broken glass. Good, so the dragons were leaving.

And not a moment too soon.

"We have the mage!" Crystal said from the bottom of the stairs. Kristen felt her heart both leap into her chest in excitement and plummet in fear. It was great to capture Constance but so obvious a location could only mean that the woman had completed whatever plan she'd gone to execute.

It turned out that the captive was Amy, not the technomage.

"Amy?" Kristen said, not quite sure of her reason for being there and while she feared the worst, she also dared to be optimistic. After all, the girl wasn't any more bruised or battered than when she'd left her.

"Larry and I got the cuffs on. Those mages aren't a threat. We left them with Drew and he's bringing them up the tunnel to the hotel."

Larry rushed into the entryway, took in his surroundings, and caught his breath. "You…have to teach me…the make your shoes…levitate trick…" he wheezed between breaths.

Amy smiled and settled on the floor. Kristen hadn't even realized she'd been floating. "We think we know where Constance is," the girl said.

"Finally, some good news," Heartsbane muttered.

While the young mage didn't let her smile slip, her eyes betrayed the terror she felt in her heart. "It's really not."

CHAPTER EIGHTY-TWO

"Tell me again how you know she's down here?" Kristen whispered as they made their way through a hallway in the basement. She wasn't entirely sure what to call the level of a hotel that was below the basement and didn't seem to house anything except generators and apparently long-obsolete gold-refining equipment.

"We combined what was left of our magical strength and were able to detect her. Well, not her exactly but something with her magical signature." Amy took a deep breath to calm herself. "It feels like… Kristen, it feels like another of those bombs like we found in their base."

"I'm only glad the two of you were able to notice it," she replied.

"It was mostly the kid," Larry whispered. "I gave her some guidance but the power's all hers."

"You're doing all right then?" Kristen asked as they proceeded down the hallway.

"I'm beyond spent." Amy grinned weakly. "I'm so tired and hungry. Fighting Constance took more out of me than I realized and that bomb earlier today was…well, that was a big drain. And this one feels bigger."

Note to self. The only person you thought capable of doing something to stop the bomb is beyond exhausted and could barely contain one that was smaller than this.

"There—I think she's in there." The girl pointed to an open doorway on the right side of the hall.

Kristen looked at Stonequest, Heartsbane, and Windlock, who all nodded. It was time to face Constance.

She sprinted forward and turned the corner to find her quarry arms-deep in a device that did look frighteningly similar to what Amy had described at the base. A large chamber was surrounded by pipes that led to and from the center of the device but this one had to be the biggest brother of the bomb they'd seen earlier. It was the size of the desk, and rather than having copper piping as Amy had described it, the entire contraption seemed to be made of dragon bones. It floated ominously in the center of the room.

"Get your fucking hands up!" she shouted as she raced toward the assassin.

Constance nodded, withdrew her hands from the device, and held them in the air.

Kristen almost hesitated in her approach—she'd never seen the woman comply with anything—but then she noticed how badly her hands were trembling.

The look on her face was also one of pure exhaustion. There were bags under her eyes and sweat dripped down wrinkles that hadn't been noticeable before. The mage even seemed to have gray hair that she previously hadn't.

"I'm coming behind you and I want you to lower your hands slowly," Windlock said and slid his hands into a pocket of his coat.

"Sure," Constance said and sounded bone-tired.

The investigator approached and continued to look suspicious despite her obvious exhaustion. She made not even the slightest attempt to struggle when he brought her hands down, nor did she resist when he put a pair of the magic-dampening cuffs on her.

Once those were in place, she fell to her knees and laughed as tears streamed down her face.

"What's so funny?" Kristen demanded.

"I had less in reserve than I thought," the woman said and tried to stand but without success. "I used too much magic, but it'll be worth it. My work is finally done."

"What do you mean, your work is done?" she asked, although she knew as well as Constance.

As if to prove her correct, the assassin only raised her chin at the device in front of them. "I had barely enough to charge it."

Stonequest was already studying the device. "It's made of dragon parts. That seems like a structural issue. This piece of crap probably won't work."

"No, no." Constance tried to shake her head but it simply sagged so her hair hung in her face, drenched with sweat. "It's made of copper and is coated with dragon parts. Plus, there are more caches—the pieces too small to be used for bullets—placed nearby. It'll be beyond anything any dragon could ever imagine. And we'll get it all in High Def."

"Tell us how to turn it off or you die as well," Kristen said.

Constance tried to laugh but only coughed out a little blood. "I'd be lying if I said I didn't enjoy our cat and mouse game. But the Steel Dragon has clearly shown where her loyalties lie, which means I won't be too sad to see her go down with the Council."

"You'll die too. Don't you see that?"

"At your hands. You've never heard of a martyr?"

"Curse you! Amy, you contained a blast earlier. Can you and Larry do that with this bomb?"

The two mages shared a look that made their answer obvious. "At full strength and with Larry's help, I might have been able to. But after a day like today? I'm sorry, I can't."

"Tick-tock, Steel Dragon," Constance said. "Do you see those black holes at the top of the device?"

Kristen grunted an affirmative.

"When those are all filled with light, time's up."

There were eight holes and four of them were already glowing. Before she could ask how long it took one to charge, another blinked on. That only left three.

"Your mages can't do anything about it, even if they did have the energy," the assassin said from her place on the floor

Kristen scowled at her and retrieved her radio. "Hernandez, I need you here. We have a bomb we need disarmed."

"You got it, boss. How long do we have?" Hernandez asked.

In response, another of the black circles filled with light. Two left was not encouraging.

"A minute? Maybe two?"

"It'll take us more time than that to get there," the woman said dubiously.

"Shit!" Kristen cursed while Windlock pulled his out radio.

"Emberwing, we need those dragons out of here now. If they don't get clear, it won't be pretty."

"Yes, sir. Most have already left sir, but—"

"Spit it out. We don't have time to soften bad news!"

"Some of the senior members… Seven of them have locked themselves in a room and are talking about finishing deliberations. I'll try to…" The sound of knocking at a door was followed by obviously negative replies. "Sorry, sir. They won't agree."

"Then break the damn door down!" Windlock snarled. He looked at the device. Two holes still needed to light up, but they wouldn't remain dormant for much longer.

Kristen had already moved beyond thinking about the Council. If this bomb detonated, they were dead, but so were all the people who had come to help her. So was humanity's chance at peace. She had to stop it. Fortunately, she had a bomb expert on the radio.

"If its anything like the other one, I think you should be able to deactivate it," Hernandez said. "I looked at the remains of the one at the base, and I think it's more like an engine than a bomb. If you can disconnect a portion, it won't be able to build the pressure it needs to overheat. See if you can use those steel fingers of yours to snap the part that's not active yet."

She looked at Constance, who watched her from the floor, but the woman's expression offered no clues.

Cautiously, she looked at the two tubes with the holes that had yet to fill with light. She wondered briefly if it mattered which she tried to disarm when the hole in one of them lit up.

The assassin began to laugh.

Kristen ignored her and stretched her hand toward the bomb. It would be simple. All she had to do was break a pipe. The Steel Dragon's specialty was breaking things.

But when she came within a foot of the device, her hand bounced off an invisible barrier.

Constance laughed so hard she couldn't breathe. "Did you really think I would make it that easy for you?"

She moved quickly around the bomb and tried to touch it from any angle, but her efforts proved fruitless. It was inside some kind of floating sphere of force.

"I'm sorry. I said I would defer to you, but we're out of time," Windlock said and transformed into a dragon.

"What are you doing?" Larry asked him, his voice pitched high with panic.

"Something I learned from the Steel Dragon's book." The investigator wound his tail around the invisible barrier. Even in his dragon form, he was unable to reach the bomb but that didn't seem to be his intention. Instead of trying to touch it, he banged his tail against the sphere, which rolled the bomb into his waiting talons.

"That won't break it," Constance fumed.

"I know," Windlock said. He sounded incredibly tired but also proud. "Sometimes, there's nothing to do but let a bomb blow up."

He pushed the ball with his nose so it rolled down the hallway to the stairway they'd come down. Before it reached the end, he exhaled a blast of fire that ripped a hole in the ceiling of the hallway and opened it to the basement above it.

Kristen was able to see the last hole fill with light before he closed his talons around the sphere and treated it as carefully as she had handled a greased egg in her third-grade track and field day. The dragon lurched through the ceiling of the hotel's basement and into the hotel itself.

"He can't stop it now that it's charged. Once it overloads, we're all done. The corrupt Dragon Council has seconds left to live." Constance tried to shout but mostly coughed on her own words.

She didn't seem to be lying, though.

A high-pitched whine emitted from the sphere and grew louder and higher by the second.

Kristen raced after Windlock and followed the sound through the kitchen to see that it had shattered a shelf of crystal.

The investigator didn't release the sphere and simply bulldozed out of the hotel and into the snowy night. His dragon limbs cradled the sphere awkwardly like he tried to hold onto a bubble.

She realized then which page he tried to steal from her. "Windlock, you won't be able to get clear. Drop that bomb and get out of there."

"No can do, kiddo. If I drop it now, it won't be as far away as it needs to be. You taught me that at the party when you saved my life. If I drop it, the whole damn mountain might come down."

Over the radio, she could hear the whine of the device. The keening pitch grew louder and higher until it seemed that was all she could hear.

Still, Windlock talked to her as he pumped his wings and tried to fly higher and higher. "You were willing to sacrifice yourself to save others. How can I do less than that?"

"I had a vest!" she yelled into her radio, but he either couldn't let go of the speaking button or wouldn't as he didn't seem to hear her.

"You must continue your fight. You have the right of it. Dragons and humans can destroy one another or learn to coexist with mutual respect. Those are the only two options, although I guess I'd prefer the latter course." He chuckled, an ominous sound when mixed with the piercing shriek of the bomb that drew ever closer to destruction. "You gave me faith, Kristen Hall. Steel Dragon, you can save both races of your heritage. You're the only one who can."

"Windlock! Dammit, Windlock, drop the bomb! You're far enough away. Windlock!"

Kristen continued to yell into the radio even after the device exploded high above the hotel and the surrounding mountainsides. The flash of light was as bright as the sun and reflected off the snowy mountains. It cast everything in an eerie, harsh light for a moment before the shockwave radiated out, struck the mountains, and caused snow to avalanche down almost all of them.

The windows of the hotel rattled but none broke, neither from the shockwave nor from any errant shards of dragon.

Everyone was safe except for her mentor and one of the most respected Dragon investigators in the world.

Windlock was dead.

CHAPTER EIGHTY-THREE

Kristen didn't let herself cry for Windlock, although others did. Stonequest had shed a tear or two and Larry wept inconsolably, but she couldn't, not yet.

Instead, she helped to escort Constance to the main entrance of the building. There, they met the rest of the technomages still under the guard of the human SWAT team as well as the two wounded dragons. Emerald's eyes were healing. He still couldn't read text but he could see well enough to help watch the prisoners. Despite their magic prowess and work to try to destroy dragon kind, they hadn't fought against their captors. Apparently, Constance was the devoted one.

When the entire team was together again and she was finally convinced that the threat to the Dragon Council was over and the spark that might start a war extinguished, she let herself mourn Windlock for a moment.

She hadn't meant to, but she hadn't really had a choice.

Once everyone was safe and Emberwing's guards were called to reinforce the security to ensure that the mages wouldn't break free, Kristen made her way up the stairs to the ballroom. She wanted to check on the dragons who'd decided to remain behind.

Halfway up the steps, she stopped, frozen in place because she wondered what Windlock would have done in this situation. She thought he'd treat this as he did everything else with cool, calculated indifference and that he'd try to convince the Dragon Council not to do anything rash without weighing all the evidence. Then Kristen remembered that he was dead and she'd been unable to go further.

She stood on the stairs, her tears streaming down cheeks so scratched and bruised that even in her steel form, her wounds could be seen. Her mind couldn't believe he was dead. After everything he'd done for her, she thought bitterly, he'd finally done too much. She silenced the thought, though. To stop the violence Constance tried to commit, she would have done the same. Only now did she see how cruel that decision could be for the people she was doing it for.

"Are you all right?" Emberwing asked and placed a scarred hand on her shoulder.

Kristen nodded, wiped her tears, and forced herself to return to her regular skin.

"I think I will be."

"He was a real sonofabitch," he said and rubbed the scars on his face absently. "He does things to folks, makes a mark…" Emberwing chuckled as if he'd made a joke he hadn't meant to. "He changed you. I can tell. He was a good dragon." He sniffed and grimaced and she wondered if he'd maybe shed a tear too for his old friend.

After a long moment of silence, he said, "I told the Council what happened."

"What'll happen to Constance and her mages?" she asked.

"They'll be interrogated, then executed for their past murders," he stated.

"There should be a trial," she said and surprised herself with how much she felt like that was the thing that needed to happen.

Emberwing raised an eyebrow. She couldn't really tell from his scarred face but she thought it might have been in disbelief. Either that or he was actually impressed. "Tell that to them yourself, Investigator. They want to see you and thank you for saving them."

She nodded and continued to the second floor where she pushed the big door at the top of the stairs open to reveal the ballroom. Within, eight dragons were seated at a large table in eight ornate chairs. Behind them, the wall and windows were destroyed from the escape of the other members of the Dragon Councils. The floor of the ballroom—still shiny even in its current condition—had been severely scratched by the massive dragons claws all pushing off it to take flight.

Yet the eight council members still held themselves with the pride of kings and queens. Their clothes were like snapshots of periods of history from the world, pristine despite the destruction all around them. While the wall behind them was missing, the room was still warm as if the eight dragons before her radiated more than enough energy to fill the area.

"May I present Lady Kristen Steel," a dragon with the appearance of an extremely well-kept, silver-haired man said. Decimus Aurelius wore a silver tuxedo and black tie, the same as he had the last time she had seen him. It seemed a lifetime ago that she'd saved his life from another of Constance's bombs and he'd knelt before her and sworn her a debt.

Kristen stepped forward and bowed. "Thank you…er, Lord Aurelius—sir," she added hastily. "But it is Lady Hall, as that was my father's name."

"Forgive me," Aurelius said easily. "May I present Lady Hall to your lords and ladyships."

The others exchanged glances and pulses of auras too rapidly for her to follow at the use of her human name, but no one spoke.

Decimus Aurelius sat at his place at the table. Of all the dragons in the world to find in this room, she couldn't have asked for much better. She wondered if he'd stayed because he felt he owed her a debt or if it was because he trusted her to stop Constance. It didn't seem like the time to ask.

Instead, she saluted as she'd seen others salute members of the Council. Windlock had shown her how—not a pleasant thing to remember.

"Lady Hall," another dragon said, this one in the form of an older human woman with long silver hair who spoke in an accent that might have been from somewhere in the Arab world. "I am Lady Shimmerclaw. I speak for the Full Council, and I would like to congratulate you on behalf of this deliberative body for your quick action."

"Congratulate me?" she responded. She thought a big thank-you-for-saving-our-fucking-lives was more in order, but she didn't tell Lady Shimmerclaw that.

"Indeed!" another dragon interjected. He was a jowly man in a tight coat with brass buttons. His accent placed him as northern European. "Without your swift action, this meeting might have had to be held in the snow. I daresay we might have lost a couple more of our members."

The dragons continued in that vein for a while and told her how well she'd done and how courageously she'd acted. All of it felt phony to her like they thought they were the president pinning a medal on a police officer for saving a kitten in a tree.

As they made the rounds of congratulations, another dragon came in through the window. He landed and despite having faced Constance and her technomages, Kristen felt a pang of fear. His form was terrifying, hardly more than a skeleton with skin wrapped tightly to it, the color of leather left out in the sun. He transformed into a man in a black suit with an oddly marked face, pulled out a ninth chair, and sat.

The dragons welcomed him as Lord Boneclaw—an odd name to be sure, although in human form, he didn't seem any more or less imposing than the others. He too held himself with god-like confidence. The group returned to their congratulations.

The only ones who didn't have a vaguely condescending tone were Aurelius—who genuinely and profusely thanked her—and Lord Boneclaw. He said little, although the way he appraised her made her almost feel violated. She felt like he was looking at her as if she were a piece on a gameboard to which she didn't even know the rules.

"I would also like to officially honor Investigator Windlock," Shimmerclaw said and once more took control of the meeting once every dragon save Boneclaw had said their piece. "We will definitely be sure the history books will show that it was his heroism and sacrifice that saved us all."

Kristen had to bite her tongue at that. It made her want to rip into these fat cats. Windlock hadn't needed to die. For one thing, they could have taken the threat seriously from the beginning. Or they could have continued to assume there was a threat until they'd actually cleared the hotel. Windlock would still be alive if either of those options had been chosen.

She said nothing, though, and chose not to ruin this small honor they tried to bestow on him, but she was quietly furious.

"Investigator, we look forward to working with you further and wish you the best success in finding out if this mage had any more allies." Shimmerclaw nodded at Kristen—an obvious dismissal—and turned to the other dragons.

"Now, back to the matter at hand," Shimmerclaw said as if Kristen had already left. "I'm quite sure all of you talked with all of your other council members before this meeting, so the eight—"

Boneclaw cleared his throat.

"Pardon me, the nine of us present can vote on what we should do about the threat these weapons pose to the security of the Dragon State."

"I speak for the North American Council when I say we do not believe that dragons should go to war," Aurelius said. "The dwarves are to our north, no one else's, and they will not like it. Furthermore, many of the attacks—and indeed, most of them—took place in North America. We have the most to lose and therefore our opinion should be heeded. We have Lady Hall to stop any more of these mages. War is not wise." He nodded to Kristen at the end of his speech. At least he still cared that she was there.

Boneclaw cleared his throat. "With all due respect, Decimus, you do not speak for the North American Council as I disagree with your assessment completely. These mages have proven themselves to be a real nuisance to security. They must be crushed before their attempts at chaos can go any further."

"Decimus, do you really still hold to these arguments despite this last attack? You saw the explosion as well as us," Shimmerclaw said. "If Windlock had not done what he did, we might have all perished. Surely some of our other members would have. I am not sure we can still seriously consider peace. What says the council?" She looked around at her peers.

Glances were exchanged between the various members along with more pulses of aural power before the jowly dragon spoke again. "I think I speak for most of us when I say that for Investigator Windlock and the two dragons murdered in that tunnel, the humans must be culled. They have gone too far. Of course, we should exercise caution and only cull those who pose a political or security risk—and maybe some of the more troublesome celebrities too, probably—but leave the workers, craftsmen, electricians and the like as unharmed as we can manage. I would hate to see more than fifty percent losses in the working class."

Shimmerclaw nodded at this but there was something in her expression that Kristen couldn't quite place. She almost seemed disappointed that the rest of the council had agreed with her. But no, that wasn't quite it, Kristen thought as the dragon looked at each of the members. She seemed to want to see which of them really did agree that it was time for war.

Obviously, Boneclaw and the jowly dragon wanted action while Aurelius was against it, but how split were the others?

Shimmerclaw apparently wanted the answer to this question as she put it to a vote. "Then let us decide democratically what we shall do. May I remind you to vote not for political gain but for what is right. Whatever we decide will be binding, for all dragons follow the will of the Dragon Council."

"All dragons follow the will of the Dragon Council," the other eight dragons responded in chorus, even Aurelius. Even though he didn't look pleased at the prospect, he looked like he took the oath quite seriously.

"Wait!" Kristen yelled, no longer able to help herself.

"Forgive Shimmerclaw. Perhaps she was not blunt enough given your upbringing," a dark-skinned female dragon with a shaved head said, "You are dismissed."

"That's it? You'll vote to go to war just like that?"

"It won't be a war but a culling," the jowly dragon explained ponderously.

"That's disgusting. All of you are disgusting!" she shouted, no longer able to keep her aura in check. It lashed out like hot flame and the dragons recoiled at the uncouthness of it.

"If you would all get off your thrones and pay attention, you'd know that you don't have to go to war. If you'd notice what's going on, that people—human beings—are fed up and sick of your kind—our kind—hoarding the power, we wouldn't be in this mess. You treat humans like cattle and sheep until they to dare stand up for themselves, then you treat them like weeds. It's disgusting. All of you—"

"Are disgusting, yes, we got that part," Aurelius said, although at least he was still smiling.

"Are you quite finished?" Shimmerclaw asked her. She seemed to be shocked by the impertinence of someone speaking to her so. The dragon probably hadn't had anyone so much as fart in her presence for fifty years.

"No! As a matter of fact, I'm not," Kristen answered, quite amused that the Council member had invited her to speak once again, whether she'd meant to or not. "Also, frankly—as my dad used to say—I'm not sure you'll win this scrap. We raided a mage base today. Did you read Windlock's report? Let me summarize it for you since it looks like you've been busy here eating hors d'oeuvres or whatever. The technomages had a dragon chained underground for more than twenty years—a dragon like me. They harvested its body to make the weapons that have killed dragons."

"We read the report," Shimmerclaw said and sounded ashamed.

"And we didn't appreciate the vulgarity of it then any more than we do now," the jowly dragon said, quite affronted.

"Well, that wasn't all we found," she went on. "That mage base we raided revealed other locations as well. There are more cells like

Constance's, each of them with their own captive dragon and each producing as many dragon bullets as they can and as quickly as they can. If it comes to war, humans will have thousands of dragon bullets. They already have thousands of dragon bullets, but if it comes to war…" She laughed darkly. "That's all Constance wanted. If dragons attack people, the technomage terrorists win. They reach out to the army and soon, we have fighter planes armed with dragon bullets. Grenades manufactured with dragon scale fragments. We have every hunter and gun-rights enthusiast in America carrying bullets to kill us. Is that what you want? Because a vote to cull humans is a vote to cull yourselves."

Kristen took a deep breath to say more and realized that one, she needed to breathe again after all that, and two, she didn't have much else to say.

While most of the dragons did nothing but mutter about her impertinence, Aurelius looked intrigued. "What would you have us do?" he asked.

No one else paid him much mind, but when Shimmerclaw repeated the question, all the side chatter stopped.

"What would you have us do?" she asked. "Do you truly have an option that can stop war?"

She was proud of herself for not letting her jaw hit the floor. Her hope had been that they'd vote no, not turn to her for a solution, but she didn't hesitate long before she seized the moment she was given, short though it might be.

"Give me the job," she said.

"Pardon?" Shimmerclaw said and a smile grew at the corners of her mouth.

"Give me the job of stopping these mages before we go to war," she said and her thoughts gained momentum. "I'll create a team to solve this existential threat to both our species. We can all agree that both humans and dragons are at risk if war happens. A task force with both sides included will be able to find a better solution to a threat to us both."

"Do you truly think working with common humans will be of

value?" Shimmerclaw asked. She sounded more intrigued than anything, despite the rude words.

"We're all alive because of a mixed-species team," Kristen said with a shrug. "I would bet it will work again. Give the job—and the responsibility—of this to me."

"And if you fail?" Boneclaw asked. He didn't seem particularly bothered by the idea of her failing to prevent a war. He didn't seem indifferent either but…eager. Kristen decided that it wasn't the eerie name and strange dragon body that made her dislike Boneclaw. It was the way he looked when he spoke about war.

No one else moved. All eyes watched the tension build between Boneclaw and the Steel Dragon.

"I dunno." Kristen shrugged. "If I fail, I can see that war will probably be inevitable and neither side will rest until the other loses. I know you think it will be you who wins, but I can think of quite a few humans who would feel the same way. But it won't come to that—not as quickly, anyway—if you let me try to stop it."

"Then we vote," Shimmerclaw said.

CHAPTER EIGHTY-FOUR

Kristen left the Council meeting in a state of disbelief. She found her friends—human, dragon, and mage—waiting for her outside.

They all cheered when they saw her, but she couldn't share their enthusiasm.

She was quiet and even subdued as she closed the door to the Dragon Council meeting behind her. It clicked shut ominously.

Jim stepped forward first. "Are you okay? It sounded kind of… loud…in there for a while. You had us worried."

From their smiles, it was obvious that they had been able to tell it was she who had done the yelling.

All she could do was nod absently in response. Her mind was awhirl. Seeing all her friends there—especially Larry—without Windlock gave her an intense, overwhelming feeling of grief. She hadn't realized how much he'd meant to her and now, he was gone and he'd never know. The grief mixed with the sense of what was coming and the responsibility she'd been given—no, the responsibility she'd asked for.

"They voted for it," she said.

"For war?" Jim sounded horrified. The expressions on everyone's faces said the same.

"They voted to put me in charge of hunting the rest of the mage cells. I'm going to...that is, I have to stop them all. I'll free all the captive dragons—my...my siblings—and end this threat to both dragons and people."

"How long did the Council give you?" Stonequest asked. "Before they decide to cull the humans?"

"That's sick," Butters interjected.

"That's how they think of it," Heartsbane said. "They've been in power too long to view humans as a threat."

"They said if anything else happens, they'll reconvene and vote on it. Until then, I'm in charge."

Silence hung in the air for a second before Stonequest uttered a whoop of triumph. "Kristen, that's amazing. The Council didn't set you a deadline for this? For them, that shows a ton of confidence."

"They said I'd have to report back in a week," she said dubiously. "They want to know how many cells the technomages have, where they might be, and what continents they're on. I need to have answers."

He nodded, still impressed.

Jim was less enthusiastic. "So basically, you're talking about going up against a damned army. A number of small armies, in fact. Small, magic armies."

"I know." She shook her head at the idea. "I know it's crazy, but Windlock was right. It has to be me. Now that the Council has given me this opportunity, I won't blow it."

Drew put a hand on her shoulder. "At least you know you won't be alone, right?"

"Huh?"

"This is too big for you to mess up and too important. I'm in," he said and smiled.

"Seriously. We can't let the rookie mess this one up for the rest of us," Keith said to an echo of "You're the Rookie," from the rest of the team.

"I'm in too," Jim said.

"Of course. We are as well, right, Beanpole?" Butters said.

Beanpole shook his head as if to show how crazy he thought it was, but he was smiling. She thought that was a yes but wouldn't push him.

"I'm with you too," Amy said. "I said I'd be your mage and I meant it."

"I guess you'll need a dragon," Heartsbane said begrudgingly.

"Or two," Emerald added.

"You guys…thank you… Really, but this is too much." Kristen was overwhelmed. "To do this right, it'll be more than a job and I can't ask you all to commit that much time to this. Plus, I can't afford to pay anyone. I can hardly afford to pay Amy."

"You can pay me less," the mage protested.

"You don't need to worry about all that," Larry said and stepped forward. His eyes were red and puffy from how much he'd been crying.

"What do you mean? Even soldiers get paid," Kristen said.

"So pay us."

"Okay, I looked at how much investigators make. It's good—better than being a human cop, for sure, but it's not enough to support you all."

"You mean Windlock didn't tell you?" Brockton asked. He had the first smile she'd seen on his face since his boss had died.

"Tell me what?"

"That old bag of wind…and after all the times I said I would tell you and he kept saying no. He must have planned this in case he died because he knew how badly I wanted to tell you. That sonofabitch!" Larry laughed at his old boss's death and Kristen was quite confused.

"Larry, please explain why you think Windlock dying was funny?"

"Because he knew I'd be a wreck if he died," he said and grinned like a fool, an odd look with still-wet cheeks and his red puffy eyes. "He knew this would be the only thing to cheer me up. He told me he told you. I still can't believe this."

"Spit it out, Larry," Drew said.

"Windlock filed a new will just in case. He wanted to make sure Kristen continued to have whatever resources she needed to fight her battles, even if he was gone. Kristen…he gave you everything."

She tried to smile at the mage. He'd lost so much…but Windlock hadn't really been rich, had he? "You mean…like, the cases in his office."

"No, no. Windlock…well, he was quite old and fairly wealthy. He paid me his entire investigator wage and only did the job out of a sense of duty. You…you have a castle, Kristen, land, and a pile of gold."

She couldn't do anything then but break down and cry.

The fresh wound of losing Windlock was still too raw and his gift too precious. She couldn't believe that he'd sacrificed so much for her.

Now, she had everything she needed—wealth enough to build her own army and equip it well and enough allies willing to help.

He had given her everything to complete the mission she'd pursued since she'd first learned she was a dragon. Kristen Hall, human woman and the Steel Dragon, was finally ready to fix a world that had been broken for far too long. Or, at the very least, not allow it to shatter beyond repair.

The End
(for now)

Steel Dragon 4 is coming this spring from Kevin and Michael.

If you loved Steel Dragon, you might also enjoy the Federal Histories series, from Michael Anderle. Book one is Witch Of The Federation and it's available from Amazon and through Kindle Unlimited.

The future has amazing technology. Our alien allies have magic. Together, we are building a training system to teach the best of humanity to go to the stars.

But the training is monumentally expensive.

Stephanie Morgana is a genius, she just doesn't *know it*.

The Artificial Intelligence which runs the Virtual World is charged with testing Stephanie, a task it has never performed before.

The Earth and their allies, may never be the same again.

Will Stephanie pass the test and be moved to the advanced preparatory schools, or will the system miss her? Will the AI be able to judge a human's potential in an area where it has no existing test data to compare?

Available now at Amazon and through Kindle Unlimited.

Hi there! Wow. Just...wow.

You are awesome. The Steel Dragon has been a smash success. I am having tons of fun working on it, and clearly folks are having just as much fun reading it! I can't tell you how valuable that sort of feedback is to me.

Well, actually... I can. I can say thank you in the best manner that a writer possibly can, and that's to give you more books. Ideally, a lot more books, am I right?

You've inspired me to get back into urban fantasy storytelling in a much bigger way. It's a genre I left behind ages ago, and I wasn't sure when or if I was ever going back to it. I'd become mostly a science fiction author. Spaceships and ray guns replaced werewolves, mages, and dragons. But the level of enthusiasm folks like yourself have shown for this series has got me motivated to give you more.

I'm in the process of doing an update on the old Blackwell Magic novels. These stories were OK, for my early writing period, but they could use a little love at this point. The new editions will be longer, much more fun to read, and feature everything I've learned about writing in the couple million words I've put in since then. I also have the long-awaited seventh book waiting in the wings; it's done, ready to go, and will be coming out with the relaunch of the first six books. I picked up covers for books eight and nine as well, and plan to extend it to at least twelve books before calling it a day on that tale.

Dragons? Yeah, we definitely want more dragon stories. I have three brand new series in some stage of completion that revolve around dragons. Because they're fun to write, especially when you try to do something interesting and new with them. Kristen's story is just the beginning.

Here's the thing: I love telling stories. I write down the words, pour the books I write out onto the page. The work is a lot of fun for me. It's the kind of job that doesn't make me shudder at the thought of sitting down to work. Ultimately, it's folks like yourself that I tell these stories for. I might still be a storyteller without readers, but I wouldn't be able to write nearly so many. Thank you for that.

You've already met Michael via his author notes in so many books, but here's a little more about me.

I live in Boston these days, but I grew up in Vermont. We moved around - a lot! - so I don't really have a home town there. Because we were moving so often, making friends was a challenge. Books offered the sort of friendship that I could take with me wherever work carried my family. I started reading when I was three, but really took off when I was five. I fell asleep one night listening to my parents and a couple of their friends talking about Middle Earth. It was love at first sight. I was enthralled. I needed to know more.

So I picked up a copy of "The Hobbit" my parents had and tried to read it. Mom was amused at first. After the fiftieth time I asked her what some word meant, she was less amused, and showed me how to use the dictionary. After that I took off like a bullet. I finished "The Hobbit" in kindergarten and read the Lord of the Rings trilogy in first grade.

Not coincidentally, first grade was also when I wrote my first short story. I wrote or told stories one way or another ever since.

It's been a wild ride, and there are so many more tales to tell. I hope you'll continue to join me for them, both the Steel Dragon tales, and the others to come in the future. As always, I'd love to hear from readers. You can reach out to me at author@kevinomclaughlin.com

Thanks for reading!

Kevin

MICHAEL'S AUTHOR NOTES
FEBRUARY 28, 2020

THANK YOU for reading our story! We have a few of these planned, but we don't know if we should continue writing more after that and publishing without your input.

Options include leaving a review, reaching out on Facebook to let us know, *and smoke signals.*

Frankly, smoke signals might get misconstrued as low hanging clouds, so you might want to nix that idea.

The first dragon stories I really got into were *Dragons of Autumn Twilight* by Margaret Weis and Tracy Hickman back in about 1986. I hate to admit it, but I'm not really a large J.R.R. Tolkien fan. *The Hobbit* and the *Lord of the Rings* trilogy were (for me) too slow in the action department, and I wanted MORE magic than Gandalf produced.

Explosions! Magic! Arrows and swords! That was what I wanted to read, *not* the descriptions and slow machinations of the Hobbit.

Please don't send me hate mail. I'm just a person who wants to microwave my reading, not have the story slow-simmer before I read it.

(The real reason I don't like some of those stories is I *hate* stress. Anytime a story goes too long before the resolution of the stress event, I will read ahead to make sure I know a character I like is okay and going to live.

Or has died, and I will then put the book down and never read it again.)

Diary Sunday Feb 23rd to Sat Feb 29th. (Mostly the same for all books coming out during this week.)

Well, this is a little early (I'm not quite into the week yet), but I can admit I'm going to be out of the office for a couple of days.

Where are you going, you ask? Why, to the White Label World Expo. I know, it clearly gives you goosebumps up and down your arms just thinking about it, right?

No?

Well, color me surprised. (In case you are super-curious, here is the link: https://www.whitelabelexpo.com)

I've now reviewed the list of those exhibiting, and I'm not sure if I'll last beyond a couple of hours. I'm pretty sure this should be renamed the CBD Conference for those not yet involved.

I did notice there is a class on leveraging Amazon's algorithm for growth. That looks interesting.

On to other topics!

We have plenty of cool books coming out next week, including *Scions of Magic* Book 05, *Hunter Cadet* Book 03 (this series has been extended to 06!) We have a brand-new series *WAR MAGE* Book 01 (3 in 1) on Wednesday. We finish the week with *Goth Drow* (3 in 1) on Friday and *Steel Dragon Book* 03 (3 in 1) on Saturday.

All in, that is about eleven (11) books' worth of reading. So, I hope you don't treasure your sleep!

#Sleep Is Overrated.

#Read all Night, Sleep all day.

#Don't Be A Quitter – Finish the book!

#Your boss will NOT understand, I guarantee it.

I will be editing *OpusX* Book 06 this week, so if you are in Vegas, you might find me at the Aria Five-50 bar typing into the night, trying to pound their iced tea (I swear that stuff has 3x the caffeine of any other tea) and finish just one more chapter or three of editing.

Today, I visited the Aria barber (in the Spa) for the first time. The barber (a Russian lady, Luba(?)) talked me into a true barber shave.

Dammit, that hurt!

I only ever do a dry electric shave, and my beard was NOT pleased with the experience. It wasn't too bad (yes, it was.), until the last towel.

Those who have done this are probably chuckling.

You see, the first towel in a barber shave is hot, or at least nice and warm to open the pores. She flicked the first towel back and forth a few times to cool it, then settled it on my chin area (this was going well), then wrapped it all the way around my face leaving an opening for my nose.

HOLY D@#%R that was a bit warm!

But really nice after the shock. The towel was infused with something that smelled spa-ish and very outdoorsy.

The actual shave was a bit harsh (ripping hairs out at the roots it felt like) at times, but I expected that to happen.

It was the last towel, the one to close the pores, that made me bounce out of the chair.

It wasn't just "a little cold." No, it felt like she laid ice water in a nice circle on top of my face. As if I were in the sea off of Iceland, with only my nose sticking out above the frigid water.

In short, it *sucked*.

I'll do it again, but probably once a quarter. There is very little that can provide such a close shave as a razor blade. Besides, the thought of only one small jerk of the hand to end your life gets the blood flowing, #AmIRight?

Yeah, even I could have done without that last thought. See you next book!

Ad Aeternitatem,

Michael

** I went to the White Label event yesterday. Stayed four (4) hours, took one class on Amazon ads, and met a really interesting guy who does tattoos (very talented.) Judith, my wife, and I had lunch with Wayne and Kia, his wife, and I'll see if we can help them publish their books.

Who knows, you might see future art from him at LMBPN, and we can blame CBD oil .

Book 3 - Vengeance Over Vanaheim

Book 4 - Hel Hath No Fury

Blackwell Magic Series (Urban Fantasy)

Book 1 - By Darkness Revealed

Book 2 - Ashes Ascendant

Book 3 - Dead In Winter

Book 4 - Claws That Catch

Book 5 - Darkness Awakes

Book 6 - Spellbinding Entanglements

By A Whisker (short story)

The Raven and the Rose - Free novelette for email list fans!

Dead Brittania Series:

Dead Brittania (short prequel story)

Book 1 - King of the Dead

Book 2 - Queen of Demons

Raven's Heart Series (Urban Fantasy)

Book 1 - Stolen Light

Book 2 - Webs in the Dark

Book 3 - Shades of Moonlight

Other Titles:

Over the Moon (SF romance)

Midnight Visitors (Steampunk Cat short story)

Demon Ex Machina (Steampunk Cat short story)

The Coffee Break Novelist (help for writers!)

You Must Write (Heinlein's rules for writers)

CONNECT WITH THE AUTHORS

Connect with Michael Anderle and sign up for his email list here:

Website: http://lmbpn.com

Email List: http://lmbpn.com/email/

Facebook:
www.facebook.com/TheKurtherianGambitBooks